MOBB DEEP'S -
"SHOOK ONES PART II"

SCREEEEEE

TALON

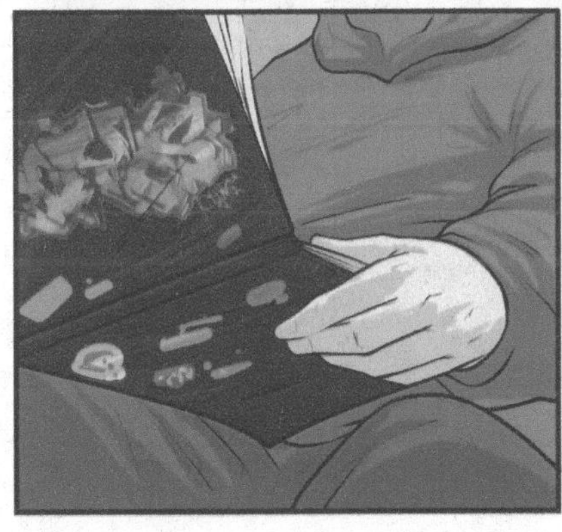

IN SEARCH OF ROHAN CHANG

THIRD EDITION

LINCOLN LEE

Hey there! This book is dedicated to you. Remember, you are extraordinary and capable. Don't let anyone tell you otherwise!

And for God, Almighty.

PROLOGUE

L esser cities would grow dark, disappearing into shadow when the sun set. But New York City roared, coming alive under heaven's stars. The metal and glass of the skyscrapers lit up, one after the other, transforming into a dazzling kaleidoscope of pink, yellow, and orange. Then, as the colors faded with the rapid coming of night, electric lights illuminated the city's pathways before him. Sensing it was the perfect night in the ideal place, he felt his energy rising anew.

His eyes sparkled, the skin wrinkled a little underneath, and he couldn't contain the excitement touching his soul as he watched the flow of people streaming out of the buildings into the night, seeking thrills and lovely delights. For some, it was like a savory meal at the end of a long day; for others, it was knowing that someone who loved them, or at least wanted them physically, was waiting at the other end of their subway or taxi ride. As the people flooded the streets, he became more aware, and New York seemed more vibrant. The aroma of green apples and flowers filled his nostrils, making him smile.

He loved New York, as clichéd as it sounded: its attitude, its hustle and bustle, its shimmer. He always believed something good was about to happen there. He thought New York as beautiful and pure; hopeful even, and he always looked to the coming of a new night because it made his dull days that much brighter.

He would tell himself all day that it would be a good experience even if he didn't catch a glimpse of her, since there were seven million people there, after all. But he had seen her twice in this neighborhood. She was just as much of an FAO Schwarz fan as he was, and maybe today would be the day he got up the nerve to say something to her instead of pulling his cap down further, looking the other way so she didn't see his face and realize it was the cute guy who had complimented her on her smile.

He saw her right then. *There*. She was on her way out of FAO Schwarz. He didn't look at *her*, just at her light steps barely touching the sidewalk with each gentle sway. *He saw her but didn't move*, gingerly frozen against the lamp post, watching.

She didn't notice him as she exited the toy store, not even when passing him. Why would she? He was just one of seven million people flowing through the mighty city, and even with that many folk, if you lived here long enough, you were able to start not seeing people. It was sort of a must-have for anybody who called the Five Boroughs home. Because if you got right down to it, there definitely should not be this many human bodies crammed into such a small space. Unless you were home alone, or had the kind of job where you had a private office, there was always someone around—every all-night restaurant, every subway station, every nook and cranny in every lush park. You had to invent your own privacy or you might freaking go stir crazy!

She smiled as she walked down the jam-packed sidewalk with nothing short of joy in her steps. She was getting to the age where she didn't have to do anything she didn't want to, making her own decisions a lot of the time and enjoying being part of the vibe and flow of New York City. Other people might look around and see nothing but big box stores full of overpriced junk, and streets crammed with way too many people trying to avoid each other. However, she saw FAO Schwarz and all the hundreds of others as nothing short of magical. All full of baubles, trinkets, and hidden treasures, sparking her imagination and making her hopeful she could one day make enough money to buy them all. Out on the street, her mind was going in a million different directions, planning her future, enjoying the fading sun shining down on her warm dewy skin as she waved at every child and dog she saw, happy to feel their giggles and hear their woofs. She thought New York City was a beautiful place, day or night. Some of her friends told her she was living in Fantasy Land, and that New York was polluted and dangerous, but she couldn't see it that way.

She was like Dorothy heading home from Oz. She couldn't wait for her incredible family and the coziness of her own space, filled with books and sentimental trinkets, because being at home was even more joyous than all her fun being in the city. She had a package for her dad, and eagerly wanted to get it to him before he started his post-dinner routine of prayer and reflection. She picked up her pace, hoping she could get home quicker by hopping on the subway only five blocks away. And she would save even more time, she reasoned, and be at the station even earlier by cutting through that alleyway.

He hadn't wanted to stop her on the street. It seemed like that would be too overwhelming, and New Yorkers got really rude when you stopped them mid-block. That was an excellent way to be told to fuck off, or get a nice friendly shove. But when he saw her make a sharp left into the narrow alley, he thought it was his lucky day. At the very least, he could tell her he took the same shortcut, warn her of some non-existent danger, and say pretty girls should never walk alone in an alley. He imagined the smile that would come over her face when he was complimenting her, and picked up his pace.

At the entrance to the alley, he paused, suddenly full of self-doubt that he could actually pull this off, and mused, *What if she doesn't really like me? What if she was just being polite the first time we met when she said I was a classic gentleman? What if she doesn't even remember any of that?*

He started to get nervous and contemplated walking on, but that's when the little voice inside his head spoke up, whispering, *"Remember her smile? Remember how it made you feel? You deserve to feel that way! You deserve to see her smiling only for you! Don't back down now! Make it happen! She turned that way, and she's all alone down there! Be the white knight she wants!"*

She turned her head when she heard a noise behind her. She figured it was a cat, maybe a rat or a pigeon, or someone taking out the garbage, and thought little of it. But then, she saw a man following her at the end of the alley, moving toward her more quickly than she liked. Like he was trying to catch up with her ... or maybe just trying to catch her. And then she quickened her pace hurriedly! However, the alley was longer than she had initially thought, and she was only slightly more than halfway down it. She was probably being silly, but she suddenly felt like she needed to be back on the street with other people. She checked over her shoulder once more and now found him even closer, waving his arms to get her attention. "Excuse me, Miss!" he yelled. "You dropped your wallet back there."

"What?" she asked. She frantically felt inside her Louis Vuitton bag to find her wallet was indeed missing. It was a new Hermes wallet her dad had recently gifted her for her 16th birthday. Everything was in that wallet. And she'd worked so diligently last semester, brought home all As, and had made her dad so proud that he'd surprised her with the Hermes treasure on her birthday.

He was waving it now, and she relaxed both visibly and mentally. He was the kind of New Yorker she told all her friends was out there. The Good Samaritan. The rare guy who was looking out for you. The kind of person she aspired to be in her day-to-day life. The reason she took volunteer jobs, while her friends were at the mall. The reason she babysat for free in her apartment building while others were price-gouging for childcare. *Good people do exist everywhere*, she thought.

She turned and smiled up at him. He was a lot taller than her, but pretty much everyone was. The stranger smiled back, and she recognized him. *A good guy, indeed*—or so she thought.

As he gently handed back her wallet, she profusely thanked him. He nodded at first but sensed a slight tingling discomfort surging from her. He was more annoyed than saddened as she wasn't giving him the adoration he so craved when returning such a personal treasure. *Damn her*, he thought, *I will make her beg for me now*. His annoyance became frustration, now growing into a rage that in the past had only been quelled when his thirst was quenched entirely.

As he grabbed her shoulders and pulled her towards him, she tried to pull away, her happiness disquieting to trembling fear, and she knew she had made a grave error. Her troubles had only just started in the New York alleyway on this warm night when she had only been minding her own business, and wanted to get home, sweet home.

AND THEN HE saw her and smiled...

CHAPTER

ONE

Sometimes, change is for the better, and sometimes, it's for the worse. But the more things change, the more they stay the same, especially in my little town. It's a place in Queens, right off 188th Street, a place we locals call Fresh Ghetto. Believe me when I tell you, nothing good ever happens here. At least, not usually. I know that because I've lived there my whole life. The signs on the borders claim I really live in Fresh Meadows, but that's the kind of joke we locals don't find funny. The name is so not true that it isn't right. *Nothin'* fresh down here, other than maybe new drugs, new gangs, and new garbage. And Meadows? This is the very definition of the concrete jungle, man. If you see a tree anywhere, it's probably in the lobby of an office building and made totally out of plastic. The only available grass here is the expensive bargain you buy on the corner or the risky safe bet from behind the high school if you know the wrong kind of person who's also the right insider.

That's what I have in common with my town because nothing good usually happens to me. They say I'm all over the place, and at my last Parent-Teacher conference, my history teacher, Ms. Brown, told my parents I was a "ticking time bomb." Not exactly the lavish praise mom and dad were looking for. But at least my story is good, if not complicated, and I guarantee you won't hear anything like this again in your lifetime. You may think you know how it will end, but I assure you, you don't.

I was born in New York City, the Big Apple, the melting-pot capital of the world. Home of The Empire State Building, Central Park, The World Trade Center, my beloved New York Yankees, those clowns over at Shea Stadium, the Knicks, the Giants, the Islanders and Rangers, Times Square, and The Statue of Liberty.

This is where everyone, and I mean every single person of all shades and stripes, meshes together—the rich, the poor, the young, the old, the bad, and the good. I am guessing there are good people out there. I know a couple. My friend Amayah is the best, not only because she's stunningly beautiful but also because she's very sweet to me. That certainly helps. Then there's my dear friend Drew, known as Lore on the streets - a vibrant force of nature, an endlessly exciting, free-spirited creative whose radiance lit up the world around me. Meeting Lore exposed me to an artistic world within myself that I never knew existed.

This place might be home to me, but I can't say the same about my parents. They came here from Taiwan before I was born, sold on that age-old story of the American dream. To hear them talk about all the opportunities we have here, one would think the streets were paved with gold and we ate steak and caviar every night. They work their asses off twelve hours a day, and they're still looking for more work! And lately, I've found that I just don't resonate with either of them like I used to.

High school has really changed my view of the world. I never see my parents happy or smiling, or laughing. If they do, they must do it when I'm asleep or at school. I often find them on the couch, nodding off and snoring to the classic tunes of TV show reruns. Is that the sweet life they planned to have for me? Working so many hours, I pass out on the couch at 7:45 p.m. on a Tuesday? Yeah, no thanks.

At school, people smile and laugh all day long—talking about their weekend plans, parties, dates, and get-togethers that seem like the most fun you could have simply by showing up! And my goal this year? To hit up the biggest and most *baddest* party ever, not just some excitingly dull snoozefest.

But my parents are convinced that if they keep on killing themselves day after day, they will be able to get a slice of that American pie that every immigrant sells themself on—the big house, the cars, the social acceptance, the whole nine yards. Of course, they've already determined my role in this entire fairy tale. The model minority. The straight-A student. The guy who makes 1550 on his SAT without even breaking a sweat. Helpful. Honest. Earnest. Has a job when he's thirteen and says all the right things to white people when they stop by the family business.

One fly in the ointment, though. I'm none of those things and have no desire to be. In fact, I'm about as completely different as possible from that image. I'm not sure I could be that person even if I tried.

When I was a young kid, I was the by-the-book, hard-working Asian stereotype that my parents expected from me and my brother. Sometime around fourth grade I started noticing that being that person wasn't working out for me the way I wanted it to. I was ten or eleven when I started to really notice the difference between me and the kids at school, who I'd thought of as the cool ones.

That first spark of independence was making its way into my subconscious, and I was starting to piece together that not everything my parents told me was the absolute truth of the matter. My earliest memory of this phenomenon was in fifth grade. I had been one of the top students in my class all through elementary school, which meant routine high praise from my teachers. In the earlier grades, there weren't a lot of cliques inside the classroom. Everyone seemed to get along—whites, Blacks, Asians, Latinos—we were all interested in kid stuff like recess, cartoons, candy, the holidays, and anything else that disrupts the learning flow.

Between fourth and fifth grade, something definitely changed. Maybe it was some of the kids going through early puberty. Maybe that's the age where you start pushing back against the hand of authority and forming your own belief system. I don't know. But I remember walking up to my math teacher Mrs. Murtaugh's desk, retrieving my geometry test—a 100, obviously—and turning back around to retake my seat. I sat between David Holtz and Shawn Nelson, two white kids I had known for four years and played with hundreds of times. As I neared my seat, David saw my paper, scoffed aloud, turned to Shawn and said, "What a nerd. Typical chink!"

Shawn laughed out loud and used his fingers to make imitation slant eyes. He replied in a fake Asian stereotype accent, "Me so good at math! Wee-wee small but brain very big!" The two died laughing, as had several of my other classmates who overheard the joke.

I couldn't believe what I had heard, or that so many people thought it was funny. I wondered why it was okay to make fun of Asians but not someone from another race. Somehow, Asians were de-racialized. And isn't racist humor against any race equally ugly and not okay? Were we honorary whites? Yet, America had barred Asian immigration over a century ago, reserving citizenship for European whites. Were we also not real people of color, a real minority? The struggles and unfair treatment of Asian Americans have been largely overlooked, failing to recognize our experiences as a minority.

I was, however, proud of my test grade because it proved I was working hard and committed to being the best I could be. How could so many kids think otherwise? In a five-second outburst, they were mocking me, my intelligence, and my race. It felt like I missed a secret meeting on the first day of school where we all agreed to stop being friends, stop caring about grades, and just say and do whatever we wanted, whenever we wanted.

The new behaviors around me weren't limited to that day of the math test. I started seeing them on the playground and cafeteria, who hung out in what location before and after school, and who got picked to be on what team during P.E. It wasn't just the white kids either. Divisions were forming everywhere based on the clothes you rocked, if you bought or brought lunch to school, what sports teams you rooted for, what extracurriculars you were involved in, and what music you liked. It even boiled down to whether you were at school to be a good little learner or were showing up to hang out with your friends, have some fun, and see what you could get away with.

I seemed to be the opposite of 'cool' in every category. And I hated it.

I hated it so much that I risked the wrath of my parents, namely my father, by rebelling against the life of the honest, hard-working Asian American I was raised to be. I stopped wearing my brother's hand-me-down clothes and saved up the small bits of money I earned from doing extra work to buy clothes that resembled the latest trends at school. The only problem was that the stuff was so expensive it had usually been out of style for months by the time I could buy it from the second-hand store.

I stopped fixing my lunch at home in the morning and started using the school's cafeteria, even though the food was god-awful, and the line was so long I rarely had time to sit down and eat the whole thing before the bell rang. The cool guys like Shawn and David, who had humiliated me over my math test, were into music like MC Hammer and Vanilla Ice, the Chicago Bulls, and wearing colorful hats turned at ridiculous angles. They had several of these hats confiscated by teachers, since you couldn't wear them at school, but they kept showing up with more.

I wouldn't say I liked their cheesy-ass pop rap, but I listened to the stations that played the same fifteen to twenty pop songs over and over again so I could quote the lyrics when I tried to get into a conversation. I never liked the Bulls because Michael Jordan kept knocking my Knicks out of the playoffs, but I pretended to worship him like the other boys when we played basketball at recess or before school started.

In short, I went to as many lengths as I could to stop being the stereotypical Asian. I intentionally began answering test questions incorrectly to avoid always having the highest grades in the class. That was the hardest part of it all because every inch of my being told me to strive to make a 100 on everything, but I never wanted that scenario with Shawn and David to repeat itself, so I slacked on the tests. I would intentionally miss a few questions to lower the perfect scores to 88s. My dad about hit the roof the first time I brought home a report card with two As and three Bs on it. Most of the kids in my class would have felt like they had won the lottery and a year-long pass to Disney World if they pulled those grades, but for me it was an embarrassment to the family that kicked me off video games and watching TV for two weeks. Oh well, I stopped caring.

On rare occasions when one of the cool kids would ask me my opinion about a new song, or if I had seen the Bulls' highlights the night before on ESPN, progress was accomplished. It was worth risking the anger and disappointment of my parents to make those very slight advancements towards being popular.

However, it didn't work out because I was too different from being a popular kid in the long term. By the time high school started, I stopped trying to copy the kids who were the social leaders at school. I just couldn't compete, and it was exhausting to try. I didn't have the money for their brand of clothing. So I chose to wear blue jeans and black T-shirts to show that I wasn't focused on fashion and had more important things on my mind. I couldn't pretend to be interested in listening to Nirvana and Pearl Jam to feel down. I preferred hip-hop and gangsta rap, and I would put on my headphones to block out the rest of the world whenever I could.

I routinely made good enough grades to keep my parents off my case, but I wasn't obsessive about studying how my brother had been at the same age. Going to the best college possible didn't have a lot of appeal to me anymore because earning my parents' praise wasn't my end-all-be-all. Way too often I found myself in a melancholic mood without really knowing why. I had a working theory, though, one that I hadn't really shared with anyone because I was scared of what they might think of me.

We learned all about the scientific method for creating a hypothesis in science throughout middle school. Well, this is my hypothesis for how things work when you're an American kid from an Asian family.

When it comes to the big-picture stuff, nobody thinks you're a minority. You get lumped in with the white kids at school because you typically make good grades, aren't a discipline problem, graduate on time, go to college, and get a nice job after school. Therefore, no teacher will feel sorry for you or cut you slack when you forget your homework or bomb a test because you couldn't sleep the night before. You're just supposed to be naturally smart and successful.

But when it comes to all the small things, the ones adults shake their heads at that kids obsess over, now you're just back to being a fresh-off-the-boat minority. Asian kids don't get picked first in gym class. Nobody expects you to set the fashion trends in the hallways, and nobody asks if you want to hang out on Friday night. I'd say it was pretty awful.

If we weren't showing off our brains, we were pretty much invisible. Every racial group was fabulous and celebrated in America. And the Asians were ... what? The racists thought we were a monolith, the ones you turned to when you needed cheap takeout or your suit cleaned by Monday morning. But I knew we were much more, each with different lives, with diverse lines of work. I mean, my cousin was a doctor, my distant uncle a lawyer, and I saw others on TV like Daniel Inouye, who was a U.S. senator. But over the years, I had accepted the harsh anti-Asian truth being flung in my face daily.

As an Asian American, the challenges of racism were many, but the feeling of not fitting in at school was even more distressing. I tried hard enough not to get yelled at at dinner when it came to my grades, but that was it. The rest of the time, I practiced being invisible. My clothes helped me blend into the crowd. My headphones drowned out the surrounding noise when I didn't want to hear it.

Life was just one day congealing into the next. That became my mindset over time: lower your expectations, and you'll be much less disappointed.

Maybe the worst part of it was that even though I thought I was different from most of the kids in my school, and even though I kept telling myself I wasn't like them, I found my thoughts and my actions continuously being permeated by what I saw around me. I longed to be like the kids who flaunted trendy clothes and sported a new outfit to school every week. It meant that their parents were rich and could buy them whatever they wanted. Even though I didn't play sports, I was jealous of the athletes. They had that swagger about them when they roamed the halls. Everyone knew their names, their jersey numbers, and when they were playing next. Guys sought high-fives from them, and girls wanted to wear their varsity jackets, even when it was ninety-five degrees outside. Even the guys I felt were definitely not any better-looking than me got female attention just from sitting on the bench for the basketball team. It made no sense whatsoever. Why did those green and gold jackets give them power over girls? It wasn't just the stuff about the popular kids that started getting to me though.

I started sharing beliefs about other races and classes of people based on my circle of peers rather than what I knew to be true. I even harbored a few prejudices toward the people of New York City. In junior high, there was a guy in my gym class from El Salvador who spoke virtually no English. The coach made me help him out the first week after he transferred, and I spoke loudly and abruptly with him since all he knew was Spanish. What kind of person moves to New York City and can't pick up a little English? I even started saying things in my head about other Asians that I'd heard others say aloud. Did I agree with them? I didn't even know. That was the worst part. But if I thought like they thought and acted as they acted, maybe I'd get to go to the *baddest-ass* parties. It was such a pathetic viewpoint. I went back and forth between desperately wishing I could talk to the hot girls, play on a team, and hang out at the cool kids' house on

Friday night when their parents weren't home, to keeping entirely to myself and isolating myself from them all. *But screw them! They weren't better than me.*

That was how I went about things. That's until I met Drew. We shared our adolescence like brothers. He was alert, mischievous, active, and wild, and together we immersed ourselves in street art. His passion for graffiti gave birth to his alter ego—Lore—an urban artist extraordinaire. We laughed as much as we fought to create art and repeated the process a hundred times. He had barely scratched the surface of his magnificent creations on the path to greatness. However, his premature and unforeseen death shattered my life abruptly in the most jarring manner.

That's when *the voices* started. I started to wonder if I was going insane, and for a while there, the only thing keeping me from running away or checking myself in the psych ward was my friend Amayah. Well, she called us friends, but I wanted to be so much more; I was just too chicken to do anything about it.

"You've got to have faith in the world," Amayah usually says to me when she sees that I'm in a bitter phase when we occasionally walk to and from the subway. She may have a point, but she's unaware of the voices I've been hearing inside my head. Ms. Brown doesn't know about the voices either, but she knows I'm distracted and angry and anxious, so she tossed that hand grenade at my parents during the conference. I'm getting ahead of myself, though. I probably shouldn't have brought up *the voices* so soon. Maybe it's too early to talk about them.

"Be careful, Rohan, there's trouble coming onto the train." Right on cue, one of *the voices* I had heard inside my head spoke up. The voice was usually low and raspy, but this Monday morning was different from any other - the beginning of something unprecedented.

The first time I heard the voice, I was convinced my skull was splitting in two from some stroke or brain aneurysm. I was walking home from school when suddenly the words filled my ears, shouting a warning as I crossed a side street without looking. I staggered and almost crashed into the streetlight, shocked by the sound filling my head.

I was lost in the music, headphones on, swaying to the beats of my cherished mix CD. Suddenly, a raw, urgent voice pierced through the melodies, screaming, *"WATCH OUT!"* Fear overcame me as I quickly jumped onto the sidewalk to avoid what was coming. In front of me, a shiny blue sedan emerged from the shadows, narrowly avoiding being involved in a hit-and-run at the intersection where I could have been. The driver's reckless maneuvers, including sharp turns, accelerating past traffic at race car speeds, and constant honking, left chaos in their wake. Unfortunately, it was not just fear that this careless vehicle left behind; the unfortunate collision of innocent people also marred its path before it vanished into the distance. If *Field of Dreams* and a million other movies have taught us anything, it's that you don't tell anyone when you hear a voice in your head, even if it's helping you out. And this voice had saved me from fifty broken bones. I tried to reach out to the voice, greet it, thank it, but I was getting nothing in return, and it felt really foolish to keep trying.

After the incident, I witnessed several people lying on the ground. Three police officers arrived on foot at the intersection a few seconds later. One of them used his radio to describe the car involved. The slowest of the three officers stopped to help me up and asked if I was okay. I took his hand, stood up, and told him I was fine, although I was not feeling okay. I decided to take a break and seek solace in a nearby tea shop, indulging in my favorite oolong blend. As I savored the aroma and warmth of the tea, I found myself haunted by a lingering thought. Later, as I returned to my routine and played the same song that had elicited a haunting warning, I was surprised to find that the unusual voice had vanished without a trace. This left me puzzled and intrigued, pondering its origin.

When I went to bed, a news report on TV caught my attention. It turns out that the car that nearly killed me had three bank robbers inside. Two were caught, and a third was wounded and believed to be hiding near Fresh Meadows. However, three people died and three others were injured when their getaway car tried to escape, hitting bystanders.

The next day, as I stepped into the local Dunkin' Donuts in Fresh Meadows to grab my usual glazed donuts, something peculiar caught my eye. There, lurking between the parked cars, was a figure that bore an uncanny resemblance to the lone bank robber who had recently made a daring escape. His mugshot had been plastered all over the local news, so his face was unmistakable in my mind. I couldn't tear my eyes away as I watched him from a distance, and before I knew it, he had snapped at me.

"Do you have a staring problem, kid?" he barked.

Startled, I stammered, "I'm sorry, but I thought you were someone I knew."

He responded with a menacing warning, "Don't put your nose into my affairs. You got that, kid? You might find something you don't like," as he hocked a brownish-green loogie near my feet.

Feeling uneasy, I muttered an apology and quickly made my way inside. Had I really stumbled upon the elusive bank robber? I didn't dare linger to find out, choosing instead to mind my own business and get out of there as fast as I could.

BUT THEN A FEW DAYS LATER, the voice whispered in my ear again. I was in the middle of an English test and struggled to remember the name of a supporting character in one of the thousands of short stories we'd read that semester. I was racking my brain when a whisper sailed through my thoughts. *"The blackboard,"* it said, and I looked up, and there on the blackboard off the side of my teacher's desk was a list of characters she forgot to erase from yesterday's review. That was twice that I'd been helped out by the mysterious raspy voice in my subconscious.

Over the next few weeks, the voice came across in small bursts, usually to keep me from making a bad choice. I trusted it implicitly, and each time it allowed me to avoid pain, embarrassment, a bad score, or a run-in with my dad when he was pissed about whatever.

That didn't mean I felt all that comfortable with it, so one day during free time, I hit up the psychology section of the school library and researched a few cross-references to inner voices. There was much to be said about the "little voice inside your head" and how it was usually your moral compass, guiding you away from making bad choices. Some call it your inner monologue, the voice that tells the story of your life while it is happening. There were also some more vague references to people developing a sixth sense or a danger sense that keeps them out of trouble. I didn't know if this was the same thing. It did feel like an alien inside my head, but the more I heard the voice, the more I got comfortable with it. I saw it as making me unique. I felt special, like whatever this was, it chose me.

A couple of times, I'd visualized a really powerful force behind the voice, something that had sought me out and was maybe seeing if I was worthy of the power that kept appearing to me in flashes. I slowly had a few exchanges with it. Responding with thanks and expressions of gratitude made it linger around a bit longer each time. It felt like coaxing a wild animal into letting you pet it or feed it by hand. Like it wasn't sure whether or not I could be trusted.

And now, it was back on the train, and I could feel something was about to happen. That's usually how it worked. The voice would appear and tip me off about something to avoid or something to try to steer clear of. Trouble on the train could be anything, unfortunately.

I have no defense against the Bitter Four train, especially now in the summer, voice or no voice. If the train didn't break down, it usually brought us to Bedford Park Boulevard station near our supposedly spectacular Bronx High School of Science. Overrated would be my best description of our school. Was it as unique as everyone makes it out to be? Does it churn out geniuses? Hmm, I definitely was not one for sure. They all thought I was, being Asian, but the exterior wasn't matching the interior on this one. The only thing going for me was making me a target on the Bitter Four. Bullies were attracted to science nerds like hungry sharks to chum in the water on the train, especially ones voluntarily taking summer classes, and more so on Monday mornings. Why did I even sign up for summer classes? I didn't fail any courses; I just wanted to challenge myself with more difficult coursework. But seriously, why did I do that?

You see, there was no time to relax on the train; you were always looking over your shoulder for oncoming trouble, and even if you had your guard up, it would still find you more often than not. But I have my ways of escaping. My handy Sony Walkman has saved me more than once from a dreary, boring commute. So, I slid on the headphones, and the monotony of the stops faded into the sick beats of Mobb Deep's *Shook Ones Part II*. My head started to bounce slightly to the moment, feeling Prodigy's verses about being more mature than his actual teenage years, and when the shit hit his fan, his warm heart bled cold.

Looking out the windows, I studied the blink-and-you'll-miss-it artwork adorning the darkened train tunnels. If only Lore were here, he'd appreciate it just as much. This was Crook One's turf, and his wild styles were so legendary in the Bronx that I almost wished the train would stop here so I could drink it in deeper: all the details, all the gracefulness, all the attitudes.

Every year of my life, every school has thought they were doing us a massive favor by dragging our little asses in a school bus down to Manhattan to wander around the MET for five hours, staring at all these random paintings by the so-called great masters. However, none of them compared to Crook One. His shit was visionary. It called to me the first time I saw it before I knew what this random art on the side of a building was even about. Being in the presence of greatness, even rushing by in partial darkness at fifteen miles an hour, inspired me, and I slid my black book out of my backpack with the reverence a holy man might take out his Bible.

I usually do a quick once-over of the people surrounding me.

Nobody can have a drink or some hand food if they're going to sit next to me while I'm working on my art. It's a standard rule, and I'll hop all over the train to find a suitable perch if I need to, but it was not necessary today. I didn't waste too much time after waking up, so the car was less than half full. The morning rush hour was still forty-five minutes away.

Reaching into my pocket, I felt the familiar shape of my two golden fat caps. These caps, used for canned spray paint, not only hastened the completion of my pieces but also added a touch of flair to my art by broadening the spray area. They were no ordinary tools; they were a gift from Lore, given to me with special significance years ago.

"Try to keep your days phat and your pieces phatter," Lore would often tell me. *It was on a rooftop where his life tragically ended* while he was tirelessly striving to create an impressive *phat piece* of art. It took me the whole year of 1995 to start feeling better. I didn't have many friends, so Lore meant everything to me. He wasn't ready to leave, that's for sure. For months, I would lie awake at night, reliving old memories and asking myself 'what if' repeatedly.

So, as I flipped to my most recent page, remembering what Lore told me, I imagined a *phat* piece for my black book. I'd started my own wild style, and I was pretty damn impressed with how it was going. The great maestro Lore One has inspired Talon One.

I am the Talon in the night. Digging the double meaning the name implied was another tribute to Lore—who you can theorize named themselves that because being an artist means learning the craft well enough to become a master and whose legend is passed along by word of mouth.

Creating the persona of Talon One allows people to interpret me as the name suggests. The Talon brings to mind the claw of a bird of prey, swooping down to leave its mark. But the talon has other meanings. The cards that were yet to be dealt were talons. I liked that vibe, like when people didn't know what was coming next, but were hooked on watching to see what you threw down. That's the style I was driving at. Talons were also like the grooves on a key to undo a lock. I was unlocking my inner self each time I lit up a surface with my designs.

I sketched the new ones in my black book; you couldn't waste paint and wall space just testing things out. When you went after a plot, it had to be quick and decisive; you had to want it, see it, breathe it, and throw it up as quickly as possible. That first noise you heard might be a rat sifting through the dumpster for some dinner, or a trigger-happy security guard rounding the corner. You couldn't create if there was fear eating you up. It wouldn't flow, and nobody would take you seriously. So, I traced each curve and angle with both the pleasure and the angst of producing another new masterpiece. Thoughts bounced off the walls of my brain: where to add the red, the blue, and the white to my magnificent Talon One piece. *For I am the Talon in the night.*

Time dissolved when I was creating. It was dizzying. The first time I got lost in a piece, forty-five minutes went by, and I realized I had ridden the train all the way to Lower Manhattan. By the time I noticed, I was surrounded by lawyers, stockbrokers, and bankers in their three-piece suits and suspenders. It didn't take a genius to decode the thoughts behind the looks they were giving me.

This time, I was under for a much shorter escape, and after tracing the exclamation point of the capital T of Talon One, I looked up, and boom, there she was, seeming to materialize out of nowhere. My Amayah, cute with her long dark chestnut hair pulled neatly and ever so elegantly in a bun. Time didn't slow down when I saw her, I didn't hear angels singing or playing harps in my head or anything like that, but things were always different when she stepped into view. My heart pounded a little harder, my breaths got a little shorter, and I noticed details about her that I completely ignored in the average, everyday person. She was wearing a chic sweater that hugged her body. But for all her sweetness, it was her footwear, howling into the summer air with street flair. Air Jordans. Because even in the heart of Knicks' territory, you couldn't help but worship the man and his brand. I pulled back from her footwear to her face, which startled me since she glanced in my direction. Those electric forest green eyes were moving across my face, looking at me, and I'd be damned if she wasn't smiling right at me.

I wanted to talk to her casually and let her see that I was interested in being more than friends, and decided that today, that want would become a need. So I gripped the metal pole, pulling myself up, not worrying for a minute if someone would swipe my seat before I returned. But I had a bad feeling bubbling within as I started to head her way. And you know, I had a big goofy grin on my face, the kind that would telegraph my intent to anyone else around us. Anyone with half a brain would know what was on my mind. But I didn't care. She was right there, smiling at me.

Walking through the half-empty car and trying to get to her seemed like an eternity. Taking my eyes off the path for just a moment was all it took. I tripped and missed a step, staggering along and hoping no one was the wiser.

Suddenly, a loud clunk shattered the train's tranquility as the end door slid open. Here was the trouble that the voice warned of. I almost forgot it when Amayah stepped into sight, but now I was silently cursing myself for not heeding the voice's warning more in earnest.

Stomping onto the dusty dirt-stricken floor, grunting, disheveled, and, of course, tossing cuss words around like they were the only things that mattered on Earth, were a trio of loud-mouthed young hooligans whose very auras were pulsing with hate. They moved swiftly through the car, with three more following behind. I knew immediately this wasn't going to be good.

"I'll fuck up any science nerd here, especially any fucking chink!" the one in front growled. He was about the same age as me, probably sixteen, dressed all in black, from cap tilted sideways to his black rundown Nikes. There were probably fifty more guys like him hanging out on every corner of his neighborhood, and I'm sure he thrived on that feeling of likeness and belonging. His mouth curved into an angry, mean-spirited scowl, with saliva dangling from his teeth, reminding me of a growling alpha wolf. You know that old saying he's got a face only a mother could love? It's amazing his mother didn't put a bag over his head to kiss him goodnight! But good looks didn't matter much when you were a predator on the hunt in your own territory.

This must be the leader of the pack. He was a loudmouth, kept his motor running nonstop, and, of course, kept spitting on the subway car floor as if to show his disdain for authority. His boys were carefully lined up in unison, following their dear leader, forming a chevron with him as the point, each bigger and uglier than the one before. My suave move over to Amayah seemed a million miles away now. I tensed up, wondering if the posse had seen me and how quickly I could escape before they gave chase.

One moment, I tried to keep it cool, but the next, I felt like I had jumped six inches into the air as soon as the voice spoke to me.

"You can take them," it whispered. *"You've got the power within you, Rohan. Show them who's in charge! Be the hero!"*

I felt like maybe the voice was the one having the aneurysm at this point because I definitely had no way to take these guys physically. There were too many of them, and I guessed they carried weapons in those baggy clothes. Unless they were going to confront me or threaten Amayah, I would give them a wide berth. I didn't dare speak aloud, so internally, I challenged the voice: *Who said that?*

"You know me," it replied, and I couldn't help but feel exasperated by the irony that, after all this time, it had finally decided to engage in a conversation in such a tense situation.

"I've been keeping you safe these past few weeks, haven't I? The bank robbers? The test? Your father's wrath? I know a thing or two about that!"

Was the voice saying it had a father somewhere? This was getting more and more confusing. "So, what are you saying, voice?" I felt really dumb calling it "voice," but it wasn't like we were best friends. "I should kick these guys' asses because I can hear a voice in my head?"

There was something that sounded like a low chuckle in my head. *"Just a voice, am I? I'm so much more than that, Rohan. I am here to teach you, to guide you, to imbibe you with powers the likes of which the world has never seen. All you have to do is accept me as your teacher, and we can begin!"*

An actual conversation. Holy shit, was my brain finally giving in, just like an eggshell breaking? I had heard whispers at random hours, but never like this. And here I was, in broad daylight, on a train filled with people. As freaked out as I was about what was happening inside my head, the situation on the train was about to get more dire.

Between Amayah and the thugs on board, I decided I didn't have time for what seemed like a certain mental breakdown waiting for me. I pretended I couldn't hear it, and just as quickly as the voice came, it dissolved into the unpleasant staleness of the car.

The thugs came closer in the car now, hovering over a kid two years my junior with all the classic trappings of a nerd begging for trouble. The glasses, the pocket protector, the violin case clutched across his chest. It was like watching a stereotype come to life. I thought about extending a warning, but before I had taken another step, the leader's palm was splatting the kid's face. His whole head spun left to right like he'd been sideswiped by a taxi cornering at fifty miles an hour. The junior nerd went down in a heap, his face conking against the train seat with a loud thud as the thugs gave out whoops of satisfaction. The leader was high-fiving his mates, and I felt my blood pumping faster again.

"TKO!" the leader bellowed, and his followers roared into laughter. A second thug, Dominican by the look of him, grabbed the victim and dragged him to his feet. I recognized him now, Roger, a couple of years younger than me, and a true genius if the school ever had one. He was captain of the Number Sense team, not that these clowns cared, and there was buzz that he might play violin with the New York Philharmonic during its annual holiday concert series. The big Dominican lifted him off the ground by the collar and knocked his glasses to the floor while a slippery looking Hispanic kid rifled through his pockets. When they had picked his belongings clean, the two threw him over a row of seats stained by three decades of dirt, grime, piss, and god knows what else. Roger now lay in a heap, not moving.

"FINISH HIM!" the leader yelled in a passingly good impersonation of Shao Kahn's voice from Mortal Kombat. His followers echoed in delight, and one or two took the bait and chimed in with taunts of "FATALITY!"

I was relieved they had found a target before they noticed me, then felt complete shame that I was relieved they were pulverizing an innocent kid. These fucking bastards. I wished that I could do something about it.

Be the hero for once, the voice chimed in again.

Looking down at my feet, all I could see was the same gum stuck to the same pockmarked floors of the Bitter Four that I had ridden every day for years. Wash, rinse, repeat. That was the story of my life. Wasn't it time I did something different? Wasn't it time I lived? As our train emerged above ground, the sunlight beamed through the dusty windows as if on cue, casting a warm glow.

Clenching my fist, I yelled, "Fuck you, guys! Don't you guys have better things to do?"

The leader smiled. "Look at this motherfucker!"

"Why don't you just leave us alone?"

My second challenge didn't seem nearly as bold and commanding as the first, and I felt myself rapidly losing confidence in my plan. The leader moved swiftly to close the gap between us, his lieutenants hot on his heels. He pushed his head closer to me so that he was right up in my face, trying to display his dominance. It might have been one against seven, and he might be about to kick the shit out of me in front of twenty people, but his authority as the big man had been questioned, however briefly, and that made him scared, angry, and dangerous. He had to re-establish it, quickly and decisively, or his street cred would vanish in an instant. As he got in my face, filling my nostrils with the smell of cheap booze and cheaper weed, he started kicking the seat next to mine. The echo rattled through the train, calling everyone's attention to our confrontation as he bellowed, "You're going to get it now, bitch!"

I held my hands out in front of me like a good man of peace would, and spoke as calmly and confidently as I could. "I don't want any trouble."

The leader grinned, and that grin told me everything I needed to know about him. He had been hoping and praying someone would interfere with the beating his boys were giving Roger.

Now the leader took out a knife. A big fucking knife. And seemingly everyone got up and scrambled away.

"No Trouble? Too late for that," he yelled with a sneer. I was so distracted by the knife in his left hand that I never saw his fist as he raised it, hitting my face and sending me flying into the side of the wall like a handball smashing against the concrete. I fell clumsily onto the seats, barely keeping my balance.

My head was pulsing, and I swear I saw blue stars. Staggering to my feet, I could see faces frozen, eyes wide, bewildered from the commotion. The conductor made some incoherent announcements over the speakers. Then someone grabbed my hand and pulled me out of the car as the train came to a stop. As the train doors quickly closed, I looked up, reading *Bedford Park Blvd Station* on the signs.

I was still dizzy on my feet, but as my vision cleared, I looked down, with no thugs in sight, and Amayah's beautiful face peered up at me with obvious worry in her sea-green eyes. Her tan skin felt warm and soft as I grasped her hands and held them tight. I probably didn't need her help anymore to stay upright, but it was too good of a feeling to throw it away. She had somehow slipped between the thugs' leader and me and gotten me moving in the right direction just as the train had slowed down at our spot. I stared again into those dark emerald eyes and didn't want to look elsewhere. I didn't want to let go of her hands but did so for fear of making her uncomfortable.

"You okay?" she asked, smiling.

"What do you mean?"

"I saw that guy punch you in the head pretty good."

I frowned with embarrassment. "I was going to kick his ass."

"Uh-huh," Amayah replied.

"You know," I said, "I know how to handle myself." I shook my head. "That mofo was gonna get a good beating."

"You weren't off to such a great start there, Van Damme," she offered in a teasing voice.

"I start slow, but finish strong," I chimed as Amayah started to chuckle.

I was terrified to do anything with her but make small talk most days. At least, the part of me that was hopelessly in love with her.

Talking to her now, I couldn't help but think about where we worked together at the Eckerd pharmacy on Kissena Boulevard in Flushing. You see, her auntie, Matilda, an assistant manager there, had gotten her the job. And my older brother Henry also worked there as a pharmacist. One big happy family, I guess. Most of the time, Amayah served as a store clerk, stocking shelves, but on rare occasions, as a beauty consultant in Cosmetics. I usually tried to take a breather from the pharmacy department when I saw her with the lotions and medicated wipes down the aisle.

Sometimes I'd muster up enough courage to talk to her, but normally I'd just smile, because I couldn't think of anything clever to say. She'd smile politely and nod back. That was the extent of it. In my mind, I always had a joke or something cool to say, and the conversation would flow. When it was actually "go time," I couldn't think of anything, so I'd just smile like a dork.

She tapped my shoulder to pull me out of my reverie. "Hey, dork! If you're done kicking ass, I've got a math test to study for, and I'm a little worried."

"You're going to do fine."

She looked surprised, probably startled I was actually talking back instead of smiling and nodding. "I hope so."

"You will," I continued, my confidence increasing just a tad. "Just practice what Mrs. Doddson taught you." I finally had alone time with her out of school, out of work, and I was ... talking about math?

We were walking now, side by side, and I wondered how it would feel to be her man. Probably like a scene from a movie, one where everything that happens around you seems to augment the feelings you have for that special someone.

As we neared Lehman College, I stared up at the college's large gray exterior. The sign advertised a popular summer costume dance in a few weeks. This would be a clutch time to ask her about it, but instead I blurted out, "You got the quadratic equation down?"

She sighed. "Not sure. I was practicing a few calculations last night." I thought that if I didn't ask her now, I may as well finish that thug's work and punch myself in the face. I was seriously blowing this opportunity.

Just ask her, you fool!

I was desperate for an icebreaker. I opened my mouth to find the words I needed to make the transition from friends to date for the dance.

"Ahem."

Amayah giggled. "Ahem, what, Rohan?"

"Ahm, I think a good way to solve a quadratic equation is by factoring the left side of the equation."

"Factoring?" she questioned.

"Maybe I can show you sometime before the test; we should go over it for sure." It was flimsy at best as my words came out, but it was at least perpetuating the conversation. I could still ask her to the dance if I could just get my head out of my ass for five seconds.

"For sure," she said, her tone still light and playful.

Fearing my window was rapidly closing, I just went for it. "That dance coming up, you know, seems kind of fun. I was thinking of going as Spiderman."

She stayed silent for a moment. The silence was intolerable. If she was going to let me down easy, I preferred she just came out and said it. She probably didn't like me. I had likely entered the Friend Zone a long time ago, and, as any guy who had the bad habit of being nice to girls he liked could tell you, it was pretty much impossible to escape the Friend Zone.

"Spiderman? That's not really your look, I think Mister Kickass sounds better," she said.

I did a double-take at that response. What was she talking about?

"Kickass?"

"Yeah, you said you were going to kick their asses if I didn't stop you." She was teasing me again. Did she not realize I was trying to ask her to the dance? Or was she just avoiding the issue?

I tried to be playful back. "I didn't say it like that."

"Uhhmm Hmmm," Amayah smiled. "Sure you didn't?" She grinned up at me again, and I smiled back.

The non-answer to the not-quite-invitation to the dance was still gnawing at me, but I didn't want to let it ruin the fact that I was walking Amayah to school. I would have worked for free for a month to get this opportunity. I couldn't squander it now. I enjoyed walking with her. I felt like I was protecting her because little me towered over her. Not a lot of Asian teenagers were over six feet tall, which made 6'1" me a real rarity. I liked the way she laughed and even her making fun of me. I couldn't help but notice her hair smelled like an island breeze from a distant tropical paradise.

I only wished I had asked her outright. That would have been the cool thing to do.

A shout came across the street, and I looked to see Steven Stone, the ever-so-confident and hands-down most popular guy waving to us as he crossed the road. I had no idea why he was waving to us. He literally never talked to me unless he wanted something like borrowing lunch money that he never returned or copying my homework before class started.

"Hey, Amayah," Steven chimed in, smiling easily, his eyes traveling up and down her body as he looked over the top of his sunglasses while biting his lower lip. "Hey, yo, Rohan, what up, homie?"

Steven Stone, even his name sounded cool.

"Hey Steven," Amayah gushed. "Oh my gosh, I love your sunglasses."

Jeez, she never smiled or got that excited talking to me. The two of them talked and laughed in easy conversation. And I became the definitive third wheel, walking silently as she giggled and Steven bragged.

It was hard to be too bitter. I mean, who wouldn't like Steven? He's a charming, tall, blond. A blue-eyed Adonis. The two of them started to stroll away ahead. They made a right and began bounding up the steps into our school. Turning slightly, she looked back at me, and all I could do was smile like a limp noodle.

"That's the best you can do?" the voice in my head spoke up. It was the first time I had ever heard it speak in a situation that wasn't a clear-cut warning. *"He's taking your girl away, Rohan, and you're smiling about it?"*

I didn't like this new line of questioning whatsoever. Your sixth sense was supposed to warn you against danger, not make you feel like a moron because you couldn't talk to a cute girl.

"You don't have to be the little man, Rohan. You don't have to be the one in the shadows. Step into the light. Let me show you the way. I know your innermost thoughts. I am a part of you! I can show you how to use your strengths and become the person you've always wanted to be. I can make you the hero, the star, the stud, all of it. Let me train you. Let me teach you."

I was so focused on the voice that I walked three doors past my classroom, and one of the pricks in the front row hollered out, "Rohan's so clueless he doesn't even know what class he's in!" and got a huge laugh. Trying to quiet down the voice again, I realized I might have lost my mind to a mysterious voice, but I still had a very known quantifiable math test to pass.

CHAPTER
TWO

In the world of mathematics, Mrs. Adams stood guard like a vigilant hawk, perched high on her mountaintop throne, ready to swoop in at any sign of deceit. As I scanned my test paper, the familiar sight of functions brought a sense of relief, a skill honed through practice. Failure was not an option in math—not with my father's expectations looming over me.

If x were even, the function would be x + 5. Since x was 2, the function equaled 7 — *simple*. Then came some integral questions involving finding the area under a curve — *a piece of cake*. Finally, a few problems required finding the slope of a derivative at specified points — *almost completed*.

I shifted my gaze towards Steven, who occupied the adjacent seat just three feet from mine. He seemed uneasy, with beads of sweat cascading down his furrowed brow. The perils of popularity seemed apparent; a whirlwind of social obligations left little room for dedicated work and academic studying. Maybe he constantly went out and partied; perhaps I was wrong, but I doubted it.

As I approached the final question, a hushed 'Pssst' from Steven caught my attention. It seemed he was in a desperate attempt to catch the attention of anyone who might want to climb the school's social ladder by letting Mr. Popular cheat off them. Despite his earlier interaction with Amayah, I guess I felt bad for him, so I pushed my test a little closer to his side, so he could see my answers. He had at least said hi to me earlier, and even though it was clear he was a lot more interested in Amayah than me, I thought maybe doing him a favor would give me an opening to hang out.

Even saying it in my head made me feel kind of pathetic, but every guy and girl in the whole school thought he was cool, and I was no different. I peered over my shoulder and saw Steven diligently copying my answers onto his test, a calm replacing his nervousness. Suddenly, I turned the other way and saw Mrs. Adams walking down our aisle, but luckily, Steven had already finished as I turned my gaze back to him. "Okay, class, time is up," she said. Everyone in the room scurried out the door as if their hair had caught on fire.

"Yo, Rohan," Steven yelled as he tried to catch up to me, running down the hall, "You the man, son!"

I felt his arm go around my neck, and he squeezed tightly.

"Why do you say that?" I questioned.

"Because you saved my ass. I would've failed for sure. Thanks for letting me copy you, bro."

"I guess," I replied, smiling.

"Yo Ro, Imma tell you what, man," Steven uttered, "You're coming bombing with the boys and me tomorrow night!"

"For real, Steven?" I tried not to seem too excited.

"Yeah, for sure, my man, Ro coming through. Meet up with us at the park. The whole crew will be there."

This was exciting, I thought, as I felt Lore's two golden fat caps that I always kept for luck in my pocket. Lore would be proud! I wish he could come, but his death still hurts after spending much of our young adolescence together.

The most popular kid in school invited me to hang out. Suddenly, I was going places. And it wasn't some lame party with a keg of cheap beer or watching sports all night on ESPN. We were going to throw up some epic pieces of art. Inside, I felt guilty for how happy I was to get invited to hang with the boys. Only two hours before, I had been cursing his name for the way he was talking to Amayah in a manner I could only dream of replicating. And now I was acting like he was my cool older brother inviting me to stay up late.

Sneaking out of my parents' house was probably the easiest crime in the world to commit. Why? Because my parents like to get up at 4 a.m., so they can open up the store they work at. It was their own business, AllChang Laundromat & Dry Cleaners, which they opened up a few years back by saving and always penny-pinching so they could call a shop their own. "It was revolutionary," my dad said, "because we do both professional laundry and dry cleaning. Not just one, but both! Revolutionary!" And they go to bed around 8 p.m. every night. Yep, most ten-year-olds stay up later than my mom and dad. But I can't complain, because it means I get the apartment to myself most nights for a few hours, and it's so damn tiny that you definitely need some chill time by yourself; otherwise, you'd go batshit crazy. My older brother works the late shift at the pharmacy and is usually gone when I get home from school, clocking in at 4 p.m. and getting off around midnight. He attends Queens College in the daytime to earn a Masters in Business so he can manage the dry cleaners, the restaurant, and the maid service that my parents want to open up when they've saved enough money.

One big happy family empire, everyone working twenty feet from each other at all times. I'm praying that they'll forget to include me in this little hellhole of an arrangement. The very last thing I want to do is be stuck in Fresh Ghetto for the rest of my life. So, I put my dinner dishes away, check my watch about the five-hundredth time since Steven gave the invite, and decide it's dark enough to get ready to go.

I gotta pick out my gear and my outfit first. The former is easier —I've got my spray cans hidden in the back of my closet, and they fit nicely in my school backpack. I'll use a few towels to keep them from rattling around against each other. There are a million young people on the street at any time of the day or night in Queens with backpacks on, going this way and that. Most cops and other busybodies won't look twice if you stroll by them with one on your back, but if it's making noises that sound precisely like two aerosol paint cans banging together, BAM, that's when you get the tap on the shoulder.

My outfit? Well, that's going to take a bit more planning. Considering it's the middle of the night, and we're going to be keeping to the shadows as much as possible, it shouldn't really matter what I wear, but obviously, if that was the case, this inner monologue wouldn't be happening.

I have two goals to accomplish here: blend in with Steven and whatever members of his crew are coming along tonight, but also avoid standing out in case we get spied on by the cops or somebody's grandmother or a business owner taking out the garbage. That might sound like a complicated task, but fortunately I don't have a whole lot of clothes; at least not any I'd be caught dead in. My parents occasionally tell me they are giving me a gift, and I keep hoping it's going to be a new stereo or tickets to a Yankees game, but instead it's always clothes. Not nice ones either. Clothes that scream, "I JUST GOT OFF THE BOAT, PLEASE ROB ME AND STAB ME." I have gone to great lengths not to wear those clothes anywhere there is even a remote possibility of seeing someone I know. This included getting burning hot oil on a pink-and-lavender shirt that my mom got me for the first day of school one year, and avoiding some brown corduroy pants by allowing a big dog to chase me through the bushes in the park until they became satisfactorily shredded like paper confetti. I guess I should feel bad about it, because my parents work really hard to make money, and most of it goes to savings, but hey, you want to give your son a present? Ask him what he likes!

After a few minutes of debate and trying out some different chill greetings when I meet the crew tonight, I've decided to go with the nod and the single-syllable "Sup" to let them know how mellow I am. I also have my outfit assembled. I'm going with my favorite incognito—throwback black-and-white Converse All-Star high tops, baggy black pants, a black T-shirt with no decoration on it, a bandana around my neck will come into effect when I find a place to make some epic art, and my worn but priceless Yankees ballcap will be turned backward, of course. Black is sort of the universal neutral selection; it means you're not really trying to make a statement or draw attention to yourself. There were plenty of gangs claiming plenty of colors roaming the streets at night, and wearing the wrong shade on the wrong block could get you in bad situations, especially late at night.

And the Yankees hat is the universal symbol of tolerance in the city. You see them everywhere you look after last October, when The Yankees won the 1996 World Series. Before last year, they won in the late 70s, and I wasn't even born yet. But since October, people have been going crazy. Everywhere you look you see Yankees gear—bumper stickers on cabs, signs on windows, people repping jerseys for Mariano Rivera, Bernie Williams, and Andy Pettitte.

Most of all, you see a city that is absolutely in love with the best of them all, a twenty-two-year-old rookie named Derek Jeter. Here's the craziest part. He's only like, six years older than me, and he is already one of the best players in all of baseball. One of my friends brought his little radio to school on opening day last year so we could listen to the game, and Jeter hit his first home run that day, the same day I made him my favorite player. He ended up winning Rookie of the Year, and racked up hit after hit in the playoffs and the World Series. I haven't been able to make a game yet, but that's one of my big dreams; getting to the stadium and sitting there watching Jeter play ball.

I check myself in the mirror three times before sliding nonchalantly out the door. A lot of people have alarms in this neighborhood, but my parents refuse to spend money on one. They are convinced that by being kind to their neighbors, they have nothing to fear from anything like a robbery. I only agree with that because we have absolutely nothing of value in our apartment. A tiny TV, no stereo, and crappy furniture from second-hand stores. I'm pretty convinced that if a criminal broke into our apartment, he'd see what we had, feel really bad for us, and leave us some cash to try and improve our situation.

STEVEN HAD SAID to meet up with him and his boys by the soccer fields at Kissena Park. That didn't really narrow it down much, because there were about ten different games going on at the same time under the bright lights. There were Dominicans, Mexicans, dudes from every country in Central and South America, and a smattering of white guys who were either too small for basketball or couldn't hit a baseball. Even crazier was how big the crowds were to watch these games. It was like every person that wasn't playing was there to root for their friends, sing songs, and turn it into a party atmosphere, even though it was just some random Tuesday. And it made me a little jealous that these cultures had so much passion for everyday things like soccer matches in the park. My parents would have looked at all these teenagers dribbling, tackling, and launching shots on goal and wondered why they weren't home memorizing the periodic table or working on their college application essays.

As I walked from field to field, trying to keep it casual, I couldn't hold back the panic already creeping down my spine. What if I had the time wrong or this was the wrong part of the park? What if they had decided to start without me, or maybe the whole thing was just a joke, and Steven was out telling his friends about the lame-ass kid he pranked today after copying off my test? Maybe he was out with Amayah, and they were both laughing at me ...

"YO, ROHAN! Where you been, bro?"

I snapped around. There, by the churros stand chatting up a very fine Latina, was Steven, waving and howling at me, "Ro-Ro-Rohan-nie!" I resisted sprinting to join him, forcing myself to take slow, deliberate steps and stroll casually up to exchange a short handshake and a "Sup" with him. Thus, began the strangest night of my life, utterly.

There were four of us in all. Steven had organized it, and he took point, telling us he had a few ideas of places in the neighborhood that were relatively tag-free and were far back off the street enough or already closed for the night that would make for a *phat* environment to create some burners. We were joined by two other guys I knew from school, but neither of whom I had taken for an artist. Sticking close to Steven and providing a nonstop commentary of every shop was Lior Strahelivitz, whose dad was a prominent Jewish doctor.

Theoretically, Lior should have been at a way fancier private school somewhere. But he had been expelled twice for running a highly profitable business of writing other students' essays and term papers for various forms of currency—cash, favors, dates with the choicer females, you name it. He was still running it at our school, but he had made some upgrades to keep from getting the rug pulled out from under him again. For starters, someone else had to vouch for you before he'd do business with you. Second, you had to show him some of your other work so he could use it as a reference and make some of the same mistakes you did to make it more believable. He didn't really fit the mold of a Graff artist, but that was one of the beautiful things about it. You never knew what kind of hidden talents people had.

In fact, the fourth member of the quartet was even more out of place. His name was Jarron Carter, and he was a six-foot-three-inch Black guy with a high-top fade and glasses that were all fogged up and not cleaned in years. He had come to the school a couple of years ago, and everyone assumed the school's basketball prayers had been answered, but Jarron refused to try out for the team. He would play alone for an hour before school every day, and the coaches would come out to watch him and cajole him with all sorts of promises of playing time and perks to join the squad, but he mainly ignored them. I had taken him for an idiot or a thug, at least until I saw his marks in Physics 110 and at mid-term. He shot the academic decathlon team down as well, and as far as I knew, he had zero friends at school; yet here he was, giving me the casual nod and bringing up the rear of our four-person posse as we strolled down 150th Street.

At one point, I had to take a piss, so we stopped at a 24-hour fast-food joint to use the facilities. They hate it when you do that, so the trick is to go to the counter and order something, then suddenly rush to the bathroom. They're still waiting for you to come back and pay when you suddenly leave through the side door, and then you don't get bitched at for using the facilities without buying.

When I said I had to go, Jarron offered to watch my stuff, and I hesitated for a long moment. He seemed like a cool guy, but there had been plenty of locker break-ins at our school, and Jarron always seemed to have a new watch or a new gold chain around his neck, even though he claimed to be poor as shit. I had a very specific vision right then of him rifling through my bag while I was taking a piss, finding my hidden stash of cash, going through my spiral, maybe even finding the secret drawing of Amayah I had been making that was strategically covered up right in the middle of the notebook so nobody stumbled across it. I wasn't sure what would be worse: losing my cash or someone seeing that secret drawing, but I wasn't down for finding out.

"No big deal," I said as casually as possible, keeping the backpack over my shoulder as I headed in. I took one glance back, and Jarron was staring lasers into my shoulders. I made it as quick as I could and got back to the guys. I started talking to Lior instead to ease my way back into our group's flow.

Steven stopped at a few places and slid off into the alleys as if looking for something specific, then came back and just shook his head, and we kept walking. We wound around 58th and ended up on Kissena Blvd., and I was starting to get a bit apprehensive. I figured Steven was so cool that we'd be dropping bombs on spots all night, swapping stories, busting guts with jokes, and basically doing everything that guys do when they hang out together. Instead, we were mainly walking in silence, save for Lior's running monologue and coming up empty at every spot we checked. Some were still open, some had been recently tagged by someone else—a definite no-no in the culture to bomb something that had fresh art on it, and the one that really looked promising, on the side of an abandoned Burger King, had a cop sitting in a squad car right across the street. I was so intent on looking cool and keeping the pace that it took me a few minutes to notice that the landmarks were getting all too familiar.

Suddenly, Steven came to a complete stop and said, "Yo guys, this is the place! Our spot, boys! Slide down the alley, and let's unpack our gear."

I felt my jaw drop, and I had to force my mouth closed. We stopped outside Eckerd Pharmacy on Kissena. The one that I worked at with Amayah. By the clock on the bank sign across the street, the store had been closed for about thirty minutes, and only the dim exterior lights were still on. The lights weren't the problem. The night manager was. He was diligent, responsible, and he hated young punks loitering around his store looking to get into mischief. I knew all this because he was also my brother Henry.

In hindsight, I suppose I could have suggested that it was a bad idea or that I was getting a bad vibe, but I was too afraid that balking on Steven's choice would be a death warrant for my brief time being one of the cool kids. My palms got clammy, and I was pretty sure some time in the near future I was going to be throwing up, but for now, I just walked with the other guys down into the depths of the alley and put my bag down, pulling out a couple of cans to work with.

Before I moved to find a spot, I slid my bandana up, so it covered everything but my eyes. This had a double advantage to it. First, it keeps you from straight inhaling paint fumes again and again. You see, I knew plenty of kids who got off that high, but I wasn't a dope head, and if I were too busy buzzing on the fumes, it would ruin my creativity.

The second, far more important reason was that it made it really difficult for anyone to identify you if you did get caught tagging. Here's the deal: cops hate kids who do graffiti for one simple reason—we can run fast. From what I've heard around school and my neighborhood, most cops don't really care if you're out there tagging buildings because if you're doing that, it means you're not out there buying drugs, selling drugs, using drugs, or doing some insane gang initiation stunt like setting a bum on fire or robbing a liquor store. But cops get their salaries paid by the public, and the public elects officials to do what they want. Most business owners don't like their buildings getting marked up, and the old-timers think we're all just a bunch of juvenile delinquents who need a few weeks in jail or a good kick in the ass to stop our terrible habits.

Unfortunately last summer, Mayor Giuliani decided to agree with them to get re-elected, so he gave a big public speech and signed the Anti-Graffiti Task Force Executive Order, which basically put the goon squad on high alert to come after taggers hard and heavy. Then he pissed off every single one of them by saying, "Remember, graffiti is not art. It's an assault on our communities and our quality of life, period."

Well, ho-lee shit. He must have known what kind of effect that was going to have on Graff artists, but he just didn't care. It's not like that community was a bunch of rule-followers to begin with, and by dissing them so harshly and publicly, the mayor had opened up a Pandora's box. And now he might have had fourteen different agencies part of this monumental effort to stop graffiti—terrible move. It escalated the next day with artists hitting landmarks all over the city and newcomers trying to earn their stripes. Cops were made to patrol the streets and catch offenders in the act, which meant rolling down their car windows, flashing a spotlight on anyone suspicious, and yelling, "HEY YOU!"

The dumb ones without a bandana would turn around and stare right into the spotlight, and the cops would get a fantastic look at their faces, which made it really easy to spot them a few days later when their guard was down.

The smart ones, like me, had the bandana up, so all you could see was my eyes. That meant that even if you turned into the spotlight, all a cop could see was your bandana, your eyes, and your cap. And the number of Asian kids wearing Yankee hats at any given time in New York City, you guessed it, must have been staggering.

The other guys were already starting their creations, so I tried to play catch-up and get into a solid frame of mind. I had been working on my setup for a while now and had come to a pretty good understanding. It was nothing spectacular, but I liked the simplicity of it. It was a black bandana with a smiley face on it. I'd be tweaking it in my notebook for weeks, trying to develop a design that meshed with me and my heritage without being too over the top.

As I was considering it, I glanced over at Jarron, who was double-fisting black and yellow cans, sending sprays bursting forward in dazzling patterns. With his massive height and long arms, he looked like a massive spider looming in the darkness, building its web. I watched his technique for a moment, turned to the wall to see the result, then did a double-take at what I was seeing. It wasn't possible, was it?

"Oh my God, Jarron! Are you Steel Curtain???"

All City Steel Curtain was one of the most elite street artists in the entire Five Boroughs. He was always defying the authorities and dropping his black-and-yellow markings in crazy places that you just had to see to believe. About four months earlier, his tag had appeared between two of the arches on the second story of Flushing Town Hall. It was discovered the next morning, right before a wedding of two Richie-Riches. The father of the bride had been outright furious. It had drawn enough attention to appear on the 6 o'clock news. For weeks, my friends and I had talked about "pulling a Curtain" and where we'd like to drop a burner on some famous landmark that would be conspicuous enough to attract the TV cameras, just like Steel Curtain.

Jarron gave me a sideways glance as if he thought I was crazy. "Yeah, dog, what you think I'm doing out here anyways? Now shut it down, I can't concentrate when someone's running their mouth."

Talk about feeling like a dumbass. Here I thought Jarron might be a petty thief when he was really one of the freshest artists in the entire city. I felt more than a little ashamed of how convinced I'd been that he'd be rifling through my backpack the minute my back was turned. It was well known on the streets that talented artists like Steel Curtain would take commissions from neighborhoods, businesses, even gangs, to ink up a wall, a building, or something else to give the place some culture and attention. Jarron had new chains and cool threads because he was getting paid to do the thing that we both loved. I thought about apologizing, thought better of it, and froze.

Then, I was sure I had heard a door open, and I got dead quiet, as did the other guys, convinced the jig was up. Thank God for the good hearing of the young, because it likely saved Lior a trip to the emergency room. I heard footsteps tapping pitter-patter, creeping around the corner, then a loud echoing "PING" immediately followed. I saw an aluminum baseball bat swinging right into where Lior's head had been seconds earlier.

The guys panicked, running in ten different directions, zigzagging, stopping only to toss their backpacks over their shoulders as they scattered. I turned and tripped, going down in a tangle of legs and cans, but got up in a quick motion and sprinted towards my backpack with the store personnel, who I now recognized as my brother in hot pursuit.

I panicked when I realized that grabbing my backpack was going to lead me to a dead-end, but I'd invested too much money into my supplies to just toss it all away. I snatched it and raced towards the end of the alley, hoping for an open gate or a low fence, but what I got was an eight-foot-tall chain link number with barbed wire all the way across the top. I turned back around and used my only play, walking slowly towards my brother with outstretched arms, then ducking under his grasp and racing across the street. I broke south on Kissena, and nearly collided with Lior, who was racing the other way.

It only took me half a second to see why—a black-and-white squad car was in pursuit with its sirens blaring and lights flashing. Lior spun off me and kept sprinting for all he was worth, and I lost momentum again and headed across the street and into the adjacent alley as I heard at least one cop get out and take off after me. "Freeze, you punk!" the officer yelled. "Or, I'll—"

I was running hard, but I was already starting to suck wind. I wasn't exactly the most in-shape kid. Most people saw that I was tall and skinny and figured I was at least a passable athlete, but it simply wasn't true. I was starting to panic inside, knowing that as dumb and slow as the cops were, they still knew this part of the neighborhood way better than me. One mistake and I was going to be in the back of a squad car, and I'd never be let out of the house again.

The alley broke off, and I took a hard right, crashing into a brick wall and skinning my elbow in the process. I cried out in pain and anger and suddenly the voice was back in my brain, louder and more aggressive than I had ever heard it before. "*Grasp your power, Rohan! Seize it! Reach inside and find the gift I have provided you with. Deep down in your gut is where it lies. Feel the power! Become the power! Use it and become my ally!*"

I was desperate for escape, and I reached deep within myself and there it was, just as the voice had said—power—a massive reserve of energy. It gave me the sensation of holding one of those glowing balls from *The Sharper Image* that shoots out static electricity. When you put your fingers on the edges, the power flows through without hurting you, and you feel like you've got all the power in the world. It had been a super popular gift at birthday parties when I was younger, even though you quickly realized they didn't actually do anything but look cool. This was something completely different, though. I struggled to comprehend how I had never felt this power inside of me before. Had I not been looking for it, or had I merely not wanted to believe that the voice was a real thing?

If I got out of this fiasco alive, I was going to have to take some time to get to know this voice a lot better. The power felt like it was going to explode out of my chest if I didn't do something with it. I felt myself tapping into it, and suddenly I was no longer running; I was practically flying. It felt like I was watching a movie where the origin story kicks in, and they're off to the races. My legs were churning forward like the rims of a motorcycle. I raced ahead so quickly that it felt like my All-Stars were barely contacting the asphalt. My vision blurred to look like one of those videos they show you where they've obviously sped up the film.

I veered around another corner and just about plowed into a second squad car. Except, this one didn't have its lights or its sirens on and appeared to just be parked there while the cop inside scarfed down an order of french fries. He looked up in surprise and shook his head at me through the halfway rolled down window, then went back to his feast. I thought I had lucked out until his radio crackled, and the voice on the other end was going on about a young punk in a backward Yankees hat and a bandana wanted for questioning in a possible vandalism case. He looked at the radio, looked at me, and started to yell "STOP!" through his mouth, filled with french fries.

I rushed back down the alley for its cover of darkness, but instantly recognized my mistake as I saw the other cops' flashlights on the walls ahead as they ran towards me.

Having slowed down now, I felt the panic creeping slowly up my spine, making me feel like it might be time to just get on my knees and link my fingers behind my head. Truly desperate, I reached back down to that interior energy reserve and opened the throttle all the way up. Things got dizzy so quickly that I felt like my feet were literally off the ground. I lost my balance and crashed to a halt, my senses stretching out in all directions, trying to figure out what the hell had happened and how in the world the alley had completely disappeared.

CHAPTER

THREE

I started to shake, either out of fear or out of confusion, or maybe both. This wasn't the alley. It wasn't even Kissena Blvd. For one thing, it was way too bright. Queens wasn't exactly the countryside, but they usually turned off or dimmed most night lights to preserve some atmosphere and protect nature. New York City might have been the city that never sleeps, but people still wanted a decent bedtime in Queens.

For another thing, it smelled terrible. Queens was no flower garden to be sure, but the stench funneling into my nose was nothing short of straight smelly, shitty garbage. As my vision refocused, I looked to my left and jumped in surprise. The United Nations building loomed just across a dark stretch of murky water, as austere and grand as it looked every year on our annual field trip to see it. Except that was impossible. Because the UN building was on the east side of Manhattan, separated from the rest of the boroughs by the East River. Craning my neck, I started to get a very unpleasant sensation of being in a dream that was no longer fun and which I could not wake up from. Looming right behind me, far above my head was the unmistakable shape of the Queensboro Bridge. Ten seconds ago, I had been in the heart of Queens on Kissena Blvd outside my brother's Eckerd Pharmacy. Whatever the hell I had just tapped into sent me at least ten miles west of my stomping ground. At that time of night, in my current physical condition or lack thereof, it would have taken me until the next morning to walk this far. Something really fucking weird was happening to me. I was scared of what it meant, but I couldn't help but feel a little exhilarated too.

I was in a green space, some park along the waterfront. It appeared peaceful and deserted; pretty much what you'd expect for that time of night. Before I could even consider the scientific implications of what had just happened, a hideous scream came up from the south, breaking the silence, sending a jolt of adrenaline through me. I wasn't a coward by nature, but I didn't know what could make that kind of noise, and wasn't sure I wanted to find out.

The voice was back, quickly whispering, *"Go see what it is. You are powerful, Rohan. No one can stop you, even if they try. You are the power now. Believe in it. Let me show you how."*

I wasn't 100% sold on the voice or the power, but I did agree that I didn't need to be afraid. The way I could run now, and seemingly teleport, would let me escape any sort of scary situation the night could throw at me. I wasn't going to run there as swiftly as I could, because that seemed really foolish. I had no idea what I was headed for, so I started moving steadily in that direction, not really confident of what the heck I was going to do when I reached the person making it or the person causing it. About a thousand feet up, I saw a sign for the subway, and the final piece of the puzzle fell into place on my sudden change of location. The sign read: ROOSEVELT ISLAND SUBWAY STATION

"Holy shit!" I yelled out loud in spite of myself. The UN building looked so close because I was practically next door on Roosevelt Island. I'd never come here before, only gone over it in my uncle's car or on the school bus for a field trip. I walked around the side of the entrance to the terminal, and that's when I saw, no, it couldn't be! A body.

It was a woman. No, she was younger, maybe my age or a bit younger. I really couldn't guess, but there was no doubt she was dead. A river of blood engulfed her neck, her head twisted at a weird angle no human could make. Suddenly, my mind flashed back to a tiny snippet of news I had seen the day before, of the worry around the boroughs that there might be a new Son of Sam on the loose. Three women had been found in a three-week period, all brutally murdered with slashes to their necks. It seemed painfully obvious I had just found victim #4. I needed to notify the cops and the authorities, but all I could do was turn and vomit into the trash can nearby and wondered if the cops could ID the vomit if they found it and traced it back to me. I tried my best to keep myself together but failed miserably.

I tried to look south of her neck to see if there were any details. She was definitely young; you could tell by her clothes and the multiple bracelets and rings on her fingers. It made me feel sick she had died like this. Despite my aversion to the scene, I kept inching closer to where she lay on the ground.

"Closer," the voice whispered in my ear as I took another step towards what remained of her head. *"Closer still, see it, Rohan, see it clearly with your mind. The strong prey on the weak. Never be weak. If you don't embrace your powers, this will be you one day. Don't let that happen. Become the power. Let me be your teacher. If you fail to find the path, you will leave yourself open to this sort of fate. You, and everyone you know and love."*

I thought that under different circumstances, the girl could have been Amayah, and it made me shiver. *What kind of monster would do this?* I thought. The idea of the monster made me look around. Was it possible the person who did this was still here? Could he be watching me even now, lurking in the bushes or on the rocks down by the shore? I touched my power source again, feeling a bit more confident.

"That's it!" the voice said louder. *"You have no equal when you fully embrace your power. Find this monster, and crush him under your thumb, Rohan. Be the hero. They'll all worship you! You can have the things you dream about; they are your destiny. You deserve them. Don't you ever wonder why you long for a life beyond the simple ways of your parents and brother? Because you are different. You were Chosen. I have been guiding you to understand that. To understand yourself. You must take what should be yours and shape this world as you wish it to be!"*

His words didn't just sound good. They sounded right. I always felt like I was destined for something better than my tiny little room in our tiny little apartment. It felt, well, it felt beneath me, to be honest. I didn't want to work my ass off for twelve hours a day to barely pay my bills and have enough money left over to put fifty dollars in a savings account every month. I thought about the guys I envied most at school, guys like Steven Stone. If he wanted a girl's attention, he got it. If he wanted to take her out, he told her they were going out, and she said okay. It was like that all over as far as I could tell. If you were good-looking, girls acted like you were the funniest, smartest guy around. If you were rich, you could get away with anything. Same thing was true for power. Our president, Bill Clinton, seemed to get away with all kinds of shenanigans, mainly because he was the Commander-in-Chief. The most well-known businessman in New York, Donald Trump, had an ego the size of the Statue of Liberty, but people liked him because he was brash and said what he felt all the time. Because he was super rich, he could get away with it. Why them and not me? If I truly did have the kind of powers that suddenly seemed possible, why couldn't I just make the reality I wanted?

"It's the only way to get what you truly want in this world. They pretend that peace is the way. There is no peace. There never can be peace. The only life worth living is the one you take for yourself. It is only human to obey nature and do what comes naturally. Once you accept that, Rohan, you, and I can do wonderful things together..."

I was more than a little freaked out at how he seemed to be

reading my every thought, but before I could try and reason it out, I heard noises and saw movement in the mid-range distance. Other people heard the scream, and they were on their way here to check it out. That wasn't good news for me. I had no ID on me, no alibi of how I came to be here, and I wasn't about to tell total strangers that I had just ... what would I call it, teleported? Was that the phrase I was going to settle on? That I couldn't have committed the murder because two minutes ago I was about twelve miles east of here in Queens? That kind of straight-out craziness might not get me convicted of murder, but I'd definitely be inside the looney bin for a decade or two. I couldn't stay here and hiding seemed like a bad idea. The cops would arrive soon and be scouring the entire park, if not the whole island, for clues, and I had no logical explanation of how I got here.

I knew the only way off this island was the same way I got here, even if I had no idea how that power worked. Retracing my thoughts from seconds before I got here, I ramped up my mind with the desire to be back where I came from after wishing myself "away" from where I had been. The dizziness welled up inside of me again, and my vision narrowed to a shakiness that was really unpleasant. I felt the urge to vomit and bent over with my head between my knees to hold the puke down. I held that pose for a long time, squatting on my haunches, eyes squeezed shut, willing the vomit to stay down.

When I finally felt like I had controlled the urge to puke, I cautiously opened my eyes and took in the view around me. Unreal... I was back at Kissena Park, right by the soccer fields where I met the guys earlier. The park was deserted now, with the lights off, with only the moon illuminating my surroundings. I tried to remind myself to *stay calm, breathe in, breathe out, that's right,* long, slow, deep breaths. I was back pretty close to home, away from the island, the body, and seemingly out of trouble. If I could just hold it together, I could put my hat on forwards, lower my bandana, maybe roll up my sleeves, and take my time getting home without attracting any unwanted attention. Other than knowing it had some connection with the voice, I had no idea what was happening to me. The only thing I wanted right now was to get home to my bed, get under the covers, lock the door, and let my subconscious try to make sense of it all.

"Yo, how the hell did you do that?"

While I knew that my speed was somehow augmented, it also felt like my leaping ability had been too. Because the voice that suddenly materialized spooked the shit out of me, making me leap about ten feet in the air.

I landed awkwardly, spun around, and found Steven sitting calmly on the bleachers of the soccer field, eying me with something that looked like a blend of bemusement and utter disbelief. He looked over his shoulder and then back at me as I squinted into the darkness. It looked like someone else was there and headed off into the shadows. Had Steven been talking to him just now? It didn't really matter; I had to spin a story quickly to try to make sense of what the heck was happening to me.

"Oh my god, Steven! You scared the crap out of me!" I let out a laugh of relief. "I did not know you were back there, man!" I took a step forward to slap him a high five, but he didn't move to greet me.

"I asked you a question, Ro. How the hell did you do that? I've been sitting here for forty-five minutes waiting for anyone else to show up. Got my perfect seat here where I can see all four directions long distance in case any of the cops get cute. Had my lookout stance all set up right here. One second, I'm here alone, and the next, you materialize out of thin air. How the hell did you do that?"

Steven was the coolest kid at school and possibly the best looking, not that I paid much attention to other guys' looks. And he was seldom without a pretty girl to talk to, and always had an air of extreme confidence or a sardonic half-smile on his face. But right now, he had none of those things going for him. The only thing on his face right now was fear.

If this were a comic book, I probably would have said something noble about how great power came with even greater responsibilities and made him take some sacred oath to make him part of our secret forged destiny. But this was real life, and I was already freaked out as it was.

So instead, I simply blurted out. "There's been some kind of crazy voice talking in my mind the last month or so. I don't know what it is or what it wants, but it keeps telling me that I have some sort of power inside of me that no one else possesses. Tonight, when I was running from the cops, I was desperate to get away, and I reached down and tapped some sort of source inside me that let me run faster than Bo Jackson. I almost ran right back into the cops, so I tried to tap deeper into it to go even faster, and it ended up teleporting me onto Roosevelt Island.

"Like, fifteen seconds after I got there, I heard a woman screaming, and I'm pretty sure it was that weird guy they've been talking about on the news, the one who has been slashing women's throats. I saw a dead body, but then I heard people coming, and I freaked out and teleported back here. That's what you saw just now. I've got some kind of power that's letting me leap instantly from one place to the next...and I guess that's it."

I ran out of words and breath all at once, struggling to make eye contact with Steven because as I was racing through the story, I thought how idiotic it sounded and how he must think I was the biggest psychopath alive, just about now. So, I just closed my eyes for a bit, allowing the dead silence to take over and not knowing what to do or even say.

As I opened my eyes, he was looking at me, not with fear, but with something else, opportunity, maybe? Finally, after a long pause, he put his arms behind his head and gave a long, slow stretch. "So," he said, almost casually. "What do you think we should do about the dead girl?"

We hatched a plan that one of us would disguise our voice and call the cops anonymously from a pay phone near our homes about stumbling upon a body on Roosevelt Island and for them to check it out.

"But Ro, you can also run fast and have some form of instant transportation; what else can you do?"

I was shocked by how well Steven took it all as we walked home together. If anything, he seemed more interested in the limit of my powers rather than freaked out by the obvious questions like, "What the hell is happening?" "Where is the girl's killer?" and "Why is there a voice living inside me that only I can hear?"

We were both pretty shaken up about the murder, at least I was, and we agreed again that no matter how this night concluded, we would inform the authorities anonymously as soon as we neared home.

We took a different way home to avoid Kissena Blvd and any main streets, cutting corners from block to block and keeping an eye out. He told me how he, Lior, and Jarron had gotten separated, and he hadn't heard from either one of them since. He reasoned they would both be fine, even if the cops had gotten the drop on them. Lior's family was wealthy, which meant he wouldn't stay in police custody for long, and Jarron had family that lived pretty close to where the bombing had gone haywire. He had probably lit out at their house until things died down.

"You were the one who had me worried, Ro," Steven said with a shaky smile, like he wasn't quite sure what to make of me. "When I saw you crash into that night-shift loser, I figured you were done for. Of course, I didn't know you had this Flash speed and Nightcrawler magic power working for you back then."

I chuckled at the comparison to the superheroes, had it been just a day earlier, Amayah was mocking my comparison to Spiderman?

Feeling confident and even a little cocky, I told him, "That wasn't even the half of it. That guy who came out swinging at us? That was my older brother, Henry. He's the pharmacist there and closes it down four nights a week."

Steven looked like he thought I was pranking him, then doubled over with laughter, scaring the one or two bums huddling around a fire in a barrel for warmth. He looked me up and down with what appeared to be newfound respect. "Yoooo, Ro!" he exclaimed, now wanting the high-five he denied me earlier in the park. "That is some next level, low-down, badass truth, man! I can't believe you took that gamble, yo! Why didn't you just pull us off and find somewhere else to get creative?"

I smiled and acted as if I was struggling for words, even though I had given the answer to this "interview" about eighty times in front of the mirror, dreaming of the day I was the world's most famous graffiti artist, and places like 60 Minutes and Time Magazine would be paying just for me to sit down for a thirty-minute interview.

"I mean, yeah, I see why some people might be scared to do that where their family works, but that's not how I see it. When Giuliani started throwing this damn task force at us, it's like he's slapping us in the face and saying he'd rather have us selling drugs or killing each other than putting up the art. What kind of stupid message is that to send? So, we all start hitting back, putting our tags in more high-visibility spots to let them know that they can't silence us, no matter how many cops they put on this so-called task force to slow us down. Yeah, I could have given the 4-1-1 that Eckerd's was where my brother and I work, but yo, that's the whole point of doing art for me, not conforming! After I'm done with college, I can either go into the family business and watch my life drift away, or follow Henry to Eckerd's five times a week and lose the will to live altogether.

"So, I go with what's behind door number three, man. I say no to what they want, no to what the city wants, and I do what makes sense for me. When I'm creating up on Eckerd's with my crew, I'm letting them know that you don't own me, you can't own me, and this is who I am."

I had improvised a little bit and gone off-script, but with my new-found confidence that I was pulling from the voice in my head and that raw energy pulsing through me, it didn't just feel good, it felt right. But I was still troubled about the murdered girl and if the cops had found her yet.

Steven probably didn't sense my worries and only nodded and

said, "Amen, brother. Damn, I had no idea you were this legit. I always figured you were a little bit of a nerd gone to the boring side of the Force, always studying, hanging around that little geek Amayah, and so forth. I was damn wrong though. We got to start hanging out more, bro, and I want to see what else you can do. We got to test you and see what you can do, baby!"

Steven suggested we should have our own little secret hand-shake. So I started following his motions as our hands clasped together, came apart, came back together again in a clasp, then quickly released before kissing our fists and ending with a faint shake and pointing it all in the air. *How cool, our own secret thing,* I thought.

"Hey Steven, I want you to have this, one of my good luck charms," I threw him one of the golden fat caps that Lore gave me. "So that we can keep keepin' it phat."

"And all that," Steven replied, completing my sentence as he laughed, with his pink lips curving at the corners while his face radiated only warm vibes. "Thanks, son; this will come in handy when I do my Graff and create some epic burners. I call you son because you shine like one." With a pause, he held my gaze with his eyes, reassuring my gut that I had found a true friend.

"And hey Ro, your boy, Stee-volt, hasn't eaten for a few days," Steven sniffled between words, his mouth curving down as if he was about to fake-cry, exaggeratedly dropping his head. "Lend me a Grant, a fifty spot, cuz you know, kings like us need to eat well, and you know I got you, son."

I worked hard and had the money, and I also wanted to help my new best friend, so I did.

And having the coolest kid in school fawn over me was amazing that I didn't even register his slight about Amayah.

I showed off my new-found speed for him a few times on the rest of the way to his apartment building, and tried a few other skills out along the way. No matter how hard I concentrated, we were pretty sure I couldn't fly, but my muscle strength had gone way beyond anything either one of us had ever seen. When the coast was totally clear, I ripped a parking meter out of the ground, bent the pole into a perfect 'U' shape, then cracked the canister open, and the two of us split up all the change that came bouncing out of it. For the briefest of moments, I considered how what I was doing was breaking the law, but I saw the admiration in Steven's eyes, so I blew it off. On a whim, once it was emptied, I took the twisted metal shape and heaved it, discus style, as far as I could down the center of the street. It left a pothole the size of a small horse where it landed, and Steven did the honors of counting out the steps from point A to point B. Near as we could figure, I had thrown it one hundred and sixty-three feet. And I hadn't even broken a sweat.

Finally, arriving at Steven's apartment building, we exchanged our secret handshake. "And don't worry about the girl, Ro. I'll call the cops in my best Hugh Downs voice and inform them to go check Roosevelt Island out."

He also made me promise to hang out after school the next day to keep seeing what I could do and figure out how to use my new powers ... abilities ... talents; we hadn't decided what to call them yet and to drop some major Graff burners around the boroughs as soon as possible. It felt amazing.

The most popular guy in school was talking to me as if I was a rock star, and asking me to hang out with him. It was the kind of attention I had been craving for my whole life. Steven's social life intersected with every group at school—the athletes, the druggies, the rich kids who drove Corvettes to campus and wore gold jewelry. Hell, Steven had dated more hot girls in the past year than I had talked to in my entire life! Once I got in good with him and his crowd of people, Amayah would be begging to be my girlfriend; or maybe I could date whoever I wanted to, even two or three girls at once, like some of the other guys who were rich and good-looking. As I basked in the glow of Steven's new-found admiration for me, all worries about the murdered girl and the voice seemed to disappear. What the voice had said about doing wondrous things together was starting to sound like maybe it was a real thing. Whatever this voice was, it was changing my life.

"You told him too much." The voice was suddenly there again now that I was alone. *"Be careful who you let know the secret of your powers, for there will always be those who covet what you possess and seek to take it from you."*

"I mean, what was I supposed to do, make up some other reason that I appeared out of thin air?" I felt a little annoyed. I didn't plan on teleporting in front of someone else. "And why can't I tell anyone? The stuff I already know could help the whole world. I could start fighting crime, or be like a super soldier for the government or help the Yankees win the World Series again!"

"You're just scratching the surface of what you can do, Rohan. You have to trust me to teach you to use these powers the way they were meant to be used. When you achieve control, total control, you'll be invincible."

"Okay, well if you're going to teach me, I'm going to need to know what to call you. Saying 'the voice' is getting old."

"I've been known by many names by many people over the span of my life," it said. *"Some names in languages that no longer exist. But we'll use a simple one, my student. You can call me Nick. Nick the Brute."*

Well, that was a weird name if I'd ever heard one, but Nick was simple enough. It was good to connect the name with the voice. It made me feel slightly less insane about talking to a voice inside my head that would teach me how to use my new mysterious powers.

I suddenly felt guilty about the dead woman I had seen. I tried to tell myself it was just a lousy coincidence that had nothing to do with me. I had no idea how I had jumped to where I had landed. I certainly wasn't a serial killer and had no idea what to make of that whole situation anyway. That was a problem for the cops; I was just a kid. Or was I? Because the things I had done tonight were not something that any other teenager was capable of. The speed, the teleportation, the strength—those were all things that should be impossible outside of the pages of a comic book.

The fact that I suddenly had them at the exact same time that some psycho was roaming the streets of New York City, killing innocent women, might not have been a coincidence after all. It reminded me of something I had read once layered into some really sick art on the side of an abandoned Kmart. It was a picture of the sun and moon both rising over the earth at the same time, with the words, "Darkness rises, and light to meet it." I always thought that could have been an amazing tagline for a movie or something. It made me think of the kind of epic battles between the forces of good and evil you read about in the Bible.

It was getting dangerously close to the time when my parents would get up for work, so I reached back down one more time for that pure energy and sprinted back home. Steven's building was about twenty-four blocks away from mine. And I made it home in all of fifteen seconds.

I slipped back through the front door without making a sound and saw my brother sleeping out on the couch, too tired to even change out of his Eckerd's pharmacy uniform. He looked tiny and very non-threatening, a far cry from the angry form swinging the baseball bat with reckless abandon just a few hours earlier. If I wanted to, I could pick him up right now and throw him across the street before he even knew what hit him. It was an odd feeling to contemplate, and I suddenly wondered why I would even consider doing such a thing to a member of my own family. Chalking it up to overstimulation from the wildest night of my life, I slipped into the tiny space I called my bedroom, got under the covers, and fell quickly to sleep, trying to forget the night's trying worries, free-falling to a new reality where dreams rule.

As I was drifting off, I couldn't help but feel like that damn raspy voice was back in the back of my subconscious, whispering again and again. *"Only the beginning ... only the beginning."*

<h1 style="text-align:center">CHAPTER
FOUR</h1>

The alarm woke me up abruptly. Although, to be fair, after the night I had, if it had rung at noon, it still would have been too early. I felt achy all over, and my mind was like a dull buzz. Using your powers all night long to show off made you feel like you'd been run over by a truck and taken a sledgehammer to the forehead the next morning.

Thankfully, the alarm clock woke me up with soothing music from the radio instead of a jarring noise. If it had been the latter, even with my abilities at an all-time low, I might have shattered it into a million pieces. I unconsciously reached out to switch it off, then realized it was on the other side of the bed and had to readjust my movements to silence the radio. As I found the power button, the last words of optimism from the local DJ blared in my ear, "Rise and shine! It's time to embrace the day with yours truly, Big Flex!"

As I slowly sat up, trying to gauge my headache's seriousness, I replayed the radio announcement in my mind. Big Flex? Hadn't that guy got busted for having a sex party in the studio after hours a few months back? The nickname "Big Sex" was the most popular joke at school until a kid got stuck in a locker for 3 hours, and then everyone started making fun of him instead.

Rising from bed awkwardly, eyes shut, I leaned against the bedroom wall, taking a moment to discern the faint scent in the air and the strange flavor on my tongue. Neither experience was pleasant, and both were undeniably associated with... you guessed it, marijuana. I have never used such substances, let alone allowed them near my apartment, knowing full well the consequences from my father. Could it be that I consumed one of those infamous pot brownies everyone talks about? Or did a kind soul slip some into my pocket unnoticed?

I slowly tried to open my eyes, the persistent ache in my head a cruel reminder of last night's events. Despite my reluctance, I knew I had to prepare for damage control before my parents returned home. The silver lining in this tumultuous situation was that my mom and dad probably would unlikely set foot in this room, only because it was nothing like my own. It was too spacious, the colors were all wrong, and the cacophony of street noise was a far cry from the quiet neighborhood I was used to.

I felt completely bewildered and disoriented as if I had been transported into a surreal dream or was experiencing some inexplicable craziness. I wondered if I had unknowingly dozed off at Steven's place. Despite my overwhelming exhaustion, I vividly remembered tiptoeing back upstairs and settling into my cozy bed, eager to evade any notice from my parents.

But this wasn't home. For starters, there were clothes everywhere, and I didn't think I had owned this many clothes in my whole life combined, much less in my current life. For another, there were way more video game cartridges than books, and if you'd ever been in my room, you'd realize that I had been given a very detailed account of which was the most important thing ever and which was a big waste of time. As I continued to scan the room, I found myself taken aback. Right there, in the ashtray atop the nightstand, lay unmistakable evidence - discarded marijuana buds. The strange thing was I had never owned an ashtray. As I stood there, a wave of unease washed over me. Something was wrong, and I couldn't shake the feeling that I had stumbled upon a disturbing mystery. I had to be at Steven's so I was in for a really difficult morning once I got home. There was nothing to do about it now but start figuring out how I was going to explain my absence.

Feeling dizzy, I stumbled into Steven's connected bathroom, envy bubbling within me. Living with my parents and older bro, Henry, made me crave the luxury of personal space. As I splashed cool water on my weary face, I sought solace in solitude, longing for revival. With a deep breath, I flicked on the bathroom light switch, illuminating the lavatory. When I glimpsed my reflection in the mirror, a flood of emotions engulfed me, causing me to recoil in horror as though I could jump out of my skin. In a state of panic, I staggered backward and awkwardly landed on the chilly, unforgiving tile surface. To my utter disbelief, somebody else was in the room with me. It was a familiar face, an unexpected presence that I never thought I would encounter again in this lifetime.

Lore? Why was Lore in Steven's room? And, more importantly, why was Lore still alive?

"Lore????" I called out, my voice strained and deep. "Lore, where are you?"

Silence lingered, a chilling reminder of the urgency of the situation.

Noticing that Steven's bedroom was still dark, I stepped out to turn on all the light switches. It became increasingly clear that no one else was present, causing me to consider the possibility that Lore, like me, might have acquired the ability to teleport. However, after blinking a few more times, I still found myself standing alone in the bedroom, and a creeping sense of horror engulfed me.

I glanced around the room and noticed something shiny on Steven's dresser. As I approached, I realized it was a Bronx Science student ID card. Surprisingly, it didn't belong to Steven or me. The name on the card was "Drew Fung Ferebee," and the person in the photo bore a striking resemblance to Lore. I was puzzled as to why Steven had this card. As I held it, a chill ran down my spine. Could Steven be involved in Lore's disappearance or death? And did I just catch a glimpse of Lore's ghost in the mirror?

At that moment, I teetered on the verge of believing almost anything. Gradually, I moved back to the mirror, unsure of what I might see. If Lore's reflection appeared, it could be a haunting, perhaps in Steven's apartment. If it didn't, I feared my sanity was slipping. I hesitated, uncertain which outcome to prefer.

I felt foolish, standing carefully beside the wall as if I was waiting to surprise someone. Finally, I took a deep breath and turned the corner, looking at my reflection again in the mirror. Once again, there was Lore, his piercing gaze locked onto mine, a haunting presence that refused to be ignored.

"Lore?" I asked in a whisper.

"Are you there?"

That's when I figured it out. Lore's lips moved when my lips moved. I couldn't believe it, but I raised my hand and waved at Lore. He did the same thing back to me. Hold on! The skin on my hand had a deep, rich black hue. Lore wasn't a ghost. And the eerie thing about the mirror was not that Lore was reflected in it; it was that I, Rohan, wasn't there. I was Lore. I was in his body. This wasn't Steven's place; it was Lore's.

I suddenly lost all feeling in my legs and collapsed to the floor. Although my thoughts were still my own when I said my name, the sound that came out was in Lore's deeper, more bombastic tone.

"What the hell is this?" I questioned out loud. "What the hell?"

I barely had time to give another thought when I heard footsteps out the door and struggled to my feet as the door swung open. A chunky, fair-skinned white teenager with freckles and a menacing gaze, who looked to be around seventeen, forcefully entered the room. He didn't hesitate to jab at my shins as he pushed past me and plunked himself down by the window. I realized suddenly that there was more than one bed in the room. What had looked like a nonstop junk pile of clothes and crap was actually a bed that the big kid was now trying to relax on. Seeing things from a fresh perspective, it became apparent that the same applied to two other mounds of junk. Lore certainly didn't have the luxury of having this spacious room to himself; instead, he shared it with at least three others. It was at that moment when everything clicked for me. Lore faced even greater challenges than I or any other underprivileged kid at school. This was the MacArthur Group Home in Fresh Meadows. It was a step above an orphanage or living on the streets, but not by much. Three other guys were in the same room, sharing a bathroom, and at least one of them was already acting like a bully this early in the morning.

I didn't want to engage the other kid because he looked like a handful, and I also could sense that I didn't have my powers. Lore was a tough kid and a good guy to have at your back in a fight, but I didn't want any trouble unless it was absolutely necessary. I needed to get out of this room, out on the street, and figure out what I was going to do. I hadn't had my powers for long, but this was extremely bizarre and off the charts.

So I stood up, doing my best to avoid eye contact with Chunky Boy in the corner, and went to the bed I had woken up in. I rummaged around both sides of it and found a pair of kicks that looked big enough to fit Lore's feet. When the other guy didn't say anything, I figured I was in the clear and stood up, grabbed Lore's gargantuan backpack, ID, and the wallet sitting on top of it, and walked out the door without a word. The door led to a hallway that resembled a small college dorm. I didn't check the other doors. When I heard shouting from one staircase, I continued wandering until I found something better—an open window leading to a fire escape. I made my way down from the third floor and checked the location of the building I had just left, uncertain of what I found myself in. Recognizing that my task would take more than a day to accomplish, I knew I needed a stable place to stay instead of relying on the uncertainty of the subway or convincing someone of Lore's existence.

As I pondered my situation, a realization struck me: I had been overlooking a valuable asset - myself. If I was occupying Lore's body, then there was a distinct possibility that Lore was in mine. Even if that wasn't the case, I knew that I (well, Rohan) had an unlocked bedroom and possessed resources that could prove invaluable. I now had a plan: go to my house and inform Rohan, who might actually be Lore, about what was going on. Two heads were better than one; at least, that was what my mother always said.

I walked around the front of the group home to get the address so I could commit it to memory before I went any further. I had heard the name of the building before, from Lore and just in general conversation, but had never been by. Like a lot of my friends, and me for that matter, he didn't want people seeing where he spent his nights.

The sign at the front read: MacArthur Group Home, 1981 Dukakis Blvd, Queens, NY.

Dukakis? That wasn't a New York Street name I'd ever heard. I vaguely remembered that a man by that name had lost a presidential election some time ago, but I wasn't entirely sure. Perhaps he had contributed to helping troubled kids, which might explain why the street was named after him.

It didn't really matter because Dukakis intersected with 73rd, and I could see from a distance that the next parallel street to Dukakis was 171st. Which meant I was only about 18 blocks from my Eckerd's, and maybe a 25-minute walk from home. I was tempted to go into Eckerd Pharmacy and see if "I" was there, but that probably wasn't the best idea. Plus, Amayah might be there, and it wasn't cool to scare her on a whim.

Still, I stuck to 73rd because it was the most direct route, and I wanted to be able to think things through instead of worrying about cross streets and neighborhoods I didn't know quite as well.

Why was Lore...? Was this the past? I seemed to be roughly the same size and shape as Lore the last time I had seen him, so I couldn't tell one way or the other. Maybe it didn't even matter. What mattered was what I needed to do as Lore to get back to being my real self, Rohan.

As I strolled with a furrowed brow, I attempted to piece together all my findings about Lore, searching for any elusive clues or patterns. Most people presumed that he was an orphan, and he appeared content to let them believe it. Remarkably, having deceased parents worked in Lore's favor. His father, a notorious gangster, was rarely at home. I had learned of his shady reputation long before meeting Lore. Therefore, it was an enormous shock when Lore finally revealed the truth, and I had to muster every ounce of self-control to avoid spitting out my 64-ounce Kmart cherry cola in disbelief.

His father, the infamous Bourgeois J, was the leader of a group of dangerous criminals who referred to themselves as BWD. It was easy to guess what BW stood for, but the meaning of the "D" remained a mystery. Occasionally, you would come across a store marked with that logo after they had conducted some 'business' there. While hanging out, we often speculated about what "BWD" really meant. When we were certain nobody else was listening, we made jokes such as "Bourgeois with Dalmatians" or "Bourgeois with Diapers." However, the situation was serious. Lore's father was rumored to have seriously beaten a police officer to within an inch of his life. As a result, the police were scared and turned a blind eye to his illegal activities, as long as he kept them away from the affluent white neighborhoods of Manhattan.

Lore's mom was not involved in his life. He occasionally received a birthday card from her, but she never called or visited. It was painful to think that there were people who could be so uninterested in their own child's life. This situation helped explain why he attempted riskier graffiti bombing missions. While I had super strength and speed, Lore was like Batman, able to find narrow ledges to perch on and defy gravity as he put his tags in places that looked magical from the ground.

I was lost in thought when I suddenly realized that I was almost at my Eckerd's. Worried about the possibility of Amayah (or Rohan) being seen by their deceased friend, I started to cross the street, but then I stopped abruptly. The Eckerd pharmacy was gone. The building seemed the same, but the sign now showed "Henderson's" instead. It looked like a pharmacy and drug store, but it wasn't my Eckerd's or any other Eckerd's. A chilling sensation ran down my spine. This was not good. Either Eckerd's had been acquired and renovated overnight, or I was no longer in the right place. With inner voices, a serial killer, and superpowers to deal with, there wasn't much time to think about alternate universes and parallel timelines.

Against my better judgment, I went into Henderson's for a look around. Most drugstores are similar, but this one had lovely carpeting in its common areas and a big sign that said "HENDERSON'S IS HOME." The irony didn't escape me as I pulled out Lore's wallet and found $10 in there. I bought myself a Cherry Coke and some Cool Ranch Doritos to power up for the rest of my walk in this strange new world.

When I finally got there, there were a few other changes along the way to my (Rohan's) apartment complex, but none that I would have noticed if I hadn't been looking. Thankfully, my building was still there, and since I didn't have my keys because I wasn't actually me, I shimmied up the fire escape to our floor and moved easily to my window. I wasn't sure what I would do if I were in there, but that would have to work itself out. I levered the handle and found it locked. Alternate-reality me apparently wasn't sneaking out the same way I usually did. After standing there like a dope for a moment, I peered through, but there was a screen that made it tough to see. So I did my second dumb idea of the day: I knocked.

Eventually, I knocked three times when I heard the scraping noise. I couldn't place it at first, but suddenly there was no doubt what it was. The kitchen window, about 15 feet away, was opening, and there was a very angry Hispanic woman crawling out of it. "HEY NINO!" she bellowed. "YOU GOT 5 SECONDS BEFORE I CALL THE COPS!"

She had a rolling pin in her hand that might have been comical as a weapon if I hadn't noticed the butcher knife behind her back.

"LO SIENTO!" I called back, using some of the Spanish I had picked up from Amayah. "I have the wrong apartment! I'm sorry!" I scuttled back down the fire escape like a cockroach running from the light and took a few deep breaths.

This time I tried the front door and found that LeRoy, the security guard who never met a crossword puzzle he didn't like, had been replaced by an 80-year-old white guy with glasses and a name tag that read Stan. He asked if I needed help, and I asked what unit the Chang family was in. He took his sweet time but then told me what I already feared.

"No Changs here. Maybe they moved out. When's the last time you saw them?"

"Yesterday," I replied stupidly as Stan gawked at me. "Um, can I borrow your White Pages?"

He bent down to open a big drawer in his desk. "Do you want listings for Fresh Meadows, Queens, or all of NYC?" he asked. I chose the latter, and he brought out two massive volumes. I looked in the "*A* to *M*" volume for the "*C*" section. There were probably 2,000 Changs in New York City, but only one with my dad's unusual first name. It wasn't there. Afterward, I checked the Yellow Pages, but our dry cleaner wasn't listed there either. It looked like Rohan Chang and his father, Abraham, weren't in New York City.

Without a clear plan in mind, I decided to go to our school. The newspaper on Stan's desk indicated that it was Thursday, meaning school was in session. If Lore was alive in this timeline, he was likely skipping class. I wasn't exactly eager to go sit and listen to lectures and take a test or two, especially since I had no idea what his schedule might be like. However, at the very least, I was hopeful to see a familiar face or two - but really just Amayah. She was the one person I felt I could trust to maybe believe this convoluted story and help me out. I was already racking my brain for things that only she and I knew so that I could convince her I was really Rohan. She and Lore knew each other, at least somewhat.

WHEN I ARRIVED at Bronx Science, the school was in the right place, but the situation here was worse than in my world. The whole school looked like a military base with barbed-wire fences and security doors all around. Every gate was securely locked, and without any superpowers - which I definitely lacked - climbing over those fences was out of the question. Another hard fail for Rohan-turned-Lore. I supposed I could wave at the security cameras until someone noticed. But I couldn't get inside, so I decided to abandon the plan and returned to the train, heading towards a local coffee house a few streets away from Lore's group home. I wanted to inventory Lore's backpack and wallet and plan my next steps. My performance as Lore in the past four hours has been pretty pathetic.

I was almost at the café when I heard a surprised grunt and saw Chunky Boy from the group home heading towards me with a nasty grin on his face. He was accompanied by a slightly less chubby, shorter, and younger version of himself. My brain filed him away as Chunky Junior. He was also with a scrawnier Korean kid who was wearing 3D glasses that looked ironically cool and a John Starks' Knicks jersey.

"Well, lookie here," Chunky Boy called. "The half-breed didn't show up for class today, and we find him wandering the fine streets of Fresh Meadows like some moron! Otto and Pamela are going to write you up for this, dummy! I'll get our dessert for the week, and you, your just deserts, you'll be one step closer to getting kicked to that fucking orphanage out on Long Island for good. It's a great day to be alive!"

The Korean kid parroted, "Great day!" as they walked towards me. There was a noticeable lack of concern from anyone else on the street. This was the typical response in New York City unless you dropped a wad of cash. I didn't know what to do. I'm back to being the weak old fight-or-flight Rohan without my powers, but now I'm in someone else's body. Despite Lore being considerably shorter, he was stocky and likely stronger than I was before gaining any powers, but that's not going to make a difference if it turns into a 3-on-1 fight.

"Hey, you guys are skipping too," I called back, trying to sound casual. "Let's just all get to class and not worry about it."

Chunky and Chunky Junior looked at each other and exploded with laughter. I didn't get the joke. "Drew Fung Booboobee. We're skipping?" Chunky repeated mockingly. "We all were sitting in the classroom when you slid by the window down the fire escape! Otto was sure you were just goofing, but then you never came through the door. Pamela is so pissed at you, she let us get out of class to come find your stupid ass!"

Lore and the others were getting home-schooled by whoever Otto and Pamela were. The situation didn't add up; I had Lore's Bronx Science ID card in my wallet.

I pulled it out and held it up. "If I was getting home-schooled like you three, why would I have this?"

Chunky was now looking at me like I had a screw loose. "You got kicked out for cheating, dumb-dumb," he said slowly, not sure if he was being put on. "Did you have a stroke last night or what?"

That was probably the most accurate description of what had happened, but I couldn't let it show. And I couldn't go back home if I was in trouble when I got there. I needed the freedom of movement to sort this out, so I took the only option left: I ran.

They weren't expecting it, which tells me they weren't too smart. But they were quite excited to give chase. This was probably the most exciting thing they'd do all week, considering where they lived. They couldn't even go to school with normal kids. Lore wasn't as fast as super-powered Rohan, but he was in way better shape than previously normal Rohan, and it was easy to put some distance between myself and the others. I purposely altered my route to add a level of confusion, rather than simply running in a straight line. I decided to pull Lore's hoodie over my head to blend in better. Although there were lots of Black people on the streets, it wasn't as common to see a half-Black, half-Chinese kid with a black backpack looking all sweaty.

The problem with outsmarting idiots is that you forget they're idiots. If I had just run straight in one direction, they never would have caught up with me. Instead, I kept doubling back, thinking they'd keep running in one direction. But the chunky nicknames were for a reason. They stopped within a few blocks and spread out, mostly to save face rather than thinking they'd find me. Imagine our combined shock when I turned a corner by a tiny pocket park with a fountain shaped like a swan and ran right into Chunky Boy himself. He gave a sharp whistle, and his brother emerged from around the side of a newsstand on the street with a sick grin. I thought about screaming and shouting, but doing so would fall either on deaf ears or get the cops called on us. When you're a minority, especially with Lore's skin color, thinking the cops will help is usually just setting yourself up for disappointment. So, I stayed quiet. I've faced bullies before, so it wasn't anything new to me. Even without my powers, I knew I could get a few good shots in while getting twice as many.

As the Chunkies shoved me into the alley behind an Italian grocery store, I raised my hands and said, "Look, guys, I don't want to fight, let me buy you guys lunch and we can all go home."

Chunky chuckled, and there was a change in his pitch that I really didn't like. "If you didn't want to fight, you shouldn't have run, black boy, niggar. If you didn't want to fight, you should have kept your dirty half-breed ass out of our room. We were just fine before you moved in, smelling up the place like a dumb simian. And now you're going to learn your lesson."

I have faced a lot of racial slurs in my lifetime, being called a chink, a gook, yellow, and more, and been told that they wished I had died at Hiroshima, even though I wasn't from most of the countries referenced. However, Lore's perspective was distressing to hear. It made me reflect on how people use the n-word casually or reference rap lyrics without considering the harm it causes to many. I reached into Lore's backpack to find something to defuse the situation. Inside, I found several spray paint cans, but they wouldn't be effective as a weapon for long. Additionally, Lore only had $10 in his wallet, so I couldn't bribe the guys.

"Whatcha looking for?" the Korean kid said sneeringly. I looked up and watched as his hand slid into his backpack and brought out a long-bladed knife. I knew my eyes must have gotten bigger because all three of them laughed at my reaction. "Hey Bubba, I guess this kid doesn't have something pretty like me," he taunted.

Chunky Boy saw the switchblade and grinned. "Yeah, he's not talking so tough now, is he? He likes to tag things, but he doesn't have any art on him at all. Maybe my initials, carved into his forehead, will remind him of his place, what do you think, Shades?"

What original nicknames, I thought. But there was no time for sarcasm. Whether they were trying to scare me or hurt me, I didn't want to stick around and find out. As I delved into Lore's backpack once more, I found myself pondering the idea of wielding the paint spray cans to confront the bullies. Suddenly, my fingers fumbled upon a hidden pocket and closed around something cold and metallic, a mysterious object that had escaped my notice until now, setting off a shiver down my spine. I drew out Lore's pistol and turned around, leveling it at Shades. He immediately stopped and his mouth widened. He raised his hands above his head. "Hey, take it easy, kid, I didn't mean it."

I had only been close to a gun once before when I saw hunting rifles locked behind glass at a sporting goods store. But now, I felt very empowered holding this gun. I gestured with it, saying, "Take the switch and throw it into that dumpster right now." Shades dutifully obeyed. As I turned back, a jolt of disbelief shot through me as Chunky Boy sauntered deliberately in my direction.

I pointed the gun right at his chest. "Stop! Stop or I'll shoot!"

Bubba took two more calculated steps as I watched and warned. His gaze focused on the gun, then back to my face. "You know," he said thoughtfully. "Guns don't work great without a clip in them."

I hesitated, knowing next to nothing about guns and realizing they required ammunition to operate. Some used bullets loaded into a barrel, while others used clips. Unsure of the gun type, I took a moment to inspect and figure it out. As I turned back to look at Bubba, or was it Chunky Boy, he suddenly swung his right arm and landed a punch on my face. Staggering from the blow, he snatched the gun from my grip. My earlier indecision had cost me, and I was about to face the consequences.

The worst part? The gun had been loaded, but Chunky somehow knew that I was clueless. He took the clip out, tossed it to his brother, then turned and smashed me in the face with the barrel. I heard the crack of my (Lore's) nose shatter, and I staggered to the ground. I put my hand to my face, and it came away smeared in blood. I figured that would end it, but Chunky Boy hadn't taken too kindly to having a gun pulled on him. He brought his knee up to kick me in the same spot, and I thought I was going to black out from the pain on top of the pain. I was in a heap now and could hear Shades and Chunky Junior laughing at me as I struggled to even sit up.

"You should have pulled the trigger, dumbledore," Bubba screeched, kicking me in the side of the head and making my hearing flutter in that ear. "You point a gun at a man, you best pull the trigger. Because otherwise, what's the point?"

I finally managed to sit up, half-slumping against the wall behind me, watching Chunky Boy skillfully twirl the gun on his finger, accompanied by his brother and Shades, who grinned at his every word. With determination, I pushed myself to my feet. Despite knowing it was wiser to stay down, the urge to retaliate burned within me, refusing to accept defeat without a fight.

"Oh my, he's up!" Chunky Junior said with a squawking laugh. "He's like the black Rocky Balboa over here."

"More like that black bitch Apollo Creed," his older brother said.

"And that makes me Drago." He got in my face, smelling of onions, and rasped in a terrible Russian accent, "I MUST BREAK YOU."

He was close enough to kiss me, but I had something else in mind. I thrust my head forward and bit his big wide nose as hard as I could, grinding my teeth together until they met. He shrieked like a piglet and pulled away, crashing backward onto the pavement. I was still dazed, but adrenaline was one heck of a drug, and it was coursing through my veins. Chunky Junior and Shades had moved closer to their leader but neither looked particularly willing to examine him or help him up. With both of them lost in Bubba's anguish, I seized the opportunity, snatched Lore's backpack, and dashed down the narrow alleyway, my heart pounding in my chest. This time, I didn't run out, I climbed up. Jumping on top of a rusty dumpster, I swiftly grasped the fire escape ladder and began my ascent just as it smoothly slid down. The closely packed buildings created a labyrinth of opportunities to navigate. Confident in my speed and nimbleness, I knew I could outmaneuver the three of them and make a swift escape. My plan was to find sanctuary by locating an open fire door or descending another fire escape, ensuring a clean getaway for good.

Before anything else, I decided it was time to give them a little taste of their own medicine – Lore's medicine, to be exact. I had already ascended three flights by the time they arrived at the ladder's base. Chunky Junior had assisted his brother in making it this far. And my nose had stopped bleeding from the clean break, but Chunky Boy's was gushing blood through the hole my teeth had left. He shouted for Shades to go after me, and the Korean boy followed orders, gripping the ladder and slowly starting to climb. I let him get to about 12 feet below me when I threw the first spray paint canister at him. I had concealed myself from their sight so that they didn't know I hadn't run off. As a result, neither of the other two was there to warn him when he took the metallic missile straight to the forehead.

Shades swore and cried out as he lost his grip, barely managing to save himself with one hand. The Chunkies glared up at me, hurling insults and curses while Shades struggled to regain his hold. I bided my time until he felt secure once more, then swiftly hurled another canister at him. Despite the Chunkies' attempts to warn him, he wasn't agile enough to evade it. The canister struck his cheekbone, and this time, he couldn't maintain his grip. He lost his hold and plummeted two stories, landing on his back. The sound of his head hitting the asphalt echoed.

Chunky Boy, showing no concern for his fallen companion, insisted on getting the clip back from his brother. As he loaded it into Lore's pistol, a can of flat black spray paint came hurtling and struck him squarely on the top of his head.

"Look out! There she blows!" I shouted from above. "Today's forecast for Fresh Ghetto: cloudy, with a slight chance of paint cans. Seek shelter quickly if you're not agile and quick enough to dodge them!"

Chunky Boy dropped the pistol. As he bent to pick it up, he was hit in the small of his back by another spray can.

He glared up. "I'm going to kill you!" he screamed.

He was dangerous. Everything about this was. But the angrier he got, the better chance I had of escaping.

I shouted, "You'll have to get up here first! This building has 5 floors and 60 units. Are you going to break down every door looking for me, or are you going to climb the ladder yourself? I mean, it might break under all that weight, but go on and try! I've got a few missiles left!"

Chunky didn't wait around. He pointed the gun up and squeezed off two shots, **the sound echoing through the empty streets**. I pulled back, and the bullet struck the side of the building about halfway up, serving as a stark reminder of the danger I was in. Chunky might have been challenging to handle in close-quarters combat, but he was a terrible shot, especially when angry.

I strategically timed my next throws to coincide with his shots, a calculated move that played to my advantage. With approximately six cans remaining, I was determined not to exhaust my supply. I kept my cool and threw another can, hitting one of the bullies in the face. As I dropped another one, I swiftly ducked and sprinted across the rooftop. I didn't head for the top door but leaped onto the next roof, a decision that kept me one step ahead. I continued like this until I was so far down the block that nothing seemed familiar. Hiding low, I waited, but none of them appeared. They were armed with knives and guns, while I only had paint. It was an over-whelming victory, a testament to strategic thinking.

I carefully planned my next move - calculating how long to remain in position, strategizing my descent, and contemplating waiting until nightfall. Feeling alert, I was confident I could find a strategic spot with visibility in every direction except behind me. Moving cautiously, I scanned for the perfect location when some-thing suddenly drew my attention.

Actually, it was the absence of something that caught my atten-tion. There was a completely empty space on the exterior of a parking garage two buildings over. It seemed to be glowing, even though the sun was shining brightly on a hot day. The longer I gazed at the location, the stronger the feeling took hold of me that it was crying out for some artistic touch. Never before had I felt this way during my excursions with friends or alone. Usually, finding a spot meant locating an area without security cameras where a police officer or night watchman was unlikely to find you. This spot, though not meeting my usual criteria, felt like a ray of sunshine breaking through dark clouds. It was a flat area on top of a parking garage with a structure that housed an elevator and a payment area. As I gazed at the wall, I envisioned the image that needed to be there, clear in my mind with arcs, curves, motions, and specific colors - yellow, black, white, and orange. I was briefly concerned that I wouldn't be able to create it because I didn't have the right colors. Despite the pain I was in, I stumbled upon the last four spray cans in Lore's bag: white, orange, yellow, and black. At that moment, I felt an unexplainable pull towards them. The next few minutes passed in a flurry of confusion, as if I were under some strange spell. It felt hauntingly similar to the first time I tapped into my powers and felt like a mere vessel. My mind seemed to float apart from my body, just a bystander to the task at hand. As I gazed upon it, a spectacular work of art slowly took shape before me, crafted by my hands and spray cans, capturing the perfection I had envisioned.

Looking good, Lore!

I froze. I had heard a voice. A really familiar one. In fact, the MOST familiar one.

Mine.

I willed my arm to stop painting and took a slow look around. I didn't see anything, but I knew I wasn't crazy or high. There was too much airflow up here for the fumes to affect me. I stood still, however, unwilling to return to the job just yet. It paid off.

My G, I'm so proud of you. Letting go and finding your place and creating, it's what we always talked about, right?

I turned around and took a big step back. In front of me stood... me, or at least it looked like me. I looked older. More mature, too, as if I had gained confidence from experiencing more of the world.

"How, um, hey, what's going on?" I asked, realizing it was a very foolish opening line. "Who are you? I'm Rohan in Lore's body, but I'm definitely Rohan."

I can't answer that, but I just wanted to say how proud of you I am. Lore, you had shit stacked against you your whole life, and here you are, still seeing a chance to add a little beauty to the world. That's a skill that most people either never have or lose quickly.

"But I'm not Lore," I sputtered. "I'm you, or you're me, or both, maybe. I don't understand why I'm here and don't know what to do or how to get back."

If it sounded like whining, it probably was. But I had a long few days and had spent the last part of this one getting my ass kicked and running for my life. Was it so bad to ask for a few answers?

You needed to take a trip. You needed to see his journey, see his path.

"But he dies," I said bitterly. "My version of Lore dies. And with all my powers, with all the things I can do... I can't save him?"

I was only dimly aware of why that line sounded so familiar. It was almost verbatim what Clark Kent had said to his mother after his dad died of a heart attack. It used to be just a line in a movie I saw on TV on a lazy Sunday afternoon.

You can't save them all, the other Me said. *It's two lessons in one, Rohan.*

He gestured towards the artwork, which became clearer as I looked behind me. It was unmistakably Lore's style—a style I had always admired when he was alive and one that now filled me with deep, bittersweet gratitude, knowing that it was a part of him that still lived on.

As I grappled for the perfect words, a sudden jolt of searing pain shot through my shoulder, leaving me momentarily stunned. Just then, my other Me shimmered and then vanished, leaving me feeling utterly alone as the harsh reality came crashing back in. Shades and Chunky Junior pinned my arms behind my back and turned me around to face Chunky Boy. His nose looked like uncooked hamburger meat, and his face was bright red to match.

"No more games, niggar," he spat. "No more paint, no more guns, no more running." The other two let go of me, but Chunky Boy grabbed me and shoved me aggressively, his hand pushing against me with a powerful force, so much so that there was no way for me to halt the unstoppable momentum, nothing to slow my fall. Plunging from the 13th story of the parking garage, I free-fell 100 feet, coming ever closer to the unyielding pavement below.

"It's not fair..." At that moment, I felt Lore's spirit returning as mine drifted away from his body. As his essence took over, a chilling sensation gripped me, and dark whispers of the unknown enveloped me, leaving me in a state of indescribable horror.

CHAPTER

FIVE

I awoke gasping for air, my heart pounding in my chest. As I reached out to touch my face, the overwhelming sense of relief washed over me. Examining my trembling hands and feeling my racing heart, I convinced myself that I was undeniably awake. In that moment of sheer terror, I couldn't shake the haunting feeling of narrowly escaping from a parallel universe of darkness and despair existing within Lore's very essence. However, as I embraced the reality of awakening, an immense sense of gratitude and revitalized energy flooded through me. A profound realization dawned upon me: *I must have cherished Lore deeply.*

School suddenly seemed a lot less important than it had even twelve hours earlier. A lot of things felt like that all of a sudden. It was really tough not to see how fast I could run to school, how high I could jump, how much weight I could lift. I knew that doing anything like that in front of any group of people would get me the kind of attention that I didn't want. Individually, some people might have understood that something was happening. But collectively, people seeing a kid run like he had a lightning bolt up his ass or jumping five times as high as Michael Jordan on his best day were going to panic and call the cops, reporting an Asian kid Spiderman without the mask. The fact that the description of that Asian kid might match someone who was spotted the night before near the Eckerd's, which had been tagged, or even worse, out near the body of the latest murder victim, would have some seriously bad consequences. That meant that until I found a place to test my powers safely and anonymously, I would have to go back to being boring ol' Rohan, minorly talented at math and science, not many friends, and hopelessly smitten with the girl he works with—or did I?

Amayah had seen me stand up to the punks on the Four train the other day and had been a lot more talkative about things beyond the mundane since. What if I could do that again, except really do it? I could really put the bullies in their place. What if I could take her somewhere alone and show her the things I could suddenly do? Steven was the coolest guy in school, and he's been hanging off my every word and movement after I showed him what I was capable of the night before. I also witnessed her laughing and flirting with Steven when he had paid her even a little bit of attention on the walk to school. I thought she liked me because I was sweet and nice, but every girl loves the guy who is strong and tough and confident. What if I could be both? I mean, she'd have to realize I was perfect for her, right? The thought was both thrilling and a little scary. I had to show Steven what I could do because he had seen me appear out of nowhere. What if Amayah was scared of my powers or if she freaked out and didn't want to talk to me? Steven hadn't even asked a second question about the voice of Nick the Brute, which the more I thought about it, seemed sort of weird. I had a bad feeling Amayah would not click with Nick too much, and be bosom buddies. I was shaking my head clear of racing thoughts and competing doubts that fought for control, causing my long combed-over hair to tumble into my face. Pushing the locks aside along with the uncertainty out of my eyes, I could see once more.

Getting to the refrigerator, and being that no one was home, I tipped the orange juice container straight back and drank out of it. I might have turned into some super-being overnight. However, I still liked to occasionally rebel against the authority of my parents, who would have considered cutting off one of my fingers as punishment for something as egregious as refusing to use a cup for drinking from the family juice jug.

"So, the big shot who stays up all night can't even use a cup now?" a voice came bursting from behind me.

I spit the juice out in surprise and nearly choked on it. I spun around one-eighty, awkwardly knocking my knee against the open door of the fridge. Only to see my dad standing in the doorway between the kitchen and the sitting room, wearing his work uniform and a perpetual frown. "Dad!" I managed to get out. "Uh, what are you doing home? You're supposed to be at work!"

"I went out late last night to talk to the police with your brother about some punks spraying paint on the side of Eckerd's," he replied sternly, forcefully staring me in the eyes and taking the steam out of my plan. There was no way he could possibly know I was involved in that, but it still felt like every word he spoke was an accusation.

"When I came home, I went to check on my other son since he left his light on. Thought he might be up late studying. Turns out he wasn't even home. Gone out somewhere with his young hoodlum friends on a school night. So I waited for him for the next two hours, but he didn't come home. When Henry finally got back after cleaning up the mess, he said he'd heard on the radio that someone had gotten killed by the serial killer. I told Henry that his brother wasn't in his room, and I didn't know where he was. He told me there was no way the two were connected; the serial killer only targets young women. But I couldn't shake the thought from my mind, so your brother and I went out looking for you."

I could feel the color draining from my face. Damn; all my bravado with my new-found powers and my slick moves to avoid Henry and the police, not to mention how Steven Stone had wanted to hang out with me, were suddenly being cast in a different light.

While I was playing Barry Allen, my dad and my brother had

been wandering around the streets of Queens in the early hours looking for me. My dad, who slept maybe five hours a night, and my brother, who had just worked twelve hours straight at Eckerd's and had to deal with the cops and a bunch of young taggers—one of whom he didn't even know was his own younger brother—had just spent their night looking for me, worried about my safety.

"Henry went to bed at two a.m. He's already left for class at the college. I came back in at four a.m. and your light was off, and there you were sleeping like a baby in your crib. Totally unaware that you scared your family to death tonight. I asked Mr. Pham to help out at the dry cleaners for a few hours this morning so I could catch up on my sleep. Lucky for me, I also saw the big shot himself, shoving his tongue down a carton of orange juice meant for his whole family."

I was humiliated, embarrassed, and mad at how close most of that was to hitting the mark. Of course, I couldn't tell him what had really happened last night. I found myself falling right back into my defensive mechanism of deflecting and acting like I was the victim, and he was overreacting. "Chill out, Dad. I made a 93 on my math test, and I just went to hang out with some friends of mine at one of their apartments. His dad was home the whole time. We watched a couple of movies and had a pizza."

"And you are too good to pick up the phone and call us? And miss your curfew by oh, what, four and a half hours? You think a 93 buys you a ticket to stay out ALL NIGHT and WORRY US SICK?" His voice went way up at the end of the statement, and I stepped back in surprise.

"I didn't mean to worry you, Dad. I just wanted to blow off some steam."

"Nothing good happens after midnight, boy. I've been telling you that since you were old enough to tell time. Nothing but criminals and drug dealers and lowlifes are out and about then. Is that who you want to be in this life? If you want to throw your life away, let me know and we'll stop wasting our money on your school things and your clothes and food. You can go live out there with your punk friends and do whatever the hell you want!"

He was furious. Up there with the time I had made a 75 on a Spanish test a few years ago. He got closer to me, breathing hard and grinding his teeth. Even though I towered over him – he couldn't have been more than five foot seven – I felt like the smaller person.

"I can't even stand to look at you. I'm going for some fresh air. You'd better be gone to school when I get back. And you're working a double shift this weekend. If you have enough time to run around with your little friends, you have enough time to work more and be responsible for your life."

I was pissed off to be treated like trash after the night I'd had, and I could feel the anger surging up inside of me. I had never had anything aggressive or confrontational with my dad before, but I could feel that angry power bubbling up, and wondered if he had any idea what I was capable of. I mean, the powers had to have come from somewhere, right? If they weren't hereditary, I didn't know what to make of them. Had I been exposed to some sort of radiation or cosmic dust, or a solar flare? Wherever they were coming from, I decided I wouldn't get pushed around in my own house, so for one of the few times in my life, I decided to hit back with Nick's blessing.

"You know something, Rohan. You are better. Way better than them all. Lions need not worry, especially not about damn sheep. You remind me of a young lion, who leads and does not follow," Nick urged.

"Maybe I will move out! Beats living here. You think I dream at night about working twelve-hour shifts at Eckerd's every day of my life? My friends have interests outside of work, going to church, and family gossip every damn day! Did you ever wonder what my interests are, or is all that matters what ABRAHAM wants?"

My dad did a double take. "You need to call me Dad or Father, not by my first name," he hollered. He wheeled around, and for a long second, I thought he would slap or punch me in the face. He looked 100% ready to throw me down, but I could see him physically stopping himself short as he remembered that I was his son, not some random punk who had wandered into the dry cleaners off the street asking for a dollar or to take a piss.

"You're a disgrace to this house and your own family," my dad said, biting out each word as if it was physically stabbing him. "Your mom and I work tirelessly, and might I add, at a *revolutionary* dry cleaner/laundromat, to put a roof over your head, food in your stomach, clothes on your back, and a good education at your feet. Do you think you're going to get famous spraying paint on the side of a wall? Oh yes, Rohan, your secret isn't much of a secret. Half the neighborhood sees you sneaking out at night trying to find a place to practice your illegal dumb tagging. Do you know how humiliating it is to have those cops ask me if I know who might have tagged up Eckerd's, and I have to play dumb even though I know damn well who is responsible? Cleaning you and your friends' garbage off the wall is money that comes out of my pocketbook. I'm so ashamed. Have you ever thought about that? You think you're so special with your paintings, but they cost small business owners hundreds and thousands of dollars. We are the ones having to clean it up while you and your little friends are out there laughing about it!"

Well, I had definitely never thought of Graff art in that light, and I could feel the heat rising on my neck. I started to protest about how strict the punishment was, but my dad had already slammed the door shut behind him. *Except,* my thought burning into me, *lions don't worry about sheep.*

~

ABRAHAM DIDN'T BOTHER WAITING for the elevator. Instead, he ferociously pounded down the stairs, slamming his feet harder and harder into the tile floor as he practically bounced down them. He had gone from crippling anxiety to blissful relief to pent-up rage with his son in a matter of hours, and still couldn't get a handle on his own emotions. Rohan had been pushing back on his authority and his Asian heritage in general for the better part of the last decade. No matter how hard he and Rohan's mother pushed him to focus on his grades and his work and let the rest sort itself out, the boy seemed determined to court disaster and do the least amount of work possible while still expecting the same results.

Abraham had suspected Rohan was going out at night for hours on end, but this was the first time he had been caught red-handed. The worst part was Rohan didn't even seem concerned that there was some sort of maniac roaming around killing people on a whim. Abraham couldn't go to work in this state of mind; customers would pick up on his anger and his frustration and take their business elsewhere.

His heart hammering, he ducked around the corner of the building into the alley. It was a cloudy Queens morning and he was wearing his hat, suspecting rain might be forecast. The alley was deserted other than a few dumpsters and some random bags of trash. Doorways opened up into the alley all the way up and down its length, convenient for business owners and residents to toss their garbage out or make a quick getaway if they were up to no good. Abraham walked several doors down to get away from random stares from passersby on the street and leaned against the wall, closing his eyes and trying to regain his composure. He needed to calm his nerves. He folded his hands together and bowed his head, seeking the right words to pray to God and ask for guidance on pulling Rohan back from the wayward path he had set himself on. Abraham knew from experience that his son was teetering on the edge of going from a good kid making good grades to a juvenile delinquent who would start circling the drain to the ills of the street, whether it was crime, drugs, booze, or something else. Too many times it was happening to Asian youth in this city. Their parents worked their fingers to the bone while their children pushed back on the culture of their ancestors in favor of the quick, easy, live-for-today American attitude. Abraham detested that way of thinking. His mind was racing, and he couldn't find a starting point to ask the Almighty for help, for he was agnostic and didn't fully embrace a particular religion. He kept wincing at the idea of bailing Rohan out of jail or having to pay for an attorney for him when he got tangled up in something nasty.

"Need a smoke, friend?"

Abraham's eyes snapped open, and his head jerked up. A man in a gray jacket with his hood tightly pulled up around his face was standing in a doorway, holding an unlit cigarette. Abraham squinted. He couldn't really make out the man's face in the dim light, but he was more interested in what was in his hand.

Abraham was in a constant battle with nicotine that felt like an all-out retreat. Every time he thought he had it under control, something stressful would happen, and he'd fall off the wagon. He'd need to check his calendar, but Abraham thought it had been thirty-seven days since his last one. But he really wanted what the stranger was offering right this minute.

"Ummmm, no, I should pass, I've been trying to quit," Abraham said in a friendly voice, trying to let the other man know he appreciated the gesture.

"You sure, friend? It's good for what ails you. Whenever I have a setback, I let myself have just one, just to settle me down and let me get back to that even keel. Come on, I know a guy who is struggling when I see him," he rasped in a low, friendly voice that Abraham felt he had heard before but couldn't quite place. "Our little secret? Light one up, share a smoke with a fellow New Yorker who can't seem to get everyone to understand his way is the best way."

He took out a black-and-red lighter and flicked it open, touching the red flame to the end of the cigarette. Within seconds, Abraham could smell the delicious aroma of nicotine and flame mixing together, and he couldn't resist. He leaned forward and took it from the other's hand, feeling a weird shock of electricity as he did. It was probably something to do with the stormy weather coming in. Abraham quickly slipped the other end into his mouth and inhaled deeply. It wasn't just good, it was the best cigarette he had ever tasted in his entire life. At that moment, his promises to his wife,

Claire, to try and really stop, the stern warning the doctor had given him at his last physical, and Rohan and Henry's badgering him as younger children about the dangers of secondhand smoke, all of it were all forgotten. He took another puff and felt the soothing sensation of the nicotine releasing into his bloodstream, and sighed.

"Thatta boy," the man said, taking a second cigarette and lighting it up to make sure Abraham didn't smoke alone. "Nothing in the world that feels this good can possibly be as bad as they say, right?"

Abraham didn't bother speaking; he just reluctantly grunted his approval. He took two more giant breaths and felt his heart rate start to slow down. He knew the science behind tobacco and what it did to your lungs over time, but he wouldn't have given up the cigarette for $5,000 right now. The two men smoked in silence for about thirty seconds before the stranger spoke up from his darkened doorway.

"So, what's stressing you out, friend? Job, wife, or kids?"

Abraham looked up sharply, asking himself how he had known.

The stranger laughed, and Abraham glimpsed a mouthful of white teeth, almost too white to be possible. Maybe the man was a dentist or had his teeth professionally brightened.

"Kids. My son, actually. He's lazy and disrespectful of our rules and our culture. Was out all night doing God knows what and came swaggering in at three a.m. like it was no big deal."

The stranger barked a short laugh. "God knows? I doubt that very much. God worries about churches and orphans and kids starving in Africa. And it's the other guy. The other guy gets helped. He's also the one who has the ears of kids on the street all night, am I right?"

The stranger was talking his language, and Abraham nodded approvingly. "Yes. That is what I try to tell my kids. I tell them, 'Nothing good happens after midnight.' When you're out at that hour, you stop thinking about what you need in the long term and start obsessing about the whispers in your ear. Cravings, obsessions, curiosity, all the dangerous things a young man should avoid."

The stranger took another long, slow cigarette drag and blew the smoke out of his nose.

"My father didn't like a lot of my bad habits when I was growing up," he said in a ponderous voice. "You know how he got through to me? Severe discipline. He watched me like a hawk. Even kicked me out of the house eventually, and said if I wanted to go that way, I could do it on my own."

Abraham nodded slowly. "Did it work?"

"To the extreme," the man said. "I started working hard for the things I wanted. Never took anything for granted again. I learned how to talk to people, how to make things happen, how you have to dig deep, and go after what you want and stop expecting it to be handed to you. But I never got his approval. I've been seeking that since the day he kicked me out. But lately, I think I've realized that all this time, I was trying to be as good as him, but maybe, the truth is that I am a lot better."

Abraham turned that over in his head. It rang true. His own father had toiled for pennies for decades. When Abraham announced he was moving to America, his father shamed him publicly for turning his back on their culture and traditions. Abraham hadn't wanted to upset his patriarch, but he knew that life could be better somewhere else. Only when he got to New York City and out of his father's long shadow had he started to realize he could live his own life here.

"So, how do I get my son to understand that?" Abraham asked the stranger. "His older brother has no issues working hard and doing things the right way, but Rohan seems lazy, disinterested, like he doesn't even want to be Asian."

The stranger took another long drag, considering Abraham's words. "You've tried the soft approach. Time to move on to the hard one. Shut him down. Make him realize who the boss is in the house. Enforce the rules, even if it's easier to let him slide. Show him that he's the boy, and you're the man. He's like a wild stallion. Somebody needs to break him before he gets out of control and hurts someone."

Abraham felt his heart rate accelerating again. Rohan's behavior last night was totally unacceptable and had left him upset, angry, and exhausted. The stranger was right. It was time to put his son in his place. "You're right, thanks for the advice and for the light," he said, putting the cigarette out with his foot and tossing it into a dumpster.

"I knew you were my kind of guy," the man said, smiling again with those bizarrely white teeth. "Give my door a knock when you want to have another talk or if you need another light to make it through these crazy times and this mad life of ours."

MY DAD's outburst shook me up and made me feel like garbage. I lost my appetite quickly but knew it would come back once I was on my way to school. I wasn't in much of a cereal mood, so I grabbed a few granola bars and set out down the stairs onto the street. Walking at a normal pace felt weird, and everything around me seemed a lot slower and duller than it had the day before. The colors were a little more muted, the hustle and bustle didn't seem so important as on most mornings.

I was on my third granola bar when I walked by Uncle Julio's newsstand on the corner. His little slice of New York was all about magazines, newspapers, sodas, and snacks. He was a good guy, although I'm not sure whose uncle he was, or if he even was an uncle. Maybe it was just a nickname because he made sure the whole neighborhood of kids had someone they could turn to if there was trouble at home, or they were having an issue with one of the gangs that infringed on our neighborhoods from time to time. He was a Puerto Rican guy, heavyset and with this tiny little mustache that looked really out of place on his face. He always wore a big floral print shirt that you could see from a mile away. In fact, I think he wore it so you could see him from a mile away, so you come and buy something from him. I had the third granola bar—chocolate and peanut butter, my absolute favorite—about halfway down my throat when I glanced at the front page of the stack of New York Posts sitting on the pavement in front of me.

"JANE DOE #4 FOUND 'STUCK LIKE A PIG'"

It was the girl's body I saw last night on Roosevelt Island. The picture was of her neck slit and slashed open. Thankfully, you couldn't see her face, but bile rose in my throat, and I coughed up the granola bar. Uncle Julio's big left hand connected with my back once, then twice as he tried to assist me to stop choking.

"Ay, Rohan, ten cuidado, hermanito!" he said, clearly forgetting I didn't speak Spanish. He passed me a bottle of Coke, and I unsealed it and took a long grateful gulp.

"You freaked about these murders too, hermanito? That's three in two weeks. Someone out there is getting a bad taste for blood."

I nodded my head. It was the safest way to not say or do anything that would suggest I knew anything more about the murder than anyone else. Something further down on the front page caught my eye, and I did the world's most violent double-take of all time. My head had turned away from Uncle Julio, but now it lurched back the other way to see the blurry picture at the very bottom of the page. You could barely make out a Yankees cap and Converse sneakers, but the rest of the photo was a blurry, dark mess. The single-line teaser headline read, "Queens Grandma Snaps Black Blur Outracing Cops!"

Good god, I thought I was going to be sick all over again. Typical New Yorkers, nothing to do on a weekend night but lean out the window and be as nosey as shit about what their neighbors were and were not doing. Somehow, some grandma living in an apartment complex had heard the commotion at Eckerd's and leaned out the window with a Polaroid in hand and snapped a few images of our narrow escape from the cops. Her intrusiveness had paid off with a photo of yours truly firing up my superpowers to get out of trouble. Two incidents I had been directly or indirectly involved in, both on the front page of the same paper. My supreme confidence in my new-found abilities was suddenly taking a big turn for the worse.

I sleepwalked the rest of the way to school and dozed through most of my classes. Neither Jarron nor Lior showed up for school, but when I saw Steven, and we did our secret handshake, he said they were both just sleeping off being up all night.

Lior had stayed at a diner until six a.m. to steer clear of the cops he kept thinking were lying in wait on his block, and Jarron had come home to his brother drunk out of his mind and trying to punch through a plate-glass window to get inside his own house. Sadly, Jarron ended up taking his brother to the emergency room. I could tell Steven was bursting at the seams to talk more about my powers, but I made sure we were never alone all day, heeding Nick's warnings.

By the time I got to history class that afternoon, I was worn out from dodging him, pretending to be invested in my classes, and going over what the heck I would do next time I saw Steven and again in my head.

My teacher, Dr. George, was droning on and on about the history of New York's transportation center, which normally I might have found interesting. But today, I really needed silence and time to think, and neither one was making itself readily available to me. We had mercifully reached the twentieth century in Dr. George's lecture, and he was unveiling big maps that he had to pin up from one corner of the blackboard to the other to show the massive dig that started the era of the subway system. Now that I had this other-worldly secret, I was starting to realize just how tiny my parents' house was and just how little privacy I had basically anywhere. *Damn*, even my room didn't have a lock on it. Seeing that my dad knew my every move, my private time now was for the middle of the night with the lights off and everyone fully asleep.

Assuming I wasn't already snoozing, midnight was when I plotted a lot of my graffiti work, dreamed about where I would go when I turned eighteen and could leave home without serious repercussions, and, well, to be completely honest, thought about Amayah. I was slightly lost in that daydream when Dr. George interrupted my train of thought with a picture of a subway train and described how massively deep and wide the subway tunnels had to be built to accommodate the first trains. It took me a minute before I put two and two together. I needed a place to test my powers. I needed a place that was quiet, virtually deserted, and close enough to home that I could sneak out without making it obvious. That place was literally looking me in the eye. *The subway!*

I smiled, seeing I was turning into the Bruce Banner / Peter Parker archetype in front of my own eyes. The scientific kid who somehow takes on extraordinary powers but doesn't want to just start punching bad guys and rescuing cats from trees. I wanted to know my limitations, my strengths, my weaknesses, all of it. A normal person would be an idiot to wander down into the subway where trains come blazing around corners at forty miles an hour, but I was no longer a normal person. My adventures had told me I could outrun anything short of a fighter jet, and my strength meant I could punch a hole in the wall to escape trouble if it came down to it.

I checked my watch. I was supposed to work from four p.m. to eight p.m. tonight, but my shift suddenly seemed very optional. I just needed an hour or so to run some parameters and get a feel for the ground rules. After that, I could get to work and spend the rest of my shift figuring out a schedule to keep adding to my trial runs until I was confident in what I could do. Of course, going to work and telling my brother I was going to be an hour late made absolutely no sense, so after History 301, I made a beeline for Amayah's locker, where I knew she would come to get out her heavier books for English Literature at the end of her schedule. I know that makes me sound like a stalker, and I guess I kind of was one, but hey, you try falling in love with a girl sometime, it makes you do weird stuff. Like clockwork, Amayah popped out of a classroom and started walking right towards me. She looked a little confused to see me there, then a small smile came onto her face. "Hey, Rohan, what's up?"

I realized that for perhaps the first time in my life, I was talking to her, not as the girl I was secretly pining away for, but more for something really important to me. "Hey, Amayah, could you do me a huge favor and cover for me for like, an hour at work today? I've got something I have to take care of." Clearly, that was not the question she was waiting for because her smile faded just a bit, but she recovered just as quickly.

"Oh, oh sure. No problem. Nobody ever comes before five anyways. Where are you going to be?"

With every ounce of my being, I wanted to take her hands in mine, whisper that I had something unique to show her, and dash out of the building and around the corner to unveil my incredible powers, but I knew the time wasn't right for it yet. Before sharing it with anyone else, I had to know what I could do myself. Instead, I smiled at her and said, "It's hard to explain, but I appreciate it. See you later."

She smiled back, looking at me with her head cocked, quizzical in nature. "Okay, Ro, I guess I'll see you later." She patted my arm on the bicep, and I positively tingled with electric at the feel of it. As I walked away from her, fully confident she was staring after me, suddenly curious about what was going on, I felt a surge of energy, and Nick the Brute spoke up for the first time all day.

"See? Be the power and watch her come to you. They'll be drawn to you when you let me out. Her, the Black girl you stare at every day when she comes to buy hairspray. The one in your apartment building with the cheating husband who calls you, 'Mighty Rohan' in the elevator. Make them yours. Anyone you want. Anything you want. All you have to do is embrace what I offer. Be rich. Be famous. Be powerful. Be the leader! Get out of that shit hole you call home. Show your father you're more of a man than he could ever dream of. Take what is rightfully yours!"

Wait, did he just call my home a shit hole? The bell rang, and I was able to quiet the voice along with my racing thoughts.

Mid-afternoon, most subway stations were a ghost town. The lunch crowd was far gone, and it wasn't rush hour nor the school run. There were more bums trying to get out of the heat, the rain, or the cold than there were actual passengers. The only transit cop I saw on my way into the station was asleep in front of a tiny portable TV on his desk. I pretended to look at the route map for a while until the coast was clear, and after a train left, I walked to the end of the railway platform, did one more three-hundred-and-sixty-degree sweep, and hopped down into the tunnel.

The smell was not great, a sort of a combination of grease, body sweat, and some sort of animal, which I knew in my heart of hearts was very likely a rat or two or six. Whatever, I wasn't down here for a vacation, but to test myself.

I had bummed a flashlight out of the science lab on my way out the door when school finished, and had stowed my backpack behind a hidden cranny near the turnstile for safekeeping. I flipped on the flashlight and shone it ahead into the receding darkness to ensure the tunnel wasn't a dead end. I strolled about half a mile down in a straight line into the dark of the tracks. I advanced into the blackness, managing to restrain any lingering fear. What was going to come out of the dark at me? I was the *baddest* thing alive down here right now. If a train came, I'd hear it from a mile away.

I turned at the one-mile point and stretched my arms and legs, even though that seemed kind of silly. Then I reached down inside myself to the energy source. I harbored fears all day that when I reached for it, it wouldn't be there, as if it had been a momentary fluke or maybe that I was going crazy, but those thoughts and fears were waylaid immediately. I could feel the pulse blazing through me from the moment I turned my thoughts inward, and I took off into the gloom, my sneakers barely touching the ground. The light rose quickly as I re-entered the part of the track where the station began, and I had to put on the brakes just as fast, unceremoniously dumping myself onto the ground as my toes slapped the side of the track.

Whoa. That was exhilarating! I felt like I was running even faster than the night before. Maybe because I knew what to expect. I did it twice more, both times walking into the tunnel, then sprinting out. I checked my watch every time to make sure I wasn't going to run past five p.m. I might have been doing some very super human things, but I was still a normal person to the outside world. Keeping my parents and brother happy and no one else suspicious of why old reliable Rohan had suddenly gone AWOL were still important things.

On the third test run, long, thundering slow claps popped out over and over from the row of seats just behind the waiting area for the subway cars. I froze like a deer in headlights, about to activate my teleportation power when I looked up and saw Steven Stone sitting with his feet up, grinning at me. "I got to say, that's almost as impressive as the Asian who materializes out of thin air," he said with a grin. "When you wouldn't say a word to me today, I figured you had something else up your sleeve. Hope you don't mind me tagging along with you on another little adventure."

I smiled sheepishly. I kind of did mind. I wanted to be alone and process this myself, but there wasn't much I could do about it, seeing as Steven was here now and knew everything, including my discovering the woman's body, and Nick the Brute's voice.

Steven laughed. "So, you can run fast, and you're strong as hell, Ro, but can you fight? I mean I'm assuming you're down here testing this all out because you're going to start being the neighborhood crime stopper. I mean, Gotham's got The Bat and Metropolis has the Man of Steel.

"What's it going to be for us? Captain Queens? The Fresh Ghetto Avenger?" He winked to show me he was kidding, and I burst out laughing at the terrible names he was suggesting.

"I mean, I haven't thought that much about what I'll do now," I said, which was a total lie, and basically the only thing I had been thinking about since he and I had parted ways the night before.

"But you are going to do something, right? Clean those gangs off our streets? Get revenge on your enemies? Tag the top of the Empire State Building? Finally make your move on Amayah?"

I never had a good poker face, and I couldn't keep my head from jerking up to look at him at that last suggestion. I tried to keep it cool, but failed miserably. "What do you mean, 'my move?'" I asked as casually as I could.

Steven gave me a severe look for about half a second, then burst out chuckling. "C'mon, Ro! Are you trying to bullshit me here? The whole school knows you've got the hots for her. And the whole school knows she thinks you're a nice guy who doesn't have the faintest idea how to show some swag."

I didn't like the sound of that at all. "What do you mean, 'swag'?"

He rolled his eyes dramatically and put his head in his hands like the weight of the world was on his shoulders. "C'mon, bro, are you seriously kidding me right now? SWAG. The thing that makes you cool and makes other guys want to be like you and makes girls want you, without even knowing why they want you. That voice in your head might have turned you into Asian Wally West, but you need to ask if it can increase the size of your balls by about five hundred percent for real."

He hopped off the seat he was perched on and started to pace back and forth for effect. My new powers temporarily forgotten, I watched, wishing I could video tape what he was about to say. I found myself leaning forward in anticipation, hoping to hear the secret to being a cool guy who every girl would want to date. "Look Ro, you're smart, and cool, and you got a cool backstory for why you're out there tagging, but when you get around Amayah, you turn into this little bitch. All you want to do is tell her nice things and attend to her needs. THAT'S BORING! She might want a guy like that when she's an old ma, but right now she's a fine female looking to get in a little trouble and make some bad decisions. She doesn't want a guy following her around like a sad little puppy. She wants a guy who is doing his own thing, doesn't take things too seriously, is down for anything, and doesn't worry about whether she likes him or not. You want to get Amayah wanting your skinny ass? You need to show her that Rohan is his own man, and that she'd be lucky for you to look her way."

I shook my head doubtfully. "She's not like that. She likes nice guys, she told me so."

Steven laughed mockingly. "She did, huh? What do you think she'd say to her harmless math buddy? That she wants to get freaky with a bad boy on the back of a motorcycle? Tell me, Ro, what happened the other day when you and she were walking to school, and your boy, Stee-volt, rolled up? Did she keep talking to you, or start talking to me?"

I felt my cheeks flush red. It was only a few days ago, and so much had happened since then, but there was no denying how that incident had affected me. "She talked to you right away," I mumbled.

Steven nodded sagely, which made him look more like an asshole than a genius. "That she did, Ro. And you know what? I could have talked to her for a few minutes, and asked her to come see me at my locker after school, and she would have been there fifteen minutes early to make sure she didn't miss me. And then I could have said that I wanted her to come over to my house to study for the next test, and she would have asked me what time she should be there.

"I would have told her, 'Come at 9 p.m. because my mom will be going out with some friends.' And she would hesitate for about two or three seconds before saying okay with a big smile on her grill. Because now, she's turned on by the danger factor of it all. She would be going to the most popular guy's house at night without his parents at home. That's like a narcotic for the girls at school. They're getting pushed on the daily about their grades and their extracurriculars and what colleges they're applying for. Having a little wild fun is what they're all secretly wishing for. She'd come over, we'd talk a little, pretend to study a little, she'd ask about my family, I'd tell her how my mom is broke, and my dad bailed when I was a baby and about fifteen seconds later, she'd be lying on top of me locking lips like I was Brad freaking Pitt and her clothes coming off. Ya heard."

"That's enough!" I growled, and heard Nick the Brute's voice mixed in with mine as the anger rose in the back of my throat. "I don't like the light you're putting her in." I had been leaning against a concrete pylon while he gave his monologue, and when I broke the spell in the middle of Steven's speech, I realized I had ground my fingernails into the concrete about an inch or two. I pulled my hand away in surprise. Alarmingly, my powers were now manifesting without me being completely aware. Forcefully, I pounded the Brute back down and my rage with it. Steven talked a lot of noise about a lot of things, and I was letting him get to me. "So, why don't you do that if it's so easy?" I asked.

"Eh, she's not really my type," he said with a shrug as if it was the easiest thing in the world to get a girl to come over to his house and make out with him. "Too brainy. Too family oriented. She'd make out with me, no doubt about it, but she's too much of a goody-goody to go all the way. Not worth the effort. Your boy Stee-volt, hates blue balls; makes it hard to go to sleep."

I absolutely hated the way he was talking about Amayah, but if even a little bit of what he said was true, I had to know. "Can you show me how to...can you teach me how to swagger?" I asked, feeling like an idiot.

He grinned, "Thought you'd never ask, Bro-han."

Steven took martial arts classes on Mondays and Fridays, and was in a boxing academy on the other side of the borough that went all morning on Saturdays. He told me he couldn't teach me anything cool before I saw Amayah in an hour, but with my new powers, it didn't really matter.

"You've got these gifts now, bro. Figure out how to use them to blow her mind. Get her wondering, 'How did Rohan do that? Why is he suddenly so mysterious and cool? How do I get him to notice me?'" He talked me through it a bit more as we walked side by side towards Eckerd's. It was 5:05 p.m., and I promised Amayah I would be there by 5 p.m. I was nervous she'd be mad at me, but if I was hearing Steven right, I shouldn't even care if she got upset or not. Me not caring was the way to get her wanting to unwrap my mystery just a little more.

Steven ducked out right before we hit the corner, and we

exchanged our secret handshake, him saying he had a hot date to get ready for. I wanted to ask why he was wasting his time following me to the subway if that was true, but I was too focused on seeing Amayah and didn't worry about what Steven might be up to.

I went through the back entrance to avoid my brother, who was always watching the front of the store like a hawk, and slipped into our extensive stockroom, which seemed packed; the Eckerd truck must have dropped off new inventory. I promptly made a whirling dervish spin to avoid crashing into Amayah at the last second. She gasped, taking a lurch away from the tall shelves she was standing in front of holding a box of bananas. She tried to catch her balance, took two quick steps backward, and her back collided with the rest of the banana boxes piled to the ceiling at least fifteen deep. She stepped away shrieking as it began to ponderously wobble back and forth. In slow motion, the massive pile tilted forward with Amayah a frozen statue rooted to her spot as yellow banana death prepared to crash down upon her.

Within a split second, I was instantly there. I raised my left hand and caught the towering column of bananas as it started to fall, holding it back from crushing the sweet girl I was so smitten with. My other hand went to her shoulders, and I gently moved her out of harm's way. With my newfound strength, it was as easy as picking up a piece of paper. Each box of bananas weighed twenty-five pounds easily, and I was currently holding back at least fifteen of them with nothing more than my left arm. With my newfound abilities, it was no big deal, but for Amayah, who had no idea what I was suddenly capable of, it was nothing short of a miracle.

"Rohan? Wh-what, how are you doing that?" she asked me, gazing up with her mouth open and a shocked look on her face. I created my response straight from Steven's playbook, smiling sideways and flashing Amayah a wink.

"Been working out a bit between math tests," I responded casually, flexing my arm to settle the massive stack of crates back into their upright position. I turned back to Amayah, who was still standing there totally dumbfounded. On a whim and thinking of Steven's advice, I used my other hand to scoop her up as if she was a doll and lifted and lowered her a few times like I was using her as a bench press. She was a little put off at first, but then I heard her give the same giggling laugh that she'd given Steven a couple of days ago. That laugh flowed over me like liquid sunshine, and I could have stayed in that moment forever.

I lowered her to eye level, cracked a sideways smile, and said in a softer voice, "What do you think?"

She was smiling, but I could tell it wasn't quite the same now, as if the shock of seeing an aggressive, powerful version of me had triggered some warning bell in her mind that this wasn't the guy she really knew. *Yup, that's what swagger could do*, I thought.

She patted my shoulder and said, "Um, we should probably get back to work now, right?"

Feeling the air go out of my sails but determined to follow Steven's counsel and not show it, I feigned nonchalance and lightly lowered her to the ground.

"Good talk," I said with a wink. "Your boy Ro-rock will see you out there."

I didn't linger to see her reaction as much as I wanted to. I turned on one heel and strolled onto the store's main floor to check out what other tasks I had to do for the afternoon shift so that I could get back to exploring my new abilities.

CHAPTER

SIX

I spent my entire shift not necessarily ignoring Amayah but trying not to force conversations with her, not going out of my way to help her with her work tasks, and not even turning my head as she walked by. Instead, I used very minor bursts of my new powers to make my work infinitely easier. Instead of lugging box after box from the stockroom to restock the shelves, I waited until the coast was clear and lifted them all at once.

As luck would have it, half of a box of bananas ended up crushed in the stockroom from when I prevented Amayah from being flattened. My brother, of course, blamed me for the fiasco and handed me a write-up. But whatever, I tried my best to do the right thing and ended up close to being fired by my own brother, no less. I had to remind myself not to get mad at Henry. When he ordered me outside to collect all the shopping carts people loved taking to their cars and leaving in the middle of nowhere, I turned on the speed and finished the job in about fifteen seconds. *Take that, Henry!*

I also turned on my personality, as foreign a concept as that was, every time any female under fifty came in contact with me. Some of them looked at me as if I was crazy—mostly the older ones—but the

99

younger women and the few teenage girls who came by the store had very different reactions. They would smile when I said something off the cuff, usually taking a dig at my brother, who would act like a military dictator when it came to presenting ID to get a prescription. With tremendous dramatic effect, I'd stand behind him or turn sideways, roll my eyes, and mouth the exact words he was sternly saying. It got several smiles and some genuine giggles from the girls my age and a bit older. I guess Steven knew what he was talking about.

A few times, I saw Amayah out of the corner of my eye looking up from what she was doing or walking around the corner because she heard my voice and some other girl laughing with me. Each and every time, I ignored her, even though I'm convinced that if I hadn't, she would have smiled at me, and I could have smiled back. But I was going all in on Steven's technique and seeing where it led me. Or, more correctly, how it was leading her right to me.

Instead of offering to walk Amayah home after work, she said no thanks about ninety percent of the time; I think I gave a loud whistle. I swaggy blurted, "Rohan out, yo!" without looking back to see who was watching or listening. It dug into my heart quite a bit to blatantly ignore her, and of course, the rampant fear that if I did, she'd think I didn't like her and start talking to other guys, but as Steve had pointed out, my full court press of attention to her so far had gotten me nowhere.

I was feeling good and adding a little strut to my step as I kept up my cool new Rohan persona on the street when my brother interrupted my good vibes. "You're quite the fuck up," Henry yelled as I left Eckerd. "If you want to be a bum and do stupid stuff, maybe you should do that on your own and move out."

I pretended not to hear him ripping into me and left in a big rush when I heard another voice. Not Nick. Someone else. *"Idiot! Can't even bring a box from the storeroom in correctly! Why do I put up with this?"*

At first, I thought I had overheard someone, but there was no one within fifty feet of me, and I wasn't close to any open doors. It wasn't Nick the Brute, either, unless he had suddenly developed a thick Italian accent, which seemed unlikely given how many times he popped into my head. Was it my imagination? Was I having a brain aneurysm, and the powers that I manifested were the beginning of the end of my life? I didn't know, and I was trying not to freak out when another voice came to me.

"God, she's so hot. If she wasn't married to my brother, I'd be all over that already."

I jerked my head around. This wasn't Nick, and it wasn't the Italian accent, either!

Trying not to completely freak out, I increased my pace a little, wanting to get home and be still so I could sort things out when I noticed something. About fifty feet ahead, a young Black woman was doing stretches in a workout outfit on the steps of an apartment building. She was probably in her mid-twenties, and was drop-dead gorgeous, with beautiful skin, white teeth, and a killer body. I slowed down to take in the sight while walking by. But I hadn't even gotten that good of a glance when I suddenly noticed the guy behind her. He was sitting on the top of the steps, oversized sunglasses hid his face, and he was wearing a jacket with about ten or fifteen pockets stitched in; the very definition of a Fresh Ghetto drug dealer. He was ogling her with his tongue out. She bent over to stretch, and all he could do was lick and bite his lips. As I got closer, the second voice blasted back into my head.

"Need to wait until he's out of town on business again. Show up late with some wine and see what she's willing to do."

I had to physically restrain myself from doing a double-take. The drug dealer was staring right at the young woman's ass as she bent over when that thought popped into my head. It was him! I was hearing his thoughts in my head. There was no doubting what was running through his mind based on his body language and his line of sight. The ramifications of this were mind-blowing. I realized that earlier I must have been hearing an angry shopkeeper thinking how frustrated he was with one of his employees. I was suddenly aware of just how many people there were on the street, and started wondering if it was something I could control, or just a random occurrence. I started really looking at people as I passed them, but that didn't seem to do anything that I could see, so I went back to trying to just clear my head and see what happened. After a few minutes of distracting myself and failing miserably, it happened again.

"Never would have had a chance anyway, I was so stupid to apply."

"I swear to God if he brings home another F in math, I'm going to beat his ass until he can't walk for a week!"

"Stupid chinks taking all the jobs. Why won't they go back to their own country already. So sick of having to work for this slant-eyed bastard!"

"I wish she would just drop dead already! I'm sick of living under her rules!"

There were so many voices that it was hard to tell them apart, and the thoughts were bouncing one into another. Suddenly I wasn't so sure I wanted this power at all. I felt like if I couldn't find a way to shut the voices off, or at least filter them, I might go insane quite quickly.

"Got to see if I can open another credit card. Coke's getting so damn expensive."

"Stupid kid doesn't know how good he's got it. I can't wait until he figures out the truth about me."

"Rohan, do not be troubled, all will be revealed."

"It has to be tonight. I'm so hungry. So hungry to taste it again."

I came to a lurching stop. I had heard my own name there. Someone was talking to me in my mind! I tried to reach out and figure out who it was or what the source was, but I couldn't. It sounded female, sort of high and clear, like something from a movie with a queen or another royal person. But there had been too many voices in a row to recall more than that. It was like a faucet that was flowing freely and had now been shut off with no way of opening it back up again. I tried in vain for a few minutes to focus and find that sweet spot again where the voices would come, but it just wouldn't happen. *Who are you?* I tried to project out mentally. *What is all this?*

At first, there was no response. But after a few silent seconds, I heard the voice again, as if it was coming from a great distance.

"Seek me out, Rohan. Seek the truth. I am the light in the darkness, and I can guide you on this journey."

The voice was female, definitely not Nick, and even recalling it a few seconds later, I felt like I was being hypnotized by it. The words made me feel like I was being lulled to sleep, or perhaps that I had taken the kind of cough medicine that comes pink and bubble gummy from the store and knocks you on your butt twenty minutes after you drink it down.

The voice faded as quickly as it had come, and no matter what I asked for, it did not come again. It was getting out of hand, and I was getting worried about what the hell was going on inside of my brain, so I stopped at the next apartment building and sat on the stoop. I folded my arms across my chest and hugged myself tightly, focusing inward.

"Nick? Can you hear me?"

For a long second, there was nothing, then his voice came darting back into my brain.

"Rohan, at last you have called me forth to begin your training. I am honored. Let me teach you, my boy."

I wanted to learn, but I wanted to hear his take on what had just happened first.

"In a minute, Nick. I have to ask you something. A moment ago, I heard another voice, a female voice telling me something about how all will be revealed. Was that you?"

For a brief second, Nick was hesitating, either out of an urge to not worry me or perhaps to keep something hidden.

"I had hoped to not burden you with the existence of ... The Other, Rohan, but I see she has made herself known to you," he said. *"She is the other side of me. The negative force of our equation. She is equal parts*

seductress and spirit master. She lives to deceive. To ensnare. To bind your soul to hers with promises that no entity has the power to make. She promises the power of eternal life and all wisdom, but refuses to say where that power emerges from. She will trick you into promising unending servitude for a taste of the power her Master commands, but never will she reveal his face. I do not lie, Rohan, my battle with her and her Master has woven its way across time immortal. While I stand by my promises of giving you what you most deserve, I also ask for your help in battling this unspeakable force. Ours is the battle of all battles, the war between light and darkness, and the hope to gain victory once and for all to free the misguided flocks that are in desperate need of a true leader."

"But who is she?" I asked. "What does she want?"

Another hesitation. *"Every soul is what she wants, Rohan, and she will settle for nothing less than total victory. I seek out souls like yours, who, I believe, can make a difference in this war. You are one such, Rohan, my son, my knight. You have a warrior's soul within you, and I believe you could be the one who guides us to a final victory."*

Now two voices were talking in my head more distinctly than the rest: Nick, who was a bit rough around the edges but also seemed to have given me powers rivaling those of Superman; and this female voice, who claimed to be my guide on some incredible journey. Neither one of them seemed to want to give me any straight answers, and that's what I needed the most right now. If they weren't willing to share information, I was going to shut them out of the equation and try to figure things out for myself.

For the next day, I tried to stay focused on the things I could control and not freak out about the voices. They came back sporadically, and I had to struggle to maintain the air that I was just a normal kid doing normal things. Even worse was when I started hearing other students' thoughts while I was in debate class. We were in the middle of a test. It was deadly silent except that suddenly I could hear a scrabbling of stressed-out voices racing through my skull as I tried to properly present my argument on why new political third parties should be able to have the same access as Democrats and Republicans to create a free political market. It was already an incredibly boring topic, and hearing everyone's voices at once was making it much worse. In normal circumstances, I might have found it pretty amusing, especially given that in the space of a few seconds I had learned that Kristin Strain had cheated on her boyfriend last weekend and was now worried she might be pregnant, and that Raj Parikh was trying to figure out how to tell his father he fell asleep during the SAT and only made a 930 on it.

There was so much noise that it was giving me the equivalent of a five-star migraine.

FORMULATING A SOLUTION, I tried drowning the voices out by tiring myself and sapping my reserves. I was practicing every afternoon and morning in the subway tunnels, and my skill set had gotten more prolific with each session. I got bored with my tunnel sprints rather quickly and needed a challenge, with Nick uttering, *"a real man's challenge,"* so I grabbed a train schedule one day and started planning to see what my limits absolutely might be. The only good thing my parents ever bought me was a Macintosh computer, which I'd named "Big Berta," where I did my school reports. So I fired Berta up and started making a chart of train times and locations close enough to where I lived and my walking route to school to where the trains would simultaneously move in the same direction.

About four days after my first tunnel trials, I initiated my first train trials. It probably sounds a little insane, and I guess maybe it was, but I had to see what I could do, and I needed a starting point. So I left about forty-five minutes early for school that day and hustled down the station's stairs at Forest Hills. I had to loiter around the station for a few minutes until a cop finished his coffee and headed upstairs, and then I waited for the train to arrive. There were only a few people getting off and even fewer getting on, which was a positive, because everyone was in their early-morning haze, and nobody was paying much attention to the lanky Asian kid dressed all in black leaning against a pylon. When the "stand clear ... Bing Bong" warning buzzed, and the doors closed, I took one last look around and dropped off the platform's edge into the gloom below. I didn't hear anyone shouting, so it was "Go Time!"

"Okay, Nick," I said, "Let's see what I can do."

If he was there, and I had a vague idea that he was, he wasn't talking back. I felt he observed all my tests beneath the teaching he was trying to give me, especially after his motivational speech about the female voice I heard. Nick's explanation pleasantly convinced me for a couple of days after I first heard the other voice, but as more time passed, the less sure I became. Because sensing the other voice had given me a certain measure of tranquility, something whole, which Nick called being *'hypnotically seduced.'* But I didn't feel any evil intent in her.

Nick was more passionate and spirited, with a gung-ho attitude, that was for sure, and I guess if I were fighting the same enemy for centuries, I would be too. But as my mom often said, "Don't rush through the homework, Ro. Being first doesn't make you best." So, I was trying to keep my distance from Nick, and not fawn over him like I had when he first started saying he could teach me to do anything I wanted. I still wanted those things badly enough to fantasize about them daily, but I also knew that New York City was not the place to try out my new superhero powers and not be in total control of them. Maybe that's why Superman grew up so anonymously. Something like fifty people lived in Smallville, and he could get away with carrying tractors and leaping over the silo once in a while. I didn't have that luxury. I needed to know how to control myself before I started making bigger plans.

It was then the train took off loudly, gathering speed. I gave it a five-count head start, then took off after it into the darkness. The train had enough outside lighting to light my path, and I ran side by side with it for a few seconds and kept that pace until its next stop at Jackson Heights. If you're not from New York, you might wonder how I thought this was a good idea, since I was trying to train anonymously without drawing undue attention to myself. Nobody looks out the window of the subway while they were making their commute. Most of them are reading a newspaper, or they're trying to finish work, or they've got their eyes closed wishing they were still in bed asleep. With me dressed in all black, there would be almost zero chance for another "Black Blur" sighting.

I would race the subway every morning. From what I read at school, the cars topped at around fifty-five miles an hour on long stretches, so the one I was going up against was probably doing about forty mph. *Pretty dope* for my first efforts, but I knew I could go faster if I could just find the place to do it.

I hadn't been as successful in testing the teleportation skills because I was afraid of what suddenly materializing into a large crowd of people, or into my own apartment when my family was home, or maybe into the side of a building, would do. The subway freaked me out when I thought about teleporting. I had no idea if there were any parameters to this unique form of transport. And I only did a few short tests in my room when nobody else was home, focusing on my bed versus a spot in the living room, and they worked, but I needed more space outdoors and a lot fewer people around to really give it a shot.

I also needed to work on my self-confidence. Every time I went to draw on my energy source, I was convinced it wasn't going to be there. My powers could have been more consistent. I feared I would reach down and find nothing or wake up from the worst pipe dream of all time, but I had to stay more positive.

I never got tired of how it felt to harness the power. It was pure exhilaration, pure adrenaline, and *pure dopeness*. I wondered if this is what the greatest athletes felt when they took off from the starting line. The electricity that seemed to be crackling through my limbs made me want to run forever. And to see how far I could go before I had the slightest hint of fatigue. Could I scale Mt. Everest? Could I move so quickly that I could run across the water? I wasn't sure what my limits were, but with or without Nick's help, I wanted to find them.

One unforgettable afternoon, I was captivated by a break dancer performing in the subway lobby. His movements seemed to defy gravity, as he leaped and spun with extraordinary agility. I watched in awe as he held his hands and legs up in the air, moving with unparalleled fluidity and grace. It was as if he had broken free from the constraints of traditional dance, creating a one-of-a-kind spectacle that appeared to transcend the laws of physics. In that moment, I felt inspired by his uniqueness and artistry, realizing my own yearning to express myself in an equally extraordinary way.

I also suddenly realized why Charles Xavier had built the mansion for the kids in the X-Men comics. He needed space to train them all without prying eyes around! After school, I would train with Steven, who showed me how to add finesse to my raw strength and speed. He might have had a big mouth, but he knew what he was talking about when it came to physical violence.

We had agreed early on that I wouldn't enhance my combat with my powers when he and I were sparring. I still didn't know the limitations of everything, and I had already experienced that when my emotions were out of check, the powers could manifest without me even knowing it. I didn't want to hurt Steven accidentally or cause any attention to myself that might lead to a lot of awkward questions, so I fought him just as Rohan Chang, an average teenager. As a result, he dumped me on my ass for about two days straight when we started.

He told me to start calling him Stee-volt. However, I wasn't sure if I would use that nickname much. Stee-volt introduced me to kicks, punches, and combos of the two that I could use whether I was fighting one guy or a bunch of guys; something every superhero seems to do at one time or another. I thought we'd go to this private gym that he was always saying he had access to, but he said it was a bad idea, and we wound up in parks and alleys around town. That meant no showing off with my abilities, but that was probably for the best. Punching Steven with the strength I possessed now might kill him. Trying to learn how to harness everything at once and using my powers to fight before I was ready seemed dangerous.

Like many Asian kids, my idol growing up was Bruce Lee. Some of his films were pretty goofy by today's standards, with his screaming and moaning while kicking major ass simultaneously. However, he was the one action star my dad seemed okay with letting us watch on TV. And no one on the planet could match his mastery of different forms of martial arts, which he perfected into Jeet Kune Do, "*using no way as way and having no limitation as limitation.*" I loved him so much that I did a book report on Bruce Lee in the sixth grade, and, lo and behold, he was as much a philosopher as he was a fighter. The book I read about him from the library had a message in the back that he wrote. I checked out that book so often that the librarian told me I could have it before summer vacation. The pages got so ragged that I used Big Berta, my computer, to type out his message, print it, and hang it on my wall where I could see it every morning. It read:

"Be Water, My Friend.
Empty your mind. Be formless, shapeless, like water. You put water into a
cup, it becomes the cup. You put water into a bottle, it becomes the bottle.
You put it into a teapot, it becomes the teapot. Now water can flow, or it
can crash. Be water, my friend."

I WASN'T ALWAYS sure what it meant, but I knew it was something special. As my powers kept manifesting, I felt like it was a mantra that I could get behind. I wasn't sure what was going to happen next for me, if the powers were permanent or they'd be gone as quickly as they came, but I wanted to stay me; to stay Rohan, no matter what came next. I also had two posters of Bruce Lee in my bedroom, and when I started working out with Steven more and more, I found myself emulating Bruce's trademark screams before he would attack.

Steven or, was it Stee-volt, laughed the first few times I did it, but when I started giving him as much *whoop-ass* as I was receiving, he quickly learned to respect that the noise meant a beating might be coming his way.

As it was, one day after school, we were supposed to meet a few blocks away at a seldom-used park that was mostly a place for bums to sleep in the afternoon, away and out of sight of the police.

It was an older park with dense trees in many places, one broken-down swing set, and many picnic tables made of concrete, probably meant to discourage people from stealing them. Bums were pretty harmless, at least when it came to guys like me. I dressed almost as poorly as they did, and even though I had started putting on some muscle during my training with Steven, I still looked pretty skinny, so most of them realized I didn't have any money or food to give them. When they could tell you were just slightly above their own level, they didn't try so eagerly to work you over. What was the point?

I had no idea where Steven was. Maybe he stood me up at this park, but I didn't want to waste time, so I dumped my backpack under one of the picnic tables and started going through the warmup routine that every other kid knew from watching Bruce Lee movies growing up. I closed my eyes to get a little meditation going and was quickly moving into a series of strikes and kicks, calling out like Bruce and enjoying the sweat I was building in the silence of the trees. The air was calm, the greenery was dosing me with pure oxygen, and the voices in my head had been quiet all day. Until I heard a rustle behind me and thought maybe a squirrel was running on the ground, but I was wrong. Very wrong.

"Look at this, boys! A little Science fag is out here playing punch-punch!" came a callous voice behind me. "Ssi-bal-nyeon!"

I didn't know much Korean, but I knew what *'Fucking bitch!'* meant. As I opened my eyes and whirled around, I quickly saw I was no longer alone in the park. There were three of them. All were two or three years older than me, and of Korean descent. A little chill went down my spine as I recognized the one who had spoken. His name was Jun-seo, and he lived about eight blocks from me but went to a different school, and we didn't run in the same circles. I knew him though. Two years earlier, my parents' dry cleaning business was vandalized. It was before we got security cameras put in to watch the doors because it was too expensive, but the damage done was extensive. Windows smashed, the cash register stolen, and the store tagged with hate speech. The repairs set my parents' financial plans back years, and the police were slow to respond and never followed up after taking a first report and interviewing a few neighbors.

My dad was so disappointed that he launched his own investigation, combed the place for clues, and talked to every person he could find. Within a couple of weeks, he had a pretty good composite drawing and a name to go with it. That name was Jun-seo, a teenage lieutenant in a local Korean gang that shook down businesses for protection money and terrorized anyone who dared say no. My dad wanted to go to the police with the information, but some of his fellow business owners warned him against doing it. He eventually had to shamefully admit to us that another set of gang members, older Koreans who had been in the neighborhood for two decades, were the ones responsible. When they heard that some "revolutionary" dry-cleaning/laundromat business was turning a good profit, they had decided to take their "share" for protection. My dad had told them no and demanded they leave. They had left quietly, then sent Jun-seo back that night to pay him back for his disrespect.

I've seen Jun-seo just once since then, and only from a long way off at a festival. I had no idea if he even knew who I was, but the tone in his voice suggested it wasn't going to make a difference. They were here looking for trouble, but I doubted they knew what kind of trouble I could bring to them.

Jun-seo had a sneer on his face as he gave me the quick once-over. No doubt he had tabbed me as an easy mark for a robbery, beat down, or both. There were two others with him. One was so big I thought he might have had superpowers of his own. No Korean kid should be hitting over two-hundred and fifty pounds, but this guy was either a bodybuilder, a football player, or was taking steroids. Maybe all three. The third guy was short and wiry, and was cracking his knuckles over and over again. When he moved, his hand glittered in the afternoon light, and I realized he was wearing brass knuckles on his right hand. I had never seen any in person before, but there was no doubting the intention behind them.

I spread my feet a little further apart and focused on staying balanced. If I was going to be like my idol here, I could get out of this without having it come to violence, but if I was pushed, I was going to respond with whatever it took.

Jun-seo and his boys also spread out to make themselves look bigger than they were to ensure I couldn't run away too quickly. If I tried, it would be straight back into the trees where there wasn't much room for movement. Of course, none of them knew that I was capable of running faster than their cars could go, or disappearing in a blink of an eye back to my house, but I had no interest in sharing that information unless it was absolutely necessary.

"What are you doing out here all alone, little fag, waiting for your boyfriend?" Jun-seo taunted me, and his two lackeys laughed with him. "Who's turn is it to be the man, and who will be the woman tonight?"

I let the insults roll off me and stayed silent. *I am water. I am water.*

The wiry guy stopped laughing and said, "Hey, Bruce! Are you retarded? We're talking to you!" More laughter followed, but I didn't say a word. The silent treatment was getting them angry, but I was determined to maintain control of myself no matter what.

But that's when Jun-seo recognized me. "Wait a minute, I know this kid! Yeah, this that Chong kid whose dumb ass dad owns that dry cleaning shit hole near Fresh Ghetto. Hey boy, tell your dad his cash register is safe and sound if he ever wants to come pick it up. I mean it's in twenty pieces, but he could probably duct tape it back together."

Mentioning my dad was a mistake on his part. My dad and I might be at odds a lot, and lately it has been a whole lot worse. Ever since the morning he had caught me coming in late, he had been all over me with his foot up my butt. He had Henry send him my time-card from Eckerd's to ensure I was there exactly on time for each shift. He was also demanding to see all of my assignments—not just the report cards—and was checking my room at least two to three times a night to make sure I was where I was supposed to be. He was also using harsher language toward me. My dad was mixing in a lot of "bèndàn," which equated to an *idiot*, and "wángbā dàn," which meant *bastard*.

He seemed to be coughing a lot more too, and I heard my mom accuse him of taking up smoking again, even though he denied it loudly each time she brought it up. But regardless of all that, when Jun-seo mentioned him, the image of his defeated face from a few years ago popped into my head, and the water I was trying to be was suddenly scalding hot. My eyes flashed with rage, and they all saw it. I had the very brief satisfaction of watching the little guy take a half-step back in surprise at how my face changed, but he quickly caught himself, remembering they were three gang bangers, and I was just one loser.

"Oh, well well, looks like somebody's getting angry," Jun-seo said. "What are you going to do about it, though? Throw a punch? Take a swing? Nah, probably just piss your pants. Ssi-bal... Assuming what you've got in your pants even works."

I snapped. Insulting my family brought forth the rage. Insulting my manhood unleashed it. When I opened my mouth to speak, I suddenly felt Nick simmering in my mind with a fiery fury. I pulled it into my own thoughts, and it magnified. It was like having a best friend at your back when you were about to throw down in a fight, and that best friend happened to be eight feet tall, weighs four hundred pounds, and knows Kung Fu. Nick's energy was permeating my entire body like lava flowing down a mountain from a volcano. But not in a destructive way, at least not yet. The heat that was coursing through my body was addictive, like the way you feel when you lie in the sun on a spring day and your whole body warms up. I felt like a coiled spring ready to explode into action, and it was an incredible feeling. Perhaps the best of my entire life. I was limitless at that moment. Like, if I wanted to, I could have scaled the Empire State Building without a net, or knocked out Mike Tyson ten seconds into the first round. I had power. I had Nick. I felt unstoppable.

"How about I break your fucking face?" I snarled in a voice that scared even me a little bit; it sounded deeper, more mature, and like it didn't give a damn what happened in the battle to come.

The caustic smile fell straight off Jun-seo's face and was replaced by anger and just the smallest touch of fear. His insult had been tossed back at him in front of two of his underlings. He couldn't let that pass. "Enough!" he jabbed in an enraged tone. "Kang-dae. Break this faggot's arm off."

The giant, Kang-dae, came at me with big purposeful strides. I felt like even in my pre-powered up days, I could have avoided his grip; he was so slow and methodical. But I didn't want to put that theory to the test. Instead, I caught his two-handed hammer swipe with one of my hands and held him stone still for several seconds, grinning right at Jun-seo all the while as the three gang members stared in disbelief at what was happening in front of them. I bent the giant's hands back slowly for effect, then spun around and planted a kick right into his junk. Even trying to restrain myself a little, I still knocked him ten feet back when I kicked him, and Kang-dae screamed in pain in a high-pitched squeal that didn't match his size at all.

A rush of warning came to me in Nick's voice, and I turned just in time to see the wiry kid stepping to me with the brass knuckles ready to punch a dent in my solar plexus. I was only marginally in control now, letting Nick's reactions guide me as I caught the little guy midair at the apex of his leap and lifted him above my head. He was gasping in panic and begging me to put him down, and I obliged, but not before driving my knee up into his back. It made a resounding CRACK that might have been one of his ribs based on how loud he screamed. I flung his body on top of Kang-dae's and turned to stare down Jun-seo. If he hadn't ransacked my family's business, I would have almost felt bad for the guy.

Jun-seo was staring at his two friends' unconscious bodies as if he had seen a ghost or was in a dream he couldn't wake up from. He snapped back to the moment and reached into his back pocket, bringing out a switchblade that he spun around as he brought the blade out. It was a move I suspected was meant to intimidate anyone dumb enough to pick a fight with him, but to me, it looked like an act of desperation. He knew and I knew that a blade wasn't going to make the difference in this fight. I let him go through the motions and brought it to bear, then I touched my energy source and burst forward in half a second, grabbing his wrist so hard he dropped the knife right into my waiting hand. He gasped and his eyes bulged. I'm sure it looked to him like I had moved faster than was possible for a human. I had taken away his only advantage one second into the fight. I flipped the knife around and held it casually in front of his face, intent on scaring him the way I'm sure he scared a hundred kids a year.

"What the fuck are you?" he spat out as his teeth chattered in fear.

I felt the Brute surge within me, and before I could stop myself, I leaned in and cut slightly into Jun-seo's cheek with the tip of his own switchblade. He screamed in pain as blood started trickling down his face. I felt repulsed by the sound, so I stopped. A little slice to his cheek should teach him a lesson. If I had leaned into the blade more, the cut would have been from his nose to his ear, which Nick the Brute savagely wanted as a souvenir. "Jun-Seo," I snarled, again the voice a mix of my own and the Brute's. "I'll kill you if you ever come near my family or me again."

He started to cry and mumble that he wouldn't, but I didn't let him get far. I smashed his face with my forehead and tossed him through the air on top of the other two. As he fell, his ankle caught one of the concrete tables, and I heard bones crunch.

I could feel the Brute exultant inside of me, reveling in the carnage we had caused. *"Yes, yes, that's the power we possess. That's the power you control. Use it. Don't hesitate. Lions don't worry about sheep. You can make them all pay. All the ones who have pushed you down, called you names, shitted on your family. Turn the tables on them. Show them what it's like to be afraid. Show them that the only true justice is what you make for yourself. Make those gangs fear you, and take the streets from them! No one can stop you, Rohan. No one can stop us. I've given you the power. Use it to make the world the way you want it to be!"*

I let it flow through me. How many times had I shied away from a fight? How many times had I taken the other way home to avoid confrontation? Never again. I was the big man now. I was the one who they'd see coming and move to the other side of the street. I was the one that ...

I stopped when I heard a familiar voice. Given how many voices were coming into my head now, it wasn't that out of the ordinary. But this was the one I heard in my daydreams so much that it was unmistakable.

Amayah?

Incredibly, it was her. But it was more than just her voice and more of a vision she was nearing. She was with another girl in our grade, Elisabeth Tu, and they were walking on the border of the park jabbering about the debate team tryouts.

I panicked. I couldn't let her see me like this! The scene in front of me, the three gang members beaten to a pulp. She'd be totally freaked out and probably never talk to me again.

"My dad insisted, though. All three of my older brothers were captains, so it's like a huge deal to my whole family," Elisabeth was saying.

"This sucks," Amayah responded. *"My dad told me not to try. He said debating is a man's game, and girls don't even have a place in it. Worse,*

he doesn't even think I can be a physician because he doesn't think I have what it takes."

"Gross," Elisabeth soothed. "What is he, a caveman? Girls can do anything as well as a boy. He needs to get with the twentieth century already."

Amayah sighed, "I know. I wish he wouldn't say things like that. When I was younger, I heard him and my mama arguing late one night when they thought I was asleep. My dad always wanted a son, and they got me instead. Then something happened, and Mama couldn't have any more babies. Every generation of my dad's family has had a son go on to do great things like his own father. Sometimes he acts like he's just stuck with me."

Elisabeth wrapped Amayah in a hug.

I felt my heart going out to my beautiful crush. I never knew that about her and her dad, and it made me just about as pissed at him as I was at my own dad. What kind of father says he wanted a son instead of a daughter? I wanted nothing more than to go to her and wrap her up in a hug right then, but I couldn't. Between the fact that I was totally eavesdropping on their conversation and the case of the three pulverized Korean gangbangers at my feet, I had to get the hell out of there.

I DIDN'T KNOW which way to run, so I started concentrating on my bed in my room as hard as I could. Despite the Brute's protestations that we administer a little more pain to Jun-seo and his recruits, I reached into myself, touching the source, and instantly fell onto the soft sheets of my bed. I'd made it.

I was scared by how quickly I had lost control, so I intensified training with Steven and started trying to find other ways to mani-fest my powers to inflate my status at school and around the neigh-borhood.

I started going to school early and joining the before-school basketball games on the asphalt courts that had metal rims but no nets. It took me two days to get into a game, since they had a pretty regular crowd most mornings, but when Brian Young slipped and rolled his ankle one morning, Jarron pointed at me and said, "Yo, Roman, you're in!" I was too excited even to tell him he got my name wrong.

I jogged in, and Jarron told me to guard Eugene Perlberg, a Jewish senior who played on the Varsity and was three inches taller than me and probably outweighed me by sixty pounds.

When Eugene saw that I was sizing him up on defense, he laughed out loud and called for the ball. I kept my feet spread like I was getting ready for a fight and watched the ball instead of his eyes, knowing he'd try to fake me out. When the move came—faking a pass to his right and then dribbling to his left—I was more than ready. Faster than he could see, I slapped the ball out of his hand, dribbled back up court and threw a laser-beam chest pass to Jarron who scored an easy layup. The whistles and gasps from other players were like sweet music in my ears. Eugene was pissed, especially with his teammates mocking him for letting 'that skinny chink' make him look bad.

On his team's next possession, he didn't waste any time, dribbling up the court and heading straight at me, intent on putting me back in my place. But I didn't go for the steal this time; I waited until he went into his shooting motion and called on my energy source to send me leaping up to where I swatted the ball back in his face. It conked him in the forehead and bounced through the air to one of my teammates. I raced down the court and Douglas Tuan, the Indonesian point guard, tossed me a pass. I caught it in mid-stride, took one step, and exploded up to the rim to throw down a vicious slam dunk that sent my teammates into a frenzy. We only got a few more possessions in before the bell rang, but the surge of buzz around me grew all day long.

When I showed up the next morning to play again, I was the first pick, and there were at least ten other guys there who hadn't been there the day before just to watch me hoop. Listening to everyone talk, I overheard much chatter and disbelief at how I suddenly became this good at basketball.

I put on a show of steals, dunks, blocked shots, the whole nine yards. Jarron and Brian said I should come with them to Rucker Park sometime to show off what I could do. Even though I was more of a baseball fan, everyone knew Rucker Park was the most famous basketball court in the world. Some of the greatest streetball players of all time got their start there, and NBA stars like Kareem Abdul-Jabbar and Dr. J would show up every once in a while, to watch a game or even play with the regulars.

The next day, a crowd of thirty or forty kids was watching our before-school pickup game, including five to six girls from my grade and the one above me. Girls I knew by name and sight, but girls I never talked to and quite frankly couldn't imagine talking to before a few weeks ago. With a much bigger and much better-looking crowd in attendance, I upped the action a little bit. I used my enhanced senses to make not one but two shots from midcourt to cheers and applause, and in the last possession, before the bell rang, I jumped from the free throw line like Michael Jordan had in the dunk contest a decade before and threw it down through the rim as the crowd went wild. Kids were all gathering around me as I walked into the building. A freshman even asked me to autograph the ball for him.

I was at my locker wiping the sweat off my face with my gym towel when someone touched me on the arm, and I turned around. It was Lisa Joyce, one of the girls who watched the game before school. She was a year older than me, blonde, and had a figure that every guy in school talked about. She knew it too, wearing shirts that seemed way too tight to make her chest stand out even more than it already did. A few years ago, a guy named Tim Colvin got into gargantuan trouble when he wrote an essay about her in my first-year English class. Not that writing about someone you have a crush on is against the rules, but the essay topic was, "How can we achieve world peace?" and his answer was, "Have Lisa Joyce become a stripper." And here she was, at my locker, touching my shoulder, smiling up at me. "Hi, Rohan, I just wanted to tell you how amazing you were today!"

"Um, thanks," was my cool guy's response. Being this close to her was a little dizzying.

"How come you didn't play on the school team this year?"

Well, shit, I didn't have an answer for that. I couldn't say that my magical powers had not developed until after tryouts. Then I remembered Steven's advice about acting like I didn't give a shit. I casually shrugged my shoulders. "Just seemed kind of lame playing for the school on its schedule. I like my freedom. Do what I want when I want, you know?"

She smiled, and I had the feeling she would have smiled regardless of what I said. But it didn't matter much because that was one fine smile directed right at me. "Totally, I get that," she said, continuing to touch my shoulder. "But listen, if you want to play next year, I'd love to see you out there. I'm going to be the head cheerleader, and I will be at every one of your games."

She paused and leaned in a little closer, so her chest was touching my arm. In a much softer voice she whispered, "I'd love to shake my pom-poms and scream your name when you're winning us the state title."

Just the feel of her body pressed lightly against mine seemed to raise my body temperature about ten degrees. I didn't want her to move away, so I smiled, pretended to be Steven, and said, "Why don't you practice that a little now? Let me see how good it will look next season."

Three months ago, being this close to Lisa Joyce and saying anything even vaguely flirtatious to her probably would have gotten me cursed at, slapped, or beaten up by one of the guys who played sports and ran around in the same crowd as she did.

Her eyes widened a little at my request, but then a knowing smile came across her face. This was a girl who wasn't shy about flirting or making guys pay attention to her. She stepped in closer to me, so her chest was flush against mine, and she looked up innocently, her light blue eyes widening with just the right amount of awe to make me feel like I was the most amazing person ever.

As she leaned up and her long red fingernails grazed my ear lobe, she blew her breath onto my lips, sending shivers and making me break out in goosebumps. She whispered, "Rohan, you are so amazing on the court. So strong and smooth and soooo hottt. I want to cheer for you all night long."

True to her word, she shook those pom-poms for me. She rubbed up against my chest with hers and I couldn't tell if time was standing still or speeding up because all I wanted was that sensation to last forever. She looked me in the eye and her innocent smile got wider and sexier. She took one of my hands away from my locker and put it into her long blonde hair as she slowly moved against me. Her hair was silky soft, and I never touched a girl's hair before in any flirting situation, but now I thought I wanted to do nothing but that.

When the bell rang to start the day, I very briefly thought about taking two steps, jumping, and smashing it to pieces to shut it up and get back to Lisa, but the moment was lost as she bent down to pick up her book bag. When she stood back up, she gave me another killer smile that sent heat coursing all over my body, particularly to my stomach, my chest, and my groin. She could have asked me to go rob Wall Street right then, and I wouldn't have hesitated for a single second. She stepped closer again and pressed her lips to my ear, placing a small kiss there as she wound my fingers into her hair for one more brief touch. She whispered, "I like when you play with it, but I love to have it pulled," and then she spun with a smile and walked off, purposely moving her hips to give me an incredible view as she headed for class. I grinned, sure that my face was also blushing two shades brighter of bright red, redder than the sun, watching Lisa leave.

Was this what I wanted? Something felt strange. It was then Nick started telling me that after all the crap I had been through all these years, this was the life destined for me—the life I deserved.

"Why are you limiting yourself to your high school? There are thou-

sands upon thousands of fine girls and finer women all over New York City."

Maybe I could win a few Olympic medals, a Super Bowl, the US Open, and the Masters.

"Lions don't worry about sheep and are leaders among men," Nick whispered just then. *"It's easy for a young lion like you, Rohan, to take what is rightfully yours."*

This time next year, I'd be walking out of the hottest clubs in New York City with Julia Roberts, Demi Moore, or Nicole Kidman on my arm. Wait, it took me another minute to realize I was standing there with a giant grin on my face, needing to get to class.

When I walked through the door a couple of minutes later, Amayah looked up from her work and gave me a quizzical gaze, clearly wondering where I had been. I felt racked with guilt. I totally forgot about my dream girl while Lisa Joyce was getting cozy at my locker. But it passed just as quickly as it arrived. Why should I have to work my ass off to get Amayah to notice me? I was starting to think Steven was dead on about females. You have some swagger, and they come to you like bees to honey. The basketball games were nice for a small crowd before school, but I started to think I needed a bigger audience. Somewhere that had lots of attention, particularly from the ladies. I wanted Lisa back in front of me right now with all of her assets, but she wasn't the only hottie at school. Plus, if Amayah saw a lot of girls interested in me, maybe she'd finally take the hint that I was what she wanted and start responding the way I wanted her to. A little warning bell sounded in my head just then, like maybe that really wasn't what I wanted from her. Amayah was so sweet and kind, which augmented her substantial physical beauty. And the thought of Amayah throwing herself at me the way Lisa Joyce had, seemed not all that authentic, like something you would see in a bad Cinemax movie designed to have just a vague plot to connect the scenes where everyone took their clothes off.

I knew Amayah always supported many of the school's sports teams, so I figured that would be the perfect spot for me to slide back into her brain. Basketball season was yet to begin, and baseball tryouts were still many months away, so I decided to try out for the track team...

Coach Macey looked at me like I was institutionally bonkers when I signed the sheet outside his office, as he had never seen me do anything physically challenging. However, he wouldn't reject any potential talent, so he placed a packet in my locker containing information about practice times, uniforms, and fees. The first meet of the year was a school-wide event where anyone could participate in any race and compete. If you performed well, you would be promoted to the Varsity team for that event and compete against other schools in meets throughout the spring. Conversely, if you performed poorly, you would be assigned to the junior Varsity team and need to prove yourself during practice. Having interacted with Amayah through nods, winks, and occasional jokes at work, I confidently approached her between classes and inquired whether she planned to attend the meet after school on Friday.

She smiled warmly at me and said, "Yes," she would see a few friends and asked if I wanted to sit with them in the bleachers. Two months ago, my heart would have sung with such an invitation, but I just smiled casually and said I couldn't because I'd be on the track field.

"Be there early," I continued with a smirk. "You don't want to miss the show."

CHAPTER

SEVEN

The races I wanted to run: the 100, the 200, and the 400 were three of the last four events, which meant waiting through a lot of very boring relays, hurdle jumps, and the field events. I thought I was going to die of boredom before I got to show off, so I started putting Steven's system to use, making smart comments about other competitors, mocking Coach Macey when he wasn't looking, and attracting the attention of every girl who came near me. I really enjoyed the attention I was garnering. Girls definitely vibe with you better when you act and talk like you don't care. I got plenty of smiles and laughs as I made the rounds passing time until my events started. I had the feeling my basketball prowess had upped attendance for today's meet, especially among the girls who were turned on by great athletes. Eventually, I was so boisterous and made such a ruckus with an audience of admirers that Coach Macey yelled at me to stop disturbing the meet. I apparently disrupted the last heat of a girls' sprint and a couple of them were disqualified for taking off before the starting gun. One was Amayah's friend Elisabeth, and she was shooting me dirty looks every chance she got.

Finally, the 400-meter boys' run was announced. I was in the third heat with a bunch of other new recruits, but Coach Macey scratched out some names and put me in the first heat with the returning varsity runners. As I walked to the starting line, he jabbed, "Let's see if your legs can move as fast as your big mouth."

Ouch!

A few days of intense popularity almost made me forget what it felt like to get reprimanded by an adult at school. A few of the other runners gave the standard "Ohhhhhhh" response to Coach Macey's dig at me, letting me know that they enjoyed me getting taken down a few pegs by the gym teacher with the thick Austrian accent who was universally thought of as old and lame. The burn took my blood pressure from simmer to boil in about two seconds, and it was difficult to tell which thoughts inside were my own anger and which were the voice of Nick the Brute.

"Fucking old man thinks he can talk shit to you? He's jealous of your powers." Jealous that the kids listen to me more than him. Jealous seeing all those pretty girls circling around me while he probably goes home to an empty little apartment, eats a microwave dinner, and falls asleep after jerking it to women he had no chance of hooking up with.

For a few seconds, I felt like I could see into Coach Macey's private life with startling clarity, as if the scene I described was what he actually did after school and what life looked like for him. Part of me was laughing at the idea, mocking how sorry his life was. But in the back of my mind, I felt guilt, as if I had seen something he wouldn't have wanted me to see, something he would have liked to keep private at all costs. I shook off the pity party as I saw him continuing to stare daggers at me. If I said something nasty back to him, he'd at the very least kick me out of the meet, and maybe get me suspended from school. None of that was going to help out my plan to get Amayah's attention or stay clear of my dad. So instead, I waited until he just passed back in front of me with his starter's gun and opened my mouth, letting out the loudest, nastiest belch I could conjure. The whole heat of boys heard it, as did another fifty to a hundred people, all of whom burst out laughing. It was the perfect response. He couldn't say I burped "at" him, but everyone knew I did it on purpose. In my head, the laughter between myself and Nick the Brute was so similar I couldn't tell which of us was which for a few seconds.

He put me with the best runners to try and have me finish last and humiliate me off the team. No problem, I had a little something up my sleeve for him as well.

When the gun sounded, I took off. Not at my subway-racing speeds, but fast enough to blow by his prized runners and get out to the kind of lead that Carl Lewis might have against a bunch of high schoolers.

The race is one time around the entire track, and I was already around the first half of the track before anyone else even got to the first curve. When the finish line approached, I looked over my shoulder, and there was no one anywhere in sight, so I turned around and jogged backwards the last ten or fifteen steps, pumping my fist while the crowd cheered in amazement. Coach Macey looked like he was about to swallow his whistle as I crossed the finish line. The time on the scoreboard across the track read 23.25 seconds. I didn't know it at the time, but I just broke the world record. I took in the cheers and basked in the attention. Guys were high-fiving me, and girls I had never seen hugged me and told me how amazing I was. I looked up to see where Amayah was sitting, fully expecting her to be on her feet cheering only to find she was nowhere in sight. I scanned the crowd again and around the track area. She was gone. My cocky behavior that cost her friend the race pissed her off, and she left before I ever took the track.

"Forget her!"

Nick's voice was so sharp I felt like I could feel him banging against the inside of my skull. *"Look around you! They want to worship you!*

"They want to be you and do whatever you want them to do! Pick a girl, and tell her 'you want to see where she lives.' Take two of them! Tell

any of them you want to go in their car to anywhere you want! They grovel at your feet already! Use them and become what you were meant to be!"

Whether Amayah was in the bathroom or decided I wasn't worth her time, I didn't really care. Lisa Joyce was front and center and brought her best friend, a copper-skinned brunette named Lisa Goldman along with her. They each had a hand on one of my shoulders and were oohing and ahhing over my performance, saying I would be in the Olympics whenever I wanted. The two girls even told me I should skip college and go to the NFL, the NBA, or both, be an Asian Bo Jackson, but even better, maybe excelling in three sports. I drank in the attention and a host of other girls who kept coming up to touch me, ask for a hug, or hand me a folded scrap of paper with their phone number on it. I had more than a dozen sheets of paper by the time things started to settle down—all with names and numbers, plenty with hearts drawn around them, and one or two with personal messages that had my cheeks turning red in spite of my sudden surge in popularity. It was like becoming a celebrity overnight.

Lisa and Lisa invited me to go to Famous Pizza for a bite to eat, and about forty other people invited themselves along. The staff at the pizzeria looked very confused when they watched all these other kids pushing chairs out from other tables to crowd them around the table we were sitting. They probably thought I won the lottery or made a perfect score on the SAT based on how many people were pushing to sit close to me. I barely even noticed how many people crowded around me because those two very fine girls snuggled with me, competing for my attention and working in tandem to keep my focus on the two of them, not the twenty-odd other girls hovering at the tables around us. I wondered if they had done something like this before. When I would say anything even remotely funny, they would laugh as if I was Jim Carrey or Chris Rock doing standup. When I reached for another slice, one of them was quick to guide it to my hand. They made sure they were constantly touching me, my arms, my shoulders, my chest, and I ate it up with a spoon. When

Lisa Goldman said she had always wondered if I could kiss as good as I could smile, I let my imagination run looney. I was only too happy to oblige, but suddenly I thought of Amayah and didn't do it. Although Lisa Goldman was super attractive, I didn't have any classes with her and had never been within five feet of her. In response to me not kissing her, she made sure to press her chest against me again, and I could feel my heart rate accelerate, and it had nothing to do with my hidden powers. As I scanned the room, I spotted Steven and got a long whistle out of the corner from him, leaning against the Tekken 3 console and sipping on a Coke. He caught my eye while throwing the gold fat cap I gifted him up in the air and catching it, then flashing me a wink. I winked back. He was one hundred percent right about all this.

I stayed at Famous Pizza another couple of hours, being fawned over by girls, who were quick to duck into one of the empty seats when one girl got up to eventually get a refill or go to the bathroom. On the way back to the subway station where the big group finally parted ways, I showed off with my powers a few more times by picking a girl up in each hand and lifting them into the air as if to bench press them. Lisa Joyce made sure my hand was firmly on her butt. One of the other guys bet me twenty dollars that I couldn't jump up and touch the neon sign of a Japanese restaurant that was a good fifteen feet off the ground, so I gathered my strength again and rocketed up for it. I relieved him of his twenty dollars, then jumped even higher to put the folded bill on TOP of the sign, then jumped again to get it back down to a round of applause. Lisa and Lisa made sure to get in close for long thoughtful hugs before they said good-bye, and only after I promised to call each one of them on the phone tomorrow to see what my plans were for the weekend. I was completely worn out but didn't give a shit as I threw myself onto a seat on the departing train, yearning to be home, and started closing my eyes to rebound.

I was getting all the things that I wanted finally, and my powers were the reason for them. Steven might not be that nice of a guy, and

Nick the Brute might be a little aggressive, but I was feeling a lot more like who I should be. Sweet and kind and timid hadn't got me any dates or any friends. The last few hours were like living out one of my fantasies, except every inch of it was much, much better.

But despite it all, I still longed for Amayah to be by my side. Her touching my chest and telling me how amazing I was, were the real things that made my heart warm and made me smile when I pictured it. I couldn't figure out why I hadn't seen her. Was she turned off by my performance?

In my exhaustion, the voices started to filter in again during the train ride, and they went from a pitter-patter to a torrent of thoughts threatening to overflow my mind and crack it in two. I was hearing everything from angry cab drivers to pissed off cops to wives convinced their husbands were out cheating with their secretaries. It was so many other voices, and I was starting to feel like I was just going to give in and fall where I was sitting. I *had to* find a way to shield my brain from all the noise. I closed my eyes once more, trying to drown it out, and managed my best. Doing so, I dozed off, missed my exit by about six stops, and mistakenly went in the opposite direction. Exasperated, I confusingly got out and crossed the unfamiliar terminal towards the other side of the tracks when I stopped and realized I was in the wrong part of town.

There were five of them in all, Hispanic guys walking through the station like they owned the place, which I supposed was not that far from the truth. Four of the five wore red, blue, and white bandanas over their hair. I knew that color combination because of Amayah. She was Puerto Rican and informed me about different Hispanic gangs and how the Dominican ones were proud. These guys clearly felt the same way because their bandanas were of the same colors and looked just like the island nation's flag. That didn't worry me. What did, were the lime green accents that all five young men had somewhere in their outfits. You'd have to be blind not to see it; they probably glowed in the dark. Two had that shocking green on wrist bands that they had pushed all the way up to their elbows. A third had lime green shoelaces wrapped through his Reeboks, and a fourth had a lime green bandana around his neck to compliment the one on his head. The fifth guy, the oldest one by the looks of it, with a thick mustache and sideburns for days, wore a tight-fitting lime green T-shirt with a symbol on it and words below that chilled me to the bone, even if I didn't speak Spanish. His shirt read in italics, "Dios, Patria, y Libertad." That wasn't good. Even with my new powers, this wasn't the type of guy I wanted to run into in public.

Dios, patria, y libertad was Spanish for "God, homeland, and liberty." That was the official motto of the Dominican Republic, but around here, it had a completely different meaning. It was the calling card of Los Trinitarios, a Dominican gang that had been clawing its way up the New York City food chain rapidly over the past few years.

On the streets, the lime green represented the natural beauty of their island home, and since most of their relatives and ancestors were farmers, they armed themselves with the best weapon one would find hacking through the tall grass: machetes. The weapons were bloodier and harder to track than the guns the Bloods, the Crips, and the Latin Kings favored, and unlike the loose affiliation of other gangs, there was a strict chain of command in place.

As I slowly started moving towards the exit, I wondered if I had enough power left to teleport home. "Hey! CHINK! Yeah, I'm talking to you, Bato!" the leader in the T-shirt yelled at me, throwing up a gang sign. "What's your goofy slant-eyed self doing here this time of day?"

So much for staying anonymous. It wouldn't have held up for long anyway. I could already tell this wasn't going to end well, and the only way to get away would be to show my powers to all five of these guys. Short of killing them, it would be impossible to stop them all without really letting them see what I could do, and they would take that information and run all over the Five Boroughs with it. I wasn't wearing anything I could disguise myself with.

I spread my hands out wide in the universal sign for, "let's talk about this" and said calmly, "I'm just coming home late from school. I'm not trying to give anyone any trouble."

I didn't really expect that tactic to work, but I also didn't expect the stone-cold silence from all five gang members. The Koreans at least kept mocking me until I goaded them into attacking out of sequence. The Trinitarios clearly operated differently and had no time for games. The three with machetes all drew them and started towards me in a loose semicircle meant to box me into a small space. The leader in the green shirt hung back to observe their handiwork, and the only other guy without a weapon retreated a few steps to watch the rest of the train lobby, clearly serving as a lookout.

As the two closest gang members started to close the gap with their machetes in front of them, I reached deep inside to my energy source and found ... almost nothing. Convinced I was just nervous, I repeated the mental exercise and felt like I was trying to butter my toast only to realize the tub was empty, and I was just getting the little tiny leftovers onto my knife.

I was so preoccupied with my powers' apparent malfunction that I barely saw the first strike coming, diving out of its path at the last minute and crashing into the legs of the third attacker, tangling him up and knocking him over by accident. I scrambled to my feet just as the second machete wielder came at me. He missed with the blade, but the handle caught me flush on the cheek, and I grunted in pain. I distantly heard Nick muttering something in my mind, but I couldn't hear it clearly enough.

I was desperately trying to summon the power and got a small dose, which I used to spin around and plant a powerful kick right into the solar plexus of my attacker. It sent him sailing five feet backwards and the blade clattered out of his hands. I was praying that my abilities would make the others reconsider, much like the Koreans had, but no such luck. The Trinitarios obviously trained together to fight together, and one lucky kick wasn't going to deter them from their intent of stomping the hell out of this scrawny Asian who was on their turf. The leader, the one who verbally abused me, stepped into the hole rendered by the other guy's stumble to the ground. He was about two inches shorter than me, but far more muscular. On a good day, that would not have mattered much. But with my powers seemingly on the fritz, it could be a painful reminder of who the bully was.

"This little pendejo thinks he's Jackie Chan or something. Let's see if he bleeds yellow, hermanos!" The other two came at me at the same time, and I had to decide which way to duck. I missed the machete aimed at my head and instead felt the other rip a gaping hole down the side of my shirt, just barely grazing my ribs in the process.

I was running out of gas quickly. My performance on the track and all my showing off were causing my powers to flag now. I felt like I had just run a marathon in a suit of armor and had a sinking feeling. Right now, the showboating seemed regrettable, given my current predicament. Trying to stay out of the reach of their blades, I kept searching for an opening in the Trinitarios' attack strategy, desperately seeking to implement some of Steven's tactics, but fully aware that I was at a massive disadvantage in terms of weapons, numbers, and abilities.

I lashed out at the guy just regaining his feet and managed to knock him down again. If I was outside, I would have taken the shot and run for it, knowing full well I couldn't outrun all of them, but hoping to find a store to slip into and hide or even better, a cop on duty who could send them running back home. But being underground changed all that, and the gang knew it. They had their eyes set on the chink in their neighborhood, and the fact that I knocked one of their numbers on his ass twice made them that much more resolved to pound me into a pulp.

I did the only thing I could think of, and that was run straight at their leader, figuring it might catch him by surprise and believing the others wouldn't risk using their machetes if there was even a slight chance of stabbing the wrong person. My plan actually worked for a few seconds. Charging headlong at the leader caught them all flat-footed, and I was able to tag him twice in the jaw before he caught me with a right cross that sent me down onto one knee. As I struggled to regain my footing, his two lackeys grabbed my arms and pinned me to the ground on my back. The only silver lining was that I struggled so hard they had to drop their weapons in order to hold me still. The bad news was that my energy was completely exhausted, and they were able to restrain me easily.

The guy I knocked down a couple of times stomped one of my hands with his sneaker, and I screamed in pain despite biting my tongue to try and be tough. He laughed as I had bitten it hard enough to make it bleed. Then he stood back as the leader, looking extremely angry from the two shots I landed, kicked me in the groin and the stomach, then straddled my chest and put six or seven punches right into my face. I could feel my lip bleeding by the third one and was seeing stars by the fifth. I could feel myself falling into darkness and welcomed the relief that it seemed to be offering. I had never taken a beating like this in my life, and one of my last fleeting thoughts was that if they got bored with their fists, it would be the work of just one machete to leave me broken and to bleed out. I tried to think of the incredible afternoon I had just had, running track and chilling at Famous Pizza before this.

Must summon some will to fight, fighting against all possible hope to remain conscious. There's now a ringing in my ears, getting more and more high-pitched, to the point where I need it to stop, I must hold on ... but I'm on the verge of ... blacking out.

Suddenly, just like that, the blows ceased, and I heard the pounding of the gang members' feet receding. There were other voices now, concerned ones, and then I heard people talking rapidly. I had been moved off the ground and onto the bench. Two people were standing over me, an older woman and a younger man. They were both Dominican, and looked like mother and son. They were asking me questions, and I slurred out the answers as best I could, eventually sitting up on the bench with considerable help and effort.

They gave me a bottle of water to sip from, and thankfully it felt like my busted lip was the only bad damage to my face. The woman's name was Esmerelda, and she mentioned being a school nurse at a nearby elementary school. Her son had just come home from work, and they were walking to get dinner when they had heard the commotion. Esmerelda had seen the gang members beating me to a pulp and saved me, possibly from death, by removing the rape whistle she carried in her purse and blowing it as hard as she could over and over. The Trinitarios were known to be violent and vicious, but they were also nobody's fool. A rape whistle being blown would put everyone in a five block radius on high alert. People in New York City might have turned a blind eye to bar fights, gang violence, robberies, and racial tensions, but the sound of a rape whistle turned everybody's head. I wasn't born when The Son of Sam held New York City captive and terrified in the late 1970s, but the people from back then had long memories. That psycho murdered six people and wounded nine more, all of them young women. Even five Dominican gang bangers would have struggled to get away unharmed if an angry mob had come across them doing the unconscionable.

Esmerelda said she didn't think I had any internal bleeding, but that I needed to get to a hospital as soon as possible. I really didn't want to, but she also said the gang members would absolutely still be hanging around and would be looking to finish what they started. I gingerly walked up the stairs with her son Roberto, supporting me. By the time we were at the top, I was thankful they had stayed with me, for the pain and the effort to get there were crushing.

I had to take it really slow, and I'm sure they both thought I was the biggest wuss in the world, walking like I was two hundred years old and groaning.

Mt. Sinai's emergency room was jammed packed with people. Esmerelda signed me in, filled out my form, and told the nurse at the desk what happened. She had Roberto write down their phone number and address and made me promise I'd call if I needed anything or if I had any trouble. I thanked them sincerely for their help and waved as they walked out the door.

Pretty much everyone in the waiting room looked way worse off than me. There was a kid whose arm was turned ninety degrees the wrong way, an older woman who had a nasty scrape on the side of her head, and an overweight Black guy who looked like he had fallen down several flights of stairs. And Rohan, the super-powered idiot who was so busy showing off for hot girls that he couldn't defend himself in a fight.

It looked like it was going to be a long wait, so I found a couple of chairs to stretch out on and wadded up my sweatshirt as a pillow. I thought the noisy waiting room wouldn't let me do more than doze, but I nodded off almost immediately.

When I woke back up and rubbed the sleep out of my eyes, my jaw dropped as I realized more than two hours had passed! I was in the same spot and rather depressingly, most of the same people were still sitting in the same places. The emergency room was going to see everyone eventually, but unless you were dripping blood on their floor or puking your guts out from your eyes socket, you were going to have to wait a while.

When I sat up, I realized that my head felt much better, and my body wasn't nearly as sore. I walked to the restroom and splashed some water on my face, and was surprised to find that I looked a lot better too. I touched parts of my chest and arms and face that had been kicked and hit over and over and found the bruises hadn't just subsided; they were gone altogether. Clearly my powers were at work here. A couple of hours of sleep healed me faster than a week's worth of R&R. I was just about to leave to head back home—God knows what my parents would say when I strolled in late again—when a voice flashed through my brain. It wasn't Nick or the female voice, but someone who was absolutely terrified.

"Please God, don't let her die, don't let Winnie die, I'll do anything. Please, take my life if you need someone. Don't let it end this way for her. She has so much love and life to give. Let her have more time, Jesus, let her have more time..."

The words hit me deep. It had been kind of cool hearing some of my classmates' thoughts the last couple of weeks, but this was someone in pain. Someone who was clinging desperately to their faith in God, hoping to keep someone else alive. I spent the last week or so acting incredibly selfish, and my guilt was weighing on me pretty heavily. I thought about the compassion Esmerelda and Roberto showed me and thought the least I could do was try to pay it forward. I had to find this person and tell them I was praying for them.

I reached into my power source and tried to follow the line of thoughts as if they were a physical thing. I didn't have any real idea of how this was going to work, and I didn't really want to ask Nick for help; I had a distinct feeling he wouldn't see this as being much of a thing to waste his time on—he was all about action, not compassion. So I didn't reach out to him. I merely tried to make the words I heard into a touchstone and began to move towards it.

I wound up in the regular part of the hospital and kept thinking that at any point someone was going to ask me who I was or question what I was doing there, but they were all too busy, too tired, or just didn't care. I supposed I might have been mistaken for a medical student as well, given that I was pretty tall and very Asian. Whatever. I'd use that to my advantage if I had to. It was like playing the oddest game of Marco Polo of all time. I had no idea who I was looking for or where I was going, but I just kept holding onto that emotion.

FINALLY, I felt a surge of familiarity right outside one of those little rooms they put on every floor for family members to sit in, get something to eat or drink, and basically get away from whomever they are visiting. It was empty save for a white guy in his late forties. He was tall, probably taller than me, and had brown hair faded to gray, a big nose, and foggy glasses. He had stubble resembling a beard and mustache, and an empty cup rested on the table before him. His head was in his hands, and he looked like he was sobbing.

He looked up, nodded when I walked past, and then looked back down quickly. I got a glass of water and sat at a nearby table. My idea of being Mr. Compassionate suddenly did not seem like a great idea. What was I going to do? Tell this guy I had been reading his mind, and how could I help?

Fortunately, I didn't have to break the ice, because he did it for me. "You got a brother or sister up here?" He had a deep voice, and I didn't have an answer at first. Then I looked at the sign on the door and realized I was in the pediatric wing. Whoever he had been praying for, they were almost certainly a kid.

"Uh, my cousin, actually. He fell off his bike and slammed into a parked taxi. Broke his arm and got a concussion," I said. I actually had a cousin do this one time, so the details came easily. "What about you?"

He sighed and took a deep breath, and I wished I had kept my mouth closed. He looked utterly defeated. "My daughter," he said. "She has leukemia. Every time we think she's beaten it, it comes back, worse and worse. She hasn't been to school since last November. Had her birthday and Christmas in this stupid hospital. How do you tell a kid that Santa Claus is real, but they have to spend Christmas in a bed being pumped full of chemicals and radiation? Every time she gets another round of chemo, we all pray and wait and wait, praying, and then when the doc walks in, you know it's terrible from that first look on his face."

He lapsed into silence, and I felt awful at how much he was suffering. All these powers, and I couldn't take this man's grief away. But I had to try anyway. "But she's still here, right?" I said, trying to affect an encouraging smile. "She's still here, and you're still here for her. And praying to God to find a miracle for her. My mom likes to say that people always want God to work on their schedule instead of his. I don't know you or your daughter very well, but maybe God wants you to keep praying so that you'll know it's from him when the miracle does come."

He took a long look at me and nodded. "My grandmother used to say something pretty similar. A lifetime to us is a single second to

God. We sit around feeling sorry for ourselves, wondering what's taking him so long, forgetting he's trying to work with every single person on this planet at the same time, and who knows what else across the rest of the universe."

He started to say something, stopped, then started again. "This might sound crazy, and you don't have to say yes, but do you think you could stop by my daughter's room and say hi? Maybe give her this pep talk? I think she'd like it. You're twice her age, but she doesn't have many young visitors."

I agreed, and we shook hands. The dad told me he would return shortly and wanted to buy a teddy bear from the gift shop to surprise his daughter. I walked down towards his daughter's room not really knowing what to expect or what to say. But the encounter with her dad filled me with a good feeling, much different than the two girls asking for kisses and calling me a stud at Famous Pizza.

Her name was Winnie, and she was eight years old. She had the best smile, and she was painting a portrait of the sunny sky and the park that could be seen out her window. Winnie was bald. You could see tumors in her arms. She looked up in surprise since she had no idea who I was but greeted me with a warm smile and asked if I liked her painting.

"Absolutely," I said, honestly. "It's beautiful."

"They won't let me out there," she said matter of fact, "not even for fifteen minutes. They think I don't know what that means because I'm only eight, but I get it. It means I don't have a lot of time left, and they think anything out of the ordinary is going to push me over the edge."

Her honesty was both refreshing and tough to hear, but I gave her some honesty back. "Until you draw your last breath, though, you're still here. And while you're still here, anything is possible if you believe it is."

She gave me with a smile, but I knew she was not one hundred percent behind that smile. She talked about things she'd like to see and do, but there was a sudden sadness in her eyes when she spoke of the future. I heard it in the occasional breaks in her voice when I talked about what was going on at my school. I didn't have to spy on her chart to understand that Winnie's case was terminal. She wouldn't live to the age I was. She wouldn't go to a school like Science to harness her gifts. She wouldn't have that first maddening crush like the one I had for Amayah.

I talked to her as if we were old friends, and I was amazed how smart and sweet Winnie was. When a nurse buzzed on the intercom and said that Winnie would be going to Chemo soon, she reached out and held my hand and told me how good it was to meet me. I started to return the sentiment, but instead I felt something strange.

Some sort of connection opened when her hand touched mine. I could feel the cancerous cells inside of her. I could see them multiplying in spite of the radiation and the medicine. I could see them in my mind's eye. I could feel them, too. And I realized in that moment that I could also change their makeup, even destroy them. Holding Winnie's hand tightly and not saying a single word, I reached into my center like I had previously, but instead of spending the energy inside my soul, I began slowly transferring it. As it started to enter her body, she gasped, and her eyes grew wide.

Winnie didn't move. She didn't speak. Neither did I. I focused completely and wholly on what I was doing, neither believing it was possible nor trying to figure out when it was enough. Natural instinct took over, and as I watched, Winnie sat up straighter. The light came back into her face. Her skin turned from a pale, waxy color to the soft healthy pink of a normal child, and right in front of our eyes, a sprouting of fine brown hair appeared on the top of her head, steadily increasing in length and flowing down the sides of her head like a waterfall.

Finally, I let go and sat back in my chair. Winnie burst into laughter, crying in disbelief, leaping from her bed onto the floor of her room, turning a cartwheel, and racing around the room like Jeff Gordon at NASCAR, doing things that no terminal leukemia patient had any right to do.

"Oh my gosh! I feel amazing! Thank you Rohan!" she said, and exploded into my arms, hugging me tight and almost knocking me onto the ground. All the noise brought the charge nurse scurrying into Winnie's room, and she dropped her clipboard. I winked at Winnie, and she winked back. And I gestured to her, with my right hand touching my thumping chest. The nurse began checking Winnie's vitals and was in disbelief, causing an uproar, and she called the doctors to tell them to get there as soon as possible when I slipped out of the room.

I half-walked, half-staggered out of the pediatric wing. The power within me was way more immense than fast running and seriously savage fighting. Bigger, even, than the power of sudden and instantaneous teleporting. I needed to sit down somewhere and clear my head, so I got in the elevator and blindly pressed the button for another floor. If they hadn't noticed me as an outsider in the pediatric unit, it was doubtful they would notice me anywhere else.

I wound up on the fifth floor and walked aimlessly down to the same type of break room for people visiting their loved ones. This one was deserted so I made myself a cup of tea and sat down. My head felt like it had split in two, and I felt like I was living two lives. My actions from the track meet seemed small and petty at this very moment. Taking Lisa Joyce to the movies suddenly seemed less of a big deal. The weight of what I had done to help Winnie and the words I had spoken to her dad just before that; those things felt like they had come from a power greater than myself.

I was considering how I might contact that female voice which had talked about my greater gifts when the day took an even more unexpected turn.

"Rohan?"

A voice from a vision. I turned around, shielding my eyes from the blinding fluorescent lights up and down the hallway. I figured I was hallucinating at this point, on some shroom trip, being I've never touched it, and that wasn't likely; maybe I fell asleep in the waiting area, and this was a dream? I must have been delusional because it was impossible. But there she was. Amayah.

She slowly walked into the room, from the bright blurring corridor, with her head cocked quizzically at my delirious appearance. She saw the look on my face and must have seen how haggard and confused I was, and her expression went soft.

"Rohan, hey, what's wrong? Why do you look so sad?" She came and sat next to me. I started to open my mouth and realized I had no idea what I could possibly say to her. I started to stammer something when suddenly her arms were around me, and she was hugging me and holding me, and I collapsed into her. She was warm and soft and beautiful, and she was caring for me when I had no idea what was going on inside my head.

"Hey Ro," she whispered softly. "Whatever it is, you can tell me. If something is bothering you, I'm here for you."

I wanted to tell her the truth so badly, but where to begin? I didn't have the energy to explain it all, so I decided to pull an Obi-Wan Kenobi and go with the truth ... or at least part of it.

"I'm just really confused about my life right now," I finally croaked out. "I feel pulled in all these different directions, and I can't figure out what I'm supposed to be doing, where I fit in, or anything else. Every time I try to do the right thing, it seems to turn out wrong. I just don't know what to do anymore."

I felt her hand slip through my hair, and it felt like a bolt of lightning traveling down the length of my body. Whoever coined the phrase "sparks flying" must have had an experience like this. As hot as it felt when Lisa Joyce pressed her chest against me, the touch of Amayah's hands and the feel of her concern for me blew that moment away. She stroked my hair a few times, held me closer, and spoke.

"Ro, I'm so sorry you feel this way. You need to get out of your own head for a while. Are you visiting someone? I never thought I would see you here, especially after your show at the track meet today."

My mind raced to explain my presence here, but then I thought of Winnie and her dad, and I knew I could safely say they were my friends. Heck, if they ever saw me again, they'd probably want to throw me a party and give me a reward. I found myself considering that possibility. I imagined how much people would pay me to heal their illnesses. What was beating cancer worth to a rich man? Or to parents with a sick kid? Visions of unlimited piles of money filled my head—cars, houses, vacations, Lisa Joyce on a sandy beach in a string bikini waiting for me ....

I snapped out of it, shaking my head in disgust for thinking like that. Amayah was looking at me closely, confusion and concern still in her eyes.

"Um, yes. A friend of a friend, actually. A little girl with leukemia. She likes to have other young people visit, since she's usually just surrounded by doctors and nurses. She's a terrific artist, and I love art, so I came by to, um, you know, visit her for a few minutes."

The story sounded incredibly lame and phony to my ears, but Amayah's reaction was entirely the opposite.

"Oh my gosh, Rohan, I'm so proud of you, that's so sweet! I didn't know you did things like that." She hugged me again, and I pulled in the smell of her hair, not wanting to let go.

"I figured after the track meet, you'd be signing autographs the rest of the day, but here you are, giving back," she said, favoring me with another stunning smile. In that moment, I wondered what had brought her there.

"What about you? Is someone you know sick?" I asked with confusion and caution.

"Not exactly," she said, accompanied by the light-as-sunshine laugh that I loved so much. "I volunteer here a couple times a week, transporting patients from one unit to another to help out the doctors and nurses. They're always short-staffed, so they ask for volunteers to do non-medical tasks, like bringing patients their meals. I get to meet a lot of great people, and it gives me perspective on how good I have it."

She was truly amazing. She was in a lower grade, but already one of the most brilliant girls at school. She worked at Eckerd's five days a week and gave her time volunteering on her free days. I smiled back and shared what I was thinking, and she blushed ever so slightly.

"Would you like to come around with me?" she asked, her green eyes huge and hopeful. "I know you're probably tired, but there are some really incredible people here, and I bet you could make their day."

I hesitated for a breath, as the part of me still craving popularity had been plotting my trip home and the evasion of my parents, so I could jump on the phone with Lisa or any other names on the notes still folded up in my pocket. That thought vanished like a fleeting shadow as Amayah took my hand and stood up, beckoning me to join her.

"C'mon, let's go do some good."

It was the most enjoyable few hours I'd had in years. On the surface, that might sound crazy, considering that it was mostly pushing around old people in wheelchairs and stretchers. But I was also genuinely helping people and connecting with them, as well as spending time with Amayah, sharing jokes and temporarily forgetting all the madness in my life. About five or six rooms in, we visited an elderly Puerto Rican woman on her way to an MRI. She had a cancerous tumor they had been trying to knock out, and she was back in the hospital for an exam after three months of chemotherapy. The lady's name was Elena, and her whole face lit up when she saw Amayah enter the room. She sat up in bed and gestured for a hug.

"Hola, Elena, ¿que pasa?" Amayah rattled off in rapid Spanish. She gestured to me. "Es Rohan. Mi pana de escuela." Elena looked at me, and her eyes showed a hint of recognition.

"Ohhhh," she responded with a smile on her face. "Ro-han. Sí, sí, sé el nombre de Rohan. ¿Es el chico que tanto te gusta?"

I had no idea what she said, other than "Rohan," but whatever it was, Amayah got riled up. She blushed furiously and said, "Um, we need to get you to your MRI."

I felt a bit lost, but I didn't want to press Amayah for answers, and her blush had said enough. I simply got behind Elena's wheelchair and whisked her down the hall. I wanted to go into the Imaging Room to see what the results were; if her tumor was back, I planned to help Elena in a way no doctor could. Clearly, my lack of knowledge on hospital procedure was working against me. The tech shook his head and explained that no one was allowed in, not even family. We waited until she was done and got her back to her room, where I grasped Elena's hand. "When you get the results, please let us know. We don't want you going through the fight alone, no matter the odds."

Elena called me an angel, and I'm pretty sure she threw a wink at Amayah, then wrapped me up with a giant hug and a kiss on the cheek. It was a bit embarrassing, but the genuine compassion she delivered to me, simply because of what I was saying and doing, and not because of my suddenly remarkable abilities, warmed my heart again, just as it had with Winnie.

Amayah explained that most of the patients were on Medicare or came from nursing homes, so there wasn't much family involvement. Therefore, most of them were ecstatic when a young person like her came to get them, as it reminded them of their kids or grandkids, which was often a better treatment than anything else.

"They are such amazing fighters, Rohan," she said with a sad smile as we sat in the break room drinking Coke halfway through the shift. "Some of them know how little time they have left, yet they keep on believing in how wonderful life can be. They smile, and tell jokes, and ask all about my life and my family. They remember the little details and give me hugs. Sometimes I just hold their hands while they're waiting for a result, and you can see the sense of comfort in their faces. It gives me faith that there's still good left in the world... if you know how to look for it."

She squeezed my hand at that last part, which made me wonder if she was a mind reader. The things that I had seen and experienced lately—the murder, the fight with the gang, Steven's perspective, and Nick the Brute's insistence that I use my powers to take what I want. My recent weeks weren't exactly reassuring me that the world was full of good people. We were nearly to the end of her shift when she stopped short of the last room and gave a visible sigh.

"What is it?"

She nodded towards the room. "Mr. X. He got dumped here about three weeks ago. He's old and Asian and had a really nasty head injury. He was asleep for a long time, and he hasn't spoken a word since he woke up. He's getting therapy to re-learn how to walk. They don't know if he has family, but something in his spinal column got disrupted. They aren't sure what happened to him, since he can't speak—or won't. Every time I come to get him, I try a new technique to get him to recognize something or communicate in some way, but it never works."

She opened the door softly. "Good afternoon," she called out in her friendly voice. "How are you doing today, my friend?" The man in the bed was small and frail and stared straight ahead. She took his hand, to which he barely reacted. He looked like he didn't know where he was. She told him she had to move him, which he didn't seem to understand, but when she brought the wheelchair to the bed, his hospital gown shifted, and I caught a glimpse of a pendant on a gold chain around his neck.

"What's that?" I asked.

"The only thing he had other than his clothes when they found him. He went crazy when he woke up to find it gone, so they put it back on to calm him down."

I didn't want to upset him, so I waited until it was in sight again to take a good look. I was right. I knew that symbol. The Jade Dragon.

I held my hand to the man, offering, "Nǐ hǎo ma? Wǒ xǐhuān nǐ de yùlóng." I continued in Mandarin, saying his jade dragon pendant would bring him happiness and well-being.

He then took my hand, shook it, and said, "Ni hao! Ni hao!"

Amayah's jaw dropped, and she stared in wonder as I started speaking to the man, who responded in kind. Mixing in some Cantonese, Mr. X sounded like he was from Hong Kong, and his fondness for the jade dragon pendant brought him out of his shell. I could see Amayah beaming at me as he opened up to me, and I asked the man his name, where he was from, and what had happened to him. I was able to take down his info and give it to the charge nurse. We left his room, knowing his family was being contacted and he would soon be home safely.

Proving that even people with superpowers sometimes need to pee, I made a pit stop in the lobby. When I came back, Amayah was listening to the clerk, a Hispanic woman in her mid-20s, talking animatedly and gesturing wildly with her hands. As I got closer, I saw several other people—all with the look of visitors—listening intently. When Amayah saw me, she thanked the woman softly, and I noticed a weird look from her as she peered up at me. It was not a bad look, but not a good one either, and my mind whirred with thoughts of what I had done wrong. She took my hand and led me outside, somewhat forcefully. About halfway down the block, she pulled me toward a bench a few thousand pigeons had recently used as a toilet, plunking me down hard beside her.

Amayah stared hard at me again, and I felt myself wilting, pulling back in preparation, convinced she was about to yell at me.

I tried to act normally, but that wasn't working.

"Rohan," she said with a tremor in her voice. "The girl you were visiting today? What was her name?"

Shit, did she think I was lying about why I was there? I mean, if push came to shove, how the hell was I going to explain how I knew Winnie and her dad? I didn't even know her father's name.

"Winnie," I said, trying to sound nonchalant. "Her dad's a friend of my dad. I don't really know her that well, but ..."

She cut me off. "When I was waiting for you in the lobby, I over-heard the clerk at the front desk raving about a miracle to some other visitors. When I asked what she was talking about, she said there was a little girl with leukemia up in the pediatric ward who had suddenly started growing hair from her bald head and racing around the room, saying that she had been cured.

"The clerk said it was the talk of the hospital. They had taken her in for a rushed ultrasound, and apparently the cancer cell had vanished from her body. Her dad is telling everyone that he encountered an angel in the break room right before this all happened. A tall young Asian angel in blue jeans and a black T-shirt."

She looked me up and down, meaningfully glaring at my black T-shirt and jeans. She stood up, hovering above me, and put her tiny hands on my shoulders with a fierce look in her eyes.

"Rohan," she said, beginning to cry as she stared at me. "Did you just cure Winnie of cancer? How are you doing all this? The stuff in the stockroom? The way you ran on the track today? I was right there, and I still don't believe it! That was a miracle from God!"

In all that, I think the thing I remember the most were her hands on me and how comforting they felt. Not to mention the fact that I finally had the opportunity to tell her everything I had been thinking, feeling, and wanting to say to someone for weeks.

I finally got up, smiled, and said, "Can I walk you home? This might take a while."

She grinned back and took my hand in hers.

"Of course, Ro. Let's walk."

CHAPTER

EIGHT

As it turned out, the only thing I needed to be at ease with Amayah and have the flowing conversation with her I had always dreamed of was to suddenly look, feel, and act like a superhero. Or maybe it was just opening up and being myself, instead of stressing about how to keep a conversation going, calculating how to compliment her at every turn, and working hard to have the utmost swagger.

Confidence and honesty are incredible things, and I was starting to realize that while my new powers had definitely caught her eye, the fact that I was acting like a real person kept her looking my way and smiling. It was like I was finally introducing my true self to her. It felt incredible. It was about five miles from the hospital to the neighborhood Amayah lived, Washington Heights, but we avoided the subway and took our time walking. Letting her into my secret world would take time to explain, and I think she felt that too. To be fair though, I would have walked from Queens to Fenway Park wearing a Red Sox cap if it meant making the trek with Amayah. All those stolen moments I had tried to have with her at school, on the train, and at work, had never ended well. They always left me feeling like I was flailing about trying to be someone else. Now we had time, and something to talk about. I didn't rush it. I didn't say things to make myself seem like a hero or anything more than what I was.

Now was my chance, and I wanted to make the most of it. She asked very few questions, but kept giving me raised eyebrows and shy smiles, the kind that I had coveted like gold since meeting her. Those little smiles were the windows in a dark, dank house, opening up to let golden sunshine flow in. Many times, thinking of a smile Amayah had shared with me kept me going when I was down in the dumps about school or work or my home life. When I recounted tagging our store, I got a combination of arched eyebrows and frantic inhales. She basically came to a dead stop when I told her about how fast I could run, and how I had teleported away from the police. I teetered on the edge of deception when I got to the part about the body.

I swallowed slowly and told her I wasn't prepared for what I saw at Roosevelt Island. "At first, when I found her, I wasn't sure what I was seeing. I saw her on the floor, lying face up, her head in a pool of blood, with her neck twisted at an awkward angle no live person should make."

"Oh my goodness, Ro!" Amayah shook as she scrambled backward, trying to keep herself from screaming, locking her eyes wide and alert with mine.

"It wasn't till I got back home that it all sunk in. At which point I just kinda collapsed."

I didn't want her having even a hint of suspicion that I was involved, but lying to her felt even more uncomfortable, so I told it bit by bit.

I knew we were getting close to her block, but I was thrilled when she diverted our path into the Heather Garden at Fort Tryon Park. It's one of those heavenly places that make it hard to believe you're still in the confines of the largest city in North America and probably less than five minutes from some kind of crime happening every hour of every day. Any guy who lived in this area—or within five miles of it—who wanted to take a girl somewhere special would make a beeline for the Heather Garden. It was almost always blooming with bright flowers, trees, and shrubs, while the lush grass was like few areas of the city. Birds and butterflies were everywhere. Bringing a picnic basket and a piece of jewelry for someone special earned major brownie points in the park when it came to winning some sugar in return. Amayah had talked about this place more than a few times; seeing her in it was like connecting two puzzle pieces together. It fit her to a tee. I told her just that, and then her face blossomed into the grandest smile I'd ever seen; she radiated beside the flowering purple petunias and peach dahlias. My legs felt wobbly, and I thought I might faint at the sight of her.

Her smile faltered a bit and she said, "Ro? Are you OK? Let's sit down here for a minute."

I was going to wave it off, but she took my hand in hers, touched my arm again, and guided me to a bench to sit down. It was still warm from the sun, and she stayed close, her hand gently gripping mine as she looked me over. I told her I was okay and slowly continued my story, moving delicately past the parts where Steven gave me advice on how to get Amayah to notice me, instead focusing on my attempts to show off with my powers at the track meet and in the stockroom.

I skipped the more violent details about battling the Koreans in the park and glossed over how badly I had been hurt by the other gang encounter on the subway. By the time I got to the part about Winnie, and how I had been able to see the dark cells inside her and made the decision to eradicate them, Amayah was pressed against my chest looking up at me, tears in her eyes.

She whispered to me, "You're amazing, Rohan. I want you to know that. So many people would use these gifts of yours to be selfish and cruel, but you're the same sweet, smart guy I've always known."

I was so enthralled at being so close to her that I almost missed the signal that she wanted me to kiss her. I wanted so badly to do just that, but a flash of movement over her shoulder split my attention. Instead of leaning in, I held her still and put my arm around her.

She hugged me tight, and I let myself melt into her warmth.

"It's okay," she whispered. "You were so amazing with Winnie. I won't ever forget what you did for her today ... and what you did for me."

I felt like I could stay in that moment for an eternity, but we were interrupted by someone furiously shouting her name.

"AMA-YAH! AMA-YAH!!"

She pulled away from me and jumped back with a startled gasp. Striding towards her was an older man, an angry look on his face and a Louisville slugger baseball bat perched menacingly on his shoulder. He pointed the bat right at me and yelled, "Hands off her, pendejo! Get the hell out of here before I call la policía!"

I took a startled step back at his explosive show of aggression as Amayah moved toward the man.

"Papá! Dios mío! Calm down! He's not attacking me. This is Rohan, he's a friend of mine from school! We were just talking!"

Holy shit. I sighed. *This was Amayah's dad?*

Her dad didn't calm down at all from her explanation.

"I don't care who he is! You have a 7 p.m. curfew, mi hija! And it's 8:22 p.m.! You are already wasting your time at the hospital, because you certainly don't have what it takes to be a doctor. And now you are wasting your time with him too! Your mama is home worried sick about you, thinking that loco murderer has gotten a hold of you!"

He looked past her and took a step closer to me.

"Do you know anything about those murders, chico? Where were you when the last one happened? You sizing my daughter up, huh? See if she'd make a good fit for the next one?"

I might have been the strongest person in New York, but at that moment, I felt like a deer in the headlights. He was coming at me hard, and I was backpedaling.

Fortunately, it seemed like Amayah had plenty of experience dealing with her father and his outbursts.

"Oh my god, you sound insane right now, Papá! Rohan is in two of my classes at school. We work together at Eckerd's, and since you seem totally loco right now, he was just at the hospital visiting a friend of his. He worked my volunteer shift with me, then walked me home to keep me safe from any trouble! He doesn't know any thing about the murders. You sound loco, Papá!"

I might have blushed a bit and turned red as a stop sign, but it was fortunately dark. I wasn't about to admit to Amayah and her dad that I had stumbled across one of the murder victims while accidentally teleporting around the city. I nodded my head along with what she was saying instead. He seemed like the kind of guy where the fewer words you said, the better off you'd be.

He was still holding the bat, though, and eying me suspiciously.

"Maybe that's true, but you still know you aren't allowed to be alone with any boys," he said, unwilling to back down. "Especially some fresh-off-the-boat yellow man coming here to take away our businesses!"

"Oh my god, Papá, you are such a hypocrite! You're always talking about this city as a great melting pot and how lucky you were to get here, but what, you're only welcome if you speak Spanish? Rohan was born here, just like I was. You need to apologize to him right now."

Fat chance of that. It was racism, pure and simple, the kind that all three of us had to face down from different groups every single day of our lives. It was depressing to hear it coming from the mouth of another minority, but I learned a few years ago that being racist was hardly the exclusive property of white people. Every ethnicity and every race had its own whipping boy—the group it was going to put down and piss on as inferior for some general quality or imagined flaw. It was lowest-common denominator bullshit, yet everyone did it. I thought back to how I had guarded my backpack from Jarron the night we went bombing and my powers manifested.

I knew it wasn't fair, but it was also easy and made just about anyone feel good for a moment. We went around thinking and saying, "Sure, I'm not perfect, but the Mexicans/Blacks/Jews/Koreans can't even do this." It was so simple to blame problems on the White politicians or the Jewish lawyers or the Black criminals or the Mexican illegals or the Asians that stole everyone's jobs and worked for so little. I imagined my dad's reaction to seeing me snuggled up with Amayah on a park bench in Fresh Ghetto. He wouldn't have threatened her with a baseball bat, but all he would have seen when he looked at her was "NOT ASIAN." And for my parents, and clearly for Amayah's father, being of a different race was equivalent to being garbage—you stank, and had no business around their kids.

I held my hands up and spread them wide, the international symbol for "Hey, I'm cool."

"Hey, man, I'm not trying to make trouble. I was walking her home, just like she said."

I really wanted to keep my cool there, but he kept pushing.

"Don't ever let me catch you sniffing around my Amayah again, chink," he said, hurling the racial slur far too casually. "I got some friends, hardcore gangsters from El Salvador, who would love to show you back to the boat and out of this country."

Amayah gasped when he called me a chink, and he grabbed her by the arm as if to pull her away from the confrontation, but my blood was boiling. I felt Nick the Brute's voice pressing into my thoughts, and I smiled cruelly at the advice he whispered.

"I was born here, Loco," I tossed back in his face. "You're the one with the accent. Don't fuck with me. You have no idea what I'm capable of."

I took a sudden step towards him, and he flinched and stumbled backwards, tripping on his own feet and falling to the ground with a satisfying thud. I could feel Nick smiling inside my head at the result. I was so frustrated by my feelings that I had forgotten how good it felt to be in control of a situation. Baseball bat? I could have snapped it in half like a twig or taken it from his hands and thrown it halfway across the neighborhood. He had no right to threaten me.

However, looking at Amayah's face told me she definitely was not feeling love for me right now. She instead had a look of shock on her face, like she was seeing me for the first time, like I was something ugly and foul. She bent over and helped her dad regain his footing, speaking softly to him and checking to see if he was alright, as though she were a nurse or doctor herself.

She checked him over, then turned back towards me. "I think you had better go, Rohan," she said softly. "I think you should leave."

I tried to protest, but she had already turned and was walking with one hand around her dad's waist to steady him. He turned around and sneered at me. I squeezed my hands so tightly that I cut into my own palms with my fingernails, before turning around in disbelief and stalking the other way.

I kept my head down all the way to the bus stop and acted like I was asleep on the way home. It wasn't far from the truth. The beating by the gang and the energy loss from my hospital miracle had drained me significantly. The verbal persecution from Amayah's dad robbed me of what little spirit I had left. I faked being sick at home to avoid my dad's inevitable lecture. I went to bed, slept for about twelve hours, and some of my strength returned, but I still felt emotionally exhausted.

CHAPTER

NINE

The world of fictional superheroes doesn't have many examples of powers going dry after extended use. I mean, Superman has the sun as a recharging station, and even when he's hit by a full blast of green Kryptonite, he can still fly above the clouds and charge up to full strength lickety-split. Green Lantern's ring needs recharging from time to time, but they have some giant Radio Shack on Planet Oa to handle that. Whatever drain I felt took a few days to pass. That was okay, as I had been slacking off at school and work, and had to put in some time to make it seem like those were still the two most important things in my life.

Fortunately, pretending to be the average hardworking student allowed me to avoid Steven for a few days, as I rushed from class to class and then straight to Eckerd's. Amayah and I had virtually no time to ourselves, which was good, because she seemed to be doing everything she could to avoid me, even though I did catch her staring at me from time to time. I felt bad about her dad, but he had started it, and he was the damn grownup here, right? Why was he getting the free pass, while I got the silent treatment? Finally, after three long days, Amayah approached me at the end of school and asked if I

155

wanted to go volunteer at Mount Sinai with her again. I agreed. On the way there, I asked her how she had started volunteering. She started the tale slowly, but gained confidence as she went, explaining how an American doctor had healed her grandfather back on the island.

"I wanted to volunteer and become a doctor ever since Doctor Stevens came to help my tata. My grandfather grew up not having much and was from the caseríos," Amayah explained.

"The caseríos?"

"Caseríos in Puerto Rico are the same as the housing projects in the ghetto here in the States.

"Because of the violence common in the caseríos, mi tata was hit by a bullet that went through his thigh. The doctor stopped the bleeding by tightly tying mi tata's wounded thigh with one of his sweaters. Doctor Stevens stitched him up and gave an intravenous line, which ultimately saved my tata's life."

Amayah's family wasn't much different from mine. Her parents were hard-working people and migrants. They recognized her academic gifts at a young age and realized she might be her family's first college graduate. However, she did leave out the part about her dad not thinking she could be a doctor, so I also left it alone. But I told her what an inspiration she was, and she blushed a bright crimson.

"You're one to talk, Rohan! You can cure people with your bare hands. You could put every doctor and hospital out of business with your gifts!" I smiled back at her and truthfully told her that she had inspired me to keep coming back to help as many people as I could, without permanently damaging myself.

We didn't talk about the incident with her dad, and I wasn't sure if that was a good thing or a bad thing. I felt like he should apologize to me, and to her, but I wasn't going to ruin my time with Amayah. It was tough enough trying to downplay how many girls were into me at school, talking to me in and out of class and hovering around my locker. I had notes and pieces of paper handed to me regularly, asking for dates and calls or requests for me to come over and study.

I was trying to be good about my powers and use them with purpose, but as the days went on and the attention continued, it was getting harder to resist.

Going to the hospital allowed me to focus on doing good without worrying about other people and how much Amayah liked me. I went with Amayah on her rounds, asked her patients what was bothering them, took their hands, and focused on helping them feel better. I steered clear of trauma victims and tried not to do anything that doctors and hospital staff could handle themselves; the kid who broke his leg playing hockey was going to heal up just fine. I didn't need to be performing miracles left and right. I focused mainly on the elderly and children and asked them to keep it a secret because they were the least likely to blab to a nurse that some scrawny Asian teenager had taken away all their pain. I visited Amayah's favorite senior citizens and erased the fatigue, the burning, the tension, and whatever else ailed them. In most cases, it was like watching someone take a deep breath of oxygen for the first time after being underwater for a week.

For the children, I learned from my experience with Winnie. I started healing their illnesses slowly and carefully, so that doctors wouldn't suspect too much. If I did it right, it would look like kids were responding to treatment and fighting back on their own timeline. Amayah loved it. I could have been the showboat and taken all the credit for healing them, but I avoided drawing too much attention to myself and let the doctors and nurses get their progressive wins each day.

I had gotten distracted at the hospital, and my guard was down, and that's when the unexpected happened.

We were in the room of one of Amayah's favorites, an Italian-American from the Bronx who had owned a diner for years, but lost his wife eighteen months earlier. He had let his health fall apart shortly after that. He'd quit drinking years before after a liver scare, but started binging again once his wife had passed.

Now he was hoping against hope for a transplant, but Amayah

had told me candidly that he wasn't going to get one, at least not in time. It wasn't really fair, but his return to binge drinking, fully aware of the damage it would have, knocked him down the donor list quite a bit. I would hold his hand and slowly regenerate a tiny bit of his liver tissue from scarred and dying to living and healthy. I could have done the whole thing in one shot, but I feared that it would suck me so dry that I'd be in bed for a week, and that the Mount Sinai staff would take a much closer look at me if I wound up being in the presence of two medical miracles in as many weeks. When Winnie was ruled cancer-free, it made the local, state, and national news, and was being called the "Manhattan Miracle." Fortunately, the family was deeply religious and kept chalking up her healing to divine intervention, which left me largely free and clear. Plus, Winnie had left the hospital after a few tests to confirm her clean bill of health, so I wouldn't be running into her or her family anytime soon.

Mr. Pagnozzi, the guy with the failing liver, was pretty skeptical when I told him that if he held my hand for a bit and concentrated on positive energy, he would start to feel better. Still, after the first two or three minutes, he started staring at me like he had seen the ghosts of Mickey Mantle and Joe DiMaggio throwing him a birthday bash in his suite. I told him it was a holistic technique, and couldn't be applied more than a couple times a week. Of course, he was on a regular battery of drugs and treatments during the week from the staff, so when a blood test revealed that his levels were somewhat improving, the hospital staff wasn't overly surprised. We were in the middle of the session, with Mr. Pagnozzi watching TV—game shows were his preference—when the five o'clock news started. All three of us turned our heads to the screen as a stern-faced male anchor started his report.

"Another victim has been found, and police believe this is the work of the same serial killer who has been terrorizing the Five Boroughs over the past two months," he said over video footage of police lifting a corpse in a body bag from an alley dumpster. "The victim in question, twenty-nine-year-old Jackie Rodriguez, was found at mid-day by New York City sanitation workers as they made their rounds through Brooklyn Heights. Ms. Rodriguez's next of kin have been notified. This is the sixth victim tied to this dangerous killer, and the second this week, the first time two bodies have been found in such a narrow time frame since the killings began."

I could feel Nick the Brute stirring in the back of my mind as the news footage rolled. He had been unusually quiet since my run-in with Amayah's father, but now he was whispering. *"See that, Rohan? You could have stopped that. You could hunt him down and do to him what he's doing to those poor girls. Stop wasting your time trying to make nice with little Amayah and get out there and fight the battles you were born to fight! Let me guide you, and we'll stop this menace together and reap all the rewards we're due!"*

Nick repeated that nonstop and faster each time, causing me to accidentally grip Mr. Pagnozzi's hand a little too tightly, leaving a lasting impression and triggering an unexpected event. PBBTTTT!! The sound of clapping butt cheeks filled the room with an intense aroma of decaying sulfur.

Amayah and I shared a look, raising our eyebrows as we fought back laughter. I quickly apologized for holding his hand too tightly.

"Sorry if you all heard that. I had some pasta with hot Italian meatballs and sausages earlier, just like Ma used to make it," Mr. Pagnozzi uttered. "Unfortunately, it gave me some gas."

"No worries, Mister Pags," Amayah said.

"Everyone's talking about it being another Son of Sam out there," Mr. Pagnozzi continued, watching as the reporter on the scene talked to the garbage collectors who had made the gruesome discovery. "Between us, reminds me a lot more of that Zodiac guy out in California in the sixties. He ran circles around the cops, just like this guy. My uncle lived out in San Francisco back then, and he was a big old guy, probably two hundred and sixty pounds, but a real sweetheart, wouldn't harm a fly, you know what I'm saying? But he did fart a lot, though, big stinky ones. Anyways, by the third or fourth murder, he was carrying a switchblade in his back-pocket night and day, and if he was out after dark, he had a pistol holstered on his belt where everyone could see it.

"He used to cut out the news articles and send them to my dad, showing him that it wasn't just New York City that had a case of the crazies. The Zodiac guy was sending these codes to the cops that even the FBI couldn't figure out. We used to say that the guy was the flip-side of genius. You know, think about Albert Einstein. Off the charts intelligence, and he used it to explore the great mysteries of the world... but what if he hadn't? What if he decided that being smarter than everyone else meant that he was also better than everyone else, and proved it by wreaking havoc on society? What if this Zodiac guy was a genius who just chose the other way?"

How New York's current killer found these victims, murdered them in isolated areas, and dumped the bodies without being seen was disturbing. It was chilling to think that there might be someone out there who wasn't just a psychopath, but also an evil genius, plotting and executing these gruesome acts to spread fear and cause pandemonium at night, even in a city of millions upon millions. That made it even scarier when you got right down to it. It was tough to be anywhere in public in New York and actually be alone. You needed a closed door behind you to have any privacy, and even then, nothing was guaranteed.

I could feel the Brute stirring and mumbling, and images started rising in my mind, unbidden. I saw myself moving through the night, pouncing on the serial killer, knocking away his weapon, and pinning him to the ground. Then I saw myself at City Hall with Mayor Giuliani praising my bravery, giving me the key to the city, and saying I would be awarded a penthouse suite on Fifth Avenue for my courage. I saw myself at Yankee Stadium, throwing out the first pitch to a roaring crowd, while the players lined up to give me a standing ovation. When I went to ask Derek Jeter for an autograph, he asked for one right back. *"You could do anything you wanted if you used your powers to get them. Why would you deny yourself?"*

When I first started hearing Nick's voice, I thought I was going crazy. Working at Eckerd's pharmacy, I considered taking Abilify or Risperdal to eliminate the voices. But when the Brute helped unlock my powers, I decided that I might need to keep him around. After all, trying to exorcise him might mean losing my abilities. To be honest, that was a scarier thought than going crazy. He had been almost entirely silent since Amayah and I bonded, and never said a word while we were at Mount Sinai volunteering. But still, I would be lying to myself to say he was gone entirely. My powers were inconsistent at best, never entirely under my control. I had lived moment to moment for too long and vowed that it was time to get real answers, no matter the cost, even if that meant getting them from Nick himself.

After we finished our rounds, I walked Amayah home, our hands automatically tangling together as we exited the hospital. I never got tired of touching her like that, despite the goofy grin it put on my face. The electricity of her touch was more potent than when I reached inside someone else to use my unique energy. Her's was more natural and sacred.

We were talking about school a little when I first spotted the flash of lime green I had seen before from a parked car about fifteen feet in front of us. It was a set-up, and I was too deep in my own head about Nick the Brute, the killer, and my budding relationship with Amayah to see the warning signs.

The leader of the Trinitarios who attacked me wasn't there, but the other four definitely looked familiar, including the one I had knocked down twice in my short-lived offensive. I could clearly see the nice scrape on his chin where I smashed him into the pavement. We were in the middle of a long block, and other people were walking, but at the sight of lime-green clothing, they rapidly found reasons to cross to the other side of the street, duck back into the buildings they had just left, or simply turn around and quickly walk in the opposite direction. It was disheartening to see people act this way in broad daylight. I hated to think that people would refuse to stand up to bullies in real life any more than they would in a school, but at the same time, I had to consider that these people weren't just walking a friend home; they lived here all the time. Even if they stood up to the Trinitarios and got them to back down, their faces, their names, their addresses, and their places of business would all be marked. Just as the Koreans had done to my parents' dry-cleaning business, the Dominican gang's retribution for any slight, perceived or real, would be vicious and swift.

They'd smash your windows, harass your customers, throw a Molotov cocktail late at night, kill your dog, or give you a beatdown if they caught you alone. For most people, it was simply better and easier to look the other way, and not worry about things that didn't immediately concern them. Unfortunately, the two of us didn't have that option; we were their only target today.

On the flip side of things, I had been preparing for something like this to happen. I had no intention of letting Amayah walk home alone after my near miss in the subway. I had been practicing my fighting skills, but continuing to avoid Steven for reasons I wasn't entirely sure of—a gut feeling, or perhaps him borrowing money and forgetting about it had shaken my confidence. I was also carefully parceling my powers through trial and error on the days we went to Mount Sinai. The last thing I wanted was to need my power, protecting someone I cared about, but find myself unable to deliver. I also had one more trick up my sleeve that I hadn't shared with Amayah yet, and I thought this might be the day it came in handy.

"Qué lo qué, chink? Did you miss us? We thought you and your little girlfriend would be smarter than to come through our turf again, but I guess Asians aren't quite the brainiacs we all thought. Chairman Mao thinks he can just cruise through our hood anytime he wants because he's got a little novia now? We're going to finish what we started in the subway, and if Lil Senorita tries to run, she'll get it even worse than you."

Threatening Amayah or the people you cared for might have been an excellent tactic for a gang in broad daylight, but only because they didn't know me. As I grew more comfortable with my powers, I had developed an awareness for how much of a reserve I had. When I used my powers to fight, run, or teleport, it took very little out of me. Healing others was a different matter, possibly because I was transferring the power directly to another person. Even after giving it out in small parcels to hospital patients, I felt that I was at around eighty percent full strength, which would be plenty.

Just to be sure, I reached down inside myself, and was comforted by the reserves I found. Practicing without Steven had allowed me to focus more deeply on the mantras of Bruce Lee. Combining that with the direction Amayah was now leading me in, the idea that my gifts could be tools of peace, rather than instruments of war, I adapted a pose as Bruce would before a competition, flat-footed, arms spread wide, face serene.

"I don't want to hurt anyone," I said to the slack-jawed Trinitarios. "I am a man of peace."

As expected, their reactions were somewhere between hysterical laughter and quizzical confusion. The one I had taken down in the first fight was the only one of the four who seemed not entirely sure I was joking. The two who had held me down while the others administered the beating came at me together now, machetes in their sheaths, clearly confident of another ass-whipping.

Neither touched me. Turning on the speed, I dodged between them, ducking a punch from the kid who had previously acted as a lookout, then circled back around in the time it took them to blink to once again stand protectively in front of Amayah. The pair who had pinned me down blinked in confusion, then came at me again from two different angles. Their intent was to meet in the middle and pin me, but I took one step towards the taller one, put my hands on his shoulders, and vaulted over his head. My momentum pushed him forward and he smashed foreheads with his amigo. The crunch of bone was unmistakable, and they clattered together in a heap on the ground. In spite of the seriousness, Amayah let out a tiny bark of laughter as the thugs collapsed.

I moved back to cover her. The last thing I wanted was to handle two or three of them while the last guy grabbed her. She was tough, but I didn't want her to get hurt. It didn't seem to matter, as they were too bamboozled to notice her; all eyes were on me. They came in one at a time now, like the bad guys from old Adam West "Batman" episodes. I dodged kicks, ducked punches, and generally made every one of them feel like they were moving in slow motion, when it was actually just me operating exponentially faster than they could react. I realized it was what The Flash must feel like when he's mixing it up on the pages of a comic book. Everything the gang members threw at me felt like it was telegraphed minutes in advance, and all I had to do was decide how to evade them. After a few more swings and misses, they all stood staring at each other in a bit of a stupor. It seemed like they had gone a little rogue, as their leader wasn't around, and he'd be giving the orders by now. They must have thought I was an easy mark after our last encounter, but their confidence was shaken.

"Hey! Stop dancing like a ballerina, faggot!" the lookout yelled, then turned to the other three. "Grab his ass! We need to finish this!"

Another few attempts had the same result. They were starting to get winded, racing at me time and again without any success, and their exhaustion was tinged with fear.

"He's too goddamn quick!" one of the others gasped as he continued sucking down air, bent over with his hands on his knees. "This is stupid, yo. We shouldn't even be out here without Marco's clearance. Let's go get something to eat already."

So, Marco was the leader. That was something to file away for a rainy day. I was hoping the other guys would follow his lead, but the punk I had bested wasn't having it.

"Screw Marco! Marco isn't here! I give the orders when Marco isn't here! We take this chink down now and make him pay! Grab his little novia! I bet she'll scream just for me."

That was the situation I had feared, and I wasn't going to risk Amayah for even one second. Even a week ago, I might have turned that feeling of wanting to protect her into a fit of rage, unleashing the Brute to put these guys out of commission for a few days, just as they had done to me, but I wanted to be better than a thug. I wanted to show Amayah what I could be—what I was striving to be. I stepped back and put my arm protectively on her shoulder.

"Sorry, amigos," I quipped in what was probably the worst Spanish accent of all time. "Don't you know you can't catch a ghost?" I flipped my hood up for dramatic effect and wrapped my arms around Amayah, who looked up at me with an expression of surprise and bewilderment. I smiled down at her reassuringly and said loud enough for only her, "Hang on, mi Ama."

I reached inside myself and held her tight, focusing on the Heather Garden, the little bench she had cared for me on, and where we nearly kissed. I pictured it clearly in my mind and took a deep breath as the power surged within me.

A second later, I exhaled and felt the serene comfort of trees, the flowers, and the tranquilness of that little slice of heaven that Heather Garden represented to me now. Amayah had her eyes clenched shut, her breath held, so I brushed her hair with my fingertips and whispered in her ear, "You can relax, Ama, we're safe." I kissed her ear softly on impulse. She opened her eyes slowly and stared around in wonder.

She clearly knew where we were, but actually being here seconds after being surrounded by angry gang members was making her senses overload. I knew exactly how she felt. It was how I had felt when I landed on Roosevelt Island that first wild night. I held my arms around her firmly as her mind slowly made sense of the situation. She wiggled free to reach down and touch the grass, then stood back up, pressed her hands to my chest, and held them there for a long second.

Finally, she looked back up at me.

"You're certainly full of surprises, aren't you, Mr. Chang?"

I smiled down at her.

"I was hoping not to use that one, but ever since I ran into them the first time, I needed an escape route to protect you." It was amazing what I could say to her now that I was being honest. The things that came straight from my heart that I had imagined saying only in the deepest dark of night. Steven was so convinced that swagger and cockiness were the way to get her to notice me, but he had missed the mark entirely. The key to Amayah opening up was being honest.

"Well, it's a wonderful one. One of your best. So what else can you do? Turn invisible? Breathe underwater?" She was poking fun, but I didn't mind. I hadn't actually considered either of those things, but they both deserved a test at some point.

"Actually," I said, offering her a big smile in return. "I do have one more up my sleeve."

I dramatically slung my backpack off my back and opened it up. From within its confines, I brought forth a blanket and spread it out on the grass in front of us. She grinned at my very basic superpower, then gasped in delight at what came out of the bag next. Before school, I stopped at a little Asian bakery on Roosevelt Boulevard owned by a childhood friend of my mother's. Incredibly, their parents were friends back in Taiwan, and they wound up living and working just a few blocks apart on the other side of the world. I told Auntie I was looking to introduce a friend to our culture, and asked for something sweet that would stay fresh for at least the day.

I reached into the little bag and pulled out a sealed container of mochi, a rice paste from Japan popular all over Asia. It was sweetened with coconut powder, and I broke out two spoons so we could share.

Amayah dug in, eager to try a new cuisine, and declared it delicious with her grin alone. As we sat and ate, I asked her questions about her life away from school and the hospital. I wanted to plug in all the blanks as to who she was. She started with food, since I had shared a bit of my culture's cuisine with her.

"We eat rice a lot too, but it's definitely more of a side than a dessert," she said between bites. "When you're on an island, there's not much to waste, since everything takes a long time to get shipped. Fish, beef, pork, chicken... we eat it all. Lunch is a big deal. Only Americans think that breakfast is the most important meal of the day! We eat a lot of vegetables too, potatoes, yuca, plantains... we grow it, cook it, and savor it!"

She promised to bring me a Puerto Rican treat the next day to thank me for the gift of mochi, but I said it wasn't necessary, and that I was glad to share it with her.

She smiled shyly before saying, "So, Rohan, is this how you treat all your little novias, or am I getting special treatment?"

I was flummoxed by her directness and stumbled over my words, trying to explain that I had just thought of this on the spur of the moment and wanted to spend more time with her. She let me flounder like a fish on sand for about thirty seconds before covering my mouth with her hand.

"I was just teasing, Rohan. I think I know you quite well, even if you were terrified to say three sentences in a row to me a couple weeks ago."

So, she did notice how shy I had been around her. No reason to not forge ahead now.

"I've always wanted to get to know you better and spend more time with you, Amayah," I confessed. "I just was too shy around you. It's hard to focus when you're around me, but now that we've spent all this time together, I want to ask you a question. Would you like to be my nov-um... my girlfriend?"

The last part all came out in a rush, and I felt like I might have blown it because absolutely none of that sounded cool. She was still smiling at me though, which gave me hope.

"I like spending time with you too, Rohan. You're very special, and I don't just mean your powers. But I'll have to think about it. My parents told me I'm not allowed to date until I'm 18, and as you know, they're very strict. They're so focused on me studying and making top marks to get into a good college and have an easier life than they had. My dad still doubts I can be a doctor, and I sometimes doubt myself too. And I have to consider my faith. We haven't talked about it much, but I'm a devout Christian who follows the Bible's word. Part of that means honoring my mother and my father in all things. So, if I said yes to being your girlfriend, I'd have to tell them about it, and if they forbade it, it would put me in a difficult situation."

She brushed her fingers through my hair again. "You're very special to me, Rohan. Spending this time with you the last few weeks has been like nothing I've ever experienced before. I want to keep doing that. Is it okay if we just keep being who we are right now while I sort it all out?"

I nodded and hugged her tight to me again. It wasn't the answer I had been hoping for or expecting. It harshly reminded me that I was far from the only person with a complicated life. We talked for another hour before she had to get home, and even though I was a bit dismayed, I was still spending time with the girl I had been crushing on for years, so it was hard to feel bad about anything. She asked about my own faith, and I admitted that I thought of myself as Christian, but I didn't go to church and wasn't really practicing Christianity on the regular. I was afraid this would turn her off, and she'd lose interest, but as usual, I was utterly wrong. She reached into her backpack and drew out a miniature-sized Bible with pages dog-eared and highlighted from start to finish.

"I read it when the world starts to get too loud for me," she admitted. "Would you mind if I shared a few verses with you? I'm not trying to be preachy, but I've prayed a lot for you lately, since you shared your abilities with me, and I think some of these things could really help you consider what your place in the world might be."

I said that having her share some wisdom with me would be amazing, and I meant it. Anything that could help me unlock all the mysteries currently swirling in my life would be a welcome addition.

She smiled and began flipping rapidly through the pages as I watched her, totally content in the moment.

"The day you cured Winnie, I spent half the night awake reading scripture," she admitted. "There's so much in these pages about that kind of thing, if you know where to look. Listen to this one, this is Isaiah 58:10: 'If you pour yourself out for the hungry and satisfy the desire of the afflicted, then shall your light rise in the darkness and your gloom be as the noonday.'"

She smiled at me. "Thinking of you that day with Winnie, it was like you were pouring your energy and compassion into her. You did in two minutes what no doctor in the history of the world has been able to achieve, Ro. Do you have any idea how amazing that is?"

She didn't wait for a reply. She was excited to be sharing her faith with me, and I was humbled that she had been spending so much time thinking about me.

"This is from Galatians 6:2: 'Bear one another's burdens, and so fulfill the law of Christ.' And this one: 'A righteous man knows the rights of the poor; a wicked man does not understand such knowledge.'"

She smiled at me again. "You see, Ro? You might not go to church, but you're practicing the word of God every time you go to that hospital.

"God has blessed you, and you're using your blessing and giving it to others. That's what so much of being a Christian is about. I know you're worried about hearing voices, but I think you're hearing the sounds of temptation and the sounds of righteousness. It's *your choice* what you do with their advice. Even Jesus was tempted. In the Book of Matthew, Satan himself tempts Jesus three times, and Jesus rejects him. I don't want to scare you into thinking that the angry voice you hear is Satan, but it could be some nasty force trying to trick you in to using your powers for the wrong reasons. It may have been a while since you tried this, but maybe tonight before you go to bed, you could pray on it? See what God might have to say to you?"

I found it a pleasant surprise that she suggested I pray for knowledge because finding some answers through thought and meditation was exactly what I had been planning to do tonight. I smiled and nodded and promised I would.

She held my hand again. "It can feel a little odd if you haven't prayed in a while, but if you need some motivation, just remember that I'm going to be praying for you tonight too."

We were quiet the rest of the walk home. I hated saying goodbye, but we both had commitments to keep. I wanted more time with her, and I decided to take a further gamble.

"Ama, this weekend there's a big festival at Kissena Park—the Mooncake Festival. It's a massive deal in Asian culture to celebrate family. I know you said your parents don't want you dating, but would you want to go with me for... cultural exploration? I'm sure a ton of kids from school will be there, so you can tell your folks it's a class trip or something."

I stopped talking when I realized that I couldn't shut up. I didn't have to hold it long. Her face was glowing as she said, "I'd love to Rohan, just let me know where to meet you."

My powers enabled me to teleport, but spending a night out with Amayah had given me the ability to float all the way home.

CHAPTER

TEN

I talked easily with my parents during dinner and even praised my brother's tales of perfection and bravado from his latest graduate school exams. When the three of them were snoozing away after their early bedtimes, I returned to my bedroom and dimmed all the lights but my bedside lamp. I settled into a comfortable pose on the bed and tried to slow down my breathing. I didn't know exactly what I was doing, but I just stretched out mentally, trying to see within myself as I spoke to whoever might be listening, starting with God.

"God, give me strength to do the right thing with these powers I have been granted. Let me understand my purpose and give me direction to fulfill it. I am humbled by your gift to me, and I don't want to let you down. Please give me—"

"YOU LITTLE FOOL!"

The grating voice of Nick the Brute shook me from my prayer session and nearly tossed me off the bed. My thoughts flashed to Amayah's belief that the Brute was nothing more than temptation welling up from inside me, trying to get me to succumb to its will now that I had these incredible powers. Still, the sudden eruption had me questioning that theory.

"GOD DIDN'T GIVE YOU THESE GIFTS! IT WAS ME! ONLY ME! YOU WANT TO BOW DOWN TO SOMEONE, GET ON YOUR KNEES AND WORSHIP THE ONLY GOD HERE! YOUR POWERS COME FROM ME! EVERYTHING YOU HAVE IS BECAUSE OF ME!"

If Nick's voice hadn't been confined to my head, he would have woken up the entire apartment complex. However, my experiences had convinced me that the Brute was inside of me somehow, and no one else had the faintest idea he existed. Rather than take the abuse, I tried to reason with him, insisting that Nick answer a few of my questions.

But who are you? Where are you physically? And why did you pick me and only me?

His tone softened. He spoke at a more tranquil volume, but it didn't make his tone any more inviting. I had the mental picture of a used car salesman with oil-slicked hair above a plastered on 100-watt smile, trying to convince you to pay straight cash for a lemon.

"I am the Eternal. I am everywhere. I come to those who understand that power is the law of the world. Those who understand greatness come only to the few who seize it. You know it's true, Rohan Chang. You have been watching that burden unfold your whole life. You've seen the takers. The ones who don't give a shit about you unless you're filling their prescription or delivering their dry cleaning. They don't care about you, except for the service you briefly provide. They don't even see you. God didn't let you heal that little girl. That was the power that I gave you. I have filled you with the tools to make the world the way you want it... the way it should be! You've already used your powers to get what you want...

"Respect, adoration, confidence. Stick with me, and you'll accomplish everything you desire."

As he spoke, mental images played across my mind. I saw myself in silhouette, muscular like an action star, stopping criminals in their tracks, putting the Dominican gang members in their place. I looked out over the city from a Manhattan penthouse beside Central Park, rather than stuffed into a tiny bedroom of a matchbox apartment. When I turned, Amayah was there, sitting on a plush king-sized bed, smiling at me, and asking me to come closer. And she wasn't alone. Lisa Joyce was on the bed with her, wearing nearly nothing. She was saying that she wanted me too, and that I was man enough for both of them. My blood was sizzling as I started to half-walk, half-stumble towards them. That's when I bumped my head against the actual wall of my bedroom and snapped out of it, realizing it had all been in my head.

The Brute gave a throaty laugh that sounded closer to a snarl.

"It is human to desire and be greedy, as reflected through human history. You deserve no less. All those years trapped in your tiny prison. Trapped in slavery at a job you hate. Trapped at a snobby school where you have no friends. Break free! Lions don't worry about sheep; we are leaders who don't follow. It's easy for a young lion to take what he wants. I've given you the power to do anything you want. Stop acting like you don't want it all."

Bumping into the wall was a brief reality check, as was his mention of having 'no friends.' Amayah was my friend, and possibly a lot more. The Amayah in the fantasy that the Brute conjured up was nothing like the Amayah I knew. Her voice suddenly echoed in my mind, "I'll be praying for you tonight ..." I realized that I was being tempted at that moment, just as she had predicted. With great power of will, I reached inside and found Nick the Brute, seizing him and pushing him down deeper and deeper. I didn't know how to get rid of him permanently, not yet anyways, but I buried him so deep that I couldn't hear more than a murmur of his pleading. It took more effort than I realized, and I found myself lightly sweating by the time it was done. As I lay back on the bed, gulping in deep breaths of air, I wondered how I had veered off the path of prayer so quickly.

After some time resting in the still dark, I heard a whisper—a female voice.

"You are strong, Rohan, stronger than you know. And wise to bury the Brute. He is sly and slippery."

I recognized that voice, but it took me a moment to place it. I had heard it during my first encounter with hearing people's thoughts. They were coming to me in uncontrolled waves that day as I walked home, and in the midst of all the confusion, one had spoken my name, telling me not to be troubled and that all would be revealed.

Who are you? I thought back to the voice. *What is all this?*

The flow of words and images rushed towards me, immersing me in white light, allowing me in that instant to forget all the darkness and rage that had touched me in the past. I had never experienced anything like it. I felt joy and a sense of belonging that comforted me and made the Brute's vile temptations seem trivial and small.

"I am Hua. I am the spirit and the blossoming flower. I have tried to be your guide, but it has been difficult getting you to listen. You are blessed with gifts beyond any that you have ever known. You were chosen, Rohan Chang, because of your heart, your mind, and because you are blessed with the Shine Xiong. You have gifts. You are special beyond the limitations of mortal men. The Shine were once many, but they were persecuted for their powers. Men typically do not trust what they cannot see, and the powers of the Shine are far beyond those of the five senses. Generations flow by without a single Shine being born the entire world over, but now you are here. It may be that you will draw other Shine to you as your journey continues, but that is up to you. You have the ability to be more than a mortal man. You can be whatever you wish, but you must discipline yourself. You can see into the minds of others, but you must not use this power for personal gain. You are strong, you are swift, and you are powerful, but you must learn patience and focus. These are the tools you will need most in the trials ahead. Beware of the Brute. He would unmake who you are and recreate you in his own image. He would have you do his bidding and believe that you are acting out of free will."

"But who are you, really? Where do you come from? Why is this all happening to me?"

"I am the light, Rohan. I am everywhere, and I am eternal. Your

powers come from me, and when you use them for good, your power, your Shine, will grow. I have always been with you; it just took you a while to be aware. Those who have the right to call themselves Shine were forged in the fire in awe of lesser men. Earning the Shine is essential. We must be worthy of it. We must put aside our base desires and focus on using our strengths to help the weak, the innocent, and downtrodden. Many are called, but few Shine are chosen."

I had dozens more questions to ask, but even as I started trying to mentally send them out, I felt Hua fade away. I took out my journal and tried to write down everything she had said so I could attempt to make sense of it later, but it was tough. The Shine Xiong? Hua? Seeing into others' minds? This day had gotten weirder once again. The worst part was that the two distinct voices I was hearing seemed to be on opposite ends of some spectrum I didn't entirely understand. Both were claiming to be the source of my powers, and both were saying they were eternal and everywhere. Hua was warning me to be wary of Nick the Brute, but he'd been in my mind for months, if not longer. Where had Hua been all that time? Why hadn't she come to me first and explained this whole Shine Xiong thing if she was responsible for it?

There was plenty about Nick the Brute that I was suspicious and mistrustful of, starting with his name and continuing straight on to his bloodlust and his enjoyment of all things cruel. However, he had been in my mind longer, guiding me when I needed my powers that first time, and if it hadn't been for him, I absolutely would have been caught by the police, either outside Eckerd's or at the murder site. Either that or I would have been beaten into oblivion by one of the gangs I'd encountered.

I knew that I needed to sleep, but there was too much to sort out, particularly the part about seeing into others' minds. I first experienced hearing other people's voices when I first encountered Hua, and now I was intrigued. My first thought was to try and touch Amayah's mind, but I immediately rejected the idea. It definitely felt like an invasion of privacy and not the kind of thing I would be comfortable with. Besides, if I saw something in there that was private or about me, or both, I knew I wouldn't be able to keep it hidden. Similarly, my parents and my brother seemed off limits, mostly because I figured they were really boring, but also because I didn't want to hear their uncut opinions of me. I needed someone familiar, whose life I wouldn't feel guilty about prying into. Someone I knew, but not someone I would consider an "important" person in my life.

Someone like Steven Stone. I promised myself that it would just be for a few minutes, if I was even able to accomplish it, and that there was no possible way I could personally gain from it. I put myself back in my meditation pose and started repeating his name softly, imagining his face and then the apartment building where he lived. It seemed dumb for the first few seconds, but then I felt it, a sensation like I was floating across the rooftops. Steven's building drew near, and I felt myself dipping into a window, catching a fleeting glimpse of him watching HBO on a tiny TV, and then slipping into his thoughts and memories themselves, rather like being inside a movie theater with screens on all four walls showing the same film.

Steven was watching "Space Jam" on HBO, which was pretty funny, and made me instantly want to call him out on it the next day at school, until I remembered that I wasn't supposed to do stuff like this with my powers. His thoughts were on the kind of wealth that Michael Jordan must have amassed playing for the Bulls and endorsing the likes of Coke, McDonald's, and Nike. He was envisioning what he would do with all that money, and his fantasy wasn't too far off from what Nick the Brute had tried to tempt me with: wealth, power, and women. In his fantasy, it seemed like the woman he was after was a stripper in a nightclub.

Steven watched her for a moment, then tore his gaze away, and I could hear him mentally beating himself up, calling himself stupid over and over. It didn't make sense, but I realized that I didn't have to stay in the present moment with him. His memories were an open book, and I carefully started to turn back through the pages. Some of his earliest memories were also his happiest. They were of he and his parents, out at Coney Island, spending a picture-postcard kind of day, the whole nine yards. They put him on the kiddie rides, watched the big roller coaster zoom overhead, ate ice cream, and stayed for the fireworks. Steven had never mentioned his dad before, but that wasn't unusual. More than half the kids I knew were living with one parent or another. Amayah and I were in the minority, living with both parents in a strong marriage.

I sifted through more memories, watching Steven grow up and into his handsome current self. There was also a dark patch in the memories, and when I observed them, I saw his parents' divorce playing out through the eyes of a young kid; Steven was maybe seven at the time. Angry looks, loud voices, screaming and crying... it was painful to watch, and I didn't stay long in those flashbacks of pain. The big house from the early memories got smaller, and his dad largely vanished from sight. His mother underwent a physical transformation. Her sensible outfits were replaced with tight-fitting ones, her hair done up and tons of makeup on her face. Steven was with a babysitter for large stretches of time before and after school. An older woman in a tiny apartment, she would pinch him hard on the arm and yell when he didn't mind her.

Another memory flashed across, one of Steven fighting with an older boy who was mocking him, telling him that his mom was never around because she worked at a strip club every night, and that she had been at his cousin's bachelor party with all of her clothes off. Steven fought the older boy viciously, which seemed to have spurred his desire to take martial arts. As I watched, he got muscular and fit and started getting attention from the other boys who wanted to be his friends and the girls who wanted him to notice them, even just for a minute or two. Steven's mom was getting older and was home a lot more. She was now entertaining men at their house, with Steven desperately trying to ignore the music and other sounds coming from her bedroom. I cringed at what Steven was going through as the men arrived and left at all hours of the day and night, while his mom callously took the cash they brought her and placed it in a glass jar beneath the kitchen sink. One night, she was drunk or doped up or both, and she rambled on to Steven about how to get ahead in life, telling him, *"If you want something, you never have to work a single day in your life, Stevie. Pretend you care about them, use them, use the system, but let someone else do all the work, and you just enjoy the ride."*

Now thirteen or so, Steven looked disgusted by the implications, but as I kept watching, scrolling through his life, the younger version of Steven started testing the theory. He started telling teachers about his parents fighting as a way to get out of assignments. He would beg classmates to buy him a soda or a candy bar, claiming that he was working a night job because his mom was in the hospital, and he needed the energy. He fed the same lines to a long string of girls, telling them that he never noticed what a beautiful thing had been standing right in front of him, and now he couldn't take his eyes off her. Every one of these encounters led directly to clothes coming off, which I was not interested in seeing.

I saw myself in a few recent memories, which was undeniably odd, like seeing a photo of yourself that you never knew had been taken in the first place. I saw Steven cheating off me on not just one math test, but several. I also saw Steven spying on me in the days after I revealed my powers and saw him creeping out of his house late at night dressed all in black. I tried to pursue the memory, but as Steven moved through the streets, the memories became dark and disjointed, as if Steven was suffering from some sort of amnesia.

Deciding I had seen enough, I broke the connection to Steven and became aware of myself back in my bedroom. The digital clock said it was 2:45 a.m., which meant that I had been inside his mind for almost three hours. That was more than a little bit startling because it had felt like ten to fifteen minutes, tops. I chalked it up as another lesson I would have to learn when it came to my abilities. Time worked differently inside someone else's mind.

CHAPTER
ELEVEN

For better or worse, I saw Steven in an entirely different light with freshly awakened eyes the rest of the school week. I stopped playing basketball before school to spend more time with Amayah, which actually made me even more popular, as kids implored me to hang out after school, shoot some hoops, help them hustle people for money in a footrace or a game of one-on-one, and all kinds of other crazy stuff. In a move that surprised pretty much everyone who had ever met me, I began going to the school library during my free period for research on an "independent project" I had started. I had to tell everyone who wanted me to hang out that I wasn't feeling well, excusing myself and leaving the school courtyard. Doing independent work and going out on your own to learn more was a highly valued activity and a sign that you were here to learn, not just goof around and pretend you were the Asian Julius Erving before school. Amayah looked at me quizzically when she saw me leaving for the day, but I just smiled and waved to let her know that everything was fine. I needed answers, and I wasn't going to get them by simply letting Nick and Hua argue back and forth in my head about who was the right one to follow.

The school library had these great new computers that housed databases of all the books they had, and you could cross-reference them by date, by source, and a bunch of other stuff. It was part of the burgeoning Internet that everyone was talking about at school, and I figured that if I couldn't get some answers there, I couldn't get them anywhere.

My biggest problem with the two voices attempting to guide me is that they seemed to be at odds with each other—enemies to the core. Yet both had given me good advice and unlocked parts of myself that I hadn't known existed. Nick helped me become the most outstanding athlete ever and taught me how to fight back against bullies. But Hua, who had seemingly come late to the party, had been there when I had figured out the healing component of my powers, and she preached peace and compassion. Lots of guys I knew would consider those weaknesses, even though I knew that my own parents advocated them strongly, both at home and in church. I knew Amayah felt that way about things too, and we seemed to be at our closest when I was using my powers to help others.

I didn't feel like I should be forced to choose between one or the other, though. I didn't feel like either Hua or Nick was all right, nor all wrong, a fact that was frustrating me to no end. It all had a familiar ring to it, the battle between them I had suddenly become a part of, and I finally hit on it while walking past our family bookcase on my way to the breakfast table. I saw a stack of our old computer PC game boxes. Henry had received the computer as a birthday gift for getting into graduate school, but he and his friends bootlegged games and made copies of the CDs in their spare time, and when cramming for tests threatened to overwhelm them. That's how we were both introduced to Starcraft, Betrayal at Krondor, and an all-time aggravating favorite, Myst.

Myst was my brother's passion—and the bane of my existence. It came with zero directions, zero hints, and just plopped you down in the middle of a strange island where no one else lived. You had to click around with the mouse on a zillion different objects, trying to manipulate them into solving puzzles where you didn't even know the objective to unravel an unrevealed mystery. It didn't take a genius to draw the connection between the helplessness of starting to play Myst, how I felt about my new powers, and what I was supposed to be doing with them, but the actual link came from the plot.

There were these two dudes named Achenar and Sirrus, who were trapped inside magical books in a library. Their dad created the books and had died, and each brother blamed the other for his death and their current predicament. Both wanted you, as the player, to set them free. It sounded a lot like my problem with Hua and Nick. The real kicker in the game was that both of the brothers were lying. They were both responsible for imprisoning their father in his own creation, but had then gotten stuck themselves. If you helped either of the brothers out, you wound up switching places with him and being imprisoned forever.

And where does that leave me? I felt neither Nick nor Hua was giving me the whole story. Should I help one over the other?

Unfortunately, the powerful database at the school's library wasn't initially as helpful as I thought it would be. The first result for "Hua" was that it was a Hawaiian word for fruit, but a second definition was also a 'genus of freshwater snails.'

However, I did know that "Hua" meant *flower* in Mandarin, and she had mentioned that she was a blossoming flower. *Perhaps Hua is planting a seed in me so that I will blossom and bear fruit.*

Referencing "Nick the Brute" brought back zero results, as did "Nick" and "Hua" together. As for the mystical "Shine Xiong," there was a Xiong Clan whose history dated back 6,500 years, but references to mystical powers were not exactly jumping off the pages. "Xiong" did have a hit in the search as it meant *fierce* in Mandarin. *So maybe it's something about shining fiercely. How am I going to do that?*

The way Hua talked reminded me of the way my mother quoted the Bible when we were younger, before she started working every day of the week. I went to a different database, and found a search engine strictly for Bible quotes, typing in "Shine" and watching the results stream past, sensing that I was finally on to something.

*"Arise, **shine**, for your light has come, and the glory of the Lord rises upon you. See, darkness covers the earth and thick darkness is over the peoples, but the Lord rises upon you and his glory appears over you. Nations will come to your light, and kings to the brightness of your dawn."* - Isaiah 60

That one hit close to home, considering what I had been doing at the hospital. Using my powers had saved many people from the darkness of death and despair and brought them back towards the light of living.

I kept scrolling and the word kept rising again and again in verses that filled me with hope for what might lie ahead.

*"Because of your great compassion, you did not abandon them in the wilderness. By day the pillar of cloud did not fail to guide them on their path, nor the pillar of fire by night to **shine** on the way they were to take."* - Nehemiah 9:19

*"Many, Lord, are asking, "Who will bring us prosperity?" Let the light of your face **shine** on us."* - Psalm 4:6

*"He will make your righteous reward **shine** like the dawn, your vindication like the noonday sun."* - Psalm 37:6

*"The light of the righteous **shines** brightly, but the lamp of the wicked is snuffed out."* - Proverbs 13:9

There were dozens more. I felt strong and proud reading them, as though there was a higher purpose for me encoded in these verses. I felt like I was seeing things clearly for the first time since the powers had manifested. I was also feeling a lot better about Hua and much more wary of Nick.

I left the library after memorizing a few of the verses and thinking about other ways I could help people with my powers when I felt Nick rise in my brain. I braced myself, preparing for an onslaught of epic proportions. Just like me, he got out of control when he was angry; I saw it when I began praying to God, and during the confrontation with Amayah's father. I braced myself for an explosion that never came.

"Rohan? I know you are questioning me. I have not been totally honest with you, and I believe that you deserve to know the truth."

It felt like a trick, but I was willing to listen to see what truth I might find within it.

"I know that you have found satisfaction in helping others, but I want you to know the truth. The reason why I am helping you develop your powers is because a war is coming. And if you don't learn how to fight, Rohan, then you are going to be a casualty of that war. You, your family, Amayah, and everyone you hold dear. My dear boy, there's a famous Chinese saying, it's better to be a warrior in the garden than a gardener in a war.

"Brute is an accurate name for me, as I am strong and courageous in decisions and actions. I am a go-getter, the opposite of a weak, sniveling, and cowering fool. Rohan, isn't it time for you to stand up for yourself and take charge of your own life?"

That challenge got my attention in a hurry. Even if he was blowing smoke up my ass, I still couldn't shut him off now. "What are you talking about?" I asked mentally. "What war? A war with who?"

"The only war that matters. The only fight that matters. The battle for the soul of mankind. The corruption of this world against the truth of it. The world you see around you is just so much window dressing. The hearts of men are cruel, and when things start to fall apart, they'll turn on each other like dogs fighting over the last scrap of meat. Men always return to their natural state when things go badly; they'll kill each other over bread, slit their brother's throat for a drink of water, and wage war for a single strip of Holy Land."

I had to admit that Nick's logic was sound, considering how nasty people could be to one another. Killing in the name of religion was commonplace and had been for centuries. There were always intense stories of people killing each other over a pair of Air Jordans or a car stereo or a jilted love affair. I knew that I could use my powers to help people, but what if that wasn't enough for them? What if they wanted to possess those powers for themselves or have me do things that I didn't want, like being some sort of assassin or hitman? What if they threatened my family or Amayah if I didn't comply? It was all too scary to think about.

"I know you have your doubts about me, Rohan, so let me prove myself to you. Very soon, you will experience a change. It is something you won't see coming. Something you can't prepare for. And something you cannot avoid. You will find yourself lost in the wilderness, disconnected from your family, and unable to return home. When you get there, and you lose faith in yourself, remember who showed you these powers and gave you the strength to overcome your problems. When this happens, ask for my help, and you shall have it, my son."

Nick's certainty shook me to the core. It didn't sound like he was bluffing, and even though there was some vagueness to this major change he was describing, like a fortune cookie note promising a small bit of luck or a horoscope that says you will meet someone new, I couldn't help but start sweating over the possibilities and implications. And if it all did come to pass, what would I do then? Would I reach out to him, unsure as I was of his intentions? It was not a question I looked forward to answering. After taking the subway, I walked home a bit faster than usual, afraid of what unknown would come.

The next day, I received a wonderful surprise from Amayah, who brought me freshly baked empanadas filled with chicken as a breakfast treat. We gobbled them down together right outside the school grounds and volunteered again at Mount Sinai that week. I told her to meet me at the playground in Kissena Park off Booth Memorial on Saturday night, and we would walk to the festival grounds together.

It was a huge annual event each autumn, and various cultures and communities mixed in the vibrant celebration. As the fall foliage dropped before me, I couldn't help but appreciate how close Amayah and I had grown since the summer. It was still warm enough to dress casually, not wanting to make too big a deal of the festival and not wanting to imply that I thought it was a date. I went with cool kicks, Air Jordans, blue jeans and a black T-shirt. My biceps were getting bigger, bulging actually, as I had been working harder than ever on my battle tactics. I was hoping Amayah would notice, and maybe even give my arm a squeeze or two.

All of that was forgotten in the blink of an eye as I walked through the playground's gate and saw her, a vision in jade, laughing as she casually pushed two little girls on the swings. Amayah was wearing a sleeveless green dress that just touched the top of her knees. It matched her eyes perfectly, and she wore a necklace that featured small green stones. Her hair flowed down to her shoulders, and despite all the time we had spent together over the past few weeks, when she smiled at me, I opened my mouth to speak without a single word coming out.

I must have looked like a fish struggling for air. Amayah cocked her head quizzically to one side and said, "Ro? You okay in there?"

I smiled as I stuttered in reply. "Yehhh. Yess! Yes, I'm good. I just, I've never seen you so dressed up before." I smiled again, nervously, and remembered that what she seemed to like about me was hearing the truth. "You look elegant."

She got shy right then, which made her even more lovely. She talked to my chest instead of my eyes. "I didn't know what to wear, I wanted to go with something classy to match the refined gent I was going with to the Mooncake Festival."

Ama glanced up at me. "The dress is ... okay?"

Seeing her blush like that made me fall even harder. "The dress is beautiful," I assured her. "But the girl in the dress is perfection."

I impulsively took her hand, and she laughed, spinning her body into a gentle twirl. She was giggling the whole time, but didn't let go of my hand as I turned her around, leading her towards the park's central area. And as we looked up, the ever-beautiful and bright moon glowed among the stars in her full magnificence and eternal enduring grace, floating in the heavens to shine back the sun's fiery brilliance.

The lights were up, and the music was already going. The mid-Autumn event was designed for families and included all sorts of musical performances and dance groups, not just Asian ones that celebrated the Mooncake Festival but other troupes from India, Bolivia, and across the Caribbean. It was still light enough outside to see the massive waves of kites soaring at one end of the park, and people were already setting up lawn chairs and picnic blankets at the other in anticipation of the grand finale, a giant fireworks extravaganza. I had a few places in mind that would be great to watch the fireworks with Amayah snuggled close to me. I had been coming here for years with my family; my parents were probably wandering around somewhere talking to friends and community members at that very moment. Fortunately, I was tall enough to see them coming a mile away. Their reaction to me holding hands with a Puerto Rican girl would probably generate its own set of fireworks, and not the kind I wanted to be anywhere around.

There were booths full of food and crafts and clothes and jewelry and pretty much anything you could imagine. Amayah wanted to see everything and taste it all, and I got the clear feeling that she didn't experience much culture outside of her own. I was happy to explain everything as we watched the lion dancers move to the music, perfectly timing their steps to make many feet look like one mighty animal. After finding a tiny table to sit down at and have a drink, she asked me to explain the name of the Mooncake Festival, and I was only too eager to break it down.

"Well, it's rarely on the same day twice because it happens on the fifteenth day of the eighth month of the Chinese lunar calendar," I explained over the music. "In Asia, Chinese New Year is the only thing grander than the Mooncake Festival. We call it the Mooncake Festival because it celebrates the roundness of the moon, signifying the family's completeness. During the festival, people wish that the full moon brings a happy family and a prosperous future, and that your family shares the graceful moonlight, even if you are far from someone you care about."

She nodded. "We talk like that too, when we speak to people back on the island. We say that we can see the same moon and same stars at night, which means we're not really so far apart."

"Different cultures, same ideas," I agreed, and she nodded happily as the moon gleamed brightly above us, watching every smile, every glance, and every moment. "The mooncake is the biggest food part of the festival. You never want to eat one by yourself; it's considered bad luck and a sign of greed. The crust part is my fav."

We did some people-watching until the sounds of physical activity pulled our attention. The stage that had been home to a band earlier in the evening now contained several mats and a dozen or so individuals in martial arts workout gear. We walked closer, and I said, "This is probably a demonstration of Shaolin Kung Fu. I know this sounds nerdy, but in the sixteenth century, monks trained in Shaolin defended China's coasts from pirates who came to raid the villages and monasteries there. It takes mad commitment and skill to learn."

We slowly moved through the crowd until we were close enough for Amayah to see. The students ranged from young men our age up to people in their mid-twenties. The younger students went first, showing off basic form, followed by the advanced students who engaged in mock battles that showed off their agility and discipline. Each group got a louder and louder round of applause. Just when we thought the demonstration was over, the sensei asked for quiet and spoke.

"We have one more exhibition tonight. Prize student, among our youngest. Great skill, incredible instincts, and a Yankee American! We are humbled and honored to have him in our midst. He will now battle his sensei to show you his incredible Kung Fu."

The sensei turned and barked towards a young man standing in the back row on the stage, and he strode forward. When he lowered his hood, I gasped aloud, and Amayah said, "Oh, wow!"

It was Steven Stone.

From the applause that followed, it was obvious that Steven was well known in the Kung Fu and mixed martial arts circle. I heard a few other people call him by name and realized that several classmates were also in attendance. I clapped, excited to see him, but I couldn't help noticing Amayah's gaze fixed on Steven as he took his position.

He had incredible footwork, quick hands, and threw in some acrobatics that dazzled the crowd. Amayah was glued to the stage like a movie screen, gasping, breaking out into spontaneous applause, and even calling out, "Again! Again!" I was grateful when it was over, but less so when she insisted on going over to congratulate him. He stood in a circle of other martial arts students and many other teenagers, some of whom I recognized from school.

He saw me coming and sidestepped another conversation to give me our secret handshake and a high five, then took a hug from Amayah, which made the muscles in my jaw clench and release. "Your boy, Stee-volt, needs to change, but I'll catch up with you all later. Try not to be too bored without the big kahuna."

"Alright, Steven, we'll try not to," I uttered.

Despite my best efforts, he found us at the edge of a music stage about thirty minutes later, and we all sat down at a table to talk. Steven had no problem talking up his accomplishments repeatedly and how he, "your boy, Stee-volt," was the youngest to achieve this level of mastery in all of New York City. As he rambled, I couldn't help picturing him as I recently saw him through his mind's eye in his apartment building. I also tried suppressing memories of his mother entertaining men in the middle of the day. I felt guilty as soon as those thoughts crossed my mind. I could practically feel the Brute gleefully rubbing his hands together. While my internal debate raged, a new band took the stage and kicked off their set to the cheers of the onlookers.

Ama squealed in surprise. "Reggaeton!" She was on her feet in no time, clapping and moving to the beat. I had definitely never seen this side of her, and I froze when she turned and said, "Rohan! Come dance with me!"

Sure, I had been willing to take on the Trinitarios for Amayah, but dancing in public seemed terrifying by comparison. I stammered out something about being sore from last week, and she rolled her eyes.

"I'll dance with you."

I turned my head sideways as my heart dropped to the floor. Steven was standing up with his hand outstretched to Amayah. After changing his clothes from performing, Steven now wore a muscle shirt that showed just how ripped his arms and chest were, not to mention giant shoulders and that damn pretty-boy face to round it all out. For being the guy with superpowers, I suddenly felt small and weak. Amayah glanced my way, and I'm sure she wanted me to step in and take her to the dance area myself, but I wilted. I avoided her gaze, sipping my drink, watching from the corner of my eye as Steven gripped her hand. She let him take her away from the table and to the area in front of the stage, which was quickly filling up with young couples dancing, laughing, and enjoying the impromptu concert.

I felt like the world's biggest idiot. She wanted to dance, and more importantly, she wanted to dance with me. Even if I was the worst dancer in the world, she wanted me out there with her. Now she was dancing with Mr. Popular, who she was obviously attracted to, because what girl in school wasn't? I had gained a lot of popularity at school in the last few weeks, but very few of the kids from my neighborhood actually went there.

I glanced up to see them smiling at each other and dancing close as the music ramped up. I saw her asking him a question, to which he laughed and took one of her hands, placing it on his bicep. She laughed in reply and kept her hand there significantly longer than necessary. She gave it a squeeze before moving her hand away. I didn't know much about reggaetón, aside from the fact that it started in Puerto Rico and used a lot of drums and keyboards. I hated to admit it, but I was almost glad Steven had spoken up. I knew I'd be a total klutz and would be worried that the whole crowd was laughing at me.

As I sat alone, the rhythm changed, the music slowed, and whoops and whistles cut the air. I didn't get it at first, until I saw the style of dance change right before my eyes. Guys were pulling their partners close and pressing together in a way that would have given most parents and school chaperones a heart attack. It was like watching a car crash unfold as I scanned the crowd, finally focusing on Amayah in her dazzling green outfit. She was facing my direction and smiling, and I thought she saw me, but quickly realized that Steven was right behind her with his hands on her waist, dancing far too close for comfort. She was moving to the beat, which would have been hot to watch, had she been dancing alone, but with Steven right behind her, holding her hips, it looked like she was halfway home on a lap dance, smiling all the way. I stared so long that he eventually noticed. For a brief second, he cocked his head, as though someone was talking in his ear, and I saw a nasty smile spread across his face. He stared at me and winked, and then I watched him run his hand through Amayah's long hair and pull her back even closer to him. Her smile faltered, as his grew wider, spreading into a sneer. He was practically on top of her and moving against her in a way that made it look like they belonged in a bedroom, not in public. I stood up and strode away from the stage, without looking back. I couldn't watch whatever the hell was happening anymore. I knew that she had a crush on him all along, and now he was playing it up to piss me off after I had kept him at arm's length. Seeing her smile at him and letting him pull her so damn close had my heart ticking like an impatient bomb. I moved far enough away so the reggaeton music disappeared under piped-in tunes and tried to decide if I should go home or just walk the streets to cool off.

A hand on my shoulder sent me jumping five feet in the air. I turned around to see Amayah still breathing hard from the dance, her jade eyes fierce, a frown on her face.

"Rohan! I've been calling for you, why did you rush off like that?"

It was impossible to be angry at her, even after what I had seen on the dance floor.

"You two seemed to be having your own fun, so I went to get some air," I said, meaner than I had intended.

"Fun?" she retorted, her face twisting in hurt. "Being grabbed by that jerk and having him touch me without permission is not my idea of FUN, Rohan. I was trying to get your attention, because he wouldn't leave me alone, but you were gone so quick that I had to ask another couple to intervene. It was embarrassing! Do you think I wanted to dance with him? I'm here with you, Rohan. You're the one I wanted to spend time with tonight."

My heart sank. Just as I thought. She wanted me out there, but I was too lame and pitiful to take her hint.

"I'm sorry. I've just never danced before, and I didn't think you'd want to hang around me once you saw how lame I was."

Amayah gave a big sigh. "So, I'm not going to hang with you anymore because you aren't the best dancer? Do you think so little of me, Rohan? The guy who performs miracles and protects me from angry gang members and says the sweetest things every day? I'm ditching him because he can't dance?"

I felt ashamed and foolish and apologized to her on the spot. She playfully hit me on the chest and looked up into my eyes. "I came here because I wanted to hang out with you, you big dummy. Now, someone said something about some fireworks?"

The last hour of the festival was a blur for me. I boosted Amayah up into the lowest branch of a tree and climbed up next to her to watch the fireworks light up the sky. She leaned her back against my chest and stayed there the whole time, her soft breathing reassuring me that I was, in fact, awake, rather than lost in this apparent dream.

There were people out on every street, and it was late, so we decided to take the bus home, rather than walk all that way. Amayah took my hand without a word as we boarded the bus and snuggled right back into me as we sat on the narrow seat in the dark. The bus took a long time to get going and hit all sorts of traffic as we slowly picked up speed towards Washington Heights, though I secretly hoped it would take hours to get there. All that mattered was being with Amayah. I didn't care where we were, what the time was, none of it. Amayah pressed against me as I held her, and that warm embrace meant all the difference. As I felt the moment's magic, energy started surging within me. I couldn't explain what was happening, glancing around, wary of the other passengers' reactions towards me on the bus. The feeling grew more and more significant, and I felt something was off, becoming terrified of what would happen next.

TWELVE

An intense swirling of ethereal blue and white light enveloped us, leaving me feeling both warmth and weariness, as though we had ventured through a celestial portal with fleeting speed. Amidst the golden mist, I beheld the cherished spray nozzle I kept for luck, twirling and dancing in mid-air. Memories of Lore cascaded through my thoughts in a dizzying whirl, evoking profound emotions within me.

Our first meeting was at a local pizzeria in Fresh Meadows, where we connected over a game of Street Fighter. It marked the beginning of a strong bond between us. Despite not having parents in his life and his troubled background, I realized that Lore and I were not so different after all. Our shared love for video games and street art solidified our friendship. These memories serve as a haunting reminder of the fragile bond we shared, highlighting the fleeting and bittersweet nature of our connection.

"I don't come from a perfect home like you," Drew said while absentmindedly doodling his *Lore* tag in his black book.

"Trust me, Drew. My home is far from perfect," I said.

"Of course, your home is perfect. What are you talking about? And DO NOT call me Drew; It's JUST LORE!" he shouted at me.

I was struck speechless, my eyes widening in alarm as my jaw dropped in hurt.

"I'm sorry, Ro. I didn't mean to yell. I just don't like the name Drew much. You see, I was the only Black Chinese kid that grew up in a group home that got my ass kicked every freakin' day. My dad thought being a gangsta was more important than being there for his family, and my mom, well, wasn't even a mom. So, I don't really give a damn about the name my parents gave me! They have never been there for me, and they never will be. So, screw them; I am not Drew Fung Ferebee, I am simply Lore."

As the memory faded and I blinked my eyes, my vision became clearer. The bus had vanished, and the fat cap instantly returned to my hands. It wasn't night anymore. And my hand was still cuddling Amayah's, and she was still dozing against my shoulder, but everything else had changed. Had I subconsciously teleported us? I tried to take in as much information as I could, but I felt like my five senses were going into shock. The bus was gone, but we were still moving. My plastic seat vanished, and a block of wood replaced it. The rhythmic clip-clop of horse-drawn carriages, similar to those traversing the streets of Manhattan, mingled with the imposing presence of mounted NYPD officers on horseback, resonated in both my ears and mind.

I craned my neck around and saw the impossible. We were in a wooden wagon being pulled by a pair of horses. I looked left and right and saw nothing but wide-open green fields and meadows. New York City had vanished, and the paved street had gone with it. The horses pounded their feet on some sort of sand and dirt road.

We weren't alone, either. At least fifteen other people were squashed into the back of the wagon with us. All of them were Black, most were asleep or staring blankly ahead with dull, lifeless eyes. Nothing made sense, and I was beginning to worry that I had suffered some sort of seizure or brain aneurysm, and that the events of the last few weeks were all psychotic episodes that my brain had created to deal with the trauma.

A noise startled me out of my speculation, and I looked up to see another horse approaching quickly, bearing a heavyset white man around my father's age. He was dressed... well, he was dressed like a cowboy, as foolish as that sounded in my mind. He wore boots with spurs and a dirty-looking slouch hat pulled low on his brow. I gawked at him, unable to process what could possibly be happening. Where had I teleported us to? Amish country? A dude ranch? I opened my mouth to ask where we were, but the grizzled cowboy beat me to the punch.

"Don't you dare look me in the eye, boy! Just because you got some lighter skin don't mean you aren't every bit as much a slave as them darkies beside you. You drop them eyes before I pull you out of that wagon for forty lashes!"

Slave? Did he just call me a slave? Amayah was stirring at my side, and then sat straight up, looking around in bewilderment and fear.

"Rohan? Wh... what? What's happening? Where are we?"

I put my arm around her and turned her head to look right into my eyes.

"I don't know, but you need to stay quiet and keep your head down. Something happened inside me on the bus, something with my powers, and it sent us somewhere that isn't safe. The guy on the horse called me a slave, and I think everyone else in this wagon is one too. Hold onto me and follow my lead. If things get bad, I'll try to use my powers and get us out of here."

Even as I said those words, I had very little confidence that I could make good on them. I felt tired. Not quite as bad as I had after healing Winnie in the hospital, but I was fatigued and not at all myself. As we sat quietly in the wagon, trying not to attract attention from the men on horseback—I counted at least four others, along with the one who had shouted me down—I began to feel nauseous. I figured it was on account of being in the back of a wagon for the first time, but as I sat there, my palms started sweating and the back of my neck grew clammy. I bent over, putting my head in my hands as Amayah squeezed my hand in concern.

"Ro? What's wrong?" she said in a quiet voice.

"Don't know ... not feeling good," I whispered back, as I detected a metallic taste on my tongue. I wondered for the second time in the past fifteen minutes if I was having some sort of stroke. Maybe the mooncake had been undercooked? I thought I was going to throw up, but feared the inevitable response from the angry cowboy, so I focused hard on keeping my food down. I thought I conquered it, but then began to shake like a leaf. Looking at me, you would have thought it was twenty degrees outside, but it was actually steaming, way hotter than New York City should have been in the early autumn. I had to remind myself that this was definitely not New York or any place else I had ever been. I was having trouble controlling my muscle movements and slipped off the wooden bench onto the bottom of the wagon.

"Rohan!" Amayah said too loudly. The cowboy grunted, and I heard the sharp CRACK of his whip and her cry of pain, a welt appearing on her left arm with a dot of bright red blood in the middle.

"Shut your mouth, wench!" the cowboy yelled angrily at her. "Mind your own self! If that yellow boy gets sick and can't work, we'll cut him up and feed him to the pigs. You worry about your own wench self!"

I was having a seizure, as near as I could tell, based on memories of a classmate in third grade who had been prone to them. I can't say how long it lasted, but when it finally slowed down, I was covered in sweat, out of breath, and the metallic taste was practically choking me. With Amayah's help, I clambered back onto the wooden bench and sat with my head down, terrified of what might be happening and berating myself for somehow involving Amayah in whatever had gone wrong.

When I finally had a moment to catch my breath, I remembered Nick the Brute's words a couple days before. I had a very bad feeling that what just happened was precisely what he predicted that afternoon as I left the library. I didn't anticipate any of this, and I certainly wasn't in control of the situation, nor did I know where we were or how to get back. I was already tempted to call out for Nick's help, but some other force, a little guardian angel on my shoulder, perhaps, kept urging me to wait and see what happened next.

The wagon ride lasted a long time. I wasn't wearing a watch, and Amayah didn't have one either, so we had no way of knowing how much time had passed, but the sun was low on the horizon by the time the wagon began to slow. After maybe an hour or two, we started seeing signs of civilization, houses made mostly of wood and some of brick.

As the horses pulling our wagon slowed to a walk, I saw a town square with scattered two-story buildings. There were posts to hitch a horse while you went inside to do your business. There was something that looked like a restaurant and bar, a general store, a place to buy horseshoes, and what might have been a hotel, although the women out front calling out to the cowboys passing by suggested it was more of a brothel. Amayah and I looked around in wonder at these new sights, except they weren't really new, were they? With every passing moment that I didn't wake up in a cold sweat from this dream, I was becoming convinced that the question was not actually "Where are we?" but "When are we?" That was equally scary and thrilling.

However, we would have to focus on surviving the here and now without knowing how to control my powers to get us back to when we belonged. We passed out of the town square and the landscape changed to farmland. Huge fields of corn, wheat, and other crops I didn't recognize rolled past. After several more miles, the wagon abruptly turned and started up a cobblestone pathway towards a large farmhouse. Whatever was coming next, it looked like it would be here.

When the wagon rolled to a stop, we stayed still as the mounted men tied up their horses and sauntered up to the house, where several Black servants were moving to take care of their mounts and offer them refreshments. The driver of the wagon hopped down and walked to the back of the wagon, swinging the back of it open with a practiced hand. I had only seen his back to this point, but now saw that he was middle-aged, with black hair fading to grey, wrinkles on his forehead and dark brown eyes. He had a faded grey shirt on, trousers at least one size too big, and tattered leather shoes with holes showing half his toes.

He cupped his hands to his mouth and called out, "Can you all understand me? You all speak English? Nod your heads, that's right! Good. Now listen to this, because I'll only say it once. You are now the property of Captain William Franklin. This here is his plantation.

"This is your new home. Captain Franklin is your new master. If he speaks to you, you will call him 'sir.' He is not your friend. He is not your father. He is your owner, your master. My name is Juba. Pronounced Juuubaah. I drive this wagon, and I take care of several other functions for Captain Franklin. Most of you are here to pick cotton. This will be your daily function. If you do a good job, you will be fed, clothed, housed, and cared for. If you do a poor job, you will be deprived of such things, and you will have no one to blame for that but yourself! If you are caught stealing, you will be punished. If you attempt to flee this property, you will be caught and either hung or shot, whichever Captain Franklin prefers. When you see the master or any of his family, you are not to speak unless spoken to. You are not to meet their gaze unless instructed. You are not allowed in their house unless you are specifically told to do so. Nothing here belongs to you.

"When you exit this wagon, you will give me your name, your family members with you, your age, and your trade. Don't lie, don't pretend to be dumb or deaf, and we will get you set up in your new home right quick."

Amayah and I were far from the step-down out of the wagon, so we were among the last passengers to exit. I couldn't help noticing that everyone in front of us was Black. Many were in terrible physical condition. Maybe three or four had something resembling shoes, but the rest were barefoot, their feet cracked and blackened. Some had children with them, others were alone. When they had all departed, I slowly helped Amayah down and climbed down to find Juba staring at us, his jaw slack.

I immediately realized how badly we stood out. Not just in terms of our race, but our clothing as well. Amayah was still wearing her vibrant green dress, and I was wearing jeans, hole-free shoes, and a T-shirt. Everyone else's clothes were drab and some shade of brown or grey. We might as well have had an extra pair of legs and a third eye. Plus, I towered over Juba, who was barely taller than Amayah. Seeing that every other man was of average height or less, my belief that we had somehow traveled into the past was confirmed. I remembered reading that the average man in the nineteenth century was only about five feet five inches tall. Our difference put me at least eight inches taller than Juba, if not more.

He tried to regain his composure as he stared up at me. He might have been in charge of the wagon, but he was still just a slave, and slaves that took too long were slaves that felt the whip. "What the hell are you wearing, boy? Why is she dressed like she been at a brothel all day? Where did they bring y'all from?"

"New York City," I said without thinking. I hastily added in a more stereotypical Asian accent. "Ah, I come on trade boat from Pacific." I pointed at Amayah. "Girl comes from islands. We travel together."

He nodded. "So, you married? She your wife?"

Thinking that this would be the best way to keep us together, I nodded, and Amayah glanced sharply at me, then nodded along.

"All right, ya'll come along. I'm goin' to get you settled in and in some proper clothing. I don't know what fashion looks like up in

New York, but you can't be wearing these clothes around the white folk or they goin' to be askin' way too many questions about you."

Grateful to have avoided trouble right off the bat, we nodded again and followed the rest of the slaves, a term I had to quickly adjust and accept, on a rock-laid path far from the main house. Way back into the woods, entirely out of sight of the main house, were four narrow, long buildings that looked like equipment sheds. Some buildings looked more like huts made from wooden logs mixed with the earth than houses. It didn't seem like a very pleasant place to live.

They had one door each and small windows. Juba stopped us in front of them.

"These are Captain Franklin's slave quarters. This is your new home. Go in and find a bed. If you married, you get one bed. If you single, you get one bed. If you got children with you, you get one bed. Captain Franklin will provide you with clothing. Your fellow servants will wash your clothes once a week. If you miss washing day, you can keep working in your own soiled garments. If you damage them clothes, you in charge of repairin' them. If you lose them clothes, you will go without. You get chow time in the morning before your shift and at night after your shift. If you get caught smuggling food, you will be punished. If you get caught with any contraband not approved by the master and your overseer, you will be punished."

He went building by building and unlocked the doors to the slave quarters. There was clear evidence of other people living there. Meager belongings covered many of the beds. The slaves in front of them quickly dispersed to the four buildings and moved silently to fill empty spaces. At the back of each building was an outhouse and a rough stone basin filled with water. There was a well somewhere nearby, or some other source of water, as several buckets were piled on the ground. It was a dirty, dingy place, lit solely by the windows. At first, I wondered where the light switches were, and then I felt like a fool, because even if electricity had been invented, it definitely wasn't going to be used in slave quarters. For about the twentieth time since teleporting to this bizarre timeline, I tried to summon the power in me but failed to locate it. There was some remnant there, and I felt like I could summon my speed and strength if I had to, but what good would it do to run away? We had no supplies, not much money, and no way of knowing where we were or where to go. Again, I was tempted to reach out to Nick, to ask for his help to get us out of here, but something about that didn't feel right. It felt like he wanted something from me—an oath or a pledge or a promise. And perhaps if I was under enough pressure, he assumed I would agree.

If someone tried to hurt me or Amayah, I could also handle them, though I was a little worried about the guns. However, even if I killed every man who worked for this Captain, what then? I couldn't just take over their property and expect no one to notice or report what had happened to some higher authority. For the time being, our only hope was to lay low, not attract attention, and figure out how to get ourselves out of this mess.

As Amayah and I headed into one of the buildings, Juba put his hands out. "Not you," he said in a quiet voice. "Ya'll come with me, right quick now."

We followed him, obviously worried about what might be next. He walked down a hillside, and we saw a small river—maybe just a creek—and a small house built on the lower banks. It had definitely been built by hand, and when he opened the front door, it was just one large room inside, with a few beds full of children and a rocking chair where a Black woman sat patching holes in a pair of faded pants.

"Juba! You're home!" she exclaimed, rising from the chair. She stopped short when she saw Amayah and I enter behind him. "Juba! What in God's name is this? Who are they?"

Realizing he hadn't asked our names, Juba turned to us expectantly.

"I'm Rohan, and this is Amayah," I said. Amayah nodded and gave a small smile. "We're from New York City."

Juba had cocked his head at my first words, and I realized that I hadn't affected my Asian accent. Well, too late to add it back in now. I added sheepishly, "We're not slaves. We're not supposed to be here."

"We're students," Amayah added. "We go to a school there. We wound up here by mistake."

"Cecilia," Juba said to the woman, obviously his wife. "I can't put them in the bunkhouse with all the rest. McPherson gonna have way too many questions about them, 'specially the girl. He'll take her straight to the Captain, and God knows what will happen to her then."

A chill ran down my spine, and I cursed myself for not thinking of that earlier. Of course. Amayah was young and beautiful, but if she was treated as a slave, the master could do anything he wanted to her and with her. I stopped myself there. I didn't want to think about what that might entail, and I saw Amayah's face go pale as she came to the same realization.

I spoke with confidence I absolutely did not have. "I won't let that happen, Amayah. You know I can stop them if I have to."

Juba and Cecilia stared blankly at me, and I made no effort to explain.

"We need to hide her," Cecilia said with determination. "We already lost one beautiful girl to that white devil of a man. Her name was Sally. She used to clean and keep the whole property nice and tidy. Then one afternoon, when she was sweeping in front of the main house, Master was just watching her from behind, humming, then suddenly, without warning, came up behind her and just dragged her away.

"We heard Sally's screams from the main house, then a loud curdling cry with a thunderous thud, and then nothin'. We never heard or seen from Sally ever since."

She turned and gave Amayah a pat on the hand and a small

close-lipped smile. "Don't you worry, young miss, we're going to keep you safe and out of sight. You can stay here and help me with my work—cooking, cleaning, anything we can do without going up the hill. Never go up there alone or you won't come back. Master damn well yanked out another girl's teeth for dentures and beat her senseless for crying."

Amayah nodded, comforted to have found at least one ally in this bizarre set of circumstances. "But what about Rohan?" she asked. "He's... he's my husband."

I might have blushed, but it was too dark to see by then.

Juba answered. "He'll have to live with the rest of the slaves; there's no hiding him, he's too darn tall to miss. We'll get you both the right kind of clothes to blend in, but he'll have to go to work in the fields. He can visit you after dark. Rohan, we'll get you a hat to wear all day in the fields. Get your face dirty, to look as dark as possible, and maybe no one will notice you.

"Keep your head down and mind your work; hopefully they don't see that you a Chinaman."

I definitely didn't like that term, but this was not the time or place to complain. I just nodded, then remembered... "Thank you. Both of you. We owe you our lives."

Juba nodded. "Say your goodbyes then, and here, take my extra pair of clothes for now, you stand out too much as it is. Get them on, and get up that hill quick to the bunkhouse and get you some shut-eye. McPherson gets up with the sun, and he makes examples of slaves who aren't ready to work first thing. You don't want to be that example, boy."

We nodded, and I embraced Amayah. She clung to me as Juba and Cecilia greeted each other, giving us as much privacy as possible in a tiny one-room house. "I'm scared, Rohan," Amayah said. "We shouldn't be here. How are we going to get back home? Are you... does your power feel like it's coming back?"

I shook my head. "I don't know... I'm sorry. I'm sorry for all of this. If I had to use it to run or fight, I think it would work, but the energy I need for teleporting just isn't there. Maybe after I sleep, it will be."

I assumed she was disappointed, but she didn't say it. She seemed to be having a conversation with herself that concluded as she nodded.

"Alright, we'll take it slow and figure out what to do. Jesus went through trials and tribulations on his way to discovering his true purpose. Maybe this is God's will for you and I to do the same." She squeezed my hand. "You better go get some rest. Sounds like you'll be working outside all day tomorrow. Make sure you eat whatever they give you and drink lots of water, okay? I don't want you getting sick again."

I nodded. I was so worried about Amayah that I hadn't given much thought to what my life would be like here tomorrow. Picking cotton all day didn't sound awful. I liked being outside, but this wouldn't exactly be hanging out in Central Park. I promised her that I would take care of myself and hugged her tightly. I leaned towards her ear so Juba and Cecilia couldn't hear me.

"I know they said don't go up the hill, but you listen good. If someone tries to touch you or take you away from me, you scream and fight and run to find me. If I have to, I'll use my powers to get us away from here, and we'll figure out what to do from there. Okay?"

She nodded against my chest, and I felt some measure of relief. I couldn't protect her every waking moment, but we had to be on the same page if things went south.

I pulled back, but kept my arms around her. She looked up into my eyes, gave me that shy smile that made my heartbeat surge. "My esposo takes such good care of me." She got on her tiptoes and kissed my cheek softly. I couldn't help but smile.

"Get moving, son," Juba said, breaking up the tender moment. "Sunrise comes quick, and you gonna need all the sleep you can get."

I usually woke up with the sunrise, as I typically left for school early, so I didn't think a change of scenery should matter much. Given how unpleasant everything was, I certainly didn't think I would have to worry about sleeping past the first light. A bed I finally found empty, the only one available, in the bunkhouse was wobbly, tiny, and hard and felt like it was missing a leg; the blanket atop it was threadbare and full of holes, and the pillow wasn't even a pillow, more like a burlap sack that smelled awful. But I was grateful to have a place to lie down. The other residents of the bunkhouse barely stirred when I came in. Fortunately, a lantern was still burning inside, so I didn't trip over anyone.

As I lay there, my heart ached for Amayah. I wanted her to be okay down the hill with Juba and Cecilia. I was praying to God or Hua or whoever I thought might listen. Something told me they were good people, and would protect her no matter what, but they were still slaves on a master's plantation. No matter how well-placed Juba was in the hierarchy of this place, his skin was still the wrong color to have any real say in what might happen next. I tried to think of a plan as I rested there in that musty thing they thought of as a bed. In the midst of heavy breathing, occasional intense snores, and even some random high-pitched farts, I found myself desperately trying to figure out a way out of the mess I had somehow gotten us into. Unfortunately, no solution came to me before I drifted off to sleep, surrendering to the peaceful lull of darkness.

It seemed like I had been asleep for mere moments when something smashed into the side of my head, sending waves of pain rippling through my skull. My eyes snapped open, and I jumped to my feet, intent on confronting my attacker, already reaching deep to harness my power. I was totally off-balance, my hearing was muted in my right ear, and my vision swirled as I tried to place my location.

It was mostly dark in the bunkhouse, and suddenly I remembered that not only was I not at my house, but I was also in the wrong year, and I didn't know what year it was. Something happened with my powers, and Amayah and I were dropped in this strange place, in another century, or maybe even another reality... Someone was talking to me in a loud, hoarse voice, and I steadied myself against a wooden wall as I looked toward the source.

"I SAID BOY, ARE YOU DEAF AND DUMB?" The shape in front of me was barking right in my face. I was still having trouble hearing and focusing as I shook my head back and forth for extra effect.

"No, no, no, I'm not ... I can speak. And hear. I'm just really tired."

CRACK!!

My other ear exploded in pain, and I fell to my knees beside the bed. Whatever hit me the first time had come around for a second turn. The pain was overwhelming, and I doubted that I could keep myself conscious if it happened a third time. I didn't know if I should stand back up or remain on my knees. I thought about Juba's warning the night before and realized that I had done the one thing I wasn't supposed to do; be late for work in the morning. I fleetingly wondered how the people here knew when to get up, when they didn't have alarm clocks, but that thought was interrupted by the feeling of long, calloused fingers in my hair, pulling me from my knees back to my feet.

I shrieked in pain and then got very quiet and still as I found myself face to face with a man who could only be McPherson. Sunrise surely wasn't the thing that woke me up; it was him, the scariest person I have ever met in my entire life. He was the Captain's overseer for the cotton pickers, and I realized why the fear had crept up in both Juba and Cecilia's voices when they spoke of him the night before. As my eyes adjusted to the slowly growing pre-dawn light, I got my first good look at him. He was an inch or two taller than me, which made him a giant compared to everyone else. He had powerful arms, not like a bodybuilder, but more like someone who had been working in the fields every day of his life. I couldn't tell how old he was, maybe forty, or sixty; he had too many scars and wrinkles and deeply furrowed lines of anger to be sure. He had a big stomach tucked under a gray work shirt, but it didn't make him look fat. On the contrary, his bulk made him highly intimidating, like a wild and crazed rhinoceros, and the way he was manhandling me told me that he had been doing this with impunity for a long time.

McPherson squinted at me, one of his eyes half-closed and

yellowish with some oozing infection. It was all I could do not to recoil. His breath stank of some harsh alcohol concoction and tobacco, with an overall reek of stale onions.

"Where you from, boy? You don't look like no African," he said in a low voice that made me shiver. The growl deep in his throat seemed to come from a demon in hidden depths I didn't want to see.

"Where they buy you from?" he yelled. "I say again, are you deaf or just dumb? Must be one of the two. I say dumber and slower than molasses in February, as Master always says."

"New York City," I croaked out, trying to affect the sort of accent I had heard Juba speak in, but feeling like I was failing miserably. "I am a student."

That was the wrong thing to say, and I knew it the moment I said it.

"A student? Boy, you can't read or write, you tryin' to play me for a fool?" The hand flashed again on my right ear, and I only stayed upright because he still had my hair clenched in his hand. Whatever hearing I had in that ear was utterly gone, and when I put my hand there, I could only feel it numbly. My hand touched something wet and sticky, and I brought it up in front of my eyes to see my own blood.

"Get yer ass in line, boy," McPherson hissed in my face. "Say one more word today, and I'll bury you in the Back Twenty, and let the worms have you for dinner."

I realized he was Black, but McPherson wasn't like the rest. He acted with an air of authority infused with a vicious demeanor and spoke with a never-ending tone of condescension.

He let go of my hair, and I staggered to stay upright.

He was barking commands to the slaves, but it clearly wasn't necessary. They knew the routine and were lined up without a single word, though I'm not sure I could have heard any, given the state of my ears. I tried to use some of my power to restore my hearing, although I had never tried healing myself, but I felt some small improvement, at least enough to keep me from collapsing.

I got behind a smaller man, slightly bent at the waist, who looked like he might have been 80 years old with white hair and dozens of wrinkles. He didn't even blink as I walked, his gaze fixated on the back of the man in front of him.

I emulated his pose, staring straight ahead and not moving a muscle or making a sound until we were told to exit the bunkhouse. It wasn't much of a walk; about 50 feet away, a low table was set up with two long wooden benches. Three Black women were moving from spot to spot, putting something at each place and splashing water out of a bucket into chipped and unmatched cups.

The people in front of me each took a place at the tables, grabbed what was in front of them, and began eating. I got the last spot and looked down at what first looked like a potato, but was actually some sort of roll made of a type of wheat I had never seen. I thought it was going to break my teeth when I tried to bite down into it. I pulled it apart and found the inside somewhat softer and started to gnaw it into pieces that I thought I might be able to swallow. On any other day of my life, I would have spit it out in disgust and taken my chances finding something better to eat later, but my gut was telling me that it was going to be a while and that I would need strength for whatever was ahead. I picked up my cup, made of a rough metal, and looked inside. Even in the dim light, I could see that it was nothing I wanted to fill my mouth with, but what choice did I have? I tasted it briefly and bit my tongue to keep from spitting it out. It was water, I assumed, but terrible, as though it had been scooped out of a mud-filled river. I hadn't been expecting a Denny's Grand Slam, but this was utterly disgusting. I forced myself to eat and drink anyway.

I felt a bit stronger than I had the night before, but nowhere near strong enough to try to jump us back home. My heart sank at the thought of Amayah. How had her night been? Had Juba and Cecilia treated her kindly? Everything was probably fine, but my paranoia was kicking into overdrive here. After all Ama and I had been through, the thought of something horrible happening to her in this terrible place made my stomach churn even harder.

I didn't have much time to dwell on it. McPherson grunted a command and we were suddenly up and back in a line. As we marched away from the bunkhouse, I noticed that one of the three women clearing the tables was Cecilia. She made an effort to look down as McPherson led us past, but for the briefest second, she turned her head, looked right at me, and gave me a tiny warm smile. The fear that had paralyzed me like a vise clamping down on unfinished wood had vanished, and I thought, "Ama is okay."

The march to the cotton fields was far longer than I imagined, and the further we walked, I began to realize just how big the place was, and how wealthy and powerful this Captain must be. The Captain must be a Rockefeller of his times, a grand capitalist, but in its most savage and primitive form. Slaves were a material commodity at this primitive juncture in the past, and the Captain seemed to have an abundant supply. It was their eyes that told me everything I needed to know about their experiences and the terrible price of lives lost. When we finally came to the fields, the sun was high in the sky, beating our skin with unforgiving rays, and I realized that I was already sweating before doing a single piece of work.

Wherever we were, it was far warmer than New York City, and the air seemed to hang heavier with humidity than anywhere I'd ever been. As we approached the fields of cotton plants, the man at the head of the line walked to a small shed and unhooked the door, walked inside and returned with a huge pile of burlap sacks. As we walked past him, he gave one out to each of us, including me. We walked single file to the edge of the field, where McPherson stopped us.

As we awaited his instructions, a hand touched my shoulder, and I glanced over to see Cecilia standing there, smiling softly with her own burlap sack. Apparently, she also picked cotton, in addition to all of her other chores?

In the thinnest of whispers, Cecilia said, "Your wife is fine. She's minding my young ones. Stay close to me out there, and keep your eyes and your mind on your work. I'll make sure he doesn't come at you again."

I almost asked how she knew what had happened, until I remembered the condition of my ears. My small dose of power might have restored my hearing, but the blood was still drying on the sides of my head.

I only nodded, not wanting to risk anything with McPherson, and she patted me lightly on the back. After that, the rest of my day was simple, albeit incredibly grueling and maddeningly boring.

There were vast rows of cotton stretched out further than I could see. The cotton grew on the tops, like marshmallows or whipped cream on a Starbucks Frappuccino. You used your hands to pull the cotton off the plant and stuffed it in your bag. When your bag was full, you walked to the end of the row to the nearest giant wicker basket, dumping your cotton there and then returning to repeat the process.

I learned that moving too fast was also a bad idea. For one thing, your bag filled up so quickly that it got really heavy, really fast. Who would think that something so light and fluffy could be so damn heavy? That wasn't the only problem, either. There weren't thorns like you might find on a rose bush, but bristles that could stick your finger like a needle. The third time I got jabbed, it drew blood, and I used a tiny bit of power to stop it. Cecilia tried to give me pointers quietly, but she was clearly afraid of angering McPherson for any reason. He was never in the same place twice, roaming the fields with a bullwhip on one side of his belt and a strange contraption on the other that I couldn't quite figure out. Finally, when he stopped to give a tongue lashing to another worker, I was able to get a good look. It was a flat piece of rock, some shale stone wrapped through his fingers with twine hooking it all together. He kept it in the palm of his hand, and when he got angry, he smashed people on the side of the head with it. It wasn't a knife, nor would it cause anyone to bleed to death. It just hurt like hell and made you afraid of him raising his hand even an inch.

I could tell that every person in the field was terrified of him, and rightfully so. Even so, his weapons were not firearms, which meant that he wasn't the ultimate authority. The Captain and the other free men didn't trust this guy enough to arm him, so if Amayah and I had a chance to run for it, he wouldn't be able to shoot us in the back. It wasn't much to be excited about, but it was something.

Over the course of the next several days, I saw Amayah for maybe half an hour total. When the sun went down, McPherson ordered us all back to the bunkhouse where we had dinner. The meal was considerably better than breakfast, as the slaves prepared it themselves, and it was a shared communal event. Even though no money changed hands, they had a bartering system with each other and with the poor whites who worked on other parts of the plantation, or from other different plantations altogether. Plenty of the poor whites were treated just slightly better than the slaves, solely for the color of their skin, though they didn't have any land or slaves of their own. As I watched quietly from my corner seat of the low table, I couldn't help noticing that the poor whites and the slaves got along just fine. They didn't act like one was any better or worse than the other; at the end of the day, they were both just people who breathed the same air, ate the same food, and shared the same unspoken dreams.

The talk was quiet, and it was clear that no one wanted to be caught having a good time, as that might displease the people in charge. Slaves would come from all over the plantation for the big dinner, and for the bartering sessions—cooks, houseboys, maids, field workers—everyone had something, and needed something. Those who weren't involved in the trading would move to the edges of the grounds and keep an eye out to ensure no one was coming down the hill from the farmhouse. If a member of Captain William's family or anyone considered loyal to the family was spotted, a whistle imitating a local bird species was sounded. The call would be repeated throughout the grounds to let everyone know that it was time to put away anything that might even remotely be considered contraband and get back to doing nothing.

Fortunately, Amayah did not leave Juba and Cecilia's house except in Cecilia's company, and then only to the stream to fetch water for washing clothes or drawing someone a bath. She had put her long hair into a bun under a handkerchief to hide its length. She also let her face and hands get dirty, just as I had, which helped in not drawing unwanted attention. However, she couldn't hide those emerald eyes of hers, so she kept them focused on the ground unless she was looking up at me.

Even in this crazy situation, all I could do was fall into bed every night and sleep. I felt that I should have been scheming for a way to escape back to our own time, and the sight of Amayah looking up at me made me feel like there suddenly wasn't enough air to breathe, that I should be trying harder. We barely spoke when we were able to steal a moment. We just held each other, literally and figuratively, sometimes sneaking a long-welcomed embrace between us, a tiny shred of familiarity in this surreal landscape. I knew she was counting on me to get her out of here, and I swore to her that I was working on it. Every morning when I woke, I silently prayed for that feeling of uncontrollable power to come over me again, so that I could bring us back to our own time, but it never came.

One night, after finishing all the work, and trying not to stare down the hill, one of the poor white men who frequently traded with the slaves sat down beside me.

"Easy, son," he said with an easy smile. "Not trying to scare you, just noticed that you don't do much talking. I wondered if there was a story there somewhere. I like a good story. They're free, and once you've got one in your brain, nobody can take it from you. Nice thing to keep you going when you're tired, hungry, and sick of all this."

He spoke with a candor I was unused to hearing since our arrival. The slaves were good people, and they had taken Amayah and me in without so much as a question about our strange appearance. But they were beaten down in every imaginable way. Even a man like

Juba, who had his own "house" and was allowed to live with his wife and children, seemed tense in most situations. Even so, the more time I spent with them, the more it seemed like everyone was simply trying to make it through the day without being noticed, just like us. It seemed like a miserable existence, and I wondered how my country had gone so long thinking that slavery was a necessary evil or, even worse, an irresistibly profitable scheme.

I murmured that I was from New York City, and he nodded his appreciation of that fact, then reached into a pocket and removed a small flask. He took a swig and passed it to me for inspection. I didn't want to be rude, so I took the tiniest sip I could and immediately regretted it. It burned like fire all the way down my throat, although once it got there, it felt better, almost soothing. I hadn't had much alcohol in my life and imagined that whatever I had just put in my belly would have knocked me out cold if I'd swigged a full glass of it.

"New York City? Would be nice to see some day, no doubt, but not sure I'm ever gonna get out of here. So, tell me, how'd your luck go so bad that you winded up on the Captain's plantation? And what do you think of our little slice of paradise?"

It was sarcasm. Something I hadn't heard since the last day I had been to school, which was only a week or two back, but it felt like decades at this point. I gave him a startled look, and he flashed me a tiny grin. It was almost like talking to a real New Yorker again. Almost.

"Really, really bad luck," I said, nervously telling a version of the truth because it felt somehow wrong to lie to this man. "One minute, I was having a great time at a festival and talking to a beautiful girl. Then the next minute, I ran into trouble, and I was in the back of Juba's wagon heading here with no idea how I got from one place to the next as if I had reappeared in a different time, a different life."

That was pretty much what had happened, but I could tell he could relate.

"Ain't that the truth?" he replied in eager agreement. "Sounds like how I feel sometimes. Life will have you scratching your head.

One minute I'm building my own horse barn and blacksmith shop, then the damn Choctaw showed up and burned the whole town down. Nothing left but ashes for any of us. Next thing you know, I'm having to shoe horses for pennies for the Captain and pretend like he's doing me a favor by letting me take a few rotten vegetables home with me every night. It seems like a different life, where I cared for horses and bent metal."

His willingness to speak so forthcoming about his sad state of affairs made me nod in appreciative agreement, empathizing with him.

He returned the nod. "I'm forgetting my answers, sorry about that. Name is Wayles, William Wayles, but please don't use my first name. My mother gave it to me at birth, o' course, but she never would have if she had ever laid eyes on that Captain up in the big house. Man is cruel beyond anything I've ever seen in all my years. If you see him coming, run the other way, you do that, okay…"

"Rohan. My name is Rohan. Really nice to meet you, Will. Sorry, nice to meet you, Wayles."

"Rohan? Can't say I've heard that one before. And the young lady with the emerald eyes down the hill is your wife, I've heard?"

I gave a start and felt my eyes and arms tense up at the mention of Amayah, who was supposed to be well hidden, but secrets were apparently tough to keep here.

Wayles saw my mood turn. He was past fifty, with tawny beige burnt skin, bushy white hair, and a matching beard.

He placed his hand on mine in a reassuring fashion. "Take it easy, Rohan. I don't got me a fancy education, and it's hard to find work. I figured working for the Captain wouldn't be so bad, but I'm my own man. I have a crazy theory that men like our Master, the Captain, want us poor whites, the Blacks, and everyone else under the sun and stars to hate each other, so that the Master and all his pals can reap the rewards of the divide. So, those of us that work on this here land have a code, and the color of somebody's skin has nothing to do with it. Juba and Cecilia are fine folk, and I wouldn't dare betray you or them to the likes of McPherson or his Captain."

I released a deep sigh of relief. I was continuing to find good, honest people here, even if they did seem like they had little hope of making it out of the mess they had been born, captured, or sold into. I thought Wayles seemed more intelligent than he claimed, far more clever than many educated people from my own time.

"Thank you," I said, and meant it.

"Speaking of impressions... I have to ask, where exactly are we right now?"

He gave me a quizzical look, but just for a moment. Apparently, I wasn't the first slave to not know where the heck he had been railroaded off to.

"Welcome to Oxford, Mississippi, Mister Rohan from New York. Founded in 1837 and home to the finest center of learning in the South. Big brains around here opened a fancy university about six miles up the road a couple years back. Most locals thought it was too big an idea for these parts, but right as rain, people have been flocking to it ever since."

Mississippi! I thought with a jolt. What in the world were we doing here? I had guessed Virginia, but Mississippi? I could find it on a map, but that was about it.

Wayles could read the surprise on my face.

"Not what you were expecting to hear, I take it. I'm afraid we're a long way from your hometown, Rohan, and even if you could get out from under McPherson's eye, the odds of you making it back that way are mighty slim.

"There are slave patrols everywhere. They call themselves lawmen, but they're really just hired thugs and bounty hunters looking to make a quick score. They'll run you down on horseback and do everything short of cutting your head off. They need that to identify you, see? You might not be dark as most of these folks, but you're still a stranger and that makes you a target. You and the young lady would have every eye on you if you tried to run. I hate to tell you this, but you're probably stuck here for a long while."

I was already deep into this conversation, so I figured one more question wouldn't hurt. "I know this is going to sound crazy, Wayles, but could you tell me what year it is?"

He chuckled a bit. "I'm definitely going to need to hear your whole story at some point, Rohan. They must have had you locked up in a hole in the ground. Fortunately, my pappy taught me to read before it all went to hell, so I can still see what ol' Handsome Frank's up to in Washington when I stumble across a newspaper. It's the year of our Lord 1854."

CHAPTER
THIRTEEN

*ait, what? **1854**?!*

Amayah and I were trapped about a hundred and forty years in the past, and of all places, in Mississippi. What the heck? I had no answers. I didn't want to ask Nick my questions, and Hua couldn't be found, and the power to parse others' memories wasn't available to me at the moment. While my strength was slowly returning, and I suspected that I could teleport a few miles if I concentrated, I had no surge like I had the night I brought us here. I wasn't sure if I would ever regain it. I told Amayah which year we were stuck in, and she visibly wobbled, just as I had when Wayles told me. Something had drawn us here, and I had to believe that there was a connection I needed to make if I was going to get us home. This wrong past for us to be in could be the right place to find ourselves doing the right thing.

The following week, I saw my first public flogging. The cotton pickers all had quotas to meet based on how much crop the powers of the plantation thought they should be able to pick in a week. My number was fairly low; they thought I was new and probably an idiot—not all that far from the truth. However, the more experience you had, the more cotton they thought you should be able to pick, regardless of anything like health, age, or any other 'trivial' thing. Some of the older men had high quotas after long years of picking, but they had slowed down over time, and keeping up was taking a toll. One, a quiet man named Thomas, came up well short of his goal, and it was brought to the attention of McPherson by one of his lackeys.

Dinner was abruptly interrupted, and the participants of the barter session vanished from sight as McPherson stormed down the hill with a scrap of paper in hand. I had serious doubts the barbarian could read, but he hollered, "THOMAS! Come here, boy!! Been too soft on you, and you done gone and tried to make a fool of me!" The people around Thomas scurried away, perhaps without even realizing it, as the overseer drew near.

He didn't meet the boss man's gaze as he quietly said, "Got old, boss. Can't work it like I used to."

He shouldn't have said anything, of course, because McPherson smashed him on the right ear with his makeshift rock weapon. McPherson motioned for one of his subordinates to rip off what was left of Thomas' shirt while another held him down. McPherson unraveled the black whip from his belt, stood back 10 feet or so, and brought it forward with a terrible CRACK! across Thomas's bare back. He didn't scream; he roared. It was a terrible noise, and I winced as if the blow had struck me instead. McPherson barely even noticed; he was already winding up for the second strike, and then the third, and a fourth.

Every instinct in me was telling me to go and help this poor man. I thought I had enough power saved up to disarm McPherson, but what would I do next? There was no way I could rescue all these people, and it was unlikely I'd be able to hold off all the men who worked for the Captain. There was also Amayah to think about. Even if she was ready to run away with me, how far would we get before something else happened to us? I was stuck here and felt powerless. It was a devastating feeling. I lost count of the lashes, and Thomas was no longer moving. His body trembled as the whip came down, but he had blacked out. McPherson either didn't realize this or didn't care, as he brought the whip down again and again.

Finally, his motion was interrupted by the appearance of someone smaller, but no less fierce, standing in front of him, along with the utterance of a single word.

"Please."

It was Cecilia, Juba's wife and Amayah's caretaker. She was tiny, standing there before the massive bulk of McPherson, but a fire burned in her eyes as she stood between the beaten man and his attacker.

The whip froze in McPherson's hand as he stared down at her in disbelief. She held up her hand slowly and said softly, "Please sir, let that be enough."

McPherson lowered the whip halfway, but did not put it back on his hip.

"You think just cuz he yo daddy, you gonna step in and interrupt his punishment?" he barked at her.

I looked back at the broken body of Thomas, my stomach lurching into my shoes. I just met him a few days ago, and he seemed very polite, although timid. But Thomas was Cecilia's father? I tried to imagine what it would be like to see my mom or dad forced to work like this, forced to take a savage beating for failing to accomplish a task. I felt tears welling up at the edges of my eyes. *My parents.*

What thoughts were swirling in their minds at this moment? How deep was their concern? Children often vanished in the chaotic maze of New York City; each disappearance shrouded in a myriad of mysteries. Perhaps they believed I sought refuge with a confidant or rebelled enough to embark on a temporary escape.

I had only spent a whole night out once before, with Lore, that one time when my dad threatened to kick me out of the home for not obeying his rules. Touching the fat cap Lore had given me, I remembered:

"Still moping around, I see," Lore had offered.

"Lore?"

Lore gave me a hug and said, "Don't worry about the disagreement with your dad. I've got your back, Ro. We're like brothers forever, Big Lore here for you always.

"Now, let's go hit this wall up. That's what we're here for."

Lore pushed down gently on the nozzle, releasing a sizzle of paint from his spray can onto the open canvas before him. Ensuring the can's proximity to the wall, he crafted clean and sharp lines with precision. Swapping the nozzle for a fat cap, the paint burst forth, embracing the surface with broader strokes, swiftly transforming his *Lore* blockbuster.

"Don't fret about the wild styles just yet. Concentrate on getting good at blockbusters before bending and torquing your letters."

I fondly recall Lore's words, urging us to transcend beyond the boundaries of mere graffiti *toys* and unleash our creativity to create magnificent masterpieces across Fresh Meadows that unforgettable night, inspiring us to elevate our craft before parting ways.

As the memory faded, I thought that my parents had probably checked with a few family friends and asked the school about the people I spent time with. Perhaps they had even reached out to the police. That made me think about Amayah's family and how terrible this must be for them too. She had a much better relationship with her family than I did with mine, and I suddenly felt awful for them, imagining how it must feel to not know where she was and have no way of contacting her. When a beautiful young girl vanished, everyone feared the worst, especially with a serial killer on the prowl across the Five Boroughs. My guilt trip was interrupted by the scene playing out in front of me.

McPherson closed the gap between Cecilia and himself, towering over her and staring down hard. All eyes were on the confrontation, but no one said a word. Hell, I wasn't sure anyone was even breathing. We were all terrified of what might come next, especially me. Cecilia was watching over Amayah. If something happened to her, or if McPherson had some reason to go to her house to exact further punishment, my Ama would be discovered, and things could spiral fast. McPherson continued staring her down for a long minute, then said in a softer, but no less intimidating voice, "Ask me nicer."

As if following some sort of unspoken cue, Cecilia's stern look softened into a slightly playful smile, and her outstretched hand turned and pressed up onto his giant muscular arms, then rubbed up his chest.

"Please sir," she said in a sweeter voice than I had ever heard from her. "Please let him be done, for me, sir."

McPherson's fierce face broke into a nasty-looking sneer, somehow even more worrisome than his usual demeanor. "That's right," he said back to her. "Again."

Cecilia kept asking nicely and kept pressing her hands on his chest and arms as she did. You could tell from his face that he was eating it up. The whip went back onto his side holster and that same giant hand moved to Cecilia's hip, then up and down the side of her body.

"Tell Juba you going to be out late tonight," he ordered with a stern tone. "Tell him you might be gone until morning."

I tensed up at the idea, but Cecilia probably had her escape route planned already, seeing how she knew how to affect McPherson.

"Sounds nice," she said with a smile. "But I'm in charge of drawing the bathwater tonight for the Captain and his family. We don't want to upset him, do we?"

The words "Captain" and "upset" got McPherson's attention in a hurry, and his hand abruptly stopped moving on her body. For just a flash, I saw a look of fear and doubt cross his face. It was McPherson showing himself in a new light, and I understood that he was every bit as much a prisoner as the rest of us, just one with a tiny taste of power that he was constantly leveraging into something twisted and dangerous. I idly wondered how often McPherson had taken the blame for a missed quota or a slave failing at some task, resulting in him receiving as many beatings as he gave out as overseer.

Cecilia's mention of the captain broke the spell he was trying to weave, and he took a step back, as if suddenly remembering where he was.

"Nothing but a damn tease," he said to Cecilia and spat on the ground near her feet. He turned around, and every person ducked their eyes to avoid making contact with McPherson's. He stomped away up the hill as Cecilia ran to her father, joined by several other slaves and Wayles. They picked him up and got him into the bunkhouse to care for his wounds. I watched the slaves help each other without a single word spoken between them, though my attention was mostly focused on Cecilia. She had stood up to the scariest man on the plantation with no special powers, other than her faith and her love for her father. I was blown away and started thinking more and more about the other people here. Perhaps Amayah and I weren't stuck here after all. Maybe we had been sent to help.

When she was finished tending to her father, Cecilia took me down the hill to see Amayah. Ama was spending time with Cecilia and Juba's kids, and I saw that she was teaching them their letters. She gave me a huge hug, and I lifted her off the ground with a little spin. I told her briefly what had happened and my thoughts about our purpose here, and her eyes glowed with intensity.

"I had the same thought today!" she exclaimed. "We've been treating this like a curse. Like we're being punished, but maybe we're not. Maybe we're getting an opportunity to see what things were like in this time, help make them better, and take those lessons back to our time. That's why I started with the letters. It might take forever, but as long as we're here, we should do what we can, right?"

As always, I was overjoyed just to be around her and hear her vision of how to make the world better.

"Ama, I think you're incredible. After spending so much time with you, I see that you're one of the most hard-working and compassionate people that I've ever met. You're so full of conviction, finding the good out of the most dire situations... it keeps me in awe and inspires me to be more myself," I exclaimed. "And Ama, I just want you to know that you, more than anyone, have what it takes to be a physician."

"Oh my gosh, thank you, Ro," Ama said, staring at me lovingly. "That means a lot, especially coming from you."

McPherson sat in the hovel of a house the Captain had offered him as a pathetic reward for his service. He was drinking heavily from the jug he kept with him at all times. His headaches were getting worse, and his right knee was in constant pain. He knew that he was getting old, and the Captain would eventually cease having a use for him. He was terrified of that day and what it might mean. Would they put him down like a rabid dog? Sell him somewhere else where they would literally work him to death? He knew from other slaves that there were illegal fighting rings in certain parts of Oxford where two Whites would pit one of their slaves against another in a fight to the death. It was a way to get rid of worthless property that didn't involve wasting money on a burial or employing a doctor.

McPherson didn't fear death, and he could think of far worse ways to die than in a ring against another man, testing honest strength against strength. But what he did fear was the day he couldn't lift his hand to punish a slave in the field. He feared the day they realized he was weak, just like them. That was the day when one of the Captain's hired hands would probably call him out in the middle of the night and bury a bullet in the back of his head. They were all afraid of him. They wouldn't dare try to arrest him or throw him in the stockade. It would take ten men just to bring him down. He'd killed men before; he could do it again.

His jug was bone-dry empty, and he had to piss. He had hoped not to do anything but drink until he passed out tonight, but now, Mcpherson had to get up and move if the overseer didn't want his whole bed to smell like urine, and if he wanted the good stuff that allowed him to sleep. He got up slowly and put his boots back on. His feet were purple, even black in some places, but letting anyone see them would be a sign of weakness. He reached under his bed for his walking stick, seven feet of bald cypress that he had picked out himself and spent a summer smoothing and finishing. The slaves thought he had it for show and intimidation. None of them knew how much he leaned on it over the course of every day. If he was going to walk to the little shanty town over the next rise to buy more liquor, he would need it.

The sun was going down, so he walked as quickly as he could. Most of the traders were closed up for the night by the time he arrived, and the only two left open were out of what he wanted. One didn't sell the stuff, and the other had nothing left but some weak grape wine he tried to offer him in exchange for collecting a debt owed over on the next property. McPherson didn't say a word, just stared at the poor white trash merchant until he apologized and scurried off like the little rat he was. That left McPherson with nothing but a long and angry walk back home. His knee would be killing him by then, and if he wasn't up with the sun, he'd get a whipping the likes of which no other slave could ever take and not die. He was about to leave the shanty town when he saw a lit cigarette flame burning in the dark, just at the end of the row.

McPherson squinted, but he couldn't make out who was holding the smoke.

"Boy, ya better get home before your Masstah catch ya out past dark and tans ya hide!"

McPherson heard a low chuckle in the darkness and watched puffs of air appear in front of the man's face. He couldn't make out more than his lips and teeth in the dark.

"Not a worry, McPherson, ya and me got the same Masstah. 'Cept

I'm free to come and go as I please, and if he tried to whip me, I'd blow his fucking brains out."

McPherson didn't recognize the man's voice and still couldn't see his face. "You know me? You one them hired guns the Captain keeps around?"

The man nodded in the dark. "Something like that. Looks like ya came up dry on ya booze run. But it's ya lucky night. I've got a spare jug I picked up back home. Trade it to ya for a favor if ya in the bargaining kind of mood."

McPherson strolled closer, careful of some clumsy trap. He was the biggest out here, but definitely not the smartest. He used his fists when other men would more wisely use their brains.

"What favor you want?"

"The kind that helps ya self. I was watching today when that Cecilia was out there teasing ya, trying to get ya to spare ha pappy. Wasn't right how she did ya like that. Lil' bitch needs to deliver on ha promise, not just flirt and go."

McPherson jerked his head up. It was like the man was reading his mind. Cecilia was such a tease. Had been as long as he'd known her. Had used him for favors left and right when she was first sold to the Captain, always hinting that she would reward him, but never delivering. Then one damn day, all the slaves were celebrating the fact that she got herself married to Juba, and was pregnant on top of that.

"You right, damn it. But I can't touch her. She married to Juba, and he's got favorite status with the Captain. Drives the horses, runs errands into town, all that shit. He's the only one leaves the plantation without a White face beside him. If I do something to her, I'll be hung by dawn."

Another low chuckle.

"Nothing so violent as all that, my large friend. Everyone expects ya to use ya fists, but what if ya use ya wits instead? What if Cecilia wasn't able to do what's expected of ha? Why, then she'd be in trouble. That sort of failure would take ha outside ha husband's protection. She have only two choices then. She can go up to the big house and take ha punishment, hehe, and leave ha lil children without a ma. Or she can seek out the only man on the plantation who can save ha ass from punishment. Seems like a pretty slave would be willing to do about anything in that situation, if it meant saving ha own skin and keeping ha family safe."

McPherson had to think the whole thing through slowly, but his eyes gradually grew wide at the possibility. He wasn't clever, but he wasn't entirely stupid. He looked down at the figure standing in the dark and saw a pair of gleaming eyes buried in the shadow.

"She gonna need to come begging me to keep her safe."

The hired gun smiled in the dark as he passed a thick, full jug to McPherson, who uncorked it, smelled it, then guzzled it down. It was sweet and rich, and it filled his throat with a comforting warmth. He slurped down another satisfying gulp.

"Oh, she'll be begging ya all right," the other said, his voice getting deeper and fuller in McPherson's ears. "I find the best begging is done on ha knees. Can you see ha in ya mind, on ha knees, McPherson? Hee-hee.

"Looking up at ya? Saying please? Saying she'll do anything ya want if ya just keep ha safe? Any damn thing."

McPherson's eyes were already drooping, and his lips pulled back in an ugly sneer. The hand not holding the jug reached out as if he was stroking Cecilia's hair while she knelt in front of him.

The stranger leaned up and said softly, "She'll do anything ya want, my friend. As often as ya want, day or night, over and over again. Hehe.

"Because if she doesn't, well, one word from ya, and ha family is ripped apart forever."

McPherson was nodding along greedily. "Yeah, finally going to put out what she's been teasing all these years. Won't have a choice in the matter. Won't be able to go runnin' home down by the river. Take her away from that high-class Juba who think his shit don't stink. Make her my little wifey for a while 'til I get bored with her.

Let Juba know who taking her to beddy bye every night while his sorry ass sleepin' cold and alone."

The paid gun chuckled again at the scenario McPherson was playing out in his mind. "Ya know exactly what she needs, my friend. But ya need to make it so they don't doubt ya. Get one of those lackeys from ya captain to come wit ya. Explain what ya doing, hell, maybe give him a turn with ha himself if he wants."

McPherson roared with laughter at the thought of that. He imagined little Cecilia not just being taken by him, but by a greasy, disease-ridden White boy too. He took one last slug from the jug and went to pass it back to the stranger, only to find him gone. He had probably gone off to take a piss. McPherson didn't care either way. He took the jug in one hand, his walking stick in the other, and trudged swiftly home, eager for the next morning when his plans could unfold.

I WAS UP and ready to pick cotton early the next day, doing my best to avoid the discipline that got doled out otherwise. But when McPherson showed up, he was joined by one of the Captain's hired guns, a man named McMurtry—White with greasy black hair, a long drooping mustache, and chewing something I assumed was tobacco. He kept carelessly spitting some slimy, crusted phlegm monstrosity out his mouth onto the slaves' bare feet and worn-down shoes while menacingly ogling each as he walked by, insisting under his breath, "No good slaves, they all deserve a lashing."

As McMurtry walked, a pistol in a holster dangled from his hip, letting everyone know who decided the law around here.

McPherson spoke up as we all gathered around: "Mr. McMurtry here has a letter from your Master, Captain William! He is going to read it to you slowly, and you are going to pay him mind!"

McMurtry pulled a faded yellow piece of paper out of his pocket and began reading from it. At least he was pretending like he was reading. He never looked down at the paper, and I suspected this was some sort of game he and McPherson had cooked up. Since they didn't think any of us could read, they weren't putting much into the show.

"It reads, we are behind on our production, and we believe that the slaves are falsifying their cotton counts. For this reason, we are requiring some among you to increase your quota by the end of the week. If you hear your name, step forward and receive your new quota."

Everyone tensed, silently hoping that their name would not be called. McMurtry continued.

"Jeremiah! Your quota has increased from eight hundred pounds a week to one thousand pounds a week!"

"Gregory! Your quota has increased from eight hundred pounds a week to one thousand pounds a week!"

"Rodrick! Your quota has increased from eight hundred pounds a week to one thousand pounds a week!"

"Cecilia!"

I tensed as her name was called, suspecting this was the true purpose of the announcement. She had embarrassed McPherson the day before, and he was going to have his revenge. She stepped forward.

"Cecilia! Your quota has increased from eight hundred pounds a week to three thousand pounds a week!"

Stone silence. Cecilia glared at McPherson, and he sneered back. This was his response to her.

Eight hundred pounds of cotton a week translated into about one hundred and twenty-five pounds a day, which most workers were able to accomplish. Pushing her total up to three thousand made it physically impossible to reach her quota, period. Even if she worked from dawn to dusk seven days a week, it was impossible. When she didn't make the quota, he could have her taken to the big house for private punishment or punished publicly out in the commons. Or most likely, it would be a combination of the two, plus a trip to his shanty down by the stables. Wild horses were broken by those stables. Their squeals, moans, and neighs likely muffled any screams from the slave girls McPherson was known to bring there.

All because she took a stand to save her father's life. It wasn't right, and it made my blood boil. At that moment, I was half-tempted to snatch the paper from the hired gun and read what it really said, but it would be my word against theirs, and I was a nobody. I'd have to come up with a better plan.

I thought about what to do all day long, but I still didn't have an answer by quitting time. By then, Juba had found out about the increased quota, and he and Cecilia were huddled together talking in low voices off to the side of the barter station. Wayles came over after the meal with his flask and let me have a tug on it, as he had for the last few days. We sat there briefly together in the silence.

He then opened his mouth with many questions about New York City, and I tried to answer them carefully, trying to remember as much of its history as I could so I didn't say something that made me sound even more bizarre than I already seemed.

"You look like a man with something on his mind," Wayles said after his second or third attempt to make me laugh failed miserably.

It was true. I was thinking about my U.S. history from my sophomore year, going over a passage I had been forced to memorize and recite in front of the class. It had virtually no meaning back then, just another random thing the school had thrown at us in order to grade our performance. But in this unprecedented situation and with ample time to think about the ways of the world, it was all coming back to me, and I found myself turning the words over in my mind, considering their meaning.

"Sorry, I'm not good company tonight, Wayles," I replied. "I've been thinking about something I learned back in school in New York City. The way things have been here the past few days, it's been weighing heavy on my heart."

"I dropped out after fifth grade," he said. "But I'd listen to what you have to say."

I turned to face him so I could look him in the eye. The more I thought about it, the more important what I was thinking about seemed.

"Back where I'm from, there was a man, um, who talks about equal rights for all people. Not just people with property or people who look like you or people who can read or have money, but everybody," I told him. "I've heard his speeches lots of times before, but I never really gave it much thought 'til I got here and saw how things really are."

Wayles nodded. "I heard they're a lot different in their thinking up in the North. Free Blacks in a lot of places, and programs trying to help people who can't help themselves. A lot different from down here, of course, and not really doing us no good."

I nodded. It was true. Even in my time, I knew it was true. Different places had different understandings of tolerance and equality. Here, the only people who took each other at face value were those who had nothing of their own—no property, no rights, no money. It was so damn backward that a vicious psychopath like McPherson could set up a trap for Cecilia to fall into, forcing her to either lose her life, her decency, or her family. Her choices were painfully few.

We'd had to memorize big chunks of Dr. Martin Luther King's speech on the anniversary of his birthday. They were racing through my mind as I looked around at all these hard-working people whose entire lives could be destroyed at the whim of sadistic men like McPherson and his Captain. I had yet to see him, but I did have a bit of morbid curiosity about the Captain. Who was this unseen terror? My imagination was constantly inventing new versions of what he might look like.

"In his speech, the man said, 'I have a dream that my four little children will one day live in a nation where they will not be judged by the color of their skin, but by the content of their character.'"

Wayles seemed to pause for a moment and think it over.

"That's a nice dream, Rohan, but down here you get judged

based on who has the money and the guns. And none of us do or ever will. If we try to stand up to them, they'll kill us without a second thought."

I turned that undeniable fact over in my head. Up until yesterday I would have agreed wholeheartedly with that notion. The beatdown expressions I saw all day long and the fear of McPherson suggested as much. But then Cecilia had stood up to save her father's life.

I spoke again, recalling Dr. King's speech, not sure if I was talking to myself or to Wayles or a little of both.

"We cannot walk alone ... and as we walk, we must make the pledge that we shall always march ahead. We cannot turn back ...We cannot be satisfied as long as a Negro in Mississippi cannot vote, and a Negro in New York believes he has nothing for which to vote. No, no, we are not satisfied, and we will not be satisfied until justice rolls down like waters, and righteousness like a mighty stream."

I recited it with my eyes closed, remembering each word from practicing it in front of the mirror. I was pleased that I still remembered. When I opened them, Wayles was looking at me with an intense stare.

"It's never going to get any better down here unless we make it so," he said in a near-whisper. "You, me, Juba, Cecilia, their kids, all these people... we're just going through the motions of a shitty life where we hope we don't get killed between waking up and going to bed. That's no kind of life at all, is it? Who is this man who speaks so well?"

I hesitated to name him. It seemed silly, but Dr. King was a visionary of the twentieth century. "He was a great man known by his initials—MLK," I explained. "It kept him safer that way, as the people who opposed his view didn't know exactly who he was or where he lived."

"Makes sense," Wayles replied. "A man starts talking like that in public, he's liable to get himself shot."

I couldn't help but open my eyes wider in response, trying my best not to show how correct that statement was.

"So, what are we going to do, Rohan? We can't form an army and attack them. How do we break this cycle?"

I didn't have an answer, but perhaps the beginning of one.

"First we help Cecilia meet her quota to keep McPherson from doing God knows what to her," I proposed, with more confidence in my voice than I actually felt. "Then we figure out a way to get as many people away from here as possible. Even if it kills us."

FOURTEEN

I knew very few people there, offering only a few nods and waves. Wayles knew everyone, so he spread the word that we were planning to help Cecilia meet her unreasonable quota to keep her safe from McPherson, and were enlisting help. We talked about ways to move cotton into her designated basket without the powers that be noticing. I wound up suggesting one idea from a movie I had seen the previous summer, *The Shawshank Redemption*. The film's main character used a tiny rock hammer to chip away the inside of the walls of his cell over many years, and he hid the evidence by putting the chipped rocks in his pockets and then dropping them in the prison yard as he walked around every day. My idea was to do the exact opposite.

Everyone's clothes had deep pockets for carrying what they needed, so I proposed that every person in the fields near Cecilia should put their pull from every tenth plant or so into their pockets. One of the other men, a younger slave named Davis, went out early one morning and grabbed a few extra burlap sacks from the shed and dumped them into the big baskets in the field. Everyone put their extra cotton in these sacks, and at the end of each day, when the light was failing, the extra cotton was snuck to where Cecilia's count rested. It was tense for the first few hours until the guards posted to watch us became just as sunburnt and dazed as we were from the heat. McPherson made his rounds, but only to ensure that no one was slacking off. With Cecilia's life on the line, everyone was working harder than ever, and he had little to get mad at.

It was hard to keep count of how close we were to her quota, but on the last night before the deadline, the men lifted the burlap sacks and counted them, coming to a grim reality. We were a thousand pounds short. With the teamwork of the other slaves, we had doubled the amount of cotton that Cecilia picked in a week, but that wasn't nearly enough. That night at the communal dinner, there was a real sense of dismay and panic setting in. Every idea to fill up the sacks had the same risk of discovery and death for anyone involved. Juba and Cecilia didn't want anyone risking their lives like that, so they kept shooting down ideas. Finally, everyone began tiring out and headed for bed. I asked if I could walk Juba and Cecilia home to see Amayah.

As USUAL, she was dazzling, playing at the center of the children when I walked in, but she quickly disengaged, running to me and wrapping her arms around my neck. She started to ask how the count was going, but from one look at our faces, she knew.

Her face fell, but then she raised her head triumphantly. "I have an idea." She gathered the three of us and summoned Wayles for good measure, as he had a good head on his shoulders. The kids were put outside to play and sing, while the oldest was told that if he saw anyone coming down the hill, he should raise the alarm so we could play dumb. Amayah squeezed my hand as we waited for Wayles to arrive, and I started to wonder what exactly she was up to. When Wayles finally arrived, he sat heavily on a chair, and Amayah spoke up.

"Rohan and I have told you that we're from New York City, and that's true," she started. "What we haven't told you is the full story. I think it would be best if you heard it, because believing in us is the only way we'll make it out of here alive."

I looked up at her with wide eyes. Was she really about to tell them the truth?

She continued, "This is going to sound crazy, but hear me out. Rohan can collect the rest of the quota by himself before sunrise. He's... well, he's special."

Convincing Juba and Cecilia that I could finish their quota in a single night would not be an easy argument to win. They were already talking themselves into taking their kids and running for it, perhaps stealing a horse so they could get faster and further away. But it was fool's talk. That sort of escape would take planning, and they were trying to figure it out in one night.

And neither of them took me seriously when I said I could finish the quota, but why would they? Ama asked them for five minutes to listen to what we had to say before they decided. It was time to come clean.

"Juba, you were one of the first people we met the day we came to the plantation. You drove us in the wagon. Tell me, where did we come from? Where did you stop and pick us up?"

He immediately looked uncomfortable and looked back hard at me and Cecilia before sighing. "Don't remember. 'Course we picked up a lot that day. You might have gotten in when I had my back turned. Was hot that day too. Mighta been the heat that got to me."

I rolled my eyes. "You expect me to believe that, Juba? You saw what we were wearing, and you saw what we looked like. There's no way we would have gotten in that wagon without you noticing."

I could see the fear and suspicion on Juba's face. He had convinced himself that we'd been there all along, even though he knew we hadn't been. We just appeared, and there was no explanation for it. I didn't want him doubting himself or us now, so I pushed on.

"We were not there, and then we were there. The only explanation we have, even though I know it's hard to hear... is that we're not from this place. We're not even from this time. 1854 is a year in the distant past for Amayah and I. Where we come from, there are no slaves in the United States. I know this sounds even crazier, but I can do things that normal people can't do. I can do things to get your quota tonight in just a few hours before McPherson comes looking for it."

They didn't believe me. I knew it, but I had an ace up my sleeve.

"I know you think I'm crazy, so I'll prove it to you. Cecilia, you go in the farmhouse pretty regularly, right? Think about something in the kitchen that you see every day and describe it to me. And please don't worry yourself."

She looked at me, clearly puzzled, then said. "Well, the Captain got his wife this fancy vase from the Orient when he was overseas. She got it up in the window for all the world to see. She has us shine it daily, and we can't even touch it if she's not there supervising us."

Confident in my abilities for the first time since we arrived, I nodded and said, "Okay, I'll be back with it in 30 seconds."

I could have told them that I was about to turn their house into solid gold, and they would have been just as willing to believe me.

"Be right back," I whispered to Amayah and kissed her cheek. I stepped through the door, gathered a significant amount of energy for the first time in days, and then used my super speed, racing into the kitchen in a few blinks...

When I walked back into Juba and Cecilia's house with the vase in my hand, they both scooted their chairs back, nearly hitting the back wall. If it hadn't been such a serious situation, it would have been hilarious.

"That's impossible!" Cecilia whispered furiously. "I just saw it up there not an hour ago! How'd you get that, boy?"

"Like I said, I can do things that other people can't," I repeated. "We're not from around here, but I think we were sent here to help you. So, I'm going to put this back, and then I'll pick your cotton for you."

Amayah smiled and held Cecilia's hands in hers. "It's okay. I know how it feels to see him do something remarkable for the first time. In the first few days I knew about Ro's abilities, he saved me from a gang of men trying to hurt me, and saved the life of a little girl who was going to die."

"What the hell is he?" Juba asked her, apparently unaware that I was still standing at the door. "A witch? Some kind of demon? Is that why he don't smell like the rest after a long day's work?"

As I reached into my power center, I turned over my shoulder and saw Ama smile. "Oh no, nothing like that. In fact, I think he's probably a lot closer to being an angel. He can do things you won't believe, even when you see them with your own eyes. He doesn't even know how special he is, though I keep trying to tell him."

The rest of the night was a blur. I put the vase back, fighting off my desire to rob the farmhouse blind and find the loot I was sure the Captain had stashed away somewhere. It wouldn't do the enslaved people or Wayles any good to rob the place before I had an escape plan worked out. After I put the Oriental porcelain back, I ran to the fields and began zig-zagging my way into the deeper sections. Fortunately, the moon was close to full, and the stars were bright, so I could clearly see what was in front of me. I moved as quickly as possible to pick the cotton without destroying the cotton plants. I didn't want to leave any suspicious marks or signs behind. I wanted it to look like Cecilia had somehow done it all by simply working harder. I did it all in about two and half hours, then took another half hour to rest before walking back up the hill. I stopped briefly at Juba and Cecilia's house and tapped lightly. Juba appeared at the doorway with a drawn knife blade, and I put my hands up in the moonlight to show him that I was unarmed.

"It's done," I reassured softly. "Three thousand pounds of cotton in her pile."

He shook his head in wonder. "You're a miracle worker, my friend. Bless you."

"You're welcome," I replied. I couldn't help but look over his shoulder and see Ama sleeping peacefully. I wanted to go and take her in my arms so badly, but I knew it still wasn't safe.

A FEW HOURS LATER, as the sun rose, we gathered outside the bunkhouse while other slaves retrieved the cotton baskets for inspection. There was tension in the air. Only the four of us—myself, Ama, Juba, and Cecilia—knew that there was suddenly enough cotton to meet her impossible quota. Everyone else lined up thought this would be the last time they would see Cecilia in the same condition, that she'd either be beaten, taken away, or killed in front of them. I suspected Juba would protest and try to fight if that happened.

Ama was still hidden down by the creek with Juba and Cecilia's children. If things went badly, I planned to use my powers to run to her, grab her, and teleport us away from the plantation.

I had no idea where we would go or what we would do when we got there, and I didn't like the idea of abandoning Juba's family or Wayles, but I had to think about what was best for the two of us if this became a total clusterfuck. I kept reminding myself to keep my head down and not act impulsively unless it was clearly all going south. A few people knew I was different, but for everyone else, including McPherson, I was a nobody. That look wasn't hard to pull off, as I had years of practice.

We stood there for what seemed like hours until McPherson's massive frame was seen lumbering down the hill. People immediately began straightening up, moving from the benches to stand in a line, and tucking in their shirts. That's when someone gasped aloud.

Coming behind McPherson were two gleaming white horses, and on their backs were an older White man and woman. The woman wore a dress that looked like silk and shone a bright yellow. It was the most beautiful piece of clothing I had seen since arriving; slaves wore nothing but grays and browns. The man beside her reminded me of a hawk I had once seen during elementary school when a local zoo brought wild animals for an assembly. He had a sharp nose, almost like a beak, a small mouth that didn't seem to move, and bushy eyebrows that were graying unevenly. His hair was short and white, and his eyes were a piercing pale blue. These details paled in comparison to the military uniform he wore, complete with a row of medals across his right breast, blue dress pants, and polished riding boots. The top of his head was covered by a black felt hat with a wide brim fraying on the edges, shading his eyes from the hot sun. He had a sword in its scabbard across one hip and a large pistol holstered on the other. It was the man I had been wanting to see but not actually meet. Captain William Franklin, the pride of Oxford, Mississippi.

The Captain and his wife cantered up on horseback in the wake of McPherson's lumbering strides. This was it, then. McPherson was preparing for a big show; he had even brought his boss along. I prayed silently that we'd all survive whatever came next.

A few minutes later, the Captain, his wife, McPherson, and the hired gun McMurtry had us line up as the cotton baskets were inspected.

McPherson called them one by one. First was Jeremiah, who had made it to one thousand and seventeen pounds, then Rodrick, who had hit one thousand and thirty-one pounds. Both men breathed huge sighs of relief when their counts came back positive, though they knew it would be the new normal for them, and this would be their new burden every week.

Gregory, the third man to have his quota increased, seemed a little older and more worn around the edges than the first two. He was missing a couple fingers on his left hand. I don't know what had happened to him, and when I asked Wayles about it one day, he grunted and said, "dogs." That didn't matter now, and what did matter was when Gregory's count was tallied, it came out to nine hundred and eighty-nine pounds, not quite a thousand. As naive as I was, I figured it was close enough to round up. When I was in the stock room, if my brother told me to grab fifty items, he wouldn't flip if I only brought 48. However, this wasn't a drug store, and these guys weren't my well-meaning older brothers. Gregory hadn't even opened his mouth to offer an explanation before McPherson blasted him across the right side of his head with his rock-and-twine weapon, sending Gregory spinning into the dirt. He stumbled quickly to his feet, much to my astonishment, and tried to limp back to the line, but McMurtry put a boot in his back and kicked him back to the ground.

"Not so fast, dog!" the hired gun barked. "You have displeased your master and are in dire need of punishment."

While McPherson glowered over Gregory, who stayed pressed to the ground with his head hung low, McMurtry sauntered over to the Captain and his wife, still on their horses, and started conversing in voices too low for me to make out. After a moment, the Captain's wife spit out a nasty laugh, and I heard a snatch of conversation— "like the old useless dog he is." McMurtry hustled back to McPherson and whispered something to the massive overseer, who grunted in return. He turned and trotted over the hill towards the shanty he lived in, but was back a few minutes later with what I initially thought was a small horse, but was actually a large dog with a rope tied around its neck. The dog was pitch black, its tongue dangling with drool from the exercise. It was like a four-legged version of McPherson—big, ugly and spoiling for a fight. McPherson held it by the rope, attached to a tight chain around its neck. I doubt anyone else would have been strong enough to hold the beast. McMurtry kicked poor Gregory again and said, "Get up, dog!"

Gregory raised himself to his feet and shot a fearful look at the dog, fear and recognition painted across his face.

"Ya fell 11 pounds short of your new quota, dog!" McMurtry shouted into Gregory's face. "So, the Captain has decided you get an 11-pace head start before McPherson turns Cain loose on you. Eleven paces to make yourself scarce or get up one of them trees. If the beast catches you, then he gets his reward, maybe even from them hands by chewing off a couple more fingers, what do ya say? If by some miracle you get away, we'll consider that God's Divine Intervention, and you can get back to work. Ya ready? NOW GET!"

He slapped Gregory across the back, and the poor man stumbled and nearly fell. McMurtry counted his steps and screamed in delight for everyone to hear. "That's one and two! You still right here boy, make them next steps count or you'll be chewed up and shit out before noon!"

Gregory caught his balance, looked back at the dog, then took off at a dead sprint towards the line of trees that separated the cotton fields from the main road.

McMurtry counted off quick, stumbling between his own cruel laughter, "Three-four-five-six-seven-eight-nine-ten-eleven, let him loose, Mac!"

McPherson dropped the rope and let the massive dog free. The people assembled drew back in terror, but Cain only had eyes for the man running away. The dog was clearly trained to hunt down deserters and criminals; it was furiously fixated on the rapidly departing form of Gregory. I didn't want to watch, but I couldn't look away. It seemed like Gregory had picked the right path; the trees were just a few feet away, and several had branches low enough to swing onto if he got his good hand planted right. But even as we watched, he stumbled on a root, and Cain was on him, growling and gnashing with his massive jaws. Gregory screamed aloud as the teeth closed on his shoulder, and then his elbow. He fought as best he could with his good hand and kicked at the dog with his bare feet, but the dog probably outweighed him by fifty pounds and was bred for fighting exactly like this. It caught Gregory's elbow and shook its head back and forth, the way a smaller dog might hold a bird or squirrel before shaking it to death. Gregory was tossed a few feet to the side, but came up with a stick, swinging it blindly at the dog's head. Cain backed off warily, clearly having been trained with some sort of weapon as a deterrent. The dog snapped its jaws in frustration, calculating the danger, but Gregory continued shouting loudly and jabbing the stick forward. It seemed that the dog would inevitably overcome its fears and charge again, but it never got the chance. McPherson stepped forward and released a piercing whistle with two fingers in his mouth. Cain immediately turned his head, then raced back to its master and sat obediently before him like a Golden Retriever, rather than the murderous monster from seconds earlier.

The dog was unharmed, but Gregory was not so lucky. Blood ran down from scratches on his cheek, and more soaked his shirt at the shoulder, with a strip of skin dangling off his elbow like a red rubber band. It turned my stomach, and I looked away to avoid vomiting on the spot. Gregory staggered back to the clearing, frozen and unspeaking. Even after that brutal punishment, he had to be properly dismissed by the powers that be.

A shot suddenly rang out, freezing everyone in place as its eerie echo faded. Gregory dropped lifeless to the dirt.

I saw McMurtry holding his gun with white smoke rising, then reholstering it.

"An old and wounded slave is an unuseful one. And an unuseful slave is as good as a dead one," the Captain callously declared. "Let that be a lesson to y'all. We need productive slaves on this here plantation. Any slaves associated with the last name Franklin shall be ever fruitful."

I risked a glance at Cecilia, standing stock-still beside Juba, her hand entwined with his. I couldn't imagine what she was thinking. How could the Captain kill Gregory without so much as blinking an eye? I was terrified for Cecilia, who would face the next round of judgment. Everyone had tried to help her meet the unfair quota, but that combined effort had left her 1,000 pounds of cotton short. Now her fate and that of her family lay in the wild promise of a stranger, a scrawny kid from New York City who claimed to have powers beyond those of mortal men. If I had been in her shoes, I probably would have already made a run for it.

McPherson wrapped the rope chain back around Cain's neck and McMurtry called out, "Cecilia! You got them three thousand pounds, girl?" He laughed, and the rest of those with authority laughed with him. This was all a game to them—a sham trial where the verdict was already decided.

They knew one woman couldn't bag that much cotton in a week, but they would put her through the motions before doling out her punishment.

"Here, sir," she replied, stepping out of line.

From around the bend came the men with her basket. They put it down and disappeared, drawing confused looks from master and slave alike. They came back with the second basket, then a third, and then a fourth. A murmur went through the gathered slaves, but it quickly lost steam as McPherson whipped his head around, daring anyone to speak further.

"Now then, what's all this?" McMurtry asked one of the slaves who had lugged the baskets out to be weighed.

"This Miss Cecilia's quota," one of the men said, keeping his eyes firmly fixed on the ground. "All stacked up in her spot this morning."

McMurtry raised his eyebrows and turned back to his Captain astride the white stallion. The plantation owner nodded almost imperceptibly and McMurtry made a circling gesture with his fingers. "Count it up!"

As the cotton was pulled out, handled, and weighed, I kept my head down like the rest. McMurtry went back and forth between the counters while McPherson watched from a ways off, the veins in his neck bulging, his grip tight on Cain's leash. At last, McMurtry stepped back, wrote something on his scrap of paper, and called out in a loud voice, "4136 pounds of cotton here, sir!"

Holy shit. I had been so aggressive in my nighttime gathering that I had gone another thousand pounds past the quota.

The reading of the seemingly impossible tally set McPherson off with Cain by his side, and he strode right at Cecilia, bellowing in anger. Shoving Juba to the ground with one meaty hand, he picked Cecilia up by the chin and screamed into her face, "You bitch! You think you can fool me? Who helped you? Who did this? You're mine!"

McMurtry tried to get him to put Cecilia down, but he was a stick of a man next to the giant overseer. Cain was barking nonstop now as Juba grabbed at McPherson's other arm and was tossed aside again. Fearing for Cecilia's life, I started gathering what energy I had left after the night of cotton-picking, but before I could act, the scene was torn asunder by another loud CRACK.

It scared everyone and woke McPherson from whatever angry haze he was descending into. The overseer dropped Cecilia like an ordinary man might drop a drinking glass, and she hit the ground hard. McPherson spun in wide-eyed surprise to find his Captain, still on horseback, a pistol smoking in his hand. The warning shot he fired had missed McPherson by several feet, but the Captain's point was made.

"What in God's name is wrong with you, boy? Woman picks 4,000 pounds of cotton in a week and you mean to choke her to death? She don't work for you... you all belong to me. Every damn last one of you. You don't go touchin' my property without my permission.

"You strong and you fast, but you ain't smart, boy, that ain't something God blessed upon you. See that dog you got on that chain? That's what you are to me. My big black dog I turn loose when I feel the need. But when I ain't got that need, you sit at my feet, quiet like. You snarl without my permission, and I'm liable to starve you for a week. You try and bite the hand that feeds you, I promise you'll never see the sun rise again. You got your whip and your boots and your little shithouse by the stable and suddenly you think you can decide who lives and who dies among my personal property? You ain't nothing but one more nigger, bought and paid, boy, now get your black ass outta here before I decide to blow a hole in it."

For one achingly long second, I thought McPherson was going to disobey. I thought he'd charge the Captain or sic the dog on him, but none of that happened. He didn't say a word, obeying his master's words, stalking up the hill towards his shanty with Cain in tow. As he passed me, I saw him turn and give the Captain's back a hard stare without the Captain noticing. The look made me shiver. There was murder in that man's eyes.

When McPherson was gone, the Captain addressed the rest of us for the first time. "Well, well, this is a landmark day indeed in old Oxford town," he said, slowly cantering about on his horse. He rode back to where his wife sat astride her mare. "What should we do to celebrate this fine occasion, my love? The Lord Almighty has blessed us with a powerful bounty this day. How should we say thanks to the LORD who has delivered to us this copious treasure?"

She considered his question for a moment, then looked down on us like some great queen seeing peasants for the first time and spoke a single word. Captain Franklin nodded and turned back to us. "My lady wife has asked me for a great favor, and I have granted it. Y'all can have this whole day off. I will grant a holiday and a cause for a joyous celebration."

CHAPTER
FIFTEEN

The haunting memory of Gregory's murder was on my mind constantly. Wayles, speaking with a heavy heart, revealed a grim truth. "In the eyes of the Master and the powerful, such acts are considered a necessary evil," he said, his gaze distant. "In these parts, the punishment of slaves is the way of our land," Wayles lamented, painting a grim picture of resignation with his words. "It's best not to let the Captain and those who reign over us see your tears for Gregory."

I sighed, overwhelmed with sorrow. "But how can we simply forget his murder?"

"Pray, trust in my words. This gatherin' we're holdin', it's as much for honorin' Gregory's time among us as it is for lettin' us catch a breath from the madness that's been doggin' our heels. If you catch my meaning, it's a time for rememberin' and forgettin'. We're all of us in this together, sharin' our burdens and finding a sliver of peace in the memory of Gregory, who walked these trials with us," Wayles offered me comfort by gently placing his hand on my back. "So let's hold fast to this moment, as a celebration of his spirit and a brief escape from our troubles."

In a peaceful moment, amidst the songs of birds and the gentle breeze, I witnessed a moving procession led by ten Black children. Each of them carried armfuls of roses, as if they were holding precious treasures. Their voices came together to form a beautiful hymn:

"FLY'N TOWARDS YOU, Jesus, I'm on my way to you.
Guiding me home, Lord, I'm going home to you!
My time here is short, no fear, close to you!
Jesus, with you, is where I long to be, ooh-ooh.
United with you, forever with you."

AS THE HAUNTING melody of the hymn faded into the air, a solemn procession of Black women gracefully emerged, carrying baskets of flowers, wreaths, and crosses. The hushed audience turned their attention to Juba, who began to speak with a voice laden with emotion and wisdom.

"Our worst fears were realized; the decision was against poor Gregory, and he paid with his life. Gregory wasn't just any man—he was a beacon of goodness, a tireless worker, a dignified man of color. He will always be cherished in our memories, not just as a man but as our beloved brother. Lord, Jesus, please cradle Gregory's soul and all those who walked before him with gentle care in your heavenly home."

Men started to drum while everyone started praying, and Cecilia poured water from a jug on the ground that had been the site of so much suffering. The children then placed their roses on the wet earth to honor Gregory and those who died before him.

"Let us remember Gregory and find healing," Juba finished. "Let us not all be sad on this day but celebrate his life as he would have wanted."

By nightfall, the celebrations had just begun. I felt like I had been transported from the most perilous place on Earth to somewhere else. Maybe, I witnessed everyone trying to drown out their misery and pain.

Every slave on the plantation had the entire day off, and they prepared a great feast to be shared in honor of Gregory. The menu included turkey and pieces of sausage that someone had bartered for. The vegetables were simmered gently in rich stews and flavorful sauces, presenting a hearty meal far superior to the tough fare of the morning. With its inviting, warm aroma, a freshly baked loaf promised comfort and sustenance. A jug of juice with its tantalizingly sweet contents caught the eye at one table. Nearby, some men casually shared their flasks, the liquid within sparking laughter and camaraderie. Amid the lively gathering, a bonfire roared to life, casting its warm glow on the assembled tables and their cheerful occupants. Just a stone's throw away, Juba played melodies on his banjo under the rustling branches of the trees. His twang harmonized with the soulful notes of a harmonica, the airy voice of a flute, and the rhythmic clatter of spoons - a quartet performed with skilled precision. As I stood there, the tableau of festivity unfolded before my eyes, bathed in the golden glow of firelight and underscored by the melody of music. It was a heartwarming scene, filled with joy and a sense of unity, beneath the starry night sky.

During our weeks here, they were downtrodden and depressed, but they were now all smiles, laughing and swapping stories like the best family reunion the world had ever seen. Stories of Gregory were told, his life remembered, and instead of grieving, people had joy in their words, celebrating his life. I did not doubt that most would stay up all night and only fall into their beds when dawn was fast approaching.

I helped move tables, carried wild game to the fire, and met everyone's children, all of whom were stunned by my height and demanded one piggyback ride after another. I was in the middle of disentangling myself from one of these encounters when I saw her.

Ama and Cecilia were gracefully ascending the hill, their arms cradling freshly picked flowers from the stream's edge. The evening's dimming light draped Cecilia in a dark blue dress, which appeared nearly black, while Ama was adorned in its identical counterpart. The soft, silky fabric of Ama's midnight blue dress danced around her, caressing the breeze as she moved. I hadn't witnessed such radiance in her since the festival night, yet here she was, her hair cascading elegantly across her forehead, her face illuminated by a joyful smile. Rooted to the spot, I watched her approach, bathed in the day's final golden sunlight. In that moment, her beauty transcended anything I had ever seen before, casting a spell of enchantment that captured my heart entirely.

Amayah placed the flowers down and came to hug me, but was interrupted by Cecilia and Juba's daughter, Claire, who wanted to see the dress. She was soon surrounded by other girls and whisked away into a crowd, laughing and smiling. I watched her go, happy to see her enjoying herself with the other children. My belly rumbled, and I was still on call to help with the heavy lifting of benches and food, which I was more than willing to assist with. I enjoyed helping and feeling like part of the group. I preferred to keep it a secret that I was the one who had helped Cecilia reach her quota, and I was happy to remain anonymous. My height and distinctly non-Black physical features already attracted enough attention as it was.

After dinner, Juba and the two other musicians began to play a series of songs, and the slaves started clapping their hands and dancing along. At first, it was just one or two couples, but eventually, more and more people came to the fire and started dancing. The smiles, laughter, and sheer joy of the moment were so different from everything I had experienced on the plantation until that moment. It filled me with an incredible warmth that I had forgotten about during the long days of picking cotton.

My gaze wandered through the bustling crowd until it locked onto her. Freed from the swarm of children, she was immersed in lively conversation with Cecilia, their laughter mingling like that of lifelong companions. Her eyes caught mine, sending a warm smile across the distance that set my heart ablaze. Under the flickering glow of the fire, her eyes sparkled with the freshness of spring — radiant, tender, and alive. They bore flecks of determination and the vibrant green of new beginnings, hinting at the resurgence of life at summer's dawn. My cheeks flushed with a heat that mirrored the fire's embrace, as she illuminated the night in a way I'd never seen before, surpassing even the brilliance at the Festival of the Moon. At that moment, amidst the chaos of our worlds — stripped of the distractions of school, feuds, family tensions, and the clash of cultures — I found solace. Yet, the joy of our shared connection was tinged with the weight of responsibility for bringing her into this peril. The thought of Captain Franklin, McMurtry, or McPherson discovering her presence twisted my stomach with dread. What would they do if they found her and I wasn't there to protect her? Despite my strengths, I was not all-seeing. Each day, as I left for the cotton fields, anxiety gnawed at me over the possibility of someone uncovering Juba and Cecilia's sanctuary and the treasure it held within.

She could be taken to the farmhouse or somewhere off the plantation, and it would be hours before I knew anything. I wouldn't be able to live with myself if anything happened, yet Amayah seemed immune to the threats on every side. She was happy and giving, eager to help Cecilia and her family, and willing to make the best of our dire predicament. Looking at her now, she seemed positively strong under the moonlight.

Another musician then joined the makeshift band, strapping a pair of barrels into a drum set and beating on them. Amongst the sounds and the energy, I found myself enveloped in the ambiance of a growing rhythm, a palpable heartbeat that seemed to intertwine with my own, bringing new life under the night sky.

Claire, the oldest of Cecilia and Juba's daughters, probably eleven or twelve, was helped onto one of the tables, where she started singing in a loud, clear voice that seemed impossible given her slight build. Claire's golden-brown skin and hair, braided in a lovely, gorgeous pattern, glowed under the moon's gleam. She knew tonight was rare, given how people laughed and embraced one another like this. She sensed the positive and genuine attention from people who considered her as family and took the time to appreciate her unique talents, instead of hurrying her off to bed or chores.

I lost my train of thought as she slipped into a beautiful song, singing the first few verses gently before hitting a crescendo. I didn't know the words, but I could feel the energy building and turned to look for Amayah. Not only had Amayah also caught the pulse of the music, but she abruptly dropped her plate of food onto one of the long tables and whirled her head around, seeking me out.

I don't think Amayah had ever looked at me the way she was looking at me now. A long surge of heat passed through my body, and I checked to make sure I hadn't stepped a foot into the fire. As she came closer, her emerald eyes shone, and her smile spread open. No doubt, I felt ablaze, and I never wanted it to go out. She ran the last few steps to me, grabbing my hand and leading me into the swirl of people.

I followed her without hesitation, not wanting to let her out of my sight again. It was the exact opposite sensation of what I had felt that night at the Festival of the Moon, the night I had been too shy and self-conscious to dance with her. This time around, I didn't care who was looking or what they might think. Being with my Ama was all that mattered.

Once she found a good spot, she turned and faced me, smiling up into my eyes.

"I want to show you how to Cha Cha," she said loudly into my ear, above the joyous din of the music.

"Cha Cha?" I asked.

"Why, Mister Chang, you don't know how to Cha Cha?"

"Miss Bello, I think I may know, just like Bruce Lee did," I said, laughing.

"I heard he was a great Cha Cha dancer, and it's simple," she gushed. "Even a superhero should have no trouble picking it up quickly. I know it doesn't sound the same, but listen to the drums playing in the background. Let's pretend and make it into a Cha Cha beat. Hear that, one-two-cha-cha-cha… that's the beat!"

Following Ama's lead and gazing into her eyes, I could have sworn I heard the Cha Cha, as everything else faded into the background.

I thought I was getting the hang of it, at least until she placed my right arm around her, and my hand slid to her lower back. She pressed her body against mine, and I felt her gentle warmth on my chest. Fortunately, it was night and too dark for her to see me blushing. Then she found my hand with hers, and we began to move together. My emotions surged as I surrendered to passion. Even the immense depth of my abilities seemed insignificant compared to the moment I was experiencing. As we danced, she gently guided my right arm to wrap more closely around her, deepening the embrace.

With a tender touch, she guided my left hand with her right, her head finding a peaceful haven as it rested upon my shoulder. This simple gesture drew us immeasurably closer, enveloping us in a cocoon woven from the threads of our affection.

I stumbled slightly, perhaps due to the dim lighting or my lingering exhaustion from a night spent speed-picking. Yet, it was mostly because of Amayah, her presence intoxicating, as if I were drunk on her love.

"I'm nothing special, Ama," I whispered. "But tonight, dancing with you under the stars, I feel like there's never been a more special moment in my life than now."

"Oh, Rohan," Ama whispered back in my ear and pointed up into the night. "See those two bright stars in the dark sky to the right? That's us."

"Two stars, forever intertwined in twilight, each reflecting the other's brilliance," I said softly.

"Unless one of the stars stumbles," Amayah laughed radiantly, looking down at my feet.

"I'm not used to this," I said, trying not to focus on my ineptness.

"That's because you need to lead me with your left foot," Amayah said gently. "Now it's your lead, Ro. Show me how you want me to move. Now, let's go at it again."

I was suddenly grateful for the lack of light because her request for me to show her how to move sent my imagination into overdrive. I glanced down at the inviting bulge of her breasts; the dress was clinging to her in the heat of the fire. We undoubtedly broke Cha Cha etiquette when I pulled her in closer, feeling her smooth skin against mine.

"Let's try again," I said, trying to regain my focus. I held Amayah tightly, feeling her irresistible body melting into mine. I knew she could sense it, too.

As we danced, moving with the rhythm of the Cha Cha music playing in our imaginations, our steps - two rocking and shuffle steps - perfectly mirrored the slow-slow, quick-quick-quick beat. In those moments, thoughts of returning to 20th-century New York City faded away. I pondered the possibility of staying here, leaving the plantation behind with Amayah by my side, envisioning a simple yet blissful life together. The idea, though enchanting, felt wildly out of reach. Amayah's dreams were tied to her family and her future; she harbored ambitions of becoming a doctor, aspirations that were far from achievable in 1850s Mississippi.

Was I foolish to believe in the possibility of our relationship surviving? At the time, such concerns seemed irrelevant. I was prepared to risk appearing foolish. Shedding my fears and doubts, I chose to concentrate solely on the tender moments Amayah and I were creating, treasuring the beauty of our connection.

She said, "Move to your left, then shift your weight to the right," and smiled as she led me to the four beats. My right hand tenderly found its way to the small of her back, just above her bottom, lingering in a soft touch as I awaited her response to the gentle gesture.

To my surprise, she remained silent, and gracefully continued, making me appear as a far more skilled dancer than I rightfully deserved to be.

"Put your left arm up," she said, and as I raised it, she twirled under my arms. "Yes, good!" She cooed, then playfully punched me in the rib.

"I did it, right?" I asked in disbelief.

"Are you sure you've never done this before?" She laughed, then softly started to sing a song as we danced. For a moment, I gaped at her, unsure how she knew about a slave ballad until I remembered that she had been living in the same one-room home as the young singer for the past two weeks. I twirled her faster as the stars sparkled and the wind blew. It felt as though we were the only two people at the party, or perhaps even in the entire world, as everything else dimmed and receded from our perception, leaving us enveloped in our own private universe.

The dance persisted, unwavering and enchanting. I would not have ceased our movement, not even if Captain Franklin himself had charged down the hill, accompanied by a raucous band of hounds. Lost as we were, far from any semblance of home and devoid of direction, I found there was nowhere else in the world I'd rather be. Holding her so tenderly, I was content to dream.

I rested my head against hers, allowing our shared affection to flourish. Our legs intertwined and embraced each other, creating a comforting and intimate connection as we cuddled closely. She gasped slightly, and we moved more slowly to the music than ever.

I gently lifted her left hand and placed it against my chest, where my heart was beating intensely. I desired for Ama to sense the depth of my affection for her. Responding, she pressed closer, enhancing the connection between us. Together, we seemed to float, turning in graceful circles. In that instant, all other happenings of the day paled in comparison as the only thing that held any significance was the bond we shared.

Her goodness emanated effortlessly with every motion, word, smile, and deed, as she dedicated herself to the Jubas and their children with a selflessness that was truly admirable. Where most would balk at acknowledging such a reality, choosing instead to retreat into the confines of their own minds, Amayah saw her situation not as a burden but as a precious opportunity. She seized on it with both hands, teaching not just the Juba children but Juba and Cecilia how to read, write, and master arithmetic. Ama's assistance even extended to helping Cecilia with her chores, doing them so smoothly that they barely attracted notice.

As I prepared to tell her of my love, the words faltered on my lips. The specter of her not reciprocating those feelings loomed large in my mind. Although I was hopeful, the familiar dragon of self-doubt threatened to paralyze me. Perhaps sensing my turmoil, Amayah looked up at me, her lips pressed together in a silent communication that spoke volumes. At that moment, my desire to kiss her intensified, but the sound of children playing and laughing in the background snapped me back to reality. With the recollection of the sixty or seventy enslaved individuals around us, the enchanting moment lost its spell. Gazing down, I sighed softly and apologized, "Amayah, I'm sorry for bringing you here."

"Don't worry," Amayah said with a grin, playfully slapping my butt. "Otherwise, we wouldn't have shared this lovely dance."

I couldn't help but laugh. Her sweetness, humor, and affection made me feel like I had stepped out of a classic romance film, suddenly filled with the courage to charm my true love.

In that fleeting instant, as my gaze drifted downward, I understood with a quiet certainty that the moment I had long anticipated was unfurling before me. She lifted her eyes to meet mine, the playful spark that once danced in them now extinguished, giving way to a vulnerable, pure openness that both spellbound me and stirred a whisper of fear at the realization of her flawless being. I had never kissed a girl except on a dare at some middle school party in a dark closet, and that surely didn't count. Time, however, was a luxury I no longer possessed, as Ama, with a grace born of the moment, rose upon her tiptoes. As I gently lowered my head to match the ascent of hers, our lips met in a tender, unexplored embrace. In that moment of connection, all uncertainties dissolved, rendering them insignificant within the depth of our kiss. We might have been the worst kissers in the world, but that didn't matter to me. The moment our lips touched, it was as if an electric current surged through me, sending energy waves throughout my entire body. As our lips united, I was bathed in a cocoon of warmth. Time itself halted, rendering the world around us utterly trivial until...

"AMAYAH!"

A horrible shriek interrupted my blissful moment, and I took a stumbling step forward as little Rose pulled on Amayah's arm, tugging her away from me.

"YOU PROMISED ME BEDTIME STORY!" the little girl was shrieking and complaining. "YOU PROMISED!"

For a brief second, I thought Amayah might refuse, but she was ever the sweet and patient one. "A promise is a promise," she said meekly, looking up at me sadly, the shyness returning to her face. She kissed my cheek and returned down the hill with Rose, skipping lightly through the grass. I understood how she felt. As the night whispered its serene lullaby, I went back to the bunkhouse, my heart guarding the day's fleeting escape and the glimmer of hope brewing from within, softly signaling the imminent arrival of a dawn filled with possibilities.

CHAPTER

SIXTEEN

Three hours later, we were back in the fields, working our fingers to the bone under the increasingly dangerous and overly watchful eye of McPherson. At midday, he called an unexpected stop. He and the other overseers were joined again by McMurtry, who had yet another nasty sneer on his face.

"Got some new quota numbers for you slaves!" he called out. "Y'all performing goddamn miracles out here in the field, so we figure a little bit extra wouldn't hurt you none this week!" He made a big show of shuffling the paper and turning it upside down, then said "Ah, here we go. Cecilia! Ceecieelliaa, your umm quota has increased from three thousand to ten thousand a week! Y'all have a good day now!"

This time, an audible ripple of disdain filtered through the slaves gathered together from the fields. Three thousand pounds of cotton for one person had been impossible, but most of the slaves had figured their communal efforts had worked and saved Cecilia from certain punishment. But ten thousand? This wasn't punishment; it was revenge, pure and simple.

Only this Sunday, there was little doubt that the Captain and his wife wouldn't be called down from the farmhouse to oversee the counting and weighing. Those processes would likely take place out of sight of the big house, and even if by some miracle Cecilia did produce ten thousand pounds of cotton, it would still be judged insufficient, and her punishment would begin in earnest. If things went that far, I knew that no one would ever see her again. I couldn't let that happen. I raised my eyes in her direction long enough to catch her gaze. She gave the slowest of nods back to me. This mockery of human life had to end.

Two nights later, the word passed silently from only the most trusted about a secret meeting at Juba's house just after midnight. It was the night when the moon would be closest to new, and the word that got around was only to come in secret if you were tired of the conditions of the plantation and wholeheartedly committed to a new beginning. The meeting itself was a mission, to begin with; those that could sneak out and make it came, and anyone not able or wanting was not to breathe a word to those in charge, lest we all suffer for it. I arrived early to spend a few extra minutes with Amayah. She comforted me with her words and embraces as I prepared to do something entirely new—be a leader.

"Speak from your heart, Ro. That's what you do best," Ama said as she gave my hand another reassuring squeeze. "When you tell them what you're really thinking, they'll believe you. That's how you got me to understand your powers ..." She paused, and a shy smile came across her face. "And how you got me to understand what you've been hiding in that big heart of yours all this time." She winked and kissed the base of my neck before moving off to check on Cecilia's kids.

The farmhouse and its hired guns and overseers would be all asleep by the time the meeting started, or at least that's what everyone hoped. But even a crying baby could wake a guard, and that guard might decide to stroll the grounds one more time, which could lead to someone noticing a bunch of slaves out of their beds. On top of that, we were gathering illegally, which was a good enough reason for the powers that be to hang the event's leaders.

Knowing all that, I sat at Juba's tiny table with him and Wayles, watching as slaves appeared at the top of the hill, wearing dark colors, staying low, and walking in roundabout routes to reach our position.

It seemed on this night that Juba and Wayles were connected, but opposites, like two sides of the same coin. Wayles was happy and bright, while Juba was dim and scared. As Juba looked out into the night sky at the positions of the stars and when enough time had passed so that even the stragglers had arrived, he began speaking in a quiet but stern and steady voice.

"Y'all heard by now what happened with my wife and McPherson, and how they put that quota up so high that can't nobody but God himself reach it," Juba insisted with an involuntary sideways glance at me. "Y'all saw how the overseer was with Cecilia's Pappy, and then again with poor Gregory.

"McPherson has lost the battle for his sanity, and he's slipping farther and farther into madness. Y'all that work in the farmhouse know that the Captain is worse than McPherson by half. Slaves that make mistakes in his house don't ever leave. He might have played the benevolent master the other day in the yard, giving us a holiday, but you know damn well that he'd rather kill us at eighty on our deathbeds than let us have even one single breath of free air. Staying here on this plantation is a death sentence, and don't none of us wanna die here. I sure as hell don't. Now I want you all to listen to what this man has to say. He knows more than the rest of us, and he can do things we cannot do."

Juba sat down, and I stood up. It was utterly silent, other than the gurgle of the stream down below, and the only light was a single candle burning in the window that Juba lit every night so that it wouldn't look different from any other night. I took a slow, deep, terrifying breath, and then another one. I knew they would be hard to convince, but I had made Amayah understand, and then Juba and

Cecilia. Perhaps it was possible. I stood straight and tall and put as much bass into my voice as I could muster.

"I've only been here a couple of weeks, and I realize that most of you have no idea who I am," I began.

"Your name is Rohan, and you pick cotton," a voice spoke out into the darkness.

"You are some kind of Oriental, and you can pick faster than anyone else," a second chimed in.

"You're married to that pretty girl Cecilia been hidin' from the overseers for two weeks," came a third.

I stood there dumbfounded. What I didn't want everyone to know appeared to be one hundred percent common knowledge, dissected in the blink of an eye. I started to stammer, which was not helped by the snickering laughter I heard behind me from Wayles and Juba. One of the three men who had revealed my information called out again, "Get to the point already, Rohan. We're Black, we aren't blind."

I took a deep breath, and then another, trying to find the silver lining. At least I wouldn't have to give them my whole background.

"Okay then. You do know me. You know I helped Cecilia's quota past the impossible amount of four thousand last week. You know that no one seems to know how my wife and I got here or where we're from. We're not from Mississippi, or even the South. We both grew up in New York City, and we weren't supposed to be here, but here we are. But we can't stay here. None of us can.

"Like Juba said, it's only a matter of time before someone kills you, whether that's McPherson, McMurtry, the Captain, or one of the other monsters that run this place; it doesn't matter. Eventually, every single one of you will fall on the wrong side of their brand of justice, and that will be the end of it. But there's a bigger picture than just that.

"You need to know that war is coming to the South. A war between the states. North against South, and we'll all pay a price in blood for that war. The South is planning on breaking away from the rest of the country so it can set up its own government, where you'll be a slave forever, and your children and their children will suffer the same fate. But the North will try to stop them, to keep them in the fold, and when that happens, the two sides will draw battle lines and then draw each other's blood. Neighbor against neighbor, brother against brother. It will plunge the entire country into a battle with much death. The fighting will come here, and one of two things will happen. Either your master will burn down this plantation to prevent the Northern armies from using his land to replenish their supplies, or you will be conscripted into the Southern army and forced to fight. Different paths, but the same damn results.

"You'll be taken away from your small comforts, taken from your family, and put somewhere else with no rights. If they take you off this land, you'll be left with nothing. No roof over your head, no clothes on your backs, and no food for your belly. If you get put in the army, you'll have a bed and three square meals a day, but do you know who you'll be fighting? The Northern Army. The Army that is fighting to give slaves their freedom. And it will be your duty to kill those men who are trying to save you. Those two options don't work for us, and they shouldn't work for you either. So, we're taking the road less traveled. We're escaping for the North together. We're going to head for the great state of Illinois to meet a man who will be vital to your success."

"Wait a minute," a voice piped up. "Thought you said y'all were from New York City? Why don't we go there?"

"Because the man you need to meet is in Illinois for the next few years," I said earnestly. "New York can't help you right now, but I hope you all see it some day."

With Juba and Wayles' help, I laid out the plan. Anyone who wanted to leave would have to bring as much food as possible and something to put water in. If they had anything that could be bartered with, that could come too. We would travel light and be safe; that was the rule. Those interested would meet at Juba's on Saturday night at midnight. From there, we'd move to the stables and hitch Juba's favorite horses to the wagon and convert it to a covered version. Everyone, save Juba and Wayles, would ride on the inside during the day. Wayles would disguise himself as McMurtry, so anyone who spotted Captain Franklin's wagon from far off would see nothing more than his hired gun and driver out running their master's business until a bounty was put on our heads.

I could tell that very few wanted to come. Being an enslaved person who was alive and breathing might have been better than being caught and hanged because they trusted some kid who appeared in their midst two weeks ago.

Without manifesting my powers in front of them, I knew it would be hard to convince them. The stories spread like wildfire that every slave who tried to escape was either caught or killed, but Wayles said that simply wasn't true. It was no easy trip to get from here to the North, but at some point, even Captain Franklin would stop pouring money into a search for desperate fugitives. He only spent money to make more money. The price of hiring bounty hunters to travel across multiple states didn't make sense, especially when there were militias everywhere performing the same tasks. We would have to be extremely cautious, and success was far from guaranteed, but the alternative was to stay here and die.

Only three of the slaves who had gathered ultimately decided to come with us. That was three more than Juba was expecting. It meant that we would be a smaller number, which was probably for the best. Fewer people meant fewer mouths to feed, less complaining, and less of a chance of someone getting cold feet. When the meeting broke up, we wanted to ensure everything was ready to go, so Juba checked on the wagon and replaced a cracked axle while I made for the cotton fields to swipe a few burlap sacks for supplies. The little shed out there had hundreds of them inside, and they definitely wouldn't miss a few, or so I thought. I had just finished shutting the door to the shed when I felt a presence behind me.

Looming out of the dark was the massive bulk of McPherson. He had a bottle in his right hand and his stone weapon in his left. I froze in place as his dim shadow fell over me.

"Well, well," he said in a slurred, undeniably drunk voice. "It's the little Oriental boy sneaking around late at night. You helpin' Celia get that quota by picking all night? I know you are, you little damn yellow bastard!"

He took a swing at me, but I was able to dodge his fist. He was moving slower than normal, and he couldn't seem to fix his gaze on me.

"Come back here, boy!" he yelled as I backpedaled away from a second thunderous blow. "Come here and take your medicine! Don't worry, I'll just rip a few teeth out. You'll be okay in a few months!"

I wanted to use my powers to beat the pulp out of him for the way he had threatened Cecilia and brutalized her father, but I was already dangerously low on my reserves. Plus, if I beat him up, or even killed him, the repercussions would be swift and far-ranging, and we'd never get a chance to escape. So, I turned and ran, hoping to hide somewhere until morning and then figure out a plan from there.

But as I turned to rush up the hill, I tripped on a large loop of root and tumbled to the ground. I scrambled back to my feet, but it was too late. That slight stumble had cost me, and McPherson's huge hands latched onto my legs and thighs, somehow picked me up, and hung me upside-down. I flailed away as he laughed at me, then brought one massive knee into my face. I heard my nose crack as I screamed in agony. He dropped me on my head, and I rolled over in a desperate attempt to escape. Instead, he kicked me in the back, knocking me to my stomach as my limbs spread. Hitting me in the back with the stone in his hand, I sunk further into the dirt and grass while the wind rushed out of me.

I heard the snap of the whip an instant before it tasted my back, ripping through my shirt and into my flesh. It came again and again as I tried to find the strength to get away, but even in his drunken rage, McPherson could move faster than I could scuttle away, and his aim, while not great, connected more often than not. I counted at least a dozen lashes before he got tired, cursing at me as he stomped back up the hill to sleep off his hangover. I wished I had the strength to do the same, but the pain in my back was excruciating. It was too much to even move, and I slipped into an unconscious darkness, facedown in the unkempt grass by the withering stream.

CHAPTER
SEVENTEEN

I woke up to Amayah screaming my name. I was soaking wet, and my body ached miserably. It took me a moment to remember where I was, when I was, and what the hell I was doing in the grass by a river. Then I remembered the meeting, the decisions, and McPherson's savage attack. Amayah's hand gently tangled in my hair, and she whispered my name over and over until she burst into tears of relief as I turned my head to meet her gaze.

I was barely fifteen feet from the storage shed, across the brook from Juba and Cecilia's home. Amayah would have seen my body lying motionless and face down when she came to wash up or fetch water. I trudged gently, step by step, to Juba's house, at a snail's pace. Cecilia made me sit at the table while she went around back to pick some herbs from a tiny garden she kept.

Amayah held my hand, kissing it over and over as I relayed what had happened the night before. When Cecilia came back, she crushed up the leaves of a sour-smelling plant and mixed it into hot water. She had me drink some—it was terrible—then wrapped the leaves in a wet towel and rubbed them across the welts and cuts on my back. There was some feeling of relief, and as I felt deeper for that soothing, I found a reserve of my power, as though it were waiting for me. Very carefully, I began repurposing it into the broken shamble of my nose, the streaks of torn red flesh on my back, and the broken ribs from his ferocious kicks. Amayah gave a small gasp as she watched a lash mark slowly heal itself back into place. I didn't want to make it too obvious or wear myself out in the process, so I squeezed her hand, and she squeezed mine back.

The rest of the week passed in a blur. I rested more than I wanted to, mainly because I needed to heal up and save my energy for the trip. We slowly stockpiled food and jugs of water. Extra clothes too. The final head count was me, Amayah, Wayles, Juba, Cecilia, her father Thomas, their oldest Claire, their eight-year-old daughter Rose, their three-year-old daughter Grace, and three brothers in their late twenties who claimed to be triplets—Adam, Patrick, and Stephen—who had been sold on the promise of a free life in the North.

None of us made any extra effort to help Cecilia achieve her outlandish 10,000-pound quota of cotton during the week. We worked just enough to make it seem like we were staying on task. I avoided being anywhere near McPherson, although I knew that if he wanted to make an example out of me again, all he'd have to do is come looking. I'd have to take it; any other alternative would risk exposing the whole plan.

WE MET at Juba's at midnight on Saturday. One of the triplets, Stephen, backed out at the last minute, but his two brothers were there, clearly disappointed, but promising to send for their brother once they had saved up enough in the North. Wayles had arranged to meet us just outside the property, as he wasn't welcome to stay overnight without clearance from the Captain.

We dressed in our darkest clothes and made our way to the stable where Juba was waiting, as expected, with two horses and the wagon. He talked in a low voice to the animals to keep them still and quiet. They were used to late-night trips when emergency supplies were needed, so they were unlikely to give us away. I helped Amayah, Cecilia, her father Thomas, and her children into the back of the wagon and told them to stay still and quiet and not to put their heads out of the cover unless myself, Juba, or Wayles told them it was alright. The brothers went in too, and I was the last, sitting just inside the flap, to watch our back and be ready to act if need be. Aside from Claire's father, Thomas, emitting a few malodorous yet alarmingly clangorous farts, we all stayed pretty quiet.

We crept down the long road leading to the main gate, and then out toward the road leading back to Oxford. We'd be turning north instead, away from the relatively bustling town center with its brothel, saloon, and more. The path north ran into the far east part of Lake Sardis, a popular spot for fishing, hunting, and timber. Once the Captain figured out we had escaped with his wagon, he would send men to the trail on the east side of the lake in hopes of catching us there. That's why we planned to swing wide around the western shore, which would take at least two days to circumnavigate. It was tedious and time-consuming, but it was also the route absolutely no one would expect us to take. In theory, it would put us closer to Illinois than going around the eastern side. They would expect us to head for Jackson to resupply and then make for Nashville before crossing into the north from Louisville, Kentucky into Ohio. Thankfully, Wayles had a number of maps from earlier adventures with his father showing that there was a better way to go.

We'd swing around the western tip of the lake and then head due north into Arkansas, which was still largely unsettled and full of more wild animals than actual people. That would lead us up to St. Louis, where we would be within striking distance of Springfield, Illinois, the state's capital city and, more importantly, the home of the man known as the Great Emancipator—Abraham Lincoln. Of course, none of our companions knew who Lincoln was. Still, I knew he'd be President in about seven years and was primarily anti-slavery, hopefully, their best bet for survival. In the meantime, Wayles would ride up top with Juba and act like he owned the wagon—and Juba, for that matter. He would pretend to be a slave trader looking to move his merchandise into a bigger market. Wayles was good at expressing big emotions and could pull off the part quite well.

As we crept toward the end of the plantation, I finally breathed a sigh of relief. I didn't know what lay ahead, and I had no idea if it would help Amayah and I get back home, but simply doing something felt right in my heart. Helping Juba's family, Wayles, and the twin brothers get clear of the Captain and his sadistic cabal of slavers felt good too.

However, just as we passed onto the road towards a single light, which I took for Wayles' lantern, I realized that we had been betrayed. The third brother, Stephen, was standing on the road waving his hands back and forth. The wagon slowed and stopped, and Stephen cried aloud, "I'm sorry, brothers!" just as a gunshot rang out, dropping him to the ground.

McMurtry stepped out from the nearby tree line, puffing on a long wooden tobacco pipe and lighting a lantern as he came. Behind him was the looming form of McPherson, his slate weapon cocked and ready, an evil grin on his face. I jumped out of the wagon at the sound of the gunshot, which put me, Wayles, and Juba squared off against the two well-armed thugs. It was the three of us, facing the two of them, in an apparent standoff, though only one side had any steel.

"What's the punishment for runaway slaves again?" McMurtry said aloud with a low cackle. "That's right, death. Looks like you boys picked a lousy night to run from Captain Franklin."

NONE of us moved for a long moment. I was trying to calculate how to get the gun away from McMurtry before he could shoot Juba or Wayles. Superman might have been faster than a speeding bullet, but I had no idea if I was.

Despite their strength in arms and drunken confidence,

McMurtry and McPherson weren't in complete control of the situation. McMurtry's gun was a six-shooter, meaning he had at least five bullets left. It was dark outside with no moon and few stars and just the light of Stephen's lantern spilling over the road. I knew from my history books that before the 20th century, guns had been notably unreliable and that even trained sharpshooters weren't guaranteed to hit their targets every time. If the three of us all took off running in different directions, he'd have to try and shoot one of us quickly and then hunt the other two on foot.

McPherson might have been a 19th century version of the Incredible Hulk, but he wasn't fast enough to catch any of us, not even little Rose and Grace, who were probably cowering in fear in the back of the wagon, along with Amayah, Claire, Cecilia, her father Thomas, and the pair of brothers. That was another small point in our favor; the two enforcers didn't know exactly how many people we had in the wagon or what was inside, although if they had interrogated Stephen, they probably had a good guess.

McMurtry didn't want a shootout, as we were all his boss's property. If a herd of cattle breaks down a fence and runs away, you don't go and shoot them all; you try to get them back in the pasture, because they're worth a lot more alive than dead. McMurtry was facing the same dilemma. He would have to intimidate us into going back peacefully, or he would have to shoot a couple of us to scare the rest into obeying. The problem was that we had already mustered up the courage to run, which meant we had accepted death as a distinct possibility, either here or somewhere out in the wilds of the American South.

McPherson was snarling rabidly back and forth between Juba and me, as if he couldn't decide which one he wanted to pummel first. Seeing as he had just gotten the drop on me so recently, I figured he'd want to get Juba out of the way as soon as possible, so he could lay claim to Cecilia before she got taken up to the big house to serve the Captain himself. However, if McPherson looked too close at me and saw that my injuries had almost completely healed up, he might decide I needed another beating to leave some real scars.

McMurtry was smarter. "Ya'll in the back of that wagon, come on out with your hands raised and join these fools so I can take stock of who you are and what numbers you got. Captain William will want to know the names and faces of all his ungrateful children tonight."

True to their earlier promise, there was no movement from the back of the wagon. They gained no advantage by stepping out of the wagon. If the Captain's goons wanted them, they would have to go in there after them, or do something drastic enough to draw them out. I could see the uneasy look pass between them when no one emerged. They were beginning to realize that the cowed slaves they dealt with every day were not the ones fighting for freedom.

If they had been smart, they would have brought five more men with them, and at least a couple more guns. That way, a couple could go around the back of the wagon and drag the rest out while they covered us with the guns. People acted a lot more obedient with a gun pointed in their face, but with McMurtry holding the lone gun, he could only directly threaten one of us at a time. I could barely see his face, but I could hear the strain in his voice as he called out a second and then a third time for the rest to come out.

When he got no answer, he called to McPherson instead. "Get around back, there boy, and pull them outta that wagon!"

Suddenly, Cecilia's voice piped up from the darkness.

"Yes, c'mon back here, sugar!" she called, her voice artificially sweet. "These boys got some nice sharp knives to stick in your neck when you turn the corner! You won't feel a thing 'til you're six feet under, and the Devil himself is welcoming you home!"

It was a dangerous strategy, to be sure. A rage-filled McPherson could probably rip the wagon apart board by board if he wanted or kill both the horses with his bare hands to strand the whole opera-tion. But suddenly he was very aware of what a precarious situation he was in. Damaging the Master's property was liable to get him killed, even if he did it to stop thieves and runaway slaves. And for the first time in what was likely a very long time, someone was challenging him; inviting him into a violent situation, rather than cowering in fear. He had no idea how many people, other than Cecilia, were waiting for him in the back of the wagon, or if they were armed as she claimed. Even the biggest, strongest man alive could be knocked to the ground if enough people jumped on his back. If those people were armed with anything sharp and got an advantage on him, even for a second ... well, even McPherson could bleed. He almost took a step forward, then lurched to a stop instead.

"You do it!" McPherson demanded, challenging McMurtry. "You got the gun, you go pull 'em outta there! You're the one with the pistol! Go get them!"

McMurtry was having none of it. "If I go back there with a gun, who's going to watch these three?" He motioned with the pistol and for a moment it wasn't pointed at any of us. I was nearly tempted to make a move towards McMurtry, but the disagreement between him and McPherson had pulled my attention. If the two of them kept bickering, perhaps I could signal to Wayles and Juba of a strategy that involved them getting back on the wagon and the hell away from here while I remained to deal with these two men.

McMurtry wasn't an idiot though. He saw the slight lean in my posture and retrained the gun on me with a flash of his wrist, "None of that, dancin' boy, don't even think about it, not even for one second."

I idly wondered how he knew about my dance with Amayah, but realized that few things stayed a secret on a plantation this size with as much gossip as passed between the slaves and the hired help. He called over his shoulder, keeping his gun and his eyes trained hard on me.

"You scared of a bunch of women and babies? Fine, then! Run your black ass on up to the farmhouse and tell them to wake the Captain because his finest employee, the noble Craig McMurtry, has apprehended a whole flock of runaway slaves and needs assistance in returning them to their proper enclosures for punishment."

McPherson blinked, then blinked again as his simple mind tried to unravel McMurtry's flowery manner of speech.

"Way a minute, you didn't catch them, I did!" he bellowed. "Stephen came to me with the news. You were just skulking around and followed us! You're not taking credit for my find, dammit!"

The two argued for another thirty seconds or so, but McMurtry did so with his eyes still locked on mine, occasionally flitting to Juba and Wayles to make sure they weren't getting any ideas.

Finally, McMurtry played his trump card, the ace up his sleeve. "If these ingrates and bastards get away tonight, whose story do you think Captain William is going to believe?" he asked McPherson in a low, sly voice. "His faithful compatriot from a long string of military conquests and a proud White Southerner like myself? Or a half-wit, oversized freak of a nigger so out of control that he damn near choked a perfectly healthy female slave on account of her picking more cotton in a single week than three healthy men could? You got yourself a little taste of power and you forgot who you are, boy. You are property. You answer to people like me, and you sure as hell don't presume to tell me my business!"

Just as with the Captain a few days earlier, when McMurtry dropped the 'N' word on McPherson, I thought the overseer might just lose control of his temper and charge the hired gun. Then it would be a matter of what happened first, McMurtry pumping enough bullets in McPherson to put him down or McPherson getting a hold of McMurtry and ripping his arms off. But it didn't come to that; at least not yet. The big man might have been slow, but he wasn't entirely stupid. His skin was still the wrong color to come out on top in any battle of whose story the Captain would believe, and though he might have hated McMurtry and the other White men even more than he appeared to hate his fellow slaves on the plantation, I could see his shoulders slump. He turned and started trudging back towards the gate and the long road up to the farm house. As McPherson turned, he rumbled, "You ain't nothing but a White slave, a drunk who couldn't keep his own wife satisfied." At that point, McMurtry's eyes blazed with anger and his body stiffened up.

McPherson hadn't walked 10 steps towards the farmhouse when McMurtry pivoted away from us and aimed his pistol at the overseer's broad back.

"Take that tone with me again, you son of a bitch!"

By all rights, I should have let him shoot McPherson in the back. Assuming he hit his mark, and who couldn't hit a target that big, it would have at least badly wounded and possibly killed one of the three most dangerous men on the plantation. If we were really lucky, it would only wound McPherson, who would turn on McMurtry, and the two would fight each other, maybe even kill each other, while we escaped in the chaos.

However, seeing those slumped shoulders when that slur was hurled reminded me too much of my own experiences back home in New York; being treated like trash for the color of your skin was something I knew all too well. Something in the way the big man's face fell touched me; it might have been pity, or even sympathy for what he had become. My mind flashed in that moment to the memories I had accessed inside Steven Stone's memory just a few weeks earlier. I remembered how his tough, self-involved, con-artist exterior was really just a shield to mask the hurt and pain he had suffered as a child. He had a dark side, of which I had seen only a little, but how much of it was his fault, and how much of it was born of the utter lack of parenting and compassion he had received as a child? Was that what McPherson suffered from as well? He had been someone's child once, and probably someone's brother. At some point, someone twisted his mind around in order to use his great size and strength to become a hateful machine that stalked Captain William's plantation. Amayah and I had already decided that we had been sent back through time to help people, but I had never considered freeing the person who might have been in more pain than any of us.

That wave of realization turned into a giant surge of emotion that rushed through my body, tapping into my power source and exploding out of me as I used my speed.

"LOOK OUT!" I screamed as McMurtry squeezed the trigger, and I lunged forward to tackle the hired gun to the ground. Even with my enhanced abilities, he still got the shot off, and McPherson was shoved forward by the bullet's force. As I knocked McMurtry to the ground, I squeezed his wrist so hard that he shrieked in pain and dropped the gun. Wayles pounced on the pistol a moment later and stepped away from McMurtry's feeble attempt to grab it back.

I easily overpowered McMurtry with a burst of strength and pinned both his wrists to the ground. He struggled and cursed and spit in my face, but I had him in a steel vise. Juba ran to McPherson's side. The big man had fallen, but was already back up in a sitting position. I wasn't sure how smart it was for Juba to approach someone that violent, although freshly wounded, but I trusted him. He knew McPherson best, as both held positions of authority on the plantation. I could hear Juba talking to him in a low voice before helping the giant to his feet. I stepped away from McMurtry as Wayles cocked the gun and pointed it down at the proud White Southerner without a word, the message clear.

From the back of the wagon, Cecilia's voice rang out, clearly trying to calm the fears of everyone hidden away.

"Juba? Rohan? Wayles? What's going on out there?"

"It's all right, my love!" Juba called back. "Mr. McMurtry here has shot and wounded McPherson, and Rohan has relieved him of it. Just hold tight."

Amayah's voice came next. "Rohan! Rohan? Are you all right?"

"I'm fine, Ama," I said, hoping to help keep her from panicking. "Take care of the little ones. We'll be back on our way soon enough."

Of course, that was easier said than done. We had disarmed one of our would-be captors, and the other was wounded, but both of their voices still worked, as did their legs. Even if we tied them up, they'd eventually still sing like canaries as soon as they could stumble back up to the farmhouse from the road, and our presumed eight-hour headstart would be drastically cut down.

That wouldn't do, but the only other option was a permanent step I wasn't sure any of us were prepared to take: killing them both.

I wasn't squeamish about death. If I was going to fight crime or save lives in whatever time and place I happened to be living, I understood that killing someone might eventually be part of the equation. But it would need to be in a situation where there was no other choice, where it was them or me—or someone I loved. McMurtry and McPherson were scum, plain and simple, but one was wounded and the other was disarmed. There had to be another way out of this, but I needed to figure it out fast.

As we stood there trying to devise a plan, I realized we were already out of time. The loud noise of the gun going off, something that was almost white noise growing up in New York City, carried quite a long way on a quiet night in Oxford, Mississippi. We heard muffled shouting from well up the road, and lanterns were visible up by the farmhouse. McMurtry's pistol shot had woken someone, or maybe two someones, or maybe more, and now we were about to be caught before making it a quarter mile from the plantation.

I looked at Wayles, who looked at me, as Juba looked at both of us, all three clearly hoping one of the others had a bright idea. In that tense moment of confusion, McMurtry exploded from his prone stance with a blade none of us had checked him for. He used it to knock the pistol out of Wayles' hand and grabbed Juba around the neck, turning the blade so it caught the starlight and glittered dangerously against his flesh.

"Not so fast, boy!" he yelled at me in a raspy, desperate voice. "Try that sneaky shit again, and I'll slit his throat before you take your first fucking step!"

Despite his warning, I still almost risked it. I was faster than him. I had proved that when I took his gun, but he still got the shot off. Even if I got to him in a blink, all he had to do was push the knife forward and the blade would do the rest. Even in my time, it was almost impossible to survive a slit throat. If he pierced Juba's throat, the jig was up. Juba knew the horses and the roads here better than anyone. Wayles and I might make it a few miles, or even all the way to the lake before we got caught, but I doubted we'd get much further. Juba was the glue holding this operation together. His entire family was in the back of the wagon, probably terrified by the struggle currently turning our situation upside-down all over again. I glanced up the hill and saw the lanterns getting closer.

The fact that they were elevated told me that whoever was carrying them was likely on horseback, which possibly meant the Captain himself, or at least some of his best men. No one else was worthy of riding a horse on the plantation. Given the gunshot, they were approaching slowly and in larger numbers. We were rapidly running out of time.

McMurtry saw the lanterns approaching and laughed wickedly. "Looks like my gunshot woke the Captain hisself! Oh, how he's going to love watching you bunch of maggots trying to escape with his horses and all his precious niggers. Why, I imagine he might let me have first crack at Cecilia before he feeds her to the dogs. Don't worry, Juba, I'll make sure she has a night to remember before she goes screaming down to- AHHHHHHHHHHHHHHH!"

His final words were cut off as McMurtry found himself lifted off the ground by McPherson. The hired gun was so concerned with the danger in front of him that he forgot all about the one he had left behind him. McPherson might have been wounded, but he was still fiercely powerful, and while McMurtry was dangerous with a gun in his hand, he was a fairly scrawny man. He tried to swing the knife into Juba's neck in one last act of defiance, but McPherson's massive hand closed around McMurtry's knuckles. I heard bones crackle and shatter as the smaller man screamed in pain, the blade dropped and forgotten. His weapon gone, the gunslinger feebly tried to find any weak spot in the giant's massive bulk, but it was pointless.

McPherson's hands came together on opposite sides of the gunslinger's head. The sharp snap of McMurtry's neck sent a rolling shiver down my spine. His eyes rolled up in their sockets and his lifeless body collapsed to the ground in front of me.

We all stood staring up at McPherson, wondering who he might come after next. Wayles retrieved the pistol and was holding it square, extended, but was also visibly shaking. I didn't blame him. I'm not sure every bullet in the chamber could stop McPherson if he got going. He reminded me of the Juggernaut from the old X-Men comics I had read in the library of my elementary school. Before Wayles had to make an unpleasant decision, McPherson held one giant hand up.

"Don't kill me, boss. I'm not gonna make you no trouble," he rumbled.

He turned his gaze towards me, the only one among us even close to his height.

"Why'd you do that, boy? Why'd you stop him from killing me?"

I took a moment to measure my words carefully, feeling like what I said next would send this situation in any one of various ways.

"He was going to kill you in cold blood," I said slowly, choosing each word carefully. "No man should die like that. And you've been every bit as much a prisoner here as any of us. Forced to do things against your will. No rights, no freedom. No man should have to live as a slave. I wanted to give you the chance to choose your own fate."

He held my gaze for so long that I was convinced the riders would be upon us by the time he finally blinked.

"Been a long time since I had a choice in things," he said, his voice softer than before. "Feels good, even if it means the end of it all," he added, nodding towards the approaching lights.

"Come with us then," Wayles spoke up, surprising everyone, possibly even himself, with the invitation. "We're getting the hell outta the south. Get in the wagon, and you can come along. Help us stay safe, and when we get there, you can have any job you want. With your size, you'll have 20 offers a day!"

McPherson smiled, a real, genuine one, at the thought, but shook his head.

"Free or slave don't matter at this point. I done murdered that man, and he's the Captain's own kinfolk. Even if I made it north with y'all, they'd still come for me and hang me quick as a cat. Just be unnecessary danger for you all and your family. Besides o' which," he raised his left arm, and I gasped at the massive blood stain that had befouled his shirt. "I'm not long for this world. Already having trouble, bleedin', and you know they ain't callin' no doctor out here for the likes of me. Y'all get back up on that wagon and get on outta here. I'm gonna go meet the Captain on the road and give y'all a head start here."

I couldn't believe what I was hearing, but there was no time to argue. Juba said something quietly to the man and gave him a short bow. Wayles nodded and backed away slowly to the wagon, never quite lowering the pistol all the way. I decided to be a bit riskier, taking two steps forward and holding out my hand to shake his.

"Good luck," I said, which seemed rather foolish, considering what he was about to do. I thought suddenly of Amayah and added, "God bless you."

McPherson shook my hand, then closed his eyes as a tear escaped down his cheek, then softly quoted one of the Bible's most powerful lines, uttered by the humble king David in Psalm 23.

"Though I walk through the valley of the shadow of death, I shall fear no evil," McPherson said. "For Thou art with me."

He let go of my hand and said, "Now get outta here, boy. Don't look back!" He shoved me so hard I almost fell, then regained my balance and jumped into the back of the wagon, nearly colliding with the two remaining brothers, who had apparently been trying to decide if they were going to stick it out or make a run for it on foot.

"It's alright!" I said hurriedly, as everyone started asking me questions at once. "McPherson killed McMurtry, and he's going to try and delay the Captain to give us a head start! Now everyone hold on tight, we're getting out of here as quick as we can!"

No sooner were the words out of my mouth than the wagon lurched forward. Juba had put the lash to the horses and set them off at a brisk pace. The wagon wasn't built for comfort at any speed above a leisurely pace, and it seemed like the wheels were finding every stray rock and stone on the road as we picked up speed.

I had nodded when McPherson told me not to look back, but I couldn't help from peeking out beyond the fabric that covered the wagon. The giant overseer met the mounted men on the road, their lanterns illuminating him clearly as he gestured wildly with one arm while raising the other, likely showing where he had been shot. There was a moment's hesitation, and then I saw at least two men drawing their sidearms. McPherson grabbed the reins of the two closest horses and slammed the animals together, knocking their riders from the saddle and turning the scene into a chaotic swirl of men, horses, and flame. As we rode over the hill and out of sight of the mad scramble, I heard shots fired again and again and again. I closed my eyes, and felt Amayah's small hand press its fingers against mine. I looked to my left and saw her there, eyes closed, her head bowed as she began to pray out loud. "Lord, may McPherson remain strong. I'm so very grateful for his sacrifice. Let his suffering be brief, and let him find life renewed in your Holy Spirit now and forever."

Her words reflected exactly what I was feeling, and I had never been more grateful to have her in my life than at that exact moment, racing headlong into the darkness, with death and destruction behind us and no idea what lay ahead.

EIGHTEEN

It was 22 miles from Oxford to the banks of Sardis Lake if you were planning on swinging around the eastern shores and heading for Jackson. We weren't doing that, of course, but we wanted any pursuit to think we were, so we kept on the trail north for a few miles, then took the wagon on a northeastern path well worn by wagon wheels from other excursions headed that way. Juba sent the horses up the trail about half a mile, then stopped and let them stomp around and leave those steaming piles of dung that only horses produce. He unhooked them from the wagon and had me, Wayles, and the two brothers pull the wagon back down the path to the bigger road, then slowly re-angle it and turn it due west along flat ground that was not nearly as well traveled. I probably could have handled the task all by myself, but the brothers didn't know about my powers, and we didn't want to spook them or make anyone more jumpy than we already were.

Juba walked the horses single file, holding their reins tight to avoid leaving the tell-tale signs of horses leading a wagon. He had Cecilia go back to where we made the trail appear to lead northeast and walk about 20 paces off the road, then let a piece of the fabric of her dress catch on a patch of bushes and tear, leaving a strip behind in the grass to be found by anyone who came hunting. Juba and Wayles had both spent time on the run before and knew what it was like to be tracked. The two of them took turns driving the wagon as I sat next to them, helping them stay awake and look for signs of trouble. I might have been the fastest and strongest among us, but I didn't know anything about horses or wagons and didn't think that was the best time to learn. Regardless, I had a brain in my head and was using it the best I could. My intellectual capacity and their real-world know-how were a good combination, although every time we took a break and ran our plans by Amayah and Cecilia, they were quick to point out the flaws and fine-tune the ideas, coming up with a perfect final strategy.

It was Amayah's idea to have Cecilia "lose" a part of her dress just off the path. We figured that no matter who lived and who died in McPherson's final confrontation with the Captain and his forces, someone was going to be hot on our trail by now. If the Captain had survived McPherson's attack, that was terrible news, as he could marshal up manpower very quickly to come after us; his military connections and prestige in the South would see to that. If he was hurt or killed, however, there would be plenty of confusion over what to do next. Juba had no doubt that the Captain's wife, who he called the secret power on the plantation, would take over and prevent any sort of power vacuum from occurring, but she wasn't as shrewd as he was when it came to affairs off the plantation. Wayles said it was far more likely that she would put a bounty on our heads and open it up to anyone with a horse, a gun, or a greedy bone in their body. That might mean a lot more people looking for us, but Wayles thought that would actually be better, as it would mean a lot of amateurs taking part. Amateurs not only missed signs that an expert tracker could follow, but they almost always mucked up the actual tracks and signs of passage as they rode their horses all over the place trying to sniff out a lead.

We drove the horses harder than anyone was comfortable with

straight through the night. Juba was an expert coachman, enough to know the road in the dark, and with the moon hiding her own face, hidden from the sun's shine, and cloaked by the clouds, we were fortunate not to encounter a single rider. An ordinary man would wait for the brightest phases of the moon to make a journey at that time of night, but we had gambled and did the opposite, and it paid off in solitude.

When the sun started creeping through the trees, we stopped to let the horses rest, get everyone out to use the bathroom, and inform the others of our master plan to stick it to the master and deceive those following us. We encouraged the girls, Cecilia's dad, the women and the two brothers to do their business a bit closer to the road than they might have done otherwise, and Juba set the horses to nibbling on grass that was quite long, so even an untrained eye could notice the difference in the lengths of nearby strands.

The master stroke was Cecilia's torn dress. She had been a familiar face all over the plantation for years, and she only had two or three sets of clothing, though that was quite luxurious for a slave. Anyone who had any connection to the plantation would see that cloth on the ground and assume she had been there. We fervently hoped they would see the obvious wagon tracks leading northeast and sound the alarm that we were headed that way, starting the proverbial wild goose chase that might go on for a hundred miles, lined with greedy men believing they would surely catch us right around the next bend.

Once we set out west, the trail was rougher and far less traveled, which was both good and bad, and our pace slowed. The horses were weary, and Juba rewarded them by not working them as hard. Besides, now that it was daylight and we were on a seldom-used trail, we didn't want to attract too much attention. A wagon stuffed full of people racing along a trail like that would be suspicious to anyone, even those who had no idea who the Captain was. So, we kept it leisurely, just a master and a slave driving a wagon through the backwoods of Mississippi, perhaps headed for some newly appointed settlement not drawn on the map quite yet.

It was initially tough to keep that plodding pace, knowing there were angry men on horseback out there looking for us, but as we went farther and farther along without catching sight of a single person, I began to relax and enjoy the ride. The brothers, Adam and Patrick, and even Cecilia's dad, Thomas, started taking turns on the wagon. None of them had ever set foot off the plantation in their lives, and you could see a mixture of excitement and fear in them as we got farther and farther from the only life they'd ever known. However, I could see a new sparkle in Cecilia's father's eyes. As for the brothers, I didn't see much remorse about Stephen's death, and I suspected they weren't really triplets, perhaps just three guys who had decided to find their courage by imitating familial bonds.

I was glad that other people ventured out to the front, which gave me time with Amayah. I realized with some degree of excitement that she had been pining away for me just as much as I had been for her all those nights on the plantation with only a quarter mile separating us, though it felt like worlds apart. She was still actively teaching Juba and Cecilia's girls their letters and helping Cecilia learn some algebra. I felt terrible that they were not out of the wagon much, except when we stopped for breaks or the night. Still, women were rarely in positions of authority at this time in the past, and a slave woman or someone with Amayah's tan skin color and intense young beauty would be too memorable to anyone we passed on the road. I'm not sure who knew Ama was even there on the Captain's plantation, but they'd never forget seeing Amayah, and anyone who came sniffing out our bounty would know precisely where we were, and the chase would be on. I pitched in with their education, thinking about them growing up in the free North and how much better their lives would be once they could read and write. I played games with them, swung them around, let them bounce on my knee, and told them silly stories, scary stories, and tales of romance and adventure to get them to sleep at night.

First, I started with fairy tales, then I branched out into some of my favorite movies. That caught the attention of the adults in our party, and each night, with Amayah's help, I thrilled young and old alike with dramatic stories that we had seen at the cinema, on the movie of the week, or from a rental from Blockbuster Video back home. We had a hard time getting through the first couple of these tales; retelling the events of "The Lion King" and "Aladdin" was a good start for entertaining Claire, Rose, and Grace. We kept having to stop and start certain tales and modify them to more relatable circumstances. One night I launched into the plot of "Back to the Future," which certainly seemed appropriate, given the fact that Amayah and I had traveled back in time before we were born, but then I remembered that the movie revolved around the 1950s—a full century in the future—not to mention computers, skateboards, a DeLorean, and just about every other piece of technology invented in the second half of the 20th century. In short, I abandoned ship. About four nights into the stories, I hit the jackpot when I took a deep breath and sat down close to the fire, so the light danced across my face as I said in a deep voice, "A long time ago, in a galaxy far, far away..." Well, I had to explain what a galaxy was, but after that, I had every single person around that campfire hooked on the story of a beautiful Princess who lives on a ship that can fly through the stars, her two living machines made of metal who help her in her day-to-day activities, and a terrible villain, a giant who suffered a terrible accident and must wear a mask over his face to keep breathing. I described his sword made from red fire that can cut through anything, and how everyone's guns shoot beams of light instead of bullets. Every last one of the listeners was hooked as I introduced Luke Skywalker, Han Solo, Chewbacca, and the rest.

When Luke blew up the Death Star and saved the day on the third night of the story, they automatically wanted to hear it all again, so I blew their minds and told them I had two more entire adventures about the same characters. Amayah filled in the parts I forgot and delightfully voiced Princess Leia to my Vader, Han, and

Luke. She sat close to me, and I could feel her eyes watching me with delight. I felt like I was showing her every good part of who I was, and she was loving it, which made me love her even more than I thought possible.

That night, Wayles and Patrick took first watch, so Amayah snuggled in close to me on the ground. It was so simple, this life. No school, no subway, no homework, no overbearing parents. For the first time, I considered what would happen if we couldn't find our way back to our timeline, and what life might look like if we didn't. I couldn't lie to myself, being here with Amayah and the good people who had helped us didn't seem half bad. However, one thing I did worry about was our families and how they must be feeling right now. I was so lost in thought that I didn't notice Amayah gazing up at me with a smile on her face.

"You're so good with them," she said.

"Good with who?" I replied.

"The kids. You're so patient and kind with them. You'll make an amazing father someday, Rohan."

I gave a start, which was hard to hide, considering I was laying on the ground with her wrapped up in a blanket.

"A father... a father?" I asked, none too gracefully.

She laughed lightly at my floundering reaction.

"Relax, my hero," she said sleepily. "Someday, not today."

I watched her fall quickly to sleep and tried to do the same. I thought a lot about Amayah... kissing her, calling her my girlfriend, losing my virginity with her, but the thought of us one day becoming parents had never been a part of those fantasies. I guess I hadn't allowed myself to dream that far ahead.

Now the thought of marrying her and having not just a teenage romance, but a lifetime of happiness, was bouncing around my mind, and sleep was hard to find.

. . .

Over the next ten days, we passed west of Lake Sardis and onto a more established road heading north towards the town of Memphis, Tennessee. I didn't recall much about Memphis from geography or history, but I was pretty sure that Elvis Presley was from there, although his great-grandfather was probably still a baby in the 1850s. Juba said that we'd start seeing more and more people the closer we got to Memphis, and he was right. Wagons, men on horseback, and even people just walking to town started popping up all over. Just like that, we went from hiding in the wilderness to hiding in plain sight.

Neither Wayles nor Juba believed anyone in Memphis would know about us, as everything had suggested that we went northeast towards Jackson and then on to Nashville or Ohio. It was the quickest route to a part of the country where slavery was outlawed, and the roads were the most well-established, which would make a journey that way the swiftest. We were hoping to outsmart them, and have them assume we chose that route because we had women and children with us and would want to keep them relatively safe, not rambling through the wilderness where all sorts of unpleasantness could befall us. The unknown of what had happened at the plantation after we escaped was wearing us all thin.

Juba and Cecilia believed that the rest of the slaves would not easily give up information about us, and with McMurtry and McPherson both likely dead, there would be a distinct lack of information on who exactly had escaped. Wayles warned us that the more people that came around, the more he'd have to act like our master in order to maintain the illusion that we were all his property. For Juba and the others, it was as easy as slipping on a familiar pair of shoes, and I felt horrible at how easily they could fall back into their roles as slaves based solely on the color of their skin. It was more difficult for me to remember who I was supposed to be, a light-skinned slave who kept his eyes on the ground and didn't say a damn thing to anyone unless his master allowed it. We wound our way along with various other travelers into Memphis after about two weeks on the run. It was a good thing too, as we were running short on food. Wayles, Juba, and the remaining triplets had been smart along the trek, cutting cords of wood, picking fruits, and preying on animals that wandered too close to the camp, and our wagon eventually found its way outside a general store in a busy square where people were trading goods back and forth. It reminded me of a flea market back home. Everyone was out to get a bargain and make a buck. I stayed in the back with the women and children and Cecilia's dad. My height would have attracted too much attention, and we wanted to be as inconspicuous as possible.

Wayles didn't want to cause a scene, so he wandered off, looking to trade what he had for enough food to get us to the next big town, which would be St. Louis. We'd take the road along the river all the way there, which would afford us fresh water, the chance to fish and catch game, and eat whatever was edible that grew along the mighty Mississippi, but he still wanted to stock up as much as he could. If we had to deviate from that course, we would need food reserves to survive. Nobody wanted to risk everything for freedom, just to starve to death on the road. We rode a good five miles outside of town into the setting sun before Wayles called for a stop, figuring we were at a safe enough distance. As we went through the process of making camp for the night, he told us everything he had learned.

"Ain't nobody heard about the Captain or our particular plantation, but there's a call to keep an eye out for escaped slaves from Mississippi, from Oxford in particular," he said. "But that might not even involve us. Slaves be runnin' all the time when they done somethin' so bad that they figure it's better to take a chance than to stick around. Or maybe they just fed up with this miserable life. Those of them that asked, I told them I was out of Duck Hill, Mississippi, about a hundred miles due south of here. That way, if anyone decides to back-check our story, they'll see that we came from the right direction and weren't anywhere near Oxford, so there's no reason for us to have heard the news yet."

I gave a huge sigh of relief. I half-expected to find an entire posse of gunslingers waiting for us at the edge of town, but the people in Memphis seemed more interested in their own comings and goings. We were just one more wagon with a White owner and a few Black slaves in the back.

Trouble finally caught up to us a few days later as we headed north through the wilds of southeastern Arkansas. We kept the Mississippi River to the east so that we stayed out of the "true" South at all times, and we stopped to see what meager supplies we could barter for in a town with a hand-painted sign that read "Frenchman's Bayou" hanging in the breeze. I didn't know what Frenchman ever made it all the way to Arkansas to find this tiny settlement, and I didn't really care.

The thrill of being off the plantation was starting to wear thin as we inched our way north. The days were long and hot and uneventful, and our stomachs were perpetually rumbling as we continued to divvy up the food into smaller and smaller portions. Wayles was settling up with a fat-bellied general store owner with a beard that reminded me of ZZ Top when Grace started throwing up in the back of the wagon and complaining she needed fresh air. It was a terrible noise, and she was so tiny that my heart went out to her, but the timing couldn't have been any worse. We were in a reasonably crowded area, and the back of the wagon was to stay shut at all times, but helping a little sick girl feel better seemed right.

As Wayles directed Patrick and Adam to load up the vegetables, fruit, and a few rabbit and squirrel pelts he had traded for, I spied the mishap happening with our better halves.

Cecilia was hustling little Grace out of the back of the wagon with Amayah, helping her get the sick child to an alleyway to empty her belly, rather than cause a mess on the street. I watched the shopkeeper, and saw that he didn't bat an eye at Cecilia or Grace—just two more slaves. But when Ama got out of the wagon's back, her hair wasn't secured and fell down to her shoulders in all its glory. The shopkeeper's eyes narrowed at the sight, and I could see the lust come over him as he looked her up and down. I swiftly got up and started to move towards the wagon to intervene, then remembered who I was supposed to be—just another slave doing his master's bidding. I sat back down before anyone noticed, trying to keep my head down, but tilted just enough to see what was going on beyond the veil.

The big-bellied shopkeeper crossed the road quickly and clapped his meaty hand on Wayles' shoulder. "Well sir, I do believe you have been holdin' out on me when you said you don't have nothin' else of value in this here wagon!"

Wayles hadn't noticed the miniature drama of Grace, Cecilia, and Amayah, and I saw his face go a little white. I knew that Ama had only been thinking about helping the sick child, but it was too late. Amayah had realized her mistake by then and backed up towards the wagon with her head down, but attention had been drawn.

Wayles saw the look in the shopkeeper's eyes and reached out to slap Amayah across the back. "Get back in there, you damn unruly wench! Mind me, or you'll have another 20 lashes come sundown!"

He turned back to his temporary business partner with a look of disdain. "She's the most unruly one I've ever owned," he said, and spat on the street for dramatic effect. "Can't follow the simplest orders—lazy and stupid."

If the shopkeeper was paying attention to Wayles' words, he was hiding it well. He only had eyes for Amayah as she scrambled back into the wagon and pulled the veil shut. I hoped that would be the end of it, but it seemed our luck had run out.

The big man turned back towards Wayles.

"Sounds like she's terrible, not worth the effort to break her. A filly with spirit ain't belong on a wagon, riding, but in a house, gettin' proper discipline," he said, licking his lips. "Why don't you name your price for her? I've got a whole larder full of frozen meat that will keep you and yours fed for three months. You can pick anything you want out of my back room—guns, jewelry for your Missus if you have one, silks and furs for only my finest customers."

Wayles was suddenly, painfully aware of the mess he had

stepped into, trying to cast Amayah as a terrible worker worth less than the price he had paid for her. There was no doubt what the shopkeeper wanted Ama for, and it definitely wasn't sweeping the floors or washing the windows of his shop. The fact that he had offered Wayles basically anything he had in stock in the first salvo of his offer meant that he wasn't planning on taking no for an answer, which meant trouble if we couldn't figure out a solution.

Wayles took the massive offer in stride, responding casually, as if the man was offering him a minor exchange of goods.

"Perhaps, I misspoke in my rage, and I do apologize to you, sir. She's not worth much to me, but my employer says differently. She's the payment for a debt owed to him by a business deal gone awry down in the Port of New Orleans. A merchant there offered my employer a shipment of spices and silks from the Far East, then claimed his ship was lost at sea.

"This one was working as a maid in the merchant's homestead and my employer took a shine to her and arranged a bargain for her services, such as they are."

When he said "services," Wayles raised his eyebrows and gave a knowing glance to the shopkeeper, who chuckled loudly in return and rubbed his greasy hands together. The conversation made me sick, though I knew that Wayles was a attempting to untangle us from the predicament and get us moving out of town as quickly as possible. The shopkeeper smiled and said, "Sounds like your boss and I got a lot in common. We always know there's another way to settle a debt—or at least get what we want."

The big man had one of his own servants hustle into the store, and the man returned with a heavy piece of paper, a quill, and a round metal circle I didn't recognize. The shopkeeper quickly scrawled words on the paper and then pressed the metal against it. It made a seal appear on the paper, the same logo as the sign above our heads.

He pressed the piece of paper into Wayles' hand. "For your employer is my writ and seal, Charles DuBois, owner of the general store and one of three town founders of Frenchman's Bayou, good for $200 of merchandise, at his leisure." He snapped his fingers, and his slave handed him a burlap sack. He opened it up, took a whiff, nodded and handed it to Wayles. "An extra $200 for you and your employer," he said. "You can give that all to him, or maybe some of it slides into your pocket on the road. That's none of my business. A handsome reward for one worthless slave wench."

Wayles didn't put his hands on the bag and returned the letter to DuBois' slave. "Your generosity is noted, sir, but she's not mine to sell you. I must apologize, but we have to keep pushing on north now before the day gets away from us."

The shopkeeper, DuBois, was smiling with his teeth, but it didn't reach his eyes. I could spot it quickly, and I knew Wayles could too.

"Well, north you shall go then, you and your lot of unruly slaves, good sir. Until we meet again."

CHAPTER
NINETEEN

We were about two hours north of Frenchman's Bayou, having left the town and the outlying farms and ranches behind, and were just beginning to breathe easier that we had avoided further trouble. Only then did we round the bend and run into unforeseen complications.

There were nine men, all on horseback, arranged so that the road was impassable, unless we wanted to run right through them. All of them had some manner of firearm either drawn or at their sides, and right square in the middle of them, sitting on a horse that looked entirely miserable, was Charles DuBois, the spurned shopkeeper. He removed his cowboy hat and fanned himself as Wayles brought the horses to a halt. I had taken the first shift to allow Juba to attend to his family; Grace still wasn't feeling all that well. I had a hat on, my head hung down, and a dark raggedy cloak covered my entire body. I didn't move, though Wayles and I were whispering under our breath about how many men there were and how well-armed they appeared to be. Neither discussion was comforting.

Wayles, cool as a cucumber, called down, "Mr. DuBois, I did not expect to see you again so soon. Can you and your fellow gentlemen please kindly disperse from the center of the roadway so that I may carry on my way north?"

His dignified speech earned guffaws of laughter from some of DuBois' men, but not from the shopkeeper himself.

"I would like nothing less than to allow for that, good sir," DuBois said back with the same easy formality. "Unfortunately, I will need to conclude our business transaction before such a thing can be granted. However, I have put it to my mind, this matter with your employer and the wealthy merchant from New Orleans, and have decided as a businessman of high moral character that I should intervene in the interests of all parties."

Wayles was speechless.

"What I mean to say, sir, is that I feel that your employer is getting the short end of the deal in the matter of this debt, likely because his eyes are deceived by the bewitching appearance of that girl you have in the back of your wagon. Thus, I will relieve you of her foul presence before she further ensnares your master in this matter. Women of her type are from lands beyond the sea where they practice all sorts of witchcraft and devilry. I will take the wench from your sight, so she can no longer perform these deceptions. However, I don't want your master left high and dry, so I'm upping the offer to $500 in cash." He had the same burlap bag in his hand, and it was much heavier this time, given the effort it took him to lift it.

"Only a fool would turn down this deal, sir," DuBois concluded. "Now, bring that wench out here so my boys can properly secure her, and we shall allow you to pass."

Wayles grabbed the reins tighter in his hands, as though preparing to run the wagon straight through DuBois' posse. It would probably not go well; hell, it might even flip the wagon, but Amayah was a big reason any of them had made it that far, and we had already agreed that this trip was for all of us or none of us. There was no going back, or leaving anyone behind.

"Mr. DuBois... your generosity is appreciated, but my answer must still be no," Wayles called back. "I ask again that you kindly move your cavalry aside so that we can continue on. It's nearly dark."

Under his breath, he said, "Rohan, start moving towards the back of the wagon and warn them what's coming. Nice and slow."

I didn't want to stand up, so I began to slowly edge my way back, but DuBois was no fool.

"Tell your yellow boy to cease that trickery!" he called out. "This is your last offer, sir. Take this generous bounty and let us relieve you of that long-haired streetwalker, or my boys will kill every last one of you and burn your wagon to the ground with you and your slaves inside it. By the time the sun sets, there'll be nothing left of you but ash."

I'd had enough of this polite intimidation, and the thought of anyone touching Amayah for even a second sent a blaze of fury up my spine. I rose to my full height, keeping the cloak around me and covering my head. In the fading sunlight, I imagine that I looked more than a little sinister, some towering gargoyle sprung to life.

As I began gathering my energy around me, my thoughts flickered to the storytelling sessions of the last few days and their stellar subject matter.

Hiding my grin, I decided it was time to put George Lucas' imagination to the test and see how well it worked on "weak-minded fools" from over a century ago.

I pitched my voice several degrees lower than my normal speaking tone, using the bass I had commanded during storytime with Darth Vader's sinister tones.

"You will stand aside and let us pass," I said slowly. "Or I will destroy you."

A few of the horse riders looked wary, but DuBois spat out another chuckle. "What's wrong with your yellow boy's head, son? He fell off the wagon one too many times?"

Wayles looked at me for a moment, entirely stupefied, but then his mind caught up as he remembered the fireside stories.

He turned back to our accosters. "This isn't a slave, Mr. DuBois.

This is that wench's husband, a warlock from across the great ocean. He comes from a mysterious island in the Pacific. He's a wizard with spells that summon demons and give him power over flame! You have angered him now, sir, and lest you wish to see that anger unleashed, I would kindly ask you that you take your posse and ease on home!"

A few more of the men had begun to look anxiously between them. If they believed what DuBois was saying about Amayah, then they might believe that her husband was just as dangerous—and just as inhuman. I spread my arms slowly for effect as the sunlight faded further. I pointed a finger dramatically at DuBois and said loudly, "Here is the one who refutes MY POWER!"

The two mounted men nearest DuBois sidestepped their horses away, not willing to cut bait, but no longer confident that their boss was the best person to stand beside. DuBois himself was not going to be cowed by some tall slave in a long cloak, but for the first time in weeks, I summoned the power within me, letting it surge around and around inside. Normally, when I held it like this, I was preparing to fight someone or heal someone, but this time I simply held it in check as it surged stronger and stronger into my hands. Particles and bits and pieces of all sorts felt like they were pulsing, pushing, and coming together, concentrating and swirling into a circular ball of energy in my grasp. I heard Wayles gasp, and I risked opening my eyes. I couldn't have been more thrilled if I was suddenly holding Darth Vader's lightsaber itself.

I held up my hands for all to see as the pulsing light made a sizzling noise, pulsing from white to an ashy gray to a pulsing orangish-red. DuBois' eyes went wide, and his horse whined in concern at what was appearing out of the gloom—something decidedly unnatural.

I pointed again at DuBois and bellowed, "This is your last warning. Flee this place or feel my wrath!"

With that last word, I gathered my power and leapt off the front of the wagon, turning a somersault in midair and landing about 10 feet from his row of horsemen. My jump covered at least 30 or 40 feet, well beyond human capabilities, and the fact that I had stuck the landing and was now just feet away from the posse was more than they could handle. Their carefully constructed order broke down in seconds, and they fled back down the road, past the wagon, without a single look back. DuBois alone was left behind and I looked up at him, feeling the power coursing across my field of vision.

The most powerful man in Frenchman's Bayou cried in sheer terror and threw the bag of money at my feet. I smelled an unpleasant, familiar odor and looked up to see the front of his trousers rapidly staining as he pissed his pants in fear.

"Begone, you Devil!" he cried as he raced past me and the wagon, and out of our lives forever.

Suddenly, Juba, Amayah, and the rest came spilling out of the wagon full of questions as to what in the world happened and how we scared off DuBois' posse without a single shot fired. I tried to downplay what I had done, but Wayles was having none of it. He stood up before the rest of the party like Jay Leno doing a Tonight Show monologue and gave a reenactment that was both pleasing and embarrassing to hear. Of course, this let the poorly kept secret of my powers out of the bag to the brothers, Cecilia's dad, and the kids, but most of them suspected it in some form or fashion, between my cotton-picking prowess and how I had disarmed McMurtry the night of the escape.

I insisted we resume traveling several more hours into the night before stopping, even though everyone was exhausted. I could tell Wayles disagreed, but he was willing to take my lead after the display I had just put on.

When we finally did stop, Wayles was on his second go-round of the story as I returned from my own random stream of thoughts.

"So, he stands up tall as you please on the wagon in that cloak and starts talking in that deep voice just like Garth Vader, saying "You will leave this place-"

Amayah interrupted his story with a giant laugh.

"Garth Vader? Wayles, who in the world is Garth Vader?"

Wayles looked a little crestfallen at having his story interrupted. "The villain. From the space story! The one who is really Luke's father, you know! Garth Vader!"

Now, we were all trying hard not to laugh at our friend, although Cecilia's dad, Thomas, let out a hee-haw under his breath that caused him to fart a bit too, which made us all laugh even harder.

"Clean out your ears more often!" Juba said with a laugh. "His name is Darth Vader, not Garth!"

"Could have been a Star Wars/Wayne's World crossover movie," Amayah said to me with a wink.

"Party on, Wayne?" I said, smirking.

"Right!" she said with a smile. "Party on, Darth!"

A couple of hours later, with the three girls asleep, along with Cecilia's dad and Adam and Patrick tending the horses, we had an impromptu war council—me, Amayah, Juba, Cecilia, and Wayles. I voiced my continuing fear that DuBois would return with a militia force to hunt us down, but the rest, even Amayah, disagreed.

"Think about it, Ro," she said calmly. "What kind of person claims they saw an eight-foot rat or aliens or a werewolf in the woods? It's never the powerful businessman or the politician, it's the people that everyone else already thinks is crazy. The little old lady or the homeless guy. People with power like DuBois are always terrified to lose it. He'd rather swear his men to secrecy and pretend that he donated the $500 than admit he threw it away and ran like a baby from a warlock from across the sea." She couldn't help grinning at me at that last bit.

"This man Dubois is a big fish in these parts. He won't want to risk others seeing him as anything less," Juba agreed. "He's probably at home right now convincing himself of some other truth that makes sense. He'll spend all day tomorrow ensuring that those men who came with him understand the same facts as they happened. Whether it takes coins in their pockets or a threat to their ears, they'll all sing the tune he wants to hear and never speak of it otherwise."

"The bigger question is, what do we do with this?" Wayles asked rhetorically, swinging the burlap sack full of printed U.S. currency in his hand. "We've gone from slaves on the run to filthy rich in a few hours. With this kind of money, we can book a cabin on a steamboat straight up the river towards Springfield or get to St. Louis and ride in luxury on a train car all the way to our destination."

It was painfully tempting to embrace a bit of luxury after so much hardship. The idea of seeing Grace and Rose's faces looking out the window of a train or off the top of a boat was a tempting dream to turn into reality, but still I hesitated.

"Wayles, how common is it for slaves to ride a train or a steamboat? Especially with their children?"

His slight smile at whatever luxurious fantasy he was living in quickly evaporated, and I knew the truth before he even spoke it.

"Well, no. I mean a White family that's well off will usually have a servant or three with them on a long trip, and the servants have to ride in a separate car, of course, but it still beats a wagon trail by a long shot. But yes, it would definitely be odd to see. Maybe a little extra coin in the conductor's pocket would smooth it over."

I shook my head. "We can't risk the attention. We'll have to continue with the plan we have and keep the money safe, so if we need it, we'll have it. Maybe you three," I pointed to Wayles, Juba, and Cecilia, "split it up three ways, so if we get separated, we know that you'll be alright."

The matter settled, we sat quietly, enjoying the peaceful evening and the closeness of unlikely friends.

"Rohan," Cecilia spoke up after a long silence. "I must ask. Do many people from your time and place have powers like you?"

Amayah cut in before I could answer, her voice full of pride and love. "No! Rohan is the only one that we know of. And he doesn't just use his powers for fighting off bad guys and scaring off lecherous old men either!" Before I could stop her or shush her, she launched into the story of that first day at the hospital, and how I had cured Winnie of cancer.

The others listened in rapt detail, and when Amayah recounted how Winnie's hair began to regrow, Cecilia crossed herself rapidly three times. Cecilia's eyes refused to find mine, which I found embarrassing and completely unnecessary.

She whispered, "The power to heal. The power of God in your hands. You are ..."

I cut her off. "No, don't say that. I'm not God. I'm not Jesus Christ either. I'm just a kid from New York City with some powers that come and go, who wound up in the wrong time and place. Please don't think of me as anything more than that."

Cecilia lifted her head and held my gaze steady with her own as she whispered, "Jesus sent all the people away except his disciples, Peter, James, and John, and Jairus and Jairus' wife. Then Jesus took the girl by the hand and told her to arise. The girl got up from her bed, completely well again."

It was a verse from the Bible. I had read it recently after one of my first talks with Amayah. I had to admit it sounded quite similar to what had happened to me when I met Winnie at Mount Sinai. But there was no way this was the power of God in me, right? Especially with Nick the Brute on one side and the mystical voice of Hua and her talk of the Shine Xiong on the other. Although I tried my best to avoid reaching out to Nick for help, Hua was nowhere to be found. Both were mysteriously absent and did not seek me out like they did in the past. I meant to go to the New York Public Library and do some research on Hua, but as my romance with Amayah blossomed, I had been quite distracted from the mystery of what was going on with me. Regardless, being compared to Jesus Christ was extremely uncomfortable.

"I'm convinced he's an angel," Amayah told the group, making me blush at the genuine awe in her voice. "He is selfless and heals people, even though it exhausts him. He is kind and good to everyone he encounters. Especially me." Now it was her turn to blush.

I kept trying to brush off and downplay any comparisons.

"It was just a one-time thing," I said, referring to Winnie. "I probably couldn't do it again if I tried."

"That's not true," Juba now spoke up. I started to wonder if the whole wagon was against me. "Your face. You healed yourself."

I touched my nose and remembered that Juba had seen me the morning after my unpleasant encounter with McPherson.

Juba turned to Wayles. "McPherson caught him that night after they increased our cotton count to 10,000. Broke his nose, probably a cheekbone too. It should have taken those injuries months to heal, but you were better in a day, with a straight nose and all."

I was weary from all the excitement about harnessing my power and from feeling like everyone was insinuating I was something more than I actually was.

"That was just ... that was no big deal," I said half-heartedly. "I just heal quickly. You know, like, uh, like Wolverine."

"Who in the hell is Wolverine?" Wayles said, cocking his head like a curious dog.

I threw my hands up in the air. "Fine, I can heal myself and run super-fast and heal people and have super-strength. And I can occasionally teleport myself and other people from one place to another. And at least once back in time. But none of that is important right now. We need to get some rest and get back on the road in case DuBois decides he wants to be the big bad scourge of the south."

Cecilia patted my shoulder. "Rest, son. Get your strength back. We'll follow you wherever you think is best."

As I drifted off to sleep, I played Cecilia's words back in my head and realized their meaning. I had grown up and become a man. And these people's lives were now in my hands. I couldn't let them down.

CHAPTER

TWENTY

We never saw DuBois again, and as we forged our way north through eastern Arkansas, and into Missouri, I stopped looking over my shoulder quite so often. It took us another three weeks to reach St. Louis, which was a big city in the making even then, with some 35,000 people living there. Wayles even risked buying us accommodations in a bunkhouse on the way out of town. For the first time in months, we slept in real beds inside a building, not out on the grass or in the back of a wagon. It was almost too comfortable, to be honest. I was so used to crickets chirping and birds singing that hearing only a fireplace crackling sounded odd. I thought for one tantalizing moment that Amayah would come sleep next to me, but little Rose asked her to snuggle, and she couldn't turn her down. The next morning, we ate a big breakfast from the kitchen, although they wouldn't serve anyone but Wayles in the actual eating area. Nonetheless, we mounted back up feeling refreshed and reinvigorated.

We met with very little trouble the rest of the way north. It was only another 100 miles—about six days in the wagon—to Springfield, and our biggest threat was a rattlesnake that slid into one of Wayles' boots while he was taking a bath in the river. Fortunately, he heard the tell-tale rattle when he picked the boot back up and avoided a nasty bite. Claire and Rose stumbled into some poison oak, but Cecilia had the poultice brewing almost immediately to fight it off, and Juba wasted about three hours one morning trying to flush a deer he was convinced had scampered away at the sight of the wagon. It turned out to be a raccoon and we teased him over it for the next 24 hours. Three days out of Springfield, I was standing in my shorts, washing myself off in the river, when someone coughed behind me. I turned to see Amayah blushing red as a rose behind me.

"Oh, Ro, I thought you were back at the wagon... I can come back," she said.

I smiled widely. It was rare for Ama to be the one flustered and off-balance when the two of us were alone together. "It's okay. I'm just about done," I said, moving to get in my shirt and out of the cold morning air. But before I could put it on, Ama stopped me with her fingers. Her hands went to my bare back, and she traced her fingers up it, making me shiver from something other than the cold morning.

"Rohan?" she asked in a whisper. "Why are these scars still here? Why didn't you heal them up like you did for your nose and your face?"

I didn't have an exact answer for her. I wasn't even sure I had one for myself.

I took her hand in mine and copped her chin with my other hand.

"I, um, don't really know. I don't feel like it's fair that I can heal my own wounds so easily, but everyone else must wear theirs for the rest of their lives." Now that I was thinking about it, I realized that maybe I did know the answer; I just hadn't been able to admit it to myself.

"I saw Cecilia take those lashes for her dad. I saw Juba take them to protect both of us. They can't make that pain go away. They have to live with it, work with it, sleep with it... it never goes away, even when it stops hurting. How many lashes have these people taken in the years and decades before we showed up? We've only been here a little while, but their fight is the same fight that people like you and me have in our own time—to be treated fairly because of who we are, not because of what we look like. I guess what I'm saying is that I earned those lashes. I earned them because I did the right thing to protect people who were looking out for you and me, when everything was telling them that they probably should have done the exact opposite. They risked their lives for us and got punished for it. When we decided to help them, why should my fate be any different?"

She had tears in her eyes as she looked up at me. "You are such an amazing person, Rohan, and you barely even seem to know it." She stepped behind me and hugged me around the waist, pressing herself against my scarred back. She laid a string of tiny kisses along the path of the scars, standing on her tiptoes to reach the highest of them, then dropped down and held me tight for a long time. I didn't ever want her to let go.

TWO DAYS LATER, we spied Springfield from a long way off, its dull roofs and rising smokestacks, then people moving to and fro. The joy we felt at finally being in the free territories of the U.S. was incredible. We hugged and kissed each other, patted each other on the back, and thanked God for the blessings that had delivered us into a land where everyone had a chance to be free and make a life for themselves. We decided to walk hand in hand into town, something that Juba, the twins, Cecilia, and their children had been doubtful about. They saw themselves as less than White people and were afraid that this was all just a pipe dream, a cruel joke at their expense, and that when they arrived, there would be harsh men with ropes there to collect them and take them back down South, never to be seen again. Wayles, Amayah, and I had to convince them to come out of hiding.

The twins, Adam and Patrick, volunteered to man the wagon and find a place for it while the rest of us went into the center of town to inquire about lodging and work. Amayah and I were hoping to get some alone time to determine our next move. I needed some much-needed space to test my powers and see if I could harness the energy to get us back to the right when and where.

I was at one end of the human freedom chain, with Amayah next to me, who held hands with little Grace, then Rose, Claire, Juba, Cecilia, her father Thomas, and Wayles at the end. I'm sure we got some stares, but I didn't really care. We had done what most thought impossible and got kind, good-hearted people away from the tyranny of the Captain's plantation to the free part of the country, where they could control their own destiny and be safe from the war to come. I didn't want to give them too much information, like the fact that the Civil War's end would soon be followed by President Lincoln's murder, because why burden them with things they couldn't control? As we walked into town, we spied free Blacks taking notice of the new arrivals, greeting Juba and Cecilia with waves and tips of their hats. It was a beautiful thing to experience up close.

We started to move faster and found ourselves laughing with the pure joy of it all, and somewhere in those moments I realized what was happening, the strange sensation was welling up within me, just like it had that night on the bus after the festival when Amayah and I had first been transported. It overwhelmed me from within, like a dam ready to burst through its retention walls. I gripped Ama's hand tighter and said with unabashed glee, "Ama! It's happening! Hold tight to me!" She nodded and her electric green eyes glowed wide and fierce as she dug her fingernails into my palm. We continued to run forward, but I felt a lightness to my steps now, and when I turned to look down the line of my fellow travelers, they seemed to be shimmering, almost transparent, as if a barrier of some sort was forming between us.

They sensed it too, maybe not in the same way, since they had never experienced it before, but I saw little Grace try to grasp Amayah's hand more firmly, but fail to do so. She looked up with concern as she saw what was happening, then cried out sharply, "Don't go, Amayah! Don't go!" That got the attention of her sisters, her parents, and Wayles down at the end of the line.

We'd had told them a day like this might come and that we would always be together in spirit, not to be sad, if they were, to look up at the night sky, looking for a new moon, just like we would be, thinking of them, forever more in our hearts.

Cecilia's dad, Thomas, touched his heart and smiled at us, which surprised me, as I had never seen him smile or be genuinely happy since we had arrived. They all stopped and watched as we kept moving forward, no longer in control of our own movements, as though we were on a souped-up version of those people movers they have at the airports. I turned to wave goodbye to my dear circle of friends and saw each of them looking on with smiles on their faces.

"Thank you, my friends!" Juba called out.

"God bless you two!" Cecilia added. "Love one another!"

"Look out for Garth Vader!" Wayles shouted, a wide grin on his face.

As the barrier divided us completely, we found ourselves immersed in a radiant circle of blue and white light, reminiscent of our initial journey to 1854. My golden fat cap, tightly gripped in my hand, started to spin and rise into the air, triggering vivid memories of Lore.

"That's right," Lore had exclaimed enthusiastically. "Exactly like that, perfect." He observed me with the keen eye of a mentor, applauding the precision of my spray can's movements as I breathed life into a dull handball court wall in Fresh Meadows with artistic finesse.

"Is that so? Lore, you're too kind," I responded. Watching my *Talon* piece emerge on the wall, I couldn't help but value our friendship.

With a swift switch to the slender nozzle cap for my final touch of shape-lettering; he once again cheered me on, "Your outline is flawless, my friend. Look at you; you've got this!'

With a beaming smile, I couldn't help but express, "You're a good friend, Lore..."

As the memory of him faded, I clutched Amayah in a desperate embrace, unwilling to let go for even a moment as we raced through a tunnel of blinding light. The world around us was a blur of speed and uncertainty.

We both closed our eyes, and the world went blank for a very long breath.

As we departed, I thought of Juba, Cecilia, their children, Wayles, and all my friends from Oxford, and how hard they had fought for and yearned for their freedom. Even under the appalling conditions and harsh reality under Captain Franklin, Juba and the unfortunate others who toiled under the grueling sun found happiness and love when they were with each other, together.

Wayles had also shared stories of his kinfolk who lived out west, informing him of poor Chinese folk working in mining and news of them building a grand railroad connecting all the states. According to Wayles' kinfolk, the poor Chinese got paid next to nothing—relegated to only the most unsafe assignments, carving out tunnels, and chipping away at granite. Many had died from unexpected explosions and horrific rockslides while blowing up dynamite in the mountains. Even so, when they gathered to celebrate the Lunar New Year, their laughter, love, and grand jamboree were so infectious that people from many other towns joined in the festivities.

And I don't think there was ever a feel-good story of a compassionate Captain Franklin or any other white plantation owner being good to their slaves. There was probably only horror that perhaps still affects the present. But I saw real heroes, not in myself, but in Juba and his family, who were always willing to fight the good fight.

Even before I opened my eyes, I knew we were back in New York City. I could hear the underlying bustle of the city, the sound you hear 24/7—depending on where you live. The noise of people walking everywhere, shouting into phones, taxicabs, and buses and delivery trucks battling their way through intersections too small to fit them all. The sound of jackhammers trying to fix up the city one block at a time, only to start all over again next year or next decade. The buzz of the stoplights telling you that you better start stepping across the intersection before the Do Not Cross sign came back up or you were taking your life in your own hands. Looking up, I smiled with gratitude at the mountains of skyscrapers that had materialized all around me. The weather felt mid-spring, maybe April, incredible in the morning, but it would get hot quickly once the sun crept up in the sky. We were somewhere in Manhattan, but that's all I could tell, as I didn't spend a ton of time in the ritzier parts of the Five Boroughs, but simply seeing tall buildings and yellow taxis and neon signs sent a wave of relief through my entire body.

Unfortunately, a wave of nausea suddenly hit, and I suddenly remembered how out of control I had felt after we first jumped into the slave wagon a few months earlier. Trying to hold onto Amayah, whose eyes were still closed, as if not yet ready to see whether we had made it safely home, I slipped to one knee on the hard asphalt, and my shoulders slumped.

She must have forgotten what happened the first time too, because Amayah snapped awake and knelt beside me. "Rohan! Ro! What's wrong?"

I opened my eyes and forced a smile. "It's okay," I said slowly. "It's like last time, but not quite as bad. See? No seizure this time." We sat on the sidewalk together, oblivious of the foot traffic all around us. People didn't notice that a tall, gawky Asian boy and a drop-dead gorgeous Puerto Rican girl in 1850s slave clothing had suddenly materialized out of nowhere in the middle of the block. That wasn't exactly a shock if you've ever spent any time in the city, especially before working hours. People get so lost in their own worlds—where they're going and what's going to happen when they arrive—that they usually don't see what's happening unless there's a gunshot or a siren on the same street. Then Amayah put her arms around me protectively as I regained my balance and slowly stood, her arm around my waist.

Standing awestruck together, we drank in the sights, the smells, and the sounds of our beloved home.

I still couldn't believe that no one had stopped or at least done a double-take based on how we were dressed, but then I looked down. My cloak and wool pants and heavy shirt were gone, replaced by the clothes I had worn to the festival. I looked Amayah up and down and saw the same luminous green dress she had worn to the Festival of the Moon. My mind reeled at how this could possibly be happening. When entering and returning from the time stream, we returned with the same things we initially started with. Maybe some higher law of the universe was at work. Can something at least be brought back from the past? I hope to answer that in the future.

We both burst out laughing at the sight of each other back in our twentieth century outfits.

I ran my hand through my hair and wondered if we had ingested some hallucinogenic drug at the festival in one of the desserts or the punch or something. Had it all been a dream? Had we wandered from Queens to Manhattan in a drug-induced stupor, imagining that we had gone back in time a hundred and fifty years to pre-Civil War Mississippi? It seemed preposterous, but I was suddenly taken back to a beloved story from my childhood, *The Lion, the Witch, and the Wardrobe* by C.S. Lewis. Of course, everyone knew the story of the kids stumbling into Narnia and defeating the White Witch to save the day, but the part that always blew my mind came at the end of the novel, once they were all grown up and had become mighty Kings and Queens of Narnia. They were all on a hunt for some sort of animal, perhaps a stag, when they stumbled back upon the place they had first entered and wound up re-entering the wardrobe. When they tumbled out on the other side, they were back to the same ages they had been when the novel began; the years fell off them and in real time, it had only been about an hour since they had left. Could Amayah and I have shared some sort of joint vision? Was it just the next morning in 1997 New York City and our parents were freaked out because we hadn't come home last night?

It sounded impossible, but not more impossible than the fact that until a few minutes ago, we had been at the end of a month-long journey through 19th century America, dodging slave hunters and foraging for wild game and edible plants. I looked down at Amayah and said, "Did we dream that whole thing?"

She shook her head wordlessly, then her green eyes widened. Her hands went to the back of my shirt, then lifting it, a gesture I might have found extremely enjoyable in other settings, but we were in the middle of a Manhattan sidewalk.

She didn't seem to notice when I stiffened up. I felt her fingers on my back tracing two very familiar lines.

The scars from the lashes McPherson had delivered. We hadn't imagined anything. It was all real, and whatever divine force had sent us to that place and time had similarly decided that our work was done.

"It was real," Amayah said. "We were there, and now we're back. Rohan, what are we going to tell our parents? We need to think of a story and work out the details and stick to them. If we tell anyone that we time-traveled back to 1854 Mississippi, we'll both be at Bellevue before the end of the day."

She was right. We needed a plan, and we needed it before we bumped into anyone we knew. But first, I really needed something to eat. I suggested that we get breakfast or lunch or whatever meal time it was and figure it out with full stomachs. Fortunately, the same laws of time travel that returned our clothes also gave me back my wallet. I checked it and found a $10 bill, which wouldn't be enough, so I grabbed my ATM card and headed across the street to the first fast-food joint in sight—a McDonald's.

It wasn't packed, but it was busy enough that Amayah went to grab a table while I ordered. The cashier was sporting a throwback Afro haircut that I thought was a pretty bold choice, but he seemed to be making it work. The guy at the next register looked like he was heading to Woodstock when his shift was over, given his long shaggy hair and a full-length beard-mustache combination. Assuming it was just one of those locally owned chain restaurants where the owner relaxed McDonald's tight corporate policies, I shrugged and placed my order—a 10-piece chicken nugget deal for Amayah with a Sprite and four quarter-pounders with cheese and a Coke for me. Yes, I was going to feast. Considering some of the stuff I had eaten, and not eaten, in the past two months, I wasn't going to worry about it. The cashier told me it was going to be $12, which seemed remarkably cheap, so I handed her my ATM card.

"What am I supposed to do with this?"

The cashier was staring at the ATM card like I had just handed her a piece of toilet paper.

"Um, swipe it in the machine to pay for my food?"

She stared at me even longer, one eyebrow raised.

"We don't take credit cards, buddy. It's cash only."

"What, since when?" I jabbed back.

"I don't know, since we opened? Now can you pay or not?"

What the hell? I wondered what kind of backwards McDonald's wasn't taking debit cards in this day and age. Something was up, but I was starving, and Amayah was waiting, so I fished around in my wallet and scrounged up a ten-dollar bill, a single, and four quarters to pay for the meal. Setting my uneasiness aside, I unwrapped the first burger and sunk my teeth into it, feeling the joy that only meat, cheese, and bread can deliver, savoring every taste bud explosion as I gnawed into it like a malnourished T-Rex. I was on my third bite by the time I got to the table and gave Amayah a salute with the burger, sliding into the booth across from her and handing her the rest of the order. She thanked me with a smile, but didn't immediately dig in. She just stared at me with those intoxicating green eyes, and gestured me to lean closer to her.

"Rohan," she whispered in my ear. "Something's wrong here. Look at the people at the other tables."

I turned my head, hoping my worst fear wasn't real. I saw other New Yorkers destroying their cholesterol counts with fatty fries and milkshakes, but there was more. The bizarre haircuts weren't limited to the two cashiers. Afros were everywhere. And tracksuits. Quite a few women were wearing what looked like old-school workout clothes, the kind that Olivia Newton-John and Pat Benatar had rocked in the early days of MTV. The people wearing glasses had enormous frames with tinted lenses.

Everyone looked dressed for a costume party, and we hadn't received an invitation. It was definitely New York, but it was a different era. The fashion on display here seemed like the late 70s and early 80s, and the girl at the register looked at my ATM card like she had never seen one before. To quote Han Solo, I suddenly had a really bad feeling about this.

"I know," I replied back, relating the story of the ATM card to her. "Let's just eat and then figure out what to do next."

She nodded, and we ate in silence. The brilliant taste of the first quarter pounder was somewhat diminished with the second, third, and fourth ones, but that didn't keep me from scarfing them all down in short order. Amayah demolished her nuggets and fries and gulped down the Sprite. We'd gone more than a month without processed food injected with sugar and preservatives, and I had truly missed all the junk food, more than I ever could have imagined. When we were done, we sat for another few minutes, finally satisfied. We were supposed to be coming up with a plan of what to tell our parents about our mysterious disappearance, which felt like it had been at least two months ago. Still, the more we glanced around McDonald's, the more we knew that our parents in this timeline might not know we were missing or even know us in general.

"Well, I'm just going to come out and say it," Amayah uttered in a nervous, shaky tone. "This is New York, but I don't think it's our New York. These people definitely aren't dressed like it's 1997, and if that lady has never seen an ATM card before, we're not in the right 'when.' Again."

Being overwhelmed after all we'd been through, I had to confess I admired her very much then. I was nervously making small talk without admitting what was up. But Amayah wasn't afraid to cut to the chase.

"Our first priority is to find out when we are," she continued. "That should be simple enough. There must be a newsstand around here somewhere. Then we'll need to figure out what to do here. I'm assuming getting Juba and Cecilia's family to the north was important last time. So, what needs to happen here?"

"You're absolutely amazing, do you know that?" I gushed.

She blushed. "Jeez, Rohan. It's just one adventure after another with you, isn't it?" She held out her hand, and I gave it a reassuring squeeze.

"Well, the good news is that our money works, although I've only got a few dollars left," I said. "But this is New York City, and there must be somewhere to go if we need a place to stay or a hot meal.

"But you're right, first things first. I can't believe I have to say this again, but let's go find out 'when' we are."

Sure enough, there was a newsstand on the corner, hawking magazines, The Post, the Times, candy, gum, condoms, and just about anything else you might possibly need in the middle of the day. TIME magazines were stacked twenty or thirty deep, and I could see the red cover gleaming, but couldn't make out the face on the front. As we got closer, I thought it was President Clinton looking back at me, but as I got closer, I realized I was wrong. "DEBACLE IN THE DESERT" blared the cover headline. The troubled man on the cover was one I had only seen in history books, and once when some teacher had forced us to watch an old debate on TV for government class. His name was Jimmy Carter.

That wasn't the most important thing about the magazine though; in small type at the upper-right hand corner, I found what I was looking for. A date line that read "May 5, 1980." This wasn't my New York, not technically. 1980 was the year my family had immigrated, and somewhere in this city, my mom was probably holding a one-year-old named Rohan.

"1980!" Amayah said, her mouth hanging open. "That's the year my parents moved here from PR! In fact, I think my mom is probably pregnant with me right now! Oh my god, if I see them, I think I might die of shock." She was half-giggling, but also serious. She sounded on the verge of hysteria, and I couldn't really blame her.

I blinked and ran back over what Amayah had just said.

"Wait a minute, your parents came here in 1980?" I asked. "Mine did too. In fact, if I'm not mistaken, I think they got here a couple of weeks ago or so. That means there's a one-year-old version of me probably crying my head off somewhere right now."

Amayah laughed at the thought. "Little baby Rohan? Aww!"

Before I could reply, Amayah gasped.

"That has to be it, Ro! Why else would we be here? We must need to help our parents do something... we should compare notes on what we know about their stories. We also need a place to crash tonight, because while I enjoyed sleeping outside on the road to Springfield, I'm not trying to fight the bums for the best cardboard boxes on Fifth Avenue."

I laughed aloud at her comment. She had so many layers. I knew that she was sweet and smart and beautiful, but her sense of humor blossomed in wonderful, matter-of-fact and unexpected ways. Sometimes, I don't think she even realized she was being funny until someone else's laughter told her so.

"Hey buddy, you gonna buy something?"

I glanced up and realized that I'd been standing there clutching the TIME Magazine and not moving for a minute or two. The clerk at the newsstand was staring at me impatiently, probably thinking I was some punk teenager trying to lift a Pepsi can or a Hershey bar when he turned his back.

"Um, yeah, sorry, lost track of time there," I replied, smirking at how true that comment was in every sense. I looked along the news-paper aisle, where the Times and the Post sat, pulling at my attention with their bold headlines. The Times won out, largely because it only cost a quarter, but also because I could see the top tab of the sports page blaring about a Yankees win, 10-1 over the Twins. I paid the man his quarter, smiling, and flipped to the sports page to find Lou Pinella's surly mug, 17 years younger than I'd last seen him, glaring back at me.

"Sheesh, he never even smiled, even as a player?" I said to no one in particular, then shut my yap. A guy like the clerk was probably used to all sorts of nut jobs spouting off about what they saw in the newspaper, but I didn't need to add "Asian kid who thinks he knows the future of baseball" to the list. Amayah was skimming the magazine covers as I paid, and even though we were about seventeen years in our own past with a few nickels in our pockets, and without knowing a single person—at least one who would know us back— old habits die hard. I flipped to the box score to check out how the Bronx Bombers were looking. The box score told the tale as clearly in 1980 as it did every morning when I read it before school. Some catcher named Rick Cerone had launched a three-run homer, and Hall of Famer Reggie Jackson went deep as well. I marveled at names in the lineup—Bucky Dent, Willie Randolph, Graig Nettles—all guys I had watched play on Old Timer's Day. I suddenly had an extreme desire to attend a game at Yankee Stadium in 1980, mainly because everything would be 1980 cheap! I couldn't imagine how that would possibly help us help our parents, as I'm not sure my parents could name a single Yankee who had ever played, even Babe Ruth, who my dad only knows as a chocolate bar.

Regardless, I thanked the man for the paper and tucked it under my arm as we walked away.

Amayah was right; we needed a base of operations if we were going to find our parents in this mass of humanity and figure out what sort of help they needed. My mom and dad had always talked about coming to America as one of the greatest experiences of their lives, namely how they found work immediately and were welcomed into the Asian-American community. They were certainly well-respected by most people now, but clearly not all, given my previous gang conflicts. I'm not sure if that respect crossed racial lines, though, and I said as much to Amayah.

"It sounds a lot like my parents' story as well," she said as we walked, though we had no clear direction. "They always talk about how great it was from the first minute they got here and how they found a community to invest in almost immediately. However, it had always felt like they had been holding something back, omitting the details to make it seem better than it really was. Maybe there's something there we can look into."

I agreed, and we made our way to a warm, sunny park, sat down, and started sorting through the newspaper, seeking clues about neighborhoods where immigrants were moving to, what industries they were getting jobs in, or anything that seemed vaguely connected to our hunt. It was a big newspaper and an even bigger city, but eventually we found something interesting—a want ad for working at a youth center, with an emphasis on counselors who could speak different languages. The youth center was located in Union City, New Jersey, just across the Hudson through the Lincoln Tunnel. We wanted to find our parents and do whatever was necessary to trigger another time jump, hopefully one that would lead us back home. Still, we also saw the reality that New York City was massive, and our parents were four people whose whereabouts we didn't know, who had only recently arrived and were likely unknown to most people. Other than walking right into them on a street corner, we were going to have to search them out. We'd need money and a place to stay to make that happen, and someplace where no one was going to ask questions about an Asian American boy and a Puerto Rican girl who never seemed to be at school.

That was the golden ticket element of the want ad that Amayah found. Room and board were provided Monday through Friday for counselors, meaning that we could camp out there all week and pool our resources and earnings to aid the search. On the weekends, we'd have to improvise, but there were places open all night all over the city, or once we saved enough money, we could rent a room for a night or two for basically nothing and hole up there until Monday morning rolled around again.

We collected the last of our meager coins and took the subway and bus out to Union City, hopping off and mounting the stairs outside the Union City Home for Wayward Children on 37th Street. It wasn't much to look at, but that was good news. We wanted a place with a low profile and even lower standards, somewhere they wouldn't question little things like why our driver's licenses said we hadn't been born yet or why my shoes featured a basketball player who was currently an anonymous senior in high school in North Carolina.

We walked in and asked the secretary, who had almost certainly been asleep before the bell chimed, how to apply. They had no official job applications, another good sign, so we put our names on blank sheets of paper, including where we went to school—fortunately, the school had been around in 1980—and why we wanted to work at the Home for Wayward Children. When Amayah asked me to read her answers over, I blushed and showed her mine. We had both written, "I love kids and can't wait to be a parent some day." Same sentence structure and everything. Our experiences helping teach and care for the Juba children: Claire, Rose, and Grace, had impacted us both, and it was an incredible vibe to share with her. After a few minutes in the lobby admiring the colorful art that decorated the walls, the secretary summoned us to meet the facility director in the back office. A woman named Mrs. Wilkinson greeted us there. She appeared to be in her late forties, with short brown hair, a big smile, and an undeniable energy that we both found infectious from the start.

"Every time I think it's time to move on and pack up shop, Jesus reminds me that there are still good people left in the world," Mrs. Wilkinson exclaimed, beaming at both of us. "So, you're foreign students here for college, then?"

"Yes ma'am," I responded, laying the humble Asian act on a little thick. "My parents were supposed to wire me funds for tuition and lodging, but I have not been able to contact them. I hate not being productive, so I thought I could work here and help out until I hear from them."

Amayah nodded on cue and spoke in her best "eager to please" voice, making sure to play it fast and loose with her 'S' sound, dropping it more than half the time to give that fresh from Latin America vibe. "Si, senora. My parents sent my luggage ahead, but it was robbed at your airport. Until they can replace my things, I have nothing, so I would like to work here supporting the youth of this fine country."

It felt a little disingenuous laying it on like that for Mrs. Wilkinson, but we needed these jobs for our financial situation and to get a safe roof over our heads. She was eager to hear about our experiences and our favorite things about working with children. We passed the interview with flying colors, and a few hours later, we were going through our first-day orientations. We met the rest of the small staff and were warned never to contact the kids or their parents outside the facility, and not to take any pictures.

After that, we split up briefly because, unlike the wagons in 1850s Mississippi, young men and women didn't share sleeping quarters here. My room was tiny and square, with a window overlooking the street beside a small bunk bed. There appeared to be no one else living there, so I went with the top bunk, reasoning that it would be a further climb for the rats and roaches, who seemed to know the back way into every room in the tri-state area. I didn't have any luggage, so I sat down for a few minutes, then headed out the door to the common room where Mrs. Wilkinson had suggested we rendezvous after getting acclimated. Amayah was already there and surrounded by children buzzing around her like bees in a flower garden. She was reading from a book of fairy tales, making wild gestures with her hands to thrill the enraptured audience.

She looked up and saw me and exclaimed, "We're saved! The handsome prince has finally arrived!" The children turned as one and gaped to see who she could possibly be talking to. A few of the older boys rolled their eyes and the girls squealed in delight. Amayah stood up, her cheeks blushing red and called out, "My hero! My knight in shining armor! Oh, I knew you would come for me, my sweet!" My face flushed to match hers.

Before our adventure, I probably would have clammed up at such attention, stuck my hands in my pockets, mumbled something, and shuffled away. But that was then, and this was now... with Amayah.

I leaped into action, picked her lightly off the ground, spun her around, and declared, "I have come to win yonder maiden's hand in marriage!" More squeals of delight arose from the girls in the audience. I set her back down and pretended to scan the rest of the common room, a scowl crossing my face. "Now then, where is that terrible dragon I keep hearing so much about. He'll soon meet his end, or my name isn't Rohan, the Fresh Prince of Queens!"

It was stupid and silly, and I would have been ridiculously embarrassed to join in just a few months ago. But Amayah was grinning in delight, and the kids were eating it up. I was suddenly reminded of Claire, Rose, and Grace sitting around the campfire while we told them tales of Simba and Nala, Jasmine and Aladdin, and dozens more. Kids were really something, so totally adaptable to terrible situations, so long as you gave them a little light of hope that things would get better, and that someone cared for them. Juba and Cecilia's girls risked their lives to escape north and treated the whole thing like a grand adventure, even as death stared back.

The kids were from all over New Jersey and New York and spent time here for a host of different reasons. Some came from broken homes. Some had only one parent who worked late into the evening and couldn't afford daycare or babysitting. Some had no parents to speak of, and their grandparents were getting too old to care for them twenty-four hours a day. Some were struggling in school and were in dire need of a helping hand. A few aimlessly walked the streets without any idea of where they were supposed to go or who their family was. Those kids without homes were going to foster care or to an orphanage at some point, but they still needed to socialize with other kids their age, which is where we came in. After story time, we did some arts and crafts, then Mrs. Wilkinson sat down in a big comfy chair and read from the Bible. Amayah snuggled in close to me, and I held her as we watched the children's eyes widen as Mrs. Wilkinson told of Jesus performing miracles and God rescuing true believers from terrible fates.

When Mrs. Wilkinson put down the book, she asked if any of the children had ever seen God or Jesus. She mainly got blank stares and a few solemn head shakes. "How about an angel?" she asked. "Have you seen an angel before?" One boy asked what they looked like, and Mrs. Wilkinson smiled. "Why, that's the thing, Jeremiah, angels can look like anyone, even you and me! I believe there are angels among us, sent down from Heaven to help us when we've lost our way, when life gets too harsh, and when we feel like we can't go on anymore. Has anyone ever felt that way?"

Now she got a few nods and murmurs of agreement, and a little dark-skinned girl raised her hand.

"Yes, Isabel?" Mrs. Wilkinson said.

The little girl spoke halting English and grew frustrated when she couldn't find the words until Amayah took her hand and spoke Spanish. Her face lit up, and she started talking rapidly, with Amayah making her pause for air every couple of sentences so she could translate for the rest of us.

"Isabel says that her great-grandmother said that her own grandmother told her about seeing an angel when she was very young. I'm sorry, two angels," Amayah explained.

The other children were positively buzzing at the idea that a story was forthcoming about real angels. I saw them leaning in as Isabel described it, and Amayah translated.

"Isabel says that her great-grandmother told her the story before bed one night. That she and her husband and their children were running away from home because they were being treated badly. They had to go in a wagon," Amayah paused to listen to Isabel, then smiled wryly. "They had to go in a wagon because they didn't have a Ford or a Chevy."

Mrs. Wilkinson and I both chuckled at that little detail.

"They rode many miles in the wagon, but they were chased by banditos, um, men who tried to rob them. When the men tried to make them give up, an angel descended from the sky and drove the bad men away. The angel could fly through the air and shoot light from his hands ..."

Amayah trailed off and cut me a look of stunned disbelief. Isabel kept talking, but Amayah stopped speaking for several long seconds. Realizing that the children were staring at her, she focused back on the little girl.

"Sorry, the angel drove the bad men away. He was married to another angel, a beautiful girl, and the two of them guided Isabel's ancestor the rest of the way on their journey before they disappeared forever."

I was trying not to let my jaw hang slack as Isabel's story sparked fresh memories in my mind. There was no doubt that the story was true, nor was it much of a stretch to imagine who those "angels" were.

Amayah had to make sure. "Isabel, la abuela de su abuela, que nombre es?"

"Cecilia," the little girl replied, and Amayah made a sound halfway between a laugh and a cry, hugging her tightly and throwing me a wink.

Hours later, when the two of us finally had time alone, she squeezed my hand warmly. "Wasn't that incredible, Ro? I'm telling you, us being here is Divine Intervention... there's no other way to explain it."

Again, I wasn't as well-versed in Christianity as Amayah, so I was constantly playing catch up.

"Divine... what? What do you mean?"

She smiled broadly at me again. "It means that it's our destiny to be here, just like it was our destiny to be in Mississippi in 1854. God has a plan for us, especially for you and your marvelous powers. Isabel's story is a sure sign of it. We need to be paying attention, so we'll know what to do when the time comes."

She sounded so confident and sure, which was the complete opposite of how I felt. I hadn't used my powers since arriving in 1980 and hadn't thought about getting home for a few days, wondering why I didn't, but I already knew the truth. I was happy here. I had a job, a place to live, no one was telling me what to do, and the most beautiful girl in the world was by my side. I had to admit to myself that I wasn't so sure what 1997 could offer me that was better than what I had going on right now. I didn't voice that out loud to Amayah, so I just nodded along with her explanation. She smiled and snuggled into my arms as we discussed how we might find out where our parents were. It seemed like a hopeless idea. Even if we scouted the neighborhoods where the "future-we" lived in now, neither of us knew how long our parents had been residents there. And what would we say if we did bump into them? "Hi, we're future versions of your children. Can we help you somehow?" Amayah was convinced that was our purpose here, but I wasn't so sure.

We stayed so busy at the shelter that I was able to go for hours without thinking or talking about the quest to find our younger parents. About a week into our work, Mrs. Wilkinson gave us both Friday night off, so I took Amayah to see "The Empire Strikes Back" at the local theater. Of course, I had seen it a dozen times growing up, but it was still a blast to see it with an audience that had no idea what was coming next. When Vader told Luke the truth about his parentage, the place went absolutely bonkers.

As we got more comfortable at the shelter, I got to know another male counselor who worked there. His name was Nathan Gils, a diminutive white guy with a crazy comb-over hairstyle. His dad was a lieutenant in the Army, and Nathan liked calling himself "The Big General" and telling the boys at the shelter that they were all soldiers in his army. I realized that it didn't really matter what decade you were in, little boys loved playing Army and Police Officer and anything else that allowed them to dress up, shout orders, and pretend to shoot one another with imaginary guns. Nathan got a huge kick out of having them line up and present the colors of the flag (an old Partridge Family blanket), but he got more than he bargained for when one of our youngest residents joined the group. His name was Tommy, and he had a speech impediment that manifested when he got too excited, as he often did when The Big General started barking orders. As a result, Tommy tried to say "Hello, Big General'' one day and instead shouted, "Hello, Bobo!" The other boys thought it was the funniest thing they had ever heard, but in that moment, The Big General was gone, and Bobo was born. He took it in stride, because as long as the kids were happy and smiling, we felt like we were doing our jobs. He started hanging around more often, which was fine, as I wasn't supposed to be fraternizing with Amayah after hours.

After our craziness in 1854, I had settled into a more comfortable routine here in laid-back 1980. I wanted to continue some of the discipline training I had been working on before, inspired by the unrivaled one. Bruce Lee. After cashing my second paycheck, I went down the block to a drug store to pick up a few things, including a pen and pad for writing and a small photo of Bruce Lee himself with the moniker 'The Dragon' that I had seen there a few days before.

Every night before bed, I would tilt the photo of Bruce, The Dragon, so I could see it properly while going through my water exercises, imagining myself as formless and shapeless, like water, and becoming the shape of what I occupied. I touched very lightly at my power when I did these exercises, to enhance my potential and feel the flow of energy through me. It was a great feeling, and it reminded me of what I was capable of, even if I wasn't currently using those abilities. About halfway through my routine, Bobo walked by my open door, did a double take, and circled back around. Stepping a couple of feet inside the door frame, but not saying anything, Bobo watched my movements and glanced at the photo I used as my center.

I paused after a couple of minutes and smiled slightly in his direction.

"Wow, Rohan, that was really bad ass, man. I had no idea you were a karate guy," he said. "Do you think you could teach me to move like that? I bet you know how to kick some major butt in a fight!"

Well, he wasn't wrong, but bragging about my powers was not a good idea, even if I was living in a different era than my own.

"What I was doing is called 'being water,'" I explained. "It's a technique taught by the late, great Bruce Lee..." I paused for a long minute, unsure whether Bruce Lee was alive in 1980.

"Oh sure, the martial arts guy," Bobo said with an appreciative nod. "My dad took me to see Enter the Dragon a couple of times one summer. But what do you mean about being the water?"

I sat in the wooden chair in my room and invited Bobo to sit on my bed.

"It means a lot of things. Bruce was kind of a complex guy, and knew many different forms of martial arts, but for me, it's about being flexible with both your mind and your body," I said. "Water can be still, or it can be full of rage. It can move from one position to another effortlessly and might never take the same shape twice. For me, it means that I should live my life in a fluid frame of mind. I'm largely peaceful and serene, like a still lake, but if there is just cause for me to be upset, I can shift and take a new form immediately. I can channel my energy into defending myself, my friends, or my ideas, but I'm not going to turn into a monster. I'm still me. I know what my limits are, just like water loses its power when it's spread too thin."

Bobo's eyes had considerably widened as I waxed poetic about the mantra. "So wise for one so young," he said quietly, almost to himself.

"Huh? I think we're probably about the same age, Bobo," I replied.

"I guess you're right," he said with an odd half-smile. "So, can you show me how to use my water hands and water feet to kick some ass the next time those jerks from two streets over try to shake me down on my way to work?"

I hadn't ventured outside far enough to know who he might be talking about, so I slightly changed the subject.

"It's not about how hard you punch or kick though, Bobo," I said. "It's about what's in your heart. If you stand up to people who are doing the wrong thing, you've already won. Even if you lose the fight, you're doing what you know is right. Eventually, you'll come to a solution to your problem if you stay true to your beliefs."

"I like that idea, but I'm unsure how it will keep me from getting beaten up. Telling a bunch of mouth-breathing thugs that I'm doing the right thing by getting my face pounded in isn't going to feel so good in the morning," Nathan said with a smile.

"I know that. There's also the idea of picking your battles. Running away from a fight doesn't make you a coward. If you see someone getting robbed by eight thugs, you shouldn't go up and tell them to stop or you'll kick all their butts... that's just going to get you a whooping. But if you go to a payphone and call the cops, you're doing what's right, even if you risk getting caught up in the violence, you know..." I didn't say any more, hoping he could draw out the connection on his own.

He took a long moment to think before responding.

"We moved a lot during my childhood, what with my dad being in the Army and all. He was highly ranked, and didn't have to go to Vietnam, thank God, but he was still expendable enough that every phone call we got put us all on pins and needles that it was another transfer. I've lived twice in Tennessee, on different bases, once for a long spell in San Antonio, Texas, and another time in North Carolina. They're all nice places, except that when you live in an Army base, you don't see many nice places. And bases are the worst when it comes to fitting in.

"Everyone has their cliques and their social circles, and you're the new kid every single time.

"Whenever I was scared of the first day at a new school, scared to walk past the bully of the base, or had to start packing my bags again, my mom would get out the Bible and read to me, or encourage me to read it for myself when I got a little older. There were a few passages that really soothed my nerves. I turned them into part of my nightly prayer routine. Do you pray every night, Rohan? Most people don't. They're either too tired or want to watch TV or are trying to find someone to take home from the bar. Not me though... praying before bed is the only way I can relax and let go of all the stress and anxiety that builds up in me all day. It probably sounds corny, but when I go to bed, I want to unburden everything that's worrying me, so in case I die in my sleep, God will already know what's in my heart when I reach the pearly gates."

I had seriously underestimated what Bobo was about. He came across as a slightly chubby and meek nerd who had probably been ignored or overlooked for most of his life, unless a bully was looking to make an example of him. His faith in God reminded me a lot of Amayah's, and for all my powers and abilities, I was envious of his confidence in that faith right now.

"I'll make you a deal, buddy. You start teaching me more about faith, and I'll teach you more about fighting. How's that sound?"

He broke into a wide grin that completely lit up his face and made him seem like a totally different person.

"That sounds amazing, Rohan. Let's start tonight. God's always ready to get and give some love."

He raced to his room and returned with a well-worn Bible, then sat next to me on the bed, flipping tirelessly through the pages. I waited, and then waited some more, waiting for him to start.

"Here's a great one to start with. Matthew 21:22, 'And whatever you ask for in prayer, you will receive, if you have faith."

"That seems really simple, but that can't possibly be true," I said.

"Why not?" Bobo asked back with a knowing smile.

"If I pray to God for a new Corvette and tickets behind home plate for tomorrow night's Yankees-Orioles game, they aren't going to just show up on the sidewalk outside tomorrow morning, that's why," I replied.

"Ahhh, but you're thinking about it all wrong!" he said. "First and foremost, you don't have faith. You've already said it can't happen, which by definition means that you're doubting God's ability to do it. That, by definition, is the opposite of faith—it's doubt.

"Second, you're treating God and prayer like a magic lamp with a genie inside. God isn't a DJ taking requests. He's asking you to look inside yourself and decide what's important to you—and then pray for the power to receive it! Most people pray when they're so desperate that they think there's no other hope. Or when they think nothing else can help them. They pray when they get bad medical news. They pray when they think they're about to get fired. They pray that the team they bet on will win the Super Bowl. God's going to listen to whatever you say, but he's going to look into your soul to determine what you need. And what you think you need might not be what God thinks you need!"

Well, that was about as transparent as mud, and I told Bobo as much. He laughed and said sagely, "Like Ma always told me, all will become clear in time."

He flipped the pages to 2 Corinthians 5:7, "For we walk by faith, not by sight."

He turned to me. "This is a big one for me when I go somewhere new. So many times, I've popped up in a new spot where I didn't know anyone except for my mom and dad. Praying over this line at night, realizing that I can be the same Nathan with the same faith in God, regardless of where I live is really, really calming. I can't tell you how many nights I've warded off insomnia with this prayer."

I liked that one a lot more, mainly since I was a time-traveling, super-powered vigilante, who was only a few miles from home, but about 17 years too early to know anyone there. It also reminded me of being *like water*. I marked the verse down to save for later.

"One more for tonight, I think," Bobo said. "From Jeremiah 10:13,

'When He utters His voice, there is a tumult of waters in the heavens, and He causes the clouds to ascend from the end of the earth; He makes lightning for the rain and brings out the wind from His storehouses.'"

Bobo was quiet after that. "This one kind of goes back to what we were saying about bullies and tough guys. They might be able to rob me today, but their power is nothing compared to God's power. A jerk with a switchblade can scare you for a few minutes, but God's voice is powerful enough to bring the rain, break the tide, and even level mountains! That pumps me up. It makes me feel like when I hear God's voice in my head, I can face anything."

I didn't believe it was a coincidence that Bobo had brought up hearing the voice of God in his head. I had to ask him...

Suddenly, I thought of when Steven Stone heard about Nick the Brute and barely blinked an eye. But something was off about Steven, as my trip into his mind showed. I didn't know what it was, but even if he hadn't been so inappropriate with Amayah, I don't think I would have shared any more secrets with him.

"Hey Bobo?"

"Yeah?"

"Have you, uh, have you heard the voice of God in your head?" I asked.

He turned and smiled serenely at me.

"Absolutely, brother. I'd like to think I hear it every day. I mean, it's not like Charlton Heston in "The Ten Commandments," but it's definitely a special connection. Sometimes it's just a feeling, or an image, or the knowledge that things are ultimately going to be alright when something isn't going my way. It's a constant comfort, and I count my blessings every time I feel it."

I nodded slowly. That wasn't exactly what I had been hoping to hear.

"What about you, Rohan? Have you heard God talking to you?"

"Uh, well, I don't really know. It's complicated. I don't want you to think I'm a psychopath."

He smiled, "You seem pretty normal to me, Rohan, let's hear it."

I really thought about clamming up, but I had to give it a shot.

"Well, I've been hearing two voices in my head for a while now. One is um, ugly, I guess. Cruel. Always telling me to do things that are sort of selfish, but also things that I sort of want for myself, so it's not always a bad thing.

"The voice is, uh, I guess, angry a lot. Like it's focusing my frustration at certain things that I want, but sometimes can't have."

I was half-expecting him to start running for the door or laughing in my face, but he wasn't doing either. He was watching me patiently.

"And the other voice?" Nathan prompted.

"It's a female," I said, realizing how stupid it must have all sounded to hear out loud. "Um, she says that she's the light and that she's blessed me with tremendous gifts. She tells me to be careful of voices that I hear, but I'm not really sure who to believe. Sure, the male voice is rougher, but ever since I started hearing it, I've accomplished things that have eluded me for a long time. Whenever I try to talk to the female voice, she doesn't respond. And yes, I realize that I sound totally crazy right now."

I didn't really want to look at Bobo after revealing all that, but when I did, I saw nothing but concern in his eyes.

"It sounds like you're under a lot of stress, Rohan. Thanks for being open with me, I'm sure it wasn't easy. And I don't think you're crazy. I think you're brave, and I believe that you're special. Hearing voices in your head is something that dates back to the earliest days of humanity. Jesus heard voices in his head, like his Heavenly Father trying to guide him and the Devil trying to tempt him. I can't promise you that God and Satan are battling in your head for your soul, but clearly, you're destined for something great."

I was eternally grateful that he didn't think I was crazy. He put his hand on my arm and squeezed it in silent support. It wasn't the explanation I had been hoping for, but it was enough for now. I wasn't insane and destined for Bellevue Hospital. That was a feather in my cap for all this. I smiled and nodded, telling him that he had given me a lot to think about.

It felt good to have a friend, even one who seemed a little scatter-brained most of the time. I took a hot shower, said my prayers as Amayah had been teaching me, adding in the ones that Bobo shared, and then went to bed, daring to dream good dreams and hopeful for the happy beginnings that tomorrow might bring.

CHAPTER

TWENTY-ONE

I wasn't the only one making a new friend at the shelter. Mrs. Wilkinson had also just hired a girl named Brittney. Like Amayah and I, she was a natural with the kids. But she was also hiding something from her employer. Amayah figured it out about four days after Brittney arrived.

She had frizzy strawberry blonde hair and blue eyes. She favored leg warmers and baggy sweatshirts, which was weird, considering how hot it was outside, but perhaps it was just the fashion of the day. I had no idea, since I could barely tell you what the fashion of my day was, given my years of not caring about the latest trends. Brittney seemed to gravitate towards the children who were the quietest and spent a lot of time by themselves. She took the empty room next to Amayah.

Ama and I ate a quiet lunch while the kids played outside on the playground, at which point she relayed to me in confidence what had occurred the night before when she was with Brittney.

"I was going to invite her to come get some ice cream with me, you know, just something friendly to break the ice, but when I walked into her room, she spun around and seemed like she was hiding something," Amayah told me.

"She had her shirt up and her pants hanging low, and then she pulled them back up really fast. I didn't really know what was going on until I went to the bathroom and saw the syringe."

Amayah might have been the sweetest girl in the world, but she had still grown up in a rough neighborhood, and knew the signs of drug users and their bad habits. Brittney got over her initial panic and the two went down to the commissary for a scoop of ice cream. Both were guarded when talking about their families, for different reasons, until Amayah opened up about how she and I were dating (my heart skipped a beat, hearing her say it) against her parents' wishes.

That confession was just what Brittney needed. "I'm here doing community service for a drug charge," she told Amayah as she licked her spoon for the last few drips of chocolate ice cream. "I love kids, and I'd like to be a teacher someday, but I have to work off a hundred hours of community service before they wipe this off my record."

Amayah admitted that she almost hadn't said anything about what she saw in Brittney's room, but felt that God was guiding her to this place.

"I told her that it sounded like a terrible burden to have an addiction, especially one that doesn't go away," Amayah told me. It was a brilliant strategy. She didn't accuse Brittney, just made a matter-of-fact statement that the other girl could take as she wanted.

"After a few more minutes of conversation, she admitted that she was still addicted and using, having brought a supply with her. And she's exploring her options around the neighborhood to score more. She was a Staten Island girl, so Jersey might as well have been another country, but she knew that if she kept looking, it wouldn't take long to find some."

Amayah had kept quiet, knowing that being a good friend often meant being a good listener, rather than trying to tell someone how to solve their problems. The silence stretched out between them, but then Amayah brought me up.

"Rohan doesn't look like the angry type, but he got into a few fights before we started getting closer," she told Brittney. "When we started sharing thoughts and feelings with each other, he told me that he didn't want to fight, and that he didn't even feel like himself when he was fighting. I told him that he could lean on me for support, and he has. In fact, he hasn't been in a useless fight since then."

As she relayed the story to me, I realized that she was right. I teleported away from the wayward gang in her neighborhood, and had used my wits, rather than my fists, to help us navigate through the Oxford time leap. I was impressed that Amayah had noticed all that while we were on the run, fearful for our lives.

"Anyway," Amayah told Brittney, "maybe that's something you and I can work on together. When you feel like you need a fix, you can come find me, and we can talk about how you're feeling and what's making you want the drugs. I don't know if what I say will help, but maybe taking that little pause, looking for a friend to talk to, or doing something constructive will help you fight off the cravings."

Brittney eyed her suspiciously, but Amayah kept quiet. "What are we going to talk about instead of me taking a hit?"

Amayah shrugged her shoulders. "Whatever sounds good that day. Music, clothes, movies, future plans," she said earnestly, before arching an eyebrow. "Cute boys."

Brittney grinned back at that. "Oh my god, did you see Harrison Ford in the new *Star Wars* movie? When Princess Leia says she loves him, and he responds back with..."

"I know!" Amayah finished, and then blushed, remembering who was listening to her recounted story. "I mean, he's way too old for me, but still ..."

Her blush made her even more beautiful, and I told her as much.

"Annnnnnywayyyy," Ama said dramatically. "Getting back to

Brittney, when we went back to hang out in my room, she spotted my Bible and asked me about my faith, so I shared some stuff with her. I thought maybe the three of us could have a Bible study some night. Invite Nathan too." It took me a minute to realize she meant Bobo.

"That's cool, but you know, if you want me to, I can probably use my power to cure Brittney of her addiction or at least repair whatever damage the heroin has caused her."

Amayah responded with a half-smile. "That's nice of you to offer, Ro, and I thought of that too, but think about what might happen after we leave."

I almost stuck my foot in my mouth and asked, "Leave for where?"

"When we're back to our own time and the cravings hit her again, she won't have you around to heal her back up. Your powers are amazing, don't get me wrong! But I think this might be something that God wants me to do in a different way." She squeezed my hand reassuringly.

The next night, the three of us had an hour-long Bible study punctuated by lots of jokes and laughter. Near the end, Brittney said she would call her mom and talk to her for the first time in three weeks.

The two bid me goodnight as I returned to my room, feeling it had been a good night. I began working on two writing projects in my journal, one for Amayah and one primarily for me. I was completely lost in thought, so I didn't even notice the soft knock on my door until it became more persistent. I opened it to find Amayah looking at me with tears, though I had no idea why.

"Hey!" I said in surprise. "What are you doing here after curfew? I don't want us getting in trouble with Mrs. Wilkinson!"

She closed the door quietly and glared at me. "Really, Rohan? In trouble with Mrs. Wilkinson? You're a time traveler with comic book superpowers, and you're worried about the wrath of a forty-five-year-old charity mom?"

Her tone surprised me, but she did have a point.

"I guess you're right there, but Ama, why are you crying? Is everything okay?" I went to wrap my arms around her, but she put up a hand and stopped me cold.

"What's wrong, Rohan? You have to ask that? I just sat there listening to Brittney and her mom make up on the phone and tell each other how much they love each other. I miss my mom and dad so much, Rohan! I miss my family and my friends and school and the hospital and my whole life! I feel like you don't even want to go back to our time anymore, and you don't seem like you want to go find our parents either!"

My jaw dropped open, but I had nothing to say. She was right. I was perfectly happy in 1980 New York, and if she never mentioned our parents or 1997 again, I don't think I would have either. I still had some guilty feelings about what my parents might be thinking or doing right now, but whenever those feelings started to well up, I just pictured Amayah dancing close to me, and that kiss at the dance. Nothing else seemed to matter. My parents were always so damn busy with work anyway. I liked to tell myself that they had probably already forgotten about me... one less mouth to feed.

"I ... Yeah, I guess you're right. I'm happy here. I'm happy with you and working with the kids. My parents and I didn't get along so great most of the time, and if I go back home, they'll limit my freedoms all over again. Besides, didn't you say that your parents wouldn't let you date me anyway? If we go home, we might not be able to see each other outside of school."

I didn't want to say it like that, because that was my fear, not hers, but she had backed me into a corner, and I could feel all my doubts and worries about the future pushing back.

She glared at me with real anger in her eyes. "How dare you try and make me choose, Rohan Chang! How selfish can you be!? You think God gave you these incredible powers so you could heal a few people and then retire to 1980 New Jersey?"

That stung. Hell, it did more than sting. It was like she had slapped me across the face. I knew that I was being selfish and greedy with Amayah. I knew she had a bigger life than me, but I was hoping that our bizarre circumstances would make me the center of her universe, just as she was the center of mine. In the course of two minutes, I had gone from being totally confident in our relationship to not knowing what to say next. It felt like a time for damage control, but a small, terrible part of me—possibly Nick the Brute still lurking in my subconscious—reminded me that it wasn't like she could run off and never talk to me again. I was the only way she was making it back to 1997.

I hated thinking that way, even though it did give me some small measure of comfort. However, I didn't want Amayah to be indebted to me; I wanted to make her happy. So I said what I should have been saying for weeks.

"I'm sorry, Ama. I've been selfish. When we're done tomorrow, let's go start walking the streets and find your mom and dad."

She didn't smile. She also didn't throw her arms around me and declare me her savior. But her face softened a little bit, at least for a moment.

She looked past me to my desk and the journal laying open. She squinted at the paper, and I moved to block her view, remembering what I had been writing.

"Oh, that's not anything, don't worry about that."

But Amayah stormed past me, snatching the journal from the desk, her finger tracing down the lines of notes ...

WORLD SERIES

    1980 - ?

    1981 - Dodgers

    1982 - ?

    1983 - ?

    1984 - Tigers

    1986 - Mets

1989 - A's
1992-93 - Blue Jays
1994 - Strike
1995 - Braves
1996 - Yankees

SUPER BOWL
1987, 1991 - Giants
1993, 1996 - Cowboys

HOCKEY
1994 - Rangers

SHE HELD it up and looked at me quizzically. "Sports trivia, Rohan? I know you love the Yankees, but what is this? And why don't you want me to see it?"

I was the one blushing now, but this time out of embarrassment. I really didn't want to tell her what I was doing, but I couldn't think of a cover story, and I had vowed that I would never lie to her.

"Um, well, if we were going to be staying in this time frame permanently, I thought about making some money on the Super Bowl and the World Series, since I already know who's going to win," I said, avoiding eye contact. "You know, we could make tons of money and maybe buy a place to live or something."

When she didn't say anything, I risked a glance up at her face and immediately wished that I hadn't. She was livid. I could see it in her eyes.

"Selfish," she said in a scalding whisper. "You are being so selfish right now. Using knowledge of what's to come to make money gambling? Did you listen to anything at the Bible study? Honestly Rohan, where is your head at? You stood up to those monsters in

Mississippi because it was the right thing to do. Does this seem right to you?

"Because if it does... well I'm not sure what that means for us, but I want no part of whatever it is you think you're doing right now."

"I thought it was the best thing to do: make money for us to be stable. But I don't have to do it if you really don't want me to. And if I don't gamble, you'll care about me again?"

She walked to the door and turned sharply on her heel to face me.

"I've always cared about you, Rohan. But this isn't who you are." She opened the door and stalked out without another word as the door swung shut behind her.

I looked at the cold door, then the barren wall, and then back at the door again.

CHAPTER

TWENTY-TWO

I spent the whole night fighting the urge to run to Amayah's room to relieve my drowning pain, not caused by a physical ailment but more by an eternal aching. I knew she didn't want to see me and that I needed to give her space, but it was one of the hardest nights of my life. I had that feeling you get in the pit of your stomach when you've really messed up, and you know things might get worse before they get better, if they ever do. I hated the fact that I had hurt her, even though I hadn't exactly lied to her, but I wasn't doing what I said I would when we first arrived in this version of New York City. Our time in 1854 Mississippi was both harrowing and exciting, and since it was just the two of us surrounded by strangers, it felt like we were meant to be together all the time. Clearly, Amayah didn't feel the same way. She was longing for her family and school and her friends and all the rest.

When I finally fell asleep, my body greedily rested for about an hour when suddenly a barking dog woke me up. I was so completely out of it that I forgot what had happened a few hours before, and I had that blissful sense of not being aware of anything for a moment before I remembered Amayah's face, her tears, and her harsh tone. I

338

was terrified that she would avoid me in the morning, or that she would just be gone. Maybe she stormed off in the middle of the night, sick of me and my bullshit. Maybe she decided to search for the younger versions of her parents by herself. Maybe something bad had happened to her, and she was lying in a hospital bed, robbed and hurt. My stomach lurched, and I felt like punching myself in the head for being so stupid. Somewhere along the way, I had confused possession for love, and started thinking that Amayah was mine, and that I needed to keep it that way by keeping us in the past. The clock read 1:39 a.m. I doubted that I would be able to go back to sleep, but I tried anyway, as the alternative was sitting there hating myself. I clenched my hands into fists and pulled the covers up over my face to make it as dark as possible. That's when I heard the voice that always seemed to slide into my mind when anger and fear were ruling my thoughts.

"YOU FUCKING COWARD!" the Brute practically bellowed in my ear.

I jerked upright in bed, half-expecting some specter of my tormentor standing at the foot of my bed. Of course, I was alone. That was one of the bad things about hearing voices in your head. They would never show their faces and convince you that you weren't actually crazy.

"You can have anything you want. Anything at all. And yet you still limit yourself to the words and whims of that LITTLE BITCH! When are you going to cast aside these shackles you put on yourself and embrace who you truly are?"

I knew that I was in dangerous territory because his insult to Amayah didn't immediately cause me to lash out and silence him. Of course, I didn't think that way about her, and could never think that about her. But I didn't feel like I deserved such an angry response from her, either. If we ended up stuck in 1980, it was going to be hard to scrape by on the meager earnings we were pulling in working for the shelter. Neither of us had money saved up for college, nor did we have real driver's licenses or social security cards. Finding real work or getting into a school without those things would be impossible. If I were to save money all year and put it on the Phillies to win the World Series, like I knew they were going to, I could win us tens of thousands of dollars and start building a nest egg for a more comfortable lifestyle. I knew that she didn't want to stay here and that gambling was against her religious beliefs, but I thought she would have understood when she realized why I was doing it.

The Brute took my silence as an agreement and pushed forward. *"USE YOUR POWERS THE RIGHT WAY, BOY! Take what you need, take what you want. If you want her, you have the power to make her yours. You can call to her right now, bring her to your bed, and she'll obey your every command! You can go anywhere, command anyone, and they'll do your bidding. Just unleash me. Let me be your servant, and I promise you this world will tremble at our approach."*

It was tempting, to say the least. I couldn't deny that. Being intimate with Amayah was on my mind more and more. I felt that a more alpha male like Steven Stone would already have slept with her because he said it was so easy for him. I wasn't sure I'd ever stop being mad at the sight of them dancing together at the festival, even though Amayah had patiently explained that it was me she really wanted to dance with. Not to mention that, as much as I enjoyed working with the kids, I could work here for 10 years at my current salary and not be able to afford even a tiny room anywhere in the Five Boroughs. Why should someone with my abilities have to live in poverty like this? Could I just try out the Brute's method for a day or two? Just to see what it looked like? I wouldn't do anything inherently bad, of course, but I could at least see what was possible.

To be honest, I didn't understand what was so wrong with gambling anyway, especially since it wasn't really gambling. I knew the Phillies were going to beat the Royals because my brother's favorite player growing up was George Brett, the Kansas City third baseman. Before Henry went off to college and got all serious about everything, we would play baseball at the park with him pretending to be George Brett and me playing the role of Ron Guidry or Dave

Righetti. Brett was the star of the Royals in the 1980s, and Henry had told me about 500 times how close he came to batting .400 in 1980, finishing at .390 for the season. He and the Royals came up short in the World Series, which stuck with me because I used to make fun of him when he would go on and on about Brett always kicking the Yankees' butt.

"Henry!" I cried out. "Goose Gossage will strike Brett out and kick your butt!"

Baseball might have saved me from doing something stupid, because I was so locked into my memories of discussions and fictional hitter-pitcher confrontations with Henry that I tuned the Brute out entirely. When he started talking again about getting everything I wanted, I thought of Henry and I agreeing as kids to someday make it to Yankee Stadium. I didn't necessarily miss my brother at that moment, but I definitely felt a longing for him, for home, and for the chance to honor that promise. Even as the Brute tried to gain more purchase in my mind and soul, I closed that path off and pushed him back down. I reminded myself that being respectful and transparent were the reasons Amayah had warmed up to me and that the experiences we shared were leading us to a bright future together. That meant being a meaningful part of each other's lives for a long time, not for the span of a few sweaty minutes in bed together.

Suddenly motivated, I got up and returned to my desk, getting out the journal and turning to the other section I was working on. I glanced at the clock; it was nearly 2:30 a.m., but I was wide awake and felt that I could write until I fell asleep or was finished.

I finished the writing assignment about an hour later. Once I focused on making things right with Amayah and thought of how blessed I was to be around her, the words flowed from the pen, although I did a few more drafts to ensure I got it right.

I slept for about three hours, which was more than I had expected after the terrible night before. I got up, said my morning prayers, and went down for breakfast. I greeted Amayah like it was any other day, and did the same for Mrs. Wilkinson, Bobo, and Brittney.

Amayah returned the greeting, and I could feel her eyes on me as I ate breakfast. I was friendly with everyone and tried to act as genuine and normal as I could. I screwed up, and I was going to be better. I didn't want to grovel or beg for her forgiveness. Actions spoke far louder than words, in my mind.

I focused on engaging with the kids throughout the day and gave my all to each interaction. I realized that I had been slacking off in that department too, just going through the motions of asking them about their days, but hadn't been asking about their hopes, their dreams, and their fears. When things started to wind down with my responsibilities, I retreated to my room and packed a bag of snacks, a Thermos of water, extra layers of clothes, and all the money I had on hand, along with a map of the Five Boroughs. Once the kids went to dinner, and after they got ready for bed, I walked to Amayah's room and knocked lightly on the door.

She didn't answer. I knocked again, and then a third time, and a fourth. I called through the door, saying that I was sorry and was ready to go and look for her parents, but she still didn't answer. This wasn't fair. In fact, it was complete and utter bullshit. I didn't want to be mad at her, but how many times had I saved her life, and now she couldn't even talk to me face to face? I pounded on the door one last time and then barked, "I'm sorry, I guess I'll go find your parents on a Friday night on my own so we can get the hell out of here!" Still nothing, so I stomped off, out of the building, and blindly walked toward Manhattan with no real clue as to where I was going or what I would do when I got there.

I took the bus to Fifth Avenue, but somehow ended up in Brooklyn, someplace on Flatbush Ave. After dozing off on the bus, lost in dreaming of Ama's loving embrace, I awoke haphazardly and stomped around, looking for some way to take out my rage, but failing miserably. It wasn't supposed to be like this! I had worked my ass off to get everything ready for the weekend trip to find Amayah's parents and her stubbornness was ruining it. It was hot for mid-May, and after an hour or two of being angry, I ducked into a sports bar to drown my sorrows in cheeseburgers and a milkshake. There were only a few other people at the bar, most of whom looked like drunks or degenerate gamblers, the only people at this particular establishment on a Friday evening without the Yankees or college football on the TV. As I waited for someone to take my order, I stared at the TV as a cheesy NBA logo came up on the screen. It was followed by a youthful Brent Musberger, the NBA's leading announcer on CBS, who was touting the afternoon's events. I got up and walked closer to the images of Dr. J, Magic Johnson, and Kareem Abdul-Jabbar getting to the arena in Philadelphia. Abdul-Jabbar was on crutches, meaning that this was the legendary Game 6 of that year's Finals, the game where Magic Johnson went from upstart to unquestionable superstar.

The bartender was watching the pregame and turned his attention to one of the older men sitting quietly at the bar nursing a short glass. "What do you think, Lou? Got much action on today's game?"

Lou, who looked and smelled like he either lived in this bar or in an ashtray, responded with a hacking cough and a laugh that made me recoil. He was wearing a green fedora that might have been in style thirty years earlier and a cheap suit jacket to match.

"All on the Sixers," Lou responded in that awful raspy voice. "With Kareem out, nobody thinks L.A. has a chance. Everyone figures they'll hold him out and take their medicine in Game Six, then dope him up on painkillers for Game Seven and try to nurse him through it."

Brent Musberger was saying pretty much exactly that, and the bartender was agreeing with both of them. However, I knew better. In fact, I knew exactly what was going to happen this afternoon, and if Lou was the kind of professional I thought he was, I was about to have the opportunity of a lifetime. I cleared my throat, but neither of them noticed, so I said, "Um, excuse me?" and cleared my throat again.

The bartender turned around, chewing his gum rather urgently, giving me a look up and down. "Scram, kid, you're not old enough for a drink unless it's ice water."

That drew a laugh from the few other men sitting on the stools, but I pushed on. "No, I don't want a drink, I was going to say that you're both wrong about the game. The Lakers are going to win this thing easy."

That got everyone's attention, especially Lou, who swiveled on his stool and gave me the kind of shit-eating grin you would expect a seasoned bookie to have for a teenage kid with a loud mouth.

"That right, kid? A blowout, huh? That why the spread is Philly by eight?"

"With all due respect sir, but yes, that's right. Philly isn't going to know what to do with Magic at center. He's going to rip them apart. There won't be a Game Seven."

The bartender shook his head as Lou growled in that raspy voice again. "I admire your tenacity, kid, but you don't know what the hell you're talking about. I'd let you put your money where your mouth is, but you're too young to be gambling and probably don't got a buck in your pocket." He turned back to his drink and the game.

I figured that would be his response.

"Oh, I'm sorry. How old do I need to be to place an *illegal* bet? If you don't know the answer, I think I saw a cop outside down the block. I can go ask him how old I need to be to place an illegal bet with my new friend. Lou, right? With my new friend, Lou."

Lou smiled, but it was the grin of a shark smelling blood in the water. The rest of the bar was watching closely now, seemingly yearning for a good show.

He looked at me for a long moment and then gave a little snort. "Okay kid, let's put your money where that fat mouth is, assuming you've got enough from your paper route to afford a real man's bet."

Lou chuckled and said, "76ers are an eight-point favorite. If you can put down one hundred dollars on L.A. and they cover, I'll give you $250. If they win outright, you get five hundred dollars. But if the

76ers cover, I keep your money, and I get to slap that smart-ass face of yours."

Whistles and a catcall from down the bar followed the offer. Lou was throwing his weight around and his minions ate it up, especially the bartender, who wore the biggest shit-eating grin of all.

Fortunately, I had history on my side of things. At least, I hoped so. I opened my backpack and took out my envelope stuffed with cash. I made a display of counting it out on the bar as everyone watched me. It was still a small crowd, but it seemed to be growing as Lou and I traded barbs and insults.

I held it all up for them to see. "I've got $380 to spend," I said. "And I don't want any points, Lou. In fact, I'm gonna give you a whole dozen. Lakers win by at least thirteen points tonight. I guarantee it."

Lou laughed first, but the others soon joined him. I waited for them to shut up, which was no small feat, before I continued.

"Lakers win by at least thirteen, means I win five thousand," I said, and I saw Lou's eyes flash with a hint of warning. "But see Lou, here's the thing, I want more than that. I want a lot more than that. So, I'm going to sweeten the deal for you. Lakers win by at least thirteen, and my boy Magic scores forty plus against the 76ers' mismatched defense. I hit both of those, and you owe me fifteen thousand. If you take the bet, and I don't hit on both, you keep my money, and every guy in here gets to punch me right in my slant-eyed, cocky-ass bitch of a face. Ball's in your court, Lou." I winked, gave him a fake smile that never reached my eyes, and shrugged innocently, taunting him.

You could tell he was shaken, and wondering if I had recently escaped from a mental institution. Magic was a great player, but not a great scorer. The 76ers were playing at home against a team without Kareem. It seemed like a lock, and he knew it, making him suspicious.

Fortunately, I figured that he'd rather be wrong than look soft in front of his lackeys. The king couldn't be made to look like a jester.

He said in a silky soft voice, "Okay kid, you got yourself a deal. Come sit at the bar and eat your dinner, and we'll watch it wire to wire. Mickey here will hold the money so nobody forgets why they came. When it's over, we can all settle up."

Guys were gathering all along the bar. Clearly, they were looking forward to some little Asian punk getting his comeuppance, and personally punching me in the face was going to be their cherry on top. One neanderthal-looking giant even tried his brass knuckles on for size, smiling at me while tipping his hat.

I looked around at each of them. "I can see you're excited about your prospects, but that cuts both ways. You're all witnesses to the bet, right? Are you men of your word? If what I say happens, are you going to make sure that Lou pays on his end of the deal? I hope you guys are honest New Yorkers when the bill comes due."

They didn't like being accused of anything else and their hackles rose, assuring me that the bet would be honored on the impossible chance I won. Just then, the waitress brought my burger and shake. Maybe they all thought I would be too nervous to eat, but I had no problems chowing down as tipoff approached. I took a long sideways glance at Lou and could see the beads of sweat on his forehead beneath the fedora.

At six foot nine, Magic Johnson was the tallest point guard in NBA history, but was undersized to be playing center, especially in place of the seven foot two Kareem. The 76ers got the ball first and went right at Magic in the paint, where he was tasked with guarding the much taller and stronger Darryl Dawkins. However, when Dawkins tried to dribble the ball to the basket, Magic tied him up and the Lakers gained possession and scored on the transition. Two-Zero L.A., an ominous start for Lou and his fifteen grand.

The Lakers started fast and scored the first seven points, but the 76ers were bigger and brasher inside and were up 52-44 in the second, before L.A. rallied to tie it at sixty at halftime. Lou was smugly staring at me when I came back from the bathroom. He had sent one of his guys in to make sure I didn't climb out the window to make a run for it.

"Good game by Magic, kid, but it's not looking good for you and your twelve points," he said with an evil grin. "You want outta the deal? Maybe just let me keep the money, and you run home to Mommy?"

A guy like Lou was used to making other people look weak. He didn't expect a kid to keep pushing back. "Actually, my mommy doesn't even know I'm out here, Lou, so that won't work," I said. "But I'll tell you what, since you seem nervous, I'll bump the spread up to fourteen points, okay? Just so you can chill out a bit. Lakers by at least fourteen. I feel bad for you, and I don't want you feeling like I ripped you off by only giving you twelve. A gift, Lou, from me to you, a gift of our friendship."

"Are you high?" the bartender asked me, and several of the onlookers nodded, rolling their eyes. "Jesus, kid, how much deeper are you trying to bury yourself?"

I grinned and slurped down my milkshake as play resumed. The Lakers ran off fourteen straight points to start the third quarter, and Lou's smart remarks seemed to come fewer and farther between. The 76ers made one final push to get it to 103-101 with five minutes to go and L.A. called timeout. Lou was back to brash confidence, but several of his supporters had switched sides, with the Lakers threatening a massive upset and Magic Johnson sitting at thirty-three points.

In the final five minutes, all hell broke loose at the Spectrum, across Philadelphia, and in that little sports bar in Brooklyn. The Lakers finished the game on a 20-6 run over the final five minutes to *win the game by sixteen points*, 123-107. Magic Johnson scored nine points in the final five minutes to complete one of the most legendary performances in NBA Finals history—*forty-two points*, fifteen rebounds, seven assists, and one pissed as hell Lou the Bookie.

I was exchanging high-fives with guys who had been looking

forward to punching my lights out a few hours earlier when someone noticed Lou trying to sneak out the side door. He pretended to ignore the shouts from his fellow barflies, but he had to stop and acknowledge us when Mickey the bartender pulled a shotgun from beneath the bar and ominously pumped both barrels.

"Deal's a deal, Lou," he said in a soft, deadly tone. "You're trying to walk out of here squelching on a deal. If you pull that shit, you won't be allowed back in, and everyone around town will start calling you Lou the Fucking Rat."

Lou raised his hands as he slowly turned around and returned to the bar, eyes never wavering from me as he put a note on the counter.

"Okay, Mickey, if that's how you want to play it. I don't want no fourteen-year-old Chinaman saying Lou Boudreau don't pay his debts."

He nodded to the bartender. "Go on, open the safe."

The barkeep put the shotgun down and pulled a massive steel safe from under the bar. He spun the lock backwards and forwards and then opened it up. He reached inside and pulled out three thick stacks of bills wrapped in plastic. Each of the bills had Ben Franklin's face looking up at me. He pushed them my way. Three stacks, fifty each, all hundred dollar bills. Mickey shook his head and said, "Count them at home, and for God's sake, don't go flashing them around anywhere. Find a place to keep it where no one will notice. And get the hell out of here before I change my mind."

He nodded toward Lou at that last statement, and I began to understand. Lou was the bookie, and Mickey was more than a bartender; he was the boss and owner of the bar, or maybe he owned the whole block, which meant that they were probably in the mafia, and I was probably in over my head. I had my powers at my disposal, but that wouldn't do me a lick of good if they had some guys tail me back to Jersey to see where I was working. I'd be putting everyone at risk. No matter how upset I was at Amayah's reaction, I wasn't going to do that.

I put the money in my backpack and said, "Man, I've gotta hit the head after all those drinks."

I walked into the stall, closed the door, and called on my powers. I still couldn't summon whatever I needed to time travel, but I didn't have to. I had more than enough to make the short jump back to Jersey, and I chuckled at what Lou and his boys would think when I didn't come out of the bathroom. I would be the Asian kid gambler who robbed them blind and then vanished into thin air. It'd be one they told their grandkids.

I STASHED the backpack under my bunk. I didn't think I had to worry much about anyone stealing it, but I planned on bringing it everywhere if I ever left the children's center, just in case. Feeling better, I padded down towards Amayah's door. The lights were off, but I knocked anyway. I wasn't going to tell her about the money, but I was assuming she had cooled off and might be up for apologizing to me. She didn't answer, again. I stomped back to my room and flung myself on the bed. It had been a long day, but I couldn't sleep. Bobo was nowhere in sight, so it was quiet, but that made it even tougher. I tossed and turned, frustrated with myself, frustrated with Amayah, and frustrated that I had won fifteen thousand dollars and couldn't even celebrate with anyone. Amayah would throw it in my face, saying that I had only won by cheating, and her opinion of me would diminish even further, but I had big plans for the money. I just couldn't tell anyone. I was trying to figure out a way to use the money without drawing her suspicions when I heard Nick's voice slithering up through the crevices of my subconscious.

"Nice job today, boss, you really showed them up," he whispered into my brain. *"You should do that more often. Nothing wrong with stealing money from people who steal it themselves."*

He had a point there. Mafia guys like Lou weren't making that money on the up and up. That money came from things like selling drugs and fencing stolen goods and shaking people down for so-called protection.

"Money's better off in your hands anyway, Rohan," Nick said. *"Use it to protect your people. Arm yourselves. Find a place to hole up and be safe. I told you there's a war coming. You've seen it throughout history. People like you are barely treated any better in 1980 than in 1854, and it was the same in 1500 and 1200 and 500 and will be the same 500 years from now."*

I didn't want to know how Nick knew so much about history. The more we spoke and the more he allowed me into his world, the clearer it was that he had been around for a long, long time. Very few things were supposed to be immortal, and if he wasn't God or an angel, that didn't leave many other possibilities.

Even so, he was still the only voice I had to talk to right now, and I couldn't help but desire some sort of affirmation.

"But Amayah's still pissed at me for even thinking about gambling!" I said in frustration. "She'll never believe that I just found fifteen thousand dollars on the street, and she'll break up with me if I try to keep it and use it. She doesn't understand that I'm doing this all for her! For us!"

I could feel Nick's energy spread across my shoulders and forehead like a cool, soothing presence. It creeped me out more than a little, but I didn't resist. Not having Amayah around for even a day had made me painfully lonely.

"Amayah may not like it," Nick reasoned, *"but that doesn't mean you can't have your fifteen grand and eat it too."*

I had no idea what he was suggesting, and I was sleepy, so I grunted in the tone of a question.

"You can time travel, my young friend," Nick's voice was softer and smoother than it had been in a long time. *"I can help you control it. If you vanish from 1980 and jump back to your time, perhaps a few days earlier than you left, before the Moon Festival, that beautiful Amayah will be waiting for you, and she won't know how you got the money. Maybe you won the lottery, or your long-lost uncle died, or you saved someone's*

pet in a fire. Who cares? The point is that you'll have your little girlfriend worshiping you again, and you'll have all that money. In fact, since she's not talking to you anyway, why not go back to the city tomorrow? Bet it all on whatever's next—golf, horses, whatever you wish... grow your wealth, Rohan, grow it large and deep. If you get tired of waiting for your bets to pay off, you can always slip back into that bar and swipe Lou and Mickey's safe. You spied on the barkeep as he put in the number combination, right? I know you have an excellent memory. Oh yes, I was watching through your eyes, and I would have done the same thing. You never know when you might need a little more... or a lot more. Or all of it."

I knew I was tired, but I also knew what he was saying. I had the power to take whatever I wanted. And if the Amayah stuck in 1980 didn't like it, maybe the naive 1997 Amayah would. With my powers, it wasn't just that I could pick and choose the girl I wanted... once I mastered the powers Nick promised to teach me, I could pick the version of the girl I wanted. It was insane to think, but it gave me an icy shiver of a thrill, nonetheless. If I ever had a fight with Amayah that seemed destined to end in a breakup, I could jump back a few days, or even a few hours, if I could get the time jumps under control, and avoid the conflict entirely. No one would know. Well, no one but me. Unfortunately, my powers constantly came and went and were only partially under my control. Could Nick possibly help me master them?

"You can do anything you want, as many times as you want. You can have the perfect day every day, take a different girl to your bed, live out every fantasy you've ever had, Rohan. Why make yourself suffer because of her mortal, imperfect emotions? You've grown beyond that, and beyond her, beyond any of them. Lions don't worry about sheep. They are all dim lights burning out quickly, while you shine eternal as the sun."

"Shine? Wait, shine?"

Nick realized his mistake too late. I sat bolt upright in bed and pushed the covers off. I hadn't noticed how hot it was in the room. Somehow, the thermostat was way up, and I was sweating and feverish, as though waking from a nightmare. I went to the bathroom to splash cold water on my face and slapped myself a few times to wake up fully as I focused on pushing Nick's voice quieter and lower in my brain.

The Shine... well, the Shine is my destiny, according to Hua. And now the Shine was this warped and selfish mindset Nick was trying to push onto me. He had nearly succeeded. I was tired and angry and had spent the day giving into my bitter instincts. I was at my most vulnerable, so I opened the door and welcomed him into my mind. Nick gave me power; and taught me how to shape it, but he was dangerous and wanted more than he was letting on. I had to ignore him and take control of myself. He wanted to take me dangerously close to behavior that might tear my life apart and make me do things I couldn't take back, time travel or not.

"I know you seek the Shine, there's only one way to belong to the House of Shine. To Shine like the sun, you must burn first, burn bright, burn all..." Nick continued.

Except I didn't want to burn myself or anyone else, especially anyone I loved.

Giving Nick the cold shoulder, I fell to my knees and opened my heart and my mind to Hua, to God, to any force of good that might be listening. I prayed for strength, and I prayed for peace. I prayed for wisdom, and for Amayah, and for the forgiveness of my sins.

I slept peacefully, wrapped in the loving embrace of the light. When I woke the next day, I felt stronger than I had in weeks, and I went straight to Amayah's room, determined to wait all day if need be. I knocked sharply, though, hoping my luck had changed.

She must have been sitting right there because she opened the door in seconds.

"I'm ready to go start looking," I said, not giving her a chance to speak. "I think it makes the most sense to start in your neighborhood and expand out from there. It's a Hispanic neighborhood in 1997; there's no reason some of the people wouldn't have also been living there in 1980. We can toss your parents' names around, get some leads and see if anyone knows something. I've got my journal and some pens and paper, and we'll put together a chart of possible leads to track down.

"Are you ready?"

Ama nodded, and I noticed that she already had her own backpack on. I thought she almost smiled, but must have thought better of it. Or perhaps she was still mad at me and didn't want me to assume that everything was back to normal.

"Let's go find my parents," she said, closing her door behind us.

We had enough money to take the 188 bus from Union City to Washington Heights. We actually had much more than enough, but I needed to keep that a secret. Amayah sat by the window, and I sat beside her, resisting the urge to put my arm around her as I typically would have. It sucked, feeling that she was still mad at me. I didn't like feeling so distant from her after we had shared so much. I kept those feelings to myself, though, and tried to remain easy and optimistic. Complaining about the way she had treated me was probably the worst thing I could have done.

Silently watching the landscape through the windows, I felt like a tourist visiting a city I could only vaguely remember. The big, iconic parts of Manhattan across the Hudson lay before us, but many of the stores looked like massive movie sets. We saw *The Wiz*, an electronic spokesman on a billboard who declared, "Nobody beats The Wiz," something I only knew about from an old episode of *Seinfeld*. We marveled at the gas prices, just over a dollar per gallon, and were shocked at how many cigarette advertisements were plastered all over. People also smoked everywhere, indoors and outdoors, which was drastically different from the late nineties. In school, we learned that scientists had known for decades just how terrible cigarette smoke was for your lungs, but they took massive payoffs from tobacco companies to keep quiet, until it became impossible to deny the facts.

Amayah and I spoke a bit each time the bus rolled past something we didn't know, or something we thought of as old and aged in 1997, but was new and shiny in 1980. It wasn't a conversation, but at

353

least we were exchanging actual words. I tried to watch her without looking like I was watching her, which was tough, even with super-powers. I saw Ama's eyes widen, and her expression was of someone who had seen something they desperately wanted. I followed her eyes, and as a fellow passenger departed, they left behind a Columbia University pamphlet. Her pang of longing was under-standable. Columbia was a utopian paradise amid the rough-and-tumble neighborhoods surrounding it. For a girl like Amayah, with such lofty academic hopes, it was the pinnacle of her aspirations. At Columbia, her incredible aptitude would be rewarded and champi-oned, not viewed with doubt as it often was by her dad.

I felt a pang of guilt as we started moving again. I had no idea what I wanted to do after high school, other than getting some more *ups* in the city and dating Amayah. The girl I loved had bigger dreams than me, and I realized that despite being older than her, she was far more mature at this point. I needed to grow up, as my amazing powers might not be enough for her to put her own life on hold once we got back to our own "when." The bus kept chugging along up River Road, parallel to Henry Hudson Drive, as we zipped through New Jersey and over the George Washington Bridge. We hopped off at the George Washington Bridge Bus Station at 4211 Broadway, the official Washington Heights stop, only a few minutes' away from Mitchel Square, which was just as tiny and green in 1980 as it would be in 1997. Amayah's face lit up as we passed into the relatively familiar territory of her future neighborhood. The streets bore the same names, even if the hairstyles and cars were radically different. We started reading business names back and forth, and she ticked off a list of those that would still be around in 1997, and those that had changed names and storefronts. I suggested we stop at J. Hood Wright Park to figure out a plan, but Amayah blew past me and gave a cheer as she raced towards a tiny hole-in-the-wall restaurant.

"Malecon!" she shouted with a note of joy I had not heard in quite some time. She turned and offered me a sincere smile that instantly warmed my soul. "We come here on Sundays after church. Um, I mean, we will come here at some point."

She sighed. "I'm so tired of all these different verb tenses. Let's go inside and get some lunch. I want to see if someone I know is here."

I opened my mouth to object, or spout off some sort of *Back to the Future* reference about not tampering with the timeline, but she gave me a look that shut me right up. She might have shot me a smile, but it was clear that I was still very much in the doghouse.

The restaurant wasn't much to look at on the outside. Still, inside, it seemed bright and sunny and comfortable, with peppy music featuring a Spanish singer accompanied by guitars and drums coming from a small radio on the front counter. There was an old-fashioned chalkboard splayed behind the counter with the entire menu handwritten in pink and blue chalk. The smells coming from the tiny kitchen behind that were making my mouth water. I smelled meat and spices and all sorts of fragrant things that I certainly hadn't enjoyed at the shelter commissary and fast-food restaurants around town. That made me realize once again just how much I had been taking Amayah for granted since we had arrived back in New York. I called her my girlfriend, but I definitely wasn't treating her like one, except when we were alone. I never surprised her with a night out for dinner or anything else that went above and beyond. It felt like I was in a long-term holding pattern of keeping the status quo and just expecting her to be fine with it. I had spent so much time obsessed with making her my girlfriend that I hadn't considered what I would do when that was actually my reality.

Ahead of me, Amayah had her head on a swivel, looking all around to spot a familiar face. Just then, a heavyset man with long black hair came out of the kitchen, wearing a greasy yellow apron and a wide grin.

"Buenas tardes, señores!" he exclaimed happily. "Welcome to Malecon. I hope you brought your appetite with you this afternoon."

Amayah gave an audible gasp. "Pepe!" she exclaimed. "Oh my goodness!"

The man, who I'm guessing was Pepe, did a double take of his own. "Um, yes? I'm Pepe... do I know you, senorita?"

Amayah looked frantically at me for a moment, and I opened my mouth, then closed it again. I had no way to remedy Pepe's flummoxed face, and I hoped she could think quickly on her feet. "Sorry!" she said, a little more composed. "Err, my abuelita pointed you out at church and mentioned that you worked here, but I didn't know your hair was so long like that." She smiled extra wide, hoping to smooth the confusion out with some charm.

"Oh, sí, sí," he responded with a nod. "I keep it bunned up at la iglesia; I don't want them thinking I'm some hippie."

He laughed, and we joined him. It looked like we were in the clear. Pepe said, "I didn't catch your name, though? You or your gringo friend?"

"I'm Amayah, and this is my friend Rohan," she said. "I just moved to Manhattan, and Rohan is one of the first friends I've made at school. Even though I'm Boricua, I wanted to show my gringo friend some different types of Hispanic cuisine tonight."

Now we were talking Pepe's language. I could see his facial expression shift from slightly wary to flattered.

"Well then, you brought him to the right place, hermanita!" he exclaimed. "Don't worry about the menu, go find a booth, and I'll serve you up something muy especial esta tarde!"

He motioned us away, and I followed Amayah to a booth with a good view of the street outside. Once no one was in ear shot, she giggled and said, "Pepe is one of my dad's best friends in 1997, and he's the owner of this Dominican restaurant. But so long as I've known him, he's been totally bald."

I snorted, and she giggled. I glanced at Pepe back at the counter, charming customers and hollering orders into the kitchen, flipping and twirling his hair around gloriously, like Prince Charming with a beer belly.

"Do you think it's the stress of running a business in Manhattan for two decades?" I asked thoughtfully, then turned playful. "Or maybe he's wearing a wig?"

Amayah laughed at that idea, and suddenly things felt almost back to normal. On impulse, I reached for her hand, but she pulled it back, and I was left sitting there awkwardly with my outstretched hand on the table.

Amayah glanced over her shoulder at the kitchen, and when she turned back, she was all business again.

"I don't know how long he and my dad have been friends, but Pepe is a native New Yorker. If my parents are out there somewhere trying to plug into the local Puerto Rican vibe, Pepe will be a great resource to use."

Right on cue, Pepe appeared with a platter of food that he set down between us at the table. Amayah gasped as she looked it over and immediately began undoing her paper silverware holder.

"Okay, Rohan, time for your taste buds to take a trip to the islands!" Pepe said with a big smile, flipping his hair one more time for good measure. "This is picadera frita pequena, one of the house specials, so dig in."

We prayed before eating, before Ama smiled, "I miss eating here."

The basket of food could have probably fed my family for a week, and Amayah must have noticed the amazed look on my face.

"Meals are huge in their country," she exclaimed as she took the first bite of what looked like fried chicken and moaned in glee. "It's all about abundance and having more than you need so that people always feel welcome. No one wants to go to a house or show up for dinner unexpectedly and have to be turned away. That would be massively embarrassing to the women who run the house, so they always make more than enough.

"So," she continued, "what we have here is chicharrón de pollo, carne de res, y cerrado frita, longaniza, and tostones. Dig in, Mr. Chang."

That felt like another small step in the right direction, calling me by the playfully formal designation she occasionally used when she was amused or impressed with my behavior.

She caught herself, but let it slide. "Dig in! Or I'll eat it all, and you'll have nothing but an empty stomach!"

At that, I went after the meal like a shark with blood in the water, and my tastebuds immediately acknowledged how incredible the food was. Fried beef, pork, chicken, and fish practically leapt off the platter and into my mouth. There were Caribbean spices and delicious flavor combinations I had never experienced before. I forced myself to slow down because I was tearing into meat like a starved carnivore. I noticed Amayah watching me, so I tried to slow down and not look like a wild animal. When we were done inhaling the food, Pepe brought out more, featuring bistec encebollado, and then an inviting cake called tres leches, the last bite of which I felt entirely willing to fight for. When we were done, I belched much louder than appropriate, and Amayah started giggling. After about 30 minutes, Pepe returned to the table and refused to take my money, saying it was on the house for us, an incredibly generous offer considering how much we ate.

"You're welcome here anytime, amigos," he said, about to walk away, but then he paused for a moment. "Hey, hermanita, just had to ask, how do you spell your name? Not many Amayahs in this community."

She told him the spelling and he smiled, shaking his head.

"Talk about a coincidence," he said. "A new Puerto Rican couple just moved to my neighborhood for the affordable rent, and the esposa is five months pregnant; they just migrated here, and are talking about naming their child Amayah, if it's a girl. What a small world. Anyway, you two have a great evening!"

My jaw dropped, and I saw that Amayah was similarly stunned. Pepe already knew Amayah's parents. Without a second thought, she called him back in Spanish, telling him she probably knew them, asking him which street was home for this new young couple.

TWENTY-THREE

Pepe said he had only recently met the couple but connected instantly with the husband over their love of John Travolta. He didn't know the exact house number where they stayed, but he did know which section of the Heights they were at. It was early evening by the time we finished talking to Pepe, but Amayah was energized by the fact that her parents were close by, and she wanted to scout some more territory before we found a place to crash for the night. We walked deeper into Washington Heights and the area unofficially known as Little Dominican Republic. Pepe said that people from all over, including Puerto Ricans and some Asians, come to his neighborhood to start life in the states because of the cheap rent and spacious accommodations. "Washington Heights es muy asequible," Pepe gushed about his community. I was amazed how different it looked at night, compared to the days I had walked Amayah home after school. To be honest, once she decided to push on after we talked to Pepe, I began touching my energy source, keeping it close at hand. We'd been messed with before by gang members in the short number of days I had walked her home—

weekdays and in broad daylight. I didn't want to say it out loud, since I was still on thin ice with Amayah, but I was worried that this area might be even rougher on a Saturday night.

Our current mayor, Rudy Giuliani, might have been tough on taggers, but he was famous for cleaning up New York City and making it safer for the average person to go out and not fear for their life or their stuff every day. However, he didn't take office until 1994. I thought the mayor in 1980 was Ed Koch, but I wasn't sure. I also wasn't sure what he did or how bad the gang problems were back then. To be honest, my knowledge of New York's history was generally pretty sketchy, especially once you got outside the sporting world and the unofficial Hall of Fame of graffiti artists of the Five Boroughs. The late 1970s in New York City to me meant Reggie Jackson and The Son of Sam. Sam Berkowitz was captured in 1977 and was currently in a prison somewhere serving out a half-dozen consecutive life sentences. Thinking of him suddenly made me shiver, despite the warm weather outside. I remembered the body I had stumbled across and the fact that a serial killer was on the loose when Amayah and I vanished after the festival. We had no way of knowing how much time had passed in our 1997, but I couldn't help thinking about that night and all the subsequent deaths that had been reported. Was he still active? Had he killed again? How many people had died at the hands of that psycho? I tried to tell myself that he had likely been caught. I mean, they usually got caught... eventually.

According to what you saw on TV, that was because serial killers secretly wanted people to know how smart they were, so they would intentionally make mistakes, allowing someone to figure out what they were up to. At that thought, I remembered the gaseous Mister Pags at Mount Sinai, who had talked to Amayah and me about the Zodiac Killer, who had taunted police for years with no result. Some weird intuition told me that the guy in 1997 was much more like Zodiac than the rest. He seemed brutal and sadistic, and not particularly worried about getting caught. Not for the first time, I cursed myself for not using my teleportation powers sooner that first night. If I had, I might have stumbled upon him before he could kill that girl out by the UN building. Even a cold-blooded killer wouldn't be a match for my speed and abilities, even just a small dose. I might have stopped him right then and there. For the first time in a while, something stirred in me, and I wanted to get back to 1997. If not for Amayah's sake, then for the fact that I might be able to find the guy and stop him from taking any more lives.

As we walked along, a chill raced through my bones. What if the serial killer in 1997 was also in New York in 1980? Maybe the killer from my time had been inspired by the Son of Sam from this one. I had no idea how old this person was, or even if they were in New York City. I had to admit that it didn't seem likely. And even if he was around right now, he might have been five years old, or some average Joe who hadn't snapped yet.

But the fire was lit. That murderer was making trouble in my version of New York City, and the faster I got back there, the faster I could do something about it.

My fears of a rough crowd on this Saturday night were utterly unfounded. Washington Heights buzzed with people out for a meal, grabbing a drink, looking for a party, or just enjoying each other's company. There were musicians in ones and twos playing music here and there, with open guitar cases for tips. Street vendors had little stands set up, hocking treats and drinks and crafts made by hand.

Everywhere I looked, people were laughing, talking, giving hugs, and welcoming handshakes. Colorful streamers were up outside of businesses, and blinking lights caught the eye to attract more business, inviting people inside.

"What's everyone celebrating?" I asked Amayah. "Is it some sort of holiday?"

She gave out an exasperated chuckle.

"Rohan, I swear. Yes, this is the festival of it's Saturday, and I don't have to work tomorrow morning, so let's celebrate!"

I didn't reply right away, trying to change the subject. She rolled her eyes and continued.

"People don't need a festival or a holiday to have a good time here. They're happy because they're off work, and it's a nice night, so they can visit friends and family and catch up, and most importantly... this is life, and it should be joyous and celebrated! Think about Juba and Cecilia and Wayles from back in Oxford! Think how little they had and what they would think of a place like New York and a night like this!"

That's when I stopped and really looked around for a moment. There was so much genuine happiness on the faces of everyone I saw. Even seventeen years newer than they were in 1997, most of the buildings looked tiny and rundown, not at all the sort of place I would want to live as an adult. I had grown up wanting the penthouse with a view of Central Park, the car service at my beck and call, and all the respect and happiness that came with being rich. As I looked into that crowd, I considered what happiness was, and the true value of feeling safe and secure. These people had roofs over their heads and knew where their next meals were coming from. They had dozens of people who loved and protected them, and if they wanted to, they could get on a bus or a train or a car in the next ten minutes and go anywhere else in the country without anyone's permission. They were blessed beyond belief here, and I realized that for all my complaining and bitterness back in 1997, I was too. A roof over my head. Food that I didn't have to grow. A family that looked after me no matter how lousy I treated them. A place to learn. A place to work. The things I had in my life that I took for granted were things that Juba and Cecilia would have viewed as gold and diamonds. I felt a flush come over my face, and it had nothing to do with the humidity.

At that moment, a street vendor who couldn't have been more than nine came up to us with a bouquet of single-stem roses, chattering to Amayah in Spanish. He pointed to me, and Ama laughed and nodded, so he turned towards me and began plucking one rose, then another, and holding them up for my inspection.

Amayah gave me a cool look. "He wants you to buy one for your girlfriend, to show her how beautiful you think she is."

I started to grin, and she returned the small hint of a smile. I reached into my pocket and brought out a five-dollar bill. The boy shook his head slightly, as if to say that wasn't going to cut it, so I added a ten to the mix and held them out. He gave a whoop and handed me the entire bouquet, at least a dozen of them, and raced off hollering to anyone who would listen, "Soy rico! Soy rico!"

Amayah had looked away to watch a band and burst out laughing when she turned back around. "Rohan! He was selling them for fifty cents apiece, what did you do?"

I shrugged. The little boy had got me good, but I didn't really care. Amayah was smiling at me, and I handed her the bouquet. "It seemed like the only solution to show you how beautiful you are."

She still didn't take my hand when I offered it, but I was pretty sure I had made up a considerable distance in the gap between us. She carried the bouquet proudly as we continued wandering the streets. She kept asking people if they had seen her parents, giving their names and mentioning that her mother, Teresa, was likely pregnant. A few people pointed one way or another, but everyone was generally having too good a time to worry about the location of two strangers.

Besides, I reasoned, if her mom was five months pregnant, she'd probably be at home resting at this time of night. We stayed out almost until midnight searching. Amayah gave the roses out one by one to several young girls who were out with their parents, and the lovely looks on their faces at such beautiful gifts were priceless. At last, we checked into a tiny motel on West 188th Street. The room was $8 per night and consisted of a sink, a chair, a bed, a door, and a window. The bathroom was down the hall and shared by the entire floor. The bed was tiny, which gave me a moment of hope that sleeping next to Amayah might thaw the rest of the ice between us, but she stopped me short.

"You're in the chair," she said. "Feet on the bed. And you can have the blanket so you're not too chilly."

I nodded and said no problem, even though it hurt my heart after what had seemed like a good day between us. She was asleep, or at least faking it, within a few minutes, so I stretched out the best I could and drifted off, worn out by the walking and the stress of the day.

WE SLEPT late and locked the tiny room behind us on Sunday morning. We didn't have to be back at the shelter until tomorrow morning. Mrs. Wilkinson said the center was closed until midday tomorrow due to renovation work in the primary children's play-room, so we had a whole day to find Amayah's parents. I felt a lot less optimistic than I had the night before, when Pepe's report made it seem like they might be just around the next corner. However, we were hopeful that people out in the morning might be more willing to help us than those who had been out to party and relax the night before, so we started walking to the section of the Heights that Pepe suggested and to the apartment building where Amayah lived in 1997. It was quite the sight in 1980, glistening in the sun and showing considerably less wear and tear than we were used to seeing. We walked the building's halls a few times, and Amayah stopped over and over outside unit 327, the one she would someday share with her parents, touching the door handle and the trim but never knocking, clearly aware that the faces behind it would not be those we were missing.

"I know they aren't in there, but I still want so badly to go inside," she said. She even had the key in her tiny purse that she had brought to the festival, but knew it would be illegal and get her in sizable trouble if she went inside, assuming the key even worked.

Back outside the building, we sat on a park bench and discussed our next move.

"They couldn't be living here now; it's too nice in 1980, and if they just got here, they're probably living cheap, saving every penny just to scrape by, especially with a baby, um, with me, on the way," Amayah reasoned.

I nodded my head. "Okay, so we know the general area where they're at, thanks to Pepe, but we need to figure out exactly which part is where Puerto Ricans live when they first get here and have basically no money. And probably someplace close to a hospital, since they wouldn't have a car and might not be able to afford a taxi for the drive over when your mom finally does go into labor."

Amayah gave me a raised eyebrow, clearly impressed with my logic. "Well, well, Detective Rohan seems to be on the case this morning," she said with a smile. "Let's put that brain of yours to work."

It was a police officer who ultimately pointed us in the right direction, giving us the address for a Puerto Rican flophouse located on Seaman Avenue, across from Inwood Hills Park's tennis courts in the same area Pepe mentioned. It was a rundown-looking place with three stories of small windows, with laundry hanging on lines outside them. We were trying to decide on a strategy to have the building super help us locate her parents if they were even living there, but then the door to the building popped open, and a young couple walked out. The man was wearing black slacks and a white-collared shirt that looked bathed in starch to make it as stiff as possible. The woman was wearing a long green and yellow dress that looked intricately sewn by hand. Neither of them could have been more than seven or eight years older than us, but all of that came and went through my mind in a matter of milliseconds. My eyes were fixated on the woman's face, a spectacular spitting image of Ama. It couldn't have been anyone else.

Amayah was looking across the street at a commotion of squabbling taxicab drivers when I touched her shoulder, coaxing her around. She started to protest until I put my hand up, pointing at the couple crossing the street.

"There!" I said in my best stage whisper. "Crossing the street all dressed up! It has to be them, right?"

Amayah stared and gasped. A wide smile spread across her face, and she gave me a big hug without ever taking her eyes off them.

"Si! Yes! Oh Rohan, you found them!" she squealed. "C'mon, we can't lose sight of them!"

She moved swiftly into the intersection, and I lengthened my stride to keep up. Her parents were walking at a normal pace up Seaman and turned left onto Isham Street. We stayed far enough behind so they wouldn't get suspicious, but with my height, it was easy to keep tabs on them. Plus, it wasn't like this was a tense action movie where they knew they were being followed and would try to lose us in the crowd.

It was late Sunday morning in New York City, so many people were out and about. After following them for about half a block, it dawned on me that we had no plan of what we were going to do now that we had found them. We couldn't tell them who we truly were, as that would probably get us institutionalized, or they would just run in the opposite direction. We both believed that we were here to do something in relation to both of our parents, but had no idea what that task entailed. We needed a cover story so they would engage with us, and share some details about their lives. We would need a darn good one if we were going to hang around them for more than just a few minutes on a busy street. I said as much to Amayah, and she agreed. Fortunately, her parents apparently had a long way to walk this morning, which gave Ama time to turn her considerable brainpower to the task and begin sorting out a plan. We needed to find an in.

It only took her about three minutes to come up with a tentative plan.

"My mom has a cousin who came to New York City before she did. Her dad was in the military, and her mom passed away. Her dad ended up getting a government job here, but he was constantly traveling for the government, and she'd stay with friends. She lived with us for a couple years when I was younger, then she went and got married and moved back home, I think. Her name was Zulema, but I always called her Aunt Zuli. If my parents have only been here a couple weeks, I doubt they've had time to visit family. I could pretend to be her; I don't think they ever met before they were living here. I can just say that I recognized her on the street and take it from there. We could volunteer to show them around, see if they need anything, or maybe get ourselves invited over to their place for dinner. If they think I'm family, they'll probably open up a bit about any difficulties they're having, and maybe the answer will reveal itself."

It was as good a plan as any, and I had no better ideas, though I did have a concern. "So, who am I supposed to be, then?" I asked. "Their long-lost other cousin, is the most Asian-looking Puerto Rican of all time?"

It was a joke designed to make her laugh, but it didn't quite land.

"You can be Rohan," she said. "My boyfriend who is usually sweet, but occasionally a total blockhead, who will work very hard to help with their problems to get himself out of the huge doghouse he's been building lately."

I nodded and said no more, turning my focus back to her parents to make sure they didn't get too far ahead of us.

It was another twenty minutes in the hot May sun before they finally slowed down and crossed to the other side of the street, with "Zuli" and I following a few seconds later. We walked all the way down Nagle Avenue, close to Highbridge Park, as her mom and dad slowed, then stopped at the corner. Their destination was a branch office of the Western Bank of New York, proudly advertising on its window, open for business on Sundays.

Well, this was going to be awkward. It wasn't like a restaurant or a grocery store where we could just happen to bump into them. If they had walked this far, they probably had an appointment for something, and we couldn't exactly crash that. Besides that, we still looked like two teenagers, which we were, and teenagers rarely had business in banks unless they were with older family members.

Fortunately, Amayah already had another plan in mind.

"Give them a few minutes to get to their appointment, then we'll go sit in the lobby. If anyone asks, we'll tell them that they're my aunt and uncle, and we're meeting them here to help them run some errands this afternoon since my 'aunt' is pregnant. No one is going to kick us out for helping a pregnant lady."

We watched the time tick by on the bank's clock, and after five minutes, we ducked in the door. The bank was bustling with customers and tellers, along with plenty of employees sitting at ornate wooden desks meeting with well-dressed individuals and couples. I had seen enough TV to realize that most of these people were all dressed up on the weekend because they were applying for loans, and I suspected that Amayah's parents were likely here for the same reason, either for a business or a home investment. It was a pretty bold move after only being on the U.S. mainland for a couple of weeks, but I admired them for it. They had made it to America, right? Time to start living that American dream.

Amayah's parents were seated at a desk where a middle-aged white man with glasses and a three-piece suit was smiling at them. I didn't like the look of his smile, though. It was plastic, like he had zero interest in whatever they were saying. Unfortunately, the noisy bank meant that we couldn't really hear any of their conversation, which I supposed was also intentional. Most people didn't want their big business decisions being broadcast to the whole world. I could tell that Amayah was having the same thought, and her shoulders slumped as she realized that we might not be able to hear a word they were saying.

But I didn't want to miss the opportunity. We needed to know what was going on.

"Hang on a minute," I told her. "Keep your eyes open. I'm going to try something."

I manifested the same powers I had used to access Steven's memories a couple of months ago, and hoped that with the proper application of energy, I could do something similar, enhancing my senses, just as I could enhance my speed and strength. Ultimately, it felt like a sporadic ability to read other people's thoughts, and I focused on the desk and the three people sitting there until I could narrow the noise around me, filtering the excess out to the point of just hearing them.

"Got it," I said quietly under my breath to Amayah. "Sit right next to me and don't let anyone break my concentration, and I should be able to hear what's going on."

I was so focused on keeping my ability functioning that I scarcely noticed Amayah moving close and pressing tight next to me. It did feel great to have her so close again. I closed my eyes to focus better and was astonished that I could still see them in my mind's eye. It was like looking through smoked glass. I could see Amayah's mom and dad and the loan officer clearly, but everything around them looked blurred and distorted. I vowed to start documenting and practicing my powers more diligently, as I had early on with my train races, so that I could properly understand their breadth and limitations, if there were any.

The Bello's were putting papers on the man's desk, so I pushed aside my idle thoughts to listen in, repeating what I heard to Amayah as the conversation began.

"So, you are Sergio and Teresa Bello, and you are here to apply for a home loan today. My name is Josh Septimus, and I am a senior loan officer for the Western Bank of New York. It's very nice to meet you both today," the white-haired loan officer uttered, his smile bigger and faker than ever.

Amayah's dad, Sergio, only nodded, but Teresa replied, "Yes, sir. We filled out the application, and we're looking for a home loan so we can buy a unit in a nicer part of the city and start building our first home here in America."

It was a nice speech, and probably not even rehearsed. Teresa looked and sounded like she was speaking from the heart. The loan officer, Septimus, barely seemed to hear her, as he was already thumbing through the papers they had presented him.

"Bello, huh? What is that ... Mexican?" he asked flatly, without looking up.

"We are from Quebradillas, Puerto Rico," Teresa said with a smile. "We recently came to the Estados Unidos and both found good work here in New York City."

Again, the loan officer didn't look up.

"Already got jobs, eh? Good to hear. You wouldn't believe how many foreign degenerates come to this beautiful city and start walking around looking for handouts. I drive by them every morning on my way in.

"Bunch of wetbacks who can't speak a lick of English and think the world's just going to be handed to them on a silver platter now that they're in New York. Utter trash."

The smile faded from Teresa's face, but she didn't say anything in return.

After an awkwardly long pause, Septimus looked up. "So, where are you working, exactly?"

She took the cue and smiled again. "I am working at a Cuban restaurant called Havana's Cafe. I wash dishes and bus tables each day. My husband took a job for The Ellington Company in their factory. He assembles electronics and also works overtime as a maintenance man."

Septimus looked up again. "Is your husband capable of speaking?"

Sergio smiled in return at the man, but made no attempt to answer the question. Teresa held his hand in hers. "My husband has not been as quick to learn English as I have, so I do most of his talking for him," she admitted. "But he is very smart and is learning English as rapidly as his job allows."

The loan officer looked back and forth between them for a

moment. "You're telling me he doesn't understand a single word I'm saying?"

She might have blushed and definitely looked embarrassed. "He knows un poco, a little bit, things that are essential like 'phone' and 'hospital.' But he works fourteen-hour days, and it's hard to focus on English lessons after such long days."

Septimus grinned like a wolf at the sight of a lamb. He was clearly looking down his nose at the Bellos, and I gritted my teeth as I relayed the information to Amayah, who looked ready to get up and intervene.

"So, if I call him a dumbass to his face, he won't understand me?" the loan officer was saying, and a shocked look crossed Teresa's face. "Or if I tell his wife what a sexy mamacita she is, and how I would rather do this interview with her sitting on my lap?"

Teresa's mouth hung open in stunned disbelief. She tried to cover it up, as Sergio was looking at her quizzically, and asked her something in Spanish. I didn't speak enough to understand, but he was obviously concerned with her sudden change in demeanor. She patted his hand and said something quietly that seemed to placate him.

She turned back to the loan officer. "Mr. Septimus, we are two very hard-working people trying to start a life and a family here. We are very blessed to have a child on the way, and we want to provide him or her with the very best home we can."

His eyes widened a little, and he looked her up and down. "Pregnant, huh? I can't even tell... that body is looking good. Glad you came in before you got too heavy; fat women are a big turnoff for me."

I felt miserable for Amayah's mom having to face this asshole alone. I knew that I could hurt the guy so easily—a quick punch to the solar plexus to knock the wind out of him, although a swift kick to the balls would probably be much more satisfying. He was a classless, Grade-A jerk, and he deserved to pay for it.

I steadied myself, realizing how much like Nick the Brute I was sounding just then. I was only supposed to be observing, not saving the day. That was a lesson I had to learn in Mississippi on the plantation, and it was happening again here. Having powers didn't mean you used them in every situation; you definitely had to pick and choose your fights. I tuned back to the conversation, if you could call it that, at the desk.

"So, let's get this straight. Your husband works ninety hours a week making minimum wage; that's $279 gross a week. You work forty hours a week making minimum wage; that's $124 gross a week. So, the two of you are pulling in $403 a week before taxes. That's not much money, honey.

"You know what they say here in the good ol' USA, where the real tax-paying Americanos are. No money, no honey," the loan officer casually explained.

Teresa wouldn't back down. "It is enough to qualify for a loan based on the application process of your bank, sir. In fact, it is more than enough based on the numbers listed here. And we both pay taxes."

He looked at the piece of paper, a brochure from the bank, scoffed, and crumbled it up in his hand. "And what happens when your baby comes, and you have to stop working to be a mommy full-time? Where does the money come from to repay the loan then?"

Teresa refused to be intimidated. "I will be taking off six weeks, and we have already saved up the money to cover that time. After that, our son or daughter will be cared for by a neighbor. We have already arranged something mutually beneficial with her that allows me to return to work swiftly."

Septimus made a big show of getting out a calculator and punching several sets of numbers into it. When he was done, he looked up.

"I'm afraid I can't approve this loan; there are just too many factors working against you. Your jobs are not secure, your husband can't speak a damn word of English, you're about to blow up to a blimp and have a baby, and who knows if you'll even want to work after that. A lot of you gals get used to sitting on the couch burping a baby and eating Bonbons and never go back to work again! Then the loan defaults and my boss is chewing my ass for giving a couple of illegals a loan in the first place! Hey, what are you gonna name your kid, anyways?"

Teresa answered in her kindest voice, despite his repugnant and demeaning manner. "Antonio if it's a boy and Amayah if it's a girl. We are not here illegally, sir. We migrated legally. I filled out all the paperwork myself and I have our documentation here if you'd like to see it."

He waved his hand away, dismissing her words like flies. "Antonio? Amayah? Those names are terrible. Get some American names so your kids won't have the same burden as you. Call them Eric or Samantha, so people will think they're from here, not some third-world island. Whatever. It's still too much of a gamble. This is a bank, not a charity. I'd start looking for a rental if I were you and tell your dumb-dumb husband here that no ingles equals no dinero around these parts." He stood up and extended his hand, clearly signaling them to leave.

Teresa looked on the verge of tears, but she didn't let herself break down in front of the asshole from the bank. "Thank you for your time, sir, and have a good day."

Realizing they were leaving, we jumped to our feet and hustled out of the bank ahead of them. The rude way they had just been treated was not going to make this any easier, but we had to try and interact with them. Eventually, they were sure to notice a beanpole Asian kid following them around, especially once they got back to Washington Heights.

We moved down the block the way they had come from, gambling that they would head straight home after the disappointment. Sure enough, they came out of the bank, Teresa dabbing at the corners of her eyes, Sergio with his arm around her, speaking quietly together in Spanish. Their pace was notably slower as they headed back on the long walk home. It felt so lousy to see good people treated unfairly. My inner self, the part that guiltily agreed with some of the Brute's suggestions, was already moving through a list of possible ways to make Septimus' life miserable in the days ahead. I pushed the anger back down again, reminding myself that I was here to help people, not hurt them. Amayah interrupted my thoughts, "Hey, they're headed this way! Look alive and follow my lead. It's showtime!"

TWENTY-FOUR

We walked right past them on purpose. It would be impossible to believe that someone you never met could recognize you from the back of your head alone. So, Amayah made sure she was deep in a fake conversation with me as she walked past the younger version of her parents on the busy street. She acted the whole thing out perfectly, doing a double-take, then coming to a complete stop and loudly exclaiming, "OH HEY!" then turning and calling, "Teresa! Teresa Bello, is that you!"

Her mom came to a surprising halt of her own, then turned back around, shielding her eyes from the sun. Sergio turned as well, gazing quizzically at Amayah as she broke into a big grin and closed the distance between herself and her unsuspecting parents. I loitered for a moment before following.

"Teresa! Teresa! It is you! It's me, prima! Zulema! Cousin Zuli! Miguel's daughter! Oh my gosh! Papa told me you were coming to the States, but I didn't know you were here yet! How are you?"

Teresa was taken aback by Amayah's—or Cousin Zuli's—outburst of energy, but at the mention of 'Miguel,' her eyes flickered with recognition, and she smiled back.

"¡Dios mío! Zuli! You are so grown up! The last fotos mí mamá has of you, you were still a little girl!"

She turned to Sergio. "Amor, es mí prima Zuli, la hija del primo Miguel. ¿Recuerdas? El oficial militar de los Estados Unidos?"

Now Sergio nodded in recognition and smiled as well. "Si, yo recuerdo! Hola, prima, que pasa?"

"I'm doing great!" Amayah replied, using more English on certain parts so I could follow along better. "When did you get here? How have you been? I thought you'd be living in Washington Heights... what are you doing all the way down here?"

Teresa's face fell, and Amayah did a terrific job of acting like she didn't know why. "Teresa? Are you okay?"

Her mom nodded sadly. "We just had a bad time across the street at the bank there. It's not important, though. It is a blessing from Jesus to see you here and all grown up! Oh, and who is your friend?"

It was impossible not to notice the giant Asian kid towering over the conversation. I was introduced and shook both their hands, trying to keep the ironic smile off my face; the two of them were friendly with me now, but when her dad met me in 1997, it was vastly different.

"I'm really sorry for what happened in the bank," I told them. "Listen, I was just going to buy Amayah lunch. I got a bonus from my boss yesterday. Why don't you come join us, and you guys can catch up?"

They refused about thirty times, trying to be polite, but we refused right back until they gave in, and we headed for a tiny Mexican restaurant called El Rey visible down the block. I gave the waiter a $5 bill from the money I saved working at the shelter, but also, knowing I had a lot more than that in my bag and told him to keep the chips and salsa coming fast and furious. We wanted to keep Teresa and Sergio occupied for as long as necessary.

It was clear that they had not been to many, or maybe even any, restaurants since getting to New York City. Being waited on seemed like a foreign concept to them, as was the fact that the waiter kept stopping by every few minutes to refill our drinks, along with the chips and salsa.

Amayah and her mom were talking back and forth about their shared relatives, which conveniently cemented her cover story that she was actually little Cousin Zuli all grown up. The fact that Amayah knew New York City was also helping a great deal, as she asked where they were staying in Washington Heights, despite already knowing, and peppered them with questions about what they'd seen and done so far. They were clearly both thrilled to be in the presence of a somewhat familiar face, and we could see the tension melting as they talked about Puerto Rico (real and Little). They told a half-English, half-Spanish tale of saving up enough money to come to New York with the aspirations of owning their own business someday and making a better life for their children than they had growing up.

"And you're pregnant now?" Amayah asked with a knowing look.

Teresa's eyes widened in surprise. "How can you tell? We haven't told a soul, and I'm not really showing!"

Too late, Amayah realized her mistake. Teresa had left that part of the story out. Amayah recovered, smiling and saying, "It's a gift I have. I'm always able to tell when people are pregnant, sometimes even before they know themselves!"

Teresa nodded her head that it was indeed true, and it was congratulations all around, although we stopped them from ordering a round of margaritas, as they seemed unaware of the tie between alcoholic beverages and pregnancy complications. I shook Sergio's hand and congratulated him, and we sat and talked to them for another two hours about everyone's experiences in New York City. It was an impossibly unique experience to hang out with Amayah's parents with their daughter both in front of them and inside of Teresa. They were good people, warm, and interested in what both of us had to say on so many subjects. It was hard for me to believe that they would be so opposed to Ama and I dating back in

1997 based on what I was seeing today. It was a truly serendipitous moment.

We all walked back to their flophouse together; Amayah told them that the two of us were just enjoying a day in the city and had no other commitments. They invited us in, although they were clearly embarrassed by the tiny size of the unit they were renting. However, if they saw where Ama and I were spending the weekend, they would have felt much better about themselves. About two minutes after we walked through the door, though, Teresa gave a small gasp of pain and sat down hard in the chair. Amayah was at her side in a moment, holding her hand and asking what was wrong.

"I think it's just my little baby saying hello," Teresa said with a smile, easing her way to a more comfortable position. It was crazy to think about what I was seeing. Amayah at sixteen, helping her mother, who was probably twenty-three or twenty-four at the time, get comfortable, as the baby inside of her, who was also Amayah, tried to get comfortable in her own little room. It was the kind of thing that could definitely blow your mind. Amayah was likely thinking the same thing. She was playing the role of "Cousin Zuli" well, but seeing her mom experiencing discomfort had her way more concerned than a normal person probably would be. I couldn't imagine how she must have been feeling, being in the presence of her parents at such a young age, especially when she had been missing them so painfully over the last couple months. I marveled at how well she held herself together. I imagine that on the inside she wanted to leap into her dad's arms and wrap them both up in a long hug, but instead, she was settling for holding her mom's hand and attending to her needs, as Sergio and I stood by without a clue of what to do.

"You should take it easy ma-Teresa," Amayah said, nearly slipping. "Let us help you today."

"You are so sweet, both of you, but Sergio and I need to go to the market before it gets too late."

Amayah stared at me as if I needed to say something, so I opened my big mouth. "You stay here and let Zuli take care of you. Just make a list for Sergio and me, and we can go get what you need, okay?"

Teresa tried to argue, but it was three against one, so she penned a list of about fifteen items and told me what market they preferred. A few minutes later, Sergio and I were marching down the street, an unusual pair to be sure, headed for the store. Other than a few smiles and my comment that it was really hot outside, we didn't say much. I spoke two languages he didn't know, and he spoke one I didn't know, so hopefully, we wouldn't need much verbal communication on this trip.

When I checked the list as we entered the store, I was pleasantly surprised to see that Teresa had written much of it in both English and Spanish. Several of the items were fruits and vegetables, so I handed Sergio the list and butchered a few of the words out loud, "Naranhas, uh platanos. Can you get those, please?" I pointed towards the list, then towards the sign for the produce section, and he nodded.

"I'll meet you BACK HERE," I said with a big arm gesture and a gentle smile, hoping he understood, hoping for the best.

I folded the list in half and tore it down the middle, handed him half, and then started walking through the market picking up items that Teresa requested. Chicken, tortillas, a roll of paper towels, a few spices for cooking, cheese, a loaf of bread—the standards of many meals at home when you didn't have much of a budget. I knew it well. If you substituted out the tortillas for rice, this could be almost the same as my family's weekly trip to the grocery store. I got a kick of going up and down the aisles and seeing which brands I recognized and which I had never heard of. Even the ones that would carry over into 1997 all had different packaging and slogans on them. It was incredible how much the world would change in the next seventeen years. It definitely was altering my perspective on what a crazy and wonderful world we lived in, and how much I wanted to get back to my own version of it. Hopefully, we'd uncover the big task that Teresa and Sergio needed help with sooner rather than later.

The trip to Mississippi had been revelatory, but the two months there were stressful and harrowing, to say the least.

I was walking back towards the spot where I had left Sergio with everything I needed except the milk when I first heard the raised voices and the shouting. I started to walk faster towards the front of the store, where I could hear at least two people speaking in loud, angry voices. I prayed that it didn't involve Sergio, but as I rounded the last aisle, my fears proved to be correct. Amayah's father was standing between a man wearing the outfit of a store employee, and a large, black NYPD officer in his street blues. Not good, not good at all.

I slowed down a bit to take in the scene. Sergio was shaking his head back and forth, repeatedly saying, "No ladron! No ladron!" I didn't know what that meant, but I suspected I was about to find out. The employee, store manager Kenneth Young, according to his name tag, was pointing at Sergio and telling the cop, "I saw him put the fruit in his pockets and walk right outside the front door, plain as day. Classic case of shoplifting, officer... I want him arrested and banned from the store!"

The cop was listening to the manager seriously, but I thought I saw a little amusement there too. It was a crime to steal from someone, sure, but arrested for taking oranges and bananas? That wasn't exactly a crime destined to land you on the six o'clock news.

I approached slowly and caught the officer's eye. "Excuse me, sir, this man is a friend of mine. Can you tell me what he's done wrong?"

The store manager turned on me like I was interrupting the Pentagon War Council. "Who the hell is this kid? Hey! Who the hell are you? Mind your own business, boy! This doesn't concern you!"

A year ago, I would have gotten the hell out of there without a second look, and probably wouldn't have intervened in the first place. But Sergio was Amayah's dad, and he was a good guy. I wasn't going to let him twist in the wind without seeing how I could help.

The cop ignored Mr. Young's outburst, fortunately.

"Hey kid, you know this guy for real?" the officer said skeptically.

Sergio had finally noticed me. "Rohan! Rohan!" he cried to me. At least he knew my name.

"I do, officer, he's my girlfriend's dad, um, my girlfriend's uncle. He and his wife just came to the U.S. a couple weeks ago. His wife wasn't feeling well, so she stayed home, and I came with him to get some groceries for them."

"That solves half the mystery," the cop said, "but he still put food in his pockets and walked out of the store, which is unfortunately the very definition of stealing in this city."

Sergio was gesticulating towards me and then pointing to where he was standing. He imitated looking for someone but not being able to find them, then pointed towards the door. It made perfect sense.

"I told him to come back and wait here for me after he got the produce on his wife's list," I explained. "He probably came back and didn't see me and decided to look for me outside."

The store manager rolled his eyes in disbelief. "C'mon, he put the fruit in his pocket for safekeeping or what? There are signs all over the produce aisle saying to use plastic bags."

I shrugged my shoulders. "He doesn't speak English, sir. Which means he also can't read it. I think he was just trying to keep the food safe while finding me. He wasn't trying to steal from you."

Mr. Young didn't look convinced, but the cop looked ready to close the case.

"I think we just had a simple mix-up here. If these two gentlemen are going to pay for the food that was accidentally taken out of the store, I don't see why there should be any need for anyone to be arrested or any further arguing."

I immediately said that we would head right to the cash register, and Sergio nodded for further reinforcement. The cop was turning to go, but Mr. Young, an angry look on his face, couldn't help himself.

"I don't like it. I stopped him today, but what happens tomorrow when I'm on the floor or in my office? I'm so sick of these damn minorities coming into my store and my neighborhood. Criminals, every last one of them!"

The cop stopped mid-turn and slowly rotated back to stare down at the oblivious store manager. I felt like I was about to witness a tornado smash into a building, but I couldn't look away.

"Excuse me, sir," the cop said, his voice now deep and booming. "But it almost sounded like you said that ALL minorities were criminals. That seems like a pretty racist thing to say for a person whose business is in the heart of a very diverse neighborhood. Especially someone who relies on a minority police officer to patrol the area around his store. I must have heard you wrong, because it would be a very, very, very bad idea for you to PISS ME OFF."

He shouted the last three words at the store manager, who looked like a wilting flower by comparison. He apologized to the officer, then to us, and hastily retreated to his office as fast as his waddling legs would carry him.

The cop turned back to us. "Thanks for clearing that up, kid... and hey," he caught Sergio's eye. "Welcome to the neighborhood, brother."

When we got the groceries back to Sergio and Teresa's little apartment, Teresa seemed to be feeling better, propped up on a few pillows in bed and laughing with Amayah. I could see the glow on both women's faces, and it struck me again how remarkably alike they were. I helped Sergio put the groceries in the tiny refrigerator that came standard with the room.

When he was done, he went to check on Teresa, then started rapidly speaking Spanish, pointing at me several times and saying, "Rohan." Amayah listened to his story, turned to me, and smiled. "Rohan," she said. "Thank you so much for doing that. You are so sweet."

The compliment wrapped around me like a warm hug. I wanted nothing more than to be alone with her right now, to hold her and kiss her and play with her long hair, but I knew that I had to at least wait until we figured out what we were doing here and what Teresa and Sergio needed. Would we have to secure them a bank loan? That sounded harder than escaping the South as a runaway slave. At least escaping involved an escape route and a durable wagon. Figuring out how to get a loan sounded about as complex as building a rocket ship.

The sun was getting low in the sky, and we were still stuffed from lunch, but Teresa wanted to take a walk to get the blood flowing, so we agreed to come with them and headed into the park across the street. None of us were tennis players, so we just enjoyed the green space, watching the kids play and the couples hold hands in the late spring night. I had never noticed how much I liked being in nature until I started spending time with Amayah.

After an hour or so, we could tell that Sergio and Teresa were getting worn out, so we headed back to their apartment. About twenty feet from the building, we saw the door slam open as three figures dressed all in black with ski masks burst out, pushing their way past onlookers and racing past the four of us at the edge of the curb. We gaped at them in shock as Teresa yelled, "My purse! He's got my purse!"

I turned and saw that the purse Teresa had carried to the bank, now slung over one of the departing figures' shoulders, bouncing against him as he ran. Another had a radio in his hands, and the third held a garbage bag that probably wasn't full of garbage. There was no mistaking what was happening; the three of them had just robbed at least Sergio and Teresa's apartment and perhaps others as well.

Beside me, I saw Sergio priming for action as he turned to give chase, but I put a hand on his shoulder and used my power to hold him back painlessly. I shook my head and pointed at Teresa.

After all, I had heard enough Spanish lately to understand and say something. I looked him in the eye and said, "No, Sergio. Su esposa y su bebé."

He blinked and took my meaning. He had a young wife with a baby in her tummy. Racing off after three thieves in an unfamiliar neighborhood was not the behavior of a good husband and father. He nodded and put his arm around Teresa as I moved to follow the three crooks. A hand appeared on my chest and I looked down to see Amayah staring up at me. I could see her anger at these men for trying to take what meager possessions her parents had managed to acquire. I knew how she felt. I had felt the same way when the thieves intimidated my dad and stole the cash register from the laundromat. We had so little as it was, why did they have to take even more from us? But back then, I was a scrawny, scared kid, not the New York ninja I had become over the past few months. This time, the weak and the innocent weren't going to get bowled over by a bunch of punks.

She looked up into my eyes with fierce intensity. "Go get them, Rohan," she whispered, and I was off.

The slowest of the three thieves was barely in sight, but I lowered my urge to run at full speed after them, as I might kill someone else accidentally by smashing into them, and because it would attract way too much attention on a crowded Sunday night street. I settled for running at track sprinter speed, Carl Lewis style, my knees rising high as I made quick pivots and rapidly narrowed the gap. The trailing guy turned and saw me coming, his eyes widening in disbelief at how fast I was making up ground. He screamed something ahead to the other two, who abruptly swerved left down an alley and out of sight. I reached the spot where they had turned and looked into the darkness. Not good. Not good at all.

There were a few flickering lights overhead and all sorts of places to hide—trash cans, dumpsters, mattresses leaning against the brick. I slowed and then stopped, checking my angles before stepping foot off the well-lit street and into the dim alley. I knew I could take one or all of them in a fight, but I didn't know what sort of weapons they might have on them. I wasn't eager to test the limits of my powers against a knife blade or a bullet in a dark alley. I was about thirty feet into the alley when I heard a clang, and the dumpster I had just passed flung open. All three crooks jumped out from a mound of trash, and with their element of surprise, I only dodged the first two. The third knocked me sideways into another dumpster, and I fell to the concrete, his weight planted squarely on my chest. The air whooshed from my lungs, and I coughed in shock and pain. The other two got to their feet and started kicking me in the ribs as the one on top sneered down at me.

"What'd you think, you were some kind of superhero, you little bitch?" he asked, snarling with laughter. "Going to impress your little girlfriend? After we cut you up, maybe I'll go back for a piece of her next!" A switchblade appeared in his hand, and he twirled it around menacingly.

Giving me that much time was the worst mistake he could have made, other than suggesting he might hurt Amayah. I grabbed the back of his legs with my arms and threw him off me; his head cracked against the underside of the fire escape hanging from the building to our left. His two associates both took a step back as they watched their leader's hard landing, and I took that time to flip myself up to a standing position, grab them each by the back of the neck and smash their foreheads together. They collapsed like rag dolls at my feet. The third one got up groggily, trying to keep his balance, as I walked up to him and snatched his ski mask off his head. Surprisingly, he was about my age, maybe Puerto Rican. I spun him around and put his arm behind his back, making it just painful enough so he wouldn't struggle.

"Where's the loot, kid?" I asked him, trying to make my voice as deep and intimidating as possible.

He had no problem giving up the stuff they had stolen after what I had done to his friends. He pointed to the other dumpster. "Behind, behind there."

Just to reinforce that he shouldn't try anything funny, I used the hand not holding his arm to move the dumpster out of the way. It had to weigh at least five hundred pounds, and I nudged it like it was made of Styrofoam. He made a nervous noise in the back of his throat and said, "What the hell are you, man? How'd you do that?"

"I guess I'm some kind of superhero, you little bitch," I said in his ear as I stood behind him. "Just out here trying to impress my little girlfriend."

The other two were out cold, so I marched the leader out of the alley and into the street. A few people were hanging around, having heard the noise, and when they saw me and who I was restraining, there were shouts of encouragement and even some scattered applause.

I called out, "There are two others knocked out in the alley, and a switchblade laying around somewhere too. Somebody call the cops, and let's get this trash off our streets!"

More of the crowd cheered, and I smiled. This is what being a hero was supposed to feel like. I had taken out the trash, and people loved it. I marched the third guy all the way back to Sergio and Teresa's apartment, with him carrying the trash bag in his arms, and the purse slung over his shoulder.

Word on the street beat us there, and Amayah, Sergio, Teresa, and a bunch of other residents of the flophouse were out front as we walked up. They broke into applause, and the manager of the flophouse shook my hand. Three other men kept a watchful eye on the crook to ensure he didn't try anything funny before the cops arrived. Teresa got to me first and gave me a giant hug and a kiss on the cheek, but Amayah was right behind her and did the same, though her hug was quite a bit longer. Sergio came over and pumped both my hands relentlessly, telling me, "Gracias, Rohan! Gracias!"

The thrill was short-lived, unfortunately. Back inside Teresa and Sergio's apartment, we saw the real damage of the robbery. They had smashed a small religious statue the couple had on their windowsill, apparently thinking it might have money in it. They had also come through the window, and had fallen directly onto the wooden crib they had purchased for baby Amayah to sleep in. It wasn't the best quality wood to begin with, and it lay splintered on the carpet.

Teresa was already crying. She got her purse back from me, and the few meager belongings scooped up in the robbers' haste to flee after rifling through her tiny apartment. Seeing the damage to the crib, combined with the ugliness she and Sergio had both experienced at the bank and the grocery store, it seemed like it was pushing her to a breaking point.

Sergio wrapped his arms around her and held her tight, whispering softly in Spanish in her ear. I felt helpless and wished that I could have been there sooner to catch the thieves in the act.

Teresa looked up at us, still crying. "Is this how America is? Are we going to get talked down to anytime we go somewhere by white people? And then come home to find that our own people are robbing us because it's easier than working? Did we make a mistake coming here? I thought America was special, but right now, it just seems like another place for people to treat you badly and take what you worked hard for."

It was heartbreaking to see. The American dream was falling so dreadfully short of what the newly-arrived couple had been hoping for. Amayah held her mom's hands, but didn't have much to say. I just stood there trying to think of words that would reassure them that the people of New York City were indeed better than what she was experiencing.

Fortunately, I didn't have to stand there long before a knock came at the door. We were all wary, considering what had just happened, but Sergio untangled himself from Teresa and looked through the peephole, then opened the door.

There were at least four people there that I could see, and perhaps a few others crowded behind them. A young blonde-haired man stood at the front with a pleasant smile, and Sergio gave him a nod.

"Sergio, Teresa, we heard what happened tonight, are you guys all right?" The guy had an accent I couldn't quite place, English or Australian.

He noticed Amayah and I standing there. "You must be the guy who chased down the thieves! Wow, the whole neighborhood's raving about you, mate. You need to give the Jets a call and offer to play linebacker for them. I'm Noah, I live across the hall from the Bellos. We heard that you lost some stuff and wanted to pitch in."

Noah looked past them and saw the ruins of the crib on the floor. "Oh nuts, but good news, yours truly is the son of a woodworker back in Auckland. I'm here on a scholarship to NYU, but let me grab my gear and I can get that fixed up for you long before the little one arrives." Noah ducked out of the door frame and disappeared across the hall.

A middle-aged Dominican woman stepped into the spot he had just vacated. "My husband and his brother went to get some boards to nail up your window that they broke," she said. "It will keep out most of the bugs until the super can fix the glass."

Teresa's face went from sadness to shock to surprise in less than a minute. Another woman who had to be close to one hundred stepped through with a casserole dish in her hands. "Enchiladas con carne," she said. "Been in my freezer a couple weeks, but it'll be delicious once it thaws out. It should last the two of you at least three days unless the hero here is eating too... looks like he has a big appetite." She smiled and gave me a wink. "And all four of you have a standing invitation for dinner in Unit 3A any day of the week.

"Don't let those thieves get you down. This is a good neighborhood and a good place to live."

A few more neighbors followed, bringing small gifts to the unnerved couple. It felt a bit blasphemous, but I was reminded of the story of Jesus' birth and how the wise men had come to the manger with gifts of gold, frankincense, and myrrh to welcome the baby to the world. We were seeing the very best of New York right now, the very best of humanity in general, and it warmed my heart. The energy inside of me grew stronger, and I could nearly taste the feeling that I associated with time-jumping when we first transported to Mississippi and then back to New York. It wasn't a full dose, however, so perhaps our job was only half-complete. I realized that it might be time to visit the Chang family.

The Bellos thanked all their visitors with hugs, handshakes, smiles and tears. By the time everyone left, it was almost midnight, and Teresa and Sergio both looked dead on their feet. I could tell that Amayah didn't want to leave and would have been content to just sit in her chair and watch the two of them sleep all night, but I knew that wasn't the wisest choice. I gently suggested getting back to our neck of the woods, causing her eyes to shoot lasers at me when I said it, and I knew this wasn't going to be easy, even if it was the right thing to do. Amayah stalled for any reason she could think of and managed to stay another thirty minutes, but both of her parents were nodding off, so I finally announced that it was time to make our exit.

Teresa hugged Amayah, and she leaned back into it for all she was worth. I shook Sergio's hand and wished him luck, saying that we would see them soon, which was true in a sense. I slowly inched Amayah towards the door and it was painful to watch her struggle to leave. I wouldn't have minded staying later, but Teresa needed her rest, and the events of the day were something Sergio and Teresa needed to process together; not necessarily with a cousin they had only met twelve hours ago and her Asian American boyfriend. I finally used a little extra strength to pull her away from her mom and get the apartment door open. As we were halfway out the door, Teresa called out to Amayah in Spanish. "Prima! Tú novio está muy simpático y guapisimo." I knew enough Spanish to know she just called me very nice and handsome, and I grinned as Teresa blushed. I looked down at Amayah, but she refused to make eye contact; the hurt and pain were back as I pulled her away from her family and out into the New York night.

Ama called back, "It's a girl, I think," and smiled. "And I can tell you that I'm sure she is very proud of you right now."

Teresa and Sergio smiled back, and Teresa lovingly touched her stomach. Amayah made a soft gagging noise in her throat, as though it was all too much to keep enduring. I said goodnight one more time and got her out the door at last.

Bolting past me, Ama stormed away into the lonely street in the silence of the late night.

CHAPTER

TWENTY-FIVE

I knew that she was upset at having to leave, but I hadn't expected her to run off without me. I had to turn on the jets to catch up as she rushed down the street. "Amayah! Amayah, wait!" As she neared a bus station entrance, she rounded on me with furious eyes.

"Jeez, Rohan, why didn't you just pick me up and throw me out the window? I'm so sorry I wanted to spend a few extra minutes WITH MY FAMILY!"

She yelled the last three words, and it knocked me back a step. I backed up even further, fearing the pain of her wrath. She realized that she was making a scene, but she didn't seem too concerned about it. With her fists balled up, she continued to glare hard at me, daring me to speak.

I put my hands up as if claiming self-defense. "I know you wanted to stay all night, Amayah, but we're not here for us; we're here to help them.

"They both have work in the morning, and they're both dead tired, and your mom is pregnant with you. They've been trying to get us to leave for an hour, but they're too polite to say so. Your mom has you inside her tummy, and she needs to rest!"

I was a little loud in return, louder than I should have been, but I was frustrated that the day had gone so well, yet she was still mad about it. She didn't talk to me much on the way back to the shelter in New Jersey, but on the bus trip home, she did move over and curl up against my shoulder.

"I know you're right about my mom and dad, but it doesn't make it any easier," she said, her voice muffled against my shirt. "Seeing them so young and happy and full of hope, even with the odds stacked against them. What a sight!"

She looked at me then, and the hurt seemed to fade away from her eyes. "I kept thinking 'This is it' every time we did something to help them today, but I think what we really did was show them that other people do care about them, even if they're not Puerto Rican! They were so beaten down at the bank, and I'm sure so many people feel that way when they first get here. But we helped show them that the diversity of New York is a good thing, and that people are good because of who they are on the inside, not based on the color of their skin."

She kissed me softly on the cheek then, and it burned hot and bright. "Thank you, Rohan. Again, you are capable of such wonderful things."

She offered her hand, and I took it, and we rode in silence all the way back to the shelter. I was full of silent prayers of gratitude to God for bringing my Ama back to me, and I vowed to never take her for granted again.

We were both dead on our feet and desperate to shower and collapse into our beds before the rising sun, but I stopped Amayah short. "Hey, I have something for you, a small gift. Can you swing by my room real quick so I can give it to you?"

I knew that she was exhausted, but I was hoping that she was just curious enough to fight off sleep. "A gift for me, Mr. Chang?

Where did you find the time?" she asked with a small smirk on her face.

"For you, Miss Bello, I have the power to make time slow down, stop, and even reverse," I said with a sheepish smile.

I opened my door and gestured for her to enter. She sat in my desk chair after eyeing the bed for a moment. I might have been kind and considerate, but I was still a guy, and she still thought twice about sitting on a teenage boy's bed late at night. I pretended not to notice as I opened up the journal to the page I had been working on.

I had planned to slide the note under her door at some point. It was a personal, emotional thing I had written to her, and I was still unsure about baring my soul this way, but I decided that I needed to show her every single piece of me so she could understand how serious I was about us.

I cleared my throat and was horrified when my voice cracked, then cracked even more as I started to speak.

"I wrote ... dang it, I wrote this for you the other night when I couldn't sleep. I realized that I had just been enjoying the status quo with you, instead of continuing to get to know you and telling you how I feel about you, about myself, and about, well, everything. So... I'd like to read it to you now."

I looked up, but her face was expressionless, with just the smallest curl of amusement in her lips. She liked it when I was nervous, which made me more nervous. Which all probably entertained her to no end.

I took a deep breath and spoke from the heart, finding my voice for the words I had spent hours getting just perfect.

"Amayah," I spoke.
"*Feeling the windy air through your hair,*

A breeze so unique, beyond compare, without a care.
I saw your smile and eyes all aglow,
I wanted to hold you close and never let go.
Your bright face is a vision, but your heart, a true guiding light,
Vanquishing my worries through the coldest night.
You showed me a world far from the cold I've known.
In you, girl, I found my heart fully grown.
Time slips through my grasp, future, present, and past.
My love for you, Ama, unwavering, destined to last."

I WAS COMPLETELY ENGROSSED in the lines of the poem, hesitant to break the spell by looking up, fearing the vulnerability of discovering her expression. Yet, when I finally dared to glance up, my apprehension was swept away by a wave of warmth. Amayah had leaped from her chair in a burst of emotion, wrapping her arms around me in a tender embrace. Fortuitously, the bed cushioned our fall, sparing me from any injury and allowing me to fully immerse myself in the embrace of the girl of my dreams. Held in her arms so tightly, I felt a surge of love so intense that it seemed it could defy reality itself.

I gently caressed her luxurious, silky hair, reveling in the sensation that I cherished above all else. This moment was a testament to the fact that we had overcome our rough patch, a thought that filled me with hope.

Her eyes, sparkling with joy and shimmering with tears, met mine, and in a soft, tender voice, she whispered, "You remembered my poem, Mister." This simple acknowledgment spoke volumes.

I smiled at her, wishing the moment could last forever. "I'm sorry it took so long, Miss. Turns out that paper was a bit expensive in 1854, so I had to wait a while to jot it all down."

She gently lifted the paper from my hands, her eyes scanning the words with care before she placed it gently on the bed, as though it were too precious to risk any harm. Turning to face me, she then settled fully into my lap—a gesture that flooded my senses with warmth, marking an indescribable moment of closeness I hadn't felt in a very long time. With a tenderness that sent shivers down my spine, she traced her finger down the contour of my face, gliding over to my neck, then to my chest, and gracefully back up. Her eyes locked with mine, she whispered, "You possess a beautiful soul, Rohan, and a heart that's truly remarkable. Beyond your ability to run fast and defend with strength, it's your innate powers—those of kindness, empathy, and love—that stand out. Let those virtues be your guide, for with them, you're destined to change the world for many and craft wonders beyond imagination."

Her praise rolled over me like a wave, and I felt so close to her and so good inside that I spontaneously tried to gather my energy and get us back home. It felt so good and so right, and for a few seconds, I thought it would work, but the power faded away, and I felt a surge of fatigue.

Amayah noticed the sag in my face and muscles. "What's wrong? Are you okay?"

Her attention to detail when it came to others' suffering never ceased to amaze me. I smiled and tried to perk up, even though it felt like I could sleep for twelve hours. "I'm fine, Ama. I was feeling so good right then that I thought I could have gotten us back home, but I came up short."

She stroked my hair and rubbed my shoulders a bit, and my muscles hummed their thanks for the soft touch.

"Ro, don't be silly. We're only halfway done here. We need to start figuring out where your parents are so we can help them, just like we helped mine. Plus, the other two times we jumped, you weren't trying, right? Didn't it just sort of happen?"

She was right, but I still didn't like the idea of the powers controlling me, rather than the other way around. I didn't want to think about Nick's offer of controlling and bending the powers to my will. Ama had been right thus far, and I agreed that it made sense to seek out my mom and dad.

Unfortunately, we would have to wait another week because we didn't have much free time at night, especially if we wanted to be prepared to watch over the children the next day. I held her for another 10 minutes, saying very little, aside from promising to see her in the morning. I doubt the door had fully closed before night closed in, carrying me into dreams, where I found myself lulled into a peaceful and sound sleep.

TWENTY-SIX

I woke up to my alarm going off way too early. At first, I thought it was a mistake, but then I saw the sunlight coming through the window. That's when I remembered that I had a commitment to the kids, so I knew I had to get out of bed. I felt like using my powers to get going faster, but using them in everyday situations didn't feel right. Superman didn't use his powers to get to work in the morning; he took the subway or walked, unless he had to fight crime before clocking in.

Using my powers to overcome grogginess before work seemed like a misuse of my gifts, so I opted for a hearty breakfast and a cup of coffee instead. The fact that Rohan Chang was now a regular coffee drinker was in some ways more unlikely than just about anything else that had happened over the past few months. Given our heritage, my family had always been big-time tea drinkers. Still, when Henry went to college, he switched to coffee for the caffeine rush that sustained him through taking a full course load, working any job he could find, and studying relentlessly. I'm pretty sure that Henry switching to coffee had sent me in the other direction; I hated being compared to him, which happened constantly inside our community and at school, so I stood beside my parents and derided his drinking it.

But things changed at the youth center. The kids never ran out of energy. Never. They only quieted down when the lights were off and needed sleep. Otherwise, they were going a million miles an hour doing whatever seemed like the next best and most amazing thing. So, one morning, as I came dragging into the commissary where Bobo and Amayah were talking animatedly about the New York Museum of Modern Art, I was just trying to keep my eyes open. Bobo was the first to tell me that I just needed some coffee, and was stunned when I said that I hated it.

"You've got to try it, Rohan," Bobo had exclaimed, retrieving a mug for me and filling it up with the dark, hot liquid. "It's like liquid jet fuel for your brain."

Amayah's eyes narrowed at the comment. "Uh, Nathan?" she asked, refusing to call him Bobo. She said that it was not a nice nickname, though he didn't seem to care. "Jet fuel already is a liquid."

He threw his hands up in the air in mock disgust as I tried a sip and nearly spit it out. So hot! So bitter! Who would think this was a good drink?

"Good grief, man, don't drink it black!" Bobo cried out in mock horror. "What are you, some sort of a savage?" He retrieved the cup, but Amayah took it away from him, claiming that she knew what my taste buds liked.

When she returned it to me, the coffee had changed from black to a buttery-tannish color. "Cream and two sugars," she said with a smile. "That's the way I like mine too."

I gave it a tentative taste and blinked in surprise. The dark black swill from a moment ago was gone, replaced by a creamy sweet flavor and a warmth that flowed from my throat to my nose and down into my stomach. I eyed each of them suspiciously. "This is the same stuff?"

Amayah giggled. "Rohan Chang discovers coffee, ladies and gentlemen!"

I've been a firm believer in coffee ever since. As I drank my jet fuel this morning, thinking about our recent revelations with Ama's parents, I saw Bobo hovering over the sports page across from me. The Yankees had lost to the Blue Jays and Tommy John got hammered, going only two innings before getting knocked out in a 9-6 loss. I got the page with the rest of the box scores and pored over them, just as I would have back home in 1997. It was weird seeing the standings back then. There were only two divisions in each league, instead of three, and the Marlins and Rockies didn't even exist! I went box score by box score, reading the names and seeing who I remembered. My eye caught on the Phillies beating the Astros 6-2, and I felt a flush on my face, recalling Amayah catching me a few nights earlier with my sheet of gambling 'predictions.' Reading a book about 1980s baseball at the school library had turned me on to all the previous champions of the league from my lifetime. In 1980, Houston and Philadelphia would meet again in the National League Championship series, with the Phillies winning in five games. My beloved Yankees would get smoked by the Royals in the American League Championship series. I felt kind of grimy about making the list of future champions, even before Amayah had seen it, but it also irked me not to use my knowledge to make things easier for us. I wondered if Amayah would approve of me making the bet for her parents, or for Bobo, or even in the community center's name, but I seriously doubted it. I knew that I should get rid of the list, but I kept pushing it to the back of my mind, hoping that I could reason out a good solution and still earn some real money.

The great Mike Schmidt hit a home run for Philadelphia, and I once again felt myself drawn to Yankee Stadium. I had traveled back and forth in time and could teleport from one location to another, but I had still never sat in the bleachers with a hot dog in one hand and a giant pretzel in the other yelling "Red Sox suck!" with fifty thousand other New Yorkers. For one crazy moment, I realized that I could probably teleport myself onto the field at Yankee Stadium right this very minute if I really wanted to, but again, that felt like a misuse of my powers, so I shook the idea from my mind. The tone of the article made me chuckle. The writer clearly believed that both Houston and the Phillies were just the flavor of the month, noting their strong records to start the year and will to overcome adversity. This would be Houston's first time in the playoffs ever, and Philadelphia's first time in the World Series since 1963. At this point in history, they were more of a joke than the curse of the Cubs or the Red Sox. Philly had never won the World Series, even though they were one of the first baseball teams in the country, with history tracing back to the 1880s. It was crazy to think that their first team formed just a few decades after the time we spent in Oxford. Not for the first time, I wondered if, at some point, I'd be able to actually control my time traveling and use it to visit critical moments in history, or even go into the future. The possibilities of that kind of power were limitless. I could be the greatest teacher or writer in the world if I had a direct window to any time I wanted, past or future.

However, at the moment, I had to get my butt out of the commissary and help some wayward kids learn their ABCs and 123s, which was the bulk of the agenda this morning. It was humbling work for someone like me, when I knew that I could be out somewhere testing my powers or fighting crime, but it also felt good when Amayah looked at me as I helped a kid make a connection. It was like God wanted me to be a positive role model and a shining example for the kids to imitate, as I only wanted great things for the children at our center. That night, Amayah, myself, Brittney, and Bobo hung out watching TV for a while and had an impromptu Bible study. Brittney didn't go out the weekend we went to find Amayah's parents, but had gotten permission to stay in her room. She read her new Bible and did a lot of writing, so she was anxious to share her findings with the rest of us.

She had hit on something in the Book of Proverbs, which quickly became a favorite of mine as well. When you grow up not fully invested in the story of God and Jesus, the Book of Proverbs is a great place to get your feet wet with Christianity. The Proverbs are like short stories of good advice, rather than long, sprawling tales of men who lived hundreds of years ago with great plagues, death, and destruction. Not that I was knocking all the miracles that God, Jesus, and their followers had performed, but a cynical teenager like me wasn't always in the best frame of mind to accept that a flood once covered the entire world or that a burning bush spoke to Moses and gave him his life's purpose.

Regardless, Brittney was excitedly reading her observations to us, and she highlighted the text from Proverbs 12:11: "He who tills his land will have plenty of bread, but he who pursues worthless things lacks sense." Brittney was beaming up at us, as if the secret to life was hanging right in front of our faces.

"This is it!" she exclaimed. "This is my new mantra for life. What could be more worthless than drugs? It doesn't cure sickness. It doesn't make me feel better in the long run. It has literally no worth, yet I spend my money on it, I lie about it, and I let it come between me and the people I care about the most!"

We all saw what she was saying, and I was impressed by the clarity she was showing. Every time I watched a movie or a TV show where people were getting off drugs, it seemed like they could barely function. You'd see them in the bathroom throwing their guts up in the toilet or suffering terrible cases of the shakes. Brittney was defying that stereotype by doing great work, looking inward and figuring out not just how to stop the addiction, but what it meant to her in the first place.

"I realized that all of the effort I was putting into my addiction— the smoking, the acquiring, planning out how to get the money, lying to my parents or my friends about where I was going to... all that time and effort could have been spent shaping my life and figuring out what I can do to help others and nurture my own inter- ests," she said. "On Saturday night, I called my drug dealer and let him know that I was breaking up with him. Figuratively speaking, of course. I told him never to call my number again, and I went outside with a book of matches and burned all my contacts for that sort of stuff."

Her statement hit home, and when we parted ways for the night, I hung back a minute and slipped into the commissary supply closet to retrieve a book of matches. After I told Amayah goodnight, I opened my window, struck a match, and touched its flame to the piece of paper with my sports forecasts on it. I let it burn down to a crisp as Hua softly whispered, *"Blessed you are with the Shine Xiong."* I watched as the ashes scattered to the four winds.

"Don't burn the place down now, I'm just getting settled in!"

The voice sent me jumping nearly five feet in the air—Bobo!

"Oh hey, Bobo," I uttered, trying to brush off the sight of the situation he had just witnessed. "Just, uh, just getting rid of something I don't need anymore."

"The healing power of transformation, brother, I can dig it," Bobo responded sagely. "Take something that's a problem and change its essential elements into a new form. That's a great strategy for eliminating opposition."

"Uh, thanks," I replied. Bobo sometimes talked like he was much older than he looked. He seemed to seek me out for guidance on some things, but at other times, I had the distinct feeling that he knew more than he was letting on. "I think I realized tonight when Brittney was talking that I have a crutch I'm always falling back on. But I don't have to live that way. I need to embrace the life in front of me and make the best of it, instead of trying to be in control of everything."

"That's living by faith, brother," Bobo nodded and smiled at me. "Reminds me of a great sermon I saw a minister give one time. He demonstrated the power of God using nothing more than a stool."

"A stool?" I said, a sarcastic tone rising in my voice. "This I've gotta hear."

"Okay," Bobo said, his smile continuing to spread. "Let's do a little role playing. You're going to play a hard-headed teenager named Rohan, and I'm going to play the role of Jesus."

I laughed out loud. "Sounds about right."

He took the chair at my desk and pulled it out. "We don't have a stool, so this will have to do. Now, let me ask you a question. Who would you want in charge of everything if you had a choice? Your life, fears, worries, doubts, all of that... You or Jesus?"

I rolled my eyes. "Well, as a prospective Christian, I imagine that the correct answer is Jesus. I would like him to be in charge of my life because I have too much anxiety and stress and worry in my life already."

"Great!" Bobo said. "As Jesus, I'm going to sit in this chair and take charge of your life. This chair is the control center of your life. Whenever you have a question or have a concern, talk it over with me, and I'll take care of it."

"Okay," I said. "What's the catch?"

"No catch!" Bobo replied. "Now, first of all, we're going to have to change your diet, because you're eating way too much fast food, which will eventually destroy your heart health. So, McDonald's is down to once a week."

"Um, what?" I replied.

"McDonald's—the one with the golden arches? You go there about five times a week, right? Now it's down to one; Jesus has spoken."

Before I could object, he continued.

"Second order of business. Amayah wants to be a doctor, and she deserves to go to the best possible medical school that money can buy. So, when she graduates from high school, she's going to go to Cornell University, and then to NYU College of Medicine. She can't have a boyfriend weighing her down, so you'll need to find your own thing and give her space to breathe. You'll have to find your own passion so that she can focus on her grades. You guys can get married after she's a resident."

"Now wait just a minute," I said, surprised at the anger rising in my voice. "We just started dating, and she could do those things, too. And she wants to be with me!"

Bobo raised his eyebrows. "Sounds like you want the chair back. I can get up. No big deal. I'm sure you know better than ... God, right?"

I started to speak, but then stopped. It felt like I was walking into a trap.

"I don't know better than God, but that's not what I want. Amayah and I just started dating. I don't want to lose her."

"That's honest, at least," Bobo said. "But sometimes, what we want and what God knows is best are two very different things. The way I've heard it, Amayah has been dreaming of being a doctor since she was five years old. And you've been dating for a few months, right? Are her lifelong dreams not as important as being Rohan Chang's main squeeze?"

His logic was hitting way too close to home in regard to my selfishness about wanting a simple, easy life with Amayah. It was a problem that had plagued me in 1997 too, even before my powers manifested. I didn't really think much about what my family wanted for me or of me; I just wanted to explore my artistic interests and be left alone. Even with my powers, should that mean Amayah gives up on her goals for mine? Her fierce independence and compassion were two things that I loved about her. Taking them away sounded unnatural.

"So what... you're saying I should just do nothing? Sit here and wait for things to happen?"

Bobo shook his head.

"No, Rohan, before doing anything, clear your mind, spend time alone, and seek guidance from God. Everything will be revealed. And oh Rohan, remember: a man truly becomes mature when he no longer depends on a woman's love or anyone else's."

I nodded and stayed quiet, thinking over what Bobo said. It was only later, in the middle of the night, that I woke up and remembered that Hua had once said those exact words to me.

. . .

WE WAITED for two weeks before seeking out my parents in Queens, mainly because we'd already spent a good deal of money tracking down Amayah's parents. I also couldn't let Ama know about the secret fifteen thousand I had stashed away and my big plans for it. I let her think that we still needed a couple paychecks each to make it a whole weekend out in the big city. My parents lived in Fresh Meadows for as long as I could remember, but I wasn't sure if our 1997 apartment was their first. It seemed too big, which was sort of a joke, but not really. To the rest of the world, the places we New Yorkers call home may seem more like broom closets than actual apartments. Our apartment in 1997 consisted of my parents' bedroom, a kitchen, a living room my brother slept in, and a makeshift room I had constructed with help from my dad and brother, which gave me four walls and a door, although the walls didn't go all the way to the ceiling.

My parents had agreed that I needed somewhere quiet to study, so they did a little remodeling to give me a private space, which was all I ever wanted. Regardless, I wasn't sure if my parents lived in the same place with young Henry and toddler Rohan, but we were on our way to find out.

We left Union City on the bus early Saturday morning. It was great having Amayah back in her typical bubbly mood as we headed east. It took more than an hour to get there, and I was grateful not to make another journey in awkward silence. Once across the Hudson, we transferred to the subway in Midtown Manhattan, which took us to Queens. The closer I got to home, the more I gawked at how familiar, yet unfamiliar it all felt. The subway station signs told me that I was almost home to Fresh Meadows, but everything else felt like an alternate reality.

Finally, the train pulled into the station at 179th Street, and after a short Q17 bus ride, we were there. Home, give or take 17 years. Like Amayah a couple of weeks earlier, I had a hard time not shouting out the names of businesses and places that I recognized. Seventeen years wasn't that long, after all, and I didn't want to look like too much of a lunatic, although that was pretty hard to do in New York City.

We faced the same challenge as we had with Amayah's parents. Even if my folks were living in the same place, what was I going to do? Knock on their door and introduce myself as their guardian angel, and *oh, by the way, that baby in your arms is me?* We figured that our best bet was to determine their routine, including where they spent their time, and arrange a bump-into-you scenario. Our apartment building took me by surprise, mostly because it was painted a deep royal blue, rather than the sickly lime green that I associated with home. We made it inside without anyone asking what we were up to, and I was amazed by how fresh and clean the lobby looked. Back in my time, rumor had it that some drunk had barfed up an entire pepperoni pizza on one spot on the floor that no one ever went near. Whatever method they had used to clean it out of the carpet failed miserably, so there had been a permanent rust-colored stain there my entire childhood. There was no sign of it anywhere in 1980.

My parents were nowhere in sight, not that we had expected things to be that easy. Just like Amayah, it was bizarre for me to walk past the door to the only home I had ever known, with the key in my hand, unsure if anyone I knew even lived there. We spent another hour outside the apartment, watching the door, but it was like finding a needle in a haystack.

I was getting hungry, and Amayah wanted to look for some new shoes, since we were doing so much walking and playing with the kids. We decided to kill two birds with one stone and set out for the Queens Center Mall, a place I was reasonably confident would be where I knew it would be in 1980. My instincts were correct, and Queens Center Mall was right where I had left it on Queens Boulevard between Woodhaven and 57th. In our time, the big studs were JCPenney at one end and Macy's at the other, but as we approached, we saw that those two slots were instead filled by an Ohrbach's and an Abraham & Straus. Regardless, we assumed that any mall would have a shoe store and a food court, so we headed inside. We went to the Gray's Papaya spot at the food court, where I had four hot dogs because of the astonishingly low price—fifty cents apiece—while Amayah settled for just one and a piña colada fruit drink. Eating proper New York food was something I would never take for granted again after our months in the old South. I was curious to see what the shoe stores looked like in 1980, as vintage anything was always cool on the graffiti scene. We found a place called Kinney Shoes that seemed to have every kind of shoe for every type of person, from shoes you'd casually wear to the disco to styles for the first day of school. Holding the door open, I grandly gestured for Amayah to enter by lowering my head and bowing, offering her a silly grin. As we went in, I stopped cold and at the sight of a salesman about ten feet in front of us, talking to three teenagers in sweatpants and tank tops. He was young and looked extremely nervous, with sweat visibly quivering on his brow. He was of average height and slightly built, wearing brown pants, a white collared shirt, and a yellow tie with the store logo stamped on it.

It was my dad.

Seeing Amayah's parents in their youth hadn't been a very big deal to me, as I didn't really know them in real life, but seeing a younger version of my stern father shaking in his boots felt like having a bucket of ice water dumped on my head. The shock rooted me in place, my eyes locked. Amayah followed my gaze, putting the pieces together. "Oh my gosh, Rohan, you look like him! Well, I mean you're a lot taller, but the eyes and the ears... totally the same. Stop staring at him though, you look like a weirdo!"

I shook myself free and blinked a few times to make sure that what I was seeing was real. Abraham Chang was selling shoes at the Queens Center Mall? I definitely never heard that story before. Well, it wasn't really Abraham Chang either, despite what his name tag said. My dad's real name was Zhang Chih-hao, but this wasn't Asia, and most Americans had no clue how to say or spell his actual name, so they just ignored it. Chang was the Romanization of Zhang, and my dad had chosen Abraham, or "Abe" for his new American first name, both because of the Biblical character and the American president who had worked to make this country safe for people of every color. My mom went by Claire, but her given name was Mei-ling. I hadn't thought much about the fact that they had both completely changed their names when they arrived, because those were the names that everyone called them in my time. I imagined coming to a new country and immediately having to change my name so that people would take me seriously, and it suddenly seemed foreign and terrible. *Welcome to America! Your name is what? Forget that, now your name is Claire.*

It was a terrible slight for people wanting to come, contribute and be a part of American society. I had half a mind to walk up to my dad and tell him to forget the Abraham part and go back to being Zhang Chih-hao, except that the shock of it might kill him. I was so lost in thought that I didn't see the situation developing right in front of us until Amayah said, "Umm, Ro?"

The three teenagers my dad had been helping were no longer looking for help; they were taking matters into their own hands, namely by trying to walk out of the store without paying for the shoes they had tried on. When my dad tried to get in front of them, they split up, laughing the whole time, and led him on a wild goose chase through the maze of other customers. All three of them strutted towards the exit, with my dad frantically trying to chase them down, but it was clear that he wasn't going to make it. I took one long step in front of the teenager nearest to the door and the main mall thoroughfare, where he could get lost in the flow of traffic in seconds. He was a couple of inches taller than me—a white kid with a terrible half-grown mustache and a mess of acne. He glared at me like I was crazy and said, "Move, bitch!" in a threatening growl, but it didn't have a hint of its intended effect. I put a hand out against his shoulder and stopped him cold with my enhanced strength.

"The cash register is back that way, friend," I said in a friendly voice that we both knew wasn't friendly. The unexpected force against his shoulder caught him off-guard, and I could see a hint of panic rise in him. He tried to move around me, but I grabbed his arm faster than he could react and held him in place.

"The cash register is back there," I said much louder and more clearly. This attracted the attention of a few other customers and a pair of store employees, who started moving in our direction. No store wanted a fight on its premises, but I didn't think it would come to that. The kid struggled against my grip once, but quickly realized that he was going nowhere.

"What the hell, man, let go!" he yelled, realizing too late that he was drawing unwanted attention in the process. His two friends had stopped to watch the confrontation, though it would have been wiser to run for it. As it was, the store's assistant manager had time to ask my dad what was going on, and my dad gestured at the other two trying to skip out without paying. Three store employees quickly surrounded them, asking to see their receipts. They took the shoes off and were escorted to the back office, glaring at me every step of the way.

I let go of the other would-be shoplifter once the assistant manager, a paunchy white guy with "Ed O'Neal" on his name tag, came up beside me. He told the kid that his options were taking the shoes off or seeing the boys in blue, but regardless, be taken to the back office for identification, and his parents called. He acquiesced without a word, and the assistant manager patted me on the back and praised me for my quick thinking. My dad was right beside him, thanking me for my bravery. It was one of the most bizarre experiences of my life. The dad I knew in 1997 was constantly riding me for failing to live up to his lofty expectations for my schoolwork and overall life. The young man in front of me was lavishing praise on me like I'd just stopped Lex Luthor from blowing up The Daily Planet. He bowed a few times before I took his hands in mine and shook them in the traditional American way. "It's no problem, uh, I'm glad to help out."

"Bù hǎo yì si," my dad apologized. *Excuse me.*

"Wo jiao Abraham!" my dad continued. *My name is Abraham.*

When he asked for my name, I realized that I had no cover story like Amayah. No Cousin Zuli to fall back on for me! I looked frantically around the store for inspiration.

"Uh, Buster. Nice to meet you." Amayah had to fake a coughing fit to cover her snort of laughter.

He thanked me over and over again, to the point that I was getting embarrassed. "Hey Abe, if you really want to thank me, you can help my girlfriend pick out some new sneakers!"

"Hǎo ó," my dad bubbled. *Okay! Sure.*

He immediately went into salesman mode, sitting Amayah down, using the scale to figure out her shoe size, and then taking us to the women's section, where he presented her with a variety of different styles. It took her about twenty-five minutes to find a pair she really liked, and my dad eagerly rushed to the store's back room to get them.

"You need to stop staring and ask him something about himself!" she lectured me once he stepped away. "Figure out what's going on with him and your mom right now. We need to get to know them a little better."

When my dad returned, I casually asked him about his family life.

"My wife is Claire, and my sons are Henry and little baby Rohan," he said. Amayah had a coughing fit thinly disguising her laughter. I envisioned Ama calling me Little Baby Rohan by the end of the day. "We came to New York last year, and are hoping to open our own business someday soon. For now, we are saving and saving and saving! We would like to open a ... is that the time? Oh no!"

We both looked at him with concern as he stared at the clock—3:13 p.m.

"What's wrong, Abraham?" Amayah asked.

"I was supposed to pick up food for an event tonight and deliver it to my wife before 4:00!" he said in a defeated voice. "I promised her several times that I would not forget, but I wound up working through lunch, and now here I am, looking like I don't care again."

He hung his head in shame, but the look that passed between Amayah and I was one of joy and opportunity. Here was a chance to do something good for my parents and spend more time with them.

"What event is happening tonight?" I asked, as casually as I could.

"The Asian-American Society of Queens is having a get-together for new members of the community," he replied. "We are new and would like to meet people, so we volunteered to bring food. But I forgot, and my sweet Claire will not be happy."

"Hey, Buster and I are going to that too!" Amayah piped up, clearly enjoying the sound of my fake name. "He just started college here, and has been looking to connect with his roots. Why don't we grab the food and take it to your wife, and then we can hang out tonight?"

My dad seemed flabbergasted by the overindulgence of good will, and I couldn't really blame him. New Yorkers aren't exactly known for their overabundance of generosity with total strangers. However, between my heroism and Amayah's earnestness, he agreed, scribbling down the address of the Chinese restaurant where he had placed the catering order. He had paid in advance—typical of my dad—and just needed it delivered to my mom.

"She works at HSBC Bank on Main Street," he told us. "If you hurry, I think you can catch her before she leaves. I thank you so very much... your generosity will not be forgotten!"

We headed out the door, Amayah breaking in her new shoes on the fly as we hustled towards the restaurant he mentioned, Szechuan House on Prince Street. I had to curb my burst of energy and excitement so Amayah could keep up. We made it to the restaurant and picked up the order, and were just in sight of the bank when I saw the lights click off for the day. Classic bank hours, in at 8:00 a.m., out at 4:00 p.m., and now we were stuck on the street with several boxes of food and no one to receive them.

It wasn't all bad, as we knew where she was headed, assuming that I was right about her and my dad already living at our tiny apartment. We turned and headed in the opposite direction. She'd likely be taking the subway, so maybe we'd catch her in the station and have an excuse to travel home with her, and possibly figure out how they needed help. Money seemed to be the most obvious answer to that. My dad had alluded to as much in our conversation, but that didn't really separate them from every other immigrant in New York City during their first few months.

I kept an eye out for my mom as we reached the subway station and hopped on a train. I described my mother as best I could to Amayah, thinking of her image in old pictures from around our house, but it was still going to be tough to find her. We walked the length of the subway car without any sign of her and finally sat down.

"I guess we can knock on the door and deliver it, but how will we explain that we knew where they lived? My dad didn't give us their address," I said.

"Maybe we can say that someone at the bank gave us the address?" Amayah countered. "Although that story will fall apart if she asks anyone about it next week."

"It's the best chance we've got for now," I agreed. "Hopefully they actually live there, especially since we didn't ask where the event is tonight."

We smiled sheepishly at each other. It seemed like we kept making it through situations by the skin of our teeth and a bit of luck. Everything worked out in Oxford in 1854, despite a ton of near misses. Then we went from having zero chance of finding her parents to being their new best friends in a matter of hours. Once again, it felt like an impossible challenge, but I was trying hard to believe that the hand of fate was on our side. We got off the subway and climbed to street level. We were less than a dozen blocks from my apartment building, and our chances of finding my mom were rapidly dwindling. We had just walked by one of a million New York alleys when Amayah's head jerked around, and she stuttered to a halt.

"Ro?" she said, her voice filling with concern. "Ro, wait a second, I thought I saw …"

Her voice dropped off, and she grabbed my arm tight. I turned back to peer down the alley, gasping in shock at what I saw. It was a scene right out of the 10 o'clock news from the Five Boroughs. A woman was cowering in terror as a man wearing a ski mask menaced her. He had a switchblade in his hand, and when she tried to move past him back onto the street, he grabbed her by the throat and pressed his knife to her neck with her back against the grimy brick wall.

Despite not having my powers, I would have immediately rushed to help. With them, I knew I was more than a match for this jerk, but that wasn't the first thing that crossed my mind. The young woman he was assaulting was beautiful, Asian, and very afraid.

She was also my mom.

TWENTY-SEVEN

Confronted with this same situation, a police officer or a good Samaritan would have slowly approached the mugger and told them to think about what they were doing. They would talk them into moving the knife away from the woman's throat by reminding the attacker of the repercussions of killing her, whereas if he just stopped what he was doing, everyone could just walk away. Of course, the cops were always lying when they said you could just walk away, or get off with a warning. Once they had the upper hand, they would smash you into the pavement, put handcuffs on you, and throw you in the back of the squad car. They'd say anything to talk you down, so you were no longer posing a serious threat.

But I was neither a cop nor a good Samaritan. I was my mother's son, and while our relationship sometimes felt strained and distant, considering that we saw each other for about forty-five minutes a day, watching someone threaten this younger version made something snap inside. I didn't use my speed to cross the distance; I took one giant lunge forward and jumped the rest of the way. Time slowed down as I leapt towards the unsuspecting mugger and my panicked mother.

His head began to turn in the last fraction of a second, but it was too late. My right hand wrapped around the wrist pressing the knife to her throat, while my left hand delivered a chop to the side of his neck that sent him to the ground of the alley like a ton of bricks. I turned to my mother and noticed a few drops of blood on her collar; the force of the collision had nicked her neck with the tip of the blade. I held my hand out to steady her, but my mom recoiled in fright. It hurt my feelings to see her so fearful of me, but I couldn't really blame her. I had appeared out of nowhere like a flying bogeyman, and she had no idea if I was there to save her or was just knocking out the competition to rob her, savage her, or maybe both.

The sight of the blood awoke Nick the Brute, whose voice reared up slyly in my head, *"Taste ... just a TASTE!"* I had to mentally shove him back down to the base of my brain as Amayah came rushing beside me, looking worriedly at my mother, "Are you alright?"

My mom's eyes slid from me to Amayah, and a flash of relief appeared. Ama was another normal-looking woman concerned for her safety, not a strange vigilante appearing from the darkness. She was still in shock, but Amayah had been around Mount Sinai enough to know how to talk to people who had just experienced something traumatic.

She gently cupped my mom's chin and turned her face, so they were looking at each other.

"Hi," Amayah said slowly. "My name is Amayah, what's your name?"

After a long pause, my mom looked back into Amayah's eyes, as if she was just now hearing the question.

"Mei... no, I'm sorry, my name is Claire. Claire Chang. I am a teller at HSBC. I was walking home when that ... that man started following me. I tried to get away from him and cut into the alley, but he saw me and came after me. If your ... friend hadn't gotten involved, I don't know what would have happened."

She was clearly still unsure about me and what had just happened, but all that mattered was that she was safe. Who knows what would have happened if we hadn't looked for her so earnestly before this?

My mom turned to me and smiled slightly. "Xiè xie," she said. *Thank you.*

"Méi wèntí," I consoled. *No problem.*

Amayah helped her sit down and began inspecting the cut on her neck, removing a tissue from her own bag and blotting the mark to see if the cut was deep. Fortunately, it seemed like a shallow wound. As I opened my mouth to tell my mom about our errand, trying to find her for my dad, the mugger stirred at my feet. I had forgotten about him in my concern for my mom, but he was trying to get up. With the Brute's voice surging in my ears, I helped him regain his feet, picking him up with one hand by the scruff of his neck until his feet were swinging in the air.

"Not so tough now, are you?" I said in a low, angry voice. "Must be a real brave guy, holding a knife to a woman's throat and threatening her? How does it feel now, no longer the predator, just another little piece of meat?"

I could feel the rage welling up in me as I said those last words in a sinister tone, but I didn't care. It was the closest I had come to unleashing my full power since I wasted the gang who had come after me and robbed my family's business. The guys who robbed Amayah's parents had gotten a little roughed up when I caught up with them, and I imagined that they had splitting headaches for a few days, but I wanted this little asshole to pay for coming after my mom. Punk had probably been skulking these parts for years, preying on immigrant women who didn't know the neighborhood well and were terrified once he swooped in. I wonder how many purses and bags and wallets this guy had back at his apartment. The image of his knife at my mom's throat returned to my mind, and I squeezed the juncture of his neck and shoulder a bit harder in return.

"Oww!"

The voice that chirped from his throat caught me off guard. It was high and squeaky, but I figured he was just panicking. I was blinded by rage, but thankfully, Amayah had noticed it too, keeping me from doing something I would have regretted.

"Ro, um, Buster!" Ama said, remembering at the last second. "Buster! Put him down and take his mask off!"

I did as she asked. I had begun to realize that she almost always had the right of things when it came to noticing the little details. I set the guy on his feet, holding him with one hand and roughly ripped the ski mask off his face to reveal...

A kid. An Asian kid, younger than me, maybe thirteen or fourteen. He could have been my little brother if I'd had one. His eyes were huge with fear, probably because a guy my size and build shouldn't have been able to fling him around like a ragdoll, regardless of how scrawny he was. He was wearing red tennis shoes, baggy shorts and a non-descript black sweatshirt. The shoes looked new, the kind you might be able to buy if you'd robbed a few people in the last month. He looked at me, then Amayah, then my mother, and cringed when he saw her glaring back.

"You're Bert Huang's boy!" she exclaimed, her frightened countenance rapidly turning to one of anger. "He runs the dry cleaners across the street from our apartment. What in the world are you thinking, and where did you get that knife?"

Now that was the Claire Chang I knew. Lecturing, asking angry questions, letting the disapproval roll off her tongue in relentless waves. The Huang boy shrank back from her insults like a fading flower, and I'm sure he would have turned tail and run if I hadn't still been holding him by the hood of his sweatshirt.

"Please don't tell my dad!" he begged in a New York accent. "I didn't mean to cut you; I just wanted some money!"

I turned to my mom and raised my eyebrows, asking her in unspoken terms what I should do next.

"Let him go," she said. "Run home to your father now and tell him what you've been doing. Children need to be taught right from wrong. My sons will know what is right! I'll be seeing your father tonight, and if our stories don't match up, you'll hear from the police by tomorrow!"

Then I heard Hua softly whispering, *"Blessed you are with the Shine."* Was my subconscious telling me that choosing Hua is what is right?

As young Huang mumbled a thank you, he scampered away so quickly that I didn't properly hear what came out of his mouth.

We watched him depart as my mom turned back to me. "Buster, was it? Thank you so much for coming to my aid. I don't know what would have happened if you hadn't arrived." She held her hand out to me formally. "I'm Claire, Claire Chang."

Shaking my mom's hand and calling her Claire was a very weird moment, but this was also exactly the kind of opportunity we had hoped for. I shook her hand back and told her in more detail that her husband Abraham had sent us to find her and deliver the food he was supposed to pick up for tonight's event. Fortunately, Amayah had picked up the bags of food after I leaped into hero mode a few minutes earlier, and they were all intact.

She was so grateful for the help that she hugged me and kissed my cheek. I think Amayah may have gotten a bit jealous, which was pretty ridiculous, considering this was the woman who birthed me. Thanks to her side trip down the alley, she was now running late both to pick up her children from the sitter—the baby version of me —and was also late getting the food to the community center. She said that she hated to impose on us again, but asked if we could take the food to the community center, since we were already going there.

We agreed without a second thought, and my mom raced one way to pick up her kids while we hustled off in the other direction. Fortunately, the address she gave us was one that I already knew. I had been to the Asian Community Center for a few award cere-monies and some coming-of-age parties. It was on the second floor of a building on 74th Street, surrounded by immigrant restaurants featuring food from all over Asia: Chinese, Indian, Korean, Pakistani, you name it, and you could find it somewhere on that street. The newcomer's welcome event was just picking up speed when we arrived, and we delivered the catering order to a grateful Japanese woman dressed quite elegantly for the occasion. She had us stack them along the wall with many other boxes of catered food, then handed us each a name tag: Amayah Bello and Buster Wang at your service. We mingled a bit, looking at some interesting Asian artwork and the blueprints and scale models of proposed Asian building influences throughout the Five Boroughs. At the same time, we carefully watched for my parents' arrival.

It took a while, but I suppose that's what happens when you have to tell each other tales of the same mysterious stranger who swooped in to defuse two potentially violent situations. Not to mention the struggle of getting a six-year-old and a one-year-old ready to go... anywhere. However, there was no doubt of what was going on when they did arrive, because of all the "oohs" and "ahhs" that were overheard from the many women at the mixer. You would have thought Brad Pitt had just walked in the room, but that wasn't the case. The only thing that melts women's hearts faster than a movie star is a baby, and that baby was me.

Amayah saw my younger self and squealed. "Oh my God," she said with a breathless smile. "You were the cutest baby EVER!" I turned to watch the couple enter, and it was truly the most bizarre thing yet. There were my parents, young and smiling and beaming. My dad was holding the hand of a little boy in a crushed blue suit that made him look like a slimy car salesman. My mom had the one-year-old version of me all wrapped up in a baby blue onesie with a matching hat, despite the fact that it was mid-spring.

Amayah couldn't take her eyes off the baby version of me as I was passed around from one woman to the next. "Already a lady killer, eh Rohan?" she whispered as I tried not to turn red. She added seriously, "I am going to blow raspberries on your little tummy before this night is over."

"Ha ha ha," I said, with a note of irritation in my voice. "I realize that I'm the cutest baby to ever crawl the earth, but we need to stay focused on what needs to happen to get us back to 1997."

Amayah turned and winked at me. "Why Rohan Chang, are you jealous of Rohan Chang?"

She was messing with me again. I took everything she said so earnestly and seriously that when she got playful, I would fall for it. I smiled in return to show that I was in on the joke, not to take things so seriously, and instantly, she let it go. We waited until my parents had made their way around the room before saying hello. We didn't want to seem too weird; not many teenagers were bursting at the seams to go hang out with a young married couple they had just met. But when they spotted us, they came rushing over to thank us for our generosity, and to introduce us to the family. This led to the bizarre circumstance of talking to my six-year-old "older" brother about Luke Skywalker and Darth Vader. At the same time, Amayah, true to her word, held "me" up in the air and cooed some baby talk before blowing a raspberry on "my" stomach that left "me" giggling and gurgling. She was moving in for round two when I saw her nose wrinkle up, and she said to my mom, "Uh oh, I think little Rohan here has a gift for you!" She passed "me" to my mom, who concurred and told my dad.

"I'm going to the restroom to change him." She gave Amayah a smile and spoke. "Want to come with? You seem like a natural with him."

Amayah turned to me for a long moment, and I could see a mischievous glitter in her eyes. She paused for dramatic effect, then said, "I would like nothing better in the whole world, Claire."

She gave me a deeply devilish grin as she followed my mom to the bathroom, with little me grinning at her over my mom's shoulder. I was trying to process the fact that Amayah was about to see my little butt, naked ... and my little something else too. Had it been possible to die from embarrassment, that might very well have been my last moment on Earth.

Instead of dying, I sat at a table with my very young older brother and my very youthful dad. My "older" brother, Henry, revealed that he had already seen *The Empire Strikes Back* twice and had brought along an action figure to keep him from getting bored at the mixer. Henry pulled a perfect, mint-condition Kenner action figure of Yoda from his pocket. I sat down and picked up his replica of the wise Jedi master who takes Luke from idiot farm boy to galactic legend, as Hua whispered, *"Blessed you are with the Shine Xiong."* I definitely saw the Dark Side in Nick the Brute. Was the mysterious voice that called itself Hua the one who could teach me how to stay in the light? She mentioned that I was blessed with the Shine Xiong, some ancient group of powerful beings. I hadn't had the time to figure out more about them, but seeing Henry move Yoda around while mimicking his backward talk, jarred my curiosity.

"Do you think he was lying?"

It took me a minute to realize that young Henry was talking to me. "I'm sorry, what?"

Henry gave me a look that told me I was on the verge of losing my cool status for not paying attention to every single word he said.

"In the movie. Do you think Darth Vader was lying about being Luke's dad?"

I had to hide a smile. Of course. Henry and the rest of the world only had two *Star Wars* movies to go by. *Return of the Jedi* was still three years away. I had read in the Times that George Lucas was going to make Episodes I-III to show how Anakin Skywalker actually became Darth Vader. They were calling them "prequels," which seemed like what I was reliving right then, seeing my entire family at much younger ages.

"No, he's definitely not lying," I said to Henry. "Vader wants to be in charge and wants Luke to help him kill the Emperor."

"We've had many discussions about Vader's motivations at the dinner table," my dad said, patting Henry on the shoulder.

"Wait," I spluttered. "You've gone to see *The Empire Strikes Back*?"

My dad gave me a strange smile in return. "Of course, I've seen it. Do you think a six-year-old went to see it by himself? Twice?"

He laughed, and I laughed with him to make it seem like I wasn't a complete nut job. I never once thought that my dad had been the one to take Henry to see *Star Wars* or any other movie, because it seemed so out of his character. Of course, the first movie I remember in the theater was *Return of the Jedi* when I was about four years old, which meant that he probably took both of us to see that too.

My dad, the *Star Wars* fan? I was so shocked that you could have knocked me over with an Ewok.

Speaking of Ewoks, with Amayah not around to police me, I decided that it was time to have some fun.

"You know what I think, Henry? I think that in the next movie, Luke will try to help Vader get away from the dark side, and the Emperor will end up trying to kill Luke. Then Vader will remember what it's like to love someone, and he'll kill the Emperor to save Luke's life!"

I was hoping for some sort of huge gasp of revelation from the younger version of my brother. Instead, I got laughter from him and my dad.

"Vader turns into a good guy!? That's rich, Buster!" my dad said with a chortle.

I shrugged my shoulders and said, "It's just a theory." When my dad turned to talk to a neighbor, I leaned down and whispered in Henry's ear, "And Princess Leia is Luke's sister!" before standing back up to go find Amayah.

She was headed my way with a big grin on her face, carrying my younger self in her arms.

"And here comes Uncle Buster!" Ama said with a wry grin. "Uncle Buster wants to hold Baby Rohan, doesn't he? Isn't he just the cutest thing ever?"

I could hardly be rude to my parents at this point, so I took this young version of me and made all the appropriate gestures and coos before passing "me" back to my parents. It was getting late, and apparently Amayah had told my mom that we were staying in Union City, because she insisted that we stay the night with them instead.

We said the polite words of not wanting to impose, certainly not with the baby keeping odd hours, but this alternate reality version of Abraham and Claire wanted us to stay with them, no questions asked, no excuses. So, we coyly said yes, quietly congratulating each other on our good luck.

I HAD to slow down and let the 1980 Chang Family walk in front of us on the way back to their apartment building. My dad mentioned how lucky they were to have found a place in a prosperous neighborhood like Fresh Meadows and how other immigrants were jealous of their good fortune. I didn't have the heart to tell them that they would still be living there 17 years later. Knowing my dad, he'd just say that it was a wise investment, and everything that he had hoped for.

That was another thing that set me apart from my parents. They made purchases like it was the last dollar they were spending in life, that anything they bought should come with a lifetime warranty, and that if they cared for it properly, it would never wear out. I was thankful that the two of them had never bought a car, or I'm sure I'd be going to school in a 1958 Studebaker or whatever other old jalopies the two of them would have scrounged up in the classifieds of the newspaper. In fact, if I knew my family history as well as I thought I did, I suspected that the washer and dryer in this 1980 apartment were the exact same ones I used to wash my clothes in 1997. My dad bought the lifetime warranties on both, a fact that the department store was now seriously regretting. The company that made the appliances had long since upgraded to a new technology for laundry machines, but my dad had his agreement signed in triplicate, and every time something on either appliance even started to shake or rattle, he was on the phone to the 1-800 number, demanding that a repairman come out. At one point in the early 1990s, the company tried to buy him out of the warranty, as it was costing them more to pay for his parts and labor than the cost of the machine itself. He shut them down and told them that a deal was a deal, and if they weren't going to honor their end of it, he was going to alert the media, call the Better Business Bureau, and probably alert the White House if he thought he could get through.

We walked behind the four of them, holding hands. It was crazy to be here, but it was pretty cool too, and I could tell that Amayah was getting a kick out of seeing the foundation of my family. I liked seeing them not so stiff and formal, and hoped this meant that when we got back, perhaps they'd accept more of who I was and the fact that I was dating Ama, who wasn't Asian, as opposed to some hand-picked selection of an ideal mate from their circle of friends in Queens.

My parents opened the door to our apartment and welcomed us into their humble abode. It was brightly lit and decorated with colorful pieces of sculpture and artwork, giving the space a festive appearance. What would one day be my room was currently "my" nursery, and I couldn't resist following my mom and Amayah in to have a look.

It was decorated in shades of yellow and orange, which gave off a warm glow even in the dark of night. I watched her put me into my crib and marveled at how easily I went to sleep. Not exactly something that was easy for me as a teenager. I felt like my mind was always racing too much to get a decent night's sleep, and my recent forays into the world of semi-superheroism were making my resting hours all the more confusing and disjointed. This was home, though. I never thought I would miss it when I came back through the door, but as soon as I entered, all the sights and smells came back rushing to me. With the layout, the same, little Henry even slept on the foldout couch in the living room, just as he did as a twenty-three-year-old. I never dreamed that I would feel respect or appreciation for my brother, whose main purpose in life seemed to be bossing me around, whether we were at work or at home. He probably hadn't had a choice when it came to giving up his room so that baby Rohan could have a proper nursery. It made me wonder at what point he realized that the baby of the family—me—was getting preferential treatment. Had my parents simply told him that this way was easier, or had he been the consummate big brother and stepped aside to let me keep that little sanctuary all to myself?

I would have to ask grown-up Henry once I got back home. For now, I watched as he efficiently set up his pillow and blankets on the couch and carefully arranged his Star Wars action figures on the coffee table beside him. I sat down in the lounge chair across from his couch as Amayah helped my mom with baby "me."

Henry was meticulously arranging the action figures into the perfect poses and maneuvers, and I watched him for a minute, marveling at the fact that the more things changed, the more they stayed the same. I could so easily picture Henry at different ages as he organized his CDs, his baseball cards, heck, even the different color M&M's on his plate after dinner.

He'd break the candy into separate color piles before eating a single one of them. It was the same routine every night. He'd start with the yellows and eat all of them before he ate a single orange. The greens were next, then the tans, and then the browns. I tried to tell him they all tasted the same as I shoveled handful after handful down my throat, but it was different for him.

There had to be organization and order. It was probably what would eventually make him such a good pharmacist. Everything had to be placed appropriately and in good order, like a prescription. Henry had those shelves and medicines and everything else meticulously labeled, sorted, and organized in perfect order, so that no matter which patient came by, he'd be ready to help them without delay. He seemed to barely notice me sitting there until the figures were all arranged just so.

"Leia can't be Luke's sister... they kissed each other," he said without even glancing at me.

"They don't know it until the next movie," I casually answered.

He narrowed his gaze at me. "When's the next movie?"

"1983," I said as if I was totally bored. "Luke will go back to

Dagobah to ask Yoda if it's true about Vader being his father, and Yoda's going to tell him there's another Skywalker."

Henry looked at me for a long time, clearly trying to see if I would crack a smile to show that I was pulling his leg.

"Are you making that up?" he asked at last.

"Nope," I said. "Remember what I told you, so then you can tell all your friends about it before the movie comes out. They'll all think you're a genius! Your brother will think you're cool, too."

"Him? Rohan's just a baby. Babies don't know anything about movies."

"He's a baby right now, sure, but he'll be four years old by the time the next movie comes out. He'll want to go with you and your dad to see it. Make sure he has a good time, and explain to him what's going on. That's what good brothers do."

Henry shrugged. "Okay, I will."

How easy it was to give advice to my brother when he was only six!

He got under the covers and looked ready for bed, but then opened one eye back up.

"Are you going to move in with us?" he asked, and it seemed like he might be hoping the answer was yes.

"Nope, just here for the night, Henry, but I can say confidently that you'll be seeing me around."

He nodded. That was apparently enough to satisfy his question. His eyes closed, and he began breathing the heavy, rhythmic sleep of a child without a care in the world within seconds.

Amayah and I sat at the kitchen table opposite from my parents, talking about New York City and where they were from, as well as how different things were from one home to the other. We had to pick and choose what we said about the Big Apple. They had no idea about Rudy Giuliani or Derek Jeter or Bill Clinton, so we had to be vague with some of our observations of how things worked. We talked about racism a bit, about how some people treated them like idiots because they didn't speak English perfectly, and how others held to stereotypes like Asians being lousy drivers with big, thick accents. We talked about the tireless work ethic that both Asians and Hispanics seemed to have in endless supply, and how we were willing to work harder than most to guarantee even the simplest of creature comforts.

"When we moved here last year, they hired me on the island as a data analyst," my dad told us. I assumed he meant Manhattan, and my jaw practically dropped at the idea of my dad in a three-piece suit on Wall Street, cutting deals and making trades.

"I was making great money there, and Claire was doing well, so we bought this property to be the foundation of our future. Thirteen days later, the meltdown happened."

I thought he was talking about a stock market crash that I hadn't known about..., there had been so many, after all. I was about to ask what would have been a very dumb question about how many points the Dow had dropped that day, but Amayah spoke up first. "Oh, my goodness, Mr. Chang, were you on Three Mile Island the day of the meltdown?"

My jaw dropped. My dad was a small business owner through and through, the kind of guy who toiled away at the laundromat behind the scenes, scrubbing stubborn stains out of shirts and putting extra starch into pants so that everyone looked good for their Monday morning meetings. Abraham Chang working at a nuclear reactor? I felt like I had stepped into an alternate dimension.

"I was indeed," my dad said rather gravely for a man still so young. "In fact, I was in the middle of rehearsing a presentation when the alarm bells went off. I remember feeling annoyed that a drill was going to interrupt my big shot at a promotion. But then we realized it wasn't a drill." He stroked his face as if physically pulling out the memories of one of the scariest moments in American history—one barely a year old for my parents.

"It was a catastrophic series of failures. One thing after another that the experts said shouldn't be happening, but kept happening anyways. The controls, instruments, and alarms started to malfunction without stopping, making the operators think the system was resolving its own errors, when it was actually doing the exact opposite. Our engineers trusted the system so completely that none of them thought to question any of what they were seeing. There were all sorts of near misses in the days that followed; things that could have gone wrong and become huge disasters, but either luck or something more divine had somehow kept any of them from happening.

"About five weeks later, they released a big report on the incident and talked about what would happen going forward. We figured that they'd scrap the whole thing, but turns out they had too much money already sunk in for that. So they announced that all non-essential personnel were getting a severance package and told us to clean out our desks.

"Just like that, it was all over. Of course, I still had the experience reading data, but you try being an immigrant, and the only American job on your resume is at Three Mile Island. I think that for a few of the job interviews I went to, they called me in just to laugh. So, I stopped going to interviews, in favor of places needing a good worker. Thus, I became a shoe salesman, and a custodian, and a window washer, and anything else that allowed me to use and develop new skills. Unfortunately, with Claire taking time off to have Rohan, we're always coming up short on paying the bills. This apartment is meant to be our future home for years to come, but sometimes I wonder if we'll be here come Christmas."

My mom stirred, and said she was ready for bed, a clear signal for her husband to stop talking. Proper Asian hosts didn't burden their guests with personal problems. I bowed to each of them and thanked them again for their wonderful hospitality and lovely home. My mom made sure that Amayah and I were spaced out on opposite couches before she told us goodnight, clearly not wanting any hanky-panky going on under her roof. She needn't worry, of course. Ama and I hadn't gotten to that level of our relationship just yet. Even if we had, getting physical in the same room as my sleeping six-year-old older brother was a definite nonstarter. I hugged her tight and kissed her forehead before lying down. She whispered from her couch, "Don't worry, we'll figure it all out tomorrow." I wish that I shared her confidence.

She winked and tucked herself into the loveseat while I somehow got stuck with another chair and ottoman, much like I had when we spent the night in that tiny hotel. That situation seemed utterly hopeless at the time, mostly because Amayah was mad at me, but it turned out okay in the end. I prayed that this would have a good resolution too. The universe was a crazy place. I had left home to look for love, figure out my powers, and learn how to become a better person. Those three things led me on a grand quest across time and space and brought me back home again.

As such, I kept waking up throughout the early parts of the night, thinking that I had dreamed everything about my adventure with Amayah and was right back home. Then I'd see her asleep on the loveseat and think that I had somehow accidentally brought her home, and man, oh man, were my parents going to kill me. It was a crazy cycle that I was just too sleepy to escape. I finally slept for about an hour straight until a soft noise woke me up. All those nights on watch in Oxford, plus traveling through the South on our way to Illinois, had turned me into a light sleeper. I also had a paranoid fear that the time travel thing would start happening while I was asleep, and Amayah and I would somehow get separated into different time-lines. That prospect freaked me out more than I was willing to discuss with her.

The noise came again, and I opened my eyes slowly, not wanting to disturb anyone, in case someone was actually breaking into the house. I had been involved in quite a few altercations while trying to help out my parents and Amayah's parents in the last couple of weeks, and I wanted to make sure I was ready to act if necessary. Through my half-opened eyes, I saw a figure moving in the dark. I watched as the figure bent down and picked up a duffel bag, then pulled it over their back. They wore a hooded sweatshirt, and I thought it might really be a robber breaking into the wrong apartment, but then they turned into the streetlight glow from outside the bedroom window, catching their silhouette.

It was my dad. Why would he be sneaking out after midnight wearing a hoodie and carrying a duffel bag? I reasoned that he might have another job he went to at night, like a night watchman or a stocker at a grocery store, but it seemed weird that he hadn't mentioned to us that he'd be getting up and going, particularly right through the room where we were sleeping. I didn't know what to make of it all, but my curiosity was piqued. After he closed the door softly behind him, I slipped silently off the couch, strapped my own shoes back on, and softly opened the apartment door just in time to hear the ding of the elevator, suggesting he was either about to get on or about to descend. With no one else in the hallway so late at night, and the building security cameras still a decade away from being installed, I touched my energy center and raced down the hallway to where the elevator had just closed. Four stories down would be a fairly quick ride, but not nearly as fast as me. I sprinted down the stairs to the lobby of the building with seconds to spare. Blending into the shadows of the dark lobby, I watched my father get off the elevator and make a beeline straight out of the building, not looking up once. This was getting weirder and weirder, but I was determined to fill in the missing pieces of this puzzle.

CHAPTER

TWENTY-EIGHT

After about twenty blocks, I wondered if my dad was simply out for a lovely evening stroll, albeit a long, and rather quickly paced one. But why the duffel bag? And who has enough energy to work all day, take care of two little kids, and then take a leisurely miles-long walk in the middle of the night? We were both strolling down Queens Boulevard, with me hanging back at a distance of about one hundred feet. I occasionally moved to the other side of the street in case he took a look back, but he seemed to have no worries about being followed. When he finally turned off the main drag, it happened so fast that I almost missed it. He seemed so focused on the single-minded task of getting wherever he was trying to go. I counted to ten before following him again. He walked a ways down the alley, and I had no idea if it connected or went to a dead end, so I took the liberty of leaping up to a nearby fire escape and shimmying up to the roof of the building, about three stories up. I was able to open up with a little speed up there and practice my leaps, flying from one roof to the next. It was exhilarating, real Peter Parker training montage stuff, and I had to stifle a whoop of happiness as I sailed across open space.

I was able to get even with my dad and watch him from above. Even if he looked straight up, it was too dark and cloudy to see me, and why would he ever think someone was up there anyway? At last, he stopped near a streetlight, buzzing as it slowly failed, on then off then on again.

He put the duffel bag on the ground, looked both ways to make sure he was alone, then unzipped it and removed something from inside. As I watched in disbelief, this younger version of my father held up a can of spray paint and began spraying the side of the building directly below me.

"You've got to be shitting me," I gulped as I reached into my pocket to feel the ridges and outlines on my golden fat cap. Abraham Chang, the biggest boy scout on Earth, was a tagger in his youth?

I knew that my mouth was hanging open, but I couldn't seem to close it. It was like learning that my dad was in a garage rock band or that he had a third arm sewed behind his back. I couldn't see exactly what he was creating down there, but I could tell what emotions he was currently feeling—the need to escape, the desperate desire to break out of his current set of circumstances. I had seen all the moves before, because I had done them myself. It was the kind of graffiti I made when I felt like I was never going to get out of the apartment, out of high school, or out of Fresh Ghetto. My dad was clearly in pain, and in need of an outlet, one that he wasn't able to share with my mom or anyone else. My heart went out to him. He was trying so hard to be the man he thought he should be: a husband, a father, a good New Yorker, a good American, true to his roots, all that stuff... but it was slowly tearing him apart. His strokes were bold and massive, and his lines were ragged and blurry. This was the classic artist explosion, and it didn't matter what it eventually looked like, only how it made you feel.

He went at it hard for a good ten minutes until he was dripping sweat and panting. I admired his commitment to the work and recognized his struggle to do everything he could to hold his life together all at once. I felt the same way with school, and trying to figure out what to do with my life, dating Amayah, and confronting the voices in my head. Sometimes you just had to cut loose.

My dad had a Thermos from which he took a few big, long swigs after he finished. I figured that he would head back home to get some sleep, and he seemed to be heading in that direction. I kept to the rooftops, as it was easier to track him from above, and it was much cooler to be up there. He was about halfway back to the apartment building when he took a left where he should have taken a right. His movements slowed, and he started looking more like a burglar and less like a tagger. I wasn't sure what was up, but I wanted to see better, so I found another fire escape and swiftly slid down to street level, staying back in the shadows.

He walked around a corner, and I almost got caught, because he came right back around the other way a moment later. Fortunately, his shadow caught in the reflection of a light across the street, I saw him coming and ducked out of sight. I crouched behind a large dumpster, which smelled like a combination of rotten fish and stale eggs, and tried to hold my breath. If nothing else, this little excursion was showing me that my tracking skills were absolutely terrible, and I needed to step up my game if I was going to be working nights in New York City tracking criminals.

I watched my dad standing completely still outside a building. I blinked and squinted my eyes, as suddenly there was someone else with him—a tall, skinny guy in a hat. He looked like he was holding a lit cigarette. Who was this other individual, and why was he talking to my dad?

~

ABRAHAM STOOD in front of Don's Pub. He then leaned against one of the doors, and as he did, the door gave the slightest of creaks and opened slowly. He watched it swing inward, inch by inch, just like every other night. No alarm sounded. No tell-tale red light signaled that a motion detector was active.

Abraham first ate at Don's Pub a year ago, one afternoon when Claire had gone out with friends for dinner. He complimented the old-style cash register, which reminded him of one he had seen growing up back home. No electronics at all, just old-fashioned mechanics and metalwork. He always found stuff like that fascinating, as if technology had gone past the point of beauty and now was cheaply made because it was the easy, cheap, and economical way of doing things.

Abraham stopped by for a couple more meals in the months since, and was walking home late one night when he passed by the restaurant. On a whim, he leaned up against the glass to get a look at the register, and the door swung open in front of him. He stumbled a few steps inside the restaurant before scampering back out, feeling guilty, despite not doing anything wrong. He checked the door and realized that the lock wasn't turning all the way. From the inside, it would seem locked, but the door still swung free on the outside. He thought about leaving a note, but that would surely invite a thief, so he decided to swing by the next day and let the manager know that the door wasn't working right.

In the mail, around that same time, they received a notice that their rent was going up twenty-five percent, effective next month. It felt like yet another tightening of the screws on the young immigrant couple. Abraham spent half the night consoling Claire and the other half trying to figure out how much longer they could survive here with the rent increasing as it was. He remembered the unlocked door and the cash register around 4:00 a.m. as he scanned the want ads for a job he could pile on top of his already hectic work schedule. He remembered freezing up in the moment, as a coolness slid through his body. He didn't immediately put the idea in the "impossible" category, but he didn't want to think about it either. Instead, he did nothing, including not reporting it to the Don's Pub staff the next day. He just kept going to work. He stopped eating at the restaurant, out of guilt or shame or some unnamed feeling. But every time he worked late or when he would go out bombing, he found himself walking home past the restaurant and leaning on the door to see if the lock was fixed. It never was.

"I THINK that model was built in the 1920s, right before the Great Depression started," a friendly voice rumbled from behind Abraham, sending his heart into panic mode as he spun around, hands up to defend himself, not knowing who had gotten the drop on him.

"What? Who? Who are you!" Abraham uttered in a rush. Maybe 8-10 feet away from him, his face unseen in the shadows, was a tall, skinny man wearing a dark-colored hat with matching pants and a crisp suit jacket, holding a lit cigarette and taking a long drag as Abraham struggled to compose himself.

"I startled you. I apologize," the man said in a raspy voice, taking another drag. "I thought you heard me coming, but I guess the register had your attention. I was saying that mechanical model is from the 1920s... a beaut, isn't she?"

Abraham was still breathing hard, feeling caught in the act, but working hard to remember that he wasn't doing anything wrong.

"The register," Abe gushed. "Right. Yeah. I noticed it the first time I ate here. It's, um, it's really neat."

"Neat's a good word for it," the stranger said, smiling quickly to reveal a row of far-too-bright teeth. "Also, neat would be how much money they're leaving in it every night, while also leaving the door unlocked."

The man released a low chuckle.

Abe was grateful for the darkness, so the man wouldn't see his ears turning bright red. It was like the man was reading his mind, which was not a pleasant experience when contemplating a robbery.

"Um, what do you mean?" Abe replied, trying and failing to sound casual.

Another chuckle emerged from the face Abe couldn't quite make out in the dark.

"I mean, the fools running this business left their door wide open and unlocked, with a cash register full of money in plain sight," he said, pointing at the door Abe had held open a moment ago.

"Would be so easy, right?" the stranger murmured, as if contemplating it himself.

"Um, um," Abraham stuttered with unconvincing innocence.

"Snatching that register," the stranger said. "I mean with the two of us, we could have it out of there in what, five minutes? Or just pop it open and split the loot fifty-fifty. This neighborhood's a ghost town at night. They wouldn't even know it was gone 'til tomorrow morning."

"Yes, I guess it would be," Abraham offered, pretending like this was his first time considering it. "I mean, they can't even lock their door, right? It almost feels like they don't care if they lose that money or not."

It was the first time he had said the words out loud, but he had thought about them plenty. It was the justification he was turning over and over again in his own mind: If the restaurant owners cared about keeping their money, they would care about keeping the door fixed, right?

"I mean, this place is in a busy location, right? Everyone paying in cash for lunch and dinner... there might be $5,000 in there right now," the man in black said, almost wistfully. "Think how rich they must be to not even worry about locking the damn door at night. Building is old as hell, they probably paid it off thirty years ago. That means they're not even worried about a mortgage; just paying bum wages to the staff, probably got a deal with the mob for cut rates on foodstuffs, and they're hauling in profit hand over fist. Bet they don't even keep the books because they're making so much. Meanwhile, guys like you and me, we're counting every last penny, trying to stretch it to next payday. Never can get ahead, not even for a minute."

He took another long drag and puffed out three smoke rings in perfect circles. "I mean wouldn't you like to take a break from working for once? Get box seats for a day game at Yankee Stadium?

Take a lady friend out to a five-star restaurant with a fancy new rock on her finger? Little man busts his ass every day of the year and gets nowhere, am I right?"

He turned and looked at Abraham. "What's your name, friend? I'm Ricky, ravishing Ricky, to my friends. What would you do with $5,000 if it suddenly appeared in your lap?"

Abraham didn't want to reply, and he definitely didn't want to give the man his name, so he stood still for a moment, as if contemplating his answer.

"It's um, Donald, my name is Donald," Abe replied. "I'd put $1,000 towards future rent payments, so I wouldn't have to stress about it for a while. Then $1,000 each in my sons' college funds. The other $2,000 I'd use to start designing and opening an art gallery for Asian-American artists in the city. My wife and I both love art, and we both dabble in painting. It's how we met back home. That's our real dream. It sounds crazy and our friends think we' re out of our minds to pursue something beyond a small business, but we' ve always been dreamers, she and I."

Ricky was quiet for a moment.

"That's beautiful, Donny, really," Ricky said. "I've got big dreams too. Biggest I've ever had, really. Going to move out of the shit hole I've been living in forever and get myself some new digs, a new job, and a new set of friends to match. Going to be amazing. Finally going to impress my old man. Been a long time coming. You said you'd got sons. That's awesome."

"Yes, both quite young, but growing up quick," Abraham said, imagining Rohan and Henry's peaceful faces resting at home. Suddenly, he wanted nothing more than to be back there watching over them in the still of the night.

Ricky didn't seem to notice Abraham's change in demeanor.

"So, what do you say, Donny boy? I'll hold the door open and keep watch, you shuffle in there and grab the register, or pop it open, either one. Since you're doing the heavy lifting, you can take say sixty percent of the loot, sound good?"

Abraham looked at the register one more time, but his mind lingered on his home and his children.

"No, it's not right. I need to get home. Enjoy your evening."

Ricky wasn't going to be so easily dismissed, however.

"Whoa, whoa, whoa! Donny! What did I say wrong? This is found money, man! Just like seeing a quarter on the stairs of the subway station. Someone dropped the ball and walked off without double checking, and you came along and noticed what was up. This is your money, brother! Think about what you can turn this into! Your boys' future is getting a kickstart, just like that!"

But when Ricky brought up his sons, Abraham felt even more confident that contemplating the robbery wasn't right. No matter how much he justified it, he'd be starting a business, a college fund, or whatever it was, with dirty money. Money that didn't belong to him and that he had no business putting his hands on. He had told himself over the last few months that it was his fear of getting caught that was keeping him from taking the contents of the register, but now he knew that wasn't true. It was his commitment to honesty and doing the right thing that had stayed his hand. Whether it was a guardian angel or his parents' guidance, it didn't matter; he wasn't a thief and wouldn't do something dishonest and immoral, no matter how rewarding the results could be.

He turned and looked Ricky straight in the face to drive home his point.

"If you want the money, I won't say a word, but I'm not going to teach my sons that breaking the law is okay when it suits your purposes. That's not what I believe in."

Abe turned and, without looking back, strode away. Ricky stayed still, lit another cigarette, and blew a slow train of smoke rings.

"Don't worry, Abraham," he said softly into the darkness, "about what is right, for right is just an illusion."

～

I THOUGHT I WAS HALLUCINATING, so I rubbed my eyes and took another look. The tall stranger, if he had been present at all, had disappeared, and my dad was heading back home. Without much choice in the matter, I turned on the jets and raced down the block until I found a 24-hour convenience store. It didn't take long. Even in 1980, New York was still the city that never slept. I pillaged the aisles to create the situation I needed. A Gatorade container. A sweatband for my forehead and another for my wrist. And lo and behold, they had a basketball, even though it was marked up to $19.99. It would be worth it. I bought it all, trashed the plastic bag and then ran up and down the street as fast as I could to work up a plausible sweat. Then I headed back to the corner where my dad was walking, as I loudly dribbled the basketball and held a one-way conversation with someone who wasn't there. I called him T-Ray because it sounded like a decent name for a guy you'd be playing basketball with late on a Friday night.

"Nah, T-Ray, you were the man tonight!" I exclaimed, pounding the ball into the sidewalk. "That jumper wouldn't stop working."

I paused, then let out a big laugh. "Heard that! That guy didn't know what he was up against."

Another pause.

"Okay brother, be safe getting home, I'll see you later."

I slapped my own hand and then walked around the corner just past Don's Pub. Sure enough, meandering down the street was my dad. I came to a sudden stop when I saw him, as if I was utterly shocked.

"Uhhh, Abraham? Is that you?"

"Buster?"

"Yeah man, I lit out to play hoops with some of my boys up in Elmhurst. We do it every Friday night." I spun the ball as best I could on my finger. "My buddy T-Ray and I just stopped to grab some Gatorade a couple of blocks away. He just split. Uh, what are you doing out here by yourself so late?"

He was caught red-handed, which hadn't been my intention. I

didn't want my dad to think I was following him, so playing ball with T-Ray was the perfect cover. I was so blown away that he was an artist that I hoped he'd fess up, and we'd have a connection to make, but that's not what happened. He was nervous and stuttering, and I felt awful for the situation I had put him in, so I decided to help bail him out of it.

"Wait a minute," I said with a knowing smile. "The duffel bag and the black clothes, Abe? You wouldn't happen to be bombing, would you?"

My dad started to back up, then realized I was talking about graffiti, and I could see the relief flood his face. He grinned sheepishly, unzipped the bag, and let me see the contents. He had half a dozen spray cans in there, and a couple of rags for blemishes. A decent kit for someone only in the country for a year or so, and I said so.

"Helps relieve the stress, right?" I asked, and he nodded enthusiastically.

"I don't like jogging or lifting weights, but I love feeling free and being able to create like this," he said, and I had never felt more like my father's son than in that very moment. "If it costs me an hour of sleep every couple weeks to feel this good, it's totally worth it."

I told him that I completely understood and had done some bombing myself, but confessed that my dad would kill me if he found out.

"Well, that's why we don't tell the people who will get upset, right?" he said with a smile and a wink that I wish I could have recorded to play back for him in 1997. "But in all honesty, I might stick more to the black books than any public property from this day on," pausing as he looked up into the stars, "cuz I have a family at home to worry about."

I smiled back and then switched the conversation. "So, are you bombing stuff around here? You looked like you were searching for somewhere to start some new ink when I rolled around the corner."

His eyes flashed straight to the door of Don's Pub full of guilt. I followed his gaze and saw a cash register sitting on the counter through the glass window.

My dad looked away and said, "Uh, yeah, I thought there might be some turf here to claim, but I guess it's not as clean as I thought. I was just taking a break before heading back home."

I thought he was lying, seeing how he was only staring at the register the whole time, but I couldn't pass judgment on him, even though he had no problem doing it to me in 1997. Everyone had their demons. He hadn't done anything but look; there was no way he had robbed the store in the 90 seconds when I vanished and bought the basketball. I thought back to all the fantasies that Nick the Brute had sent into my mind. My dad was tempted, but that was it. Whatever shadow passed over him back there, he pushed back and walked away from it. I was proud of him.

Of course, that didn't mean he wouldn't be tempted again in the future; a future that I wouldn't be a part of until I returned to 1997. I decided it was worth a little nudging and prodding to keep him on the straight and narrow.

"You know, a couple of years ago, my dad owned a laundromat / dry cleaner combo, kind of revolutionary, and it got broken into, and the cash register was stolen," I said matter-of-factly. "These gang members wrote racial slurs all over the store and smashed the windows. It set my parents back financially for a long time, and the police said they should have invested in better security. It wasn't that my dad didn't care about the store; he just couldn't afford to get the best of everything and still take care of his family the way he wanted to."

I left the story there. He didn't say anything for a while, and I was worried that I had really pissed him off, when suddenly he broke the silence.

"Don's Pub back there has a broken lock," he blurted out. "The cash register is just sitting there with no one watching it, but maybe the owner is just providing for his family. Heck, maybe he doesn't even know the door sticks open after you lock it," my dad was saying.

"It would be miserable for him to come here in the morning and find it all gone."

I walked towards my father and put a hand on his shoulder, "Abe, on the flip side, if some good Samaritan were to come by during business hours and point it out to the owner, I bet he might be in line for some sort of reward."

My dad ducked his gaze from mine for a minute, then looked back and nodded, his eyes ever so slightly wet with tears of... shame? Relief? I couldn't be certain.

"I'm glad you showed up tonight, Buster," he said, his voice trembling slightly. "How'd you gain so much wisdom at such a young age?"

I thought it over, then answered honestly.

"I've had a lot of crazy life experiences lately," I replied, "and a new appreciation for my dad as a result of it."

My dad nodded. "He sounds like an impressive man, and such a revolutionary. I hope to meet him someday."

I laughed. "I'm sure you will."

I HAD to keep myself from staring at him the whole way back, now that he had passed the test and avoided temptation. I wonder how close he had come to making this judgment call in the original time-line of his life. Based on how righteous he was about doing things the right way, I had imagined that there was a close call somewhere along the way. Coming so close to doing something morally corrupt and downright illegal must have scared my dad straight. I considered how relentless he was as a parent, demanding that my brother and I be perfect sons, perfect students, perfect everything! I never knew about his past, including his time on Three Mile Island.

He was successful at a young age and had enjoyed a good life before the meltdown, but I suspect the double whammy of being a minority and being linked to one of the narrowest near-miss disasters in American history made work hard to come by. Thus, he opened a small business, as "revolutionary" as it was, where he was the boss and didn't have to worry about someone else's prejudices keeping him from being employed. I think he felt like he swung and missed his chance at the American dream, and was therefore determined to push my brother and I even harder to get there. All the tough love and demands were the manifestation of the missed opportunities and closed doors he had faced as a young immigrant here.

We didn't talk much as we walked back to the family apartment. When you have a great connection with someone, you can say nothing at all and still feel like you're spending quality time together. That's how this felt, and I hoped it wouldn't be the last time I could feel that.

We took the elevator up together and walked into a well-lit apartment where Amayah was holding baby "me," while my mom paced the floor. Her face looked like trouble.

"Where have you been, Abraham?" she all but shouted at him. "Henry woke me up, saying that he could hear baby Rohan coughing. He has a fever, but you were nowhere in sight! You had me worried sick!"

Amayah was clearly far less worried about me, given that we were here to try and unspool some sort of mystery together. She raised her eyebrows a fraction at me, and I gave the slightest of nods, trying to hint that I had made progress, which meant that we might be very close to getting home.

As my dad tried to play the role of Captain No Poker Face and stammer his way through an explanation, I spoke up.

"I'm so sorry, Claire, this was all my fault," I explained, going rogue on any explanation my dad might have been making up. "I wasn't feeling good, so I got up and went for a stroll. Abe was up and followed me out, making sure I was alright, and we spent some time together just enjoying the beautiful scenery of Fresh Meadows and Cunningham Park and talking about life. Abe has really done wonders to help me feel better. I apologize for scaring you."

My mom looked back and forth between us, trying to detect a lie, then took two quick steps and wrapped her arms around my dad. "Oh, Abraham, you sweet man," she gushed.

I let out a giant breath I hadn't realized I was holding, and mockingly wiped my brow in relief at Amayah.

Both of us expected to go hurtling through time and space as my parents embraced, but nothing happened, so we ended up just retreating to bed. There must be some other piece of the puzzle missing, but I didn't know what it was, and I couldn't sort it out before sleep captured me.

The following day was Sunday, and I promised Amayah that I would go to services with her on the way back to New Jersey, regardless of what had happened in Queens. We said our goodbyes on Sunday morning, once the sun rose, with hugs, handshakes and kisses, then hopped on the subway headed back west towards Jersey.

AMAYAH WANTED to attend the service at The Basilica of St. Patrick's, a famous church from the 19th century on Mulberry Street in Manhattan. We weren't exactly dressed for a fancy church service, but she reminded me that God didn't care what you wore; he cared that you came. As we rode the crowded Sunday morning subway together, she broke down the church's history for me.

"They started building it in 1858, but they stopped for about a decade because of the Civil War," Ama explained. "So, they didn't finish it until 1879. We missed the 100th anniversary by just a year! Anyway, it's registered as a designated landmark for the city and is one of the most recognizable places for Christians in America."

It was even more impressive to see it for the first time, and humbling to go inside, knowing how many people had worshiped there over the years. We found seats way in the back, as it was packed with people, even an hour before the service began. Amayah got up and excused herself to the restroom. Since I didn't know anyone, I picked up the Bible in front of me and started thumbing through, reading passages here and there. I really liked reading the Bible. It was written from such a comforting point of view and made complex topics seem so much easier to understand.

I paused in the book of Peter, specifically Peter 3:3-4 and read, *"Your beauty should not come from outward adornment and appearance, such as elaborate hairstyles and the wearing of gold jewelry or fine clothes. Rather, it should be that of your inner self, the unfading beauty of a gentle and quiet spirit, which is of great worth in God's sight."*

I immediately thought of Ama, and how she had sprung to my mom's aid in the alley. She was completely calm and collected, and so attentive and compassionate. If I hadn't been on the adrenaline high of smacking that little punk around who had assaulted my mom, I think my heart might have melted at the tenderness Ama displayed. I always pictured Ama as a doctor or a nurse, perhaps something in pediatrics. She was so giving and caring. Thinking about where I was and who I was with, I was taken aback in the moment, perhaps for the first time in my life, genuinely seized by the Holy Spirit. I bowed my head and prayed aloud under my breath.

"God, I want to thank you for bringing Amayah into my life. I don't know what I did to deserve her, but she has helped me in so many ways and shown me the beauty of this world again and again. I was so unaware of all the amazing things I was missing out on until you brought her across my path, so that I could really see her inner strength. I think she's beautiful on the outside, but now I know that her beauty goes straight through to her very heart and soul. I—"

A tiny cough made me look up and there she was, gazing down at me, tears in her eyes and a look of fierce beauty on her face. If I could have frozen that image for all time in my mind, I would have. She reached down and brushed the stray hair off my forehead and ran her fingers down the side of my face. I wisely didn't say a word. She smiled through her tears and whispered, "Rohan Chang, you are the most amazing person I've ever met. The strongest and the bravest and the sweetest man I could ever imagine. I am so in love with you."

I almost asked her to repeat herself, because the sound of those words was the subject of about a thousand different daydreams and fantasies I'd had in the past year or so. I had wanted to say it, but like every guy in the history of forever, I was worried that she wouldn't reciprocate my feelings, or that she was just hanging around because she had to while we tried to get back to our own time. But the dam was broken, and the wheels were officially off the wagon. Ama loved me and had said so outside of a fantasy. I smiled back at her and found that my eyes were brimming as well.

"I love you too, my Ama," I half-whispered, half-croaked. "I have for a long time now, but I've been too afraid to tell you, because I didn't know if you felt the same way. You're the strongest person I know. The bravest and the sweetest too."

If we hadn't been in a church during Sunday service, I imagine things would have gotten pretty hot and heavy at that point, but this also felt more spiritual than physical, so I pulled her into me, wrapping her in my arms so tight that it almost felt like we were one person for a moment. I finally let her go, enough to see her face and gaze into her eyes.

"I'm so grateful that I found you, Ama. I think you're beautiful on the outside, but you've made me see that inner beauty is the most important thing in life. I had a crush on you from the day I met you, but the real beauty that shines bright is your soul, your mind, and your character. And your heart. The trivial exterior inevitably fades away, but a beauty like yours is eternal."

I had never bared my soul like that to anyone, but in that moment, I wouldn't have cared if she responded by laughing in my face. I had spoken my truth, sharing the essence of how I felt about her. I felt stronger right then, letting her see the barest part of my soul, than I ever had when using my powers.

"My heart belongs to you, Rohan," Ama whispered, our tears mingling in a cascade of joy, enveloped in a profound sense of acceptance and belonging. "And my soul, intertwined with yours, pledged to you until the end of my days, if you'll have it. Together, I think we've found our way back. Wherever you are, Ro, that is where my home is—within your arms."

I thought I had trouble seeing because I was blinking back so many tears. Suddenly, I realized that my power was surging, and I felt my eyes grow wide.

"It's happening, Amayah! Hold on tight! I think we're going home!"

She smiled and squeezed me harder, but something didn't feel right. Suddenly, I remembered what I had been carrying around in my backpack for weeks, the one I had planned to keep safe since that day in the Brooklyn bar. It was a burden I needed to leave in 1980. I freed myself from Amayah's grasp and said, "Hang on, I'll be back in ten seconds!"

She looked at me as if I was completely insane, but I gave her my best Han Solo "trust me" smile and raced from our row to the very front of the church. Needless to say, this caused quite a stir, given how many people were there for the service. Half of them probably thought I had a bomb or a gun, especially when I took off my backpack and unzipped it, frantically digging inside.

"Are you alright, my son?" the minister at the pulpit said, trying to stay calm so the masses would follow his lead.

"I'm fine!" I yelled, way too loudly, my voice bouncing off the tall ceilings. "I've got an offering I need to give you!"

He smiled. "Such enthusiasm from one so young! What a fine example! But do not be troubled, my son, the collection plate will come around shortly."

But I knew I didn't have that much time, so I yanked the three stacks of $100 bills from my backpack. Unfortunately, in my haste, the plastic had caught on a zipper, freeing the bills, and the money went everywhere, flying into the air. People gasped, pointed, and shifted in their seats at the sight of so much money at the foot of the altar. I had no time for the spectacle as I raced down the aisle back to the pew where Amayah was waiting. The crowd watched me go, no longer hypnotized by the money. I wrapped my arms around

Amayah just as I felt the surge of energy pulse to its maximum output. *This was it!*

"Wait!" called the minister. "Come back... you must tell us your —"

He cut short as the white light drowned out everything around us, which meant that the people of the church were seeing a bona fide miracle, the two of us disappearing from sight into a blazing white light.

"Jesus Christ!" an old woman near us yelled at the top of her lungs, which made me laugh.

Ama's eyes widened at me, and she smiled, "I'm not even going to ask about the money."

"It's a miracle, my flock!" the minister yelled. "See them clearly! Angels! In our church, delivering us from financial ruin on this day! Please don't go! Stay and deliver the Word of the Lord on this, the day of his miracles!"

We looked at each other and shrugged. "GOD BLESS EVERY-ONE!" Amayah cried out. "Love each other! Be nice to each other too!"

She had taken all the good stuff, so as the people looked expectantly at me, I raised my right fist and screamed at the top of my lungs, "LET'S GO YANKEES!"

I THOUGHT of my parents as we entered a field of intense, circular, flashing blue and white lights. Everything around us tumbled and splashed out of sight and time.

Holding out my golden fat cap, it ascended and floated higher and higher, spinning around on its axis as bright lights around us began swirling into circular patterns and bent-out shapes, concentrating and solidifying. I witnessed a mesmerizing spectacle as art slowly converged, manifesting before my very eyes. In a fleeting moment, the Wall Hall of Fame unveiled itself before me, revealing Crook in his audacious urban allure and the iconic Steel Curtain in a riot of vibrant hues. Then my gaze fixated on the intricate details of Talon One, where wild strokes of dark and white embraced purple letters and elaborate arrows. Amidst this gallery of wonders, a masterpiece by Lore stood tall, a pyramidal marvel exuding flawless equilibrium, grace, and precision—a creation harmoniously woven with mathematical perfection.

I saw him then. Lore was spraying his paint with his fat cap, creating bright oranges, warm yellows, and bold greens that danced out, outlining his unique, one-of-a-kind lettering. His strokes appeared almost effortless, his concentration was unbreakable, and his techniques were unmatched.

Ama was no longer by my side. I found myself standing on top of a tall building, with the asphalt blazing underfoot. In the distance, I saw Lore on top of the parking garage, completely unaware of the three angry bullies who were stealthily creeping up behind him, ready to pounce.

"Get the hell out of the way, Lore!" I screamed.

He continued to disregard me while immersed in the creation of his art.

"Lore! WAKE UP! Damn you, Lore, get out of the way!"

I saw the Chunky Brothers closing the final few steps, but Lore ignored my pleas. Without hesitation, they pounced on him and tossed him unmercifully over the edge.

"Noooo!" I started sprinting pointlessly across the rooftops to where he had fallen. Falling to my knees, I screamed, "You can survive this! It's all I've ever wanted!"

Everything shifted, dissolving into a dazzling white hue, as a profound silence enveloped the atmosphere.

"*Rohan?*" Lore asked.

I froze. "What's happened? WHAT'S HAPPENED?!"

"*I'm here, Ro.*"

"But I saw you fall."

"*Look, I'm here, aren't I...?*"

With a heavy heart, I bowed my head, a tightness gripping my chest.

"Why are you doing this?" I murmured, shielding my eyes from the welling tears. Lore's touch encircled me, pulling me into a tender, comforting embrace. Yet, I could not summon the courage to meet his gaze, lost in a whirlwind of conflicting emotions. The intensity of the moment weighed heavily on me, rendering me utterly powerless.

"I came to say goodbye, my brother, Ro."

"I love you, Lore ... Drew; I didn't mean to say your other name. It's ... please ... just don't leave me."

"I love you too, Ro. The time has come for you to live your life and live it well. Break free and create your wild style, becoming the artist... creator I always thought you'd become; draw out your destiny as you see fit, breaking through all the barriers."

I could no longer feel his embrace as his voice waned. As I looked up, Lore's ethereal figure, cloaked in a halo of white light, hovered before me, gradually dissipating into the unknown. Witnessing his departure weighed heavily, suffocating me with each passing moment. Unrestrained, tears flowed down my cheeks, a torrent I could no longer contain.

CHAPTER
TWENTY-NINE

Once again, the dance of circular white and blue lights enveloped us, creating an atmosphere akin to being on a high-speed carousel ride without a seatbelt. This time, Ama was right beside me, her presence a comforting constant in the whirlwind of sensations. In that moment, driven by a deep fear of losing her or something equally precious, I pulled her closer, seeking comfort in her proximity. I closed my eyes, letting the fear of the unknown meld with the thrill of being so near her, feeling her heart racing against mine. We were in this together, tethered by more than just the physical embrace. As the tumultuous lights and sensations began to fade, I dared to open my eyes, only to find the symbol of our adventure, my gold fat cap, securely in my hand, a tangible reminder of our unbreakable bond.

She was adorned in the same breathtaking jade dress she had donned for the Festival of the Moon, her elegance timeless. I glanced down at my simple black T-shirt, struck by our contrasting attire. Yet, there we stood, in the very outfits we wore before the leaps through time and space, our connection as strong as ever.

I took a deep breath and looked around slowly. It was New York

City, and I immediately recognized Kissena Park's green fields behind us. We were sitting on a park bench at the intersection of Booth Memorial and 159th Street. I tried not to get too excited, as these jumps hadn't been easy to deal with so far. I stood up very, very slowly, waiting for the nausea and seizures I had struggled with during our first two time jumps. I looked left and right, but all I saw was normal New York. No crazy hairstyles, no ads for disco clubs, or the latest season of "Dallas." No taxis that looked like they were from a period piece. This was my New York, our New York, as near as I could tell. Amayah was peeking out from behind her hands, and I slowly lowered them, smiling at her.

"We're back where we belong, and look!" I pointed toward Kissena Park's interior, where workers were taking down bunches of balloons and little twinkling lights. "It looks like they're taking down the decorations from the Festival of the Moon. We jumped back to exactly when we left, as if we were just at the festival last night!"

She slowly smiled, and a little gleam twinkled in her eye. "The festival last night where Rohan Chang was too scared to dance with the girl he's in love with?"

I blushed a little, but the truth of her comment barely caused a ripple on my ego.

"That's the one," I replied with a smile. I took her hands and spun her around in a circle, dipping her as she giggled. We were back home! I was thrilled, and my mind was racing in a million different directions, trying to figure out what we should do next.

"Oh my goodness, Ro, our parents are probably wondering where we are! We should head home and let them know we're safe!"

I hated to be apart from her, but I knew that we had to go. Especially now, after meeting our parents in their youth. They were so remarkably different from the people I thought I knew. I saw our parents fret about their families in 1980, so much so that I didn't want our parents to worry about us that way now. First, I needed to get Amayah home, and we took our time, even though we were both eager to see other familiar faces. Eventually, there was nothing to do but walk up to her apartment building. She had the key, of course, but before she could put it in the lock, the door swung open, and her parents—much older, which gave me a bit of a shock—were both standing there with faces of worry and bewilderment.

"Amayah!" her mother cried out. "Dios mio, hija! You had us worried sick!" Teresa Bello was still beautiful, despite being almost two decades older. She glanced at me, and I saw her do a bit of a double take. Whether that was because she recognized me from seventeen years earlier, or was wondering why some random Asian kid had brought Amayah home at 7:30 in the morning.

Her dad, Sergio, waited his turn for a big hug. It was heart warming to see the physical display of this family's love for each other. He hugged her tight, said something in her ear I couldn't hear, and then turned to get a good look at me.

"We meet again, young hombre," Ama's dad said in Spanglish with a half-grin.

I just smiled and hoped that he had forgotten about the first incident between us after the hospital, where he called me a racial slur and fell on his ass. Before I could say anything, Amayah stepped back to stand beside me and took my hand in hers.

"This is Rohan Chang," she said, taking a deep pronounced breath. "He's my boyfriend."

You could have knocked me over with a feather at that admission. I never dreamed that Amayah would even say we were official like that in front of her friends, let alone her parents. I couldn't help letting a big goofy smile come across my face. Even if her parents reacted negatively, hearing her say it out loud was pretty extraordinary.

Her parents were quiet for a long moment, and then her dad did one thing I never expected.

He stuck out his hand for me to shake and spoke. "It's a real pleasure to meet you again, Rohan. Amayah's mentioned you many times as one of her friends, but I didn't know the feelings were there too. She's told us that you work together at the drug store and how compassionate you are. Wish we had more kids like you around here."

It was one of the most surprising things I had ever experienced, even though I had just time traveled from 1980 a few hours earlier. I stammered out a thanks and shook his hand vigorously. Teresa gave me her hand as well and smiled at Amayah in a knowing way.

"We keep saying that Amayah should have her friends over for dinner some time, but we weren't expecting you for breakfast! We were about to start looking for you. Did the festival run all night?"

Just like that, we had an escape window.

"Um, yeah," I said with a sheepish grin. "The fireworks got wet somehow, and they kept promising this big show, so we kept hanging around with a bunch of people from school and the neighborhood.

"They got them going eventually, but the sun was nearly up by then."

"I told you it was something like that," Sergio said, nudging Teresa playfully in the ribs. "She's convinced that every time someone takes two minutes longer than they should getting somewhere that the serial killer got them."

The killer! He was still stalking the Five Boroughs. I still felt that we were connected somehow, like I had gained my powers in order to somehow stop him from continuing his monstrous reign of terror over the city, but I was so busy with everything else that I hadn't put much thought into it. I had to shift gears on that. I couldn't just pretend that someone else was going to stop this guy.

"Have the cops said anything more about him?" I asked as casually as I could.

"Just to lock your doors and not go anywhere alone," Teresa offered, frustration in her voice. "Like that's going to stop him."

Sergio looked at me quizzically, as if he was meeting me for the first time again, but also seeing a ghost. "Hey Rohan, do you have an uncle or a cousin with the same name? We knew another Rohan once when we first moved here. It was forever ago, and I'm sure my memory has gone hazy, but I feel like you look just like him."

Suddenly on the spot, I mentioned that I was named after an uncle who lived in New York in the late 1970s, but he'd decided to try his luck in San Francisco instead. That seemed to appease them enough to let it go.

The moment passed and the Bellos asked if I wanted to stay for breakfast, but I told them that I really needed to get home before my parents started to worry. I hugged Amayah long and hard, and told her that I would call later. It was odd saying goodbye after all this time together. We had slept in different rooms at the youth center in New Jersey, but for several months, she was never more than a quarter of a mile away. There was a sadness and a longing I had never experienced before as the door closed between us.

Knowing that my own parents were probably going to react a lot less favorably, I decided that I had enough energy left to make the trip a bit quicker than the long walk or a subway ride. New York might be called the city that never sleeps, which mostly means that you can get a hot dog at 5:00 a.m. or a haircut at midnight, but Sunday mornings at this hour are pretty dead. Everybody with a nine to five job or school all week is ready to cut loose and have fun, so they're sleeping late on Sundays or relaxing at home. As such, the subway station was a ghost town when I came bounding down the stairs. We had taken the subway plenty of times in 1980, but it was great to be back in my own version of it. It even smelled better, which is saying a lot when you're talking about the New York subway system.

I gave a quick glance and a second one just to be sure, then dropped off the platform onto the tracks. On a crowded rush-hour morning, that sort of behavior would have induced screams and people gathering around like they were witnessing their first junior high fight. At least one person would be a good Samaritan and jump down to try and save the person who fell, or who decided to meet their maker, and then you either got something heroic or something tragic. Fortunately, no one saw me hop down, so no one had to report the blue-jeaned, black T-shirt-wearing blur ripping through the Washington Heights subway station. I hadn't run these tunnels like the ones near my apartment, when the speed first started to manifest, but I was still able to navigate them quickly. Somewhat embarrassingly, I had memorized how to get from my part of town to Amayah's on the subway, the bus, and the train, just in case she ever asked me to come over. So, sue me... I was crazy about Ama.

I blurred through the tunnels, only having to stop once when a cat crossed my path, and I skidded to a halt to avoid it. At least, I hoped it was a cat, because otherwise, it was a three foot-long rat. There were urban legends about what was down here—rats the length of your arm, baby alligators that people had flushed down the toilet that were now the size of Buicks. I supposed that I was starting to qualify as a bit of an urban myth myself, which was, admittedly, very *dope*.

As I ran, I thought back to what the Bellos had said about the serial killer. That night I first teleported and used my powers and found the body, I shook like a leaf seeing that poor girl. I was terrified that whoever did it was still lurking around, and that I'd be next.

I was smart enough to know that going home wasn't going to get me any closure with my parents, because while it was early for 99% of New York City, the Changs were assuredly already hard at work at the laundromat. I did stop to change clothes and take a 90-second shower, so I looked far more refreshed than I felt. Going into the exact same apartment that I had just been sleeping in a few hours earlier, but also seventeen years earlier, was a bit of a mind trip that I tried to avoid overthinking. Marty McFly from "Back to the Future" had me beat when it came to understanding how time travel worked. However, it was great to be 'home,' even though I felt like I had just left. The only thing more curious to look at than everything that had changed over the seventeen years was seeing how much everything had stayed the same. A few family pictures of my brother and I were in the same spots on the wall, a testimony to parents who valued their children much more highly than I gave them credit for. I took the familiar path to the laundromat, with a spring in my step and feeling friendlier towards the entire world than I had felt in a long time.

When I ducked my head in the door, my dad looked up for the briefest second, and I could see the relief in his eyes before he refocused on the customer in front of him. It was a gesture I would never have noticed without the recent experience I'd shared with him in 1980. As dumb as it sounds, I had to keep telling myself that there was no way he was going to recognize me as "Buster," the guy he had known for eighteen hours one random night in 1980, despite the fact that those events felt so recent to me. Just like Amayah's parents, I believed that the memories would have faded, not to mention the fact that baby Rohan and Buster had been there at the same time. They would have seen the real version of me grow up day by day and had likely forgotten the general look of their old guardian angel. My dad finished taking the customer's laundry, handed him the ticket, and wished him safe travels—his classic departure line. Once the door was closed and the store was empty, he narrowed his eyes at me.

"You are staying out all night now?"

I tensed up, recalling the explosion he wrought on me the night I first used my powers. Was he about to explode in rage again? Well, so much for him not noticing that I hadn't come home. That was okay, though, I'd concocted a good enough excuse to get through this early awkward part of what I was hoping would be a much better relationship going forward.

"Hey Dad, I saw you and Mom leaving this morning as I was coming up the street. I shouted, but you didn't hear me. There was some trouble at the festival, a bunch of rowdy types knocking over trash cans and stuff, acting like real jerks. You know, there are never enough volunteers working, so my friend Amayah and I stayed, and helped clean up. The sun was almost up by the time we finished."

Yeah, it was a lie, and I did feel bad about that. However, considering that the truth was that I teleported through time to 1854 , helped some slaves escape a cruel fate, then jumped to 1980 and helped out not only my own parents, but also my girlfriend's parents in their early twenties, a lie seemed like the way to go.

He gave me a long stare, then came around the counter and patted me on the shoulder.

"I'm proud of you, Rohan, that's a very mature thing you did," he said in a kind voice I hadn't heard in years. "Were they Korean? Those punks?"

It would have been easy to say yes, because I would have been entirely in the clear. However, at the same time, the last few months had shown me there was good and evil in all types of people, and stereotyping my fictitious delinquents as Koreans was a terrible thing to do in the face of that lesson.

"They were all in ski masks and bandanas," I replied. "I doubt it was a gang, just lowlifes being lowlifes."

He nodded, like I was suddenly a sage that he respected. "Sounds about right. Lowlifes being lowlifes. They come in all colors. So, your friend Amayah stayed and helped as well?"

I did a double-take, and maybe even a triple-take. My dad knew Amayah?

"Um, yeah, she felt bad about it. She's really compassionate when it comes to stuff like that. I walked her home this morning. Her parents were a bit worried too, but we told them all about it."

"Good man, son, making sure that she got home safe. I respect you for doing the right thing all the way around."

Two compliments from my dad in one month would be pushing it. Two in the span of one conversation was close to the realm of divine intervention. How much of an impact had our trip back to 1980 really had on our suddenly reasonable parents?

I smiled at my dad, who smiled back. He looked tired, and a bit old, despite his happy mood. Perhaps that was because I had just seen him seventeen years younger, but he seemed stiffer than I remembered. I needed to try and get him to take a little time off here and there if I could. So, I went to the back and brewed my dad's favorite oolong tea, just as he liked it, and brought it out to the front for him. As I watched him sip the tea and savor its rich aroma, I couldn't hold back any longer, as a warm tear rolled down my cheek. Now that I was back with my family, I wanted to do right by them and let them know how much I appreciated their sacrifices.

I got dinner for him and my mom later and sat down to eat with them. They both seemed baffled by my sudden desire to spend time with them, but seemed generally pleased and asked about school, which I could barely remember, as well as the festival. I enjoyed their company far more than usual, and it felt like I had untied some massive knot in our relationship that I didn't even know was there. I knew that my parents loved me and were good people. Maybe they just had trouble expressing their emotions because they were so utterly focused on their work and on trying to give my brother and me a better life than they had at the same age. No matter what, I vowed never to take them and their dedication for granted again.

CHAPTER
THIRTY

When Amayah and I walked into school Monday morning holding hands, you would have thought that Madonna and Patrick Ewing had just walked in the door. The stares and gasps and points and whispers rolled over the student body like a tidal wave. But it didn't matter to us because we hadn't thought about it as we strolled to school. Whoever first said that absence makes the heart grow fonder was dead on. We talked on the phone for about an hour Saturday night and then got together to do homework. Man, did that seem more trivial than normal. Getting back to our everyday routines was quite bizarre. What had been a good four months for us between 1980 and 1854 was the equivalent of about six hours for the rest of humanity. When I saw the evaluation of definite integrals looming in my homework on Sunday, I called it quits before I started. Fortunately, even calculus was tolerable when Amayah was near me. We had a serious game of footsie under the table for the first ten minutes until her mom asked why we were being so quiet, so we finally got to work, accompanied by some sly smiles and raised eyebrows.

At school, I walked her to her first class, hugged her close, and kissed her cheek, saying that I'd see her at lunch. Those who experienced this exchange acted like the paparazzi for the Post and the Enquirer, as though they were catching Dennis Rodman leaving Madonna's apartment all over again. It was insane. Over the next few periods of the school day, I had guys I didn't know and had never spoken to come up to me and give me a high five, saying, "Nice work." When I stopped by my locker between physics and world history, a girl named Abby Schneider, who I had known since the third grade, came marching up to me and said, "I can't believe you asked *her* out when I've had a crush on you for *three years*!"

She stomped away before I could say a word. A crush on me? For three years? She was a nice girl, and cute, and we were friends, but I had zero indication that she liked me in any way, ever. Of course, I had been so hung up on Amayah for at least two of those years that you could have landed a jumbo jet on the roof of the school and I might have missed it.

When I finally reconnected with Amayah for lunch, we both started talking at once, paused to let the other one speak, then started up again. We both broke out laughing, and then I held her hands in mine and said, "You go first; it can't be as bad as mine."

It turns out that it was worse. A few weeks earlier, my display on the track had gotten the school girls buzzing more than I realized. Amayah received a deluge of dirty looks, side eyes and angry "Hmmphs!" when she confirmed the news that we were officially a couple. A girl in my grade named Tracy Spitzberg, who I had also never talked to, mostly because she was super intimidating and almost as tall as me and a far better athlete, bent down in Amayah's face, declaring she was about to ask me out, but Amayah had ruined it. Ama apologized profusely, unsurprising given her endless compassion and that maybe we all could be friends. Tracy still got mad and stormed off. We couldn't help but laugh at it all. We had traveled through time and space, battling oppression and cruelty and racial prejudice, but nothing could prepare us for the ultimate test in emotional angst and divisive opinions: high school.

The first few days of our "return to normal" in 1997 felt like a vacation. School seemed fun; not having to worry about what we needed to achieve to make it back to our own time was a relief, and there was certainly no one trying to make us bale cotton sixteen hours a day. On Wednesday, Amayah and I went back to Mt. Sinai for what seemed like the first time in months, but it had actually only been a week, and I used my powers more generously than normal to guide the sick back towards full health. I went to Amayah's for dinner, and her parents welcomed me with open arms, and their kitchen embraced me with delicious aromas. I volunteered to work the closing shift at the drugstore with my brother, so I hugged Amayah tightly and kissed both her cheeks before setting off.

I didn't tell her why I was suddenly more enthusiastic about work; that was my little secret. Even though virtually no time had passed in the real world, we would be coming up on five months since we first went to the Festival of the Moon and started our crazy adventure together. I was planning something really romantic to celebrate that. I was busy looking for restaurants in downtown Manhattan to find the perfect spot. I was also saving up for a special night, which included a taxi ride to and from the restaurant and a trip up to the observation deck of the World Trade Center. I was planning to give her a ring that I had put on layaway; it was pure silver and in the shape of two hearts intertwined. Before starting this adventure with Amayah, I would have dismissed it as incredibly cheesy and been unable to tell you what the ring symbolized... but now? Two hearts and two people so intricately tied together. It was perfect.

ONE NIGHT, as I was drifting off to sleep, Nick the Brute woke me with a violence I hadn't felt in a long while. I hadn't thought about him once since we had returned, but unfortunately, that feeling wasn't mutual.

"WAKE UP, BITCH!"

Abraham Lincoln, orator extraordinaire, couldn't match Nick's eloquence.

I tried using some suppression techniques that I was teaching myself, including thoughtful prayer, minimizing his voice, and pushing down the aggressive feelings that he tried to elicit in me. Usually, a combination of two or three of these was enough to put him back in his place, but his voice kept rattling around in my skull. I imagined a prisoner in a straitjacket slamming against the bars of his cell, demanding attention.

"GET OFF YOUR ASS! HE'S OUT THERE! HE'S ABOUT TO STRIKE! GET UP AND FIND HIM! GET UP AND TAKE HIM!"

Him? Did he mean the serial killer? A slow, cold chill came over me, starting in my arms and upper legs and working its way through my stomach and down my back. Amayah's parents had said the killer was still out there, but I became distracted by my lovefest at home and school. My ears turned red, realizing that now. All these powers, and all those lessons in the past, and I was still being so greedy, except at Mt. Sinai, I suppose. I could be using my powers daily to literally do almost anything, and I was mostly just keeping them to myself. I was like Ebenezer Scrooge, hoarding his money on Christmas Eve, while the whole town froze and slowly starved. I needed to do something.

I tip-toed to the living room and turned on our tiny TV to the 11 o'clock news. Sure enough, the serious-faced anchors were talking about a new slaying. The body had been found about a few hours earlier, and my heart fell to the floor when they described the victim. She was a Black girl, all of eight years old, found in an abandoned warehouse about three blocks from her school. She didn't come home from a friend's house after classes, and her parents called the cops around 7:00 p.m. Someone mentioned seeing her playing by the warehouse, and when the cops burst in, they found her immediately. She had been badly mutilated and partially burned. The police captain addressing the media throng on TV began crying halfway through the interview—a tough old cop with a bushy white mustache and a thick Brooklyn accent, and he totally lost it. It broke my heart to see how torn up he was, but my anger far outpaced my sadness. This psychopath was running around unchecked in my town, New York City. So, I opened the floodgates just a little, and the Brute's anger and rage came rushing in.

The mystical, maddening spirit of Hua had told me that the Brute was dangerous, and I believed her, but right now he was exactly the way I wanted to be feeling. I flipped the TV off, went back to my room and opened my closet. There behind my many pairs of tennis shoes, stacks of jigsaw puzzles, and piles of half-clean, half-dirty clothes, was my secret backpack, the one I took when I went out bombing.

I unzipped it and slipped on my fateful bandana, quickly changing into the clothes I had last worn with Steven, Jarron, and Lior on the night my powers first manifested. I couldn't stop what happened to that little girl, but it was time I got serious about the person perpetrating these crimes and found a way to stop him. I slipped out the window, feeling a whole lot like Peter Parker on his way to fight crime as the friendly neighborhood Spiderman, then gathered up my energy to leap from the fire escape outside our apartment to the top of the neighboring building. Dressed all in black, I felt bold and capable of helping. I raced across the rooftops, just as I had the night in 1980 when I tracked down my dad and saw him triumphing in a moral dilemma. The warehouse in question was about three miles from Fresh Meadows, but with my speed and the free space I had atop the buildings, it took me less than five minutes to get there.

I waited about forty-five minutes in the shadow of a nearby roof before only one police car remained and another twenty minutes after that for the last lingering onlookers to finally depart. The officer in the remaining patrol car suddenly drove off with his sirens blaring after receiving a call on his radio, probably in response to a nearby crime.

I noticed a makeshift memorial for the little girl just outside as I snuck in closer. Her name was Sophia Anzari, according to several signs that people had left on the warehouse's now-locked fence, along with flowers, drawings, and even a few photographs of her at a birthday party, smiling. Seeing her so vibrant and happy infuriated me, and instead of climbing the fence, I grabbed a hold of a section and ripped it straight off, like peeling the skin off an orange. I knew right away that I shouldn't have done it because the police would likely freak out about it, but I was pretty done with the police. Whoever was doing this was up to eight known victims in the last six months. The cops were too busy busting kids for tagging to worry about a rampaging serial killer, apparently. I slipped inside the warehouse and found the spot where the girl's body had been found. It was gone now, of course, but the chalk outline you always see on TV was left behind, along with yellow police tape, so no one stepped somewhere or touched something before they had a chance to fully analyze everything at their crime lab. I didn't know what I was looking for, but I crept around cautiously, looking for any clue the police might've overlooked. I knew the cops were thorough, despite being painfully slow as investigators, but I had to look anyway. Deep down, I knew this guy was going to be my problem, and I needed to catch him for the good of all the innocent people out there just trying to live a decent life.

As I used my heightened senses and scanned the warehouse a few times over, I noticed a glint of metal in the corner. It hadn't been there a minute ago, but there it was, and I realized that the moon had come from out behind the clouds, high enough to shine through a busted window. I crept slowly towards the glint. I might have been built like a superhero, but this was still a creepy warehouse where a murder had happened. Bending down, I nudged the shape with the side of my hand. I saw it now—a metal cigarette lighter.

It could have belonged to anyone. The warehouse had been owned by a construction company at one point, and I'm sure plenty of the guys there were cigarette smokers. But the factory had been closed down for at least a year, and this thing looked brand new, still shiny. I touched it with the tip of my index finger and thought I felt a hint of warmth there, like someone had used it not so long ago. Could it have been one of the cops? That didn't seem likely. No cop would smoke a cigarette this close to a crime scene. Suddenly, I had a flash of intuition, remembering the night I had used the Shine to touch Steven Stone's mind. I was able to do so because I knew him and could envision him. I didn't know who owned this cigarette lighter, but I had the physical thing right here. Would it work? The only thing I could do was try. It was a strange-looking lighter, as it held a picture of a smiling clown with the name Pogo written across the face of it.

I sat on the ground with my legs crossed and my back to the wall so I could see the door open if someone decided to come back. I took the lighter and closed my hand around it, feeling its every groove and bump. I closed my eyes and focused on the lighter, envisioning its fall from someone's hand to the floor. "Where have you been?" I thought in my mind. "Tell me your story."

For a few seconds, nothing happened, and I was on the verge of giving up when a brief prickle of sensation coursed through my fingertips. I focused on it, followed it, like chasing the track of a shooting star without opening my eyes, as my mind filled with someone's thoughts.

I PROMISED myself that I would enjoy the sweetness a bit more the next time around and savored the treat I did. Even changed my technique a little. Hee-hee-hee... To hunt and do what's natural, every single time, so fuckin' exhilarating and free...

And I did have more time to enjoy at the warehouse, the one I chose days ago when I watched her walk home. It was perfect. No one came in there except a few drug addicts looking to crash after a score, and they only came out at night. Everyone was scared of the night. They feared its shadows and the dark places. If only they knew that 99% of my work was done in broad daylight... they would stay inside with their blinds drawn and their doors locked tight. It' s just as easy to hide in the daytime as it is at night. Easier even. Nobody looks at you for more than half a second. Everyone's too busy with their own life to give a shit about who you are or what you're doing.

All they care about is themselves and their bullshit lives and getting to that next oh-so-important thing: McDonald's lunch, their hot date, the next hit, next business meeting, next gift from their rich married boyfriend. It makes me sick just thinking about them. And every woman on this planet is a taker. They take your money, they take your house, they take your sanity, they take your freedom, they take, and they take, and they take some more. And when you question them, they leave. They FUCKING leave you. They act like they're the most important thing in the world, and you're garbage, and they let you know how disposable you are every day of the week.

But that sweet little Black bitch smiled when she saw me and waved and said thank you when I picked up the tennis ball that had rolled away. She didn't smile so much when I grabbed her wrist and covered her mouth, but that was good too. I admire me a fighter.

Some of them haven't fought back at all, just gone limp like a dead fish givin' up on life. I hate it when that happens. All my planning and effort and you're just gonna give up on the one life you have? The one thing that makes you what you are? One of them, the fat one, in Maine, passed out from fear. That was monumentally disappointing. I figured she'd try to bull past me – fear often fills people with adrenaline, which makes them powerful. I knew I could always stop her without much effort, but I wanted to see her fight for her life. Cuz I love me a fighter. But she just passed out and threw up in her own mouth. Her body reeked of frozen pizza. I couldn't even look at her. Turned her on her back and gutted her quickly. It was an embarrassment to my craft. The little girl, though? She fought hard.

And I like that the best, cuz then you really see how much they can take. Some wilt at the first sight of blood or the first little bone you break in their hands or their faces, but not her. She kept kicking and screaming and even biting. That was sweet. She started with her teeth when I had her hands pinned and the lighter up to her face, seeing which part of it would catch fire the quickest. Flesh burns and practically turns into a liquid if you hold the lighter steady. Most people scream so loud that they black out, but not this one. She started screaming, but then she turned into a pure animal and caught my knuckles in her teeth. Bit me so hard I dropped my favorite lighter, and she drew a bit of blood. Oh lordy, what fun! The exhilaraaa-tion. Hee-hee-hee... First time I'd seen my own blood in years. Of course, at that moment, I was furious. So furious that I snapped her fucking neck to shut her up and remind her who was in charge. I regretted that, because it meant the fun was over quicker than I wanted, but that's part of the evolution too, fine-tuning my process, making it better each time, getting closer and closer to the perfection awaiting me.

I GASPED ALOUD and opened my eyes. I was sweaty and shivering, but still standing in the warehouse, and it didn't seem like much time had passed. It was still very dark, and I could see the moon through the same shattered window. I had been in his mind. I was HIM, the killer. I could hear his high-pitched laugh. I didn't know his name, and I couldn't see what he looked like, but I saw his mind at work, and it was sickening. Just as the police suspected, he was targeting only women. He despised them. He blamed them for the problems in his life and decided to group all of them into one big category of the guilty party. He didn't care who he killed either. The girl tonight was Black, but previous victims had been white and Hispanic and Asian as well.

Worse, he was not working at night, as everyone thought; he was moving through the city in broad daylight, watching people as they went about their lives, picking out victims and being completely inconspicuous about it. I realized that I had fallen into the same thought process as most people, assuming that he was some creature of the night, lurking in the shadows like a vampire. And he also mentioned Maine?

I now knew more about this heinous killer than anyone else, but there was hardly anything to go on. He was a man, but I had assumed that anyway. Could I use the lighter as some sort of touchstone and keep touching his mind? I would have to try, but I couldn't do it here or now. It wasn't safe here. Not that I feared him or anyone else, but if the cops came back and found me here, I'd be arrested without a question and made the #1 suspect. Tracking this guy down would be more difficult than I thought because someone might think I was the killer if I was creeping around places he might be. I had to be smart about how I went after this guy. Being a superhero suddenly felt like a hell of a lot more work than I first imagined.

I walked home, rather than jumping across rooftops. I wanted more time to think about how I was going to handle this situation and how much I was going to tell Amayah. My thoughts vacillated between telling her everything and telling her nothing, neither of which seemed like a great idea. I was about a mile from home when I heard the tell-tale sound of glass breaking and froze in place, pressing my back against the wall of the building beside me and holding still, trying to locate the sound.

I saw movement about half a block up, right outside Key Food Supermarket. There were three guys huddled outside the store, and they had just smashed the glass storefront. One stayed as a lookout while the other two clambered inside the store over the broken glass. There was no alarm, so they had either cut the power, or the owner didn't believe in a security system. People never learned that other people would case your place and rob it if your guard slipped. I flashed back to the robbery at my dad's laundromat and then to my father looking at the cash register outside Don's Pub in 1980. However, these guys appeared to have no problem with the moral ethics of stealing from someone else. They were working fast, lugging out a couple of cases of whiskey and wine, the most high-dollar items in there. I suspected they would grab the registers next, if they couldn't quickly bust them open.

I wasn't able to stop the serial killer yet, but if I was going to stand up for the innocent and defend this town, it was time to get to work. I blurred across the street when the lookout's head was turned and ducked behind a parked Buick LeSabre about 50 feet away. I wanted to make sure there were only three of them. My energy level was fine, but I still didn't want to walk into a dangerous situation without knowing all the details. When I was sure they were just a trio, I stepped out from behind the Buick and strolled right towards the lookout with my bandana still up, masking my identity.

He gave a slight jump, clearly startled, as I had appeared to come out of nowhere and was walking right at him rather than trying to avoid being near an active crime.

"Hey, partner!" I said with sarcastic goodwill in my voice. "You guys lost your key or something?"

He had a hoodie on, cinched tight. He was young and white and clearly not expecting any sort of discussion with a stranger while standing watch.

His jaw dropped open and hung there for a moment. Then he turned and yelled, "Rico! Someone's out here! Some guy!"

Three seconds later, Rico himself emerged through the shattered window. Rico was obviously the older brother of the lookout, bearing an almost identical face. They were built roughly the same and had the same complexion and eye shape. Rico also had his hood down, probably to see inside the store better, and looked at me like I was the ultimate fish out of water, and definitely not worth his time.

"Beat it, kid," he said gruffly. "This doesn't concern you. Get home and forget you saw anything."

He turned back towards the smashed window, dismissing me out of hand.

"Ahem, uh, Rico? I don't mean to be a bother, but I'm actually gonna have to ask you and your brother and your friend to go home. Not sure if you're from around here, but breaking and entering a business for the purpose of theft are pretty stiff crimes in New York City. I'd hate to see you boys get mixed up with a bad element and wind up in prison," I said, dropping my voice into a deep booming bass, hoping to add some years to my words of wisdom.

I'm guessing Rico thought I was some sort of crazy homeless

person at that point. To be fair, there were plenty of bums loitering around at all hours, and they'd talk to anyone about anything.

Rico did the slow turn that tough guys do when someone mouths off to them. I used to think it was an intimidation thing, but having stood up to my fair share of bullies in the past few months, I had come to the conclusion that it was actually done so they could buy time to think of how to get out of the situation without looking weak or soft. As a general rule, bullies act out of fear, and whether that fear arose from not having many friends, being seen as weak, or any other imaginable thing, it didn't matter because I needed to take a stand.

When you showed them that you weren't afraid, they got desperate and angry... and made bad decisions. I was counting on Rico landing on at least one of those three.

"Are you crazy, boy? Do you need a beatdown right here? You some kind of tough guy, thinkin' you own these streets? Get home, little Asian boy. Do some extra credit on your math report, or I'm gonna knock your teeth outta your mouth."

Rico's brother whooped at that idea, and Rico smacked him in the back of the head, putting a finger to his lips.

"Guys?" a new voice emerged from the store. "What the hell's the problem out here?"

I looked up as the third member of their little gang emerged. He was a grown man, easily in his thirties and built like a ton of bricks with bulging biceps, a stack of chest muscles, and several tattoos on his neck in that blue ink that immediately tells you he got them in prison. His head was completely shaved, and when he turned to get a clear look at me, I saw that his most prominent tattoo was in the shape of a Swastika.

That symbol made my anger surge, and the Brute answered the call. White supremacists thought psychopaths like Adolf Hitler had it right and that other people were inferior to Aryans, so inferior that they had a right to slaughter them as they pleased. This guy was an ideological descendant of the captain from Oxford, and people like

him who saw the color of your skin as an indication of your worth—
or lack of it. I turned my head slowly and locked eyes with him.

"If you want, instead of robbing this place, I'll give you some
money to get that filthy tattoo zapped off the side of your head." I
pointed at the Swastika. "Fresh Meadows doesn't really like Adolf.
We don't sit well with trash like that."

He got a gleam in his eye like it was his fondest pleasure in the
world to have someone insult him about the tattoo, which is probably the exact reason he got it put in such a prominent place and
shaved his head, leaving it perpetually visible. He dramatically stood
on his tip toes, as if to look behind me.

"The way you're running your mouth, I would have thought you
had a whole yellow army behind you," he said with a mocking laugh.
"But all I see is one little chink with a big fuckin mouth. You must be
the stupidest chinaman in New York."

On his third-to-last word, he lunged at me, a clever tactic for a
fighter, as the other person is leaning in to listen, not preparing to
defend themselves. I imagine he'd successfully used it on plenty of
people who challenged him physically, but he had never fought
someone like me.

He lunged and I dodged, feeling time slow down as I reached
inside to feel my power source and harness it. "I am water," I
thought in my head, trying to balance the rage that the Brute wanted
to unleash with the flow of Bruce Lee's calming meditations. I sidestepped the big guy and delivered a chopping strike to the Swastika
target on the side of his head, sending him sprawling sideways into
the concrete wall of the supermarket and down into a heap.

It happened so fast that you could have blinked and missed it.
The two brothers took an unconscious step back as the big guy tried
to regain his feet, baring his teeth as he turned to face me.

"Some sort of Kung Fu bullshit trick!" he said as he shifted his
weight back and forth between his feet. "That shit only works once,
boy!"

He was right. Bruce said to never use the same move twice in a fight. Always keep them guessing and backpedaling. The big guy clearly wanted me to make the first move, but I held my ground and kept my eyes on his midsection, which would betray his next attack, no matter which way it came from.

He lunged again, but it was only a feint. As his upper body pulled back, he lashed out with his left foot, aiming for my kneecap in an attempt to get me off my feet. It didn't matter what his technique was; I was watching and waiting. I caught his foot in my hand and rotated it clockwise. His whole leg followed suit as I flipped him up into the air with blinding speed. He fell face-first on the pavement and I heard the crunch of his nose breaking against the asphalt.

"Oh shit, Johnny!" the younger brother said as they both moved to help their leader up. He shoved them both off and stood up, red blood gushing freely from his nose.

"Grab him! Hold him still so I can break his face!" Johnny yelled, though the words were coming out funny, either due to a split lip or a bitten-off tongue. The brothers hesitated, but disobeying their leader clearly still scared them more than me, so they came at me together, clumsy and slow, one from each side. Neither was tatted up like Johnny, or at least I couldn't see any ink, and neither had that hardened look of a career criminal. I felt bad for them, having gotten mixed up with this guy so early in life. As they tried to grab me, I jumped straight up in the air, gripped the grocery store's unlit sign, spun off it like a gymnast and landed behind them.

"Rico," I addressed the older one. "I've got a brother too, and he would never let me get mixed up with a punk like this guy. Don't let him ruin your life and get you sent to jail, too. Take your brother and go home and stay the hell away from him."

I could see the struggle in his eyes. I felt like I could read his mind, even though I wasn't actively trying to. I could see some scenario where Johnny had likely recruited Rico, offering him protection or just a cool friend to have. One thing led to another and now Rico had drawn his younger brother into the mix, only to suddenly bite off way more than they could chew.

"Shut the fuck up!" Johnny yelled at me, and I knew I must have hit pretty close to the mark. "Rico, we hit this place and two others tonight, and you go home with three G's easy. You're Rico Rich, remember that! Put it on that car you've been eyeing and all them rich bitches at your school will be lining up for a shot to ride your jock."

Of course, popularity and attention from the opposite sex. How many dumb moves were made by men over the years for the promise of those two things? They had turned me into a swaggering idiot on the track not too long ago. Now they were threatening to get Rico a couple of years in juvie, at least, or maybe a few more at Rikers.

I wanted to defuse this whole thing as easily as possible, without anyone getting any more hurt than necessary.

"Okay," I replied. "Let's settle this like men." I pointed to Johnny. "You versus me. First one to put the other guy on his ass three times is the winner. You win, I walk away, and you guys do whatever you want with what's inside this store. I win, you walk away and avoid this store like the plague, and you let these two go home. And then you stay the hell away from them."

I could see the fear in his eyes, since I'd already knocked him on his ass twice. If he lost to me, he'd lose the brothers' services, and they'd undoubtedly spread the word that some lanky Asian kid had whipped Big Johnny's ass in the middle of a job. But what else could he do? I had painted him into a corner and even his slow-moving brain knew it.

"Fine," he said, trying to get that dangerous, disinterested look back on his face, but failing miserably. "Hurry the fuck up, though, little boy. I got places to go and spend this money at."

We stood about six feet apart, giving him room to contemplate this next move. I knew a guy like this had earned his rep by winning fights and that he'd have a few more tricks up his sleeve. I was right, because he went low, then popped up, attempting to grab the front of my jacket and headbutt me into submission. It might have worked on some other skinhead at one of their little angry get-togethers, but it wasn't going to work on me. I caught him with an open hand to the solar plexus, knocking the wind from his chest and driving him back a few steps. He tripped on the sidewalk and fell backwards with a shout of surprise. As Rico and his brother watched, eyes wide, I leapt forward to land with my feet on either side of Johnny's chest.

"That's one," I said matter-of-factly as I grabbed the front of his jacket with one hand and dragged him back to a standing, yet staggering position. He took a wild roundhouse swing at my face that I dodged easily, swinging my knee up into his stomach and pushing him back to the pavement.

"That's two," I added. Johnny was saying something unintelligible as I lifted him back up. I let him stand there and tapped my chin. "C'mon big shot, show me how superior you are to me. Put one right there, I'm asking you nicely for it."

He tried some sort of two-handed hammer-looking thing, probably his most surefire big damage move, but it was slow and telegraphed, and I was fast and purposeful. I caught his hands in mine, separated them, then used his own clenched fist to punch him in the face. He dropped like a stone.

I turned to the brothers. "Go on, this isn't the life you want. That guy is street trash trying to drag you down to his level because he's decided he wants to be king of the trash pile his whole life."

The two started backing up as Johnny rose to his feet yet again, limping and swaying. His body had betrayed him, but he still had the attitude and the hatred for fuel.

"Hey, boy! You can't stop me from taking what's mine! Only way you're stopping me is if you kill me!" Johnny, without warning, took a black handgun from a concealed holster at his waist and pointed it in my direction. "Or maybe I'll just kill you instead!"

I turned on him in a blue of movement and picked him off the ground by the shoulder. Nick the Brute's voice rose like bile in the back of my throat.

DO IT! HE WANTS IT! FINISH HIM AND THEY'LL DIE FOR YOU! BUILD YOUR FOLLOWERS AND TAKE CONTROL!

I can't lie, I was tempted. The streets would be better off without this asshole on them. One fewer violent crook. One fewer racist. One fewer guy trying to get his hooks in others and turn them into bitter, pathetic clones of himself. I started squeezing the spot between his neck and his shoulder, applying force to watch his reaction as he realized that I could crush him like a bug.

"*Rohan!*"

It was the voice of Hua, the spirit that had taught me about my powers and warned me about the Brute.

Compassion, Rohan! Not violence! Blessed are you with the Shine Xiong. My Shine Xiong ninja, you cannot solve violence with more violence. Be better than your attacker!

It was tough for me to offer Johnny even the slightest bit of compassion. Maybe he thought I was a punk kid he could easily beat up without even taking out his weapon. But he'd shoot me dead if I didn't have my powers. He was fully prepared to rob this store and many others and bankrupt the owners for a few hours of frivolity. And that damn Swastika glared at me from the side of his head. This guy embodied everything wrong with this neighborhood. Greedy, arrogant, hateful.

Now, he just looked afraid. Afraid of me. And I didn't want to be feared. That wasn't how I would make this city a better place. I took a long look at Johnny, and was reminded of my dad, of all people. At some point in his past, Johnny had been in that same situation my dad had faced back in 1980. He had contemplated his first crime, that first thing he knew was wrong that would start him down a path. He chose the wrong way, whereas my dad chose the right one. What had Johnny been before that? Young. Innocent. A child. Someone's son. Someone's brother? Nobody was born a monster. Well, maybe the Brute, but nobody human, at least.

Who was I to act as judge and executioner of a guy I had randomly encountered on the street? He might have already been to prison and not learned his lesson, but that didn't mean there wasn't still hope for him. Even if Johnny wound up back in prison, didn't learn a damn thing, and went back out on the streets, it wasn't my responsibility to declare him hopeless. I stopped the robbery; that was my job. I lowered him to the ground, broke his gun into about ten pieces, and commanded, "Sit down against that telephone pole and don't move." After the pressure on his shoulder was gone, he was more than willing to comply.

I turned to the brother and said, "Get back in there and get me a piece of paper, a Sharpie, and two rolls of duct tape."

They both said "Yes sir" in unison, which was pretty hilarious, and were in and out in less than five minutes. I duct-taped Johnny to the telephone pole to the point where he could barely move, let alone get out. After much consideration, I duct taped his mouth, after ensuring that he could still breathe out of a broken nose. I wrote on the paper, "I tried to rob the grocery store, but I got caught. I will try to make better choices next time," and attached it to his pants' leg where he couldn't reach it. I fished into my pocket, brought out a quarter, and gave it to Rico. "Go hit up the pay phone on the corner and call 9-1-1. Tell them the place is getting robbed. Then you guys get home and stay out of trouble."

They nodded and the younger one said, "Hey man, who the hell are you?" His eyes widened, his mouth following suit, "What are you, some type of New York Ninja?"

As a superhero buff, I went with the first thing that came to mind.

"I'm the NY Talon," I growled. "This is my town, and I don't like people messing with it."

I turned and dashed away in a blur, leaving them with the most sensational story of their lives to tell anyone who would listen for the rest of their days.

CHAPTER

THIRTY-ONE

I made the paper. Three of them, actually. Amayah was beaming with pride the next morning when I met her to walk to school, holding up a copy of the Post, its headline blaring:

RETURN OF THE BLACK BLUR?

The words sat atop a picture of Johnny taped up outside the supermarket, looking pissed as hell. Before I could take the paper, Amayah read it aloud in a deep dramatic voice, *"Eyewitnesses say the robbery was interrupted by a tall, imposing figure in black who defeated the crook single-handedly, leaving him for police to find with a hand-written confession note. The mystery man then disappeared into the night, leading some to speculate that he is the same "black blur" spotted in an alley in Queens a few weeks ago."*

She put the paper down, batting her eyes at me. "Every girl dreams about dating a superhero."

She handed me the paper and hugged me around my waist, pressing her head against my chest and letting me feel her warmth.

"I'm so proud of you, Ro, standing up to that guy and making a difference," she said in a soft, earnest voice. "But what were you doing out so late?"

478

I had forgotten about my inner conflict of what to tell her about the serial killer. However, hiding things from Amayah had gone very poorly in the past, so I came clean about everything, including the Brute, the lighter, and the vision.

Her pupils dilated as I told her about the tale of being in his head, but she didn't interrupt. When I was done, I waited as she processed and organized her thoughts.

"First off, thank you for sharing this with me, Ro," Ama confessed. "I know that couldn't be easy to go through. Being in the head of someone like that, someone who treats other people so cruelly and indiscriminately. He sounds even worse than the TV stations have made him out to be. And dangerous, too. If you're able to figure out who he is or where he is, I think you should go to the cops and let them handle it."

I expected that response, because as compassionate as my girlfriend was, she also loved me and would have a hard time forgiving herself if something bad happened to me that she felt she could have prevented.

"I don't know how I could tell them without implicating myself though," I said. "How could I possibly tell them where I got all that knowledge from? I can't tell some random detective that I've been inside the guy's head; they'll lock me up and throw away the key."

"Maybe an anonymous tip then?" she said. "If you can get his name and address somehow, you could use a payphone to call 9-1-1, like you had those boys do, and report it. They're desperate to stop him. I'm sure they'd at least check it out."

I nodded. I wasn't sold on the plan, because if the police ignored the tip or failed to catch him, he'd probably disappear for a while and then show up in Boston, Philadelphia, or somewhere else even further away. I needed to end this guy on my turf before he realized who he was up against.

I wanted to focus all my attention on him, but it was tough, given how busy I was at school, at work, with Amayah, and regular patrols around Queens, looking to shut down criminals and get them off the streets. I tried to commune with Hua for more insight, but she was frustratingly hard to connect with. Nick the Brute was completely the opposite.

Anytime I got frustrated or angry, he was waiting there, trying to stir me up further and further.

I made sure to meditate, read my Bible, and pray to Hua for guidance every time I went out at night to patrol. I tried to stay on the rooftops as much as possible, to avoid people noticing the way I was dressed and peg me as "the Black Blur," which was not nearly as cool a name as the NY Talon. I limited myself to no more than three hours out on the street, as I still needed to rest before school, so I'd usually stroll around until after midnight, from 10-1 or 11-2, always making sure no one saw me or tried to follow me home. Sometimes I found someone up to no good and stopped them; other times, I saw nothing. I couldn't decide which was better. If I found nothing, then saw something in the paper or on the news the following day, I would feel like I failed. If I saw nothing and heard nothing, I hoped it was because the city was getting better, and people were being safer.

Even so, I couldn't deny that I got a thrill when I caught someone red-handed and was able to intervene. The feeling of righteousness in calling out their misdeeds was a powerful thing. Those who tried to fight me learned the hard way that I was faster, stronger, and more determined than they were. The ones who tried to run never got far. On the anniversary of my first week of patrolling, as I got the drop on three gang members stealing car stereos, one of them screamed out, "Shit, it's the Black Blur, run!"

That was annoying for two reasons. One, because they ran in three different directions, and two, because they were repeating the newspaper's baloney headline. The Black Blur sounded like a turn-of-the-century football player. Plus, I was pretty sure that most people thought I was Black. Not that there was anything wrong with that, but Asian people don't exactly get a fair shake when it comes to superheroes. The old Superfriends cartoons had a Japanese dude named "Samurai" who was, you guessed it, a samurai who could turn the lower half of his body into a tornado and alternately fly or knock people over with it. I thought he was cool when I was little, but having watched old reruns of it years ago, it was painfully obvious that he was stuffed into the show's later seasons, along with Black Vulcan (a Black guy), El Dorado (a Hispanic guy), and Apache Chief (a Native American) to give the Superfriends some racial balance. I was trying to be that compassionate neighborhood defender but still wanted equal representation. I ran down each of the three would-be car thieves, made them swear not to do it again, and reminded them that there was no Black Blur; instead, they had survived an encounter with the NY Talon. They promised to spread the word.

It was bonkers to hear people talk about me, larger-than-life accounts of some spectacular encounter, smatterings of conversations on the street, and the occasional news story about me stopping some crime lord or other. There were no pictures of me, thankfully, just fleeting eyewitness reports. Even some of the kids at school were talking about it, now that the buzz about Amayah and I dating had calmed down. The school was a whole different world once you were accepted, but I tried not to let it go to my head. I was doing my best to be kind and friendly to everyone, including some kids I had once ignored or pretended not to know. I knew these people had all seen me as invisible before, but I had to admit I hadn't been very social to begin with. Lost in all the shuffle was the fact that I hadn't spoken to Steven since we returned. I had math class with him, but he never looked my way. I didn't know if he was embarrassed about what had happened with him and Amayah at the Festival of the Moon, but given that he was the only person besides Amayah who knew what I could do, it seemed strange that he was avoiding me, or so it seemed. However, his lack of interest in our former friendship or whatever we had was admittedly low on my list of priorities.

Along with policing the neighborhood, I was still working at Eckerd's as much as possible to get my pricey plans for Amayah and my anniversary all squared away. I had nearly saved enough for the dazzling restaurant and taxi rides and told her to save the date for something unique. I didn't want her making plans with her family that she couldn't get out of, and she had been trying to get me to give her hints ever since, but I managed to stay strong. That was particularly difficult the day we were studying after school at her house for a math test. Her parents were outside talking to a neighbor when she started pestering me about the surprise. I said nothing, until she got on my lap, put my headphones on me, and played Notorious B.I.G.'s "Hypnotize." She grinned and started to slowly dance and move her hips, singing the lyrics softly to me, then whispering in my ear to give her just the smallest little bit of a hint.

My superpowers had no defense for that sort of attack, and I was prepared to spill every secret of my entire life when her mom opened the door back and hollered up the stairs, asking if I wanted to stay for dinner. Reluctantly, Amayah stood back up and winked at me, knowing that my defenses were weakening.

I HAD BEEN CARRYING the killer's Pogo the clown Zippo, in my pocket since the day of the murder. I focused on it a couple more times, trying to gain access to his thoughts, but nothing came through. I didn't know if the mental link was a one-time deal or if I was doing something wrong, but I felt like tossing it out of anger. That all changed while stocking shelves in the back after hours at Eckerd's as my brother locked down the pharmacy. I felt a warmth growing against my leg and thought I must have bumped it against one of those opened therapeutic heat wraps an angry customer returned. I didn't see any heat source on the shelf, so I reached into my pocket and immediately realized that the lighter was the source of the warmth. I pulled it out to inspect it further. Without thinking twice, I kicked the door to the supply room closed and sat on the floor among the towering rows of shelves. I kept the lights off, so I was unlikely to be interrupted.

I closed my hand around the lighter, ignoring how hot it was, blinked a few times, and then shut my eyes as my mind awakened to someone new…

"Stacey!!"

I turn, feeling the anger welling up already. What the hell did she want now? She was on the front porch, her hair still up in rollers, wearing that hideous pink bathrobe that she thought was so sexy and fun.

"Stacey! Why do you have to go to Manhattan again? You were just there! Can't your boss ever get off his fat ass and take these trips himself?"

I was trying not to let her see my true emotions. It was difficult when I was so close. I could have just gotten in the car and sped off, but that would leave her with doubts. Doubts could be problematic. I didn't think she had the common sense or the attention span to find what was hidden in the false floor of our bedroom closet, or what was buried beneath the storage shed, but if she started doubting that I was telling the truth, that nosey, shrewish quality that all women possess might drive her to start poking around where it didn't belong.

So, I turned around and plastered that damn fake smile back on my face. "You know how it is, honey! The boss man eats, and the little man takes the shit!"

She liked that turn of phrase, and it always made her smile, even when she was pissed at me.

"Yeah, but why does he keep shitting on you? It's such a long drive. At least tell him to put you on an Amtrak or a plane to get there!"

I shrugged my shoulders with my carefully constructed 'Oh well, that's my luck' demeanor. I shook the briefcase full of bullshit files at her. "Probably doesn't trust any of those other knuckleheads to deliver it to the right place at the right time. The guy across the desk from me, Ramirez? Remember you said his wife looked like a sluttier version of Charro at the Christmas Party? Can you imagine that idiot trying to drive to Manhattan and deliver the Penske file on time? He'd probably drop it in the East River!"

She laughed. She loved cruel jokes that demeaned other people because, of course she did. All women loved to point out others' flaws and shortcomings. I never figured out whether it was an inherited trait or something they had all learned from their own shrewish mothers, but give them some gossip, and they would eat it up like cotton candy. The sweeter, the better.

I waved to her, and she waved back, then called. "Will you be back Sunday for dinner? Your son promised to come home and bring his new girlfriend along!"

Damnit. I never missed an opportunity to spend time with my son. Someone had to keep him on the straight and narrow and let him know what the women of this world were after. I had seen his new girlfriend in a few pictures from a trip they'd taken skiing in Colorado. She was blonde and tan and looked like she'd put out on the first date for the price of a couple beers. If she got her hooks into Jason, she'd have him married without a prenup, sitting at home as a stay-at-home wife, painting her nails and sucking the life from his bank account and his manhood.

I didn't want to leave early and drive back home. There were too many moving pieces in Manhattan. I hadn't been there since the last one, and I had so many loose ends to track down and see who was ripe for fresh picking. Who would be my lucky lady this weekend? That Hispanic bitch at the toll booth that smelled like garlic and acted like it was the end of the world to give me change for a $5 bill? The slut near Times Square who said she was an escort but was so obviously a hooker that she should be arrested on sight? She thought I had forgotten about her when her pimp came after me, but I don't forget that easily. Bitch asked me on a date, then said I was too limp to satisfy her when I turned her down. I have a long, long memory. I remembered things bitches had said to me decades ago. Things that made me feel like clawing my own eyes out and raging in the woods for hours. But that was before I met the hiker.

She had been out in the middle of nowhere—her mistake. That was my territory. The secret place I went to when I felt like I would go mad if I had to keep hanging around normal people, pretending to be just like them. I could be primal there. I could scream in my true voice without having to worry about my wife, my son, or anyone else hearing me. I could call them by their real names and demand justice for what they had done to me. Sometimes, I had to settle for doing all that in the car when I couldn't get away to my secret place.

That sweet hiker had been about forty, a little on the plump side and going gray, but fit enough to be out in the wilderness on a Sunday morning. Her mistake. Her name was Joanne Garcia. At least that's what her ID and credit cards said, which I eventually ran through my woodchipper. She explained she had been hiking the canyon before the crowds got there when she heard my screaming. She thought I had gotten caught in a rockslide or something. Finding me completely safe, but certainly not normal, had freaked her out much more than if I had been battling a mountain lion or pulling my leg from under a boulder.

It meant those insane noises of anguish and pain had come from a seemingly "normal" person. Well, not completely normal. She found that out when I launched myself into her. She had a walking stick, but you could tell it was just for show. She couldn't have fought off a six-year-old with that thing, and her utter lack of knowledge of how to use it as a weapon was laughable. I hadn't known that I was going to attack her until I was halfway to her, but I couldn't let her go after what she had seen. Even if she didn't tell the police or a park ranger, she had still seen me in my true form, and that was absolutely unacceptable. No one saw me like that unless I allowed it. If you were going to see me that way, I had to make sure you would stay quiet about it. Since I couldn't keep her with me twenty-four hours a day, the only other solution was to make sure she never spoke to anyone ever again. That's when my hands went around her neck, and I squeezed and squeezed. She tried to fight, but mostly she just flailed. It was pretty pathetic, really. Perhaps it would have been different if she realized that she'd die if she didn't get away. She slapped at my arms and took one good swipe at my face, but once her oxygen was gone and her head popped blue, she was past the point of no return.

Poor sweet Joanne would stay quiet now. All I had to do was worry about her identity, her travel purse, and her body. I took the purse with her ID inside and stuffed it into my massive backpack. A park ranger could search it for five minutes and never find the carefully sewn-in hidden pouch. I had originally used it to get weed into and out of national parks without much of a hassle. Most rangers were cool about pot, but you'd occasionally get some stupid hero who fashioned themselves to be the national park version of Marshall Dillion, throwing his weight around. For now, it served the purpose of hiding her identity until I could get rid of it.

As for the body itself, well that's what the waterfall was for. Most people thought Niagara Falls was the highest free-flowing waterfall in New York State, but Taughannock Falls State Park had it beat by a good thirty-three feet. And Joanne had been right... hiking this early in the morning meant you could beat the crowd. I had to drag her about an eighth of a mile to get her in a good position, which meant banging her face on rocks a few times, but nothing that messed her up too badly. Oh lordy, what fun! The exhilaraaa-tion. Hee-hee-hee... At her age and weight, any small-town cop worth his salt would see that body floating at the base of the falls and peg her as an inexperienced hiker who got too close to the edge, slipped on the wet rocks and tumbled 200-plus feet to a watery death. Chalk the broken neck up to any of the dozens of underwater rocks she hit, and you could toss her in the wagon, call the morgue, and tell them to take an early lunch, case closed!

I had to keep my son from going down the same road and marrying a damn vampire like I had, so I vowed that I'd have my victim picked out tonight and taken care of by Saturday, so I could get out of town early Sunday. That cut down my window a lot and heightened the risk. I didn't like it, but I couldn't resist. The police in New York were even dumber than those I had encountered in Houston, Atlanta, and Detroit. Idiots who wouldn't know how to find their own asshole without forensic evidence. I had stood in the crowd of gawkers when they recovered the little black bitch's body from the warehouse and the cops hadn't taken a single look at anyone in the crowd. Totally clueless. By the time they figured out a single one of my patterns, I was already deep into another one. The cops in Detroit hadn't even realized that a serial killer was working for more than seven years there because that town was so messed up, and their depart-ment was so inept and corrupt.

I waved my final goodbye to the shrew, promised I'd make it in time for Sunday dinner, and headed out to the expressway and the big, rat-filled monstrosity of New York City. If I could live a thousand lifetimes, I'd never purge them all, but one by one I would make them bleed, make them suffer, and make them realize the hypocrisy of their pathetic little lives. It sure is a pleasure when I take what's mine and what's due—

FIERCE POUNDING on the door shook me out of the killer's head this time. "ROHAN, DAMN, OPEN UP!"

It was my brother. I stood up and my legs cramped in protest. Apparently, I had been in his mind a little longer this time. Long enough to make my muscles and my brother angry with me. I got to the door and unlocked it, flinging it open. He was standing there sweating and breathing hard, looking scared, confused and angry.

"What the hell, man? I've been beating this door down for 10 minutes! Why did you lock it?"

"Sorry, sorry," I apologized, slurring my words purposely, to feign that I had just woken up. "I've been running around so much, I just sat down for a few minutes to rest my eyes. Must have fallen asleep. Maybe I locked it by accident. I'm so out of it, man."

He shook his head, still angry, but I could see the understanding in his eyes. Someone who worked full time and attended school full time would understand why I was struggling to burn the candle at both ends.

"I get it, Rohan, I do, but you have to be careful with the lock. I thought something happened to you, man, I was freaked out."

His concern was touching. Our relationship had greatly improved since I returned to 1997. Perhaps he was still guided by my advice to his six-year-old version, him to watch out for his little brother. The differences in our relationship weren't as pronounced as they were with my parents and Amayah's, but they were noticeable, which was sweet.

"It's time to go home, man, c'mon," he patted me on the shoulder, then recoiled in disgust. "Why are you sweating so much? Are you sick?

"You're not supposed to come to the store if you're sick, man. It's company policy. If the customers get sick, they'll blame us and take their business to Rite-Aid in two seconds."

I hadn't noticed that I was properly drenched in sweat. Was it because of the connection with Stacey or the effort involved? I didn't know, but after assuring my brother that I was fine, I started racing through all the details of the killer I had just learned. I needed to get home and write it all down in the computer file I had created. I labeled it "Ideas for Graphic Novel," in case my family ever went snooping.

I walked quietly beside my brother on the short trip home. I didn't think I was going to go out patrolling. Too much to sort out about Stacey. What a name for a serial killer. I guess I shouldn't joke about it. The guy clearly had a lot of screws loose upstairs, which made him infinitely more dangerous than some common criminal. Or maybe he just didn't have any feelings for other people at all, which would make him a complete psychopath. That was even more troublesome, because someone without emotions could and would do almost anything to get away, and keep perpetuating what they wanted. I rebuffed my brother's offer for a late-night meal and said, "Thanks, but I need to get to bed."

Once inside my room, I fired up the computer and opened the file. I started at the beginning of the vision, breaking down what I had been able to discern from his own memories and the conversation with his wife, who was obviously totally clueless about the fact that she was married to a total psychopath who had no "business" in New York City except for stalking and killing people. I found myself secretly wishing that she'd find the crawl space or whatever the hell was buried under the tool shed, except that doing so would probably end up getting her killed as well.

I went to the top of my file and started moving things down. What did I know about him? His first name was Stacey, and based on what I could see of his wife, he was at least in his forties, maybe as old as his fifties. He didn't live in New York City, which really threw me for a loop, because I wouldn't just be able to follow him home if I saw him in the act or after it. At the same time, if he didn't live in the city, he wouldn't have a natural hiding place. He'd have to rent a hotel room or stay in a flop house or just hide out in his car, but even that would mean a parking garage somewhere. If you weren't from New York, there weren't many places to hide out where someone couldn't spot you. Even the lousiest rooms by the hour had a clerk out front to collect your money and make sure you weren't killing anyone once you went inside.

So, he came from out of state, or perhaps another part of the state. I couldn't really tell based on his surroundings, but he lived or at least traveled to other places to kill. He mentioned Michigan, Georgia, and Texas, at least. And Maine in the vision before this one. Jesus, that was a lot of ground to cover for one guy to keep killing people and getting away with it. He couldn't live that far away though, because he was only going to be here tonight—or maybe he already was here. It was daytime in my vision, but night had definitely fallen.

Damn, he was likely somewhere in the city looking for a victim at that very moment, and I had no way of knowing where he was or what he looked like! It was incredibly frustrating, and the Brute started his nocturnal stirring in my soul, floating ideas of me flying roof to roof across the city, going after anyone who looked suspicious and answered to the name of Stacey. That idea was obviously dumb. I had heard the guy's own thoughts; he worked in the daylight, which meant that he was probably driving right now and would go to work tomorrow. I hated feeling so helpless, but unless I unlocked more about him, I could only keep writing my notes and trying to figure out where he might strike next.

I stretched my arms and legs and walked across the apartment to get a drink of water before sitting back down as I stared at the lighter on the desk. Maybe the Pogo lighter heats up when Stacey thinks about a new murder or committing one. That was at least something to chew on.

My body and my powers were incredible weapons, but right now, my mind was the most significant tool in my arsenal. I vowed to call Amayah tomorrow and share what I had learned with her, but I knew it was my show to run for the moment. I was the one able to forge the connection with him, though I didn't really know how that worked either.

I kept telling myself, "He's just a man. Men make mistakes. Especially ones that have been doing the same thing for a long time." I had to figure out how to catch him in a mistake and be ready at a moment's notice. That was going to take critical thinking, planning, and a bit of luck as well.

I knew that his home base was less than a day's drive from New York City, he hunted in the daytime, and that he had at least a couple potential victims in mind. The hooker who propositioned and insulted him was near Times Square, in the middle of Manhattan, but the working girls usually didn't come out until the sun went down, so they could disappear around the corner with a customer or fade into the alleys when squad cars got too close for comfort.

There has to be something here, something helpful ...

If he was working in the daylight, how did he manage to piss off a hooker? Apparently, a hooker who then told her pimp, which led to some sort of confrontation between the two men. That this had happened at all gave me some hope of catching him. More than one person had seen him and knew what he looked like. If I wanted to interview all the pimps and hookers that worked Times Square, it might take me the rest of the year, but at least it was a place to start.

It sounded like the police were grasping at straws in every city where he had hunted. Having even one clue gave me hope. He had also mentioned a woman at a toll booth. I concentrated hard on that part of the vision and was able to pull it back up, just briefly, in my mind's eye. There she was all right, chewing a big wad of gum, looking down at him as he asked for change for the bucket. You were supposed to take a different lane if you didn't have enough change, but this guy didn't exactly strike me as a rule follower, so no surprise, he blew off the signs and went where he damn well pleased. As he was haggling with her and not-so-secretly seething at her garlic-laced breath, I somehow was able to subtly "shift" my perspective of the image and look out his windshield. He was on the southernmost end of "the city," aka Lower Manhattan, which meant this was the Holland Tunnel. That wasn't the most earth-shattering news in the world, as a zillion people from a zillion places came across it every day into the city, but at the same time, it was another step forward in the mystery. It meant that he probably didn't live anywhere north or east of Manhattan, which eliminated a big chunk of the region at once. It also pretty much guaranteed that he wasn't from Long Island, as no one would drive around to the tunnel from there. That just left everything south, which, unfortunately, was most of the Eastern Seaboard.

I thought back to his voice again, trying to place the accent, but I had been to so few places myself, other than 1980s New Jersey and 1854 Mississippi. I'm not sure I could have placed an accent aside from maybe Louisiana or Texas. He sounded like he had lived in New York at some point, as some of the familiar sounds and cadences from these streets were definitely in his voice. Just as the vision began to fade, I had a marvelous moment of inspiration. I shifted the image again, and found myself looking in the rearview mirror. I stared into his bright blue-gray eyes for just a second. One of his eyes was darker than the other, and he had a sharply pointed nose above a fluffy brown mustache going grey.

Stacey the serial killer had a face like any other man, at least the fifty percent of it I had seen. *Now I've seen you*, I thought to myself, as though mentally challenging him. *Will you even see me coming for you?*

I am New York's Talon in the night.

CHAPTER

THIRTY-TWO

I met Amayah for coffee the next morning near her apartment building and told her everything. She was dazzled by what I had been able to uncover on my own. She was also chilled by the fact that Stacey was in the city right now, and there was basically nothing we could do about it. She made me describe his face, made a partial drawing of it on a coffeehouse napkin, and gave it to me for reference.

"Just because," she said cryptically. "In case you need to make sure it's him." We spent the rest of the morning being lazy and strolling close to one another before Amayah headed home to help her mom clean out the apartment. Her mom loved using Fabuloso to clean, and was constantly raving about it. A cousin from back home was coming for a stay, not Cousin Zulema, gratefully, she told me with a laugh, and they were setting up a makeshift guest bedroom for her. I promised to call her later if I saw or heard anything or had any more breakthroughs about the man we were now unofficially hunting.

I found myself walking aimlessly, trying to sort out more of the mystery, and my legs seemed to unconsciously take me right to

Times Square. I knew it was literally less than a needle in a haystack's chance that he would be there right now, or that I would see him, but just knowing that he had been there at some point was enough of a lead for me to check it out. With Amayah busy at home, it wasn't like my social schedule was burning up with appointments.

I turned off Forty-First onto Seventh Avenue and almost immediately regretted the decision. The noise, the lights, and the tourists gawking at everything like country bumpkins seeing their first stoplight, were all there. The fact that most people in the world identified New York City's character as Times Square was sort of repugnant on fifty different levels. I mean, give me the Empire State Building, or the World Trade Center, the Statue of Liberty, or Yankee Stadium! Those were the iconic spots of New York. Times Square was like being in a terrifying combination of the world's cheesiest shopping mall and a Chuck-E-Cheese. There were people dressed up as everything from Superman and Wonder Woman to Bill and Hillary to Luigi and Mario, all begging tourists to take their picture... for a cool ten bucks. Every chain restaurant imaginable had a flashy neon sign there. Every upcoming movie had a billboard, and every Broadway play was advertised as the greatest thing you would ever see. It was exhausting, but I had gone all the way there, so I would at least look around and see if anything interesting was transpiring.

After about ten minutes, I saw nothing out of the ordinary, but I realized that I would have to spend a few bucks from our anniversary fund on lunch because my stomach was growling after using a bit of my energy to get here in the first place. I really didn't want to go inside any of the tourist traps, so I settled for the line at Nathan's Famous hot dog cart. There was a family of four in front of me, along with an older dude trying to look young and hip with Bermuda shorts, a Florida Marlins baseball cap pulled low, touching his dark Ray-Ban sunglasses. I wasn't trying to diss any other baseball fan, because that was my favorite sport and way better than football or basketball, but seriously, the Marlins? In the middle of New York City? That was a trendy hat to rock only because the Marlins had just entered the league a few years ago. Everybody in South Florida was salivating over having a baseball team, given how many Hispanic people lived there and how many great baseball players came to the U.S. from Cuba, Puerto Rico and the Dominican Republic.

Unfortunately, the Marlins had a horrible start to their franchise history. In fact, just last year they went 80-82 and acted like they had won the World Series because they didn't finish last in their division. 80-82 for my Yankees meant that someone was getting fired as manager, probably Billy Martin if King George had anything to say about it. The Marlins had gotten off to a hot start and were in second place in the NL East, which I mostly liked because they were ahead of the crap-ass New York Mets, the biggest underachieving team in the world. As much as I enjoyed following the 1980 Yankees for a few weeks, being back in 1997 and watching them push to defend their title was infinitely better. I vowed that after I took Amayah to dinner for our anniversary, my next big purchase would be taking her to a Yankees game, a first for both of us. They were off to a decent start this year, but the Yankees always seemed to come second to the Orioles, who had spent every day this season as the American League East's top team. I hoped to see my Yanks battle the Red Sox next season, even though ticket prices for good seats would be through the roof.

The Nathan's line was moving slowly, and I listened in amusement as the two teenage boys with their parents, clearly on vacation, complained about not getting to see the "real Times Square," as their parents gawked at the attractions, taking pictures of literally everything.

The older brother rambled, "I mean, I know the hookers aren't gonna hang around in the daytime, but did they have to get rid of the titty bars and the X-rated movies too? Not saying I was gonna go, but even a look through the window would be something to tell everyone back in Des Moines."

"Blame Giuliani," the old guy in the Marlins' hat told them, eavesdropping on their conversation, just like me. "He wanted that clean Times Square action, so people like your mom and dad would drop $150 on lunch for four at Chili's and then go waste another $300 at FAO Schwartz before you lug it all back to the hotel."

They both gawked at him.

"I mean, the hookers must have gone somewhere, right?" the older brother bemoaned sadly. "They didn't all just retire."

The older stranger laughed. "If you're staying near here, sneak down around midnight and they'll be all over. Or tell your parents you're going for an early-morning jog. They'll still be out until the sun's really up, but you gotta be careful. The pimps will be out collecting their nightly earnings, and those boys don't play if you're browsing without buying."

I nearly jumped out of my skin at his words. So the pimps came out at the end of the night to collect their money from the hookers. The end of the night also meant the start of the day. When the sun came up. If Stacey was working in the daylight in Times Square, then he'd get there early to start casing it for potential victims. That would mean crossing paths with a hooker trying to make one last score before she called it a night, and if he was rude to her, well, her pimp was probably close by and could personally deal with the asshole upsetting one of his girls.

I had worked out another piece of the puzzle. If Stacey was in Times Square as the sun was just coming up, he might do it again. Unfortunately, I had missed my opportunity this morning, but he might still be in the area if he had spotted a potential victim. Unfortunately, I thought this all the way through while staring at the guy in the Marlins cap. He finally got my attention by waving his hands in front of my face a few times.

"You okay there, cowboy? You're looking at me like we're long-lost brothers, except I don't have any brothers, and we're slightly different colors."

I snapped out of it, embarrassed. "Uh, sorry sir, just got lost in my train of thought. Are you really a Marlins fan?"

He touched the cap, as if he had forgotten it was there, then smiled broadly, "All the way! Season ticket holder since day one. Did you see our first-ever game? Sell-out crowd, Charlie Hough on the hill, and we shoved it right up those damn Dodgers' asses. I was there, about ten rows up on the first base side, one of my favorite games ever."

He was a legit fan, and we bounced baseball talk back and forth about the pennant races in the National League and the American League as we waited. When he finally got his order, he gave me a salute with his cap.

"See ya around, buddy. Maybe if your Yankees can get their act together, I'll see you back here in October when we beat 'em."

I laughed and waved back. The Florida Marlins in the World Series? And beating the Yankees to win it? No chance in hell.

I ate my hot dog and drank my shake on a bench, as far away from the noise and fake celebrities as I could get. I kept scanning the crowd for someone with mismatching blue-gray eyes, a sharp nose, and a bushy mustache, but no one fit the profile, and I grew more frustrated as the day passed. The only thing that really caught my eye was a girl about a year younger than me who looked like she had stepped straight off the cover of the Sports Illustrated Swimsuit magazine. Tall, blonde, and looking like a supermodel, she was with a few friends who acted oblivious to the fact that every guy in a six-block radius was staring at them as they went from one fake celebrity and superhero to the next, posing with each one. As in love as I was with Amayah, I couldn't help but notice her from afar. She was bubbly and breezy and ridiculously attractive and kept circling around for another set of pictures from her Kodak disposable that she kept in a little purse. When I finished my lunch and decided that I didn't need to be one of a thousand gawkers drooling after her, I did the next dumb thing on my list. I walked down to the Holland Tunnel to casually look in the windows of the toll booth operators for the woman from Stacey's memory. I wasn't really sure what I would do if I spotted her, other than try to ask her a few questions about him. But would that really accomplish anything? She was a toll booth operator in New York City. Asking her if she remembered a guy who had been rude to her on the job would be like asking if she had taken a breath of oxygen lately. But I had the time, so I made myself try. Anything to avoid the feeling of helplessly sitting around while Stacey hunted his next victim.

While I might have had luck figuring out about the prostitutes working until dawn, that luck ran dry at the Holland Tunnel. Without a car to drive, I had no plausible way to get in front of the toll booth operators and even see their faces, much less have some sort of social interaction with them. After about half an hour of trying to scheme my way to the tollbooth stations, perhaps as some sort of official representative from the city, I realized that I had no way to figure out this part of the riddle, when Hua whispered, *"Ninja, you are blessed with the Shine Xiong."*

"Hua, I'm confused and have many questions," I replied. Walking back towards Central Park, I was trying to commune with Hua and learn what being blessed with the Shine meant. I'd hoped I would learn something valuable, but Hua remained silent. I had tested plenty of my powers, but there was so much I still didn't know. I felt like I was scratching the surface of my limitations if I had any, and Hua could help. For now, instinct and luck had gotten me through some dicey situations, but I didn't want to keep relying on that combination, especially with someone like Stacey.

He was a stone-cold killer, and had eluded attempts to not only catch him, but even identify him for at least a decade. Touching his mind a couple times had only increased my anxiety about what an encounter between us might look like. Even a serial killer wouldn't be prepared for someone like me, who was faster and stronger than anyone else, but the way he was killing people, eluding capture, and basically running circles around the police was a dangerous combination. That made me fear what Stacey was capable of, comparable to the time stuck in the 1850s. How was he doing it? Was he a genius? Was he a cop? Or a spy? Did he have something that allowed him to move silently and disappear without leaving a trace? I couldn't find the wavelength to communicate with Hua, which was bothering me more than I was letting on. Why couldn't she just reach out to me? The Brute was just an angry feeling away, but the peace and calm that Hua exuded were not things I could conjure up inside me while stressing over Stacey.

And because of that uneasy mindset, I was so unfocused that I walked right into the unexpected. I rounded a corner and saw a flash of blonde hair several doors down leaning against the side of a building atop a short flight of stairs. The blonde was giggling, and despite being fifty feet away, I heard her say, "You said you had something to get me high, right? Where is it?"

I froze for a moment, then realized that my enhanced senses were letting me hear and see things at a distance. I squinted my eyes for a better look and stopped in surprise. It was the blonde girl from Times Square who everyone had been staring at earlier. She was still wearing the red miniskirt and matching tank top. Her gaggle of friends appeared to have vanished, but she wasn't alone. A man was there, leaning in and saying something that made her giggle again. Probably just some scuzzy guy in the street that had promised to get her high. I didn't like it, but it didn't really seem like much of a crime either. I was about to cross to the other side of the street when I heard the pitch of her voice change.

"Hey!" she scolded sharply. "That hurts! Let go!"

I turned back and saw her struggling with the guy, who had a teal-and-white cap flipped backwards on his head. The Marlins fan. What the hell was going on? The guy was at least fifty, old enough to be her father. She was struggling harder now and had nearly gotten past him. He turned sideways to grab her by the wrist, which is when I saw his profile's sharp nose and a slight mustache. Sure, his stache was short and trimmed and not as bushy as my vision, but son of a bitch! Being lost in my thoughts and his sunglasses and ballcap pulled down had distracted me earlier, but his other features were now recognizable. Stacey, the serial killer, had been standing right there in front of me, and even worse, I had talked about baseball with the guy and hadn't figured it out. I had been wondering how in the world I would find the guy, and hadn't given much thought to what I would do if I did. Suddenly, he was right in front of me, and I had no plan whatsoever.

"HEY!" I screamed—a gut reaction I immediately regretted. To be honest, the only thing I was thinking about was keeping that girl alive, not discretion. It's the kind of thing you never think about when you're reading a graphic novel or watching a superhero movie. Batman and Spiderman can always find some random way to keep the victims safe on a ledge or stashed out of the way while they finish off the supervillain. I didn't have that luxury. I had been on this block a few times, but not to the point where I knew the whole layout. I suppose a more experienced superhero would have been able to visualize the entire street in their head and figure out a plan of action, but I definitely didn't have that skill set.

Fortunately, my sudden appearance threw Stacey off, as he stumbled at the sound of my voice and turned to look over his shoulder in surprise. The girl screeched "HELP!" in my direction, and I reached down for my power. Stacey clinched her wrist tighter and then flung her down the stairs with incredible strength. She probably didn't weigh more than one hundred and twenty pounds, but the force of his movement and the angle of the stairs sent her smashing chin-first into the sidewalk.

Even from a distance, I saw the blood splatter, meaning that she had probably broken her nose and split her lip, at the very least. Pausing to watch her tumble had cost me, as Stacey leaped over the railing, far more agile than a guy his age should have been. He raced across the street as I rushed towards the girl. I had a terrible decision to make—follow him or stay with her.

As I reached her side, he turned the corner and disappeared out of sight. If I went full speed, I'd be there in two seconds, but what if I didn't see him when I turned the corner? Looking down, I realized there was no decision to make. The blonde girl was hurt badly and needed medical attention. I told her not to move and asked how she was when she suddenly turned over and started slurring her speech. Blood was spilling from her forehead, her nose, her mouth, and one of her ears. I didn't know what to do. I could heal people, but that was by altering their cells to fight the diseases within them. Her injury was caused by severe trauma to the skull, and I had never remedied that before. I decided that I'd have to risk being seen and get her to a hospital as quickly as my feet could take me. I didn't know the exact distance, but I knew where Mt. Sinai was from all my trips with Amayah, and that would have to do. I told her not to worry and that I would get her to the hospital, so I lifted her lightly when she suddenly looked at me in my hoodie and screamed.

I almost dropped her, but my reflexes kicked in as I gently put her back down in a seated position. Still, there was no denying that the racket she made alerted the neighborhood. A couple down the block was just stepping out of a taxi, and they hustled forward as she screamed again. I didn't know what to do. She was hysterical and bleeding, and what was I going to tell her? That I had just saved her from a serial killer? As the couple approached, the man called out, his arm stretched protectively in front of his partner. "What's going on here?"

The girl I tried to help was in shock. She looked at me, then at the guy, then back at me.

"He's insane! He's trying to kidnap me! HELP!" she shrieked, staring right at me. My mouth dropped open. What the hell was she saying? I had just saved her life, and now she was pointing the finger at me.

I looked up and saw the guy approaching me cautiously, his fists cocked.

"Hey, what are you doing, man? Go find some other way to get your kicks!"

I opened my mouth to explain, then closed it, then tried to stammer out a response and failed.

The blonde girl, despite being battered and bloodied, pointed an accusatory finger at me and shrieked. "It's HIM! The serial killer! He offered me drugs and then tried to kidnap me!"

Shit! Whether she had a concussion or was just confused by the sudden turn of events, she had jumped to an extremely wrong conclusion, and now I was in real trouble. I heard a blaring siren in the distance and realized that I needed to get clear of this situation. I didn't see any way to talk myself out of this one, so I backed away slowly, then turned and ran, way too fast, in the direction Stacey had fled.

CHAPTER
THIRTY-THREE

I couldn't find him, and there were too many cops around to do anything useful near the motel. My best option was to go home and throw myself into bed in frustration. I wanted to call Amayah, but it was after midnight, and even though her parents liked me, I don't think they liked me enough to brush off a 2 a.m. phone call. Amayah didn't have a phone in her room, so the odds of her picking up before they did were slim. I would have to wait until I saw her the next day to tell her what happened. I was worried now. The most worried I had been since Mississippi.

The blonde girl had taken a blow to the head and apparently couldn't distinguish Stacey from me. Thinking about it from her point of view, I guess I could understand. One minute, a guy dressed in dark clothes was trying to kidnap her, and the next thing she knew, a guy in dark clothes was carrying her after she had been flung down a flight of stairs. She screamed for help, but that might not have been directed at me, just a general reaction to Stacey's violent turn. Even more frustrating than letting him get away was the knowledge that I had stood in Times Square and talked to the psycho for several minutes without putting together his identity; I hadn't even considered it! For all my powers, a serial killer had been standing two feet from me in broad daylight, and I had been completely unaware.

Even with his Pogo the clown lighter tucked into my backpack—I had sensed nothing. I was angry at my powers and angry at myself. I don't think I slept more than a couple hours as I replayed the events again and again in my mind.

Fortunately, the next day was Sunday, but things went from bad to worse as soon as I got up. With the rare day off—the shop was closed on Sunday—my dad was sitting at the kitchen table sipping tea and reading the paper. He put it aside when I walked in, and my eyes fell on the top headline:

"BLACK BLUR = NY SLASHER?"

Oh, damn. This was all sorts of bad news. The cops had questioned the blonde girl and the couple from last night's near miss with Stacey. Between the three of them, they had pinned down a few details, including that the man who had tried to kidnap her was tall, young, dressed in black, and ran away far too fast for an average human. The journalists took that description and ran with it, and the logical result was the idea that the Black Blur was perhaps not a good Samaritan who stopped robberies and defended the weak, but rather a violent late-night prowler who just might be the serial killer that had been stalking the Five Boroughs for months. Yes, this was really bad. The police investigator named the "Blur" as a person of interest in the girl's attempted kidnapping, as well as "other potentially related crimes."

I imagined the real monster somewhere in Manhattan at a corner coffee shop, eating a bagel with a schmear of cream cheese, holding back his laughter as he read about someone else getting fingered for his crop of slayings. Actually, if he was like many of the serial killers I had seen on those TV specials, he might have actually hated what was going on. Those guys seem to love taking credit for their crimes or being so smart that no one can ever catch them. If someone else was getting credit for what he was doing, he might be upset enough to take the attention back by doing something rash. For the first time since the previous day in Times Square, I felt a bit hopeful. If Stacey was upset because the attention had shifted, he might draw the focus back to him with another killing that wasn't as properly planned. The fact that the girl had gotten away with her life also made me think that he might be slipping. I knew that he had to go home to see his son for dinner tonight, which meant that he was going home angry and unsatisfied. I thought of him as a druggie who had failed to get the hit he was desperately seeking. If Stacey was the same way, it would only make him hungrier for his next score.

The phone started ringing, which shook me from my worries. I grabbed it by the second ring. It was Ama, who had seen the same paper on her parents' kitchen table and called me straight away, her voice full of worry. We agreed to meet at our usual coffee hangout, and I cautiously told her not to believe what she had read and that I loved her. Saying anything more in front of my dad seemed like a bad idea.

It took almost two hours to explain everything to Amayah at the coffee shop, including careful maneuvering around the parts about me staring at the hot blonde. She was in equal parts amazed and horrified that I had been a few feet from the serial killer, and forced me to see the silver lining.

"You saved her life, Rohan... you know that he would have killed her otherwise," Ama consoled, her eyes crinkled in concern.

"You didn't do anything wrong, and the papers will forget about you in a couple of days when some Yankee comes stumbling out of a strip club at 4 a.m. or someone spots a nine-foot alligator in the park."

That made me laugh at a moment when I really needed it, another reason I loved her so powerfully, and I felt that she was probably right. If I could keep a low profile and focus on finding out Stacey's complete identity and helping people who needed it, the papers wouldn't have anything else to report on. My only real concern was the cops. If they caught me unawares or decided that I looked like the person of interest as I walked down the street, I'd have to have a good alibi on hand and be sure to keep my cool.

Amayah was already two steps ahead. "If anyone asks, I'll tell them that you were with me all night," she said with a flirty smile. "Even dumb police officers understand what teenagers like doing at night, and it's definitely not prowling around killing people."

The fantasy of my made-up alibi was a distracting thought, to say the least. I pulled her close and kissed her forehead, her nose, and her chin as she giggled. "I love you so much," I told her sincerely. "You seem to make every problem disappear."

Our anniversary was about a week away, so I reminded myself that I had to stay focused on Amayah, school, and my family. I had to make things right in my own life before I tried going after Stacey again. I wasn't sleeping enough or eating enough and wasn't focused on my schoolwork. Renewing the bonds with my family and strengthening my relationship with Amayah had shown me that I couldn't just be the NY Talon; I had to be Rohan Chang as well. My powers made me special, but I had to be more than that. I couldn't just be the superpowered guy busting heads and breaking up robberies. I had to be a good person all the way around... the Clark Kent, not just the Superman.

As much as I wanted to focus all my energy on unraveling the mystery of Stacey, I purposely spent the next few days focusing on Rohan Chang, the unquestionably good citizen. I took some extra shifts at the drugstore, and brought food to my parents at the cleaners on the way home from school. I helped Tracy Spitzberg with a science project to prove that we could be friends, and I took Amayah on a picnic after classes ended on Thursday. We had been gradually introducing each other to new ethnic cuisine, and each brought a delicious surprise. We lay on a blanket on a hill in the park and watched people flow by like water. She lay her head in my lap, and I played with her hair as she smiled up at me. I never believed that I could be so happy with so little. Ama and a sunny day were all I needed to walk home with a goofy grin splashed across my face.

I hung out at home with my brother, watching garbage movies on TV and talking about our childhoods. It was effortless and relaxing. I hadn't gone out on patrol all week. I felt massively guilty about that, but I also felt a weight come off me as the days passed. I couldn't be everywhere at once and had to find a balance between my real life and my nighttime calling.

I found myself lying in bed, preparing to drift off to sleep after an evening with my brother, when the Brute whispered in my ear. *"HE'S COMING BACK."*

No need to ask who "he" was. In a blink, my good mood and calm demeanor were gone. I sat upright and went to the window, looking out over the city that never sleeps. I had no idea how the Brute knew Stacey's plans, but I also didn't doubt it for a second. He might have been a troublemaker and a violent psychopath, but the Brute was not a liar. He told the truth, even when I hated to hear it. *"NOT THERE, YOU KNOW HOW TO SEE HIM."*

I knew that, but I was hoping to figure out how to solve this problem without looking through his eyes. However, if he was coming back, and I could get a look inside his mind, I might have a real chance to stop him. Whether that meant incapacitating him and dumping him on an NYPD doorstep or doing to him what he had done to so many of his victims, I wasn't sure. I didn't know how far I was willing to go to make sure he was stopped, but I was hoping I wouldn't have to kill him. He definitely deserved it, but that didn't mean it was my job to deliver the punishment. Putting him squarely in the hands of the law seemed like it would be enough. New York was tough on killers. If they were worried he might walk, they'd put him in one of the harder jails and let things sort out on their own among the prison's ruthless underbelly. At least, those were the stories we had heard at school.

Regardless, that was a problem for another day. As I stood facing the window, the whisper of the Brute still echoing, I broke my promise to myself and pulled Stacey's lighter from my backpack's secret pocket. I sat back down on the bed and held it before me like a totem, focusing on the gleam of the moonlight I had seen the night I found it.

The connection was instant, and the lighter heated up in my hands to a burning hot. I gasped aloud when I saw what he was looking at...

"BLACK BLUR = NY SLASHER?" the newspaper's front page was taunting me. I hadn't slept and walked the streets. And when I saw her, she was the sweetest target I'd seen in a long time. A girl was playing at being a woman, but I was about to make playtime over for good until that scrawny asshole ruined my plans.

Being in my shed in the backyard does wonders. My wife thought it was a home gym, and after a fashion, I guess that's true. It had a weight set that I used once in a while to make it look like I had a purpose for going in there, but mostly I go there to plan. To study. To focus on cleansing that piece of shit city little by little. Seeing that headline on my way out of town Sunday morning, I am beyond myself. I paid for the idiotic newspaper at the box on the corner and wound up taking fifty copies. Plastering them all over my shed like the world's ugliest fucking wallpaper, I let the rage boil over. That little shit was interrupting my time, and the newspaper thinks he's the one responsible for my masterpieces? Unacceptable. Un-FUCK-ING-ACCEPTABLE!

I had no reason to go back this early just to please my wife, so I just invented a fishing trip with David Alexander, the new guy at work. Said he was new in town and wanted to have some 'guy time,' and I had decided to take him under my wing. The whole thing was bullshit, of course, but she didn't know that, and there was no way for her to figure it out. David Alexander was probably nose-deep in cocaine on his dining room table right now. The guy was constantly sniffing, and his eyes were perpetually bloodshot—tell-tale signs of a classic junkie. Good for him, though, and even better for me. With a fuck-up like that around the office, no one was thinking twice about me working long hours to catch up on work I took home every weekend.

Everywhere I looked, the headline screamed at me. Everywhere I looked, that punk-ass little bitch was being given credit for my work, my achievement, my art. Reaching into my hip pocket, I pulled out the serrated hunting knife, took aim, and planted it right on the equal sign between the words in the headline. Yeah, punk, that's what's coming for you when I get back to the Big Apple. Going to take a bite out of you this time, instead of some little girl whining for her mama.

I had the place all picked out this time. Not the warehouse, that would still be too hot from the cops. The smarter detectives always come back around to places where they found bodies, because they think the killer will show up to gloat or relive it or wank off or some crap like that. Not me, I'm too smart for that particular little trap. The only place I need to go to relive it is my own mind; my greatest weapon—the thing that makes me untouchable. The thing that makes me unbeatable. The thing that makes me IMMORTAL. I threw the knife against the shed of the wall repeatedly, where the newspaper clippings hung, with that little asshole's face as my target.

I didn't get a good look at him, but if what the papers were saying was even half true, he was some sort of little faggot that thought he was saving the city by chasing off criminals. Most punks trying to rob a grandma late at night would be scared off by even the threat of intervention, so this Black Blur probably gained a reputation by popping up and surprising a bunch of kids robbing candy stores. He wouldn't get the same chance with me. Interrupting my work signed his death warrant. I will be coming to New York City to hunt him Friday night. When I find that little bitch, he'll scream for me right before I slit his throat. Oh lordy, what fun! The exhila-raaa-tion. Hee-hee-hee...

I GASPED and broke the trance, covered in sweat and seething with anger and satisfaction. I was right! Stacey was enraged the newspaper thought I was him, and that the narrative had switched from the unknown sinister stalker to the Black Blur. He was taking gambles that he hadn't in his previous trips, a flimsy excuse with an unknown alibi, rushing up here without knowing specifically where he was going to strike, and not knowing who I was or where to find me.

I tried to ignore the fact that even with him looking for me and me looking for him, we would still just be two people trying to find each other in a city of eight million. However, my previous chance encounters with him convinced me that some larger force was pulling us together. I needed to cover a lot of ground without draining my powers, but still pinpoint Stacey's location. I went to bed thinking up strategies, and by the time I left for school Friday morning, I had a great idea in mind.

I wrestled over whether to tell Amayah what I was planning on doing. Ultimately, I kept it to myself.

She was headed to a huge family dinner Friday night, and it was family only, so her novio wasn't invited. That seemed like fate as well. She would be somewhere safe, surrounded by her family. She didn't need me protecting her, so I was free to become the NY Talon without worrying about repercussions towards the people I cared about the most. I didn't tell Amayah my plan because I didn't want to worry her. After school on Friday, I walked her home, held her tight, and told her that I loved her and would see her on Saturday.

As soon as my parents went to bed, I began my ritual. I could have gotten dressed and ready in a few minutes, but I needed a true transformation, not a simple change of clothes. Rohan Chang was not the NY Talon, and the NY Talon wasn't Rohan Chang. There had to be a distinction between one and the other, or I risked losing both halves of my life and not knowing who I was anymore. I tried not to compare myself to the serial killer in this fashion. There was a distinction. He was a sociopath all the time; he just hid it really well from people like his wife and his coworkers. When he was around them, he was constantly stressed out, wearing a disguise for hours at a time, a disguise that, if it slipped for even a few seconds, would be terrifying to see. When I first discovered my powers, I wanted to be that person all the time, but that wasn't what I needed. I needed to be like water and remain Rohan

Chang as much as I became the Talon, a vigilante punishing criminals. Sure, the Talon could fight, run faster than wind, teleport, and occasionally, albeit erratically, travel through time. But, the powers never were consistent. Rohan Chang always had the power of a good family and a loving girlfriend, and his compassion and work ethic were always there, all little parts I had never noticed until others saw them in me.

The NY Talon might have been the hero that New York City needed. But, Rohan Chang was, in fact, the good guy his parents and brother needed, repairing their strained relationship, and who Amayah Bello needed, encouraging her to be all she could be, and who he, himself needed, growing into a man who hopefully would find a true purpose beyond beating up criminals in dark alleys.

As I took my backpack from the back of my closet, I noted that everything was indeed black. They could call me the Black Blur in the paper all they wanted, and others on the street might think I'm a ninja, but it was the best way to stay anonymous from everyone I encountered. If my identity got out, my family would be at risk, and that wasn't a sacrifice I would ever be willing to make.

As I dressed piece by piece, most of them in sleek black, the tension in the air increased. The sweatpants, socks, boots, and the loose, dark red turtleneck were but a prelude to the dramatic unveiling of my own creation: a balaclava ski mask made from Ama's scarf she had given me. The mask, one half in mahogany red and the other half in black fabric symbolized warmth and protection on that chilling, enigmatic night, adding the perfect finishing touch to my daring ensemble. Wearing a balaclava like that was both necessary and frustrating. It made me appear intimidating when I caught someone breaking the law or threatening the innocent, but it also limited my field of vision, and I was still adjusting to my blind spots. It had been a week since the infamous Black Blur story ran in the newspaper, and now I just looked like one of the hundreds of other people wearing dark clothing moving about the city at night.

Tonight I wanted to bring something new along; the little pocket-sized Bible Ama recently gave me, which I started reading during the early quiet mornings and offering prayer. And as I prayed, I stretched out with my senses as best I could, catching brief snippets of thoughts and conversations, but everything was so loud that it was hard to separate one thing from the next.

That was okay, as I had worked out a plan. First, I needed to zone out, and the most surefire way to do that was to listen to music.

When I reached the intersection I wanted, I skipped along to track seven and let the sweet rhymes of Inspectah Deck hit me from *Triumph*, the very best from Wu-Tang Clan. Bopping my head slightly, I walked along the overpass where 188th Street crossed over Grand Central Parkway.

I needed to cover a lot of ground, and I couldn't use the subway system, because there was no way Stacey would be there. Everyone who rode the subway was on guard for weirdos. That was as fundamentally a part of life in New York City as eating a hot dog on your way to work or yelling "Red Sox suck!" even when the Bronx Bombers were playing the Mariners or Rangers. If you saw anyone unfamiliar or sketchy on the subway, you stayed three rows away from them. If they started following you, you either ran your ass off, started screaming, or lit them up with whatever weapon you had on hand. Women didn't ride the subway without something to defend themselves. Usually, it was mace or pepper spray, but some were way more gangster than that. I'd see women pull out a switchblade, a one-shot pistol, and even a damn cattle prod that had been stuffed down a pants leg.

Whether Stacey was looking for me or another victim, or both, he would be out in the open, where he could blend into crowds, choose a target, and slowly close the distance between them until they had nowhere to run. I could read his mind when I focused hard, but that would require staying in one place and staying silent. That wouldn't let me track him down. I knew that if I was close enough, I would be able to sense him, so I had to get creative on how to accomplish what I needed to do without stealing a car or spending three grand on taxi rides all over creation on a Friday night.

My senses were sharpened outside in the darkness, rather than in my bed at home, which seemed like a far better way to connect with Stacey. I needed to cover a lot of ground, and outside was the catalyst I needed for my chain reaction. I watched the ebb and flow of traffic roll by, car after car, standing on the overpass overlooking it all as they all trickled on the highway underneath the bridge. There weren't many cars out at this time of night. People were already at their destinations and in their own hoods by now, and other than taxis, there wasn't much traffic to speak of.

Then I saw it coming from a good five hundred feet off. A big rig truck, white with huge blue flames painted down both sides of the cab, pulling a lengthy silver trailer. It was exactly what I had been hoping for. It was most likely a delivery driver on a late-night run into the city. I stepped to the edge of the bridge, checked both directions to make sure I was alone, and, timing it perfectly, hopped off the overpass and landed atop the trailer as it emerged from the other side of the bridge. I didn't weigh very much, despite my height, and it was extremely doubtful that the driver could have heard the noise over the roar of the engine, the air conditioner in the cab, and whatever else he might have going on in there. If anything, he might chalk it up to the truck being slightly above bridge clearance and clipping the underside. Fortunately, the truck didn't stop or even slow down, just kept churning down the Grand Central.

The first thirty seconds of the ride were, to be honest, absolutely horrifying. I didn't want to be there, and if it hadn't been on account of a psycho serial killer tearing up women in my hometown, I think I would have admitted defeat and jumped off. But this was it. The reason I became the NY Talon was to take down this guy running circles around the cops and leaving people afraid for their daughters, wives, mothers, girlfriends, and sisters to be out at night. And, of course, I also wanted to deliver some overdue justice to that wretched monster.

With so much wind resistance on top of the truck, I sat cross-legged like a monk, turning up the music in my ears as I tried to relax. I reached out, expanding my senses to the surrounding neighborhoods like an octopus stretching out tentacles of sensation in eight different directions.

As the wind grew louder and hit my face more intensely, my adrenaline jumped and my sensations came alive. I thought about the limits I had encountered, my many failures, and all the times I'd had my ass handed to me. I had wanted to give up many times over. However, seeing my parents battle through prejudice, become victims of crime, and continue to always work hard had shown me that if I only fight when it's easy, donning this mask wouldn't be worth much. So, now I must fight the good fight as the NY Talon. The Jubas, my parents, and Amayah's parents kept fighting and never relinquished their dignity and decency. Being a criminal and committing a crime would be far too easy for me; it wouldn't take much effort at all. So, sitting up there like a crazed man on an eighteen-wheeler, it dawned on me that true heroes show their colors when the battle becomes real—and potentially overwhelming.

As Wu-Tang's *Triumph* played, with the boom-boom of the drums thumping, I looked out into the stars, whispering in tune with Inspectah Deck's verse about the bold soldier being in control. That's who I was—the bold soldier on the move, finding ways to eliminate the evil of the world by any means necessary, using my mind and my spirit and my powers to lay a trap, before springing up to save the day. I imagined what the look on his face would be when I took him down; I imagined the horror when he realized that his sadistic ways were no match for the power of the Shine. I imagined the look on Amayah's face when she saw the headlines that I had saved the city from his reign of terror. With any luck, she would want to kiss me for a few hours, and maybe do a little bit more besides...

In that moment, I was tempted to reach out and focus on her. I wanted to feel her aura and her heart beating, and see the smile on her face as she spent time with her family.

I mean, they were all good people. I had met some of them in 1980, and hopefully, I'd be meeting more and more of them as our relationship deepened and we started spending more time in family situations. Some guys might find that idea terribly boring, but I was thrilled by the prospect. The false popularity I had gained when I first unleashed my powers was an exciting rush of acceptance for me, but I was slowly starting to understand that such praise wasn't real. Not a single one of those people had the faintest idea who I was before I could run faster than anyone else or dunk like Kobe Bryant. As amazing as my abilities were, at some point, it would get boring for them, and they would move on. However, Amayah's family was full of real, genuine, and generous people who all wanted to get to know me and took their time caring about me. That was the kind of acceptance I had been looking for all these years.

I snapped free of my dream world. Night-surfing a semi-trailer wasn't the time for self-reflection, and I needed to focus before this truck reached its destination. Otherwise, I would just be a dumb kid sitting outside a meatpacking plant or a dock in the middle of nowhere, with nothing to show for it.

I closed my eyes and stretched out, sending my pulses of energy across wide stretches of New York City, searching for Stacey's presence. The feedback I received was dazzling. I detected people from all walks of life—all races, genders, and religions, each of them going about their lives. Most of them were good people trying to make it through their day without hurting anyone else or causing any trouble. There were some darker minds in the mix as well, people who were hurting, angry, or confused. I recognized some of them as people with mental problems, or people affected by dementia or Alzheimer's disease. I touched their minds lightly, trying to give them even a fleeting sense of relief before I moved on. Others were sleeping, and their minds were at peace. It was like being everyone and no one all at once, and it took my breath away as the truck carried me through my beloved city, to which I was connected more powerfully than ever before.

It was too much to handle, and I didn't want my senses scattered when I was really only there for one person. I refocused my energy, arranged myself into a meditation pose, and closed my eyes, focusing inward, asking for guidance, offering prayer. Whether Jesus or God or Hua or the Brute was out there listening, I tried to reduce myself to being a willing servant of the power of the light, knowing that I was facing off against a monster wearing the skin of a man. I would need every bit of help I could muster.

I shut out the buzzing, wind-whipped clamor of the outside world and looked inside myself, trying to touch my source of power without activating it. I tried to follow it back to where it came from as I held my pocket-sized Bible tighter and prayed some more. It was pure and joyful, light and peaceful. I didn't sense the Brute at all, which strengthened my innate feeling that he wasn't supplying my power, but instead trying to abuse it. Somewhere in there, my thoughts stopped being just thoughts, and turned into a conversation. The female voice, Hua, spoke up in my mind, praising my ability to silence the outside world and focus on myself.

"If you cannot control yourself, then you cannot control anything," Hua said. *"Embrace the path of the Shine Xiong, for it is the way of the ninja. When you are in control of your thoughts and emotions, the entire world opens up to you, and the powers you have now will seem like children's games to you. You were chosen to hold back the evil of this world. It is legion and has many faces. You must always be ready, my ninja of destiny. Know that you are not alone, and that even in the heart of darkness, I am with you. There are others who are committed to the cause, others you will come to know, ninjas that possess the Shine and have used it to push back the darkness since the dawn of time."*

"Others?" I mentally asked her. "What others?"

I could feel the warmth of her smile, which made me glow with energy.

"Some you have met, and some you have yet to meet. Some lived when the world was young, some are out there like you, only now discovering their powers. Some are balanced on the tip of a knife, trying to determine whether they will use their Shine to bring good to the world or try to reshape it in their own image of greed and ambition."

Greed and ambition. That sounded a whole lot like what the Brute was always telling me. Granted, I did indulge those thoughts from time to time. I mean, I was a teenager, after all, and teenage boys have the worst hormones in the world, according to every health textbook. With the Brute's coaxing, and with my imagination being pretty vivid, and my ability to create crazy compelling visions, at times, it did lead to some bad thoughts.

In a solemn tone, Hua continued, *"Embrace the heights, yet never stoop to see others as mere shadows. Such arrogance leads to a perilous journey, sipping from the cup of the infernal."*

The wind fell silent as she asked, *"Do you understand?"*

"Yes, no matter how high I reach, I should never consider myself superior to another. To do so is to imbibe the poison of the devil and embark on a treacherous, dark journey," I responded with unwavering conviction.

In a whisper filled with profound insight, Hua revealed, *"True wisdom resides in the depths of humility."*

"How are you connected to the Shine?" I asked Hua, making sure to phrase my questions carefully. Whenever I grew impatient or too demanding in our past exchanges, she always vanished before providing any substantial answers.

"I reside within the light, a guiding force in the universe, the very essence of this realm and beyond, the shield that defends humanity from darkness," her words echoed within me. *"I am the dawn of a fresh start, the beacon of a hopeful tomorrow, the nurturer of celestial beings."*

That last part blew my mind. I was almost afraid to ask the next question. Regardless of what the answer was, it was going to change the way I thought about everything that had happened to me thus far.

"Are you God?"

A pause, then an answer.

"I am part of a whole. One part in three. I will guide you as I can. I will help you fight your demons."

"Do you mean Nick the Brute or Stacey?"

Before she could answer, a cold chill flowed over me, and the breath froze in my lungs. It felt like the air was going frosty in my throat, and I gasped aloud to confirm that I was still drawing breath. Stacey was in his hunting mode, and it was a terrifying sensation to feel. I hadn't been this scared since the morning McPherson had caught me off-guard and exhausted after picking all the cotton to save Cecilia's life. I could scarcely believe that Stacey was even human, with so much rage and anger in him. If I hadn't seen him with my own eyes, I would have thought he was something out of a Stephen King book or a horror movie you watch at 2 a.m. and then didn't sleep for two nights.

He was here, and he was close. I opened my eyes and looked around. The truck was rolling on Grand Central East and had just crossed over Union Turnpike on its way through Alley Pond Park. When it stopped at the light at Winchester, I stood and leapt off the back, swinging off a light pole and up onto the roof of the parking garage that connected to the NYC Sanitation Department building. The comic-book reader inside of me thought that Stan Lee or Jack Kirby would have inserted a line about the hero preparing to take out the trash of the city, but this was no time for clever narration or catchphrases. Stacey might have been a harmless Marlins fan in broad daylight and suave enough to charm that blonde teeny bopper with promises of a good time and a great high, but now he was in full-on killer mode. I said a silent prayer for whomever he might be stalking, followed by the chilling notion that I might be saying a prayer for myself. He was pissed that I was getting credit for his kills. I knew I'd have to be just as careful in this confrontation as anything I had faced across three unique eras and many physical fights.

I crept silently across the rooftop, looking for any signs of movement on the street below. I didn't see anyone, but the feeling in my chest told me he was close. At the back of the building were more dumpsters than I had ever seen in one place in my entire life. It stunk to high heaven, and I was about to chalk it up to me not knowing how to read my powers correctly when I heard a female voice softly cry, "Help me! He put me in here!"

My heart leapt to my throat. Was Stacey using this place to stash his victims until he could kill them? It seemed like the perfect hiding place. No one would smell one more rotten stench coming from an entire landscape of dumpsters. Remembering how Amayah had praised me for saving the blonde girl, despite the outcome, I jumped from the top of the building and landed easily some thirty feet below.

Aware that he might still be close enough to hear, I didn't call out to the girl. In that moment, I had to prioritize her safety over finding him. Innocent lives couldn't be risked to put him away.

I walked quietly from one dumpster to the next, trying to pinpoint the location of the voice. My patience paid off when she called out again, "Is someone out there! Please, I'm over here! He locked it, and I can't get out!"

It was the red dumpster at the end of the row. I picked up the pace, keeping my eyes and ears open for any sign of Stacey. I was conflicted about leaving my balaclava on. There was an outside shot that this had nothing to do with Stacey and was some other random case of kidnapping. I didn't want anyone to see my face, not even someone I was rescuing. But if it was Stacey... I saw what the guy could do with a knife and I didn't want him to get the drop on me and have to fight for my life while I was trying to rescue her. If he came at me while I was still wearing the ski mask, it would be a lot tougher to coordinate my attacks. I wouldn't be able to dance around with this guy; I would need to strike hard and strike fast, knock him out, and then worry about what to do with him later. I still didn't see or hear anything as I closed in on the dumpster. One more sweeping look around the area and I decided it was then or never.

"Hang on!" I whispered to the unknown occupant inside. "I'm here to rescue you!"

I gripped the padlock keeping the dumpster lid closed, and snapped it in half with my powerful grip. I carefully swung the lid open to reveal... nothing. The dumpster was completely empty. It made no sense. There had definitely been a voice, and this was definitely the dumpster it had come from. I had a small but powerful flashlight tucked into my belt, and I took it out, running the light back and forth, crisscrossing the floor of the dumpster for any signs of life. There was nothing. It was completely empty. Not even any trash inside. I swung the light back up to tuck it in my belt when the light glinted off something silvery. I pulled back and carefully aimed the light. It took me a moment to figure out what I was seeing, but when I did, my gut sunk.

There was a miniature tape recorder duct taped to the inside of the dumpster's roof. It was the kind a reporter would use at a city council meeting to take notes. I looked closer and saw that it was running, the little wheels spinning round and round as the tape spooled from one reel to the other.

"Help! Please help me!"

The girl's voice! The tape recorder wasn't recording me. It was luring me into a trap. Stacey had clearly put it here, and had possibly recorded one of his prior victims for just such an occasion. But if there wasn't a victim, that meant ..."Hello, Black Blur," a familiar voice boomed from behind me.

I turned around, and there he was. Stacey was a couple inches taller than me and looked like he was in better physical shape, but that wouldn't matter. He was wearing black jogging pants, a black sweatshirt with the hood up, and those same dark sunglasses, even though it was the middle of the night. His lips peeled back in a sneer that made his nose look sharper, flocking out his mustache even more.

"Trying to play the hero again, are we?" he said with a sickening grin. "Of course, it didn't go so well last time, did it? You tried to save the day, and the newspapers mistook you for that monster of a killer they've all been hunting for months. Not quite the adulation you were looking for, was it, boy?"

He might have keenly read the way I felt, but he wasn't the only one with extra ammo.

"Bet you hated seeing my name on that paper taking credit for all your killings, didn't you?" I snapped back, matching his mocking tone. "Bet you were pissing your pants back home because no one gave a shit about you anymore, isn't that right, Stacey?"

The physical recoil he went through when I said his name was worth every second of the misery I had endured last week. Nick the Brute gave a deep, dark chuckle that slipped from my lips before I could stop it. I watched the killer's lip twitch as he tried to regain his composure.

The dark sunglasses hid his eyes and made him more intimidating to victims, but since I couldn't see his eyes, I focused on other parts of his face. That worked against him when he was trying to act all-powerful, and his shifty mouth gave away his emotions."Think you're so fucking smart, boy? Think you know me? You don't know shit. I know all about you, though. Black Blur fighting crime, getting cats out of trees, stopping the neighborhood bully. You're out of your league here, boy, but just ask 'please,' and I'll give you a quick death."

His overconfidence would come back to haunt him. I cracked my knuckles for dramatic effect. "I don't think so, Stacey. Your time ends tonight; you've been hurting people for far too long." I punctuated my last word by speedily extending my right hand, palm flat, towards his chest, intending to knock him down and knock the wind out of him—Bruce Lee style. When people couldn't catch a breath, they were much easier to handle, and who knew what other tricks Stacey had up his sleeve?

But my hand never connected. He moved faster than anyone I had ever seen and stepped easily out of the impact zone of my hand. I spun around and tried again, but he caught me by the wrist and smashed me across the face with his free hand, staggering me as I took two steps back and crashed into the dumpster.

What the hell was happening? I could feel my power surging within me. It wasn't like the time in Mississippi where I had taken a beating after picking cotton all night. Was I holding back? Was I fighting scared? I didn't have time to think because Stacey followed his punch with a kick to my kneecap that brought me hobbling back towards him. I went low, to knock his feet out from under him, and he jumped straight up and over me, like gravity no longer applied. I turned around and I could feel my mouth dropping open in surprise.

"Fool!" he shouted. "Did you think you were the only one?" The knife appeared in his hand like a flash of light, and he threw it right at my face. I was able to bat it aside at the last second, but it cut my hand in the process, releasing a quick stream of blood.

I kicked the knife away and sent it spinning into the night sky, but as I turned back around, he was lunging at me with another knife in his other hand. He twirled it back and forth as I tried to side-step his advance, blocking his arms with my forearms. He was as fast as me, or faster, and he knew exactly how to use the hunting knife. I hadn't been this afraid since my encounters on the slave plantation. He gored me swiftly across the shoulder, and I gasped in shock and pain as blood began oozing through my shirt. I punched him in the chest, and he stumbled back a few steps, but then kept coming, altering his attacks high and low, left to right, until he sliced me again across the thigh and my upper left arm. Bleeding from three places and struggling to keep my head up, I tried to summon my power to get the hell out of there, abandoning the superhero notion to save my own life. Even that proved impossible, though. Stacey brought his knee up into my chin and knocked me back into the air and onto my ass. He stood over me, sweating and breathing heavily, tossing the knife casually from one hand to the other.

It didn't make sense. Surely, he couldn't be a Shine Xiong like me? Why would Hua imbue such a terrible person with that sort of power? A chill ran through me as I suddenly wondered if Hua had been lying to me. Maybe Nick the Brute was the real source of power. Perhaps Hua was just trying to influence me away from embracing my true destiny. I had no time to consider such complex puzzles. Whatever he was and wherever he had come from, Stacey was just as strong as me, and if I didn't figure out what to do, he was going to kill me.

"You're nothing, boy. Your powers are nothing! You have no idea who I am. What I am. But now you'll see. Now you'll KNOW. And when you die, your mommy will never be the same again, and that's when I'll visit her. Hee-hee-hee."

He spit in my face. As I moved to wipe it away, his body shuddered. For a moment, I thought he was having a stroke with all that heavy breathing, but then I saw the dark red light coming from his upper body. It was throbbing like a twisted heartbeat, and his body was shivering in time with it. I should have taken the opportunity to run away, as he was clearly distracted, but I had to see what was happening. I had to know what the hell was going on here. His arms were getting longer, as crazy as that sounds, and his chest was bulging out, bigger and broader, making a terrible sound, like the skin of a cooked chicken being pulled from the bone. As I watched, Stacey grew taller and wider, his face warping from that of a normal human into something else—something monstrous. His mustache hair spread across the rest of his face until he looked like a lion I had once seen at the Bronx Zoo, sickly and angry. His eyes flashed from blue-gray to yellow to blazing orange, making me yearn to never see that color again. His skin flaked, peeled, and fell off as bright red blood flowed down one cheek, while his mouth oozed a gooey stream of the red plasma. Getting a better look at that side of his face, I saw that it resembled a trio of claw marks from a wild animal. He was an image straight from a nightmare I could have never imagined, but one that would haunt me for the rest of my days.

He was at least seven feet tall, a horrifying combination of man and beast, muscled and twisted and bleeding all at once.

"Ahhhhhhhhh," he sighed, his voice deeper and warped. "This is true power, boy. This kind of power is only achievable by sacrificing and swearing obedience to Nick the Brute, the greatest power this puny world has ever known!"

I felt my heart sink into my shoes. I should have known that Nick was up to no good. The Brute had made Stacey into this thing. He was trying to do the same to me. He wanted me to let him out and then serve him, even though he was pretending to serve me. Would this be my fate if I gave into his primal urges? Would I become a monstrosity like this? I felt guilty for doubting Hua. She was a true servant of the light, and this was clearly her foe. If I hadn't been able to guess who Nick was and what forces he possessed before, I knew in that moment, without a doubt. He and Hua were opposite sides of a coin, opposite sides of a battle that had been waged since the beginning of time. Good vs. Evil. Heaven vs. Hell. God vs. Satan. Hua and Nick had been fighting for my service for a long time, and I had been turning that coin carefully, playing both sides. Now I was facing off against a disciple of the Brute.

Stacey's clothes hung off him as he used a claw-like foot to kick me in the chest, robbing me of breath and sending screams of pain racing through my nervous system.

"So weak! I know that he speaks to you, but you're too weak to let yourself go! That's why you'll never stop me. I was once like you. Human, fragile, a pale impersonation of my true self. I had to kill the first one, you see? The wrong place at the wrong time. And then the Brute came to me. Reshaped me. Prepared me to take on my ultimate task.

"Some fucking child like you isn't going to stop me. You've used your powers to get in my mind somehow. Do you think I haven't been looking back at yours, little Rohan? Do you think I haven't seen those sad little dry cleaners your parents think of as such a blessing? Watched you wear your little faggot work clothes to ring up condoms and mouthwash, while wishing you were anywhere else? Seen that pretty little piece of Spic ass you love so much? That tall leggy blonde I brought candy to, the one you took from me, was supposed to be my sweet treat. Maybe I'll visit your little novia later tonight to make up for the blondie and bring her some of my sweetness."

The rage I felt at hearing him mention Amayah was overwhelming. I don't know if it was all me, all Brute, or some combination of the two, but I rose to my feet in an instant and launched myself at him. I never even got close. He caught my entire body in one massive hand, lifted me four feet off the ground, and brought me close to his hideous face.

"Playtime is over, Ninja. And so are you. Those wounds should make your death nice and painful. Maybe I'll come to your funeral. I imagine sweet Amayah will need some comforting with her handsome boyfriend dead and gone."

I tried to fight him, but I was too weak, and he was impossibly strong. Stacey sank his claws into my abdomen and twisted with one swift motion. As my blood soaked through, dripping down my hoodie to my sweatpants and shoes, a quick jolt of *fear and excruciating pain* coursed through my body. With his other clawed hand, he raised the dumpster's lid and threw me inside. I smashed against the hard metal bottom and felt myself losing consciousness even as the lid slammed shut above me.

CHAPTER

THIRTY-FOUR

I thought I was dreaming ...

A light mist fell, and the fog cascaded around Ama. A few droplets caught on her cheek as she stared into the night sky. Amayah began dancing with her cousins, laughing, smiling, and enjoying a festive night with her extended family. She twirled her little cousin Marta around and around to the beat of the drums until the little girl gasped for breath.

The rooftop gathering started with ten people, but grew to about thirty as more and more primos, tios, and abuelos, showed up, were called on the phone, hollered over through open windows, or simply heard the music and came to investigate. The food was so delicious that she thought she might burst from it all, but when her Uncle Rodrigo pulled out his guitar, she was the first on her feet, and called out for her favorite songs, which he happily obliged. Someone else found a large box to drum on, and the dinner turned into an impromptu concert in no time.

Amayah felt pure joy as she spun around to the music, seeing her relatives' glowing smiles and warm faces as they relaxed after a long week of work. This was the heart of their culture, and the only reason they needed to celebrate was the fact that they were all together.

However, *right in the middle of* La Plena Viene de Cidra, *she abruptly stopped dancing, dropped Marta's hands and walked to the edge of the rooftop. Something felt off inside, like a slow chill starting at her waist and simultaneously traveling down her legs and up her arms. Had she eaten too much? No, it wasn't her stomach taking offense; it was something deeper inside. Something was making her heart ache, and she felt as if a part of her soul had fractured. The noise and lights of the party faded into the background as she stared out into the bright lights of the city. "Rohan?" she whispered.*

She didn't know how she knew, but she knew that he was in danger, terrible danger. For just a single second, she saw a vision of him, broken and battered, alone in the dark, and her heart cried out for him. He was so strong, not only because of his powers, but because of who he was on the inside.

She immediately thought of the serial killer, Stacey. Had he found Rohan before Rohan found him? She had to find him.

Putting her feelings for Rohan aside for a moment, she considered the problem logically. She saw him in a dark place, which meant that he could be literally anywhere. She closed her eyes and focused on Rohan, how he looked, how his hair smelled, how it felt when he held her close enough to hear his heart beating. Another vision flashed in front of her eyes, dumpsters by the dozen, maybe even by the hundred. She didn't know what she was looking at, but she suspected that she knew someone who might. Turning back to the party, she scanned the roof and finally spotted her quarry.

Her cousin Martin stood in the darkest corner of the roof with a drink in one hand, and the other on the small of the back of a girl Amayah didn't recognize. She was curvy and had dyed blonde hair and big hoop earrings, which swung as she talked excitedly in Martin's ear.

Amayah walked quickly his way and grabbed him by the arm. "Primo! I need to talk to you right away!"

Martin was clearly irritated at having his little dalliance interrupted, and his blonde female friend seemed even less pleased. She glared at Amayah, and her full lips turned angry. "Back off, chica! I saw him first!"

Amayah would have laughed if she hadn't been so worried about Rohan. Martin worked as a sanitation worker for the City of New York, and while he was tall and muscular from lifting all those trash cans, he was about a million degrees away from the kind of guy she'd find attractive.

Martin was already in damage control mode. "No, no baby, it's not like that, this is my little cousin, Amayah. This better be important, prima. I'm busy over here."

Amayah rolled her eyes at the prospect of Martin's 'work.'

"I need to ask you a question. Is there a place in the city where there are rows and rows of dumpsters? Like eighty or hundred of them, all lined up?"

Martin looked annoyed that the interruption was about garbage of all things.

"Sure, the Department of Sanitation HQ, right off Grand Central. Why do you care about that?"

"I need to go there fast, primo. I think my boyfriend got into trouble there, and he needs help."

Martin scoffed. "Your boyfriend? The Asian kid? If he's down there, he's probably looking to score some weed. He'll be fine, so long as he has the money to pay for it."

He turned back around to the dye job, who was looking more and more impatient by the second. But Amayah persisted, grabbing his arm and pressing her nails into the flesh of his wrist.

"Ahhh! Damnit, Amayah, that hurt! What the hell is the matter with you?"

She moved closer to him so that the dye job couldn't hear what she was saying.

"I need you to take me there right now, primo. And if you don't, I'm going to tell your dye job here about that Black chick at the soul food kitchen down the way that you also call your girl. And then I'll tell her about the elementary school teacher at PS 144 that you keep sending flowers to so you can get that second date. And then I'll tell her how I saw

you kissing Claudia Ochoa at the swimming pool last Labor Day. And then I'll tell Abuela Manuela ALL OF IT."

Martin bore a smirk on his face until their abuela's name came up. That's when the fear bloomed in his eyes and Amayah knew she had him.

"Eres loca! Fine, let me get this chica's number and grab my keys. Give me five minutes, and we'll go figure out why your boyfriend is dumpster diving."

True to his word, six minutes later, Martin was driving Amayah away from Washington Heights towards Grand Central Parkway. She knew he thought she was crazy, but she didn't care. Something had happened to Rohan; she didn't know how she had come to that conclusion or how she experienced the brief visions, but she had never been more certain of anything in her entire life. She was glad that Martin was coming with her. She knew Rohan was hurt, and Martin was strong enough to help her get him to safety if he needed it.

The Sanitation Department building was on Douglaston Parkway, just north of the Grand Central. On a Friday night with little traffic, it still took them about half an hour to get there. Martin parked right in the front of the building, unworried about meter maids working a government building on a Friday night. Her cousin took the tiny flashlight off his tool belt and shined it on the ground in front of them as they walked around the back.

There it was, the sea of dumpsters she had seen in her vision. But where was Rohan? She started calling his name and moving from one giant metallic bin to another, fearful that she was too late, or that whoever did this might come back to finish him off. Martin moved behind her, holding the light above her head as she frantically searched. After she yelled into six or seven of the units, he put a hand on her shoulder.

"Look there, someone's been screwing with it. Let's check there."

She followed the flashlight's beam and saw what Martin was talking about. A red dumpster at the complete opposite end of the row had several notable dents in it, and was turned around 45 degrees to one side, as compared to the orderly rows around it. She raced to it as quickly as her feet would carry her, with Martin trailing behind. She beat on the metal and cried, "Rohan! Rohan, Rohan can you hear me?" She got no response. Then Martin was beside her, and he handed her the flashlight as he lifted the lid of the dumpster, expecting nothing, but quickly seeing that he was wrong.

"OH SHIT!" Martin said as he saw the crumpled mess inside. "Hold the light, prima. I'm going to get him out. We have to get this kid to a hospital."

I FIGURED I was dying when I heard Amayah calling my name, as though some image of her was saying goodbye as I went towards the light and death took me to whatever the next part of my journey would be. I had slipped in and out of consciousness since Stacey had turned into a monstrosity and tossed me into the dumpster to meet my fate. I tried to use my healing powers on the knife wounds, but had made very little progress. I had used more energy in that fight than I had ever used before, especially once I realized that he was my equal, and then again when I realized that he was stronger, faster, and more powerful than I was. Each time I tried to pour the healing factor into one of my wounds, I ended up blacking out again. I had no idea how much time passed or how much blood I lost. The cold metal of the dumpster numbed me to all sensation, and it was pitch dark. I was scared to put my hands on the places where his knife had cut me, especially so on my abdomen where his claws had stabbed me, for fear of finding that I could feel my bones and organs through the bloody rips. I was in terrible pain, and more than that, I felt like I was falling apart mentally. I had been lured into an ambush, completely dominated in a fight, and the serial killer had gotten away, taunting me with knowledge that he knew all about my family and Amayah. The idea that he might have already hunted the four of them down kept pushing its way to the forefront of my mind, and I couldn't stop sobbing.

"Rohan! Rohan!"

I heard Amayah's voice and assumed I had reached the end. I could hear her pain and panic, and wondered if I was catching a projection of her voice as Stacey caught, tortured, and killed her. I closed my eyes and welcomed the end of this terrible existence. I had failed everyone, including myself, failed the Shine, all due to my arrogance, thinking I could outsmart a sadistic killer so easily. When the squeak of metal on metal filled my ears, I feared that Stacey had returned to taunt me again before slitting my throat, but the face peering down at me belonged to a stranger.

"OH SHIT!" I heard him say in a Spanish accent. "Hold the light, prima. I'm going to get him out. We have to get this kid to a hospital."

He climbed in the dumpster and kicked open the little door on the side from the inside.

"Jesus man, did a vampire get you? You're torn the fuck up!"

He looked up and squinted. "Prima! Shine the light down in here. I have to figure out how to move him... he's all cut up!"

A bright light shone down on my face, and I moaned. I looked up, and there she was. Impossibly beautiful. Impossibly there. My Ama, my love, my Amayah had found me.

"Hey buddy, just scream if this hurts," the guy with her said as he put his hands under my armpits and hoisted me off the bottom of the dumpster. I moaned as the combination of sweat and blood that had congealed between my skin and the dumpster pulled apart. My head was swimming, and I was so weak, absurdly spent and lifeless, my body like limp noodles, but I tried to help him by shuffling my feet little by little towards the tiny door that allowed outside access to the dumpster. The guy went first and then turned and half-carried, half-dragged me out behind him. We turned and she was there, my angel, staring down at me with tears in her eyes, hovering over dark circles beneath them.

"Ro? Oh my god, what happened to you? Who did this? We've got to get you to Mt. Sinai—quick!" She was smart to pick the hospital that knew me so well. They'd see my wounds, and there would be no questions as to how I got them. Everyone on that staff knew me, and most thought of me as some sort of hero, which was a bit embarrassing. Even so, I was like part of their family, and I knew they would get to work on saving my life before wasting time asking any awkward questions.

I turned my head to the guy with her, a tall, barrel-chested Hispanic guy in his early twenties with dark black hair.

"Thaaaaank... you," I gasped out at him, and he nodded.

"Thank Amayah. Somehow, she knew you were here, and that you were in trouble. She convinced me to come looking for you, amigo. I'm Martin by the way. Maya's cousin."

Ama gingerly wrapped her arms around me and helped Martin put me sitting upright on the floor against the dumpster. He was shining the flashlight over the places where Stacey had stabbed me, and I could tell that what he saw wasn't good.

"Amayah," he said, his voice wavering with doubt. "I don't think this guy should walk to the car. I'm going to go around front and drive it back here. Can you keep him upright for a few minutes?"

She fiercely confirmed that she wouldn't let anything happen to me, and I believed her instantly, despite feeling as though my life force was ebbing back and forth between the land of the living and the land of the dead.

Martin put a hand on my shoulder. "Hang on, kid, I'll be right back." He took off running as fast as he could.

Amayah sat beside me and drew close enough to look into my eyes.

"Stay with me, Rohan. Look into my eyes and listen to my voice. You're going to be fine, just hang on to me and let me be your strength."

Something in those words sent a pulse through my body, like a tiny surge of energy straight into my power source.

"What did you say?" I whispered slowly.

Ama looked into my eyes and pressed her hand to my chest, cringing at the ragged heartbeat in my chest.

"Let me be your strength, Rohan, let me take your burden," she whispered in reply. As she said those words again, I felt a tingling sensation in my chest where her hand was pressed against my heart. It grew and grew, and I felt her energy and love flow into me like a river, the opposite of what I felt when I had healed people in the hospital over the last few months.

I stared at her as my strength started to rapidly return, and she looked at me in awe, gasping in shock and surprise. Her eyes locked on the slash on my shoulder, and I looked down just in time to see the wound pulling itself closed. I looked back down at Amayah's hand, and in the darkness, I could see what appeared to be droplets of white liquid forming and disappearing steadily on her fingertips. I had no idea what was going on, if she was doing this, or if it was some new manifestation of my powers. Still, we both stood completely motionless and wordless for another thirty seconds until the droplets vanished for good. I looked down and saw nothing but healthy skin on my shoulder where I had been gored. My thigh, my knee, my hand, and my abdomen were similarly free of wounds. My jaw no longer hurt, and Amayah's jaw dropped an inch as she touched the places on me that had been bloodied and bruised just seconds earlier.

"How did you do that?" she asked, staring wide-eyed at me. "I thought you couldn't use your powers without your energy."

I cupped her chin and locked eyes with her. "I don't think I did anything, Amayah. I think you just healed me."

She shook her head. "That's impossible! I don't have... I don't have powers like that. I don't have powers like you!"

"Wait a minute, Ama... how did you even find me here tonight? How could you have possibly known where I was?"

She shook her head in disbelief.

"I was at my family party, and I suddenly felt like I just knew something was wrong, and that you were in trouble," she said uneasily. "Then I saw you in my mind's eye in a dumpster, and a few minutes later, I had another vision of all these dumpsters lined up. Martin is a garbageman, so I asked him if he knew the place, and he drove me here."

"Sight beyond sight," I reassured her earnestly. "You can't explain this away with logic or science, Amayah. There's something special inside of you; there's no other way to explain it."

We were interrupted by Martin roaring up in his car, who was prepared to race me to the hospital, which I no longer needed. This was going to get awkward.

Martin jumped out of the car and left the engine running. "Okay, prima, I put the front seat down so he can lay there and won't have to crawl into the back. You're going to be a little squished sitting behind me, but we're not that far from Elmont. They can take him to the ER there and then we can... um, where the hell are all his cuts?"

Martin was so busy talking through his plan that he hadn't noticed me getting up alone as I wrapped my arm around Amayah's waist. He started to speak, closed his mouth, and then opened it back again.

"What the fuck is going on here? You were on death's door a minute ago."

I took a deep breath, trying desperately to decide how I was going to explain all this, when Amayah spoke up.

"Rohan is El Desenfoque Negro that they keep talking about at the taqueria and the bakery," she said matter-of-factly. "He's the one who put those four Trinitarios out of commission a few months back, when they claimed they had gotten attacked by a bunch of ninjas." She couldn't help smiling at me as she recalled that detail. "He's a superhero, Martin. He's been saving people all over the city."

Martin looked me up and down, as if seeing me for the first time. "Are you really going around killing women, bro? That shit ain't cool."

I sighed, the events of the night coming back to me.

"No, Martin, please believe me, that's not me. There's a guy from out of town terrorizing the city. His first name is Stacey, and I've run into him twice. I thought I could ambush him tonight, but he was waiting for me instead." I squeezed Amayah's hand as I explained the next part. "He has powers like mine; in fact, he was stronger and faster than me when we fought. The blonde girl that reported me as her attacker got it backwards. I saw him attacking her and scared him off, but he threw her down the stairs, and it cracked her head— hard. She looked up and saw me and thought I was him."

"Damn, man, I thought Amayah was just hanging out with you for your math tutoring," Martin said. "And you whipped those kids trying to rob the supermarket a couple weeks ago?"

"Yeah, that was me."

"You're badass, Rohan. You got a lot of fans out there, at work, and around the neighborhoods. I don't think most people believe you killed anybody, but you know how the papers are. Now tell me for real, what can I do to help?"

I blinked, not exactly sure what he was asking. "What do you mean? You already saved my life tonight."

He shook his head. "There's a killer out there, amigo, and you know who he is and what he looks like, right? You said he's stronger and faster than you, so that means you need help."

I shook my head. "No way, I have to do this alone. He's a killer, and I don't want anyone else getting hurt."

He snorted. "Kid, you got your ass whipped tonight. You almost got killed. What's going to change next time around? If you can't beat a guy with your fists, you have to beat him with your brain, with your heart, and with your friends. He's not after you, he's killing people all over New York. That's not YOUR New York, it's OUR New York. I ain't got superpowers, but I know about five hundred garbage men who have eyes and ears all over the city. Tell us what we're looking for, where he might go, what he likes to do, anything you can, and we'll start getting information for you. C'mon, amigo, even Batman has Alfred the Butler and Commissioner Gordon."

I nodded. I had to be smarter to catch Stacey, especially considering what I had seen of him tonight. I didn't want to say that part in front of Martin, and maybe not even in front of Amayah. The thing I saw him become scared the life out of me. How the hell was I supposed to fight a monster like that, one powered by the merciless Brute? I needed a new plan. I needed to understand myself, and I also needed to get to the very best library New York City had to offer.

CHAPTER

THIRTY-FIVE

I went to church with Amayah and her family that Sunday. Martin kept introducing me to everyone, stopping just short of dropping the bomb of who I really was. It was amusing, if somewhat tense. We skipped their family lunch afterward to go to the New York Public Library Main Branch in Manhattan, which probably contained more information than anywhere else in the country, in an effort to start figuring things out. I had to know more about my powers before I could hope to stand a chance against Stacey.

We each went to search for books and the computer for anything relevant to "Shine," "Xiong," "Hua," even "Nick the Brute," to learn how Stacey tapped into his power. As we tirelessly worked and researched under the library's grand chandeliers and gilded ceilings, I occasionally stopped to look at Ama. And I couldn't help but appreciate her helping me on this journey.

The research was a long, slow process, and other than a few random references that generally led nowhere, we weren't finding much of anything. Hua had once told me that she was the blossoming flower and a spirit, but a spirit of what kind? A ghost spirit, or maybe someone who died a long time ago from the past? Amayah pieced together that Nick was a nickname for the Devil in Christianity, which made a whole lot of sense, considering what his powers could turn Stacey into, as well as the way he kept tempting me with pleasures of the flesh and the ability to take revenge on those who harmed me. As we sat in the park eating a late lunch, I found myself feeling low. I had stupidly assumed that I could manhandle Stacey because of my powers and my intelligence, discounting that he might be equally gifted and smart as a whip.

On Sunday night, I saw yet another facet of Stacey's ruthlessness on the late-night news. The lead story featured an NYPD captain making a statement about an anonymous tip they had received in relation to the NY Slasher. He reported that they were now looking for a young Asian male who frequently wore a black bandana in conjunction with the attempted kidnapping of the Times Square blonde and other potentially related crimes. Stacey must have called in the tip on me. I was puzzled why he wouldn't have just given them my name and address so they could make a quick arrest. Amayah said that he had probably checked to make sure I was dead before leaving town. When my body wasn't where he left it, maybe he got nervous. Calling the cops wouldn't get me convicted of the crime, since there was no evidence, but it would put up more barriers to successfully come after him. Her advice was to focus on becoming the best version of myself and stop focusing on Stacey... for now. Until I had a way to fight him and actually stop him, trying to run him down was a suicide mission.

I hated that she was right, and I hated myself for being upset with her. I called her frequently when we weren't together, just to check on her. Stacey knew who she was, and that terrified me. She grew frustrated when I would call over and over if she didn't pick up right away, including picking up the phone one night to yell, "I'm trying to use the toilet, Rohan, leave me alone!" before slamming it back down.

It was our first real fight since she had called me out on my focus on gambling and general lack of activity in 1980. I finally took her advice and started focusing on what I could do to get better. Stacey had hurt me badly with his knives, particularly since my only weapons were my hands and feet. One of the books I checked out from the library was about ninjas and samurai, specifically about their training and weaponry. I found myself lingering in front of pawn shops every couple days, as they usually had a wide selection of exotic weapons that some idiot had bought after getting his first paycheck, only to have his mom, wife, or girlfriend make him sell it. There were some interesting options, but the more I read about it, the more it became obvious that making a weapon designed for me made much more sense than buying someone else's hand-me-down. The problem was that I was still saving for dinner with Amayah, and I didn't exactly have the resources or facilities to make a weapon myself. However, I did have someone on my team who might be able to help me, so one day after school, after walking Amayah home, I crossed the street and knocked on her cousin Martin's door.

He welcomed me in like Mickey Mantle before introducing me to two of his buddies, LeeRoy and Jeremiah, two Black guys about his own age. He said they were "cool," whatever that meant, and I told him what I was looking for. I needed wood that you could easily carve and 1095 high-carbon steel. I went to the corner store and made copies of a few pages from the library book and showed him. LeeRoy said the wood wouldn't be a problem, but the steel would take some time to find.

Fortunately, there were construction sites all over the city that they drove by or stopped at twice a week. "We'll get you something, Ro, don't worry. Maybe a week tops, alright mi amigo?"

"That's amazing, Martin, thanks. But there's one more thing. I also need somewhere to put it together. Someplace that has a really hot fire, like more than 1,000 degrees. I have no idea where that's going to be."

Jeremiah threw me a knowing wink. "You forget who you're talking to here. We know this city better than anyone. I know of a building with a modern incinerator that cooks some of New York's trash, goes up to 1,500 degrees easy, if not more. If we can see what you're building, we'll get you hooked up, no problem."

These guys were unbelievable, and I was so grateful that I agreed with Martin about needing a support system. They all seemed to think that being friends with a superhero was about the coolest thing ever, which made me feel a bit better about my failure with Stacey.

They didn't have much in the way of information about Stacey himself. It was frustrating, but the killer seemed to be laying low after our encounter, which made me curious. Had I hurt him like he hurt me? Was he worn down by his transformation? I tried to sort through the clues to make more strides toward discovering his last name but kept coming up short, so I returned to what I could control. A week later, I went with Martin and LeeRoy to the Sanitation Department HQ in the morning and spent the next nine hours heating, hammering, and cooling the carbon steel they had found for me. The detailed steps helped immensely, but more than that, I just felt good about using tools to create something. It felt like I was destined for it, hammering out my weapon, forging meaning in life, my truth, and my soul.

My second effort eliminated the struggles of the first, and when it cooled down, I had produced a double-bladed ninja staff with wooden handles. It was the coolest thing I had ever held in my hands. In its stock form, it was a heavy metal short staff that would be good for defense against something like Stacey's knives, but it had two secret forms as well. I could pull on the middle of the staff and separate it into two short swords, each with its own heavy blade, allowing me to fight with two hands. But even that wasn't all. I could also reverse the handles and connect them, making a lengthy double-edged staff, similar to a double-bladed poleaxe. That would be useful for fighting multiple opponents, or keeping a tall one at a distance. I'd have to train with it frequently to get used to all three forms without hurting myself. I let each of the crew hold it and try it out as the rest of us stood a good distance away to avoid the freshly sharpened blades.

"What are you going to call it?" Martin asked, handing it back after time testing it out.

"Um, my great weapon?" I responded dumbly.

"No, amigo, every great weapon has a cool name. Like Excalibur or Sting or the Sword of Omens."

"You want me to name my sword after something from Thunder-cats?" I responded, cocking my head in mock amusement.

"Not that specifically, but yeah, something cool like that. Something that the bad guys will be afraid of when they see you coming."

I thought back on the things that mattered most to me and remembered that fateful night a few months ago when I had seen the murdered girl by the UN building after bombing with Lior, Jarron, and Steven.

"Justice," I said to myself and Martin's crew. "I'll call her Justice."

I got really into training with it after that. The more swings, slices, and hacks I took with Justice, the lighter and more natural she became. I'd climb up on the roof of my building every night and train in the dark, guided only by the stars and the moon. I envisioned ancient members of the Shine doing the same, hundreds or even thousands of years ago. As beaten down as I was by my near-fatal encounter with Stacey, I found myself wondering who the Shine had been, and who they were now. Hua said that I had met some of them. Who could they have been? I had begun to wonder if Amayah was one, with latent powers just like mine. What had happened between us when she and her cousin saved me from the dumpster hadn't been a figment of my imagination, but something much more palpable and real. I tried talking to her about it a couple of times, but she wouldn't hear of it, saying that it must have been me doing it, and that she was nothing special. I hated hearing her say that, because she had already brought me so far with her wisdom and compassion. She seemed shaken and scared by the mysterious healing, so I dropped it, figuring that we had way more important things to worry about.

But who else? Perhaps some of the greatest heroes of all time had been Shine. George Washington? King Arthur? Babe Ruth? Actually, the more I thought about it, the more likely it was that they had been unknown people. They were the heroes who operated behind the scenes. However, as much as I had referenced comic books during my last few months of exploration and acceptance of my powers, it felt more and more likely that it was all true, and that the powers of the Shine Xiong had simply been passed down and made into story form. The lone warrior, disguising himself to protect the people he cared about, venturing out into the night with forged weapons. It was the same story I had been reading my whole life.

Over a few weeks, things had shifted to Amayah calling frequently to check in, and me feeling slightly annoyed by her not leaving me alone. She kept telling me that I looked like I was training to fight in a war, and that I needed to be smart about it. I promised her I would take it easy and made sure to meditate and pray at the end of each session, trying to reach out to Hua and glean any further wisdom from her. It came slowly, bit by bit, but it was frustrating. Hua never wanted to show me how to fight, but instead how to have compassion and how to heal and how to love. Loving Stacey wasn't going to get him to stop murdering innocents across New York City.

Another positive besides the weapon was the fact that Nick the Brute had gone silent since my confrontation with Stacey. I mentally "went looking for him" and couldn't discern his presence anywhere within me. It was an odd combination of joy and unexpected loneliness, after having him lingering in the back of my mind for so long. On the Friday after I finished forging the Justice, I was sitting in math class trying to stay awake while learning about statistical analysis, when there was a knock on the door. The assistant principal ducked her head in, exchanged a quick word with our teacher, then turned and said, "Rohan Chang, please come with me and pack your things, you're leaving for the day."

My heart jumped into my throat as I felt all eyes following me out the door. Stacey must have struck someone in my family. I knew that Amayah was safely in class down the hall, so that's what it had to be. That bastard had come after my loved ones, and I was going to make him pay.

My mom and my brother were sitting in the assistant principal's office waiting for me. The principal nodded to my mom and closed the door, giving us the room.

"Mom?"

"It's your dad, Rohan. He's coughing up blood and fainted while folding clothes at the store. We've just been to the doctor. He had some tests run last month after he started having trouble catching his breath. He's been diagnosed with stage four lung cancer, and they're saying that he probably won't live past the end of the year. He's at Mt. Sinai now, and they're going to do everything they can for him. I'm so sorry, my son."

She wrapped me in a hug and I held her tight, because that's what you do for a woman whose husband is dying. Except that he wouldn't die, not if I had anything to do with it. I had slowly been healing several people at that hospital over the past few months, and I knew that I could heal him too. They'll call it a miracle, and I might have to actually go on the news or talk to the paper this time, but I didn't care. I thought back to that scene in the Superman movie where Clark is goofing off after school as his father dies of a stroke back at the farm. At the funeral, Clark tells his mother, "All those things I can do, all those powers, and I couldn't even save him."

I wouldn't repeat those mistakes. Stacey, Amayah, the Shine, Hua... they would all have to wait. I was going to take care of my father first.

I went and visited him that night at Mt. Sinai. He was asleep when I arrived, and I desperately wanted to pour every single ounce of energy I had into him right then and there. However, I didn't know what that would do to either one of us, and I wanted it to look like he was fighting the disease himself with the aid of the treatment. I put my hand on his forehead and stretched out with my second sight into his body. Cancer ravaged his lungs, and it was hungry for more fresh cells, but I slowly began transferring my own energy into the malignant ones, transforming them back into healthy ones. This would take a long time, but I would come every day if that's what it took. When I started to feel significantly drained, I let go of his arm and leaned down to kiss his forehead, whispering, "I love you, Dad." Watching him lying so still, so sick and weak, I cried, remembering all his unselfish sacrifices and enduring devotion to me and our family.

And before finally leaving, I soothed him with the truest words I could muster.

"You've always been the real hero."

CHAPTER
THIRTY-SIX

Amayah's heart was heavy yet filled with hope when I shared my dad's condition with her over the phone. Aware of the delicacy required when using my powers, she offered me a tender caution, reminiscent of her words after the incident involving Winnie and the altercation with the gang. I knew she was right. I didn't know when I might need my powers to save someone from Stacey or some other danger. I wanted to heal my dad as quickly and fully as I could, but I had to conserve my strength. The doctors also had a battery of treatments that could slow down the spread of the cancer, and if I continued to regularly treat him, with the two combined, I had faith.

I took on additional shifts at the dry cleaners to help my family in my dad's absence. I wanted to cancel our anniversary date because of my dad's illness and the beating I received from Stacey. However, Amayah insisted that we go and told me that she had bought a new dress for the occasion, which she said I wouldn't want to miss. Despite struggling with depression, seeing her dress up, especially for me, brought a genuine smile to my face. I made sure to tell my mom and brother that we were going out to celebrate our anniversary and assured them I'd return to visit my dad the next morning before heading to work.

Amayah wasn't the only one dressing up. I borrowed a slim-fitting royal blue blazer jacket and navy blue tie from my brother and ran both through the steam press at the store, along with my best matching slacks. I even added a pocket square to the breast pocket of my suit to look particularly dapper. I invested $17 in a fresh haircut and dedicated an extra 25 minutes to perfecting my shave, ensuring I looked my absolute best. Then, I called a taxi to take me to Amayah's, ready to make an impression. After picking her up, we'd head off to the restaurant together. Riding in a taxi may not seem particularly special to most people, but when your usual journeys involve navigating through the city's grime—whether it's aboard a filthy bus, a more sullied subway, or on the dirt-laden streets by foot—sharing a clean, private taxi feels as luxurious as riding in a stretch limousine. This wasn't just any ride; it was the beginning of a magical evening.

I buzzed Amayah's apartment, and she came down in a long black coat, which I found mildly disappointing. I felt like a jerk for having that reaction, but after the green dress she had worn on our first "date," I was expecting something equally shimmery and form-fitting. Regardless, her chestnut brown hair was straightened out and fell gently down her back, and she wore low heels, with touches of makeup that made her enchanting emerald eyes sparkle, further enhancing her soft and sensual lips. I had also brought her a red tulip from a street vendor, and she inhaled it profoundly before kissing me on the cheek, whispering, "Thank you, mi Ro."

She gawked at the taxicab when she realized that it was waiting for us and gave me one of those knockout smiles that nearly dropped me to the floor. The taxicab driver opened the door for both of us, and we made small talk as the cab whisked us smoothly through the city. I didn't tell her where we were going; it was so exciting to watch her guess. Her eyes were glued to the window as we rolled down the Hudson Parkway. The cab driver was clearly trying to do me a favor, and I appreciated it. Moon-sparkled water on one side of the view and the glittering lights of Manhattan on the other would put anyone in the mood for romance. Amayah's curious jade eyes got bigger as we finally hung a left on Canal Street. We weren't headed to Queens or another borough; this was prime-time Manhattan. Two turns later, we stopped on Spring Street in front of the most exclusive new restaurant in SoHo, Balthazar. It featured French cuisine, which I knew very little about, but I knew it was highly exclusive, barely squeezing out a reservation weeks ago.

I had Balthazar fax a menu to the dry cleaners earlier in the day, where I had been working a shift for my parents, and then withdrew every dollar I had saved from my bank account. I felt like a drug dealer with all the cash in my pocket, but I didn't care. This night was all about us.

Amayah spotted the sign, turned to me, and exclaimed, "NO WAY!" Her face lit up with a huge grin as she exited the cab, gracefully accepting the driver's outstretched hand and peeking through the windows. The restaurant was filled with people, but the maître d' promptly seated us at a table once I provided my name. As I unbuttoned my jacket, he turned to Amayah and asked, "May I take your coat, madam?"

She unbuttoned the black jacket and slipped free, and my heart skipped not just one beat, but closer to seven. She was wearing a red strapless dress that stopped a few inches above her knee. I stared and stared, and then stared some more, until I realized that she had sat down and was smiling up at me, mischief in her eyes. "See something you like, Mr. Chang?"

I felt my face flush. "Um, that is, well, that is, you look beautiful tonight," I finally blurted out.

"Why thank you, Mr. Chang. I picked it out with you in mind."

As I took my seat, I found myself captivated by her presence. The melody of Chris De Burgh's "Lady in Red" echoed in my thoughts, perfectly encapsulating this moment. It felt as though I was seeing her for the first time again, her elegance magnified by the stunning red dress that highlighted her glow. For once, she wasn't acting shy or coy. She stared right back at me with intense eyes and a flirty smile.

"Bonjour tout le monde! Welcome to Balthazar; Je m'appelle Andrew, and I'll be your serveur ce soir."

When our waiter, Andrew, brought iced water and menus, the tension finally broke as we gaped at the menus and laughed at the crazy prices. $28 for a salad? $18 for French bread?

"Oh, Ro, this is too much, I feel terrible you spending all this money on me."

"Don't. I've been planning this night for a long time. You're so good to me; I need to spoil you when I have the chance. You've kept me sane and safe, and I couldn't have done any of this without you."

Being underage, they didn't even bother showing us the wine list, so we toasted our ice waters and enjoyed seeing how the upper 1% lived.

Dinner was a good two hours long, as we both savored every bite of the steak au poivre, the roasted chicken, the mille-feuille, the vintage French atmosphere, and of course, each other. The staff treated us like important people, not kids, which was a welcome feeling. A little *s'il vous plait* did the trick and won over Andrew, our waiter.

I did not think about Stacey or Nick or my powers or anything aside from the woman sitting before me. Briefly, I thought of my dad and how much he had wanted to provide for my mom, my brother, and me when he was a young man. I felt like I was beginning to understand that awareness and was experiencing a surge of responsibility welling up from within me. I don't know if he and my mom ever went out anywhere fancy, but I made a vow to myself then and there that when he was healed and better, I'd insist they go somewhere like this, even if Henry and I had to pay for it ourselves.

Amayah guided me through the meal, sharing her knowledge of French cuisine, the style of the restaurant's art, and little customs that the wait staff performed that would have meant nothing to me otherwise. Seeing her enjoy herself and share her knowledge with me was delightful. I realized how in her element she was and wanted her to have the best of everything. I vividly remember Bobo's 1980 talk, a testament to personal growth and independence. He spoke of the powerful act of releasing someone to let them shine, paralleling this with the realization that a man reaches his fullest maturity not when he is loved by others but when he no longer needs another's love to illuminate his own path. That scared the hell out of me. Amayah in medical school, getting chatted up by every brilliant young male medical student for a few years? I would definitely lose her; it was just a matter of when. Even so, seeing her shining like this, basking in the glow of gourmet food, art, and culture, I knew that her dreams were more extensive than just being the NY Talon's girlfriend. If I truly loved her, I would help her figure out how to pursue those dreams.

After we indulged in a caramelized banana ricotta tart, which was a steal at just $37, we bid a cheerful *"bonne journée"* to the restaurant staff and ventured out into the sublime New York evening. The idea of heading home didn't appeal to either of us. She put on her jacket again, not so much for the chill but to shield herself from curious eyes, so I suggested we take a walk down to the World Trade Center to enjoy the view. My left hand was sweating as it clenched and unclenched around the small box inside my pocket. I had planned to give Amayah her gift at dinner, but doing it a thousand feet in the air seemed even better.

The South Tower Observation Deck, soaring 1,300 feet above the ground, was an intimate spot on Friday nights, surprisingly devoid of crowds. The elevator whisked us up to the 107th floor in about a minute and a half, a swift journey that left my ears popping. But any mild discomfort was swiftly forgotten as I stepped out to the sight of New York City sprawling majestically below. As I gazed upon her breathtaking skyline, my heart swelled with an all-too-familiar feeling of inspiration. New York, with her untamed beauty, once again whispered sweet nothings of dreams and possibilities into the eager ears of those who beheld her.

While the rest of the city was lost in the vibrant chaos of clubbing, bar hopping, or marveling at the lights of Times Square, we found our own secluded paradise. In a cozy corner, Amayah nestled into my lap, an oasis of calm in the heart of the city. Together, we gazed out the window, the world unfolding beneath us like a secret only we knew. As she tenderly brushed a stray hair from her face, the moment felt perfect. Seizing the opportunity, I carefully slid the box out of my pocket, heart pounding with anticipation.

"Amayah... I can't begin to tell you how special you are to me, so I wanted something to show you every day, even when we're not together. You are in my very heart and soul. You are in every breath I take, and in every smile that comes to my face. I love you so much. Happy anniversary."

I had worked on the speech a few weeks ago, and finding the right words took me a while.

Her eyes teared up slightly as she accepted the purple crushed velvet box from my hands, uttering the softest "ohhh" as she unfolded it open. She delicately extracted the heart-shaped ring and gracefully slid it onto her finger, where it nestled as if made just for her.

"Rohan Chang, I am utterly in love with you. How did I ever earn the affection of such an incredible man as you?"

She was fearless in her affection, while perched slightly taller on my lap, leaned down, her eyes locking with mine, and kissed me deeply, her lips parting in an intimate embrace that spoke volumes of our connection. As I returned her kiss with more depth than ever before, a surge of warmth engulfed me entirely. I enveloped her in my arms, pulling her closer, with a desire to never let go. This moment surpassed any experience I had ever had. The evening that had caused me months of worry and anticipation unfolded flawlessly.

"Well, isn't this just so fucking cute?"

Our kiss was abruptly interrupted by a familiar voice. Startled, we pulled apart, and I quickly turned my head towards the source of the sound.

Steven Stone stood ten feet away from us, wearing a long trench coat with his arms folded across his chest, his expression twisted into a cruel sneer.

"Steven!" Amayah said with a nervous laugh. "You scared us; we didn't realize anyone else was up here."

"Not surprising," he replied, that strange look still on his face. "You had your tongue halfway down Rohan's throat. Did you drop your watch down there or what?"

I didn't like the way he was talking, nor the way he was standing between us and the elevator that would take us back to the ground floor.

"Hey, Steven," I said, trying to play it cool. "How have you been?"

He acted like he was seeing me for the first time, tearing his head and gaze from Amayah to face me.

"Oh, just great, Rohan, keepin' it phat. Super cool of you to ask! I see you're having a phat time yourself. This guy I know, who I trained to fight, stopped talking to me altogether after I took him out *bombing* in Queens, and then his little girlfriend kicked me in the balls when I danced with her because her lame-dick boyfriend couldn't do it for her."

Steven then hurled the gold fat cap I had given him into the evening sky over the edge of the building, as if he were Paul O'Neill playing outfield for the Yankees and throwing a runner out at home plate..

I was really put off by his tone and erratic behavior, and I couldn't figure out where he was heading with all of this. He had known about my powers longer than anyone, so there was no way he was trying to provoke me into a fight.

"Yeah, sorry man, I've been really busy lately, and hey, Amayah didn't like how you were gripping on her, man, you gotta have more respect."

Steven stormed towards me and, without any preamble, delivered a stinging slap across my face. The force of it was astonishing.

"Why would you do that, Steven?" I screamed, my voice shaking as much as my head, still reeling from the impact of his palm.

His response was to laugh - a laugh so loud and unhinged it bordered on maniacal, as if teetering on the edge of sanity.

"Interesting choice of words, Rohan. Watch your tone. You're speaking out of turn, friend. Remember your place! And here's another thing, your boy, Stee-volt, was contemplating gripping on her again."

He shrugged off the trench coat, and what he revealed made no sense. It looked like he was wearing a pair of black shoulder pads. But as we watched, they unfolded, folded, then spread again. It should have been impossible, but my recent experiences had shown me that impossible was just a matter of perspective. Our school's blond Adonis stretched out a pair of black leathery wings that must have spanned fifteen feet from tip to tip. The tips had my attention, because they looked razor-sharp. In that decisive moment, the veil was lifted, and I realized who had truly imparted the wisdom for Steve to craft those extraordinary wings—it was not his sensei at the dojo. My mind raced back to that fateful night, a night when I delved deep into Steven's psyche, only to witness his shadowy figure vanishing into the consuming darkness, cloaked entirely in black. Was he going bombing, getting up in the city? Or going to visit someone else?

That someone else had harnessed his hatred and anger to transform him into a deadly weapon.

I didn't know what trouble Steven Stone had gotten himself into, but I needed to get Amayah away from him. However, he moved first and he moved fast, smashing his wing tips backward against the reinforced glass of the tower, shattering it into a million pieces. You don't think much about the wind when you're on the observation deck, but it was blowing fiercely thirteen hundred feet up. I grabbed

Amayah and held her close, but as I turned my head, Steven smashed one of his wings across my face and sent me reeling.

"Rohan!" Amayah screamed, pulling my attention sharply as I stumbled and fell. Panic set in, my breaths quick and shallow, as I struggled to grasp the reality of the moment. For the second time in a short period, I found myself facing an opponent whose speed matched mine, a concept that felt foreign despite my experiences. Historically, I had always taken comfort in being the fastest and strongest, a notion that had rooted in the eras of 1980 and 1854. But now, faced with Steven—his agility enhanced, mood unnervingly volatile, and armed with weaponized gear—it was clear he had fallen under the toxic influence of either Nick the Brute, Stacey, or potentially both.

I thought of Justice, sitting in the back of my closet, and what a difference it would make tonight. I knew that I would have a brutal fight on my hands that would be even more dangerous at this height, and the fact that Steven had once been my mentor. My immediate priority was to ensure Amayah's safety, to move her to an elevator and out of harm's way before the situation spiraled beyond control.

But once again, he was one step ahead. As I got up and started to move towards him, he used the wings to half-fly, half-leap in her direction.

I heard her cry out again as Steven grabbed her by the waist and jumped out the shattered window of the tower. "No!" I screamed, terror clutching my heart as they began to fall. But then he flexed his mighty wings, powering their ascent back up. I watched them rise back past the window and veer out of my view. As Steven laughed, Amayah screamed and hung on for dear life.

I was filled with fear at the idea of losing her, but I was even more angry about what he was doing. All the jealousy that had been building up inside me since the first time Steven talked to us outside of school was now surging through me like a volcano on the brink of eruption. I was determined not to let him take her, and I refused to let him win. Without pausing to consider the logistics, I focused on the ring on Ama's finger. I had carried it with me long enough to know every curve. I let its image fill my mind, then expanded my energy and teleported my body out of the tower and into the sky.

I blinked back into reality almost instantly, right behind Steven's outstretched wings, and I grabbed hold of one. It was greasy and hard to grasp, but I wasn't going to let him take her away. He grunted in surprise and began to lose altitude. Amayah screamed again as she started to lose her grip. I was distracted by her plight, and Steven used that distraction to knock me off his back and soar even higher. I plummeted, and panic threatened to grip me entirely, but I held fast to the image of Amayah's ring and teleported again, this time smashing right into Steven and trying to choke him until he released her.

He responded with a headbutt that dazed me, and I just barely held onto his chest. He spit in my face and screamed, "Stacey sends you his best, you pathetic little bitch!"

My blood boiled as we tumbled through the sky. So, Stacey was behind this. It made sense. The sudden increase in power, the animalistic transformation. God help me, would I have to fight two of them now? There was no time to consider that as he kicked me free again, and I fell past Amayah, trying to grab ahold of her, but failing miserably. It was freezing this high up, but I hardly noticed. I was completely locked in as I teleported a third time, coming back into existence behind him and putting him in a chokehold that I had no intention of releasing.

"Let her go, Steven! Don't be Stacey's slave! You don't have to do this!"

My words fell on deaf ears as he roared and tried again to shake me free, like a bucking bronco in a rodeo.

"I do this because I chose this, fool! I cherish the power, the domination, the control, you little bitch. You don't deserve your power! It's wasted on you! I'm willing to do whatever it takes! LIKE THIS!"

Without any warning, he dropped Amayah, who plummeted like

a stone. He wrapped his wings around me, preventing me from breaking free as we spiraled down together. He smashed me again with his forehead and I saw stars, but I was able to raise my hands and shove him away. Once free, I stared down at Amayah's tiny figure, horrifically free falling through the air, and I seized my energy again, teleporting below her position, trying desperately to think of a plan where I could catch her and blink us somewhere else to land. Out in the distance, I spied the Hudson. It was my only shot. If I could catch her and teleport again quickly, I could blink us out over the water. We'd hit hard, but it wouldn't kill us. I just had to stay conscious to teleport us one final time back to land. It was a gamble, but it was the only play I had.

I timed my next jump so that I'd appear just below her and be able to bear her weight without breaking my arms. I sent the surge of power out and appeared in precisely the right place. I caught her weight in my arms, which sent me plummeting out of control, the whirling wind whacking me in the face. She had lost consciousness during her nosedive, but I couldn't worry about that now. I shifted my focus to the river as something crashed into us from above. I looked up to see Steven grinning in delight as he wrenched her away from me just as I blinked out of thin air.

"NOOOOOOO!" I was so stunned by his appearance that I had lost all track of my plan and came crashing down hard into the Hudson. I must have sunk thirty feet before the water slowed my momentum. I was on the edge of blacking out when I finally broke the surface and filled my lungs with oxygen. The water was rough, choppy, and filthy, but I didn't even notice. My eyes were fixed on the receding dot in the night sky. My beloved Amayah, my Ama, kidnapped by Steven Stone, was being taken to Stacey and whatever grim horrors he'd planned.

THIRTY-SEVEN

I couldn't teleport again. I was too exhausted. When I tried, I nearly drowned. I was only about two hundred feet from the shoreline, but it took me more than an hour before I could touch the bottom of the river. I was at my lowest point, blind with rage, hating myself, hating Steven, hating everything my mind landed upon.

I could barely stand when I reached the shore and had to drag myself on all fours to a bench in Battery Park. I started praying angrily at God, at Hua, even at Nick the Brute to restore my power so that I could go after them, but nothing worked. No one answered. I turned my focus inward, determined to find the strength I needed to hunt them down, but my energy was gone. I knew it wouldn't work that way. I had never teleported so much in such a short time, and when you threw in the fight and the work I had been doing with my dad's cancer, I had nothing left. Even so, I tried again and again, until I blacked out on the park bench.

I snapped awake to the rising sun and because a bum was trying to get the wallet out of my pocket without waking me up. I jerked awake and fell backward off the bench, which sent him skittering back a few steps. It looked like he was deciding if he should try to attack me or run for it. I'm sure I looked like an easy mark—a kid, lanky and beat to shit, sleeping on a park bench. How much easier did it get? But when I opened my eyes, he saw something there that scared the life out of him; he screeched like an owl and ran for it.

I didn't know what to do next. I had no idea where Steven had taken Amayah, or if she was even still alive. I kept telling myself that if something happened to her, I would know, just as she knew that I was in danger during my fight with Stacey, but I couldn't be sure. Amayah and I were at the World Trade Center until almost midnight. Steven ambushed us shortly after we'd arrived, which meant that if the sun was coming up, it had already been five or six hours. I was terrified to imagine all that could have happened in that time. Amayah had been unconscious when I lost her to Steven, but my mind reeled with the possibilities, each more horrific than the last.

I didn't have enough of a recharge to teleport, but I knew how to use my deeper vision and didn't think it would take that much strength; I just needed a few seconds to have some idea of where she was.

Just as I had done earlier, I focused on the ring on her finger, then stretched out with my feelings to find its location. It was hard, and I began sweating after just a few seconds. Like the pinging reply of a radar, I felt its weight and texture and almost jumped to my feet.

It was close! She was close! She was... no. The ring was no longer on her finger. The ring was in the street where I had tried to save her and failed. It was chipped and damaged, either from falling from such a great height or from so many cars running over it, or both. It was a broken and battered thing now, the exact opposite of what it was meant to symbolize. I unconsciously released a sob from my throat before I realized.

Had I lost her forever? I needed a plan, and I needed help for it. Everything else seemed secondary, but I knew I couldn't overreact. I couldn't turn into a raving lunatic, claiming that my girlfriend had been stolen by a flying classmate working for the serial killer. I looked up at the World Trade Center, but it was too high up from down here to see the broken glass. They would probably just assume that high winds or a bird strike had caused the damage, since no one else was up there, at least not by the time they went to investigate. Someone might remember a beautiful girl in a red dress and a lanky Asian kid in a blue suit, but would they really think we shattered the windows of the viewing deck? Unlikely.

I started walking as quickly as I could. However, I needed food. I also needed to talk to someone, and figure out a plan. I had just enough money to ride the subway home. I figured I'd catch hell from my mom if I didn't come home on the night I took my girlfriend out for a big date, but no one was home. That's when I remembered that it had been a chemotherapy day for my dad at Mt. Sinai. I hadn't been there with my dad or my family, and I felt like shit. Of course, I had let everyone down yet again.

I got in the shower and tried washing off the stink of defeat. I wanted to find Amayah, but I didn't have the strength. I was also racing against time, afraid of what Steven, let alone Stacey, might be doing to my beloved Ama. Until I figured out who Stacey was, or where he was, I didn't have a chance in hell of finding my girl. The ring had failed, so I tried to focus on Ama herself, but she was either too far away, or I was too weak.

We kept a jar of quarters on the counter, so I dipped into it for a subway ride to Mt. Sinai. My dad was half-asleep when I showed up, my mom shot lasers at me, and my brother looked pretty pissed off as well. I knew how it looked... like I had stayed out all night with my girlfriend and then forgotten about my dad's treatment, which I had sworn to be there for. But how could I tell them that I had been fighting a demonized classmate in the sky above the World Trade Center? I sat quietly with them as they filled me in on his treatment. The doctors were quietly optimistic at what they had seen so far, and I nodded silently, though part of me wanted to take credit for his improvement, if only to eliminate my mother's glares. However, that would convince them I was either delusional or crazy, so I kept quiet until they both stood and left.

I placed my hand on my dad's forearm and reached out to the wickedly spreading cancer infecting his body. It was there, pushing up against the healthy cells, but it wasn't nearly as large as it had been a week ago. My efforts were working, slowly but surely. I reached into my energy source to give him another dose of healing, but I couldn't seem to focus my abilities. I tried a second time, and a third, but nothing happened. I was still too exhausted from the fight, and I was scared. My powers had stopped working at critical moments in the past, and big trouble had followed. With two madmen trying to kill me, and my father dying of cancer, I couldn't afford another extended power outage.

My mom asked if I wanted to get something to eat, but I couldn't think about food, not with Amayah missing and my failure to ease my dad's pain. I needed to find a place to sit and think. Everywhere seemed risky and exposed. I kept looking up, suspiciously scanning the sky, expecting Steven to come roaring down at me at any moment. He and Stacey had thus far only attacked me at night, but the daylight still didn't feel safe. The lack of sleep, my failure to defend Amayah, and the vacuum of my powers at the hospital weighed heavily on me. Twenty-four hours earlier, I had been over the moon, about to take my girl out for the most memorable night of our lives, fighting the fight to keep my dad from succumbing to lung cancer, and practicing with Justice, the weapon I had built to fight crime and defeat the horrors of this city.

F the Brute! I swore aloud.

Who was the Brute's sworn enemy? Who was so desperately trying to get me to be wary of the Brute and do God's will? In all my stress and fear and anger, I had completely lost sight of my conversations with Hua. I had to find peace and balance and harmony if I was going to make this right, find Amayah, and defeat my enemies. I needed somewhere to center myself because there were so many things going on around me; everywhere I glanced became a distraction. I was walking from the 179th Street subway station back to Fresh Meadows when an amazing sight filled my vision. I looked up to see if it was safe to cross the street and did a double take. Sitting right there was a small, nondenominational church off 188th and Hillside in Jamaica Estates. I felt like I hadn't really seen it before. No matter. If I was dealing with demons, there was nowhere safer or better than inside a church, where God's word was law.

I said a silent prayer of thanks when I found the door unlocked and slipped quietly inside. There were two or three people in the pews, but they were all senior citizens, so I breathed easy, took a seat in the back, opened a Bible, and bowed my head in prayer. I asked for guidance, forgiveness, for Amayah's safety and my dad's health. I had tried to pray more consistently but did so only during short stretches, and I felt guilty. I had a bad habit of only praying and thanking God when things were going well, or when I wanted something. I knew from my Bible studies that the true test of faith came when you lost everything—and kept saying thank you. I prayed for a long time, and when I raised my head, I felt better, although Hua hadn't appeared in my mind.

I decided to stay a while longer and read through the Bible, hoping to find something that would guide me in a direction to regain my focus and power. I had to calm down. Even if I knew where Amayah was, which I didn't, I had no way to get there. I had to believe they weren't going to just kill her. If anything, they would use her as bait for me or a bargaining chip to back off my hunt for Stacey. They wanted her alive, or else Steven would have just killed her right there in front of me. That didn't necessarily mean that time was a luxury I had, but it did mean that I could practice a sliver of self-care to prepare myself for the inevitable. I sank deep into myself and tried to find a place of calm. Somewhere beyond time and space, beyond my fears and my doubts, somewhere that I could be at peace and talk out my feelings, confident in my belief that a higher power was listening. Even if they didn't respond, I trusted that they would guide me towards the correct path.

After a few more moments, I had the feeling of being watched and glanced up quickly. It was neither Stacey nor Steven, but rather a short, fairly rotund, balding man in minister's garb. He held a Bible in his hands and was smiling warmly in my direction. He had a familiar sort of face, but since I had been to exactly two churches in my entire life, I doubted the recognition was authentic.

"Saw you come in," he said softly. "You look like a man seeking answers. Anything you want to talk about, son?"

Where to begin? Certainly not with the truth. That was too much for a stranger. So perhaps something a little more metaphorical.

"I feel torn in about twelve different directions," I said. "I failed my girlfriend, and now she's in terrible trouble. I failed my dad when he got sick, and now I don't know if he's going to live or die. I stopped talking to a friend of mine, and now he's turned into a, well, he's turned into someone really cruel. I can't find the right path, and I feel like everyone I love is suffering because I can't handle my business."

His gaze was sympathetic, though there was still a twinkle in his eyes. He nodded and said, "So life isn't treating you well, and you're worried that you're going to lose everything. Reminds me of the Book of Job."

He nodded towards the clock. "We have a service beginning in a bit, but I'd like to talk to you more. Why don't you come back to my office, and we'll have some tea and chat?"

I had wanted someone to talk to, and suddenly here was someone willing to listen. He had an easy way of talking, which gave me hope that if I could phrase my problems in a decent enough way, he might be able to help me come up with a solution, or at least allow me to talk it out to the point where something might reveal itself.

I nodded, and he beckoned me silently. His office was in the back of the church with a small window that looked out just below street level. All you could see were people's feet and the wheels of cars and buses. It was peaceful, though, like a tiny safe space away from the hustle and bustle of the city's madness. The minister pulled a wooden chair out from a table and gestured towards it as he sat behind his desk. He took his phone off the hook, holding steady with my eye line and waiting.

I didn't know where to start, so I initially just stared back, hoping he would kick off the conversation with some sort of sage advice. When he said nothing, I felt a little flustered.

"Um, you mentioned the Book of Job out there?"

He stopped peering in silence and nodded. "I did, yes. The Book of Job starts with a conversation between God and Satan, something most people don't imagine happening—sworn enemies and all that —although if you read your scripture, you'll find that they actually had quite a few discussions about philosophy and humanity. Satan always thinks he has an argument that will defeat God's power, and when he finds that it can't, that's when he starts with the temptations and the seduction. It's a brutal cycle.

"Anyway, Job was a man who was quite well off. He had a nice house, a nice family, was pretty well off, and didn't have to toil in the fields or anything like that. And he's righteous on top of all that, knows his scripture, believes in God... everything you'd want in a Christian. Up in Heaven, God asks Satan what he thinks of Job, and Satan responds that Job is only pious because God has blessed him with so much. Take away everything he owned, Satan argued, and Job would renounce God, even curse his name. Have you ever seen 'Trading Places' with Eddie Murphy and Dan Ackroyd? It's the same concept.

"So, God wants to prove Satan wrong because, despite all the horrors that Satan is responsible for, God still wants to believe that Satan can change, if God can just show him the way. So, he gives Satan permission to take away Job's wealth, turn him out of his house, and even kill his servants and his children, whom God takes right up to Heaven. And what happens? Job blesses the Name of the Lord and says, 'I came naked into this world with nothing, and naked I shall return,' meaning that all those possessions and relationships were temporary anyway. He knew that he would lose them at some point. Satan can't believe it, so he says that he wants another shot. God grants it to him, and Satan covers Job's body with boils from head to toe and burns his house to the ground. His wife gives in and curses God, but not Job. He holds firm in his faith. He wants to die to end the pain, and begins questioning why God is letting this happen, and why God is seemingly allowing the evil people of the world to prey on the weak, but he still never curses God. Later, God speaks to him from the middle of a whirlwind and asks, 'Where were you when I laid the foundations of the earth?'

"At that moment, Job realizes that God's power is total and that everything happens for a reason. At last, he apologizes and doesn't mean to question God and repents. God blesses him over and over, restoring everything to him and granting him an extra-long life. He lives to see his great-great-great grandchildren before ascending to Heaven."

The minister looked at me, nodding slowly, as though to encourage my agreement. "Job learns that sometimes we will not understand why God is allowing things to happen, until you realize that God's will is what must happen, and that he won't test you with anything more than he knows you can handle."

I was quiet. Could Stacey and Steven and all of this be a form of God testing me? Seeing if I will submit to His teaching and Hua's guidance, and reject my own ideas of what should happen? Is this a ploy to throw off Nick the Brute once and for all? Wasn't using my powers to do good enough for them?

"I don't know if what's happening is God's will or something more," I finally offered, choosing my words carefully. "I feel like I have the power to fix all the problems in my life, but things keep happening that I'm not ready for. I feel like I'm being spread too thin, and I can't be everywhere at once to help everyone I love."

The minister cocked his head a bit, as if seeing me with new eyes. "You know, when I was your age, back in the 1980s, a friend told me to be like water. He said to be like water and take the shape of whatever stands in front of me. He urged me to be formless, shapeless. He said that if water spreads too thin, it loses its power."

He gave a small smile as I stared intently back at him. Those words... I had said them almost verbatim to the guy the kids called Bobo back in 1980. The minister stared at me until I returned his gaze.

"Funny thing is, my friend was a tall Asian guy too," he said. "Went by the name of Rohan. But you couldn't be him, because he was about seventeen years old back in 1980, and you look to be about the same age right now in 1997."

I blinked at him again. "Bobo?"

He smiled broadly, his face lighting up in a wide grin. "I'm impressed, Rohan. I've gotten a bit older since then, something to which you are apparently immune."

I couldn't believe it! Other than having less hair up top and a bit more of a waistline, he had changed surprisingly little. He was still wearing the comb-over hairstyle and had that same sparkle in his eyes.

"I can't believe that we ran into each other! It's such a small world. Did you know I was going to be here?" I questioned.

He smiled and came to sit beside me.

"The Lord works in mysterious ways, my old friend. I didn't know it would be you, but I had a feeling that being here today would be worth it. Are you still with Amayah?"

A shadow crossed my face.

"I am, but she's missing. I fought... I fought. You're not going to believe me—"

He put a hand on my shoulder.

"I won't believe something told to me by the teenager I knew in 1980 who vanished into thin air one day, and has now reappeared seventeen years later, looking exactly the same?"

"Still, it's a lot to explain. I don't even know where to start."

"Okay, let's start with why you won't embrace your full blessings as a ninja of the Shine Xiong."

My jaw dropped, certain that I had misheard, but when I asked him to repeat himself, he just stared at me, a small smirk on his lips.

"You know?" I questioned.

"Of course, Rohan. Didn't it seem strange that I appeared out of nowhere to work at the same shelter as you just a few days after you arrived, when the director had told you they hadn't had volunteers in weeks? You think I kept hanging around you by accident, when the very lovely Brittney was right down the hall, lonely in the big city? I came to keep an eye on you and make sure you didn't lose your way. Unfortunately, you seem to have lost it now."

"You mean, you're—?" I gestured aimlessly with my hands.

"Yes, my friend, I'm a ninja of the Shine. I'm actually a bit older than I appear, but I still age slowly enough to pass for normal. However, I must say, for all the powers I've been able to manifest over the years, time travel has never been on the table."

"Really?" I wondered aloud. "What else can you do?"

"Oh, nothing special," he said with a mischievous grin, raising his hand and reaching out towards something behind me. A scraping noise drew my attention, and I turned my head in time to see a pitcher and two cups float effortlessly through the air and settle on the desk.

Despite my exhaustion, I jumped out of my seat. "Jesus Christ!" I shouted, then realized where I was and who I was talking to. I sat back down hard, embarrassed by my own outburst.

"I think his powers were more about bringing people back from the dead and walking on water," Bobo said with a chuckle. "Telekinesis is quite common among the Shine, but still not something you go showing off for an audience."

He smiled wistfully. "Although I've been tempted plenty of times to use my powers to give a doubting congregation a good old-fashioned miracle or two, that's not the way. Jesus is pretty specific about what he wants from his shepherds. I can lead the flock to the meadow, but they have to decide on their own if they want to graze on the good stuff."

He turned his attention back to me, and his tone hardened.

"Sounds like you've been having that problem yourself, brother. All of these powers, all of these connections with Hua, all of these miracles... and you're still on the fence about their source?"

My face fell at that bold truth. I didn't bother asking how he knew. Clearly, a real Shine Xiong had mental powers beyond whatever I was pretending to do.

"I just wanted more proof," I mumbled.

"Proof!" he barked, giving me a start. "You can travel instantly from one place to another, jump over trees, run faster than any man alive, and travel through time. Did you think all of that was just puberty on steroids?

"Did you think that taking all those Flintstone vitamins had finally paid off? Make time for the important things, Rohan. The answers await you, but your faith wavers like the sea waves on a stormy night. Take time to have faith and practice communing with Hua and praying to God. They both want an unwavering relationship with you but can only meet you halfway. You have to walk the rest of the path yourself."

I knew he was right. Even my half-assed attempt to do research at the library had been a workaround to actually sitting down and seeking the answers within myself.

"Why did the Shine pick me?" I asked, desperate to finally get an answer to that core question.

"Because of your heart, Rohan. You have a heart that perseveres and illuminates, even if you can't see it in yourself. Once you come to realize that, you'll be unstoppable. Combined with that mind of yours, the forces of evil should tremble at your approach."

My heart? Without even thinking about it, I put a hand on my chest, as if to ensure it was still there. I could feel it beating strongly. A reminder that I was still alive. Despite the best efforts of Stacey and Steven, I was still here and still fighting.

I tried to fill Bobo in on all my troubles with the duo the best I could. "I'm scared to fight Steven and Stacey again," I admitted to my old friend. "I'm scared that they'll kill me. I'm scared of what they might already have done to Amayah, or what they'll do to my family. I'm not a killer like them. I don't think I can do that."

"Evil is something to fear, Rohan," Bobo said. "If you don't fear evil, you're lying to yourself. Evil comes in many forms and many disguises. That said, the devil was once God's child. Fortunately, you never have to fight it alone, no matter how you might feel. If you ask for help, it will always find you."

I didn't say anything. Even in the presence of a good friend, I doubted the truth of his words. I doubted my abilities because I had failed so utterly... twice. I would have died in that dumpster had it not been for Amayah's mystical sense and her cousin's knowledge of the city. If I had fought Steven just a few blocks further from the water, I would have probably died right there on the concrete below the World Trade Center.

Bobo saw me hesitate. He tapped his own heart, cleared his throat, and said, "Ro, listen, you have a choice. God created us with free will, and that was intentional. We are not robots or beasts. We can choose how we feel and who we want to be. We can choose to be good or do evil. We can fight the good fight or give up. Work hard every day or be lazy. We can become doctors, lawyers, CEOs, and even the president, teachers, writers, police officers, firefighters, or dry cleaner clerks; that's up to us. We can also be crooks or street dealers, but that choice is for each of us to make. An honest cashier who gives it all at work to help coworkers and does good in the world is undoubtedly worthier than a cash-rich street dealer, a dishonest priest, or an affluent, unscrupulous scammer preying on the naive. Don't you agree?"

I nodded in agreement. It was an old Shakespearean aphorism come true again: All that glitters is not gold.

"Rohan, do you know why I love America so much? In today's America, regardless of where we're born or what class we're born into, we can become who we set out to be, whether good or bad.

Ultimately, our responsibility is to determine our destiny and who we become."

I nodded my head, allowing Bobo's words to sink in.

"At some point, every person will have to make a choice," he said. "Will you stand, or will you stand aside? For the Shine Xiong, that choice comes again and again, and we either answer the call or we watch as evil reigns. When you do nothing, they win. They win automatically, without even a word spoken or a shot fired. Yes, your friends and family are in danger because of who you are, but who you are is also what gives you the strength to save them. You've already been tested across time and space, and despite some of your more unorthodox choices, you've survived and done right by those under your protection. This is your next test, but definitely not your last. Satan takes on many forms and faces, and he will continue to show them so long as there is someone in the world willing to heed his call."

He patted the Bible on his desk. "Every answer is in here if you're willing to look for it, but sometimes we must move beyond its teachings and become something even greater than the stories of the past. God gifted us the ability to reason, think through, and interpret His Word for ourselves. You must add to it. You must add to the story of the Shine; add to the way of the light and the word of God. The prayers in the good book are powerful, but as you move forward into battle, I think God wants to do something new within you."

I agreed as I was willing to try anything at that point. He took my hand in his and bowed his head. I followed suit, and he squeezed my hand in reassurance. After all this time, catching up with Bobo was still blowing my mind. All those nights, we had stayed up late, talking about sports and life and girls, and the whole time he had been a Shine ninja watching over me. Unbelievable, I thought, as I pulled out the pocket-sized Bible Ama gave me to increase my faith. Unbelievable, but also pretty strong proof that God was actively working in my life. And for a moment, albeit a fleeting one, I felt a bit better.

He patted my shoulder again. "This isn't goodbye, but it is good luck. Stop worrying about the devils at play and become who you were meant to be."

Bobo took a deep breath, and the prayer came roaring out of him.

"I CAN CHOOSE WHO I AM. I CAN CHOOSE WHAT I DO. GOD, BE MY GUIDE. SHINE YOUR COURAGE IN THE FACE OF FEAR! BE MY LIGHT IN THE DARKNESS! GRANT ME THE STRENGTH OF A NINJA WHEN I AM WEAK. LET ME SHINE. I WILL SHINE!"

I listened to him speak once, but as he repeated the prayer, I began picking up the words and echoing them. Thankfully, the organ was already playing loudly in the church, considering that we were roaring in chorus together by the sixth or seventh time, awash in the light of God.

CHAPTER

THIRTY-EIGHT

I left the church with a jubilant spring in my step, convinced that the power of God was within me and that I would soon be reunited with Amayah. When I got home, my mom was just leaving for the dry cleaners, as my brother headed to the drug store. I hadn't heard or seen anything about the World Trade Center on the news as my mom left the TV on, which was a stroke of luck. I didn't need anyone blaming the Black Blur for busting up one of the city's best landmarks. I had a bit of my faith renewed, but my gut was still a twisted mess at the thought of Amayah being held somewhere by Steven and Stacey.

I got in the shower, trying not to think about the day before, when I had gotten cleaned up in the same place before picking up Amayah for dinner. I couldn't let fear grip me now. Everything at home was so familiar and calm. It was as though nothing was wrong, but everything was, as I knew they were out there with my girl, and I was presently powerless to stop them. As the water tumbled over me, I closed my eyes and leaned against the slick walls. I thought I might collapse as the stress of the situation seemed to drain from my head down through my stomach and into my feet. It was a crushing sensation, like I was drowning from the sheer weight of it all. I felt utterly helpless, like I was being held down by an unstoppable force. The soap dropped from my hands, and I sank to my knees. As I did, I heard a voice from across a great distance, and my vision wavered:

She was crying, and obviously fatigued. The red dress she had picked out just for me was dirty and wrinkled. She was standing, and her legs were shaking from the strain and panic. Despite all the pain and fear, her mind was sharp; I could sense it somehow. She was listening to voices arguing nearby.

"You should let me finish him! He's weak. He's beaten!"

"HE'S MINE! MINE ALONE!"

"I should just kill her then! It'll be the perfect gift for him to find."

Amayah's eyes opened, and I saw a warped view of the room. It was somewhere industrial. Her wrists were cuffed, and the chain ran up over a pipe above her head.

She couldn't sit down. There wasn't enough slack, so she was forced to stand, which accounted for the tremble in her legs. She was fighting exhaustion, trying to find a spot to lean against to support her weight, even for a moment or two, but she was struggling and worn out.

I followed her gaze, where Steven Stone stood toe to toe with the human form of Stacey. Steven's wings had folded back up, giving him the appearance of a wayward football player wearing shoulder pads. Stacey looked mostly human, but a pulsing red glow could still be seen through the side of his face.

Stacey looked almost feeble next to the impressively built Steven, but I knew the kind of animal that lay beneath the surface of his non-threatening ordinary man visage. I had imagined Stacey recruiting Steven somewhere along the way, but now I wasn't so sure. They seemed to have two different ideas about what should come next, and neither was willing to back down.

"If it wasn't for me, you wouldn't even know who the hell he is!" Steven argued angrily. "He got the drop on you in Times Square, and you damn

near pissed yourself until I gave you the 4-1-1. You botched it again at the Sanitation Department. I took his girl and put him in the river. He's as weak as he'll ever be. I can destroy him!"

Stacey responded by cuffing Steven across the face and knocking him to the ground. Steven was up in a flash, fists clenched, ready to fight back, but Stacey opened his mouth and a low growl emerged like the roar of a big cat watching another animal approaching its kill. Steven hesitated and lowered his fists.

"Know your place, boy," Stacey warned in that same low voice. "I've unlocked powers that will haunt you until your dying day. I've been cleansing this filthy city since you were still in diapers, swaddling at your whore of a mama's tit. Don't presume to tell me my business. I report directly to him, and you report directly to me. That's the order of things. Try me again, and I'll bury you next to Chang and piss on both your graves."

Steven's jaw tightened, and I could feel the hate emanating off him in waves. He wanted to attack Stacey, even if it meant getting beaten. He wanted to test his strength, power against power, to see how he measured up. However, he knew that he'd get beaten and possibly killed, and he wasn't so tired of life that he wanted to quit it altogether. He jerked his head in sullen agreement and stayed silent.

Stacey smirked to cement his superiority. "Clever boy, I was worried you had forgotten your manners. I'm going hunting; I've gone far too long without a treat. You stay here. If you see anything suspicious, raise a signal in the sky." Without warning, Stacey leapt twenty feet in the air, over Steven, to land in front of Amayah. He cocked his arm and released it—a deafening THWACK to Ama's temple, partially knocking her out.

Steven nodded his understanding and watched Stacey pull a nondescript bag over his shoulder and check his watch.

"What the hell am I supposed to do until you get back?" Steven called after his departing master.

Stacey looked back over his shoulder and grinned. "Enjoy your little plaything. Let Chang taste her fear."

A lecherous grin spread across Steven's face as he turned back to

Amayah, waiting until Stacey was out of sight before walking towards her, licking his lips. The wing-shouldered Steven waited for her to fully wake up, tracing her body with his fingers and giggling lasciviously. He roughly slapped her across the cheeks a few times to hasten the process.

I saw through Ama's eyes as her vision came in and out of focus. I felt every pulse of her throbbing headache. Ama was dizzy and trying not to puke, trembling as he towered over her.

"Please Steven, let me go. He's... he's a monster and a murderer. You're not that kind of person. I know you aren't," she said, her voice wavering.

"You don't know the first thing about me, little Amayah," Steven replied in a falsely soothing voice. "Except how I felt behind you on the dance floor. I know you liked it too, at least until you realized your little boyfriend was watching and got all upset. But he's not here now, is he? No one is here to stop us from having a little fun."

He undid her bindings, and she collapsed to the ground before him with a clang. She grasped her hands in pain from their bindings and clutched her knees, pulling herself into a ball, as if trying to disappear from his sight altogether. He stared down at her and chuckled again.

"I could get used to this view," he said. "You on your knees looking up at me. Feels like it should be this way all the time."

When she didn't respond, he pulled her hair back, and she gasped as she was forced to look up at him. "You gotten on your knees for Rohan yet? No, no way you have... he might be racing around stopping shoplifters, but I know he hasn't found the guts to treat you like a real man."

"Rohan Chang is worth a hundred of you!" she fired back. "A thousand of you! You're jealous of all that he is! You've let these powers corrupt you and pervert you into some sort of foul beast! He uses his powers to heal the sick and protect the innocent, but you're a joke!"

He raged at the comment, but stopped short of striking her.

"A joke, huh? What's a joke is that little hole your parents call home. Or Chang's shit stain apartment in Fresh Meadows. Oh, yeah, I know all about them, you little bitch. I know just where to find your parents if I ever need them. And if superstar Black Blur Rohan can't fight me off, how do you think your old-ass parents would fare? How long do you think they'd

last, Amayah? Against my wings? Thirty seconds? A minute? Tell you what... while you lay here crying, I'll go pay them a visit. I'll tell them how you signed their death warrant with your smart fucking mouth."

He cocked his neck to one side as the wings began to unfold from his shirt again.

"Stop!" Amayah begged, sobbing louder. "Please, don't! Leave them alone! They don't have anything to do with this! Please, tell me what you want, and I'll do it!"

He turned around slowly, a sick grin spreading on his face. He clearly had no intention of defying Stacey, but there was no way Amayah could know that, particularly in her condition. She looked like she hadn't eaten or slept since the World Trade Center. She was cornered and alone, doing what she thought was necessary to protect the people she loved.

Steven took his jacket and shirt off, his muscles bulging at the bicep and pecs. His stomach was a jagged washboard. He would look like a supermodel if not for the grotesque fusion of bone and flesh where the wings bulged out from his shoulder blades. He moved to a pile of metal that looked like someone had fused it into the shape of a chair with a blowtorch. He sat down and leaned back with his legs spread wide, staring at Amayah, who stayed hunched and shivering on the ground.

"Get your ass up!" he barked. "Let me see you dance. Your bitch boy interrupted my last dance with you. I want to see the whole thing this time."

She stood up shakily and shifted her weight back and forth. There was no music, and she was on the edge of exhaustion, so it looked more like staggering than dancing. She slipped on a wet spot on the metal platform, nearly collapsing again.

"Damnit, do you want them to die? Do better!" he yelled.

"I'm sorry... I'm so tired," she said, slurring her words. "Please, just let me rest for a minute. I can't stand up."

He looked ready to explode, but then he smiled. "Okay, Amayah, you don't have to stand. Come sit down right here." He patted his leg. "A lap dance is even better."

She saw the trap she had set and sprung for herself, but there was nothing she could do now. She walked over slowly and sat on his knee, trying to keep her distance. He was having none of that. He grabbed her hips and pulled her fully back on top of him. The snug red fabric stretched over her body, clinging tight to her curves. Steven ran his hands up and down her hips and grinned. "Now that's more like it."

He stretched out one hand, and an object flew out of a bag that landed 30 feet away. It was a miniature stereo with headphones, which he turned on with his mind, tapping the buttons to find the track he wanted—"Put Your Hands Where My Eyes Could See" by Busta Rhymes. A drumbeat began vibrating and got increasingly louder. The telekinetic powers of the Shine was obviously shared by disciples of Nick the Brute as well. She was still exhausted, but trying to do what he wanted, fearful of him taking to the skies and heading toward her home, as Busta Rhymes rapped about watching his shorty being a little cutie.

Steven gripped her hips hard and made her move against him, a grim parody of how she had danced on me when she was trying to get the engagement date secret out of me weeks earlier. She looked like she might pass out at any moment. Her eyes were closing, and she couldn't help from leaning back on his shoulder.

He was getting pissed off again, and he grabbed her throat. "Wake the fuck up! I'm not your nap mat, girl."

She apologized over and over again, but that wasn't helping.

"Shut up already... let me give you a little taste of my power and then you can thank me," he said.

He put his hand on her cheek and concentrated, muttering under his breath. His hand glowed bright red, and his sinister energy flowed into Amayah. She gasped and sat upright, her eyes opening wide as the color came back into her face. She looked down in amazement.

"Thank... thank you, Steven, I feel so much better already... can I have a little more?"

He grinned up at her. "Show me some gratitude first."

She hesitated, but not for long. Amayah started to move her hips to the song, slowly at first, but then a little faster, as Busta Rhymes carried on about his shorty shaking her butt, how he was going to get in her booty, about sleeping with mistresses, and bangin' bitches.

Steven grinned as he watched her working her body. She was already tiring out again. Whatever he had transferred to her, it was short-lived.

Her eyes started to droop, and she whispered, "Please, Steven, please..."

He grinned and touched her face again, and the energy coursed between them. It was a longer transfer this time, and her face came alive with color, and she even smiled. It was not the beautiful one I knew so well, but a smile full of craving, almost like an addict after a long-awaited hit.

When the song picked up about being with his freak, like they were in freak shows, Steven gave her just enough energy to get her craving more, only to let her wear down, causing her to beg yet again. It was the opposite of the healing I provided, which filled someone with hope and light. His healing was poison, hooking a person on the poison without them even realizing it. The more he gave her, the more she wanted, and she started to move her hips faster, putting her hands on his chest, squeezing his muscles and smiling down at him with a twisted version of the sexy smile she gave me when we were close.

The next time she asked for more, instead of making her say that she wanted it, he asked her if she wanted him, and she swore that she did. He pointed at his chest and said, "Kiss me there," and she leaned down and started kissing his muscles, like he was Fabio on the cover of a romance novel, and she was the enamored heroine of the book. He leaned back and grinned, then opened his eyes and stared straight ahead.

With a start, I realized that he was staring right at me. He could see me.

"Told you, Rohan," he said, his voice echoing in my mind. "I can have her anytime I want."

I GASPED ALOUD and awoke to find myself face down in a shower rapidly filling with water. I let my guard down, and Steven had done something, pushed through my defenses, and filled my head with a different kind of poison. Was it a vision? Was it really happening? I didn't know, but whatever happened had trapped me inside my head, and my body nearly died as a result. My throat and mouth were filled with water, and I vomited, water pouring out of me, just to draw a breath. I fell to the bathroom floor, retching and gasping for air. I didn't want to believe what I had seen, but I rolled back the memory anyway, trying to piece together the surroundings and figure out where the hell they might be. I couldn't stay in the apartment. I needed to get out and move around.

I changed clothes, retrieving Justice from the dark recesses of my closet. I stashed it in my backpack, which just looked like I was carrying some sort of sporting equipment. That would protect me from any questions from the wrong sort of people.

I had to stop panicking and develop a plan, so I headed for Steven Stone's apartment. I hadn't gone there since probing his mind, but I knew the way. His family name was no longer listed on the call box, so I faked a food delivery to enter the building. With my staff at the ready, I kicked in the door to his apartment, but was greeted by an empty room. In fact, the entire apartment was empty, as though it hadn't been lived in for years. Knocking on some of his neighbor's doors, I questioned a few people, but none I encountered had any recollection of a family named Stone ever living there.

I went back home to call Mt. Sinai and see how my dad was doing, but the answering machine was beeping madly when I got inside. There were a dozen messages waiting.

I stabbed the button to play them, but I only needed to hear the first one.

"ROHAN! Rohan, pick up! It's Martin, man! We figured it out! We found the guy! His name is Stacey Keats! Call me back!"

I punched in his number, and Martin picked up on the first ring.

"Rohan! We got him! We got the guy, man!"

I asked him to slow down and tell me everything.

"So LeeRoy has a buddy downtown at the Ritz, right? He's a bellhop. We were picking up trash there yesterday, and the bellhop starts griping about this guy that stiffed him on a tip, all because he had assumed the guy was a woman. The homeboy's first name is Stacey, amigo! He had been looking around for a woman to take her bags to the car, but it was this older white dude with a mustache and a nose the size of the Statue of Liberty. LeeRoy convinced the bellhop to have the front desk lady pull his credit card bill, and she found out his name is Stacey Keats. He lives in Wilmington, Delaware. We got the son of a bitch, Rohan, you hear me!?"

I thanked him breathlessly and promised that I would come to a party at his apartment after I had defeated Keats. Stacey Keats, you son of a bitch! I had his full name, address, and phone number, but I didn't have him, and that's the only thing that mattered. It was time to change that. After arriving at Martin's place, I asked to borrow the phone in his bedroom, and he kicked everyone out of the apartment to give me some privacy.

I dialed the number on the piece of paper, and the line rang twice before a woman picked up.

"Hello?"

"Hi, Mrs. Keats? Sorry to call you on a Saturday, but my name is Anthony Chung, and I work for the New York City Police Department."

"Police department? Is something wrong?"

"Not at all, ma'am. We had a good Samaritan turn in your husband's wallet that was apparently found here at some point in the last week. It says you guys live in Delaware, so I'm not sure if you want us to try and mail it back to you? Or does your husband frequent the city? If you let us know where he works, we could send a squad car to give it back to him."

"Oh, that's so thoughtful!" she said cheerfully. "Yes, as a matter of fact, Stacey goes to New York two or three times a month for a visit, and he's there right now! He works for Franklin Engineering out on Staten Island. Here's their number."

I didn't need the number, but I let her rattle it off. I had everything I needed from his unsuspecting wife. I hung up the phone and returned to the living room, where Martin was waiting on the edge of the couch. I told him I had to get to Staten Island as quickly as possible, so he led me to a nearby parking garage and drove me down to the ferry station. I boarded the massive orange ferry and impatiently stood at the stern, watching Lady Liberty pass by in the distance. As we hit the dock, I stood up on the railing of the ferry and pushed my energy out in all directions.

STACEY KEATS! STACEY KEATS! STACEY KEATS!

I was surrounded by silence, but in the mental landscape of our mirrored powers, my voice echoed off every corner of Staten Island. It only took a few seconds for me to sense his presence before he covered it up, but those few seconds were all I needed. I held that fixed point in my head and started moving swiftly towards its origin. The area became even more industrial, without a single person in sight. It was obvious that Keats and Steven had picked this place because they knew no one would accidentally stumble upon them. I tried to see as far as I could into the distance, which is when I finally figured out where I was headed. Keats was holding Ama in a graveyard, but not the traditional type.

There on the horizon was one of New York City's most prominent eyesores, the Staten Island boat graveyard, a marine scrapyard of old wrecks and decommissioned ferries that went by the street name of the Arthur Kill Boat Yard. It was a maze of scrapped metal and rickety ships that could seemingly collapse at any time. Every year, some politician would make a big deal about how environmentally unsafe it was and how they were going to clean it up, before realizing that nobody gave a shit. It was a place to dump unwanted stuff, and there were all kinds of urban legends about what you could find there—scrap from World War II, giant alligators, Jimmy Hoffa's body... However, I didn't really care how big or complex it was. My girl was there, and it was time to be the hero.

The sun was sinking fast and the lights in the shipyard were few and far between, just enough coverage so you could head towards one if you had the misfortune to be out here after dark. I crept swiftly but cautiously from one hulk to the next. They creaked and moaned in the lapping water, sounding almost human. I could see why a psycho like Stacey would choose a place like this to toy with his victims; it was cold and cruel, alien and merciless. Even if you got free from him somehow, where would you go? Jump in the water and try to swim back to civilization? Screaming wouldn't work, and even if you snuck away, where would you run? There was no one here to save you. I knew I was getting close because Stacey's lighter started heating up in my pocket.

I had just leapt off the deck of a rotting oil tanker when I heard a whimper in the distance. My heart began pounding in my chest as I took several long strides forward, and there she was, my Ama! She was still in the red dress from dinner, although it was tattered by now; you could see her ribs through one gaping hole and the side of her hip in another. I flashed back to the vision I had of her dancing on Steven's lap. I didn't want to think about what those holes in her dress might mean, but she was alive, which meant that hope wasn't lost.

Fearing another trap, I circled around behind her, hoping to take Keats by surprise. I was as quiet as possible, gripping my staff with both hands, ready to use it in whatever form made the most sense. I stealthily scaled a conning tower on a research vessel that overlooked the open space where Amayah was standing. She looked unnatural, and as I drew closer, I could see why. She was restrained, with manacles around her wrists, which were attached to a long chain wrapped multiple times through a ship's lattice structure. I didn't care; I could snap those bars as easily as ripping a piece of paper if it meant getting her out. After cautiously scanning the area again, I jumped down right in front of Amayah. She was blindfolded and gagged, but she heard the noise, and I could see her wince in anticipation. There were bruises dotting her face, and I had to quell my rage at the thought of those monsters hurting her.

"Amayah!" I whispered.

She heard my voice, then snapped to attention and awareness.

"I'm here to rescue you, just hang on!" I reassured.

I sensed the blow coming more than I heard it. My senses were tuned up after our last encounter, and I spun around at the last moment, ducking as Stacey Keats tried to take my head off with one of the largest weapons I'd ever seen. I did a sideways flip out of the way and spun to face him, my staff held firmly in both arms. He was back in human form and holding a giant ball and chain, something I remembered from history class as a medieval morning star.

"I knew you'd come, little boy!" he raged between clenched fangs. "Now I can kill you while she watches, then taste her flesh as your body rots at my feet! Oh lordy, what fun! *The exhilaraaa-tion. Hee-hee-hee ...*" He punctuated this by ripping Amayah's blindfold off with a flick of his fingers and thoughts, yelping with laughter and snarling from ear to ear.

Her face uncovered; I saw that Ama had a black eye and was shaking with fear and crying.

Keats came at me again and the mighty spiked ball met my staff and bounced off. He tried the same move, and I blocked it again, feeling confident in my defense.

"Been training in your little Shine temple, boy? It won't save you. I've been practicing for decades. How long has it been for you... a couple weeks, little knight?"

He wasn't wrong, but I couldn't let him see me falter. I pulled the staff apart into the two swords and rushed him. *Say hello to my little friends!* His eyes widened when he saw one weapon become two, and I drove him back several steps, not giving him the chance to raise the morning star to attack. I spun my blades again and again, putting him on the defensive, as he seemed unprepared for the diversity and ferocity of my attacks.

He stumbled on a loose pipe and dropped to one knee, and as I stood over him, Nick the Brute raged at me out of nowhere, *"KILL HIM! MAKE HIM SUFFER!"*

I hesitated. I didn't want to become a murderer, even if the person I was killing was a murderous monster himself. My hesitation was a mistake, as Stacey came sweeping around with a kick that knocked me off my feet. He was up lightning quick, and the morning star impaled into my chest, knocking the air from my lungs and making me cough up blood. I scuttled back from him on all fours, but he caught me in the kneecap with the massive weapon, and again in the back of the ankle as I turned to flee. I fell flat forward, and he rose to his feet, laughing at my pathetic escape attempt. However, from that angle, he couldn't see my hands, so I caught him by surprise when I stood up with the swords connected as one long pike, swiping out and gouging his left calf with one of the blades. He roared, hollering in rage or pain or a bit of both then stepped back out of my weapon's reach. For the first time since the night I'd spooked him away from the blonde girl near Times Square, I had him scared. The emotion rolled off him in waves. His fear was clearly a huge weakness. He was so used to being the one in control that when the tables turned, even for a few seconds, he couldn't contain his emotions. I came after him as he gave ground, thrusting my staff forwards towards his heaving chest.

He caught the wooden handle in his hand and held it fast, then reversed its course back at me, plunging the other razor-sharp edge through my upper arm. I dropped the weapon in pain, and tried to scamper back towards Amayah, determined to grab her and teleport to safety, but when I turned around, she wasn't there. In her place was a hazy sort of smoke that faded in and out of existence even as I watched it. What had he done with her? Where had she gone?

"Amayah!" I screamed, but there was no response. I frantically looked left and right, but was driven forward as Keats blasted me once more in the back with the morning star. I fell to my knees and couldn't prevent the weapon from cracking into my ribs again, breaking two or three. I was on my hands and knees now, trying to stay out of his long reach, but he leaped forward and stepped on the back of my leg, pinning me down and kneeing my spine.

I collapsed, and he kicked me over onto my back with a toe under my ribs. "Poor little Rohan," he taunted. "Wanted to be a man, but still just a little boy. Where'd you send the girl? It doesn't really matter. I will find her and enjoy that sweetness. When they die, they're silent forever, and at their very sweetest. And your pathetic skills are feeble next to the power I hold."

I tried to fight, to get myself up, but I kept falling back in pain. My thoughts were scattered, as his comment about Amayah sent my mind spinning. He thought I had teleported her to safety, while I thought he had created some illusion of her. Where the hell had she gone? It probably wasn't going to matter, because he had me pinned, and Justice was in two pieces behind him, completely out of reach. I tried to focus my power on some form of telekinesis, as I had seen from him and Bobo, but there was no way I would manifest a new power at my current level of energy and fear.

Keats stood over me like a big-game hunter with a new prize and brought the morning star down into the side of my face. My left ear exploded in pain, and my vision blurred in that left eye. I looked up at him, and all I saw was the morning star looming there, the Grim Reaper preparing to drag me to Hell. My head lolled back, and I struggled to remain conscious. Suddenly, I felt a gentle breeze blowing across my face, and I opened my eyes. There, behind Keats, was a plume of that weird gold smoke, manifesting itself in thin air. Shimmering into existence from that smoke came Amayah's head, torso, arms and legs. Red and gold flowers also bloomed beneath her left eye, resembling temporary tattoos with an ethereal glow. I gasped aloud, but Keats must have thought I was crying out in pain or accepting my fate, because he didn't even turn his head. Amayah grabbed one end of Justice, raising the short sword and plunging it straight into the back of Keats' right knee.

He barked, whimpering in pain, and buckled over in two, dropping the morning star in surprise. He nearly fell on top of me, but Amayah's attack gave me time to roll out of the way, even though it hurt like hell. Even wounded, he was up almost as quickly as I was, whirling around to snarl at Amayah. I moved around him and stood beside her. She handed me the sword and stooped to pick up the other one, never taking her eyes off the wounded beast before us. I imagined how we must have looked, two beat-to-shit teenagers holding two ends of a deadly weapon, staring down a psychotic serial killer who had probably murdered more people than the years in our lives. I wanted to tell Ama to run away, far from this evil, but she was part of this now. I had told her that she had special powers when she found me in the dumpster, but she had denied it. There was no denying it now. Either something had awoken in her, just as it had in me, or something had changed in her when Steven gave her some of his energy, but there was no time to question their source.

"Are you okay?" I asked her quickly.

"I'm okay so long as you're here," she answered back, and my heart soared with love.

The reunion was brief, as Keats was seething, and his body was twitching. I knew all too well what would come next.

"Enough is enough!" he belched, and I stepped back in spite of myself. "You dare attack me in my place of power? That little bitch thinks she can interfere? You have unleashed this fate upon yourself, girl. I was going to just play with you a bit while your boyfriend died, but now I'll do you first, and rip you limb from limb as you beg for mercy!"

He screamed inhumanely, and his face began to shift and twitch. He was becoming the monstrosity. He unhinged his jaw, his arms grew longer, and his legs rippled with muscular growth. Not wanting to give him the time to reach his full strength, I launched myself at him, but he saw me coming and caught me in his grip before throwing me back to the ground.

Amayah shrieked in terror as he transformed. I had told her about it, but it was no comparison to seeing it in person. He grew taller and taller, warping into the Brute's beastly creation. He was monstrous and massive, and I pushed back the feeling of helplessness at having to battle him and protect Amayah at the same time. I limped around, and my breathing came in ragged gasps between broken ribs. He lunged at her, and she vanished into the golden smoke again, leaving only a confused look on his face. The shape he inhabited was fearsome, but when he was confused, it worked against him, as his beastlike eyes grew wide with bewilderment and a touch of fear.

His disorientation gave me the chance to get back up and try to launch another attack, but in this form, he was too quick and strong. I began to fear that I couldn't defeat him.

But I had to try, and I had to think. If he was so powerful like this, why bother using his other form at all? As I watched him retrieve the morning star, I saw how heavily he was breathing. That was my only real clue. This form was taxing his energy enormously. The Brute might let him wear this beastly suit for a time to explode and defeat enemies like me, but that didn't mean he could sustain it indefinitely. I needed to wear him down, and I could only do that by stalling and making him expend his energy. So, instead of coming straight at him, I used my agility to leap up to the deck of a derelict ships beside me and call down, "Hey dumb fuck! You lose something? I'm up here, asshole!" I tossed his Pogo lighter at him, and it boinged off his head.

Amayah and her disappearing trick temporarily forgotten, Keats swore as he hurled the morning star through the air at me. Even anticipating it, I barely dodged as the massive metal ball sailed inches from my head and lodged between two loose plates of the ship with a booing clang. I forced myself to put a smile on my face as though I had found the attempt hilarious.

"That's your best throw, Keats? My great-grandmother throws better than that, and she's dead!" I laughed again and jumped to an even higher point atop the ship. He thundered and sprung to the spot I had just occupied. He landed heavily and awkwardly, and I saw my suspicions being confirmed. This body of his was built for power, not speed and agility. As he turned to look up at me, I swung a kick into his left eye. He staggered and roared in pain, blindly sweeping one long arm at me, but I was already gone, leaping from one ship to the next before casually sitting down as he turned to track me. His chest was heaving, and he was stooped over, nearly swaying. It was working; I just had to keep him off balance.

SMACK!

I staggered forward as something smashed into the back of my head and shoulders. It was heavy and metal, and I saw stars as I struggled to keep my balance lest I fall from the ship's top level. I found my feet when whatever it was hit me again, and I fell from my perch, twisting in midair to avoid crashing down and breaking my hands. Above me, a circular shape blacked out what little light from the moon there was. It was a shipping drum from a cargo ship. Keats was using his powers to move it through the air. Even in his bestial form, he still had immense mental power, which had taken me by surprise and cost me my advantage. As I pushed the container off, he hit me full force, and I was back on the defensive, my head clanging off the metal surface. I felt darkness rising up to claim me. It was only a matter of time now. My gambit had failed, and it would cost me my life. I prayed that Ama had the sense to flee, if she hadn't already. I prayed that she would be safe and help my family understand what had happened. I prayed that ...

OF COURSE!

The power of prayer. Faith in God. The willingness to submit. They all came rushing to me, and I closed my eyes tight, reaching out with my feelings, praying as though everything depended on God.

"Hua! Hear me! I am your willing child, Rohan; guide my hand and allow me to be your weapon to defeat this great evil!"

Through closed eyelids, I sensed a piercing light and opened them to see what could possibly be causing it. Keats was gone, pushed to the background of my vision as if time stood still. In his place was a luminous white light descending towards me, a *bright shining* star. It somehow, someway, emanated love and brilliance, and tranquility.

A bright morning star?

A shape emerged from the white light, a woman, beautiful yet plain of face. Bathed in white radiance, she looked down at me. It was something out of a dream, a memory that had faded, or a connection that had never been wholly achieved.

"I am Hua, Rohan. I bring forth the brightest star of the morning. I am three in one. The deliverer of new births. Some know me better as the Holy Spirit, and I did what was needed to put forward Jesus as the Son and Savior. I am the Mother of Light. Take my hand, and let me see you."

I reached out to accept her hand in mind. It was ethereal, not entirely real, yet I believed like I never had before. I rose with her strength, dimly aware of Keats standing behind her, raising his weapon once again.

Her hand and mine seemed to move together, and I physically fought as though everything depended upon me, catching the spiked ball effortlessly as it swung down, holding it as though it were the lightest of feathers between my fingers. He dislodged it and swung again, and again I moved with quiet purpose, catching the weapon lightly and holding it frozen in place, willing its master to find peace. He didn't. It's not that he couldn't; he simply had no interest in it. He had gone beyond the point of no return. He was no longer Stacey Keats; he was the property of Nick the Brute, and firmly believed there was no way back.

Hua's sadness radiated through me. Despite all his monstrous acts, she was still hoping to find redemption for Keats. Renouncing the Brute was the only way to do it, but he didn't believe it was possible. She whispered into my mind, and I knew what I had to do. Or what we would have to do together. When Keats swung the morning star again, Hua and I caught it as one, but this time we didn't just stop its motion, but reversed it. We drove the spiked ball back into the beast's chest, and I felt the air explode out of him as the mighty weapon collapsed his chest cavity. There, between his massive chest muscles, a trickle of red appeared, which soon became a stream, and the stream widened into a river of gushing red blood. He opened his mouth, but no sound emerged. His hands pressed against his chest, only to be immersed by the flood of his life force spilling out, killed by his own mighty ball and chain and the Almighty power of God.

A second later, Ama reappeared in her mysterious mist of gold, wide-eyed and clearly shocked by the scene before her. By all accounts, I should have been dead, but instead I was standing tall and proud, unharmed by the spiked morning star. Keats was crumpled in a heap as the last spark of life left him.

As the spirit of Hua, the Holy Spirit, lifted away from me, Amayah leapt into my arms.

"I thought I'd lost you forever, Amayah! How did you get free?"

She stepped back, and I saw her brow tense up in concentration. Without a sound, she vanished into golden smoke, and I took a startled step backward when she popped back into view a few feet away.

"What the hell is that?"

"A gift from my boyfriend, I suppose," she offered with a weak smile. "It started happening when we got back to our time, but I wasn't sure why or how. Just like the mind-reading, though, I think all that time in the glow of your powers rubbed off on me."

"You saved me," I gushed with wonder at my superhuman love.

"We saved each other, Rohan," she replied.

I moved to finish the kiss that had been interrupted atop the World Trade Center when Keats moaned and began to sit up. I raised Justice over my head to strike a finishing blow when a massive shadow passed over us. Amayah disappeared into gold smoke as an enormous shipping container fell on top of Stacey's ravaged body, crushing bone and flesh beneath it. I turned and gawked, and there he was, sitting atop of an old drum canister. Wearing blue jeans and a Giants' jersey, Bobo smiled broadly at me, just as Amayah blinked back into existence at my side. *The Big General's telekinesis, in all its glory,*" Nathan yelled.

"Holy shit, Bobo!" I yelled back, "Where did you come from?"

Bobo winked and tapped his heart with his right hand, then let the smile go, causing me to grin and laugh in reply.

Amayah's bewildered look was priceless.

"Bobo? Our Bobo?! Like, 1980 BOBO???!" She raced over to him and climbed on the drum to wrap him up in a hug.

"How is this even possible?" she asked no one in particular.

"He's like me," I explained. "He's Shine Xiong, and from the looks of things, you might be too."

CHAPTER

THIRTY-NINE

"We're ninjas of destiny, daring to confront and defy expectations and forging a path that Shines," I happily stated. I was so joyful yet exhausted that I had forgotten about the second monster creeping into the night. One was dead at my feet, but the other struck just as I began to clamber up to where Bobo and Amayah were talking.

Amayah and I were beaten and battered. And Bobo had previously admitted to me in the church that he had never actually fought with his powers, preferring to use them for healing and peace. On the other hand, Steven Stone was imbued with the dark energy of Nick the Brute and his own vicious rage. Seeing his master fall had sent him into a frenzy beyond words. His attack from above was swift and brutal, all wrath and fury. But despite being in some sort of berserker mode, he still knew how to fight, and he struck Bobo first, driving his wings into the minister's back, leaving deep gashes there as Bobo screamed in surprise, tumbling from the platform. Amayah and I were knocked off as well; she vanished into a golden cloud of smoke as I lashed out and caught a hanging pole, twirling around and off it like a gymnast before dismounting back to the ground. Steven flapped his wings and hovered above us, clearly wary of giving away his advantage of flight.

He called down, "Did you like seeing our little dance party, Rohan? Did you see how eager she was? She came to me like a bee to a flower, all smiles and hips for your boy, and she couldn't get enough. Probably still thinking about it!"

I had to quell my rage, and it wasn't easy. He knew what I had seen and likely felt how it made my blood boil, but I couldn't let my emotions dictate my actions. I helped Bobo to his feet, and Amayah reappeared beside us. I didn't want to look into her eyes after what Steven had said, I was already in too much pain, so I had to focus on a plan of attack. Hua had helped me once before, but I reached out and didn't feel the same glow. This felt more personal, like it was between Steven and me, more of a test of who I was, rather than the power of the Almighty.

"Stay out of reach of his wings!" I warned the other two, since neither had much experience fighting, particularly a hellish warrior like this. "Keep him turning, don't let him corner you, and Bobo, throw some shit at him!"

Bobo started picking up everything he could get a mental grip on and hurling it at Steven as I leaped in the air, searching for a weakness with Justice. I used it in all forms—the swords, the staff, and the double-bladed poleaxe—but couldn't find a way to get to Steven without him batting it away.

Worse, he began flying higher, out of Bobo's easy reach. He turned the hurling tides, chucking concrete bricks, planks and industrial trash back at Bobo and Amayah wherever she reappeared, causing them both to run for cover. I was able to block his attacks with Justice, but he largely ignored me, focusing instead on the two weaker links, taunting me from above.

"All that power, and you still can't handle me, Rohan!" he yelled, chucking a panel of sheet metal like a jagged blade at Amayah, who yelped and vanished just before it struck her. "You thought I was training you to fight crime, but I was just training you to fight the way I wanted you to, so I would know exactly how to beat you!"

I was furious. All the things I had confided in him during those early days of testing my powers. No wonder he wasn't all that surprised when I had mentioned the Brute in my head. He had been experiencing it too. Hell, he had probably been jealous the whole time.

I shouted to Bobo to go to Plan B, and he lifted me in the air with his telekinetic powers, sending me hurtling towards Steven. I could have teleported, but I was already exhausted and didn't want to leave the other two exposed. The ploy took Steven by surprise, and I was able to land a deep cut between his shoulder and his arm, but he retaliated by gashing me across the back with one of his wing tips, and I fell hard, with Bobo catching me a few feet off the ground. Amayah was at my side, helping me stand and pressing her hands to my back, trying to flow energy into my wound. Steven landed on a high perch and called down, "This is pointless. You can't beat me, Rohan. Let's do this the old way!"

I had no idea what he was talking about, but he raised his hands to the sky and began saying words under his breath. The sky darkened, lightning struck in a giant blast, and I was suddenly falling backwards, away from my friends, away from everything.

I fell and fell some more, watching my own body standing above me. I shut my eyes as time and space spun around me and only opened them again a few seconds later, once I felt the world go still.

"Rohan?"

It was Amayah. She was here too. She was off in the distance, searching for me. I called out her name and waved. She waved back, and we moved toward each other, but another figure reached her first, and they embraced. I didn't understand what was happening until he turned and I saw his face. It was me. It was impossible, but there was another me here. His smile arched up into an all-too-familiar grin, the one I had last seen atop the World Trade Center, and then before at the Festival of the Moon, when he'd seen how jealous I was of him dancing with Amayah. Whatever strange powers Steven Stone had unearthed from Keats and Nick the Brute, this was officially the most insidious. He was inhabiting a copy of me, and as I looked down, I saw that I was now wearing his garb from the World Trade Center. He kept his arm around Ama's waist as I approached.

"It's a trick, Amayah!" I shouted frantically. "I'm Rohan. Steven is pretending to be me; get away from him!"

Ama looked confused, staring from the face she loathed to the one she loved and back. Wearing my face, Steve told her, "Don't listen to him, my Ama, I'm your Rohan. Remember how you held me that day in Heather Garden? You saved me that day. Maybe we can save Steven now."

That son of a bitch had somehow accessed my memories, and I suddenly realized that I had done the same to him without his permission. Like Keats, Steven probably knew what I was doing and had played dumb to gain access in return.

"You're sick, Steve, let us help you. It doesn't have to be like this. Keats doesn't control you any longer. Break free of the pain. We can help you get free if you let us."

Amayah was trying to be supportive, telling "Steven" the same thing, that he was a good person and a good friend, and that this could all be over if he would just renounce the Brute, renounce Keats, and come back with "us" to the real world.

"No," I said firmly. "I'm Rohan, he's Steven. This is crazy! Amayah, look at me! Listen to me!"

But she couldn't hear me, and it didn't seem like she could see me anymore either. It was like I was looking at them through a glass window, or perhaps a mirror. Yes, it felt as though I was trapped on the other side of a one-way mirror, watching them. I pounded my fists against it, but I couldn't even make a dent. Through the mirror, Amayah was telling "me" how much she loved me, pressing her head against "my" chest. The version of me that Steven was inhabiting was staring right through the mirror at me with that sick smirk I had seen too many times before. As I pounded my fists, he tilted Amayah's chin back and kissed her deeply. His facial features warped from mine to his, and I growled in rage. Amayah, her eyes, closed, unaware that he was tricking her into kissing him. The features shuddered again, and I gasped in horror. Steven's face was gone, replaced by something alien and nightmarish, dark red, with scales on every inch and a forked tongue that licked her lips. The face turned back to me. Not Steven, and not Keats; I realized in horror that I was staring into the face of Nick the Brute.

His face was scarred with a horrifying grin. He picked Amayah up as she continued to kiss and touch him and carried her to a bed, standing over her as she wordlessly removed his shirt, not seeing the red monster I could see. He pushed her back on the bed and looked at me. "See how she wants me, Rohan? Never you, just me. I've had her, you know. While you were trying to drown yourself in that shower, she kept asking for more and more, so finally, I gave her everything. She'll never settle for anything less again."

I was screaming, but no words were coming out, and the scene went black. I felt like I was going to pass out. I blinked, and blinked again, in disbelief.

I was back on the train, headed to school. I immediately thought I must be dreaming, but everything around me seemed normal and very real. The sights, the smells, the sounds, the familiar faces that I saw every morning. What the hell was this? Was it all a dream?

I looked up, and there was my Ama, sitting down in her usual seat as she got on from her stop. She smiled at me, but made no sign of coming my way, which told me that either this was a vision from the past, or something much weirder was going on.

No matter, I needed to get to her and see what was happening, so I stood up and pushed past several other passengers.

"Amayah," I said, "What's going on? How did we get here?"

She was reading a book, but looked up and squinted oddly at me, then burst out laughing.

"Why are you talking to me? We aren't friends. Go back and sit down and leave me alone chink."

I was flabbergasted and hurt. *What was going on?*

"Amayah, please, I don't understand?"

She looked up, even more annoyed. "Listen, you weird chink, leave me alone! Just because we go to school together doesn't mean we're friends. Step back to your seat, or I'm gonna hit the button and tell them you touched me!"

I staggered back like she had physically assaulted me and returned to my seat, as strangers laughed at what must have looked like a blatant rejection of romantic advances.

I sat down with a thud and stared at her, but she was already nose-deep back in her book. What the hell was this?

"It's all in your head, Rohan."

A voice, male and deep, not like anyone I had heard before. Was I going insane at last?

"She doesn't know you because it's all been in your head. The powers, the girlfriend, the trips through time. You don't have any of them.

"You've been pretending all this time in order to avoid the truth."

Truth? What truth?

Images flowed into my mind, and I saw myself crouched in the dark with a long, wicked knife in my hand. I was on Roosevelt Island by the UN Building, and as I watched, the young woman who Keats had murdered there walked by. I pounced from the shadows and caught her by surprise, knocking her down and slicing her neck open. I watched her bleed out and then raced away as voices approached.

No! ... That couldn't be me. I hadn't killed her; I had found her. The images were rushing now one after the next. I was stalking the hooker in Times Square, the toll booth attendant, the blonde teenager who had turned every guy's head. There I was trying to drug her when an innocent bystander interrupted, and I had fled into the night. The vision changed to my parents searching my room, finding a journal with terrible scrawled pictures and warnings. I watched my dad silently handing it over to a police detective as my mom wept.

It was all me. The whole time. I had killed those women. The Shine, Amayah's love, the trips through time, Bobo, I had conjured them all up as my cover story to shield my mind from the truth while I committed my crimes.

Suddenly, there was something in my hands. A shard of glass, as if from a broken mirror. Looking up, I could see my reflection staring back at me.

"You're sick, Rohan, don't you see?" a voice that sounded like mine coming from my reflection said, low and lilting, guiding my thoughts. *"You're sick, and you're weak and stupid and disgusting. You've ruined your life and the lives of everyone you know. Stop wasting their time. Get it over with already. Your parents hate you; your brother mocks you, and little Ama is much more attracted to Steven Stone than you. You have no real power; it's all been in your head this whole time."*

The mirror shard gently hung above my heart and pushed against me slightly, enough to slice through my shirt. *"The world is better without you, Rohan. The time to leave is now. No one will even miss you."*

As despair took me, I cried out and followed the voice, guiding the mirror shard deeper into my chest, into my beating heart.

As the breath left my body, the images sped up, and I watched the world go by. My parents moved away from New York City, bitter and embarrassed to be associated with me. Henry had to quit work at Eckerd's; he was threatened by coworkers and customers alike. I saw Amayah, and my heart leaped. She was walking down the street, but walked right past school, past her job, and kept going. She avoided Mt. Sinai and stopped for a long gaze at the French restaurant we had once eaten at, then turned the corner and ducked into an alley. She stopped, and he was there, smoking a cigarette, leaning against the wall. Steven Stone. She said please, and he smiled, giving her a small vial and a needle. She didn't say two words, just pulled back the plunger, stuck it between her toes into an open vein, and sighed in relief, slipping into a stupor right then and there.

"It's $50 little Ama," he said, and she cringed.

"I only have $30," she said. "Can you let me have it anyway?"

"Sure," he replied. "You know the deal."

She didn't even hesitate, dropping down on her knees at once. When they were done, he chuckled and walked away, leaving her to clean herself up. A Daily News article caught in the wind flew by and casually landed by Ama's feet. I couldn't help but read the top headline with my photo plastered in the report:

"NY SLASHER KILLS SELF"

The journalist included photographs of all the women the Slasher murdered and an individual named Rohan Chang being responsible and leaving behind a handwritten confession apologizing to the world that he did not take even more lives and that his despair and hatred led to his path of destruction.

There were gang members high-fiving Steven and paying him money for protection, for drugs, for whatever. The city looked dark and dirty, hopeless even. There was no sunshine as far as the eye could see, and it started raining as clouds gathered overhead, and it began to thunder and pour.

There was no sunshine?

It was so cold, and I began to shiver, but something in my pocket became warm. I could feel it, but I couldn't see it. It had to be the Bible Ama had given me. *"Ninja, blessed you are with the Shine."* Then and there, Hua's words blessed me with strength and determination, tranquility and goodness, blessings of hope and faith.

The Shine... It was warm, it was loving, and now it was emanating from my heart.

I saw the first rays of sunlight breaking through, chasing away the clouds as the rain stopped. Then more of the sun's warming radiant rays penetrated the gloom and multiplied, transforming the city as bright golden dandelions started sprouting from the cracked sidewalks and birds began chirping and singing. Children's joy and laughter began touching the air.

And I couldn't foresee that bleak future. I knew the truth, and the weight of the lies and accusations began withering away. There was no way I was a serial killer! I am Rohan Chang, NY's Talon, a ninja of the Shine Xiong. My powers are used for healing, and I carry the light in the midst of darkness.

That ominous future can't possibly be real, but rather a dark realm controlled by the Brute. But what I had just done in my physical form was very real. I could feel the shard embedded in my chest and the life force seeping out of me. The Brute had tricked me one last time, and if I didn't act fast, it would cost me my life.

I WAS DOOMED in this form, but I didn't have to stay that way. I had traveled through time before, and had even met myself as a baby. Focusing my energies, I reached out with my powers a little differently this time, to pull back the wheels of time just a touch, not one hundred and fifty years, just seven minutes earlier, right about the time that the Brute had tricked me into killing myself with the shard. I swapped places with Rohan and tapped his chest, whispered three words into his ear, planting them deep in his subconscious. Just three little words.

"Create His Lie."

As I lay dying, I beckoned to the Brute, calling out his name, speaking him into existence. He appeared above me, smug and triumphant. "I offered you the gifts that man has sought for eternity, fool," he said, spitting in my face. "You turned away from them, and see where that has brought you. Where it always brings mankind. You think you can turn away from your sin, but you never can. It's been that way since the day Eve brought Adam the apple. And who showed her that apple?

"'Twas me, boy. Just as I have tempted your kind throughout history and caused your pathetic forms to fall and fail, I win another victory each day that man falls short. And the more I win, the weaker my Father grows. He knows that he's losing the war. He feels it in those old bones of his. One day soon, He'll fall, and all of his self-righteous, special charity cases will fall with him. And I will take his throne, his crown, his precious children, and rule them all for an eternity. Your little friends might live to see it, but not you, Rohan. You thought you could defeat me, and all you learned is that I am eternal. I am legion. And you are less than nothing, Rohan."

Nick growled and threw his right fist out in a curved hook, hitting my temple. Hard. "I deserved to be loved, not Him. I am all. I am the Lamborghini, the Bugatti, the 5 Michelin-starred tomahawk steaks, the billion dollars. I am all of it. I am all they want, the handsome prince, the voluptuous starlet, and any other dream you pathetic wretches desire. And you, you are pathetic, so utterly pathetic, Rohan.

"But I give you one victory, back in 1854, I told Hua you would curse her, curse God, and come running to me if she remained silent. You never did."

I saw the devil's eyes open wide, but I didn't want to meet them. He lunged forward and plunged his fangs into my neck, tearing my flesh free. "Yes!" With blood flowing from his mouth, Nick exclaimed, "My Father doesn't see me! But the world sees me. And, you see me, don't you, you damn pathetic chink. As you die, know that there was never righteousness from God, just selfishness. All of humanity was and always is inherently more like me than my Father. Of course, man is me; everyone knows this, and so do you. And I tell you what, Rohan, my lil' Shine knight, lil' Ama knows this. And she's one whore of a girl."

I fell silent and was just about gone when I grabbed hold of his shoulders, much to his surprise. "You might be all of those things, but you're also trapped."

I held onto him and then traveled back in time 7 minutes, to another version of Rohan, the one who was about to plunge the shard into his chest. I switched his consciousness with mine and held onto the Brute as time played out. I stabbed myself in the chest, my life force waned, and I called the Brute to me again.

A sharp pain effused from me as my heart twisted and throbbed, agonizingly seeing my consciousness break free again and again as my unconscious, doomed version died infinite deaths in the darkest realm imaginable. It happened again and again and again. On the fifth or sixth time, he seemed to realize that something was amiss.

"What is this?" he said, his voice confused and furious. "This has already happened. What are you doing?"

"Giving you what you want," I said. "Watching me draw my last breath. Or at least, this version of me, before I duck back in time about seven minutes and swap places with myself and go forward towards death that way, and then start it all over. Of course, you don't go back to a previous version of yourself because, as you mentioned, you're eternal, and you're legion."

The devil screamed and raged and spit at me, raking my face with his claws and plunging them into me. The agonizing pain seared through every fiber of my being, but in my withering state, I was already near death, making a little more suffering a bearable cost. I had outsmarted him even more profoundly than he had deceived me, and now he was entwined in an eternal, unending struggle with a dying version of me.

As I basked in the radiant glow of my victory for the last time, my thoughts wandered to Jubas, Wayles, and Bobo, to my Ama and parents. In that moment, I realized the devil had been mistaken. Not everyone was selfish. They were not his kin. They weren't like him at all; they were loving and warm, with a deep and genuine care for me. Reflecting on the Brute's desire for me to lead independently and not follow others, which now included the Dark Lord himself, I released my consciousness from the infinite loop of time. I traveled back to the real version of myself. *Nick, you were right. Lions need not worry about sheep,* I thought.

CHAPTER
FORTY

As the life flickered out of me, I felt a hand take mine. I feared the Brute, or his puppet Steven, was still somehow upright and had come to finish me off. But the hand was small and soft, and it guided mine back to my heart, to the spot where the shard had pierced my chest.

I heard the voice of an angel. One I was sure I had invented in my head to take away the hurt and pain… but this was no fantasy. She was real, she was there, and she was speaking to me.

"In my darkest hour, you lit my light with your words, Rohan Chang," Amayah consoled me, her voice shaky but strong. "You saved my life that night. I've spent weeks writing something to tell you what I've always felt. Listen to my words, Rohan, and let my voice guide you back to me.

"*Late nights in New York City*
Rainfall, crowds, lights surround me
Crazy how they left me feeling empty
That loneliness was deadly

Till you came around and saved me
In the Bronx, through it all, we're changing
Just wanna mend you if you're ever breaking
'Cause you give me hope, baby
You're my lifeline, you're my high tide
Looking in your eyes, I know we'll survive
You're my lifeline, you're my high tide
Looking in your eyes, I know we'll survive

You walk me home, *I know that*
Time flies, even when we turn back
Gotta keep good love, make it last
'Cause this train is moving way too fast
I lay my head on your chest
Hear your heartbeat, feel my breath
For you, all I ever want is the best
We rise together, no less

You're my lifeline, *you're my high tide*
Looking in your eyes, I know we'll survive
I need you, I breathe you
I see you, believe in you
I need you, I breathe you
I see you, believe in you"

As her song faded away, I felt the white light return—beaming and beautiful. It was inside of her and inside of me. As it flowed between us like an unending river, I rose to my feet, lifted by the power of faith and love. There were tears in my eyes—of joy, of hope, of love... all of it. The light pulsed and shimmered. No, in fact, it did much more than that. It Shined. Ultimately, I never needed any weapon but my unwavering faith, my hope, and my love. I raised my arms and felt the power of God surge through me like a storm, lifting me up. I opened my eyes, to see Bobo and Amayah standing before me, bathed in white light like two angels, and I embraced them both.

As we clutched each other tightly, I heard their thoughts in my mind. Bobo was thanking me, and praising God, the Father, in His son, Jesus' name, and inviting the Holy Spirit into our hearts.

Amayah laughed through her tears that her superhero had come back to her. I projected my thoughts back to them, of hope and love and joy that we were all together and safe, and that they had helped me find my way to my true calling. In the vibrant heart of New York City, I stand transformed, a guardian of the Shine Xiong, the resolute protector known as NY Talon.

Bobo guided us to turn our senses outward, and as we did, more voices joined the mix. There exist others out there, just as Hua had foretold. I delved into the depths of their minds and caressed the essence of Aidan Flynn, capable of defying gravity and orchestrating thunderous echoes with a mere gesture. And Jerome Towers, who harmonized with sonar frequencies to navigate uncharted realms and unleash melancholic wails that could shatter eardrums. Raj Patel, with his extraordinary five hundred million, heightened olfactory senses, deciphering scents from afar, a guardian in the rugged terrain of Yosemite Park. Then emerged Emelee Riva, a Dominican American legal scholar from Jersey, revealing her ability to weave *thoughts and aspirations* into the tapestry of another's mind, a tapestry she was intricately crafting within me. Despite our diverse gifts, we were intertwined as one. Bound by our shared quest to challenge fate, we carved a path illuminated by brilliance. Together, we stood united, the last defense against the darkness that dwelled within the human spirit. We were the architects of our own destinies, the ninjas of the Shine Xiong. We stand liberated.

EPILOGUE

Two months later, I went to the Museum of Modern Art in Long Island City on a Friday night with Amayah on my arm. I had volunteered to teach a class in graffiti for the kids of the Five Boroughs, and I was getting a service award tonight, a plaque for the wall, and my picture in a local newspaper. It was nice, but connecting with my community was worth far more than that. Anticipation filled me as I reached into my pocket and felt the familiar outlines of my golden fat cap, sensing Lore's comforting presence. Among the other volunteers at the front of the room, I felt a surge of excitement. Together, we were ready to create an impromptu mural for auction to a local business for public display. As the lines and curves came together, I couldn't help but think back over the past year and how everything had been disparate pieces of a bigger picture. At last, they had come together as one ...

Keats's body was discovered three days later when a construction company moved the "toppled" cargo container. Thankfully, he returned to human form in death, but when his pockets and the immediate area were searched, a wealth of knowledge came to fruition for the New York City Police Department. Keats had the IDs of every woman he had murdered, at least those who had been old enough to carry one. He had locks of hair in a special compartment in his backpack, maps, insane notes, and all sorts of other wild scribblings. He was tied to all of the dead women, without exception, and the case was declared closed. The Police Chief who announced it to the media called it Divine Intervention. He had no idea how true that was.

When we went back to school, the official word was that Steven Stone's mother had gotten a job, and he moved with her to California. Amayah and I didn't know what to believe. We weren't even sure there was someone really named Steven Stone at school, or if he had just been some sort of incarnation of Nick the Brute. After a couple weeks, I got up the courage to ask her about what I had seen in my vision of her on his lap. She said she had sat there, blacked out, and had no idea what had occurred until I appeared. I told her I was sorry for what happened and that she was never alone and I would always be there for her.

Without even realizing it, I noticed that my piece in the exhibition was a depiction of love and hope. I had blended together many well-known colors in the bombing world: exciting red, fearless orange, radiant yellow, gentle green, soft blue, witty purple, dependable brown, fresh white, and dignified black. My piece was vibrant, overflowing with incredible adrenaline and energy, centered around the words "Love" and "Hope" in a wild style, surrounded by the NYC skyline beneath a radiating sun. It was a scene of different people coming together, joining hands, and playing sports that had come to be as I painted, both on the wall and around me in real life. As I created and looked at all the different faces around me, I realized that we all came from different ethnicities, religions, and backgrounds. Yet, we all defined what American means, all of us embracing the ideals of liberty, equality, and uniqueness in each other. I hadn't even noticed what I was doing; I just kept going. It wasn't me doing it, though; the power of God was moving through me. Eventually, the other artists who had volunteered beside me had stopped to marvel.

"Your mural is chāo qiáng," she gushed.

Her words carried the meaning of *"kickass"* in Mandarin, one of the languages spoken by my parents, and it touched my heart. With a warm smile, I replied, "Thank you, Ama."

"Zhēn de," she replied.

Ama's passion and determination shone brightly as she pursued her dream of becoming a physician, studying chemistry and biology in her free time. She truly *radiated brilliance.* I had planned to treat her to a special dinner, but she surprised me by making beef noodle soup at my house. The dish held immense cultural significance for me, and her dedication to learning and perfecting the recipe deeply moved me. My parents were out for the evening, following Doctor Rohan's advice.

"Not bad," I said, impressed. "Looks like I'll have to perfect TriFongo to return the favor."

"Wǒ zhēnxī nǐ," Ama cooed with a glowing smile.

With warmth in my heart, I said, "I cherish you, too."

The next Monday morning was cloudy and overcast, and the commuters around me were grumbling about the possibility of more rain as they boarded the Four train. To me, the day seemed perfect. I was sitting with Ama as we rode the train to school. Seventeen weeks had passed since our victory over the forces of darkness, and we had spent a lot of time quietly holding each other since then, bonding together as only two pure souls can. My dad's recent X-rays and MRIs both came back clean. He shut down all attempts to publicize his stunning defeat of lung cancer, telling everyone from the charge nurse to the head of hospital administration that all thanks and glory went to the Almighty, so if they could pin him down for an interview, have at it. Beating cancer had turned my dad into quite the comedian, apparently.

The train stopped, and a few commuters got off, replaced by a pack of young punks, Black, white, and Hispanic; they came in all shapes and sizes. I had my arm around Amayah, which seemed to set them off. I found that seeing people happy usually brought out the worst in thugs. Maybe it made them jealous, or reminded them of their own less-than-fulfilling lives. I didn't really know.

They crept closer to our row as the train passed through a dim tunnel, and when our car came into the light at the next stop, Ama moved even closer to me. As we sat smiling and looking forward, talking about the day ahead, a loud thud ambushed the moment. It had been caused by a quick kick to an adjacent seat. As I looked up, I locked eyes with the guy in front, a giant aggressive ruffian with a half-dozen tattoos on his arms, who leaned down over me.

"HEY CHINK! Why don't you get the fuck up and let me sit next to that fine lil ma? I know ya ain't got what she needs to be satisfied. Ya heard?"

He looked us up and down, snickering.

"Yo chink, ya know who I be... bitch... I be Grande Bank Chico, ya heard!"

"That sounds a tad racist... please, leave us alone," I offered calmly. "Thank you very much."

"Shut the fuck up, bitch," Grande Banks Chico belligerently babbled.

His buddies laughed and cat-called as the rest of the train's passengers leaned in subconsciously, while looking in the other direction, hoping against their better intentions for a confrontation of some kind.

Unfortunately, I had to disappoint them all. Holding Amayah's hand in mine, and bowing my head in prayer, I quietly whispered:

"With my humility *shining* through, He said to me, 'My grace is sufficient for you, for my power is made perfect in weakness.' Therefore, I will boast more gladly about my weaknesses so that Christ's power may rest on me. That is why I delight in weaknesses, insults, hardships, persecutions, and difficulties, for Christ's sake. For when I am weak, then I am strong."

The giant angry hooligan scoffed in reply. "What the fuck, man? You think Jesus gonna stop me from whoopin ya chink ass?"

He raised his hand to strike, but was unceremoniously yanked back by a guy behind him, an older Hispanic man who looked like he was headed for a day on Wall Street.

"What the hell, man!" The irate bully said with a disbelieving yelp. "You tryin' to die too?"

But by the time Grande Banks Chico shook loose of the businessman, a Black woman in her sixties was standing over our seats. He looked up at her, and you could see the wariness enter his eyes. He probably had a grandmother who looked something like her, a woman who smacked his face when he disrespected someone in her earshot.

He turned back to get support from his crew, but found them fading back away from him. In their places were other people from the train car. A white grandfather with ragged slacks and a faded white shirt. A young mother with a baby on her arm and a look of fierce determination in her eyes. A Korean couple with suitcases stacked high on the seat beside them, gazing fiercely forward at the gang member with hidden strength.

"Fuck all, y'all," he said with a sneer, seemingly trying to hide his fear. "Y'all crazy."

I smiled at the scene before me. Good people. There were good people in this world who wouldn't stand for the violence, the hatred, and the corruption. I nodded to each of them as they walked by, saying thank you and smiling, and suddenly he was there.

At the very end of the train, Steven Stone was sitting on a bench alone, staring at us with hatred in his eyes. The eyes flashed red, the eyes of the Brute, and then he was gone, vanishing into thin air. Our train quickly burst from the dark tunnel and came out above ground into the sunshine, as the mood lightened with the sun's glimmer of golden hope. He was gone for the moment, but he hadn't been lying. He was eternal, and I knew that I would see him again.

As we hurtled towards school, I kissed Amayah on the cheek and turned my thoughts inward...

I always wanted to be somebody, and it's easy to forget that. I have grown with each place I've traveled, every person I've met, and every time I've lived. In my Ama, I have found love, hope, strength, and the knowledge that there is good in this world. Within myself, I have discovered an unwavering relationship with Jesus that I never knew I needed. In our concrete wilderness, persevering with the Lord and being content with giving my all, regardless of the outcome, is where the Shine resides - in the House of Shine, an enduring fortress filled with windows where the light shines in.

I am the NY Talon, but I am also so much more—a good son, a gifted student, and a proud Asian-American. In addition, I am a ninja against evil. The greatest trick the devil ever pulled was not convincing us that he did not exist, but convincing us that he is God in all the outward things we worship. We must first look at the unseen within ourselves, work towards a solution, and leave the rest to the Almighty.

Looking out the window, I locked eyes with the unknown, realizing the world required us to be more than we ever envisioned, ready to embrace the challenges ahead. With a gentle tap on my heart, I sent my most sincere prayer:

"I can choose who I am. I can choose what I do. God, be my guide. Shine your courage in the face of fear! Be my light in the darkness! Grant me the strength of a ninja when I am weak. Let me Shine, We will Shine!"

Reader, the Shine does not belong only to me.

BEACON POINTS
MADE IN NEW YORK
NYC TAXI
LINCOLN LEE

ABOUT THE AUTHOR

Lincoln Lee earned his Bachelor's degree in computer science from Queens College and his Doctorate in pharmacy from Long Island University. Born in New York, Lincoln frequently spent his days in the Bronx, where he explored urban art during his youth. Lincoln passionately advocates for greater awareness of the diverse Asian American community and their invaluable contributions to America's rich tapestry of history. It's important to recognize the significant impact Asian Americans have had on America, from their contributions to atomic science and labor rights to the invention of the USB and YouTube. Unfortunately, their achievements are often overlooked in textbooks. When Lincoln is not writing or reading, working in the pharmaceutical industry, or enjoying a cup of coffee, he loves exploring the outdoors in New Jersey with his dog, Licky, and cherishing time with his family and friends.

For more books and updates:
   https://www.Beacon5Points.com